THE GILDED HOUR

A *Seattle Times* Best Book of 2015

PRAISE FOR THE NOVELS
OF SARA DONATI

"Lushly written . . . Exemplary historical fiction, boasting a heroine with a real and tangible presence."　　　　　*—Kirkus Reviews*

"From page one, the action is nonstop. The more you read, the better it gets."　　　　　*—Tulsa World*

"Each time you open a book, you hope to discover a story that will make your spirit of adventure and romance sing. This book delivers on that promise."　　*—Amanda Quick, New York Times* bestselling author

"A splendidly drawn cast of characters."　　　　*—The Seattle Times*

"An elegant, eloquent word journey . . . The author has [a] gift for capturing the history and the lives of the people of that time and place."
　　　　　—The Tampa Tribune

"Powerful . . . gorgeous, vividly described."　　　　　*—People*

"Epic in scope, emotionally intense . . . an enrapturing, grand adventure."　　　　　*—BookPage*

"This hugely satisfying novel is a page-turner."　　*—Orlando Sentinel*

"A powerfully good read."　　　　　*—Toronto Sun*

THE GILDED HOUR

SARA DONATI

BERKLEY BOOKS, NEW YORK

BERKLEY

An imprint of Penguin Random House LLC
375 Hudson Street, New York, New York 10014

Copyright © 2015 by Rosina Lippi-Green.
Penguin supports copyright. Copyright fuels creativity, encourages diverse voices,
promotes free speech, and creates a vibrant culture. Thank you for buying an authorized
edition of this book and for complying with copyright laws by not reproducing, scanning, or
distributing any part of it in any form without permission. You are supporting writers and
allowing Penguin to continue to publish books for every reader.

BERKLEY® and the "B" design are registered trademarks of Penguin Random House LLC.
For more information, visit penguin.com.

Berkley trade paperback ISBN: 978-0-425-28334-9

The Library of Congress has cataloged the Berkley hardcover edition as follows:

Donati, Sara, (date–)
The gilded hour / Sara Donati.
p. ; cm
ISBN 978-0-425-27181-0 (hardcover)
1. Women physicians—Fiction.   2. New York (State)—
History—19th century—Fiction.   I. Title.
PS3554.O46923G55 2015
813'.54—dc23
2015007901

PUBLISHING HISTORY
Berkley hardcover edition / September 2015
Berkley trade paperback edition / May 2016

PRINTED IN THE UNITED STATES OF AMERICA

10   9   8

Cover photographs: Washington Square Arch © Hulton Archive /
Staff / Getty Images; Floral elements © snowflock/iStock/Thinkstock.
Cover design by Sarah Oberrender.

This is a work of fiction. Names, characters, places, and incidents either are the product of
the author's imagination or are used fictitiously, and any resemblance to actual persons,
living or dead, business establishments, events, or locales is entirely coincidental.

Penguin
Random
House

Young as she is, the stuff
Of her life is a great cargo, and some of it heavy:
I wish her a lucky passage.

RICHARD WILBUR, 1921

PRIMARY CHARACTERS

The Quinlan Household on Waverly Place

Aunt Quinlan: retired artist; widow of Simon Ballentyne and Harrison Quinlan

Anna Savard: physician and surgeon

Sophie Savard: physician; originally of New Orleans

Margaret Quinlan Cooper: Aunt Quinlan's adult stepdaughter

Henry and Jane Lee: groundskeeper and housekeeper; in their own residence

The Verhoeven/Belmont Households on Park Place and on Madison Avenue

Peter (Cap) Verhoeven: attorney

Conrad Belmont: attorney; Cap's uncle

Bram and Baltus Decker: Cap's first cousins; twins

Eleanor Harrison: housekeeper

The Russo Family

Carmine Russo: Italian factory worker, widowed; Paterson, N.J.

Rosa, Tonino, Lia, and Vittorio Russo: his children

The Mezzanotte Family

Massimo and Philomena Mezzanotte: originally of Livorno, Italy; florists; University Place at 13th Street

Ercole Mezzanotte and Rachel Bassani Mezzanotte: originally of Livorno, Italy; horticulturalists, apiarists; Greenwood, N.J.; their adult children with families

Giancarlo (Jack) Mezzanotte: detective sergeant, NYPD, and his sisters Bambina and Celestina Mezzanotte; 45 East 13th Street

Elsewhere

Oscar Maroney: detective sergeant, NYPD; 86 Grove Street

Archer Campbell: postal inspector; his wife, Janine Lavoie Campbell, and their children; 19 Charles Street

*Anthony Comstock: secretary, New York Society for the Suppression of Vice; postal inspector

Sam Reason: printer; his wife, Delilah; Weeksville, Brooklyn

Sam Reason: their adult grandson, also a printer

Giustiniano (Baldy, or Ned) Nediani: former newsboy

Father John McKinnawae: priest and social reformer

Sister Francis Xavier: procuratrix, St. Patrick's Orphan Asylum

Sister Mary Augustin (Elise Mercier): nurse, St. Patrick's Orphan Asylum

*Sister Mary Irene: Mother Superior, the Foundling

Lorenzo Hawthorn: coroner

Michael Larkin, Hank Sainsbury: detective sergeants, NYPD

Dr. Clara Garrison: Woman's Medical School

*Dr. Abraham Jacobi: Children's Hospital

*Dr. Mary Putnam Jacobi: faculty, Woman's Medical School

Dr. Donald Manderston: Women's Hospital

Dr. Maude Clarke: Woman's Medical School

Dr. Nicholas Lambert: forensics specialist, Bellevue

Neill Graham: intern, Bellevue

Amelie Savard: daughter of Ben and Hannah Savard; midwife; off Bloomingdale Road

Asterisk indicates historical character

1883

EARLY ON A March morning on the cusp of spring, Anna Savard came in from the garden to find a young woman with a message that would test her patience, disrupt her day, and send her off on an unexpected journey: a harbinger of change wearing the nursing habit of the Sisters of Charity, standing in the middle of the kitchen.

Anna passed four eggs, still warm from the nest, into Mrs. Lee's cupped hands, and then she turned to greet her visitor. The young woman stood with her arms folded at her waist and hands tucked into wide sleeves, all in white, from a severe, unadorned bonnet tied tightly beneath her chin to the wide habit that fell like a tent to the floor. No more than twenty-three by Anna's estimation, hardly five feet tall and most of that composed of sharp corners: a chin that came to a point and a nose and cheekbones to match, elbows poking out at noncongru- ent angles. Anna was put in mind of a nervous and underfed chicken wrapped up in a napkin.

"Sister . . ."

"Mary Augustin," she supplied. She had a clear voice, all polite good manners, and still there was nothing timid in her manner.

Anna said, "Good morning. How can I help you?"

"I was sent to fetch the other Dr. Savard, but it seems she's not in. Her note said to wait for you."

People who came so early to the house were almost always look- ing for Anna's cousin Sophie, who worked among the poor women and children of the city. For a scant moment Anna thought of lying, but she had never learned the art, and there was the promise she made to Sophie.

"The other Dr. Savard is attending a birth," Anna said. "She told me you might come and I agreed to take her place."

The pale forehead creased and then, reluctantly, smoothed. Clearly she had strong opinions, but had been schooled to keep them to herself. She said, "Shall we go?"

"Yes," Anna said. "But I have to write a note first to say I won't be in this morning."

"While you do that," said Mrs. Lee, "I'm going to feed Sister Mary Augustin. If I don't, I'll have to explain myself to Father Graves in confession." She took in the nun's hesitance but pointed at a chair. "I know that you wouldn't want to lead me astray. So sit."

Fifteen minutes later, finally ready to go, Mrs. Lee took the note to be delivered to the hospital and delivered a statement in return.

"Your cousin Margaret wanted to talk to you about your costume for that ball." She said *that ball* as she would have said *the fires of hell*.

"Margaret should talk to Aunt Quinlan if she's worried. She's the one who made all the arrangements for my costume."

Mrs. Lee's small round face could produce a tremendous depth and variety of wrinkles when she was irritated, as she was now. "And what is a proper young lady, almost thirty might I add—"

"I'm not yet twenty-eight, and well you know it."

"—an educated woman of good family, an unmarried lady, a physician and surgeon, what business do you have at a ball on Easter Monday—Easter Monday!—given by that greedy, vainglorious Vanderbilt woman? Why—"

"Mrs. Lee." Anna interrupted in her sternest tone, tempering it with a smile. "I made Cap a promise. Would you want me to disappoint Cap?"

All the irritation crackling in the air was gone, just that simply. Mrs. Lee loved Cap; everybody did. Muttering, she marched back to the stove.

"You and your auntie with your heads together," Anna heard her say. "Only the good Lord knows what will come of that. And on Easter Monday."

◆ ◆ ◆

ANNA SET OFF at a brisk pace along Washington Square Park and then, realizing that Sister Mary Augustin was almost running to keep up, stopped.

"Please don't slow down or we'll miss the ferry," she said. "I can run all day."

"We'll be there with five minutes to spare, even at this pace."

A flicker of doubt chased across the angular features. In the sunlight her complexion was like buttermilk, with a scattering of freckles and eyebrows the deep red-brown of chestnuts. Anna tried to remember if she had ever seen nuns wearing bonnets before, and then let the question go.

Sister Mary Augustin was saying, "And may I ask how you know that?"

"I grew up here, and I walk almost everywhere. And I have a clock in my head."

"A clock," Sister Mary Augustin echoed.

"A talent for time," Anna said. "The ability to keep time without a timepiece. It's a skill a surgeon must develop, you see."

"Surgeon?" The little nun looked both confused and horrified, as if Anna had claimed to be a bishop. "But I thought—isn't your cousin—"

"The other Dr. Savard specializes in obstetrics and pediatrics. I'm primarily a surgeon."

"But who would—" She stopped herself and two spots of red rose in her cheeks. She was pretty, Anna noted, when she forgot to be solemn. She wondered how much information she could supply without causing Sister Mary Augustin to fall down in a faint.

She said, "Women generally prefer a woman, physician or midwife or surgeon, when they are very ill or in labor. If they have a choice."

"Oh," Sister Mary Augustin said. "You operate on women only. That makes more sense."

Anna said, "I am qualified to operate on anyone, but I am on the staff at the New Amsterdam Charity Hospital. Just as the other Dr. Savard, the one you hoped to find, is on staff at the Infant and Children's Hospital and the Colored Hospital. And yes technically, I am not allowed to operate on men. Or so says the law."

After a moment Sister Mary Augustin said, "I suppose my training is quite narrow. I've never even seen a surgery."

"Well, then," Anna said. "You must come by and observe. And we are always in need of trained nurses, if you should ever rethink your"— she paused—"calling."

For a moment Mary Augustin was struck speechless by such a shocking suggestion. Sister Ignatia would be outraged, as Mary Augustin herself should be outraged, but instead she was struggling with a sudden blossoming of curiosity. She had been in this terrifying, exciting city for less than a year; during all that time questions had piled on top of questions, none of which she could ask.

But here was someone who would not scowl at her if she put one of those questions into words. Someone who would likely even answer. She could ask this Dr. Savard what kind of medicine obstetrics might be, and how it was that a woman could become not just a physician but a surgeon. Hot on the heels of this came the realization that Sister Ignatia was right, it was a mistake to let curiosity run riot. It would drag a person to places best left unexplored.

And she still could not stop watching this very odd and unsettling woman doctor—surgeon, she corrected herself—from the corner of her eye.

It seemed to Mary Augustin at first that Dr. Savard was wearing makeup, and then realized that it was simply vivid coloring that rose and retreated in her cheeks as they walked into the wind. Her mouth was a deep shade of pink, but the full lips were also a little chapped. She wore her dark hair smoothed back and twisted into a coil underneath her very practical hat, without the stylish bangs that most young ladies wore these days. As Mary Augustin—Elise Mercier, as she still thought of herself and always would—would wear, were such a vanity allowed. She resisted the urge to touch the faint pox scars on her forehead.

With her strong features and high coloring, few would call Dr. Savard pretty, but it was an interesting face with intelligent eyes. And she was clearly well-to-do; the neighborhood, the four-story house of a light-colored stone, the heavy oaken front door with carved lilies and cherubs, lace at the windows, all spoke to that. But both of the Savard cousins had given up a life of leisure for medicine.

Sister Ignatia would tell her to turn her attention elsewhere. The rosary, for example, which swung at her waist with each step she took. If she could get up the nerve, the first question she would ask the lady doctor would have to do with her clothes.

Dr. Savard wore garments of the very finest materials, beautifully tailored but without ornament and as austere as any nun's habit. Her hat was dark blue lined in gray; a matching, widely cut coat fell in folds straight from a high yoke below her shoulder blades to the top of sturdy boots. Her leather gloves were of a deep glossy black with small brass buttons at the wrist. She carried a bulky leather bag as all doctors did, and she let it swing a little at her side as she walked.

There was an occasional glimpse of skirts swirling back and forth with every step she took, very oddly. That Dr. Savard was not wearing a bustle was not such a surprise—few women who worked with the sick bothered with fashions. But the way the skirt moved puzzled her. Mary Augustin's own skirts swung wide with every step, so that the toes of her boots peeked out, first one and then the other. Dr. Savard was walking just as fast, but her skirts seemed to restrain themselves to a much smaller arc. With a start she realized that the lady doctor was wearing a split skirt, like a man's trousers or sleeves for the legs. Widely cut so that she could walk without constriction, but trousers, without a doubt.

In the midst of Lent Father Corcoran had given a thunderous sermon on the Rational Dress Society, which he took as proof of the continuing decline of the weaker sex. He predicted physical illness, infertility, and damnation. To her surprise and unease, Mary Augustin saw that such skirts were not immodest, no matter what Father Corcoran or His Holiness Pope Leo himself might say. They looked, she could admit to herself at least, both modest and comfortable. Something so shocking and interesting and once again, she would have to keep her questions to herself.

As they walked Dr. Savard greeted almost everyone by name: the street sweeper and the baker's delivery boy, a young girl minding a sleeping baby swaddled in quilts and tucked into a crate, a pair of laundry women arguing in Gaelic. She called out to a very grubby newsboy to ask after his mother and got a smile in return, everything taciturn chased away in that moment Dr. Savard spoke to him.

In Washington Square the trees were reaching toward spring, fat buds putting out the first pale green to shimmer in the sun. The city was full of such contrasts: beautiful homes on wide streets lined with linden and elm and plane trees, and tenements so filthy and over-crowded that the stench filled the throat with bile. Little boys dressed in velvet toddled along under the watchful eye of nannies in spotless aprons, and a half-naked child crouched down to watch maggots roiling in the open belly of a dead cat.

Every day Mary Augustin asked herself what she had imagined when she was first sent to this great noisy city. In theory she had understood what it meant to take in the poorest and most desperate; she knew that many of the infants would be sick unto death and few would survive their first year. But she had never understood what it meant to be truly poor before she came to this place. Every day she was frightened, overwhelmed, and at the same time consumed by curiosity, needing to understand things that could not be explained.

She cast a glance at Dr. Savard and wondered if it would be a very terrible sin to talk to her, and what penance such an act of defiance would earn once she put it into words in the confessional.

Bless me, Father, for I have sinned. I asked unseemly questions of a well-bred, overeducated lady in split skirts. And I listened to the answers.

At the corner of Fifth Avenue they came to an abrupt halt while oxen pulled two huge drays through the intersection. Florid red lettering on the first one declared that the profusion of potted trees—some twice Mary Augustin's own height, at least—came from LeMoult's Conservatory. The second dray had a lighter load: buckets and buckets of flowers, gorgeous deep colors and lighter spring shades. On the side of this wagon was a smaller sign:

MEZZANOTTE BROTHERS
GREENWOOD, N.J.

Mary Augustin couldn't help staring, but then she was not the only one.

"I wonder what that's about," she asked in a voice low enough to be ignored. Dr. Savard looked at her and lifted a shoulder. "The Vanderbilts," she said. "And their costume ball."

She had ventured a question and got an answer, but that only brought a hundred more questions to mind. If this went on much longer, Mary Augustin told herself, her brain would be riddled with question marks, hundreds of little hooks set so deep they'd never let go.

•   •   •

THERE WAS A small market at the Christopher Street landing, but most of the stalls had already closed for the day and the ferry was ready to board. A great throng of people were waiting to cross the Hudson to Hoboken: workmen of every description, farm women hung about with empty baskets and exhausted babies, towing young children on braided strings, still whey-faced as they shook the winter off. Draymen leaned on towers of crates or huddled in groups that belched tobacco smoke.

In the middle of all that, a nun who had been identified as Sister Ignatia stood waiting for them. She was the exact opposite of Sister Mary Augustin, from her habit—everything she wore from bonnet to shoes was a stark black—to the round cheeks and sturdy frame. Anna wondered what the difference in color was meant to convey—young or old? Good or bad? And had to bite her lip to keep from smiling.

The ferry let out a shrill blast of its whistle, which saved the trouble of another awkward introduction.

On deck, voices rose high and higher still to overcome the noise of the water and wind and the engines. German, Italian, Yiddish, Gaelic, French, Polish, Chinese, and still other languages Anna didn't recognize, all in competition. Inside the cabin it would be far worse and so Anna began to look for a spot on the open deck upwind of the smoke and cinders, but Sister Ignatia had other ideas. She cast a stern eye in Anna's direction and so she followed, suppressing a sigh. Somehow Sister Ignatia managed to make her feel like a first-year medical student, always waiting to be told what she had done wrong.

The cabin air was thick with coal smoke, rapidly aging fish, souring milk, pickled cabbage, wet swaddling clothes, and above all of these, sweat. The smell of hard work, not unpleasant in and of itself.

"Now," said Sister Ignatia, leaning close to talk directly into Anna's ear. "How much do you know of what is before you?"

That this nun found it within her authority to question a qualified physician did not come as a surprise. Anna might have said, *I have seen and treated smallpox many times*, or, *I have vaccinated hundreds of men, women, and children and even a priest or two.* Or, *In the four years since I qualified, I have signed some five hundred death certificates, more than seventy percent of which were for children less than five years old.*

The factory towns near Hoboken seemed to always be on the brink of a new epidemic: smallpox, yellow fever, typhoid, influenza, measles, mumps, whooping cough, sometimes overlapping. There were measures that would have put an end to many such episodes, but the mill owners saw no reason to invest in the lives of the workers; there were always immigrants eager for a place in the silk and thread factories. It was only the intercession of the Department of Health that had brought about any change at all.

Now the mill owners were supposed to supply hot water and soap—hygiene was the first line of defense in all matters of communal health—and see to it that newly arrived immigrants had clean drinking water and were vaccinated before taking up work. A few mill owners even complied, for a little while at least. But the epidemics still came, as regular as the seasons. With the result that Anna now sat on a ferry bracketed by nuns.

To Sister Ignatia she said, "Vaccinations are not difficult. As long as there are translators to help explain, I anticipate no trouble. I am assuming there will be enough vaccination quills wherever it is we're going."

"Vaccinations." Sister Ignatia sent a sharp look to Sister Mary Augustin, and when she spoke again her German accent had thickened. "Who is telling you of vaccinations?"

Anna paused. "Wasn't Dr. Sophie supposed to go with you to vaccinate the mill workers?"

Once the face framed by the bonnet had been very pretty and still was, in the way of many immigrants from northern Europe. Round-cheeked, flawless skin, eyes of a grayish blue. In this case there was also a chin set in the way of a woman who did not tolerate sloppy habits. Clearly irritated, she said, "We are the Sisters of Charity. It is our mission to see to the welfare of orphaned and abandoned children."

Anna managed a small smile. "Well, then," she said with deceptive calm. "What is it you need me to do?"

"We are fetching the children whose parents died in the last smallpox outbreak, but the law says no one is being allowed to cross into New York without—"

"A signed certificate of good health," Anna finished for her. "Italian orphans?"

"Yes," said Sister Ignatia. "But you needn't worry; Sister Mary Augustin has been studying Italian and Father Moreno will be there to translate, as well. Unless you speak Italian?"

"No," Anna said. "Too busy with physiology and anatomy and bacteriology. But I do speak German. I studied in Berlin and Vienna both."

Had she imagined Sister Ignatia would like this reference to her mother tongue and homeland? The older woman pursed her lips in a decidedly unhappy way.

From Anna's other side Sister Mary Augustin said, "What is bacteriology, Dr. Savard?"

"Study of the origin and treatment of a certain class of disease," Anna said, relieved at the change in subject.

"Bacteriology," said Sister Ignatia, "is nothing to do with us, Sister. We do God's work among the poor children of this city and do not presume to aspire to anything else."

Another time Anna might have taken up this challenge. She had sparred and debated all through her education and beyond, often with people as intimidating and inflexible in their certainty as Sister Ignatia. A woman practicing medicine had many opportunities to hone her debating skills. But they were within sight of Hoboken, and in a few minutes she would have to take on dozens of children who had lost everything, as she had herself at a tender age.

There had never been a moment's uncertainty about her own future, but the best these new orphans could hope for was a place to sleep, food, basic schooling, and the chance to learn a trade or enter a convent or seminary.

A bell was ringing on deck, and all around them people gathered their packages and boxes and baskets and began to move.

Anna picked up her Gladstone bag and moved with them.

◆　◆　◆

OUR LADY OF Mercy Church lacked the fine statues and gilded angels and stained-glass windows of the bigger Catholic churches in Manhattan, but it was full of light and very clean. Even the cavernous basement smelled of lye soap and vinegar with no trace of rot or mold.

To this unusual state of affairs came the presence of some thirty children, all of whom stood quietly, as if it were a matter of life and death not to draw attention to oneself. Anna took stock and estimated that the oldest children were no more than eleven, while the youngest were not even out of clouts. And all of them were underfed and hollow-cheeked, confused, frightened.

At the front of the room were three tables: Anna's station, where she would conduct her examinations and write the health certificates; a table piled with used clothing watched over by a tall, gruff-voiced nun who wore a tight wimple underneath a gray veil and who was never introduced, and Sister Ignatia, who ruled over soup and bread.

The first boy to stand before Anna to be examined clasped a bundle in his arms as though he expected her to grab it away. A piece of paper had been pinned to his shirt, which Sister Mary Augustin took and smoothed out to read on the open page of the heavy register book on a stand.

"Santino Bacigalup," she reported. "Twelve years old. Both parents and two sisters died in the epidemic last week." She squinted as she made notations.

Anna took in the hard set of the boy's mouth and his unblinking gaze. She had the idea that if she were to reach out to touch him, he would lash out like a feral cat.

Sister Mary Augustin said a few words to him in Italian, and he answered in a storm of syllables that left her blinking.

"What was that about?" Anna asked.

Sister Mary Augustin held out an open hand and shrugged. "I wish I could tell you."

"He wants to go home to Sicily," said a voice behind them. Anna was examining the boy's abdomen and didn't look up. This must be Father Moreno, who had promised his help as a translator.

The priest was saying, "He has grandparents and a married sister in Palermo. He wants to go back there. It's what his father said he should do before he died."

The priest asked a question and the boy's face lit up with happiness and relief. When Anna put her stethoscope to his chest and listened, he paused, only to let go with another stream of Italian as she nodded her permission. While the conversation went on between the boy and the priest, she palpated his abdomen and lymph nodes.

He was undernourished but very strong, as tough as a bundle of twisted wire. Through the priest Anna confirmed what she could see for herself: Santino had not been vaccinated, but somehow he had evaded the smallpox that robbed him of his parents and sisters. While the priest continued his conversation with the boy, Anna walked across the room to a surprised Sister Ignatia.

Anna said, "That child hasn't had his smallpox vaccination."

Sister Ignatia frowned. "And this is important just at this point in time?"

"Is it important?" Anna took a moment to summon a reasonable tone. "If his parents had been vaccinated, they would be alive and he wouldn't be here frightened half out of his mind."

Impatient, Sister Ignatia shrugged. "We cannot change the past, Dr. Savard."

"But we can do something about his future. If you had just told me this morning, I could—" Anna stopped herself. "Never mind," she said, and before Sister Ignatia could speak: "Tomorrow I will be at your door as soon as I have finished with my own patients, and I will vaccinate that boy and every child—every one—who requires it. Should it take all day and all night."

◆   ◆   ◆

SANTINO BACIGALUP WAS still in deep conversation with the priest when Anna returned.

Except the man who straightened to address her wasn't a priest. Instead of a Roman collar he wore the clothes of a man used to heavy labor. A tall, well-built man with a heavy beard shadow and unruly dark hair that fell over his brow.

He said, "This boy wants to work. He'll work to earn his passage home to Italy." His expression was neutral, or, she corrected herself, simply unreadable.

"You are—" Anna began.

"Giancarlo Mezzanotte," he said, inclining his shoulders and head very briefly, as if her insistence on his name was untoward. But then he made a visible effort to soften his expression. "Please call me Jack.

Most people do. Father Moreno was called away to give last rites, and he asked me to help here with the orphans."

His English was fluent and without any Italian inflection that Anna could hear. More than that, there was something about the way he expressed himself that belied the clothes he wore and his callused hands.

Anna touched the boy's head, and he looked up at her.

"Is there no possibility of finding work for him here in New Jersey?"

Mr. Mezzanotte leaned down to speak to the boy again. When he rose he said to her, "There may be something. I will talk to Father Moreno."

There were bellyaches and sore ears, rashes and ringworm, head lice and broken teeth. A girl of eight had the vaguest of rales in one lung while her older brother had a shallow puncture wound on his calf that was infected. While Anna cleaned and bandaged it, the boy told the story of how he had fallen down a long flight of stairs, consulting with Mr. Mezzanotte to get just the right phrases. His expression was so studied and sincere and his manner so studiously dramatic that Anna might have laughed out loud. When she did not, he shrugged. A philosophical actor with an audience that would not be won over.

Few of the children were so eager to talk. These quiet ones she treated with as much gentle efficiency and respect as she could muster, answering questions with the thoroughness she herself had appreciated as a child. She looked up to catch Sister Ignatia watching her with an expression that was, for once, devoid of impatience. What she saw there was curiosity and surprise and a particular kind of empathy that made Anna vaguely uneasy for no good reason at all.

◆　◆　◆

THE LAST CHILDREN came in a group of four. The oldest was a nine-year-old girl carrying an infant against her shoulder while she nudged two more forward. Rosa, Tonino, Lia, and Vittorio Russo all had masses of curly, dark brown hair and fair eyes that stood out against skin the color of lightly toasted bread. According to the note, their mother had died in the epidemic, and a distraught father had turned them over to the church and disappeared. No one had any idea where he might be.

Rosa Russo stood very straight with the younger children gathered close by, her free left hand on her brother's shoulder.

"I am American," she announced before any questions could be put to her. "I was born here. We all were born here. I have perfect English," she said in a rhythm that contradicted her claim.

She was a slight child in a dress two sizes too big, but despite ragged hems and collars, all four of them had been scrubbed vigorously, necks and faces and hands as clean as Anna's own. There was a dignity about her, in the line of her back and the tilt of her head. Frightened beyond all comprehension, but determined, first and foremost.

"Come," Anna said, gesturing them forward. "I promise I won't hurt you. Come."

Her voice quaking for the first time, the girl said, "We must go to find our father."

"I understand," Anna said. "But if you want to look for your father in Manhattan, I have to give you a certificate." She held up the printed form. "Otherwise they won't allow you across the river."

"There are other places to cross," the girl said calmly.

"Yes, but how will you get there? Do you have money to pay for the ferry?"

After a long moment Rosa shepherded the two middle children before her.

The older boy was very somber but cooperative, while the little sister chirped and talked nonstop, mostly in Italian with a smattering of English. When Anna's attention slipped, two small cool hands landed on her cheeks, and she looked up to find herself almost nose to nose with a very serious Lia Russo.

The little girl dropped her voice to a conspiratorial whisper and said, "*Hai occhi d'oro.*"

"She says you have golden eyes," translated Sister Mary Augustin.

Anna smiled. "My eyes are brown and green, and sometimes they look golden depending on the light."

This time Mr. Mezzanotte stepped in and translated for Anna.

Lia shook her head, firm in her opinion. "*D'oro.*"

"Well, then," Anna said. "Let me use my gold eyes to make sure you're healthy. Can you take a deep breath and hold it?"

When Mr. Mezzanotte leaned over to explain, Lia drew in a breath so fiercely and with such drama that her eyes crossed. She was healthy, and Anna was relieved. What she didn't know and couldn't tell was more complicated: did the child not know her mother was dead, or did she simply not understand what the word meant?

Finally Anna turned to Rosa Russo, who presented herself and her infant brother with an expression that was meant to be composed.

Anna said, "May I hold your brother while I examine him?"

"Mama says, no. Mama says—" She paused. "Mama said you will take him away from us, and we must stay together."

Anna considered, and then she leaned forward and lowered her voice.

"My mother died on the day I turned three, and my father a few weeks later. Every day I think about them, and what they would have expected of me."

The girl's eyes focused on Anna's face, looking for something specific there, some answer. "Did you have brothers and sisters to care for you?"

"A much older brother, who was away at school. Too young to raise a little girl. So an aunt brought me here to raise with her family."

"Your brother let you go?" Her expression was torn between shock and disdain. "Why would he give you away?"

"It was a difficult time," Anna said, her voice catching. "Much like this time is for you all."

"There is no excuse," said the girl. "He should not have let you go. Where is he now?"

"He died," Anna said. "In the war."

"He should not have left you," Rosa said, almost incensed. "He failed you, but I will not fail my sister and brothers."

Sister Mary Augustin cleared her throat, ready to speak up in defense of a brother many years in his grave, someone she had never known and could not imagine.

Anna said, "Rosa, I hope you are right. I hope you can do for your sister and brothers what my brother couldn't do for me."

◆　◆　◆

BY MIDAFTERNOON ANNA was back on the ferry with the sisters and the healthier orphans, half of whom had had their hair cut almost to the scalp to stop the spread of lice. The children who were ill—a possible case of tuberculosis and another of measles—had been left in New Jersey to be cared for, though no one could tell Anna exactly what that meant, to her disquiet. Also absent was Santino Bacigalup. Mr. Mezzanotte had arranged work for him on a farm somewhere in the countryside.

When Father Moreno returned, he voiced the same objections to this arrangement that Anna had heard from Sister Ignatia, in a tone only slightly less irritated. The pledge of a significant contribution to the poor box finally swayed him.

The priest looked at her suspiciously. "Are you trying to buy forgiveness for some sin? The Church no longer sells indulgences, Dr. Savard."

"I'm not Catholic, Father Moreno. I would guess my idea of sin isn't much like yours."

She blotted the bank draft she had written out on his desk and handed it to him.

"And Sister Ignatia? Who will explain this to her?"

"I suppose it will fall to me," Anna said. "I hope that will count as sufficient penance."

The priest's mouth quirked, stopping just short of a smile.

"The boy needs to be vaccinated," Anna said. "Before he goes to his new employer. That is possible, I trust?"

Father Moreno said, "It will be arranged."

As she was leaving he called to her, and Anna paused in the doorway.

"I don't doubt that your concerns for these children are real and your intentions good," he said. "But you are more like Sister Ignatia than you might like to admit."

• ◆ •

ON THE FERRY, surrounded by the children and the other passengers, Sister Ignatia did not hesitate to raise the issue of the Bacigalup boy. "You interfere," said the older nun. "You interfere in ways that could have terrible consequences."

"Doing nothing has terrible consequences, too," Anna said calmly.

"Do not congratulate yourself. This is not a charitable act."

"Of course it isn't," Anna said.

Sister Ignatia pulled back a little, surprised.

"No one ever does anything out of charity," Anna went on. "Every choice we make benefits ourselves directly or indirectly. Even if it looks like a sacrifice, the alternative would be unbearable in some way. If I hadn't helped I wouldn't sleep well, and I need my sleep."

Gray eyes moved over her face, looking for some clue that would account for such an odd and disturbing philosophy. "Such cynicism is unattractive in a young woman."

"That may be. But it is necessary for a doctor and a surgeon." Anna tempered her tone with a small smile.

After a moment Sister Ignatia said, "It was a mistake to ask for your help. I won't do it again."

"That would probably be best," Anna agreed. "But I will still come and make sure everyone is vaccinated."

• • •

ONE BENCH FARTHER on, Giancarlo Mezzanotte was in deep discussion with Rosa Russo. Wedged between the man and girl were Tonino and Lia, while Rosa still carried the infant.

There was something familiar about the man's posture, though Anna was certain she had never met him before. When he inclined his head toward Rosa to listen more closely, she realized that he held himself like a doctor taking a patient's history, weighing and measuring each piece of information, not because he thought the child was lying, but because her tone and expression told him more than her words ever could.

It was an odd thought. The man was still dressed in his work clothes; he might be a carpenter or a stonemason or even a mill worker himself, but unlike most men of her acquaintance, he had a talent for talking to children. Which probably meant he had children of his own or had grown up with many brothers and sisters. Or as an orphan.

He looked over his shoulder as if she had reached out to tap it and raised one brow. Somehow he had heard her unvoiced questions.

Anna gave a brief shake of her head. When he turned away again she asked Sister Mary Augustin the question she couldn't hold back. "What kind of farm is Santino Bacigalup going to be working on?"

But Mr. Mezzanotte had heard her. He turned around again, hooking his elbow over the back of the bench to speak to her directly. He had a very deep and resonant voice, but he still had to raise it to

be heard. "I sent him to my parents. They are floriculturists and apiarists. Beekeepers."

The urge to tell him that she knew the meaning of *apiarists* and
didn't need a definition was strong, but she bit down on it, banishing
with it the long list of questions that sprang to mind. Such as, if this
man farmed in New Jersey, why was he on his way to Manhattan? And
why did he speak as though he had been educated for work other than
farming?

"I see I neglected to introduce you properly," Sister Ignatia said
dryly. "Dr. Savard, this is Detective Sergeant Mezzanotte. Of the
New York Police Department." Her jaw set hard, as though she had
to bite the words off to let them go.

An unexpected turn, but it made sense to Anna. He had a natural
authority and an air of quiet competence. What he lacked was the
condescension that she had encountered in police when she dealt
with them professionally.

"I was under the impression that most of the detectives are Irishmen."

He flashed a smile that changed the very shape of his face. A
wide, honest, open smile that felt to Anna like a physical touch.

He said, "That's true, the police force is primarily Irish."

"Just as most physicians are men," said Sister Ignatia, which put
an end to the conversation.

Anna had the distinct feeling that the older sister liked the detective
sergeant and thought well of him. More than that, she seemed to believe
that he needed to be protected from her, Anna Savard. She might have
calmed the nun's uneasiness by assuring her that she had no interest in
the detective sergeant, and even if she did, she had never learned how to
flirt with any degree of comfort. It occurred to her then that she wished
she could flirt with him, just to see Sister Ignatia's reaction.

Sister Mary Augustin brought her out of her thoughts. "I'm glad
Detective Mezzanotte is here to explain things to the little girl. To
prepare her. It's terrible when it comes as a surprise."

Anna's attention shifted to the four Russo children. Despite Rosa's
sincere intentions, they would not be able to stay together. The orphanages were segregated by sex, so that Rosa and her sister would go in

one direction while her brothers went in another. Most likely they would lie to her to make the separation less troublesome, Anna was well aware. They would tell her that she'd see the boys again soon.

People told lies to children as they told fairy tales, with complete certainty that disbelief would be suspended. Rosa Russo was not likely to be so easily misled. Anna wondered if she would lash out or beg or weep, or if she would keep her dignity as a way to protect the three children she saw as her responsibility. She would fight, that Anna knew with certainty.

The agents of the health department were waiting at the dock, middle-aged men with great showers of facial hair, scowling even before the first of the orphans came onto the dock.

Anna set off at a brisk clip, not stopping to take leave of anyone at all.

◆   ◆   ◆

AFTER FOUR YEARS of study at the New York Woman's Medical School and another four years in the clinics, hospitals, asylums, and orphanages of Manhattan, Sophie Élodie Savard had earned the title of doctor. And still, when the door of the clapboard house on Charles Street opened to her knock, Sophie introduced herself to the man standing there without any title at all.

Archer Campbell had an unruly head of red hair and skin that was almost translucent, as tender as a child's. He was a slight man, the kind who would never grow fat no matter how well he ate. His hands, large and as hard as a drover's, were ink-stained.

A man might be distracted or distraught or coolheaded when his wife was in labor, but Mr. Campbell seemed mostly irritated. He scowled to learn that the doctor whose fees he had been paying was not coming. Instead there was a woman, and worse still: a free woman of color, as Sophie had been taught to think of herself as a girl in New Orleans. One with a calm, professional demeanor who was well spoken and willing to look a man straight in the eye.

Mr. Campbell was the kind who would have just closed the door in Sophie's face had the note she held out not tripped his curiosity. This one was scrawled under the letterhead of the New York Women's Hospital and was short to the point of rudeness:

My dear Mr. Campbell:

Miss Savard is come in my place because I have been unavoidably detained. She is an excellent practitioner with much experience, and she asks only half my fee.

Dr. Frank F. Heath

As was usually the case, the combination of the low moan issuing from the back of the house, the note, and the lowered fee bought her entrance.

Sophie glanced back at the driver who had brought her. She had paid him to wait an hour in case she needed to send for assistance, but she wouldn't be surprised to find him gone as soon as she turned her back. She would have to send Mr. Campbell himself, if it came to that. It almost made her smile to imagine the affronted face he would make if she had to give him orders.

The house was small but beautifully kept, nothing out of order, every surface polished, fresh curtains at the windows. While Sophie went about the business at hand, her patient's husband blustered at her and muttered to himself, his eyes turning again and again to the clock on the mantel as he paced up and down, chewing on a cigar stump. He wouldn't allow her to close the door to the room where his wife labored, and so he was there every time she looked up. Sophie wondered whether it was his wife's labor or the fact that he had no place to sleep that accounted for his growing irritation.

"The first three gave her no trouble." He stopped in the doorway to interrogate her some hours later. "Why is this one taking so long?"

"This child is very large," she told him. "But your wife is strong and the baby's heartbeat is steady. It will just take longer than you might have hoped."

It was a relief when he left for work.

Mrs. Campbell said, "I never wanted Dr. Heath. He's so rough." She had an accent Sophie thought of as New England, her vowels abrupt and all r-sounds clipped away. "I wanted a midwife, but Mr. Camp-bell"—she glanced into the empty hall and still whispered, as if her husband could hear her from anywhere in the city—"Mr. Campbell thought the wife of someone of his high position must have a doctor."

Because there was nothing she could say to such a statement, Sophie asked instead about swaddling clothes and clouts and a basin.

"You sound strange," Mrs. Campbell said to Sophie. "Not American."

"French is my first language."

"Mine too."

Sophie turned in surprise.

"I was born and raised in Benedicta, in Maine," Mrs. Campbell said. "Lots of Francophones in Benedicta, but I moved to Bangor when I was fifteen, and I gave it up for English."

Sophie said, "I came here as a child from New Orleans." She hoped that the contraction that began to peak would distract her patient from this line of questioning, but Mrs. Campbell picked up where she had left off.

"I've never seen anyone with your coloring. Your eyes are such an odd shade of green, and your skin—"

"I am a free woman of color," Sophie interrupted. And at the blank expression Mrs. Campbell gave her: "My grandparents were French and Seminole and African, but I have never been a slave."

A frown jerked at the corner of Mrs. Campbell's mouth. "Not white," she said. "But your hair—they've got a name for somebody like you, I just can't—"

Sophie interrupted. "I was very young. I remember almost nothing of New Orleans."

Which was a lie. She had been ten full years old when she left the city of her birth, and she remembered far too clearly what New Orleans had been, the smell of seawater and bougainvillea, how cool the tile was under her feet when she played in the courtyard, the children's rhymes that still came to her now and then when she was very tired. She remembered the sound of her father's voice and the way he cleared his throat before he said something he thought would make her laugh. She remembered her mother's tone when she was happy and when she was worried and when she decided she had enough of work and wanted to go exploring and Sophie to come with her. She remembered the baker's wife who came from the islands and told stories of the Iwa of Saint-Domingue, and Jacinthe who had only

three teeth but ruled the kitchen and could make the servants tremble with a look. She remembered the quality of light that fell across
her bed when she woke in the morning.

She remembered the war and the way the ground shook and the
air itself seemed to scream. And when the worst had passed and
everything and everyone was gone, she remembered the day Mrs.
Jamison came to fetch her away from home. They boarded the steam-
boat *Queen Esther* on the big wide muddy green Mississippi and she
watched the city disappear behind her.

Sophie would not share her story with Mrs. Campbell because
people—most especially white people—born and raised in the north
could not, would not understand what New Orleans had been. Sophie
hardly understood it herself.

But her unwillingness to answer questions roused her patient's
suspicions. Between contractions she wanted to know how long
Sophie had been a midwife, how many births she had attended. A
deep line had appeared between her brows. "You do have training, I
hope. Dr. Heath wouldn't send someone without training."

"Yes," Sophie said, unable to keep the sharp edge out of her voice.
"I am a fully trained physician."

There was a startled pause. "Oh come now," Janine Campbell said
with a half laugh. "You don't believe that yourself."

Sophie could have recited the names of the seven black women
who graduated from medical schools in Philadelphia and Montreal
and New York before her, but it would do no good; she could no more
relieve Mrs. Campbell of her willful ignorance than her labor pains.
Instead she said, "I'm going to make you some tea that will help
move this child along."

• • •

MIDMORNING SOPHIE PUT a large, very loud boy with tufts of gin-
gery curls in his mother's arms. Mrs. Campbell, panting still, lay
back against the pillows and closed her eyes.

"He's a fine healthy baby," Sophie said. "Alert and vigorous."

"He is disgustingly fat," said his mother. "I wanted a girl."

The baby rooted and found the nipple; she arched her back as
though to dislodge a pest and let out a small shuddering sound.

As Sophie worked to deliver the afterbirth Mrs. Campbell lay staring at the ceiling and ignoring the infant at her breast. From the window Sophie had opened came the sound of the street on a busy Monday morning. Horse carts, omnibuses, hand trucks; knife sharpeners and fishmongers calling out for customers, the wind rocking the spindly apple trees that took up most of the tiny yard behind the house. Nearby a dog barked a warning.

Sophie hummed to herself while she bathed the baby, cleaned his umbilicus, dressed and swaddled him. He was solid and hot and full of life, and he had been born to a mother who could see him only as a burden.

There were tears running down Mrs. Campbell's face to wet the pillow when Sophie put her child back into her arms.

Women cried after giving birth for all kinds of reasons. Joy, relief, excitement, terror. Mrs. Campbell's tears were none of those. She was exhausted and frustrated and on the edge of the dark place where new mothers sometimes went for days or weeks. Some never returned.

"I don't like to cry," she announced to the ceiling. "You'll think me weak."

"I think no such thing," Sophie said. "I imagine you must be very worn out. Do you have no sisters or relatives to help you? Four little children and a household is more than anyone should have to manage without help."

"Archer says his mother raised six boys and never had a girl to help. He told me so when he first came courting, back home, that was. I wish I had thought it all through right then and there. I'd still be working at the Bangor post office. In my good shirtwaist with a sprig of forsythia pinned to my collar."

The most Sophie could do for her was to listen.

"The worst of it is, he wants six sons of his own. It's a competition with his brothers, and I fear he won't let up. He'll keep me breeding until he's satisfied. Or I'm dead."

As Sophie worked, Mrs. Campbell told her things she would be embarrassed to remember in a few hours. If Sophie said nothing, the new mother would be free to forget about the secrets she had whispered, and to whom she had said them.

Mrs. Campbell was drifting off to a well-earned sleep when she suddenly shook herself awake.

"Have you heard about Dr. Garrison?"

Sophie was glad she was facing away in that moment, because it gave her a chance to school her expression.

"Yes," she said. "I've followed along in the newspaper."

There was a long silence. When she turned around Mrs. Campbell said, "If you are a physician, could you—"

"No," Sophie interrupted her. "I'm sorry."

Mrs. Campbell heard only the regret in Sophie's voice, and she pushed harder. "Another one too soon will kill me, I know it. I have money saved—"

Sophie set her face in uncompromising lines as she turned. "By law I can't even talk to you about contraceptives or—anything similar. I can't give you a name or an address. If you know about Mrs. Garrison, you must know that the mails are not safe."

Mrs. Campbell closed her eyes and nodded. "I do know about the mails," she said. "Of course I know. Mr. Campbell makes sure that I know."

Sophie swallowed the bile that rose into her throat and reminded herself what was at stake.

2

WHEN THEY HAD shepherded the children off the ferry, Mary Augustin let out a sigh of relief to discover that there were three omnibuses waiting for them. Even better, as far as she was concerned, were the four sisters who had come to help with almost thirty desperately frightened and unhappy children. Ten children and two sisters in each omnibus was manageable. Sister Ignatia was difficult in many ways, but she had no equal when it came to planning.

Mary Augustin had just crouched down to encourage a trembling and teary six-year-old called Georgio when an older man came off the ferry, walking very slowly. As soon as he was on solid ground he simply sat down where he stood and began to fan himself with his hat. There was sweat on his brow and his color was ashen. This might be simple seasickness or something far worse; Mary Augustin tried to get Sister Ignatia's attention, but at that moment a scuffle broke out in the crowd of people waiting to board for the next crossing.

Two dockworkers stood nose to nose shouting at each other, both of them strapped with muscle and both decidedly drunk. Punches were thrown and bystanders darted out of the way, some laughing and others looking disgusted, while all the time the old man sat and fanned himself and tried to catch a breath. Mary Augustin divided her attention between moving the orphans farther away and the old man who might be having a heart attack, and so she only saw what came next from the corner of her eye.

One of the longshoremen shoved the other with such force that he went staggering back with an almost comical look of surprise on his face. Bystanders jumped out of the way of his pinwheeling arms, and in fact the man seemed to be losing momentum when his feet got caught up in someone's canvas sack. In his last desperate attempt to regain his balance he flung out both arms, and one fist slammed into Salvatore Ruggerio, eleven years old, newly orphaned, who had gone closer to watch the fight but now stood frozen with shock.

Man and boy went over the edge of the dock, backward. There was a single heartbeat of utter silence, and then the crowd erupted.

Sister Ignatia was shouting, her voice like a bullhorn over the noise. "Move the children! Get them away!"

And still Mary Augustin hesitated, turning to watch as three men, one of them in the long navy coat of a patrolman, jumped into the water. Just beyond him the old man Mary Augustin feared was having a heart attack had jumped to his feet to watch the drama, as nimble as a boy of ten.

• • •

ONE OF THE omnibuses had already left and so Mary Augustin got her charges onto the second one as quickly and calmly as could be managed. She was hesitating about whether to go see if she was needed on the dock when Sister Ignatia came marching up and grabbed her by the elbow to turn her around.

Her color was high but otherwise she wasn't even breathing hard. "The boy knocked his head. That patrolman"—she pointed with her chin—"wants the third bus to take him and that idiot drunkard to St. Vincent's." She paused as if an unwelcome thought had come to her and then shouted over her shoulder, as forceful as a general.

"Officer! We'll take the boy to St. Vincent's and nowhere else! Do you understand me?"

The patrolman, young enough to be Sister Ignatia's grandson, swallowed visibly and nodded, but she had already turned her attention back to Mary Augustin. "So you'll have to get all the rest of the children into this bus. Sister Constance will come along and you'll just have to squeeze together. I'll see about the boy—" She hesitated.

"Salvatore Ruggerio."

"Ruggerio," Sister Ignatia echoed. "And send word when I've spoken to the doctors. Now get these children away. They've seen enough."

• • •

ROSA RUSSO CONFRONTED Mary Augustin as soon as she had climbed up into the omnibus. Anger and sorrow and disappointment all vied for the upper hand, but anger won.

"My brothers," she said. "They took my brothers away."

The separation had been inevitable, but it would have been handled more sensitively if not for the chaos on the dock.

Mary Augustin said, "There are two buildings at St. Patrick's. One for girls and one for boys. You can see the boys' building just across the way, and that's where your brothers will be."

At least to start, Mary Augustin added to herself.

Since she had come to the orphan asylum she had seen children handle such separations too often to count. More often than she cared to remember. Some of them were too numb to react at all, while others collapsed or struck out. Rosa simply stood her ground. Her eyes were swimming with tears but she didn't allow them to fall. She seemed to be struggling to say something, or not to say something.

"Come sit by me," Mary Augustin said. "And I'll answer your questions as best I can."

But Rosa went back to sit next to her little sister, the two of them sharing their seat with other girls.

It was just then that she realized that the omnibus had turned from Christopher Street onto Waverly Place. She was wondering if the driver knew where he was supposed to take them when Washington Square Park came into view and she made her way forward to the box, swaying with the jerking of the bus over paving stones.

The driver was no more than a boy, but he handled the horses with ease and took no offense at her question.

"Your little ones need quieting," he said, keeping his eyes on the road and the traffic. "Upset as they are. I thought I'd take them through the park, distract them a little from that sad business at the ferry."

It was something Mary Augustin had yet to figure out, how it could be that some city dwellers were so coarse and rude, while others showed tremendous kindness and generosity of spirit. She thanked the driver and went back to her place, signaling to Sister Constance that all was well.

And in fact the children had quieted. All of them were turned toward the windows, leaning against each other to make the most of the space available, pointing to things they couldn't name. With some effort, she summoned her Italian and tried to put names to things they asked about.

They pointed to trees and walkways and children being pushed in prams, to the houses that lined Waverly Place, tall redbrick homes that must look like palaces to children who grew up in tenements.

Rosa Russo wanted to know what kind of people would live in such a place, if they were kings and queens.

"Just people," Mary Augustin told her. "Families."

Her eyes narrowing, Rosa said, "Do you know any of those families?"

Mary bit back her smile. "Not in these houses. But down the street"—she pointed down Waverly—"you see the building with the towers?"

"A church," Rosa said.

Mary Augustin was sure it wasn't a church, but neither did she know what such a grand building might be. The driver rescued her by calling over his shoulder.

"That's New York University," he said. "Looks a lot like a church, I'll grant you that."

"Rosa," Sister Mary Augustin said, "I do know somebody who lives just ahead, and so do you. Dr. Savard, who examined you before we got on the ferry. She lives a little beyond the university, with her aunt and cousin in a house with angels over the door, and a great big garden, as big as the house itself. With a pergola. And chickens."

There was absolute silence while Rosa translated for the other children, and then a dozen more questions came shooting at her. Mary Augustin answered and Rosa translated while the horses plodded forward under trees heavy with buds just beginning to open to the sun.

♦ ♦ ♦

THE DUTY SERGEANT at 333 Mulberry looked up through a twisted thicket of graying brows and ran his gaze over Jack Mezzanotte, from beard stubble down to the highly polished shoes and back again. Then he shook his head slowly, like a long-suffering teacher.

"Better get a move on, Mezzanotte. They're about to start the meeting without you."

"Had to change," Jack called over his shoulder as he sprinted up the stairs two at a time. Really he should have stopped to see the barber— he ran a hand over the bristle on his jaw—but better unshaved than late. He paused long enough to make sure that his collar was straight and slipped into the back of the room, where thirty of New York's detectives sat talking among themselves, steadfastly ignoring the men at the front of the room.

He found a chair next to his partner in the last row. Oscar Maroney had a dearly held theory, one Jack had never been able to disprove: it was best to be humorless and forgettable while in the station house. Invisibility was a valuable skill that had to be practiced. But today Maroney was violating his own rule, because the expression on his face was anything but blank. Oscar was not just unhappy, but unhappy in a way that he would not be able to keep to himself.

"Brace yourself, Jack." Maroney could summon, temper, or banish his brogue as needed, and now it simmered just below the surface. "Comstock's on the hunt for victims. Pardon, I mean volunteers." He wrinkled his substantial nose and lifted a lip at the same time so that his mustache jumped. He had a wide range of insulted, angry, accusatory, and reproachful expressions, and he used more than a few of them now.

Jack turned his attention to the front of the room, where the captain stood leaning against the wall, arms folded, chin on his chest. Front and center was the focus of Oscar's hate. Anthony Comstock, dressed as he always was, summer and winter, in a black wool suit somber enough for a pulpit.

The postal inspector was a squat, solid plug of a man with muttonchop whiskers that stood out like bristles on the face of a boar, a shiny pale pate, and a small mouth as well defined as a woman's. He had the censorious gaze of a bantam rooster, his eyes darting back and forth, ready to draw blood to keep his flock in line. Eager to draw blood. He was a bully of the first order, the worst Jack had ever seen in a career populated by bullies.

Baker knocked on the wall to get their attention, and Comstock threw his shoulders back and raised his arms like an orchestra conductor.

"My name and mission will be well known to you," he began. "I am Anthony Comstock, senior inspector of the Society for the Suppression of Vice *and* special agent to the post office by appointment of the postmaster general of the president's cabinet. I'm here to talk to you as officers of the law about a matter of grave importance."

He drew in a ponderous breath that filled his cheeks and escaped with a soft hiss.

"Any God-fearing, thinking man knows that lust is the boon companion of all other crimes. In their wisdom the Congress of this great country has vested me with the responsibility to stop the posting, sale, loan, exhibition, advertisement, publishing, dissemination, or possession of the obscene and profane. You will all be familiar with the kinds of materials I'm talking about—" He paused, brows raised, as though he hoped someone would contradict him. Jack saw now that there was a small box beside him on the desk on which he rested a fist as if to keep some vermin safely within.

"His own personal treasure chest," Maroney said in a low voice, following Jack's gaze. "The Larkin brothers are determined to have it before he leaves the building."

There were five Larkin brothers on the force, two of them sergeant detectives sitting in the front row, two more roundsmen on duty somewhere in the city, and the youngest new to the force. Good officers, for the most part, but irreverent practical jokers of the first order, a leaning that would have cost them friends if they had not practiced on each other with such obvious enjoyment. But they couldn't be called incorruptible.

Of course, Comstock was by far the biggest crook, and worse, he was spiteful, vengeful, and mean to the bone. In Comstock's case Jack could not begrudge the Larkins whatever larceny they were planning.

Comstock was saying, "It is also my duty to seize any drug or instrument of any kind that may interfere with conception or bring on abortion. Items I have seized range from informational booklets to objects made of rubber and designed for immoral purposes. The punishment for the guilty is severe. Anyone engaged in these pursuits is subject to a sentence of hard labor for a minimum of six months and a maximum of five years, and a fine of up to two thousand dollars."

He paused to survey the room. Most of the squad looked back at him as if they were deaf and hadn't taken in a word, while a few others—Maroney among them—were openly contemptuous.

"In the last years we agents of the New York Society for the Suppression of Vice have seized and destroyed more than twenty-five tons of obscene tracts and photographs, six hundred pounds of books, some twenty thousand stereopticon plates, almost a hundred thousand rubber articles, six hundred decks of indecent playing cards, forty thousand pounds of aphrodisiacs, and eight tons of gambling and lottery materials." He looked around the room but did not find the acknowledgment he believed his due. He coughed nervously and went on in a grimmer tone.

"Today I am here to recruit detectives to assist in fighting an epidemic that is raging across this country. A disease being spread by medical practitioners themselves. And not just charlatans or low men, no. Doctors, nurses, druggists, and midwives supply information and instructions on contraceptive methods to any woman who asks—and worse, they will sell syringes and rubber caps and the like without compunction or shame.

"And then there are abortionists. I have been able to bring only a small portion of these criminals to justice. It is a slow process. Regrettably slow. Our success rate must be improved, by whatever means necessary." He smirked, openly prideful. "You'll remember the abortionist Madame Dubois, I'm sure."

Jack had allowed his mind to wander off to other matters, but with the mention of Madame Dubois his attention snapped back to Comstock. The man had hooked his thumbs in the lapels of his coat and was rocking back and forth on his heels, delighted with himself.

"Rather than submit to the authority of the court," Comstock went on with his satisfied smirk, "Dubois put a bullet in her brain and saved us the cost of bringing her to trial. She was not the first such sinner to end her own life, and if I have my way, she will not be the last."

Oscar jumped to his feet.

"And you call yourself a Christian, you sanctimonious overweening godforsaken bag of shite!"

Oscar was a big man with the look of a brawler, the kind who dealt out pain but didn't feel his own broken knuckles and torn flesh until the storm was done. Comstock, shorter and softer, still didn't flinch, which went along with his reputation as a brawler of another kind. He carried a pistol, and he liked to use it.

Baker put a stop to it with a shout. "Maroney!"

Oscar's posture relaxed just enough to let Jack know he was in control of himself. Then he turned on his heel and pushed past the row of men on his way out, cursing in the most spectacular manner. The door slammed behind him with such force that the glass in the windowpanes rattled.

"Did you hear that man?" Comstock barked at Baker. "I demand that he be officially reprimanded for his foul and profane language!"

"That's one of the officers who found your Mrs. Dubois in a bathtub full of her own blood," Baker said. "His first day on the job, it was. Now why don't you just get on with it. We don't have all day."

Comstock huffed, his mouth twitching. With a voice gone hoarse he said, "I'll do that, but assured. I'll report him for his profanity and you for failing to check it." He scowled expressively at his audience, as if he had demonstrated an important lesson they should remember.

"As you are aware," he went on, "police officers do not always see through the elaborate screens set up by these medical practitioners who are so contemptuous of the laws of God and man. But I believe that detectives are equal to this challenge and I would like all of you to volunteer to serve as agents of the Society for the Suppression—"

Baker said, "The time, Mr. Comstock."

Comstock whirled around to glare at Baker—captain of New York City's detective squad—as if he were a young boy caught with his finger up his nose.

"Captain Baker! You agreed to let me address the detectives. There is a meeting of the society this evening and new volunteers must attend."

"And I specifically told you that you could not ask for volunteers, not tonight. More than half these men are working double shifts and none of them will see their beds until tomorrow. They are on special assignment."

"Special assignment? Special? By whose definition? May I remind you, Captain, that the Congress of the United States has vested me with—"

"Mr. Comstock—"

"Inspector Comstock! Inspector!" he roared, spittle flying. "You will give me my title!"

"Inspector Comstock," Baker said, coolly. "Allow me to answer your questions one at a time. I find it hard to believe you don't know what's happening on Fifth Avenue tonight. The Vanderbilts' costume ball begins in a few hours. A third of the city's uniformed officers will be there to control the crowds, and more than half these detectives will be patrolling the area in plain clothes. Those orders came to us by order of the mayor, the governor, and the senators of the state."

Comstock's fleshy mouth jerked and puckered. "Where are your priorities, sir? Do you put the petty concerns of the dissolute rich above the welfare of the youth of this city? These men are not needed on Fifth Avenue, I can assure you. Where are your morals?"

"My morals are as sturdy as your own," Baker said dryly. "And my priorities are set by my superiors. I suggest you take this up with them, because I cannot accommodate you or your society."

◆ ◆ ◆

In the detectives' squad room Maroney sat slumped, his legs stretched out before him like felled trees. A cigar was anchored beneath a mustache as glossy and thick as a badger's pelt.

Jack said, "Sometimes I regret the captain's sangfroid. I think with very little effort he might have caused Comstock's head to explode just where he stood. An opportunity missed."

"I would have liked to see that." The cigar jerked with every word.

Jack sat at his desk to contemplate the stacks of paper needing his attention.

"I'm sure we could sell tickets at a premium to see that baboon's head fly apart like a pumpkin," said Maroney. "Set up chairs for the audience. Parasols, for the splatter."

"The man has friends," Jack reminded his partner.

"Not true," Maroney said. "He has lackeys. He has compatriots. He even has admirers. But if he didn't carry that pistol in his vest and the postmaster general in his pocket, he'd be easy enough to squash. As it is I wait daily for someone to put a bullet in his noggin."

Jack said, "You're forgetting about the Young Men's Christian Association and his Society for the Suppression of Vice."

Maroney waved his cigar like a magic wand that could make short work of such pallid adversaries. He was hoisting himself up and out of his chair when the door flew open and Michael Larkin dashed in, Comstock's box of confiscated dirty pictures clamped under one arm. Without a word to either of them he leapt onto a desk, unlatched a high cupboard with one hand, and shoved the box in with the other.

Larkin was sitting at the same desk bent over a piece of paper when a patrolman came in, not a week in uniform. The kid ducked his head apologetically.

"Baker wants the whole station house searched," he said. "Can I come in?"

He made a quick and superficial job of it, only glancing in Michael Larkin's direction before he excused himself again and left.

There was a long silence.

Maroney cleared his throat. "Michael, my friend. Not on duty tonight?"

"No," came the answer. The eldest of the Larkin brothers looked up at them and winked. "All of a sudden I've got quite a lot of reading to do."

"Just out of the blue," said Jack.

"Fell into my lap," Larkin agreed amiably. "So to speak. Would you care to have a look yourself?"

Jack leaned back in his chair and propped his feet up on the desk. It had been a long day, starting at dawn in the greenhouses at home. He thought of the ferry, of ferocious Sister Ignatia and the orphans, of the lady doctor. Savard, they had called her.

He bent over the report in front of him but his mind stayed focused on that unusual face, Elizabeth or Mary, Ida or Edith or Helen. He fished the city directory out of a drawer and flipped through the pages until he found two listings: Sophie E. Savard and Liliane M. Savard living at the same address. Another mystery. One he would be looking into as soon as he could get away from Oscar.

◆ ◆ ◆

WHEN ANNA CAME within sight of Washington Square she realized how tired she was. Surgery was hard work, physically and mentally exhausting, but even the most challenging case had nothing on Sister Ignatia and a crowd of orphans.

Coming home was like shedding a coat with bricks loaded into every pocket and sewn into the hem. The tension that had collected in her shoulders and back began to abate even before the house came into sight. Some days she might lament the demands of her profession, but she loved the house and garden on Waverly Place without a single reservation. During the year she spent in Europe, Anna had worked herself to exhaustion every day so that she could sleep at night in strange houses in stranger cities. In the end she had learned a great deal, about both surgery and herself. She belonged here, and nowhere else.

Anna went around the back, past the small carriage house and stable and the icehouse, stopping in the garden to say hello to Mr. Lee, who was turning soil in a steady, studied rhythm. Mr. Lee was a serious, fastidious, and deeply affectionate man. He had taught her how to tell weed from seedling, to button her shoes and tie a slip-knot, how to slip eggs from under a hen without being pecked, and he knew a hundred ballads that he was happy to recite or sing. With a perfectly straight face Mr. Lee had taught her and Sophie a dozen tongue twisters that still made them laugh. Anna knew that if she was patient, he would observe things in his quiet way that he meant for her to hear.

Now he looked at the sky and predicted that contrary to appearances, winter had not given over. It was an odd turn of phrase, as though the winter were a bear getting ready for a long hibernation. To his shovel he remarked that neighbors who had already begun to clear away mulch would regret it. One more hard frost was coming, and it would take every unprotected tender new thing in the world. It would mean the end of the crocus and delicate Turkish tulips that had begun to raise their heads, a scattering like jewels all through the fallow beds and lawn.

Mr. Lee was seldom wrong about the weather, but just at the moment Anna couldn't worry about such things. Not while she stood in the garden, knowing that in another month it would be warm enough to sit in the pergola in the soft shadow of blossoming apple and tulip trees.

The garden was her favorite place in the world. As a little girl, before Sophie, she had had the garden to herself until the war took that away, too. When their father fell in battle, Uncle Quinlan's grandchildren were at the house most days, and from them she had learned what it meant to share more than toys and books and stories.

Someplace along the way Anna had fallen into the habit of calling Aunt Quinlan *Grandma*, but the summer she turned nine Uncle Quinlan's grandson Isaac Cooper, just a year older, had taken it upon himself to correct her. In a quavering and still strident voice he made himself clear: she had no grandparents, no parents, nobody, and he would not allow her to claim his grandmother as her own. To Anna she could be nothing more than Aunt Quinlan.

She hadn't been a child given to weeping or one who retreated when play got rough. What kept her temper in check was the look on Isaac's face, and the brimming tears he dashed away with an impatient hand. Anna told herself that he hadn't really meant to be so mean; he had lost father and grandfather and two uncles to the war, after all, and news of his father's death had come not three months ago.

Beyond that, he was both wrong and right. Isaac's mother was Uncle Quinlan's daughter and Aunt Quinlan's stepdaughter, which meant that Isaac and Levi were not related to Aunt Quinlan by blood, as Anna certainly was. On the other hand, it did no good to pretend that she still had what was lost, and so she kept the sting of Isaac's words to herself.

But Aunt Quinlan knew, because Isaac himself told her. He went to her, teary eyed, righteous in his indignation that Anna would try to take his grandmother from him. Anna never knew what Aunt Quinlan had said to him, how she had put his mind to rest, but that evening she called Anna into her little parlor, gave her a cup of hot chocolate, and waited while she sipped it. Then she simply pulled Anna into her lap and held her until the tears came and finally ended, leaving her boneless and trembling.

Anna said, "I want Uncle Quinlan back."

"So do I," said her aunt. "I still hear him coming up the stairs, and it's always a terrible moment when I realize it was just wishful thinking. You know he would have come home to us if it had been in his power."

Come home to us. To us.

Anna nodded, her throat too swollen with tears to allow even a single word.

Then Aunt Quinlan had hugged her tighter. "You are my own dear little sister's sweetest girl," she said. "And you belong here with me. When we lost your ma and then your da, every one of us wanted you, all the brothers and sisters. But I was the lucky one, you came home with me. And you may call me anything you like, including Grandma. My ma, your grandma, would have wanted you to, and I would be honored."

But Anna couldn't. After that summer the word wouldn't come out of her mouth, whether Isaac was there or not. From then on the woman who was as good as a mother and grandmother to her was Aunt Quinlan, no more or less.

The garden might have lost its magic for her then, but for Cap. He wouldn't allow her to withdraw. Her friend, her schoolmate, another war orphan living with an aunt. Together they spent every minute in the garden planning adventures and launching schemes, reading stories out loud, playing croquet and checkers and Old Maid and eating, always eating whatever the garden had to offer: strawberries, persimmons, quince, apricots the color of the setting sun, blackberries that cascaded over the fence in late summer heat and stained fingers and lips and pinafores. When it rained they were in the pergola, which was outside and inside at the same time, a shadowy bower that smelled of lilac or heliotrope or roses, according to the season.

And then Sophie had come from New Orleans, and together the three of them had made an island where Isaac held no sway. And so it had been long after they left childhood behind, until just two years ago.

Mr. Lee broke into her daydreams by clearing his throat.

"Do you mark me, Miss Anna?" He smiled at her, a lopsided curl to his mouth. "Don't put away your winter things yet," he said. "Spring's in no rush this year, and neither should you be."

And now she had to go into the house and have tea and then dinner, and instead of going to bed she would have to dress in the costume Aunt Quinlan had arranged for her, and go out into the night with Cap, to the Vanderbilts' fancy dress ball. Because Cap was her friend, and he needed her.

3

AUNT QUINLAN'S PARLOR was comfortable and completely out of fashion; no slick horsehair sofas or rock-hard bolsters encrusted with beadwork, no bulky, heavily carved furniture to collect dust and crowd them all together. Instead the walls were crowded with paintings and drawings and the chairs and sofas were agreeably deep and soft, covered in velvet the dusky blue of delphinium in July.

Sitting together with her aunt and Sophie and her cousin Margaret, Anna was glad of the respite. For a few minutes there was no talk beyond the passing around of seedcake and scones, teacups and milk jugs.

Her stomach growled loudly enough to be heard even by Margaret, who was bound by convention and simply refused to hear such things.

She said, "You haven't eaten at all today, have you." Margaret was, strictly regarded, not a cousin at all. She was Aunt Quinlan's stepdaughter, raised in this very house by Uncle Quinlan and her mother, his first wife. Two years ago her sons had come into the money left by their father, and set off for Europe almost immediately. Because Margaret missed them so, Anna and Sophie must bear the brunt of her frustrated maternal instincts.

"She'll eat now," Aunt Quinlan said. "Mrs. Lee, could you please bring Anna a plate of something filling?" Then she held out an arm to gesture Anna closer.

At eighty-nine the symmetry of Aunt Quinlan's bone structure was more pronounced than ever. It didn't matter that the skin over those perfect cheekbones worked like the finest silk gauze, carefully folded into tiny pleats and left to dry that way; she was beautiful, and could be nothing less. Her hair was a deep and burnished silver, a color that set off the bright blue of her eyes. Her very observant eyes.

Right now they were full of simple pleasure to have both Anna and Sophie home for tea at once.

When Anna leaned over to kiss her cheek, Aunt Quinlan patted her gingerly. Her arthritis was very bad today; Anna knew that without asking because Auntie's teacup sat untouched on the low table before her.

To Sophie Anna said, "Difficult delivery last night?"

"Just drawn out." Her tone said it was a topic that should wait until they were alone. If Margaret were not here they could talk about things medical, because Aunt Quinlan was always interested and nothing surprised her. But Margaret was alarmingly weak of stomach and squeamish, as if she had never borne children herself.

"What about you?" Sophie asked. "Any interesting surgeries?"

"None at all," Anna said. "I spent most of the day with the sisters from St. Patrick's picking up orphans in Hoboken."

Sophie's mouth fell open only to shut again with an audible snap. "Sister Ignatia? Why on earth—"

"Because I promised you that if one of the sisters came to call I would go attend."

"Oh, no." Sophie was trying not to smile, and failing. "I was expecting Sister Thomasina from St. Vincent de Paul." She pressed her lips hard together but a laugh still escaped her with a puff of air.

"What an interesting turn of events," Aunt Quinlan said. She looked more closely at Anna. "You and the infamous Sister Ignatia together all day long, I wonder that you're still standing."

"Maybe Sister Ignatia isn't," Margaret suggested. "Anna might have been the end of her." Margaret's tone was a little sharp, as it always was when the subject of the Roman Catholic Church was raised. She folded her hands at her waist—corseted down to a waspish twenty inches though Margaret was more than forty—and waited. She was looking for an argument. Anna sometimes enjoyed arguing with her aunt's stepdaughter, but she had things to do.

"I suppose it is funny," she said. "We certainly . . . clashed. Now should I worry about Sister Thomasina? Did she come to call this morning?"

"No," said Aunt Quinlan. "Apparently our daily allotment of nuns was met with the Sisters of Charity."

Margaret cleared her throat. She said, "I had a letter from Isaac and Levi today. Would you like to hear it?"

It wasn't like Margaret to give up an argument so easily, and now Anna understood why. She loved nothing more than letters from her two sons. They all enjoyed the letters, which were long and entertaining. This time Levi had done the writing, and they heard about climbing in the Dolomites, a difficult journey to Innsbruck, a long essay about laundry, and how each nation distinguished itself on the way underclothes were folded and how the bedding smelled.

It was good to see Margaret so pleased about her letter. And maybe, Anna reasoned to herself, maybe while she was distracted it would be possible to slip away before she remembered the ball and more to the point, the costume Anna was going to wear to the ball.

She was almost out the door when Margaret called after her. "When is Cap coming to fetch you, Anna?"

"I'm going to stop for him, as he's on the way," Anna said, inching away. "At half past ten. Things don't get started until eleven."

• ♦ •

ONCE UPSTAIRS SOPHIE said, "The longer you make Margaret wait and wonder about your costume, the more outraged she's going to be."

"But she does so enjoy ruffling her feathers," Anna said. "Who am I to disappoint her?"

She followed Sophie into her room and stretched out on the bed with its simple coverlet of pale yellow embroidered with ivy in soft gray-greens. When they were schoolgirls they did this every afternoon, meeting in one bedroom or the other to talk before they launched themselves into chores and homework and play.

Sophie took off her shoes with an uncharacteristic impatience and fell onto the bed, facedown.

Her voice came muffled. "How bad was Sister Ignatia really?"

Anna crossed her arms over her waist and considered her answer. "It's a sorry business, what goes on with orphans. It reminds me how fortunate I was. We both were."

"We were," Sophie agreed. "We are."

"I knew in the abstract, of course. But those children were terrified. And Sister Ignatia—" She sat up suddenly. "I'm going to vaccinate children tomorrow, at the orphanage. I have no idea how many." When she had told Sophie about her confrontation with the nun, there was a small silence.

"Anna," Sophie said. "You know there are at least ten Roman Catholic orphanages in the city, small and large. St. Patrick's is the biggest, and it has beds for two thousand children or more."

That brought Anna up short.

"I'll have to come with you," Sophie said finally. "If there are less than a hundred, we can manage."

"And if there are more," Anna said, "I will pay a call to the Board of Health."

Sophie gave a soft laugh. "Sister Ignatia will regret underestimating you."

"I doubt Sister Ignatia has many regrets."

There was a long silence and then Sophie said, "Have you ever seen your face when you're angry at the way a patient has been treated?"

Anna collapsed back against the pillows, and a low laugh escaped her.

"You are not saying that I frighten Sister Ignatia, of all people."

"Of course you do." Sophie yawned. "It's why you're so effective."

"So then we'll go tomorrow afternoon," Anna said. "I need to be in surgery in the morning."

"Clara's hearing is tomorrow afternoon at the Tombs. Did you forget?"

For a long moment Anna was quiet, trying to think of a way to do two things at once in different parts of the city. She had to be at Dr. Garrison's hearing, to show her support and respect for a colleague and former professor. There was no help for it.

"I'll write to Sister Ignatia and reschedule for Wednesday afternoon. Unless I'm forgetting something else?"

When Sophie didn't answer, Anna turned on her side to look at her directly. She said, "What happened today, really?"

"Mrs. Campbell asked about Clara."

Anna felt herself tense. "And?"

"I can dissemble when necessary," Sophie said. "I said that yes, I had read about Dr. Garrison's arrest. And then I made it clear that I do not have contraceptives—"

"—or know—"

"—or know how to find them or information about them, and that I observe all laws to the letter."

Which was no protection at all, both Anna and Sophie knew. Just the previous week Clara Garrison had been arrested for the third time simply because she had answered the door to a man distraught about his wife's health and offered him a booklet of information. But the next knock—not five minutes later—brought postal inspectors and uniformed police officers.

After Clara had been arrested and taken away to the Tombs, the inspectors had searched her home and practice in the most destructive manner possible. They found an envelope sitting in plain sight on her desk with a half dozen of the same informational pamphlets she had given to Comstock's undercover inspector, as well as two new female syringes.

Clara Garrison had been the lecturer in obstetrics at the Woman's Medical School when Anna and Sophie were students. She was an excellent practitioner and teacher, and utterly uncompromising when it came to patient care. Sophie had a theory that Clara Garrison had once been a nun; she had the energy, high standards, and quiet efficiency Sophie associated with the sisters who had taught her as a child in New Orleans. It was from Clara that they had learned what it meant to care for the most vulnerable.

It was Clara's good fortune that for both her previous arrests the grand jury had simply refused to issue an indictment. This time she had not been so lucky, and tomorrow she would appear in court to answer the charges Anthony Comstock had gone to so much trouble to secure.

"I want to send a pamphlet to Mrs. Campbell anonymously," Sophie said. "She is truly desperate."

"Yes," Anna said, resigned to the necessity that they do at least this much. "And then what will we do when she comes looking for pessaries or a syringe or a dutch cap?"

It was the most difficult problem they faced. A problem without a solution, and repercussions that were all too real: at one extreme another child might be born into a family of six or eight or more, living in a single room without a window or a privy. On the other extreme were the midwives and doctors who might be sent to prison or harassed until nothing remained of their careers. One day Sophie or Anna could very well misstep and end up in front of Judge Benedict, Anthony Comstock's partner in his endless crusade against empty wombs. The two of them would smirk and frown and see to it that the defendant suffered the maximum possible embarrassment and personal and professional damage.

For a half hour she and Sophie spoke very little, drifting in and out of a light sleep. The house was peaceful, and Anna might have fallen into a deeper sleep and stayed there until morning, if not for the wail rising up the stairwell. It catapulted them out of bed and into the hall, where they leaned over the banister.

•   •   •

COUSIN MARGARET STOOD in the foyer with a delivery boy who was holding a flat, square box in both hands.

Brown packing paper had been torn away, revealing the gilded frame of an oil portrait familiar to everyone in the household.

"Oh dear," Sophie said. "Isn't that Mrs. Parker's delivery boy? What is he doing with one of Auntie's paintings?"

"Returning it," Anna said. "Mrs. Parker was using it as a model for—"

"Your ball gown." Sophie bit her lip, but the smile was there and would not be held back.

Cousin Margaret looked up and caught sight of them. "Not Countess Turchaninov!" Horrified, as Anna had known she would be.

"I'm afraid so," Anna said.

"But you'll be half-naked!"

The delivery boy shuffled his feet.

Margaret said, "But your aunt Quinlan said she sent Countess Turchaninov out to be cleaned."

Anna didn't doubt that at all; Aunt Quinlan wasn't above misdirecting attention if it helped her with a plan.

"I believe the canvas was cleaned," Anna told her. "Before it went to the seamstress. Mrs. Parker had it for two weeks, at least."

Margaret threw up her hands in disgust and disappeared down the hall to the kitchen.

"I wanted to go as the warrior queen Boadicea," Anna said on a sigh, "but Aunt Quinlan talked me out of it and into Countess Turchaninov. What there is of her."

The boy cleared his throat. "You'll pardon me, but I'm after getting this receipt signed. It don't matter which one of youse signs it. It don't matter that your countess here is wearing a night rail; if I'm not away with a signed receipt the mistress will box my ears, so she will."

Mrs. Lee came marching down the hall, took the receipt from the boy, fished a pencil out of her apron pocket, and signed with a flourish. The boy grabbed the receipt and the coin that Mrs. Lee offered with one hand, tipped his cap with the other, and dashed down the hall to the service entrance in the rear.

Mrs. Lee looked up at Anna and shook her head in disapproval.

"I won't be alone," Anna reminded her. "There's no need to worry about me."

Mrs. Lee scowled. "If you're Countess Turchaninov, who is Cap going to be?"

Anna lifted a shoulder. "I have no idea."

"You can be sure of one thing," said Sophie, her mouth twitching toward a smile. "It's not Cap people will be looking at."

❖ ❖ ❖

AT TEN SOPHIE went with Anna to watch as Aunt Quinlan examined her.

She was sitting in the upholstered chair that allowed her to look out onto the street, with a gaslight flickering on the wall behind her and a book in her lap, unopened. This was the way Sophie always thought of her aunt, sitting in the high-backed chair, turning toward the door to see who had come to call.

She said, "Take off the wrap, Anna. Let me see you."

"She promised Margaret she would wear the shawl all evening," Sophie volunteered even as Anna undid the clasp. The shawl fell away and she caught it over one arm, the beading clicking softly.

"And wouldn't that be a waste," Aunt Quinlan said. She made a turning gesture with her hand, and Anna complied, catching sight of the painting of the countess, returned to her usual spot on the wall. Countess Turchaninov had blond hair wrapped in ribbons, a pert mouth like a strawberry, and a tiny dimpled chin. Anna looked nothing like her, but the gown suited her anyway.

"Mrs. Parker had to work on it full time for a week, but it was worth it," Aunt Quinlan said. "Let me feel the fabric."

And then, without looking up, "Have you seen yourself?"

"That's what you're for," Anna said, teasing gently.

"Sophie, dear. Please turn the long looking glass this way."

Sophie did just that and watched Anna as she examined her own reflection.

"Now tell me what you see, and do not be coy."

"I see a beautiful gown of shantung silk the color of ripe wheat in the sun," Anna said. "With a high waist, and beading and embroidery and clever caplet sleeves made from filigree lace interwoven with gold thread and twisted fine gold cord. The same lace forms the flowers across the bodice, which is a good thing as otherwise my breasts would be completely exposed. If I come across Anthony Comstock I'll end up in the Tombs charged with degenerate behavior and you'll have to bail me out."

"Stop changing the subject," Auntie said. "And look at yourself."

Anna sighed and patted her breasts. "Like two loaves of bread set out to rise."

"You are hopeless." Aunt Quinlan laughed.

"But honest."

Sophie said, "The embroidery is very beautiful but Margaret is right, she is half naked."

"Nonsense," said Aunt Quinlan. "That's not what people will see at all. They'll see how lithe she is, how well she holds herself. They'll see the line of her throat and the shape of her head. They'll see her eyes."

"That is also true," Sophie said. "Few people can look beyond your golden eyes, Anna."

The Russo children had been in her thoughts for much of the day and now she remembered Lia's hands on her face. *Occhi d'oro.* The last sight she had of them was on the ferry, Rosa standing very erect with the baby on her shoulder and her free arm around Lia, as focused and determined as any soldier on guard. By now they would be separated, the girls from the boys. She had spent such a short amount of time with them, but she knew that Rosa would not admit defeat. Not easily. Not until it was forced on her.

"Where has your mind gone suddenly?" her aunt asked.

"Hoboken," Anna said. "Italian orphans."

There was a short silence, one her aunt would not fill with empty promises or fictions about the fate of orphans.

Finally her aunt turned to Sophie. "Please fetch the box from the dresser, would you?"

• • •

IT WASN'T OFTEN they saw Aunt Quinlan's small but very fine collection of jewelry. Sophie opened the box and held it in front of her aunt, who pointed to a necklace and bracelets and matching hair ornament. Sophie touched the twist of small, perfect pearls intertwined with oval gold disks.

As she helped Anna with the clasps, Sophie saw more evidence of what she knew in theory: Aunt Quinlan had no peers when it came to putting a picture together.

Mrs. Lee called up the stairs. "Carriage's here."

"You must give Cap a kiss from me," said Aunt Quinlan.

"And me," Sophie said, more quietly.

Aunt went on, "Tell him to observe closely; I'll want to hear about all the costumes and the new house, too. Ostentatious and uncompromising bad taste, of course, but they have a good collection of paintings."

"I can tell you about paintings and costumes too," Anna said, a little affronted that she wasn't charged with such a responsibility.

"Oh, no," her aunt said. "You'll come home and tell me who has dropsy and who looks bilious and which of the ladies are increasing and about the evidence of Knickerbocker inbreeding. I know you, Anna Savard."

Anna leaned over once again to kiss both soft cheeks. "Yes, you do. Nobody knows me better."

• • •

WHEN ANNA WAS gone Sophie went to sit on the low stool where she could lean against Aunt Quinlan's knee. Very gently the old woman rested a hand on Sophie's head, and for a long while there was just the sound of horses in the street and the fire in the grate.

Her aunt said, "Cap does love you, and he will forgive you. You must give him time to grieve."

"That's the problem," Sophie said. "His time is very short."

She hesitated for a moment and then drew a closely written sheaf of papers from a pocket.

"I had a letter I wanted to talk to you about," she said. "It's about Cap."

It was almost exactly a year since the bacillus *Mycobacterium tuberculosis* had been isolated and identified as the infectious agent responsible for consumption, and with that Cap had withdrawn completely from his friends and family. Since that day Sophie had been writing to pulmonary specialists as far away as Russia, inquiring about promising new treatments for tuberculosis. The letter she held in her hand was the first answer that offered even a vague hope.

Aunt Quinlan had seemed very sleepy but now she roused, sitting up straighter. "From one of the specialists?"

Sophie had a moment's guilt for keeping her aunt up, but she also knew that she would have no rest until she spoke to someone about it.

"Yes. A few months ago I wrote to a Dr. Mann in Zurich. He forwarded my letter to a Dr. Zängerle in the upper Engadin Valley."

Sophie paused in the hope that her aunt would have something to say, as she had traveled widely in Europe and lived there for ten years as a young woman.

"It's a very beautiful area near the Italian border," Aunt said. "Very remote and quiet. And your letter is from this Dr. Zängerle in the Engadin?"

"He has a very small treatment facility at his own home, just five patients. A trial, he calls it. He and his wife hope to open a sanatorium if their success holds. He read the case history I sent and he's offering Cap a spot."

"He doesn't have a cure." Aunt Quinlan was not prone to unrealistic expectations or denial of hard facts, but she was also careful to mask whatever she might be feeling for fear of casting either hope or doubt where neither was warranted.

"He makes no such claim. On the other hand, his patients are much improved after treatment."

She described the protocol, reading short paragraphs from the letter when her memory failed her.

"It sounds as though it is mostly good common sense," Aunt Quinlan said finally. "Proper nourishment and rest and fresh air at a very high altitude. Do you think it might do Cap some good?"

Sophie raised a shoulder and let it drop. "It's possible. Even likely, if these figures are accurate. But the real question is, could he be persuaded to go so far?" Her calm was countered by a twitch at the corner of her mouth that she could not control, the perfect demonstration of why medical professionals weren't supposed to treat family members. In fact, she knew that if Anna were here, she would insist that they hand the whole business over to another physician.

Purposefully, she had excluded Anna, and on Aunt Quinlan's face she could see that this fact had not escaped her.

"You can't take this proposal to him."

Sophie swallowed a grimace. "You know I can't. I can't even write to him about it; he doesn't read my letters."

"Anna?"

Sophie turned her face away. "She would disapprove. She wouldn't want him to travel so far."

Her aunt might have challenged this assumption, but she seemed satisfied to let it stand for the moment. Instead she said, "It is true that Cap couldn't make this journey alone. Someone will have to go with him. I can see that you've already sorted this through in your mind. Who are you thinking?"

"I don't know," Sophie said, frustration creeping into her voice. "I find I can't think clearly about this." An understatement of the first order.

"But you think he should go."

Sophie took a deep breath. "I do. I can't explain exactly why, but it feels to me like a chance worth taking."

"You are so much like your grandmother," Aunt Quinlan said after a while. "Medicine was more than science to her."

"What do you mean by that?" Sophie asked, her temper welling up, something that happened so rarely that Aunt Quinlan was looking at her with both alarm and concern. But now she must go on. "Am I less of a physician than Anna, or is she less than I am?"

Aunt Quinlan did not hesitate. "It is not a criticism, but an observation. Anna is in the first line a scientist." And then: "I see I have upset you."

"Anna is an excellent physician," Sophie said, her voice catching.

"She is an excellent surgeon."

Sophie folded the letter and slid it back into her pocket, her hands shaking a little.

"You think I am being unkind, or disloyal, or both," Aunt Quinlan said finally. "But that's not the case. I am not finding fault in Anna; I am pointing out to you that in a case like this, you have an advantage that she does not. You understand it in the bone, you know it with a part of your mind that you deny because it frightens you."

She raised a hand to stop Sophie's protest. "When you say that Cap should go to Switzerland but you can't put words to the why of it, I understand what you are trying to say. And I know that you require help. That I can provide."

It was what Sophie wanted to hear, but it still brought her up short to hear it stated so plainly.

"He will resist."

Aunt Quinlan gave her one of her sweetest, most disturbing smiles. "I have lived a long time," she said. "And I have come up against walls far higher than the one Cap's built. He'll listen to me. He surely will."

◆　◆　◆

SOMETIMES SOPHIE DREAMED about knocking on Cap's door. In these dreams that simple gesture caused the door to swing open, revealing rooms that had been emptied of every familiar and beloved thing, a shell as clean and cold and impersonal as an operating theater. In her dream she went from room to room desperate for some sign of him, any sign at all, and then woke, bereft.

She had loved him for as long as she could remember, but she had refused every marriage proposal for reasons she had explained, again and again, in great detail. Sometimes she felt she might give in and accept him, because she could not deny to herself that she wanted nothing more than to marry Cap. Then in the quiet minutes before sleep she would see how his whole life would change. He claimed to know what he would be giving up, but he didn't. He simply could not. He was the son of Clarinda Belmont, a descendant of the Dutch who had founded New Amsterdam, a Knickerbocker, and all that word implied. She was a mulatto. A mongrel.

It was an ugly word. Cap could reject the mind-set that came along with it, but he couldn't make others do the same. She would never be free of it, and their children would bear it too, an indelible mark on the skin. He could not see that truth.

Cap's diagnosis had not changed her mind, but it had changed his. On a chilly wet day last April the truth had been waiting for her at the breakfast table.

A parcel wrapped in brown paper and tied with string, in and of itself nothing unusual; it wasn't the first such parcel from Cap or even the fiftieth. It seemed there was a packet at least once a week, sometimes addressed to just one of them, and sometimes to *The Ladies at 18 Waverly Place*.

Over the years there had been rare fruits, books about Mesopotamia or windmills or German philosophy, pens of ivory inlaid with pearl, confectionery, beautifully etched and painted ostrich eggs, tiny carvings from Japan, watercolors or sculptures by young artists whose work had caught his eye, a canary in a wrought-iron cage, cuttings from a wild rose, yards of lace from Brussels, bolts of figured damask from India, sheet music, concert and lecture tickets. When they protested he listened politely, nodded, and then carried on as always.

That morning Sophie's name alone had been written across the wrapping paper. It was a slim parcel that contained a short biography of Dr. René-Théophile-Hyacinthe Laennec; a stack of lecture notes tied with string, dated the twenty-fourth day of March 1882 and titled *Die Ötiologie der Tuberculose*; and a letter.

The biography needed no explanation. Dr. Laennec had been a talented, widely respected researcher who died at forty-five of tuberculosis, contracted from his own patients. On the other hand, at first she didn't know what to make of the notes. A pile of papers, closely written in a neat, sharp hand. Only after a quarter hour of reading did she realize that Cap had paid someone—most likely a medical student—to travel to Germany specifically to attend Dr. Robert Koch's lecture on the tuberculosis bacillus. The notes—painstaking, exacting—must have been sent by special courier.

Cap left nothing to chance. It wasn't in his nature.

She put the notes aside, and when she had gathered her courage she opened the letter. For all its brevity it cut as surely as a scalpel.

Sophie, my love,

*Forgive me. After four years of earnest effort to convince you to
accept my proposal of marriage, I withdraw my offer with the
greatest sorrow and regret. As the enclosed will make clear, the
research of the physicians you study and respect is now unequivocal.
I may live a year or five, but I cannot live even a day with you
without putting your life in danger. This I cannot, will not do.*

    Forgive me.

She had written, to no avail. He allowed only Anna near enough in
order to examine him once a month, as long as she wore a mask that
had been treated with carbolic acid and observed the strictest hygienic
measures. The housekeeper and maids who had served first his grandmother and then his mother would not be sent away, but he spoke to
them only through a closed door of the chamber he rarely left. His
secretary could sit in the same room but only at the opposite side, and
turned away. A few of his closest friends were so persistent that he
finally allowed them to visit if they too kept to the far side of the room
where Cap himself never went, and on these visits it was Cap who
wore the mask.

Cap wanted her to think of him as already dead because he thought
of himself that way. In fact, Sophie woke up every day and went to
sleep every night thinking about him. She missed him, she was furious
with him, she mourned the time she might have had with him.

The Vanderbilt Easter Monday ball was the first time he had
appeared in public since his diagnosis. Sophie wondered if his friends
would realize he was saying good-bye.

• • •

ON ANY OTHER March night at eleven o'clock the north end of Fifth
Avenue might be mistaken for a row of mausoleums scaled for giants.
The great bulk of the new cathedral on one side of the street with
schools and rectories and orphan asylums gathered around it, like
chicks to a sleeping hen. On the other side, one mansion after the other,
ornate, looming, as sterile as they were imposing. A wide street without
a single tree or even the suggestion of a garden, just high walls and hundreds and hundreds of windows sealed shut, the eyes of the dead.

But tonight the newest mansion—maybe the fourth or fifth the Vanderbilts had put up over the last ten years, Jack couldn't remember exactly—was awake. It seemed to glow, marble and granite reflecting the light that poured from every window. The first personal residence completely lit with electricity, at a cost that beggared the imagination. With its turrets and balconies and galleries it shone like an unwieldy and ill-begotten star set down among its dull red- and brown-brick neighbors.

A double canopy had been constructed over the Fifth Avenue entrance to protect the partygoers from both weather and the crowd of curious passersby. Footmen in pale blue livery and powdered wigs stood ready to help the guests from their carriages onto the deep red rug that ran from the huge double doors down the steps and all the way to the curb.

Tomorrow the personality of the house would retreat like a turtle into its shell; the stained glass would go dark, blinds and draperies closing off all light and fresh air.

His sisters sometimes tried to calculate how many thousands of yards of velvet and brocade and satin had gone into the draperies of even one of the Vanderbilt mansions, but the numbers quickly grew so large and absurd that they simply gave up and turned back to their own needlework. Their endless, precious, beautiful needlework.

Every evening they waited for him, sitting knee to knee facing each other over an embroidery frame. They would jump up to take his coat and offer him food and more food and again food until he accepted the plate they had ready for him. They wanted him to have the best chair by the fire, the day's newspapers, to hear their family gossip, worries about the weather, observations on the comings and goings of the neighbors, dire predictions about the prospects of the butcher's new clerk, admonitions about the dampness of his coat or shoes. His sisters ran his household and aspired to run him with the same painstaking and exhausting perfectionism.

From the corner of his eye Jack saw a familiar figure, a woman of at least sixty, carefully groomed and dressed to convey nothing more threatening than genteel poverty. Few would guess that a multitude of hidden pockets had been sewn into her wide skirts, ready to be filled with the fruits of the night's labor. Jack had arrested her three or four times at least over the last year. Meggie, she called herself, but her true name was unknown, maybe even to her. He was about to step off the curbside to intercept her when a hand landed heavily on the woman's artfully slumped shoulder. Michael Hone out of the twenty-third precinct, just two years on the force but he had the eye. She gave a heavy sigh and let herself be marched off.

"Meggie must be feeling her age," Oscar said, coming up beside Jack. "Twenty years ago she was slippery as waterweed. She'd be halfway to Brooklyn before you realized she was gone. O-ho, look now. Tell me, would that particular fat-assed Roman emperor there be an elected official who shall remain shameless?"

For a time they amused each other trying to put names to costumes: Cardinal Richelieu and the Count of Monte Cristo, a Capuchin friar, Chinese merchants with eyes outlined in kohl, wizards, cowboys, Queen Elizabeth, the goddess Diana with bow and arrow, a trio of young women with staffs and lifelike lambs fixed somehow to their wide skirts.

"Money is wasted on some people," sniffed a young woman whose clothes were threadbare but carefully mended. "I'd come up with a better costume than Bo Peep, you can be sure of that."

A young man dressed as a knight of Malta followed the trio out of the carriage. Covered head to foot in hauberk and chain mail and armor, he clanked his way up the walk, listing to one side and then the other like a ship in a storm.

"Look now," a man's voice called out loud enough to carry over the noise. "Won't somebody get that poor mope an anchor?"

The appreciative roar of the crowd did not slow the crusader in pursuit of his Bo Peeps, but every policeman within earshot tensed. The draft riots were twenty years ago, but it would be another twenty before they rested easy in the presence of any crowd; moods could shift from high spirits to violence without warning. Now shopkeepers and factory workers, clerks and charwomen, men with tool belts and lunch buckets, they all cooed at the sight of a cape embroidered with pearls and rubies, but people just like this had burned down the Colored Orphan Asylum and hung innocent men from light posts to vent their rage.

There was only one reliable barometer of a group ready to go sour.

Jack turned his attention to a half-dozen children slinking through the crowd as easily and unobserved as cats. Six in this group, the youngest maybe seven, and if he had to guess he would identify them as part of the pack that slept in an alley alongside a German baker's place of business on Franklin Street. The brick wall there was warmed by the ovens, which made the alley a coveted spot in the winter. It was one they had to fight to keep and could lose at any time. If there was real trouble in the air, the street urchins would disappear so quickly that they might have been an illusion.

"They're settling down," Maroney said. The crowd's attention had turned to a modern-day Shakespeare whose hat kept sliding down over his eyes, so that he tripped repeatedly over his shoes. The urchins laughed, widemouthed, gap-toothed, children still and in want of amusement.

Earlier today Jack had watched more fortunate orphans being taken into the austere custody of Sister Ignatia. In shock, overwhelmed, many of them had hung back, torn between the promise of food and the numbing familiarity of the filthy tenements where their parents had died. The doctor had done a lot to calm them, her manner so matter-of-fact, without any trace of condescension or pity. Chances were a few of them would still try to slip away from the orphanage, but none of the children he had seen today would survive long on the city streets.

The Children's Aid Society estimated that there were as many as thirty thousand orphaned or abandoned children in Manhattan, while the orphan asylums could take no more than twelve thousand at a time. The rest lived on the streets underdressed, mostly shoeless, infection- and lice- and worm-ridden. They ate only what they could steal or scrounge or beg and had nothing so grand as a tenement to call home. Most of them refused to ask for shelter at any of the charities that were there to put them up, for the simple fear they would never be allowed to leave again, or would find themselves on a train headed west and a future even more uncertain than the bleak one before them. And so they slept huddled together in doorways or perched on fire escapes, and many of them died over the long winter, defeated by hunger and loneliness and the weather.

One by one the carriages pulled up and came to a stop, and footmen and coachmen lined up to open doors and assist ladies who could not see their feet over skirts and petticoats. Then they followed the walkway lined with potted trees and statues through the marquee and into the house, where they would eat too much and drink even more.

The early high spirits had cooled a little. The crowd began to mill around, bored and eager for distraction.

Farther down the block the doors of a carriage opened suddenly. Two young men jumped down and then turned to help the ladies, all of them too eager to wait in a stuffy carriage. In response other carriage doors began to open, at first only one or two and then in a rush. Ladies in silver and buttercup yellow and blazing reds and deep purples let themselves be directed by their husbands and fathers and brothers, lifting skirts high to avoid puddles and manure and trash, giggling nervously and turning their faces away from the crowd, as if that would be enough to spare them the very attention elaborate costumes were designed to engage.

The uniforms and roundsmen would be here the rest of the night, but as soon as the last party guests had disappeared into the house, the detectives could be away home. As if he had heard Jack's thought, the captain came around the corner and pointed at them.

"I need you two inside." Baker jerked his thumb over his shoulder as if there might be doubt about where. "Talk to Beaney, he'll point you in the right direction. Thinks he saw some rogues' gallery faces in the crowd."

"Dressed as priests, no doubt," Oscar muttered. "Pranksters every one."

Baker gave a surprised and reluctant bark of laughter and then intensified his scowl to offset that small lapse.

"You'll stay at your posts," he said, "until I send word." And he stomped off, cursing under his breath.

They crossed the street, passing a carriage that had seen better days. Inside two very old ladies in powdered wigs sat waiting, their painted faces so somber that they might have been on their way to a funeral.

A couple had just stepped out of a far more elegant and fashionable carriage. The gentleman was older, his form narrow and posture brittle, and he leaned on a cane. His costume was simplicity itself: over one shoulder he had tossed a black cape with red silk lining. The red set off the tight black breeches and short jacket over a white shirt.

"I think he's supposed to be one of those Spanish grandees," Oscar said. And as the man turned his face to the light he let out a soft grunt. "That's Cap Verhoeven," he said. "Poor sod."

Verhoeven's eyes were a vivid bright blue, his complexion flushed. People sometimes called such extreme high color the red flag of the white death. Consumption was said to be gentle, even a romantic death, but Jack could see nothing benign in the way it dragged the strongest and most promising out of the world.

"A damn good lawyer, and strange enough for one of his ilk, fair-minded. His mother was a Belmont."

Oscar had an encyclopedic knowledge of the old Knickerbocker families his mother had worked for all of her life.

Verhoeven had stepped back to reveal the lady beside him, one hand on his raised arm while with the other she tried to keep a shawl in place. She let out a little cry of surprise and irritation as it slipped out of her grasp and fluttered away.

Above layers of silk gauze that moved with the breeze, her shoulders and long neck were now bared to the night air. In the light of the carriage lanterns her complexion took on the shifting iridescence of abalone: golds and pinks, ivories and smoky blues. The heavy dark hair twisted into a coronet and wrapped around her head set off the curve of her cheek.

All of these thoughts went through Jack's head in the few seconds it took the footman to catch up her shawl and drop it over her shoulders. As she half turned toward the footman to smile her thanks, he saw her face for the first time.

Oscar caught his jolt of surprise. "What? You know him?"

"No," Jack said. "Don't know Verhoeven. It's the woman I recognize."

"Huh." Oscar could fit more doubt into a single syllable than any man alive. "Where did you make the acquaintance of somebody like that?"

"On the Hoboken ferry," Jack said. "Surrounded by nuns and orphans."

Oscar's brow shot up high. "The lady doctor you told me about? What was her name—"

"Savard. Dr. Savard."

There was a small silence between them.

Maroney said, "Let's go see what the kitchen maids can spare us in the way of fancy food."

But he had something else on his mind, Jack could see it. A lady doctor dressed in silks was an oddity, and Oscar Maroney's curiosity, once engaged, had to be satisfied. For once Jack was feeling just as curious as his partner.

•   •   •

ANNA ENTERED ALVA Vanderbilt's white marble reception hall at 660 Fifth Avenue on Cap's arm, arriving late, as planned. They had missed the promenade through the house, the receiving line for which hundreds of people had to be announced, and to Anna's quiet disappointment, the dancing of the six formal quadrilles.

Mrs. Lee had been reading about the dancing in the newspapers and was especially excited about the Hobby Horse Quadrille. She told Anna exactly what to look for: a two-part pony costume of papier-mâché and velvet that fit around the middle of the dancer. Anna could admit to herself that her own curiosity had been aroused. Now she was as disappointed as Mrs. Lee was going to be.

Coming out of the cool night into the great hall they were enveloped by overheated air thick with the scent of roses and freesia and aged oak from a fireplace large enough, it seemed to Anna, to consume a small cottage. Overhead crystal chandeliers hung from the carved arches supporting the vaulted ceiling, supplemented by dozens of electric light sconces. Indoor electric lighting was an innovation, another example of the Vanderbilts' need to be first in everything. Light reflected off the polished marble floor and the multitude of jewels this class of people wore like war medals, embedded in buttons and hair combs, sewn onto skirts and bodices and capes, displayed on throats and wrists, fingers and ears.

So much light and warmth and noise, but marble floors and walls paneled with ornately carved stone robbed the room of any hint of welcome or comfort. At the top of a staircase wide enough for ten men to stand shoulder to shoulder there would be a gallery full of treasures gathered from all over the world: paintings by the masters, sculptures and tapestries from China and Egypt and Greece, jewels and inlaid cabinets and musical instruments. Later, if Cap felt strong enough, they could make their way up the long sweeping staircase slowly, at a suitable pace.

They followed a footman who took them on a winding route through the great hall, across salons and a gold and white music room. Every object was made of the rarest woods or finest stone or marble, gilded, carved, inset with ivory or pearl or the wings of butterflies, draped in velvet, damask, embroidered silk. It was meant to be overwhelming, and it was.

With the footman's assistance they found the comfortable corner one of Cap's Belmont cousins had arranged for them. Tall vases overflowing with full-blown deep red roses and honeysuckle bracketed silk upholstered chairs, a settee with a wealth of beaded and embroidered pillows, and a low table that was crowded with fine crystal wineglasses and goblets, gold-rimmed platters of crudités and canapés and caviar en croute. On a side table were more platters heaped with petit fours and tartlets topped with strawberries, far ahead of season, sugared plums and nuts, and punitions, each adorned with a V made out of gold tissue, in case the guest forgot that this was the home of a Vanderbilt.

Flowers tumbled over each other in every corner: roses, tulips, lily of the valley, freesia, whole branches of dogwood and magnolia forced into early bloom. Every greenhouse and hothouse in a hundred miles had to have been stripped bare.

In their little alcove Anna and Cap were close enough to the dancing to watch without being overrun, and Anna found herself laughing out loud at the sight. Robin Hood waltzed with a bumblebee, wings fluttering with every sweep; a Roman emperor had as partner a dairy maid; Frederick the Great danced with a phoenix, and a Russian peasant with Marie Antoinette, who, Anna noted with some satisfaction, wore a gown even more revealing than her own.

They sat watching, Anna with a flute of champagne in her hand and Cap without. He wouldn't eat or drink and he never took off his gloves outside his own home. Now he touched his handkerchief to his damp face and throat.

"It is far too warm with the electric lights and so many people. You must drink something."

"Only if you'll let me drop the glass once I'm done," Cap said, one brow raised in challenge.

"I doubt she'd miss one glass," Anna muttered. "No matter what kind of crystal it is."

"But an under maid may take the blame," Cap said. "You wouldn't like that."

There was no evidence that the tuberculosis bacillus could be passed by touching inanimate objects, but Cap had rules for himself that were inviolate. And in truth, Anna could not fault him for his concern.

She was pulled from her thoughts by two pirates who flung themselves onto the settee in mock exhaustion. Bram and Baltus Decker were Cap's cousins; they had read law with him at Yale and remained stubbornly devoted to him despite his insistence on physical distance. Now they fell over the food and drink with enthusiasm, interrupting themselves to comment on the champagne, the caviar, the pâté de foie gras and smoked trout mounded on toast points, on the orchestra, the quadrilles, and to relate everything they had seen and heard and thought since they had last seen Cap.

Bram flipped up his pirate's patch and blinked owlishly. "Where is Belmont? Never mind, silly question. He'll be here somewhere, chasing a skirt around the dance floor. Look there at that costume, who is she supposed to be? Curled-up toes, must be something oriental."

"Reasonable guess, given the fez and the golden veil," said his brother. Then they both turned to Cap, waiting to be told. Because Cap had a prodigious memory, and would share what he knew if prompted.

"I believe that is supposed to be Lalla Rookh of Persia," he said.

"Damn funny rooks they've got in Persia," said Baltus. "Ours are plain black."

"Not the bird. *Rookh* is a title."

"Book or play?"

"Neither. Poem and then opera."

"Damn me," said Baltus. "Who has the brains to write poems with one hand and opera with the other?"

"Nobody," said Anna, who couldn't resist the silly back-and-forth. "First it was a poem by Thomas Moore."

"Damn Irishmen." Baltus tipped up his champagne flute to empty it. "Bram, have we seen an opera about a girl named Rook in Persia?"

"As a matter of fact," said his brother without opening his eyes, "we did. *The Veiled Prophet*."

Baltus looked up at the ceiling, as if something there might jog his memory.

"Poisoning and a stabbing both," added Cap, and Baltus's face broke into a smile.

"Oh, yes. I remember." Then he looked out over the dancers and his smile disappeared. "Just when I had a way to start a conversation," he said sadly. "The rook has waltzed off with the pope of Avignon."

He fell back against the cushions and snagged another glass of champagne from a waiter who stopped to offer his tray.

"Cap, I swear you're looking very fit tonight."

"Liar," Cap said with an easy smile.

"I would call you more of a blind oaf," Bram said to his brother. "It's Anna who is looking spectacular."

On that they agreed, toasted each other and her, and took great pains not to stare at her breasts.

"And where is the other Dr. Savard this evening?" Bram asked.

He was looking at Cap, but Anna said, "Sophie is working." And just that simply, she was tired of half truths. "Sophie is working," she repeated, "and she is uncomfortable in this company."

"Uncomfortable?" Bram rumbled. "With us? Not with us."

Anna sent a pointed look at two men who were walking by. One wore what she supposed cardinals wore, while the other was dressed as an ancient Greek.

"Old Twomey?" Bram leaned forward to whisper. "What does Sophie have to fear from that pile of rags? Who is he supposed to be, anyway? Aristotle?"

"Plato," Anna said.

"Really? How can you tell?"

"Because Professor Twomey reveres Plato," Anna said.

Cap caught her eye and shook his head. If the Decker twins were sober, she might undertake explaining the retired professor's public lectures on Plato, Francis Gaulton, and the theory of hereditary genius. As it was, Cap took over.

"Bram," he said. "Wake up. Do you see anybody here who isn't lily white?"

Anna looked at the dancers and tried to imagine Sophie in this company. She was elegant and beautiful and exotic, as graceful in the way she spoke as she was walking across a room. Had she come with Cap tonight, no one would have cut her openly—at least not with Cap nearby—but she would have been treated with an aloof condescension, if not disdain. Anna would wager the entire contents of her bank account that Sophie could outreason and outargue anyone here—not excluding a hard-drinking former president, senators, princes and dukes, Supreme Court justices, industry giants, and a half dozen of the wealthiest men in the western world, not to mention bigoted professors of philosophy.

And if they had been willing to overlook her ancestry, they could not or would not pretend to ignore her unapologetic self-sufficiency, her unwillingness to be impressed by their self-importance. To be accepted in this company Sophie must first admit that she was not worthy of it. If she had been capable of such a thing, Cap would not have allowed it. Nor would Anna.

"Goddamn Philius Twomey to hell," Baltus muttered. Then without explanation he sprang up and dashed out into the dance floor, his sword thumping against his leg in a way that was likely to raise bruises. He disappeared into a small crowd of young women gathered in a corner.

"He's caught sight of Helena Witherspoon," Bram said. "Visiting from Princeton. Cap, you've got to meet her; I've laid odds that Baltus will marry her before the year is out. There she is."

Cap said, "A redhead. At least he is consistent."

"And here come Madison and Capshaw." Baltus smiled broadly. "Now we're in for a good time."

Anna watched Cap as he relaxed back into his chair and propped his elbows on the embroidered velvet arms. With his hands tented over the lower third of his face, the contrast between white kid gloves and the hectic color in the hollows of his cheeks and temples could not be avoided.

She dropped her gaze to the plate on her lap. She could not rest her eyes on Cap for any amount of time precisely because there was so little time left; day by day there was a little less of him, his body and mind pulling away and away on a tide that could not be turned.

• • •

MISS WITHERSPOON WAS very young. Anna wondered if she had a mother, because it seemed unlikely that any lady of wealth and standing would allow a daughter to come out in public as . . . a fairy queen? An empress? Someone with more jewels than good sense. The gown was a waterfall of gold tissue and wine-colored velvet with a row of clasps from neck to hem, circlets of diamonds with an emerald at the center of every one. Golden bracelets wound from wrist to elbow, pinned to the heavy brocade with more emerald clasps. Her hair had been plaited with ropes of black pearls, and a matching crown sat above her brow. Her waist was unnaturally narrow, the result of tight corseting from early girlhood, night and day. Anna winced to think about the damage done.

Miss Witherspoon was her father's princess, if no one else's, and she understood the ways of the rich. She made deep curtsies to each of them as she was introduced, her jewels flashing in the light. She listened to the introductions, looking first at Anna and then at Cap, back and forth, trying to make sense of what was outside her experience of the world.

Anna knew what was going through the younger woman's mind, the questions that burned to be asked but could not be voiced in society. Anna had been introduced to her as a Miss Savard. It was true that Miss Savard's manners were exactly what was expected in such company, and her gown was quite pretty, but she wore very little jewelry. More confusing still, she clearly had no husband. She was too young to be a war widow, and so, Miss Witherspoon would surmise, she must be a spinster. Far too old to get a husband, and yet she was here with Cap Verhoeven, who was regarded as exceedingly eligible husband material. The obvious fact that Cap was in poor health didn't seem to concern Princess Witherspoon, but then women were always drawn to Cap, despite—and sometimes because of—his health.

Bram was leaning over her like any hopeful lover. Did she care for champagne? Madeira? Punch? And how lovely her hair smelled, how beautiful her complexion.

"Mr. Decker," she said, finally tearing her gaze away from Cap to look at Bram.

"Yes, Miss Witherspoon?"

"Can you explain to me why your friend Mr. Verhoeven is called Cap? I understood his name to be Peter."

She topped this off with a lowering of the eyes and lashes batted prettily in Cap's direction.

"Oh, that's a good story," Bram said.

"Oh, it's really not," Cap countered.

He might have spared himself the objection, because his friends all stood up. Arranging themselves in a semicircle, they stuck out their chests and spread their legs like sailors on the high seas. Andrew Capshaw gave a tone and they broke into song.

> O Captain, My Captain! our fearful trip is done;
> The ship has weather'd every rack,
> the prize we sought is won.

For all their silliness they sang a very decent four-part harmony, getting all the way through the first stanza to then collapse, thumping each other's backs, greatly pleased with themselves.

"Got that out of your systems?" Cap said.

"It's a poem, isn't it?" Miss Witherspoon addressed Cap directly. "Did you write it?"

There was a small silence in their circle, and then Cap answered her with his usual good grace. "You are too young, I think, to remember the assassination. The poem these idiots were trying—and failing—to set to music—was written in honor of President Lincoln a few months after his death. The poet is a Mr. Whitman."

"Cap recited that poem at a public lecture at the Cooper Union," Anna supplied. "It was on his eleventh birthday, just by coincidence. He recited it and brought the whole hall to their feet. How many times were you asked to repeat that performance?"

Cap cupped his cheek with a gloved hand. "I lost count at thirty or so."

"Which is how he came to be called first Captain, and then Cap," Anna finished. Her voice came a little hoarse, something that wasn't obvious with all the noise of the musicians and dancers. Others didn't notice, but Cap did; she saw it on his face. For that moment she had him back, the boy who had once been her brother.

Then Cap's cousin Anton Belmont came sailing across the dance floor with his younger sister on one arm and one of the Schermerhorn debutantes on the other. A scramble for more chairs and champagne took a quarter hour, all the while the conversation went forward at a steady gallop, the men doing their utmost to make the girls laugh. Other friends joined them, and Anna decided she could absent herself without worry for a short while.

She rose, interrupting a perennial argument about a poker game played years earlier, and excused herself. The simple truth was that if she did not have a quarter hour of solitude in the fresh air she would seal her reputation as an overeducated spinster unsuitable for company by falling asleep in the middle of the biggest social event of the decade.

It took a few minutes to find the right kind of hallway—one used by staff alone to reach the back of the house—and from there she found a door that led into an unoccupied courtyard enclosed by a limestone wall, lit dimly by a set of workroom or pantry windows. Here music and voices were reduced to an undercurrent of sound much like a mosquito shut in a nearby room, persistent but still possible to ignore. Oh, she was cranky. And for no good reason.

The space was half filled with bricks, lumber, nail kegs, a ladder, a pyramid of roofing tiles. Odder still, there were at least a dozen tall gardening buckets filled with roses of every color and shape. She took a deep cleansing breath that came to her filled with shifting fragrances: apricot, heliotrope, honey, oak moss and vanilla, musk and myrrh.

She was far happier here in the dim quiet, but Cap had always loved fancy parties like this one, the more ridiculous the better. He would be laughing about them for weeks afterward. In good health Cap would be on the dance floor or chasing from room to room to examine a painting here or a tapestry there, telling stories and jokes and the riddles he was famous for. Emptying one glass of champagne after another as he went. Sweet-talking old women and their eligible granddaughters with equal ease.

It was Sophie who should have been here tonight with him. It was Sophie he loved, and who loved him, who knew him best. When Anna thought about the impasse between them she sometimes daydreamed about tying each of them to a chair and leaving them face-to-face until they remembered how to talk to each other.

They wanted to marry, but in the end Sophie couldn't bear the thought of what such a marriage would do to Cap, and so she refused him again and again. Anna had the idea that if he were to ask now, Sophie would say yes; she missed him terribly, as he missed her. But he would not ask.

The scent of the roses was very strong despite the cool air, and Anna thought how sad that they should be out here, unappreciated. She could take Cap a rose, a single perfect rose, and let him read into that whatever message he might.

Behind her she heard the rough strike and flare of a match. A familiar noise, nothing extraordinary about it in the course of a normal day. She turned her head and saw that a man was leaning against the far corner of the courtyard wall. He lifted the cigar to his mouth and drew on it and Anna saw the round red cinder flare in the dark. He was dark complexioned, big, dressed not in a costume but in a conservative suit, and he was watching her. Deliberately, calmly, watching her and taking in her awareness of him and the alarm that rose on her skin like a rash.

"You needn't fear me, madam. I'm Detective Sergeant Oscar Maroney of the New York Police Department." His tone was pleasant, his voice slightly rough with tobacco. "Contemplating a bit of larceny? A rose or two, perhaps."

Anna wasn't easily flustered, but she was cautious by nature and unwilling to play games with a stranger, police officer or not. She turned and walked back to the door, which was opening even as she reached for the knob.

The man who stood in the doorway was just as tall as his counterpart, and together with the solid width of shoulder and chest he seemed as all-encompassing and absolute as a wall. And oddly, in one hand he held peach, round and full and blush-colored even in the dim light. On the edge of spring, so odd that he might have held the moon itself in one cupped broad hand. Anna tore her eyes away, took one step back, and limited herself to three words, spoken calmly but with an iron core that could not be overheard: "Please step aside."

"Dr. Savard," said a familiar voice. "I didn't expect to see you again so soon."

Anna stopped just where she was, unsure but curious, too. Almost afraid to raise her eyes to the man's face.

Detective Maroney said, "You didn't make much of an impression, Jack. She doesn't recognize you."

Jack. That small hint was enough to make her look again, to take in the flash of a smile. Detective Sergeant Mezzanotte. Giancarlo. Jack.

"Is that so?" In one smooth movement Mezzanotte sent the peach sailing across the small courtyard, where his friend caught it in an upraised hand. Then he looked at her directly, a question in his gaze.

"I recognize you now," Anna said. "You are dressed very differently than you were earlier today, Detective Sergeant." He was dressed impeccably, in fact. A well-cut short-tailed jacket in the current style, a matching vest. The color could not be made out in the half-light, but she thought it might be black. Nothing flamboyant, but something more elegant than she might have expected of a police detective, even one who worked in plain clothes.

Anna said, "You're on duty?"

That overwhelming smile, again. She wondered if she still could smile herself, her face felt so oddly frozen.

He was saying, "When we met at the church I was coming from the greenhouses at home," he said. "I was there over the weekend, and I spent the early morning trimming rose canes."

He looked over her head to the roses, and she followed his gaze. He had said his parents were floriculturists, she remembered now.

"Those? Those are your roses?" She didn't try to hide the doubt in her voice.

"Most of those are from Klunder's nursery, but the very pale ones to the far right are ours. Cut yesterday, on Easter Sunday after sunset, brought in this morning before dawn."

Because she was uncharacteristically at a loss for words, Anna said the first thing that came to mind. "How very wasteful. Mrs. Vanderbilt wanted every flower to be had, whether she could use them or not."

Detective Maroney said, "Aha. That's what my sister was on about."

Anna turned to look at him.

"She wanted flowers for the Easter dinner table, but there wasn't a daffodil or a violet to be had, so she tells me, as if I plucked them all out of the ground and hid them to vex her. The best she could find was a single rose for a dollar and a half."

"A dollar and a half," Anna echoed, truly taken aback. "Our nursing students pay two dollars for a week's room and board." She realized that her tone was accusatory, but she found it impossible to sound otherwise. To Detective Sergeant Mezzanotte she said, "Is that right, a dollar and a half for a single rose?"

"No," he said. "Or I should say, no honest florist would charge that much, but some will make the best of supply and demand. I can tell you that last week my uncle had to pay fifty dollars for a hundred General Jacqueminot roses."

"Mrs. Vanderbilt pays such prices," Anna said. "Her greed means Detective Sergeant Maroney's sister had no flowers for her Easter table. She would have valued what Mrs. Vanderbilt squanders." She sounded pompous to her own ears but seemed unable to govern what came out of her mouth.

Instead of responding, Jack Mezzanotte walked across the courtyard and crouched down for a moment. When he stood again he had a spray of three small rosebuds in one hand and a pocketknife in the other. He trimmed thorns from the stems as he came closer.

"Dr. Savard is right," he said to his partner, though he kept his gaze fixed on Anna. "It is a shame for the roses to go to waste. Let me put at least a few to good use."

He stopped in front of her, so close that she could feel the heat of him. One brow quirked up, as if to ask permission; Anna could have stopped him with a word or a raised hand. But she didn't. She raised her face and looked at him to show that she was not intimidated or frightened or even embarrassed, and then she canted her head slightly. An invitation.

His attention was on her hair, one finger moving in a curve just over the silver hair clasp that Sophie had fixed there earlier this evening. Such a light touch, but she felt it moving down her spine in clear notes. Very gently he slid the stem into place, paused to consider, and moved it slightly. And then he stepped back and smiled at her.

"This rose is called La Dame Dorée. The breeder was trying to achieve the perfect white bourbon rose, but he didn't succeed. When they open you'll see that the inner petals are a very pale pink at the edge. The color isn't perfect, but the scent is truly beautiful. And before you ask, we sell these wholesale, a hundred for ten dollars."

He said, "I don't know your first name."

Her voice came hoarse. "Liliane. But I'm called Anna."

There was nothing untoward in his expression or tone, and still she felt his regard. This morning she had been a different creature to him, only nominally female. That had changed, or more exactly, Countess Turchaninov had changed that. Anna found that this both irritated her and gave her a perverse pleasure.

She said, "Your hands will smell of La Dame Dorée all night." Shocked at the impulse to put her face to his palm to test this assertion, she stepped away. "Pardon me, I have to go back to my friends."

Then she slipped through the door into the hallway and out of sight. As soon as she had turned a corner she stopped and leaned against the wall to catch her breath.

Anna touched the rosebuds in her hair with a tentative finger, sure for one moment that she had imagined the whole odd encounter in the walled courtyard.

• • •

MR. LEE WAS waiting with the carriage at one thirty, a time worked out carefully to make sure Cap did not overextend himself and that Anna would be able to see her patients the next day. Helping Cap into the carriage, Anna thought of the day ahead of her—surgeries and then Dr. Garrison's trial—and all the excitement and high spirits left her immediately.

Cap had begun to cough into his handkerchief even before they were outside. Now he collapsed into the seat, turned his whole body into the corner, and hunched over, shaking violently with each paroxysm. If he turned to her, Anna knew that she would see that his face and neck were drenched with sweat. His complexion would have darkened to purple with veins standing out on his forehead and temples and in his neck. And there would be blood.

He wanted no help and would be angry if she offered, and so Anna gave him the privacy he needed. She closed her eyes and reached for the calm she had trained so hard to achieve. Cap struggling to breathe; there would be no worse sound in the world.

Finally he sat up a little straighter, folded his handkerchief in the shadows and out of her line of sight, and immediately pulled another out of his pocket, a fresh white flag in the darkened carriage. He blotted perspiration from his face.

He said, "Thank you for coming with me." His voice came very soft and hoarse.

A minute passed and then another.

"She misses you," said Anna. "I don't think you are ever very far from her thoughts."

He said nothing, but he had heard her. His head dipped a little more in her direction, an invitation to tell him the things he wanted to hear. But because Anna could not give him what he wanted so desperately, she said nothing at all.

4

DR. GARRISON'S TRIAL was about to start, and Anna was running late. Sophie paced back and forth in front of the Hall of Justice; she wanted to go in and find a seat, and she wanted to run in the opposite direction.

People called this place the Tombs, an appropriate nickname for a building that exuded a miasma of open crypts and leaking sewers. Sophie was sure that anyone who spent any real amount of time in one of the offices or courtrooms or—worse still—jail cells must come away with sickened lungs and an aching head.

Children playing on a beach understood that sand castles must give way to water and wind even as they were being built, but the men who built the Hall of Justice had simply ignored such inconvenient truths and put it directly over a swamp. As a result the building had begun to sink before its doors ever opened. It continued to decompose like a living thing, even as people came and went, oblivious or deadened to the atmosphere.

Tenements had a stench that could make the eyes water and the gorge rise, but to Sophie's mind the Tombs were far worse. Repeated flooding and permanent damp meant rotting timber, slimy plaster, chunks of masonry that fell without warning. The stink sat on the back of the tongue and was not easily gotten rid of, even hours later. Worse still were the jail cells below ground level, where fungus and moss sprouted from walls overpopulated with vermin and water bugs.

Anthony Comstock had arrested Clara Garrison and had her thrown into one of those cells, and more than once.

A cab came to a quick stop and Anna almost catapulted herself out onto the cobblestones, turned to stuff money into the cabby's hand, and then grabbed Sophie's arm to rush into the building.

The Special Sessions courtroom was cavernous and unheated, and Sophie was chilled even as she followed Anna to empty seats on the far side of the room, where, thankfully, the ceiling was not water-marked and thus less likely to leak onto their bonnets or shoulders.

"You're shivering," Anna said, and handed Sophie a pair of fur-lined gloves from her Gladstone bag. Sophie had never acclimated to New York weather but still regularly overestimated her tolerance for cold. Anna, who knew her better than anyone, had packed the gloves, a scarf, and even a pair of the heavy wool socks Mrs. Lee knitted for each of them every winter. Sophie was a little embarrassed, but not so vain as to pretend she didn't need the things Anna handed her.

The room was filling up quickly, though the judges' bench on the stage at one end was still unoccupied, as was the jury box to the right. At a slightly lower level but still well above the main floor were chairs meant for witnesses, defendants, and attorneys. Now Clara Garrison stood there with her lawyer to one side and Maude Clarke to the other, talking quietly, a small island of calm in the noise and constant move-ment of the gathering crowd. Clara was carefully dressed, confident and professional but unassuming. Dr. Clarke too was dressed to con-vey both her profession and status, but she was a smaller woman, quite matronly in both shape and persona, and thus was usually overlooked or underestimated by the men she came into contact with. The sight of Drs. Garrison and Clarke talking together was a familiar one, some-thing Sophie had seen many times every day while she was in training. It was disconcerting to see them here, ready to be examined rather than to conduct an examination.

As Sophie looked through the room she realized that most of the prominent female physicians active in the city had come to sit in watch-ful support, including Dr. Mary Putnam Jacobi, the most demanding and uncompromising faculty member at the medical school for women.

Mary Jacobi had taken a close interest in Sophie's education and career and had gone out of her way to support and encourage her. At first Sophie suspected that Dr. Jacobi's interest had to do with the rarity of black women in medical school. That thought had proved wrong when she was invited to the Jacobi home to meet her hus-band, Abraham, an internationally acknowledged expert on diseases of children. He happened also to be the president of the New York

State Medical Society, and thus wielded a great amount of influence. Mary Jacobi had presented Sophie to her husband like a prize specimen captured against all odds in the wild.

"She has a natural and quite astounding talent for pediatric and obstetric medicine," she told her husband. He was a slender white-bearded man with a serious but kind demeanor. Gently he took Sophie's hands in his own and smiled at her as he examined them.

"You must forgive Mary," he had said in his heavy German accent. "She is always on the lookout for talent to nurture, but her approach can be abrupt. Now that she has brought you home you must sit and tell me about your studies."

Sophie didn't know if Abraham Jacobi's acceptance and support of female physicians was a consequence of his marriage, or if it had won his wife over in the first place. What she did know was that he was one of the few male doctors who welcomed women into his lecture hall, and Sophie had learned a great deal from him even before she was introduced. She still called on the Jacobis regularly, and might have sat next to Mary if there had been space for herself and Anna.

Her cousin sat in an uncharacteristic and almost moody silence, filled with a thrumming tension. Sophie put a hand over Anna's folded fingers and pressed. There was reason to be worried, and to claim otherwise would not help.

A small commotion near the door had heads turning to see Comstock coming in, flanked by his colleagues from the Society for the Suppression of Vice and the Young Men's Christian Association. They marched through the room to take the seats reserved for the prosecution, all of them dressed as Comstock was in somber black wool, identical hats tucked under their arms, all of them with mustaches and beards that shone with pomade. Sophie's dislike of these men was so extreme that she felt it like a mass in her throat.

Anna roused herself a little, her brow furrowing as if she were remembering some crucial task left undone.

Sophie wondered if she was going to finally talk to her about Cap. This morning she had planned to draw Anna aside to get whatever news there might be to share, but for once Anna had risen first. She was already in the kitchen when Sophie finally roused, deep in conversation with Margaret and Mrs. Lee, who had had a never-ending list of questions and an even longer list of grievances, because Anna had failed to observe the very things they most wanted to hear about the costume ball. Sophie would have been amused, under different circumstances.

Cap was dashing, Anna had told them. His costume was something Spanish dancers wore for a formal performance; he had had it made in Spain when he visited a few years ago, very elegant and understated and emphasizing his long, wiry form. His spirits were good; he had laughed at the outrageous stories told by his cousins; she even recounted one of the stories herself, something to do with a goose, the color of goose shit, and Mrs. Decker's treasured Aubusson rug. Anna described the more ridiculous costumes, answered endless questions about the house, the draperies, the carpets, the furniture and fireplaces and pictures and sculptures. She recounted the names of all the friends who had stopped to visit with Cap, what costumes they wore, and all the conversations she could remember. She did not say, did not need to say that Cap had kept himself apart, touched nothing and no one, permitted no one to come near, and wore his gloves all night. Nor did she talk about his health, the one thing Sophie wanted most to hear.

Instead Anna recollected quite suddenly that she had patients to see, and she was off. Sophie didn't see her again until she arrived at the front entrance to the Tombs at just before two in the afternoon, and they walked together into the courtroom. She would have to wait until Anna was ready to talk, as difficult as that was to do.

With some effort she pulled her thoughts together and turned to her cousin.

"You are very far away in your thoughts. Difficult case?"

Anna frowned extravagantly. "I have to say, that's not the question I was expecting."

"But I would like to know, nevertheless."

"A new mother came in this morning, she can't be more than fifteen. Stillbirth, and I think she might have been unattended. That she didn't die is a mystery. One of the worst fistulas I've ever seen, severe damage to the bladder and urethra."

Tearing was not uncommon when a young girl, slight of frame and undernourished, gave birth unattended to a child of even normal size.

In such cases patients were often in such extreme pain that they had to be anesthetized before it was even possible to examine them.

"But at least there wasn't a delay," Sophie said. As bad as an obstetric fistula could be, women often didn't come for treatment out of shame and embarrassment. They hid themselves away, as unwelcome as lepers in their own homes, swallowing agony until infection had turned into peritonitis and there was nothing to be done.

"Three hours in surgery," Anna said. "And I'll have to go in again. Tomorrow, if she's strong enough. I fear she won't last that long."

She turned toward Sophie; her gaze was diagnosis sharp. "I wish you'd just go ahead and ask what you really want to know."

"And I wish you'd just go ahead and tell."

After a long moment Anna said, "He is in decline. He won't admit to much pain, but the signs are there."

"Ulcerations?"

"Not that I could see in his mouth or on his face. Not yet."

Sophie was so long in trying to organize her thoughts into coherent sentences that she was startled by the cry of the bailiff bringing the room to order and announcing Judge Micah Stewart's court in session.

The judge came out of the antechamber, his head of snow-white hair standing out not just for its abundance but for the contrast to a mustache and brows that were still a carroty red. He paused before taking his seat, looking over the spectators, nodding to bailiffs and roundsmen and colleagues. Then his gaze came to rest on Anthony Comstock, and even from halfway across the room Sophie saw the disdain darken his expression.

"Mr. Comstock," Judge Stewart said in a dry voice that still managed to fill the room. "Up to your old tricks, I see."

• • •

IF IT WEREN'T for the seriousness of the situation Anna would have enjoyed watching Judge Stewart sparring with Anthony Comstock. Comstock could not hold his temper or keep his opinions to himself; what he lacked in rational argument he made up for with posturing, thundering rhetoric, and Bible verses, a tactic that was not serving him well.

"You can't summarily dismiss the charges," Comstock was saying in a patronizing tone. "The grand jury handed down the indictment, and you must proceed and allow me to prosecute this case."

Stewart leaned back in his chair. "You might be right."

Comstock looked genuinely surprised.

"In fact, if there were a legal indictment, you would be right," the judge went on. "But District Attorney Wilson found insufficient cause to let you bring your complaint before the grand jury, as he told me, just an hour ago. So you snuck behind his back, didn't you. Crept into the grand jury room like a thief in the night and approached the foreman directly with your complaints."

Comstock sputtered. "The district attorney was very busy, and I—"

"You took it upon yourself to wheedle an indictment out of the grand jury even after you were told the case wasn't solid enough to prosecute."

"Judge Stewart," Comstock began again. "Have you looked at the material we seized from Dr. Garrison's office?"

"You ignore my question to ask one of your own?"

"If you have looked at those materials you know that the defendant's purpose is to distribute—unlawfully distribute—immoral and obscene tracts and implements and thereby to pollute the public and cast the innocent into mortal danger. The first indictment concerns the booklet that Dr. Garrison herself pressed into Inspector Campbell's hands, one that instructs women how to prevent conception."

Sophie sat up straighter, craning her neck to catch sight of Comstock where he stood.

"What?" Anna whispered.

"That's Mr. Campbell there with Comstock. It was his wife I was attending yesterday when you went off to Hoboken."

Judge Stewart was saying, "As it happens, I have read the pamphlet you mention here. Read it twice, and nowhere did I come across the word *conception*. Plenty about hygiene and health, but nothing about procreation or conception or anything along those lines."

"You read the word *syringe*, did you not?" Comstock demanded.

"Certainly."

"Well, then."

"Well, then, what?"

"You know what syringes are used for, sir."

"I think I do, yes. But maybe it's time we allowed the defense a word or two. Dr. Garrison?"

Clara raised her voice to be heard clearly. "Female syringes are first and last a therapeutic tool, Your Honor. The syringe is indispensable in the treatment of disease and for applying local remedies to preserve personal health. Syringes are also used in the irrigation and cleaning of wounds and body cavities—"

"Hogwash!"

The judge drew back sharply. "You forget yourself, Comstock. Dr. Garrison, do you have anything to add?"

"No, Your Honor."

Comstock's voice rose to an indignant wobble. "But the publications Dr. Garrison distributes so freely are an incentive to crime to girls and young women!"

"I don't see it."

"Great evil," Comstock shouted, "is often very subtle!"

"Too subtle for me," Judge Stewart said. And to Anna it seemed certain that he was trying not to smile. "I find nothing unlawful here. The first indictment is hereby struck."

"Your Honor! I am a representative—"

"Mr. Comstock. Listen closely: I do not care to hear about your society, and if you interrupt me again, I will find you in contempt."

"If you'll permit me to share Judge Benedict's rulings—" He put his hand on the papers before him.

Stewart's expression hardened. "You may not," he said. "I am not bound by Judge Benedict's rulings."

"The Society for the Suppression of Vice—"

"I think you must be hard of hearing, Comstock. Unless you have something worthwhile to say, I'm going to dismiss the rest of your charges."

Comstock grabbed a book and held it overhead, turning to show it to the room.

"*Niemeyer's Anatomy*," he bellowed. "Found on Mrs. Garrison's shelf, plain as day. Mr. Campbell, is that not so? Did you not find this book on Dr. Garrison's shelf?"

A man much shorter and leaner than Comstock came to his feet and removed his hat to reveal a head of frizzy red hair. "It is."

"Independent verification," Comstock thundered. "I submit to the court that this is an obscene publication, unsuitable for sale or purchase. Most especially unsuitable for students of any kind, even students of medicine. I refer you to color illustrations on pages sixteen and seventeen and throughout chapter four. And"—he paused dramatically—"it was printed in London."

Judge Stewart's brows lowered. "Is there a law that forbids importing medical texts from England?"

"There is most definitely a law that forbids sending obscene materials through the mails. And if this book was printed in England, it had to get here somehow."

"A reasonable assumption. Mr. Wall, will your client stipulate to the claim that a book printed in London was not printed here?"

A low laugh ran through the room, but Clara's attorney kept a professional demeanor. "We so stipulate."

Judge Stewart turned his attention to Clara, who stood with her hands folded in front of herself, her expression watchful but calm.

"Dr. Garrison. Did you send to England for this book?"

"No, sir. I did not."

"Did you cause it to be mailed to you?"

"No, sir."

"Do you know how it is that it got to this continent from that one?"

"Yes. I purchased it from a bookseller in London and then I carried it, in my valise."

Comstock said, "What proof does she have of that assertion?"

"What proof do you have of yours?" Stewart said. "If you read the law with as much avarice as you read those books you find so offensive, you'd know that the burden of proof is on you, sir. You alone. Now sit down before I have you thrown out on your ear."

Stewart waited until Comstock had followed this order, and then he looked out over the courtroom.

"There are two issues here," he said. "The first has to do with the nature of the material itself. What I have here before me is a collection of medical illustrations such as might be used in teaching anatomy to students of medicine. Mr. Comstock has decided that such illustrations are not educational, but obscene. I find this a ludicrous claim. If there is any crime here, it is solely in the mind of the beholder."

Comstock jumped as if poked. "That's not for you to say."

"You'll hold your tongue," Stewart said. "Or I swear I'll fine you and have Roundsman Harrison throw you into a cell. Huffing and puffing will do you no good with me, Comstock. Now tell me, have you ever been a student of medicine?"

Comstock admitted that he had never studied, taught, or practiced medicine. He also agreed, reluctantly, that a doctor should be able to locate and recognize the different parts of the brain, the eye, the larynx, the arteries and tendons and muscles, and all the internal organs.

"These aren't the first books or images of the human body you've impounded because you find them indecent, are they?"

"I have seized thousands," Comstock said, pulling the small amount of dignity he could muster around himself. "Many thousands. Once a month they are incinerated."

"And in the meantime, they are stored in your office for safekeeping?"

"Yes. There are several hundred at any one time. The forces of evil in this city know no bounds."

"And they are locked away, never to be seen by human eyes."

Comstock frowned elaborately. "They are seen only in as far as I must show them to the court to support charges."

"No other occasion to display them."

Comstock hesitated for the briefest moment. "Am I on trial here, sir? The Postmaster General of the United States—"

"—isn't in my courtroom. There's a question before you, Mr. Comstock."

"On occasion I am asked to speak to police officers about the work of the Society for the Suppression of Vice. The younger officers often cannot even imagine the filth waiting for them on the streets and back alleys. I sometimes use seized materials as a tool in the education of professionals."

"You are an educator as well. As is Dr. Garrison."

Comstock's face went very still.

"Mr. Comstock. If I understand you correctly, you use the materials in your possession to illustrate and instruct professionals. That is your word, *professionals*. You find those materials to be necessary to carry on your work. Dr. Garrison makes the same claim and in her case, I would even agree. Do you have anything to add, Dr. Garrison?"

Clara said, "I do. I would like the record to show that my concern is first and always the health of my patients. My responsibilities to the women who study medicine I take just as seriously."

Stewart looked long and hard at Comstock, who had flushed to the roots of his hair. His whole body was shaking with rage. Comstock amused Stewart and many of the other men in the courtroom, but Anna was less dismissive. In him Anna saw a man who was controlled by the most basic and childish of impulses, a man who had convinced himself that dealing out pain and humiliation was a sacred mission granted to him by a loving and discriminating God. Because he had earned that right. Most of all, Comstock was a man who had just been humiliated and who would not forget or forgive. He would vent his anger on Clara if he could, and if not, on someone like her.

The judge's gavel gave one sharp rap.

"All charges are dismissed. Dr. Garrison, you are free to go. Court is adjourned."

Anna turned to Sophie. "Tell me about this Mr. Campbell."

Sophie stood up but lowered her voice. "It was his wife who asked me about contraception. She was very low."

The details came to Anna right away, and with them her voice caught, her voice gone dry. "Did you realize—"

"No," Sophie said, her voice low. "I had no idea he works for Comstock. Of course I had no idea."

"Have you already sent the pamphlet?"

"Yes."

"Do you think his wife could be working with Comstock too?"

Comstock did make a habit of setting up elaborate traps for physicians he suspected of providing patients with information about birth control, but Sophie could not imagine that a woman in labor would have been part of such a scheme. She remembered too well how overwhelmed Mrs. Campbell had been. Desperation like that could not be feigned so easily. She shook her head.

The crowd inched forward, and they went with it at a pace that threatened to bring them face-to-face with Comstock and his associates. The crowd shifted and Anna found herself suddenly close enough to Mr. Campbell to see flecks of tobacco caught up in his red whiskers. At that moment his gaze turned to her and he stilled, as if the sight of a woman in the crowd was more than he could explain to himself. Then he saw Sophie—Anna watched his gaze shift and then focus.

Without looking away he spoke a word into Comstock's ear and the two of them pivoted like puppets. Anna looked away, but not before her eyes met Comstock's, as calculating and distant and dark as a bird of prey.

♦   ♦   ♦

WHEN SHE GOT back to the hospital Anna found that her patient was just coming out of the state of unconsciousness that had made her surgery possible. Two of Anna's best medical students were with her, but the girl was confused and in pain, and she batted fitfully at the glass being held to her mouth. The other women on the ward were watching with interest, and Anna jerked the privacy curtain shut behind herself.

She said, "No luck finding someone who speaks Hungarian?"

"Here and gone," Naomi Greenleaf said. "She talked to the patient and I took notes. She has an odd name, Aleike—"

"—Gyula," Ada Wentworth finished, pronouncing the unusual name carefully. "Sixteen years old. Her husband is a laborer on the new bridge."

There was a pause while they all looked out the window, a habit that had dug itself in over the last years as the Brooklyn Bridge neared completion. It was so improbable—its size, the idea that anything man-made could span the expanse of the East River—that the sight of it against the sky might be taken for an illusion. And still the newspapers claimed that this spring it would open for traffic.

Ada went on, "He brought her here and went to work for fear of losing his spot. She asked through the translator if she can still have children. We were careful to make sure she understood about the surgery. She wanted us to know she doesn't have any money and she asked for a priest again. The translator said there's a priest who speaks Hungarian up near the Foundling; she'll send word. And we got a good amount of broth into her, but as you can see, she won't take the laudanum."

The girl settled a little when Anna came to sit beside her and put a hand on her brow, damp with fever sweat. She was so young, and still in her expression Anna saw that she had already resigned herself to one kind of death or another. Despite the exacting measures they took to achieve and maintain hygienic conditions, in a case like this infection was very likely and might well claim her life. If it didn't, if they could save her, she would fall pregnant too soon with the same outcome, or worse. She had only one purpose in life, to bear and raise children. If she was brave and determined enough to seek out a way to avoid pregnancy despite such expectations, the law would punish her.

But Anna would not resign herself to failure. Maybe the girl felt some of that, because now when Anna held the glass to her mouth, she drank the water laced with laudanum, her expression contorting at the taste.

"This will help you sleep," Anna said quietly. "It will relieve the pain for a while, and make it possible for me to examine you."

The girl shuddered as the tension left her shoulders and her pulse began to slow.

"We will do our very best for you," Anna said. "Now sleep for a while, Mrs. Gyula. Let us do what we can for you."

• • •

EVEN AFTER THE longest and most strenuous days Anna looked forward to the walk home, for the simple pleasure of movement and the chance to be alone with her thoughts. Most usually she used this time to go over the day's cases and debate with herself the decisions she had made, but the events of the last two days were playing havoc with her powers of concentration. When she managed to put Comstock and his witch hunt out of her mind, Cap took his place; Cap left only to make room for Rosa Russo and her sister and brothers, who stuck like a bur in her mind, as persistent as the patients she had lost to typhus and smallpox, dysentery and sepsis.

They made up a club, it seemed to Anna, and divided among themselves responsibility for keeping her aware of her failings.

She walked down Stuyvesant Street to Astor Place and slowed down as she went by the Cooper Union, as was her habit. It felt like home to her, this place where she had spent so much of her girlhood.

Before arthritis put an end to her work, Aunt Quinlan had taught classes here. Anyone with a sincere interest in the sciences, engineering, or the arts was welcome to enroll in the school Peter Cooper had founded, and Aunt Quinlan's classes in art theory, drawing, and painting were very popular. As a little girl Anna had come along, first to sit nearby while her aunt taught, and then as she got older, to explore.

Wandering in and out of classrooms and lecture halls, she had absorbed talk about chemical reactions, architecture, light and shadow, and the golden mean. When she was sleepy she made a nest in a deep reading chair in the faculty meeting room, and that was where Aunt Quinlan often found her. On the way home they talked about what Anna had heard that day and how it all fit together.

One February evening when she was not quite five years old, Anna had gone with Aunt and Uncle Quinlan to hear a politician give a talk at the Cooper Union. The lecture hall was crowded and overheated and no place for a fidgety child, and so she was sent out to play in the hall. And that was how she met Cap, who had not yet earned his nickname and introduced himself as Peter. He had brought a box of tin soldiers and he was delighted to tell Anna about every one of them.

At first Anna wondered if Peter didn't realize that there were boys' stories and girls' stories, and then she understood something about him: he made no such distinctions. It was a revelation to her, and made an instant bond between them.

It would take another five years, two epidemics, draft riots, and a war before Sophie came to join them, but then she slid into place like a last puzzle piece. Together the three of them made the Cooper Union their own, taking lessons there along with other children of the faculty, exploring classrooms and laboratories and lecture halls. At twelve they ventured out into the neighborhood, and finally by fourteen they had most of Manhattan by heart. Now when Anna passed the main entrance she was overcome with an almost unbearable sorrow, for Cap and Sophie and for herself and the children they had been.

Evening classes—always oversubscribed—were about to start. Anna watched small groups of students as they picked up the pace for fear of being late. Most of them were men intent on engineering classes, but there were women too, here and there. None of them were expensively dressed and all of them looked as though they had a long day's work behind them.

Someone dropped an armload of books and crouched down to gather them together, his dark hair lit by the gas streetlamps. Anna stopped, catching her breath, until he stood again and saw that he was a stranger, a man she had never seen before.

Flustered, irritated with herself, she hurried on. How very silly, to imagine Detective Sergeant Mezzanotte would cross her path again so soon, less than twenty-four hours since he had put rosebuds in her hair. She couldn't imagine how she might see him again in the wide expanse of Manhattan, as unbreachable now in her imagination as the Atlantic.

5

DESPITE HER ORIGINAL intention to vaccinate the Hoboken orphans the day after she had first examined them, Anna's week had been so busy that she had had to postpone from Tuesday to Wednesday and again to Friday. Worse still, Sophie was called away to an emergency, and so Anna would have to deal with Sister Ignatia on her own.

The cab was drafty. Anna tucked her scarf more firmly into the neck of her cloak and counted herself lucky to be out of the weather. Mr. Lee's prediction had proved correct: winter had returned and swept away every trace of spring. From her relatively dry and warm spot in the hired cab, Anna watched men walking into the wind hunched over, hands clapped tight on hats lest they be torn away. Sleet pooled in the gutters and streets and dripped off ledges, and every doorway was packed with bodies huddled together out of the wet, faces creased in some combination of discomfort and irritation and dull acceptance.

In the street, vendors and deliverymen vied with each other for right of way, all of them jumping out of the path of omnibuses and drays, oxen bellowing bass as if to harmonize with the screech of iron on iron. An omnibus shouldered through the intersection, the horses enveloped in the steam that rose from their broad backs. Urchins slipped through the crowds with clear purpose, alert and nimble despite the weather. They were making the best of the late storm; twice the usual number of pockets would be emptied of wallets and watches by the end of the day.

Going through Madison Square, she saw that the weather had not discouraged the beggars, who claimed spaces around the park that they defended with violence, when necessary. She saw three or four who were familiar to her but many others who weren't. A woman with a disfigured child in her arms, both of them wrapped in a dripping blanket coat. A man on crutches who wore an old and much abused uniform he was too young to have worn in the last war.

Anna had a reputation among the poor who lived on the streets, the people the city government dismissed as *the outdoor poor*. Those who were truly destitute she would stop and talk to for as long as time permitted, but the others—the professional beggars who made a living by faking injuries or, worse, by sending lame or injured children out to beg—knew that she would see them arrested and testify, if necessary. The streets of Manhattan were overrun with the poor and the merciless both.

Less than a week ago she had been out on these streets in a gown that bared her shoulders, with only a shawl to keep her warm and on her way to a party that had cost a million dollars or more. There was nothing predictable in this life, and very little that was fair.

◆ ◆ ◆

THE CAB PASSED St. Patrick's Cathedral and turned onto Fifty-first, where the orphan asylum took up two entire city blocks, with a building for boys and one for girls. Between them was a convent, a fortress of stone hulking in the rain.

The cab stopped in front of the girls' building and Anna dashed for the entrance. Once inside she took out her handkerchief to pat her face dry, and then looked around herself for the porter.

Instead she was intercepted by an ageless, humorless nun who introduced herself as Sister Peter Joseph. She reminded Anna of Sister Ignatia simply because she wore a black habit rather than a white one, in contrast to the younger Sister Mary Augustin.

Sister Peter Joseph's spine had begun to curve with old age, but she moved as quickly as a girl, gesturing to a young woman in yet another habit, this one gray, who came to take Anna's coat and scarf and hat to be whisked away to a cloakroom, she supposed, well out of sight.

Anna followed the old nun down hallways, her boots slipping a little as they rounded corners on the highly polished floors. They stopped in front of a door with two words printed across it: *Mother Superior*.

Anna said, "Is there some problem?"

Instead of answering, Sister Peter Joseph opened the door and gestured Anna inside, followed her, and then adjusted the skirts of her habit as she took the chair behind the desk. Anna was a little amused to realize she had assumed that Sister Ignatia was the head of the orphanage. She was glad to have been mistaken.

"I first want to thank you for the interest you took in the welfare of our charges," Sister Peter Joseph began. "As you are aware, Sister Ignatia does not approve of vaccinations; she believes they are dangerous."

"Yes, I gathered."

"Nevertheless, it is our policy to vaccinate and I was surprised and displeased to learn that this had been neglected. I have had more than a few surprises this week. At any rate, the children—all of them—have been vaccinated against smallpox. This was done by staff from St. Vincent's Hospital over the last two days."

She took a folder out of a drawer and pushed it across the desk to Anna.

"The vaccination records, if you would like to examine them."

Anna didn't open the folder, and she didn't try to hide her irritation. "If everyone has been vaccinated, you might have sent a message—"

"—and spared you the trip in such unpleasant weather. Yes, I might have. But I am hoping that now you are here, you would be willing to examine some of the sisters."

"You don't have a physician who visits regularly?"

Eyes the color of autumn oak leaves assessed her coolly. "Am I asking too much?"

Anna felt herself flush. "I would be happy to be of assistance."

Another folder appeared and was pushed across the desk. "These are the records for the sisters who need to be seen. There are two novice nursing sisters waiting for you in the infirmary to assist. If there is something you need that you don't find, send one of them to me and I will see what can be done. The convent infirmary is at the end of this hall, then to the left. It's clearly marked."

At the door Anna hesitated. "Is Sister Mary Augustin available this afternoon? I was hoping to speak to her."

There was a long pause, as well as a new set of furrows between the sparse white eyebrows.

"Or do I ask too much?" Anna finished.

She had earned herself an amused smile. "I will send her to you before you leave."

• • •

THE INFIRMARY WAS a large rectangular space, as clean as any treatment room at the New Amsterdam. Along one wall were supply cabinets, a table for the preparation of medicines, a tall glass-fronted case of instruments, sterilization equipment, and a deep sink. A pair of examination tables took up the middle of the room, each surrounded by a privacy curtain that could be pulled closed. She had a moment to wonder whether the children's infirmary was as well equipped, and then she chided herself for assuming the worst.

Her first patient was a nun about thirty years old with a sprained wrist. After that she treated an eye infection, lanced a boil, wrote out a receipt for a liniment that would loosen stiff joints, and finally diagnosed what was almost certainly the start of tubercular kidney and would need to be closely monitored. She wrote her observations and advice on a sheet of paper left in each nun's folder and hoped they would be read.

The sisters were all quiet and cooperative and utterly stoic; they asked no questions but answered the ones she put to them without hesitation. It was all very routine until a fifty-two-year-old Sister Francis Xavier introduced herself as the orphanage and convent procuratrix. At Anna's blank expression she explained.

"Food," she said. "Drink. I'm the one who makes sure there's enough to feed all these little faces, like birdies in the nest they are, always peeping and opening their mouths wide enough to see right down their pink gullets. And the sisters, too." She patted an ample belly. "I like my work."

Sister Xavier had a mass in her breast the size of an apple. As Anna palpated it the sister asked, "Do you think I'd get a blue ribbon at the state fair? Hurts like the devil. Waxes and wanes like the moon."

"How long has this been with you?"

The smooth brow creased as she thought. "Twenty years, maybe. Seems to me if it was the cancer it would have killed me long ago, but now it's got so big it throbs like a rotten tooth. Can it be got rid of?"

"It can," Anna said. "Or at least, I can do a needle aspiration today and then remove it for you surgically sometime soon. With any luck it won't come back again after that. You'll have to come to the hospital for the procedure."

"Hospital!" Xavier huffed a laugh. "Not me. You can draw it out with a needle, didn't you say? That will do."

"I can drain it for you here, but that will only give you relief for a short time. Surgery is called for. I'll talk to your mother superior about it. Unless you'd rather someone else operated."

Sister Xavier scowled at the ceiling in a way that made Anna feel sympathy for the sisters who worked under her in the kitchens. She puffed out an irritated explosion of breath.

"If it must be done, better you than one of the doctors at St. Vincent's. I don't care to let a man take a knife to me."

"Good," Anna said. "For the moment, let's see what we can do to give you some relief. It will take me a few minutes to get a sense of the mass, and then I have to sterilize my instruments and the operating field. The aspiration itself will take less than a minute."

"Endless bother," Xavier said. "Get on with it."

But while Anna worked, Sister Francis Xavier couldn't keep quiet. She talked and asked questions but never lost sight of what Anna was doing, stopping her now and then: what was in that bottle and could she smell it and if the hypodermic needle had been used on someone else before and how it was cleaned.

Where the others had been adamantly silent, she was determined to fill the room with words. It was an opportunity Anna could not ignore, this nun who was so willing to talk.

"I wanted to ask about some Italian children who came in from Hoboken this past Monday, orphaned in a smallpox epidemic. Two boys, two girls, Russo is the family name. Would you know anything about them?"

She got a partial shrug as a reply. "Monday is as good as a month around here, and the boys would be in the other building, if they're still here at all."

That gave Anna pause, but she focused on what seemed nearer to hand. "And the girls?"

Sister Xavier said, "There's talk of sisters coming over from Italy to start an orphanage for their own, but in the meantime the Guinea girls are usually sent down to the old place."

She used the word *Guinea*—a terrible insult, even Anna was aware of that much—as easily as she might have said *house* or *child*. It took Anna's breath away for a moment, and then she steadied. "There will be a pinch now, but please hold still." And then: "And here it is."

Sister Francis Xavier let out a great sigh as Anna pulled back on the plunger and a cloudy yellow liquid filled the syringe.

"That's better already."

While Anna cleaned the puncture site and bandaged it, she considered how best to ask what she needed to know.

"You're as bad as the novitiates," Sister Xavier said, her tone grumpier by the minute. "Can't spit out whatever it is you need to say."

"I don't know what you mean by 'the old place'—where is that?"

Sister Xavier sat up with some trouble. "This is the new St. Patrick's, the cathedral buildings. The old place got too crowded, you see, and so the bishop got after the mayor until he gifted this land for a bigger orphan asylum."

"But the older asylum is still in use?"

"It is. The Italian girls are more likely to be sent there."

"And why is that?"

The shoulder under the black habit lifted in a shrug. "They're more at home down there on Mott Street, among their own kind."

◆ ◆ ◆

IT WAS SIX by the time Anna finished with the last examination. She found her own way back along the corridors, passing darkened offices and classrooms. Somewhere in another part of the building bells chimed, but otherwise the halls were far too quiet to house hundreds of little girls. Little girls who learned their letters and their prayers and how to polish wooden floors along with other, harder lessons.

At the next window she paused to look out and saw the reason for the quiet. Two lines of girls were walking, quick-step, along a well-traveled path to one of the cathedral's side entrances. Apparently evening prayer services were in order. She wondered how many times a day this process repeated itself, and whether the girls minded. She thought probably not; they wore sturdy shoes and hooded capes, and their bellies were full. Some of them had probably put up with much worse for far less.

Anna was dry and warm now, but her stomach growled and she

wanted tea and a sandwich and a place to sit quietly for a few moments before she went back out into the weather. There was no sign of the young sister who had taken her wraps to the cloakroom but Anna found them, neatly folded, on a chair in the empty hall.

It seemed that Sister Mary Augustin was not available, after all.

For a long moment Anna waited, standing beside a window to watch as a spring rain replaced the sleet. She would have to go hunt down a cab. The thought was still in her head when she felt a light touch on her elbow.

"Pardon me," said Sister Mary Augustin. "I didn't mean to startle you, but I'm so glad I caught you before you left."

They sat on the visitors' bench in the little lobby as the light rain gave way to watery sunshine, light falling in stripes to make a checkerboard on the cool gray stone floor.

"Mother Superior gave me permission to talk to you," Sister Mary Augustin said. "But I don't have long and there are things you should know"—she swallowed, visibly—"about the Russo children."

"You sought me out to give me bad news, I take it."

Many emotions moved over the younger woman's face. Fear, regret, guilt all came and went, but finally she nodded and the story came out quite quickly. She told Anna about the drunken brawl on the docks and the rush back to the orphan asylum. Somehow, she said, the boys had gotten separated from the rest of the children.

"Separated?"

"They never arrived here."

Anna sat back, and Mary Augustin went on. They had instituted a search once this was discovered, but without success. The boys had last been seen four days ago, on Monday. Rosa was beside herself with worry.

Anna offered to talk to the girl, and color rose in Mary Augustin's face.

"They're gone," she said. "They were transferred to the old St. Patrick's on Wednesday. The priest there is Italian." She offered this as if it were explanation enough, and in fact it did lend credence to what Sister Ignatia had told her. Mostly Italians and Irish lived in the tenements crowded together along the East River.

"All right," Anna said. "I'll go there straightaway and talk to them."

She was very tired, but she would not sleep if she let this stand while Rosa waited for word.

"That's the trouble," Sister Mary Augustin said, her voice taking on a bit of a wobble. "You won't find them."

"I think I can find a Catholic orphan asylum on Mott Street."

"No doubt," Sister Mary Augustin said. "But they aren't there anymore. Sometime after eleven at night and six in the morning they went out into the weather and disappeared. The whole area was combed multiple times, but there's no trace of them."

Struck silent by surprise, Anna asked herself why Rosa would do such a desperate thing.

"Were the girls punished or treated badly?"

Mary Augustin looked as though she had been anticipating this question. "I don't know. My guess is that Rosa wouldn't stop asking about her brothers and one of the sisters lost her temper and was harsh."

"Harsh," Anna echoed. "And you have no idea where they might be. So now all four children are missing."

"Yes," Mary Augustin said. "I'm afraid so."

Anna, at a loss for words, stared for a full minute. "Then we'll have to find them. Immediately."

◆   ◆   ◆

SUPPER BREAK AND Jack sat at his desk in the detectives' squad room watching Oscar pace back and forth, grumpier with every step. He was hungry and required feeding, and soon Jack would have to get up and go out into the weather or simply resign himself to Oscar's mood.

"You'd think you'd never got wet before in your life," Oscar muttered. And: "Now we're in for it."

A runner had appeared at the door waving an assignment sheet: on Washington Square a patrolman had come across Italian trespassers on university grounds who wouldn't be shifted. He had called his roundsman, who was requesting a translator.

"I'll miss supper," Oscar groused.

With a pointed look at Maroney's middle, Jack grabbed his overcoat and hat and headed for the door.

◆   ◆   ◆

THE WET SNOW gave way quite suddenly to a warmer and gentler wind, and with that the feel of spring had come back into the air. In

Washington Square Park Jack felt the subtle stir of things growing, as tangible as sunlight on the skin.

New York University sat across from the northeast corner of the park. More like a church with its tall arches and spires, to Jack's mind, except for the noise that a crowd of undergraduates were making trying to get a game of baseball going in the park. They'd be covered in muck and mud in no time, but Jack understood the urge to be moving. Oscar did too, from the looks he threw in the direction of the players. He would join in with very little encouragement.

They entered the university through the main doors and heard the argument from across the foyer. The porter's desk was empty, but the door behind it was open and provided a view of Harry Pettigrew facing off with a small woman who stood close, her face turned up at a sharp angle to scold the roundsman, the traditional posture of mothers with sons twice their size and a bone to pick.

"It's Harry who's needing rescuing, so it seems," Oscar said. "That's the porter's wife got him backed into a corner."

It wasn't until he stepped into the office that Jack caught sight of the two little girls who sat side by side on the counter. So not intruders, after all, not even street children. These two were too fragile to survive on the street, and so, Jack reasoned to himself, they had run away, or been put out. One of them was crying softly while the other sat stony faced, her arm around the smaller girl.

"Mrs. Conway," Pettigrew was saying. "No one means these girls any harm—"

"So say you!"

"Hold on, Mrs. Conway," Oscar said. "Don't be in such a rush to draw and quarter the poor roundsman."

While Oscar negotiated a peace between the parties, Jack got a better look at the two children. They were both dripping wet and filthy, hair straggling over threadbare clothes. They shivered with the cold despite the towels that had been wrapped around them and the coal heaped up in the stove.

The older of the two raised her head to look at him directly, and in that moment Jack recognized her. Rosa, if he remembered correctly. The last he had seen her was getting off the Hoboken ferry, her brothers and sister gathered in close. She had been determined to keep the little family together, and she had clearly failed, as he had known she must. Now the last name came to him as well. Rosa Russo.

She recognized him too, because her expression shifted to puzzlement and then, quite quickly, relief. Jack remembered that she had been proud of her English, and he started with that.

"Miss Russo," he said. "We meet again."

The argument stopped abruptly as Roundsman Pettigrew, the porter's wife, the porter, and the patrolman turned to look at Jack.

Pettigrew regained his composure first. "She doesn't speak English."

"Of course she does. Don't you, Rosa," Jack said, keeping his gaze on her.

The girl drew herself up with great dignity, a small queen finally recognized by one of her subjects. "Yes," she said. "I am an American."

"Hoboken," Jack said to Oscar, enough to clue him in to the circumstances without divulging information to the porter or his wife.

Jack said, "Why didn't you tell these good people that you speak English?"

"It would not have mattered," she said, looking at the adults. "They won't listen to me no matter what language I speak. And I knew if I told them what they want to know"—she frowned at Pettigrew—"they would send us back to—"

She took note of the way Pettigrew leaned toward her, and paused. In Italian she said, "*Il orfanotrofio*. It took us so long to get this far and Lia is very tired."

"You ran away." Oscar spoke his Neopolitan Italian, very similar to the language the girls spoke.

Rosa glanced at him nervously, taken aback by the combination of an Irish face and the language of her home. Finally, she nodded.

With patient questioning Oscar was able to pinpoint where the girls had started, and when. They had left the orphan asylum at Prince and Mott before light and started north, asking directions from an Italian street musician with a monkey who wore a hat.

"But how did you ask for directions? Where is it you're trying to go?"

"Here," Rosa said, spreading out her arms. "Sister Mary Augustin described this place exactly."

Sister Mary Augustin from St. Patrick's; the face came back to him quickly. But he was missing something, so he thought for a moment and phrased his question carefully.

"Sister Mary Augustin told you how to get to here, to this place?"

"No," Rosa said, irritation starting to rise again. "On the journey from the ferry—" She stopped herself. "On the way to that place, the omnibus went past this church that isn't a church after all. Sister Mary Augustin pointed to it and told us that Dr. Savard lived just nearby. She told us about the house that has a garden bigger than its own self behind a brick wall, and fruit trees, and a pergola, and hens and a rooster."

"*Un gallo!*" her sister echoed, as if a rooster could only exist in Italian.

"I was sure I could find it because Dr. Savard has to help us. They took our brothers away, and I have to find them. I was so sure I could find a house with angels over the door," she finished.

To Lia Oscar said, "*Angeli sopra la porta?*"

"*Si. Putti e gigli.*" It struck Jack that the little girl was trying very hard to be exact.

He turned to Pettigrew. "Is there a house nearby with lilies and angels carved above the door—"

"More likely cherubs or cupids—" Oscar suggested.

"Coo-pids," Lia mimicked.

"—carved into the stone lintel. Does that sound familiar?"

"It's Mrs. Quinlan they want," the patrol officer said. "If they had said about the angels and lilies before, we would have solved this right away. The Quinlan place is half a block away."

At that Rosa's composure finally cracked and tears began to leak down her face. There was something very formal about her even in her despair, but the little one was less bound by pride. Lia might not have understood the exchange, but her sister's tears were more than she could bear.

When Oscar held out his arms, Lia collapsed toward him, pushed her face into the wool of his coat, and sobbed openly.

"She could have told us she was looking for the Quinlan place," Pettigrew said to Jack, gruff embarrassment in his tone. "Everybody knows the house with the walled garden. All they had to do was speak English."

◆ ◆ ◆

COUSIN MARGARET WAS reading aloud to them from the paper, something she liked to do because, Sophie understood, it was the only way to introduce the subjects she wanted to discuss. Margaret, raised in this house by Uncle Quinlan and his first wife, had only a few interests: her sons, the way she was perceived by the other old Knickerbocker families, keeping the memory of her husband alive, and crime.

She read many papers every day and kept a ledger detailing all the crimes that happened within a square mile of home. Now she sat in an elegant but understated day dress, her posture perfect, her head held erect, and read to them about a burglary on Greene Street, just two blocks away, in that neighborhood she referred to as *French Town*. If she went on any longer in that tone there would be an argument; Aunt Quinlan could tolerate only so much of Margaret's fearmongering and even less of her distaste for immigrants. Eventually she would be compelled to remind her stepdaughter that her father's grandparents had been immigrants. It was an old and exhausting argument, and Sophie was thinking of ways to deflect it when she saw two men coming up the street, the older of the two carrying a very little girl in a ragged coat far too big for her. A second girl of eight or nine years was looking up at the houses as they passed, pointing to gates and lampposts and doorways and explaining something. The girls looked as though they had been living on the street and had had a hard time of it.

Margaret said, "Sophie, have you lost your hearing? I was asking—"

The strangers had stopped and were looking at Aunt Quinlan's door with its frieze of angels and lilies.

"We have company," Sophie said.

Aunt Quinlan sat up, cheered as she always was at the arrival of visitors. "And still no sign of Anna. I wonder if Sister Ignatia has taken her hostage. Maybe we should send Mr. Lee with a ransom."

◆ ◆ ◆

JACK COULDN'T QUITE believe that Anna Savard might actually live in this particular house, but there was the door with angels and lilies, finely carved along the stone lintel. He had gone down this street hundreds of times and always he had wondered about this substantial limestone house of four stories, with mature pear and plum trees visible over the garden wall.

"Do you know that lady?" Oscar pointed with his chin to the window where a young woman stood.

Jack didn't recognize her and neither did Rosa, whose whole face collapsed. "No," she said. "That's not Dr. Savard. But the angels and the lilies—"

"Remember Sergeant Pettigrew said there were two ladies named Savard living here." There was no sign of Maroney's legendary impatience and volatility; he had been tamed by a little girl with a dirty face.

The door opened. The woman standing there was not Anna Savard, though she had the same bearing and the air of confidence. This woman's features were fuller, and her eyes were a color he couldn't name, not green or blue but somewhere in between, just as her skin was somewhere between old honey and copper. While these thoughts went through Jack's head, Oscar was dealing with introductions and explaining what had brought them to her door on a spring evening. Jack heard the words *Hoboken* and *orphan* and *Sister Mary Augustin*.

As it turned out this was also a Dr. Savard, another female physician. Jack had gone most of his life without ever encountering such a creature and now they seemed to be everywhere.

Rosa was saying, "Is the other Dr. Savard here? Can we see her, please?"

This Dr. Savard had a kind smile, one that would put a child's worries to rest. "She isn't here right now, but we expect her any moment. Would you like to come in and wait for her?" And then her gaze shifted, first to Oscar and then Jack. "Detective Sergeants, please do come in."

She introduced them all to another woman, this one called Margaret Cooper—middle-aged, a little nervous in disposition, a war widow, if Jack was any judge—and to the older lady, Mrs. Quinlan.

"I sense a mystery and its unraveling all at once," Mrs. Quinlan said. "Very exciting. Come in and sit down. Mrs. Lee, we will have guests for supper once Anna is come, but right now we're in dire need of tea."

The parlor was large and comfortable, but Jack felt as though he had stepped, unawares, onto a train that was gathering speed. Odder still, he was too curious to even think about getting off. Instead he watched as the Russo girls were stripped of their wraps and swaddled in blankets to sit together in an upholstered chair close to the hearth. They were telling their story to the three women, Rosa in English with commentary from Lia in Italian. Little by little Rosa's hectic tone quieted and she began to hiccup between sentences, quick sharp gulps of air. A little girl after all, ready to hand over her burdens to these women who listened so closely with such serious expressions. Looking at her now it was hard to believe she had dared so much, and survived.

In Jack's experience most men gave children little thought; they were distractions to be ignored or resources to be trained and put to work or burdens to be fed and clothed, and often all three at once. As a police officer Jack had come to understand that the children in circumstances such as these required more—demanded more—than willful ignorance or benign disregard.

Rosa was terrified, angry, confused, despairing, but at the same time she distinguished herself by an iron force of will. There was a simple, undeniable fact she would make these women understand: her brothers must be returned to her. Their father had deserted them, but Rosa would not.

Jack let his gaze wander over the room, full of color and well lit by gaslight from crystal wall sconces and hanging lamps. Paintings and drawings crowded the walls and overhead a mural in jewel-like colors spread over the entire ceiling. There were tall bookcases filled to overflowing behind glass fronts, a basket of needlework set aside, plants in tiled pots, shiny leafed and vigorous. It was an unusual room in an unusual house, peopled by women who seemed unshakable, who took the appearance of wet Italian orphans and police detectives at their door as nothing out of the ordinary.

His sisters would look around this room, at the clothing and draperies and tablecloth, and tell him what it all meant. They might be affronted or charmed.

On a side table in a prominent spot, a dozen framed photos were grouped together. He counted eight men in uniform, the youngest no more than eighteen. On a cabinet card, elaborately framed, was a man of at least seventy.

"That is my father," Margaret Cooper said, coming up behind him. Jack realized just then that she stood out from the others primarily because of her clothing, quite fashionable and conservative, which meant that she was trussed like a leg of lamb bound for the oven.

"Did he return to active duty for the war?"

She smiled, happy to have him open the conversation.

"He was an army surgeon, retired. The next photograph is my brother James. Aunt Quinlan—as Sophie and Anna call her—is my stepmother."

"The other men?" he asked.

She pointed to each face in turn, her finger hovering but not touching. "This is Andrew—my husband—he fell at Chickamauga. This is Nathaniel Ballentyne, Aunt Quinlan's son by her first husband. He died at Shiloh, fighting beside my brother. Nathaniel and James went to school together; they were the best of friends. These five"—her finger skimmed—"are some of my stepmother's nephews. None of these men came home. Not one."

Oscar had been standing aside but paying attention. Now he made a soft sound in his throat. "I'm sorry to hear it. My sincere condolences."

Jack glanced at Mrs. Quinlan, still deep in conversation with the little girls, and then returned to the collection of cabinet cards. A wedding party, a fat little boy standing with one hand wound in the coat of a huge dog, two young blond women so much alike that they had to be twins. A small painting on an easel showed an Indian woman with high cheekbones, her hair threaded with white. She was laughing, her arms wrapped around herself.

Oscar touched his shoulder and inclined his head to a portrait that hung on the opposite wall. There were dozens of photographs and paintings of President Lincoln that appeared every so often in newspapers and magazines, but Jack couldn't remember ever seeing an oil portrait, one in which the man came to life.

"That is my stepmother's work," Margaret Cooper said. "Mrs. Quinlan is well regarded as an artist. Or was, before arthritis put an end to it all."

It was hard to fathom, at that moment. The old lady who spoke so kindly to the little girls had been beautiful as a younger woman, that was still clear. But she had also been capable of painting like this, President Lincoln as Jack liked to think of him, alive, sharp energy in the dark eyes. Everyone had their own memories of the day of the assassination, stories that had been told again and again and would be told today and tomorrow and all the days of their lives. The conversation could start up among strangers in a train car or at Sunday dinner.

Jack's attention moved to a photograph of two young girls and a boy of ten or eleven. After a moment's study he realized one of the girls was Sophie Savard, and the other was Anna. He supposed the boy might be Cap Verhoeven, with a mop of blond hair and a grin of the kind so rare in photographs.

Oscar said, "It looks as though they grew up together like brother and sisters."

"Not quite." Sophie had come to help the housekeeper with a tea cart. "I was ten when Aunt Quinlan sent for me, as soon as it was safe to travel after the war. Listen," she said, turning. "She's so pleased to have the chance to speak Italian; see how her face lights up."

The old lady's language was quite formal, and by listening to it Jack knew that she had traveled or lived in Italy long ago and learned from tutors who placed more value on formal grammar than conversation, but still she had an ear for the language.

She must have felt him looking, because she raised her head and smiled at him. And took his breath away. Beautiful as a young woman, yes. The beauty had gone with the years but left something just as powerful behind.

And just then Jack heard the sound of the front door opening and closing, and then she was there. Liliane-called-Anna. Her color was high, but Jack had the idea that it was agitation rather than the weather at fault. Standing in the doorway she pulled her hat off and her scarf away to reveal the tripling pulse at the base of her throat.

She had caught sight of the Russo girls and moved forward without pausing, dropping her things as she went. The others were talking to her all at once, but Anna seemed not to hear them. She made a visible effort to straighten her back and steady her expression, but it was clear that she was shaken.

"I see we have company," she said, her voice a little rough.

"Indeed," said Mrs. Quinlan. "You've met Rosa and Lia, I believe."

The girls were leaning forward, as interested in Anna as she was in them.

"We met in Hoboken, yes," Anna said. "In fact, I was about to go out searching for the two of you. You have entire convents up in arms." She crouched down in front of the girls and touched them lightly: heads, faces, shoulders.

Her aunt said, "We have other guests, Anna." She nodded toward the alcove where Jack and Oscar stood.

Anna pivoted, her expression suddenly guarded. Jack tried to smile and found himself able to muster no more than a twitch at the corner of his mouth.

"Good evening," Oscar said, clearly enjoying both the situation and Jack's carefully masked interest. "Dr. Savard, I hope you will forgive the intrusion."

A new wash of color rose along her throat and crept into her face, only to fall away just as rapidly to leave behind mottling, something Jack had seen only rarely in his life, on the faces and throats and breasts of the few women he had taken to his bed. The image took him by surprise and made him turn his face to hide his own expression, which he feared would give away as much as a woman's blush.

Oscar was talking about Pettigrew, the children in the porter's office at the university, how they had come to find the house. Jack heard only bits of this, he was so flustered by the workings of his own mind. Then he turned his head and saw that Anna Savard was watching him. For a split second he had the idea that she had read his thoughts and seen a picture of herself, stripped bare, in his embrace, breathless.

She smiled, a half smile, a weary but welcoming smile such as she might give anyone.

"Rosa," she said. "You must promise me never to run away again."

"They lost my brothers," Rosa said with great calm. "And they don't care."

"Nothing was done out of malice," Anna said. And seeing the girl's confusion: "They did not set out to cause you harm."

"But harm was done."

Such presence of mind, in such a young girl.

Rosa said, "You won't send us back, will you?"

And there was the question. Before anyone could respond, Margaret Cooper stood abruptly. "Of course not," she said in a tone that brooked no discussion. "What these little girls need is a warm bath and a good meal, and then a bed piled high with pillows and blankets and comforters where they can sleep through the night without fear. Where they can sleep as long as they like and then have a large and filling breakfast."

The most maternal of the group, then. The younger Savard women seemed satisfied to have their cousin take the little girls in hand. Lia, biddable, came off her chair with a thump, trailing blankets. Even Rosa got to her feet without question, her face slack with weariness now that she had finally reached her goal.

◆ ◆ ◆

THEY WERE GOING into the dining room before Anna had time to make sense of the situation or her own state of mind. Or minds, because she seemed to have more than one. She was exhausted and exhilarated, angry and in the grip of an almost preternatural calm, agitated and focused. Part of that had to do with the turmoil of questions that had occupied her during the cab ride home: how to best search for the missing girls, if there were friends who could be called in to help or if that would further complicate an already fraught situation, if the police should be notified and why the Sisters of Charity had not done so already, if it would be sound reasoning to start by inquiring at hospitals, all of these questions and more. And underlying all of this, a dread that sat heavy: had she shown even minimal interest instead of just walking away from the ferry, this whole situation might have been avoided. She should have done something. Anything.

All of that, only to be relieved of the burden by the simple act of coming home to find the girls in her own parlor. The sight of them safe had worked like cold water on a hot afternoon.

And then she had turned to find Detective Sergeant Mezzanotte looking at her just when she had resigned herself to forgetting him.

He was still looking, sitting across from her at the table in her own home, quiet and observant as his partner told the story in more detail. Now that the little girls were out of the room, they talked more openly about the things that might have gone wrong but didn't.

Anna applied herself to her food with such focus that it took a moment to realize that someone had asked her a question. Mrs. Lee stood beside her with the soup tureen, one brow raised and a quirk to her mouth that did not bode well. Nothing escaped Mrs. Lee. There would be questions, but Anna would not give her answers because a lie would be sniffed out immediately, and the truth was too tender to be handled.

Aunt Quinlan said, "Anna, did you mention Detective Sergeant Mezzanotte when you told us about your trip to Hoboken on Easter Monday?"

"She mentioned him to me," Sophie said. "You translated for Anna, isn't that right, Detective Sergeant?"

Anna knew that Sophie was willing to intervene on her behalf, but it was too much to ask and, moreover, doomed to failure. They would not be distracted, these old women to whom she belonged, heart and soul. She took hold of the conversation.

"Sister Mary Augustin wasn't quite up to the challenge of so many dialects," Anna said. "And the priest was away at—" She looked at Jack Mezzanotte directly. "The term escapes me."

"Extreme unction," he supplied. "Last rites."

"So I was very glad of his help. But I first met Detective Sergeant Maroney at the Vanderbilts' masked ball later that evening," she added. "They were there on duty."

Sophie had been participating in the conversation with her usual good manners, but now she stiffened slightly. To Detective Maroney she said, "Did you meet our friend Cap?"

"We didn't have the pleasure," he answered. "I was sorry to learn that he is so ill." It was phrased in a way that could be taken as a question or an observation.

"He is consumptive," Aunt Quinlan said.

Anna was glad of the change in topic, but it also confused her; it wasn't like Aunt Quinlan to talk to strangers about Cap's health. Something else was going on.

She was saying, "Sophie has had a letter from a specialist in

Switzerland—" She raised a brow in Anna's direction. "We planned to tell you about it this evening."

"Hmmm," Anna said, doubtfully. She wondered when exactly this letter had arrived. More important, she understood that she had been outmaneuvered. The subject of the letter had been brought up because the company at the table would force her to be patient and keep what would otherwise be sharp questions to herself. For the time being.

"A specialist who can cure consumption?" Oscar Maroney looked both impressed and doubtful.

"No," Sophie said. "Not yet. But he is opening a clinic—too small to be called a sanatorium really—to launch a trial for a new therapy."

Anna said, "We'll have to go over the details later. That is, if Cap indicates an interest." *And there,* she thought. *That should be enough to end the conversation, both at this table and at any other time.* Cap would have nothing to do with such a scheme. Except now Aunt Quinlan was looking at her thoughtfully, with something in her expression Anna didn't like at all.

"But he is interested," her aunt said. "He asked for you to come by on Sunday, to discuss it."

◆　◆　◆

JACK HAD BEEN watching the back-and-forth between the older women and the younger ones, seeing affection and respect in the way they talked to each other, but also challenges and long-held disagreements.

"So may I ask, what do you plan to do about the Russo girls?"

All eyes turned to him.

"Would you like us to take them back to the asylum?"

Beside him Maroney moved uneasily.

"You would do that?" Sophie seemed genuinely surprised.

"If you asked us to, we would have to take them."

"Where?" Aunt Quinlan wanted to know. "To Mott Street?"

Margaret Cooper appeared in the doorway as if her name had been called. "You cannot be serious. We can't send them back there," she said. "Not in good conscience."

"Margaret," Anna began, but her cousin had already walked away, her back stiff and straight.

"She wants to take them in?" Oscar looked at each of the women in turn, one brow raised in polite surprise.

"She is very maternal and misses having children to look after, but of course, this is something we need to think about and discuss at length before we undertake something so—important," Mrs. Quinlan said.

Then Margaret was back, a newspaper in her hands. "'Chinese opium den raided,'" she read aloud. "'Young girls living in the neighborhood have been decoyed for immoral purposes.'" Her eyes scanned the page. "'A brawl outside Mayer's tavern at Cherry and Water Streets ended in a fatal stabbing . . .' And oh, yes, this: 'The body of a young boy found in an outhouse on Prince Street, marks of violence.' Shall I go on?"

Oscar was clearly surprised and delighted at this unexpected source of information. "You subscribe to the *Police Gazette*?"

"I do," she said, as if she had been challenged.

The old aunt shook her head. "Margaret, we are all aware of the dangers in that neighborhood, but that's not the issue just now. We have to send word to the sisters that they can stop searching. It doesn't mean we'll send the girls away."

"We might not have a choice," Sophie said. "The Church will have an opinion."

Margaret Cooper's expression turned sour, but Anna got up from the table before the conversation could continue.

"I'll write that note now."

◆   ◆   ◆

ONCE THE DETECTIVE sergeants had gone off to the convent with the note and a message, Anna let herself be drawn into a fraught conversation about the little girls and what it would mean to keep them.

"These are not stray cats," she said aloud to no one in particular, and with that sparked a sputtering maternal declaration from Margaret: she, Margaret Quinlan Cooper, knew far better than Anna what it meant to raise children, the responsibilities, the work and effort and potential for heartbreak. If Anna didn't like the idea of being tied down, well, then Anna should continue just as she was and leave the poor little girls to others, who knew the business best. Margaret's two boys were evidence enough that she was equal to the task. Margaret glanced at Aunt Quinlan as she came to the end of this speech but didn't get the agreement she sought.

Instead, Aunt Quinlan said, "Margaret, do you sincerely want to dedicate the next twenty years to the raising of these two children?"

"And the two brothers, if we should find them," Sophie said, quietly.

"Are we looking for them?" her aunt asked.

Anna forced herself to take three deep breaths. She knew what she needed to say but not exactly why she needed to say it. "I will look for them," she began slowly. "I intend to find them, if that is possible. I feel as though I owe Rosa that much. And please don't ask me to explain myself, because I'm not sure I can."

"That's quite clear, Anna," her aunt said. "She reminds you of yourself."

Flushed with irritation Anna said, "My situation was nothing like hers. I had family. There was never any uncertainty about who would look after me."

She didn't like the look on her aunt's face, and so she went on. "Even if the girls go back to the orphan asylum, I will make an effort to locate the boys."

"The chances of finding them are very small," her aunt said, gently.

Sophie said, "But if we should somehow find them, we'd have four young children on our hands." Her expression was calm but her tone was unmistakable: she would support Anna in her decision, but first she would be sure that the decision was not made rashly.

"Whatever we decide to do, we have to tell the girls in the morning," Aunt Quinlan said. "The uncertainty is too much for them."

It was another hour and a half before they had come to any kind of consensus, and still Anna lay awake once she finally found herself in bed. She got up and lit her desk lamp, got out paper and pen and inkpot. She had gone over the wording so many times in her head she wrote quickly and without pause.

Detective Sergeant Mezzanotte,

I write to thank you for your kind assistance to the Russo sisters, and for bringing them to us. After long discussion we have decided to ask the Sisters of Charity to give us custody of the girls while we

*apply for guardianship status. We will take full responsibility for
them and agree to raise them as Catholics should that be required.*

*If you are willing, we would like permission to use your name as
a reference in writing our petition to the Church authorities. Please
let us know if this is acceptable to you.*

*We will also commit to taking in the two Russo boys, should we
have success finding them. I recognize the difficulty of such an
undertaking, but I feel an obligation to at least try.*

Thank you once again for your understanding and kindness.

Sincerely yours,
Anna Savard

A half hour later, almost asleep, Anna sat up suddenly in bed. The
first shimmer of dawn was in the sky, but she lit the lamp once again,
because she had made an error that had to be corrected. She began
the letter once again: *Detective Sergeants Mezzanotte and Maroney.*

The next morning Anna sat across from Sophie at the kitchen
table studying a letter that had come with the first mail delivery. It
was very brief and, unfortunately, not the first of its kind.

Dear Dr. Savard,

*I know a number of ladies who have been treated by you, and who
speak of your wide knowledge and consummate skill as a physician
specializing in women's health. Today I write in the hope that you
might be able to provide me with that particular kind of sensitive
information the mother of many children must sometimes have. I
have recently seen one such pamphlet which I believe you supplied a
friend, and I would gladly pay for my own copy. Indeed, I would like
to buy any pamphlets you have on the restoration of menses and
good health. Please write to me at Herald Square Post Box 886 with
a list of available pamphlets and their cost. Thank you in advance
for your kind assistance.*

Yours most sincerely
Mrs. C. J. Latimer

On the table between them was also a larger sheet of paper with a single line of writing at the top:

Latimer == Campbell

It was the way she and Sophie and Cap had always tackled a difficult problem in geometry or chemistry. She and Sophie continued the practice at college and in medical school studying pharmacology and physiology. And now they sometimes discussed a difficult case.

The letter from the lady signing herself Mrs. Latimer was nothing out of the ordinary, but it had roused Sophie's suspicions. Given the timing, she feared it was connected to the pamphlet she had sent Mrs. Campbell. If her husband had intercepted the envelope, this could be a trap, yet another effort to manipulate her into violating the Comstock Act.

At Sophie's elbow was a pile of newspaper clippings that dated back five years, all of which had to do with Comstock's arrests of physicians, midwives, printers, and druggists for distribution of contraceptives or information about contraceptives. There was a handwritten chart attached, on which Anna had calculated the number of arrests according to the type of evidence, and the outcome of the case. Comstock was not terribly successful in prosecuting these cases, but he was persistent and sometimes, with the right judge, he got what he wanted.

She recognized in herself a kind of compulsion to keep track of Comstock, and a general irritation that such a thing should be necessary. For all they knew other physicians all over the city were just as worried about the possibility of being entrapped, but they were all so afraid of Comstock that they didn't raise the subject in company.

"We don't have enough information," Anna said when they had been going over the facts available to them for ten minutes. "I don't see any real connection to Mrs. Campbell."

"Maybe not, but I think we have to assume the worst," Sophie said. "Mrs. Campbell would have received the pamphlet I sent on Wednesday, probably in the first mail delivery of the day. That was two days after I attended her delivery, and one day after her husband looked at me, directly at me, while he stood next to Comstock. At Clara Garrison's trial. We have to warn the printer," she said. "If the pamphlet was traced to me, it could be traced to him, and I will not take that chance."

"Think about it for one more day," Anna said. "And think about this too: if Comstock does have someone watching you, that person could follow you to the printer they otherwise would have a difficult time locating and might never suspect."

Sophie gave her a pointed look. "Why do you want to talk me out of doing what I know is right?"

Anna sat back, picked up her cup, and thought for a moment.

"I don't. Really, I don't. But the thought of that man—my hackles rise."

"You can be sure I'll take every precaution to avoid him."

Anna would have to be satisfied with that much.

6

EARLY SUNDAY MORNING Anna came in from checking post-op patients and stretched out on her favorite divan in the parlor, putting her head back to study the mural on the ceiling. It was the work of a visiting artist who had painted because he had no other way, he explained at length, of repaying Aunt Quinlan's extraordinary hospitality.

Aunt Quinlan was known as a gracious hostess, a supporter of young artists, and an easy touch. Any close friend could write a letter of introduction that would open her door, and she had many close friends. Over the years dozens of young artists had come to call, in need of encouragement and regular feeding and a bed. These young people would stay a few days or a few weeks, and almost all of them left behind a painting or drawing or sculpture of some kind.

Mr. MacLeish had decided that nothing less than a mural would do, and banished them all from the parlor for a full month while he worked.

"And ate," Mrs. Lee pointed out at every opportunity. Mrs. Lee did not like being shut out of the parlor, and she liked even less that Hamish MacLeish wouldn't allow her to supervise his progress. By the time the unveiling came around she was determined not to like whatever he had created, but she gave in with good grace as soon as she saw it.

MacLeish won Mrs. Lee over by putting Aunt Quinlan—a much younger Aunt Quinlan, extracted from an early self-portrait—in the center of his mural as Mnemosyne, the goddess of memory.

"Just so," said Mrs. Lee. "Queens and goddesses forget nothing, except when it suits them."

"He was a student of Rossetti's," Aunt Quinlan reminded them.

They were sitting in the parlor studying the mural after MacLeish had gone on to try his luck in the west. "Obsessed with hair, masses of it. All of Rossetti's crowd were."

He had painted the muses, too, in a circle around their mother, all draped in flowing jewel-colored robes and each of them with more hair than any human woman could possibly want.

"The hair is well done, but he didn't get your faces quite right." This from Cousin Margaret to Anna and Sophie, delivered with a small sniff.

"We didn't know he was using us as models," Sophie said, because it was clear now that Margaret felt ignored.

Anna said to her, "I suppose we should be offended that he didn't ask for permission."

"Or for forgiveness," said Aunt Quinlan, dryly.

Over the course of the year Anna had come to like the mural, though she had yet to admit as much to anyone. She liked it, she told herself, because MacLeish had cast her in the role of Euterpe, the muse of music. Anna had a tin ear, and a great appreciation for both irony and nonsense.

She might have slipped back into sleep if not for a little hand that latched on to her wrist. Lia Russo staked her claim and then clambered like a monkey to tuck herself into the crook of Anna's arm. She came straight from bed, a small bundle of flannel smelling of sleep and lavender talc and little girl.

Lia put her head against Anna's shoulder and joined her in her study of the mural.

Not yet two full days in residence, and the Russo girls had taken over. Or better said, Lia had taken over; Rosa alternated between hanging back and trying to rein in her sister. When Anna left for the hospital the morning of their first full day on Waverly Place, the moving of furniture had already begun, and when she came home the discussion of redecorating, of what could be fetched from the attic, of shopping and dressmakers and shoes, was still in full voice. Anna had the sense that this unexpected upheaval in the household was going to suit all of them. Once the legalities were worked out.

She had the first draft of a letter to the sisters in charge of the asylum sitting on her desk. The writing of letters was something she did a lot of, and easily, but not this time. This time she had to explain the unexplainable: why these two girls in particular, when she saw so many of them, day in and day out.

To Lia she said, "Have you had your breakfast?"

In response the five-year-old pointed at the ceiling. "Heaven," she said. "*Cielo*."

"Very good," Anna said, resisting the urge to correct the child's misinterpretation. The scene above their heads had nothing to do with a Christian heaven, but she was not about to discuss schools of art, Greek mythology, or perspective, whether geometrical or philosophical, with this little girl. If Lia wanted to think of heaven as a place where young women took their ease in a meadow beside a brook, Anna would not try to dissuade her. She wondered if Lia imagined her mother in a heaven like the one overhead. Anna had only the vaguest memories of her own mother and couldn't imagine her anywhere at all.

"*Cos'è?*" Lia pointed again, and Anna realized she had learned her first sentence in Italian. Lia was asking the question young children never tired of: *What's that?*

"I'm not sure," Anna said. "Do you mean the apple tree?" She pretended to bite into an apple, and got a nod.

"Apple tree." Lia pronounced it perfectly.

"In Italiano?" Anna ventured. "*Cos'è?*"

"*Melo.*"

Anna repeated the word and Lia nodded her approval.

"There you are." Margaret swooped into the parlor, all bright energy. The little girls had given her purpose, something no one had realized she was missing, which struck Anna as a little sad.

"Lia," Margaret said. "Come now and have your breakfast. Eggs and bacon and toast and jam." She repeated this in something that sounded vaguely like Italian and held out a hand.

Lia climbed down willingly enough and let herself be steered away, looking over her shoulder at Anna as she disappeared. Sophie took her place, coming in with a breakfast tray.

"Is this a bribe?" Anna turned onto her side to examine the offerings.

"Do you need to be bribed?"

Anna went back to studying the ceiling. "That depends."

Sophie was still firm in her intention to warn the printer, and Anna realized now that there was nothing that she could do to dissuade her. She wasn't even sure that Sophie was incorrect.

Sophie said, "When are you going to see Cap?"

"As soon as I can rouse myself." Anna gave an exaggerated yawn.

"And when is Detective Sergeant Mezzanotte coming to call?"

Anna felt the irritation blossom on her face. "It's not a call." And then: "It's not that kind of call. I'll see him on Sunday afternoon."

"I'm wondering," Sophie began, and Anna swallowed a groan.

"I'm wondering," she began again. "If you have been so irritable since Friday evening because the detectives stayed too long, or because they left too early."

Anna got up, smoothed her skirts, and with every ounce of self-possession she could summon, she said, "I'm off to see Cap."

•　•　•

THE DISCUSSION ABOUT Sophie's trip to Brooklyn had unsettled her more than she wanted to admit. To Anna it was all theory: somewhere out in the city there was a printer who might or might not be Comstock's newest prey. Anna knew his name but nothing more, while Sophie had met the man and liked him.

It had happened entirely by accident on an icy winter morning soon after Anna had left to study in Europe. Because the roads were so treacherous and she had many stops to make, Sophie had agreed to let Mr. Lee drive her for the day.

They went first to the German Dispensary where she had been asked to consult on a difficult case. The only physician in attendance was Dr. Thalberg, difficult himself and uncompromising; he stayed nearby while she examined the forty-year-old woman deep into her twelfth and troubled pregnancy. The discussion that followed had required another hour, and by the time it was clear that there was nothing she could do for the patient, Sophie was late for her next appointment. She was pulling on her wraps as she came into the waiting room, where she stopped short.

The dispensary had been established to serve the needs of Kleindeutschland, some four hundred city blocks where English was rarely heard on the street and shop signs and newspapers were in German. It was a city within the city, with Avenue B serving as the commercial life-line, while beer halls and restaurants and oyster bars lined Avenue A. What outsiders rarely realized was that Little Germany had its own strict internal boundaries. Sophie was aware of it herself only because of Dr. Thalberg, who often wished out loud for a second dispensary where the southern Germans could be sent, far away from his Prussian sensibilities.

Sophie wasn't often asked to consult here, for reasons that were never discussed but clear nonetheless. While most sick women who couldn't afford a doctor studiously overlooked the color of Sophie's skin, the patients who came to the German Dispensary were more likely to voice an objection. Dr. Thalberg and the other doctors on staff only called on her when the patient was too sick to care.

She left through a waiting room crowded with the kind of people she would see in any other clinic: a harried mother trying to console a miserable toddler; another who looked like she had had no sleep for days; a workman cradling an injured arm; a fragile old man sound asleep, snoring softly; a stable hand in mucky wooden clogs with such a high fever that Sophie could feel it radiating off him as she passed.

And standing to one side by himself, a hand stemmed against the wall so that he could hold a foot up off the floor, was a man of some seventy years. Beside him was a leather portmanteau that had been nearly ripped in two, but he himself seemed to be unharmed beyond the need to keep the weight off his foot. He was a businessman by his dress, and one who employed a very good tailor. Everything about him was understated and of first quality, but he had the broad fea-tures and rich color of African ancestors.

A black man of property, injured. In this clinic, in the middle of Little Germany. Either he was a stranger to the city and did not realize his situation, or his visit was unplanned. She wondered if he had any idea that he would be left standing here while all the rest of the patients were seen, and would still be standing when the waiting room was empty.

Nothing of worry or anxiety showed in his expression or the way he held himself. Whether he was preoccupied by his injury or simply unaware of the dozen people who radiated distrust and dislike in his direction, that was impossible to say. All this and more went through Sophie's mind in the two seconds it took her to wind her scarf around her neck. Without conscious thought she stepped toward him, holding out an elbow for him to take.

"Can I help you to the carriage?"

He hesitated for less than a heartbeat, nodded, and took the arm she offered.

◆ ◆ ◆

HIS NAME, SHE learned as soon as they were out the door, was Sam Reason. Sophie introduced him to Mr. Lee, who helped him into the carriage in a way that did not put stress on the injured leg. Before he was properly settled, he apologized for the trouble he was causing. "Thank you kindly for stepping in. I really didn't know what to do."

The distraction that had begun to build once they were safely away gave way instantly. He sounded like home, like New Orleans. Sophie was so taken aback that she listened without comment while he told her of a cab that had been overturned by an omnibus just a block away.

"The poor cabdriver was thrown and killed outright," he told her. "And his horses had to be shot on the spot. I came away with this ankle and I've lost nothing more than my sample book." He seemed to remember something and touched his brow. "And a hat."

"But why here? Why this dispensary?" Sophie asked him.

"A delivery boy who was going by with a cart brought me here. It was out of his way as it was and the police ambulance was busy with the more seriously injured." What he didn't say, and didn't need to say, was that they would hardly have bothered with him anyway.

The delivery boy who had brought him to the dispensary had done the best he could, and hurried off to complete his work. The Colored Hospital was sixty blocks away, and would have required two hours at least, time the young man could not spare.

Mr. Reason held out his hand, which Sophie took automatically. Large and callused, a firm, dry grip, and she returned it in kind. Both Sophie's father and Aunt Quinlan put great value on a handshake and had introduced her to the subtleties at a young age.

"I'm a printer," Mr. Reason was telling her. "From Brooklyn. If you could see your way to taking me to the Fulton Street ferry, I'd be more than happy to pay you for your time and effort."

"There's no need," Sophie told him. "And we must see to that ankle before you try to walk on it. It may be broken."

At his surprised expression she explained by introducing herself. "I am Sophie Savard," she said. "A physician."

He looked more relieved than he did surprised, and with that won Sophie's respect and gratitude both.

• • •

WHEN MR. LEE left to take Mr. Reason to the ferry, Sophie turned to the men who were waiting for her help. Four of them today, none with serious injuries. As she worked she went over the morning's events in her mind, thinking of questions she should have asked Mr. Reason about his home in New Orleans, and how he had come north, and if he ever went back to visit. A disproportionate sense of loss sat like a weight in her throat, something too big to swallow.

She treated a scalp laceration, a cracked rib, a thumb crushed by a poorly aimed blow of the hammer. More men came, some with nothing more than a deep splinter, but one with a cough and rales in both lungs. She wrote him a script and suggested that he go to the Colored Hospital to be examined, knowing that he would not, could not spare the time.

At two she was back in the carriage eating the sandwich Mrs. Lee had packed for her. The traffic was even worse, stopping and starting, and it would be a half hour at least before they reached the Colored Children's Dispensary. She moved her bag aside so she could recline and sleep for whatever time the trip allowed her, and that was when she noticed the business card.

It was printed on heavy paper, smooth to the touch, the lettering raised:

Reason and Sons Printing
Atlantic Avenue and Hunterfly Road
Brooklyn, New York
Samuel Reason, Master Printer

On the back, in a fine, clear, and very small hand, Mr. Reason had written a message.

Dear Dr. Savard: My family and I would be proud to have you join
us for services at Bethel Tabernacle and then for dinner, this or any
Sunday. At your service, with gratitude—S.R.

Six months later Sophie heard Dr. Garrison mention that she was looking for a new printer, and so she recommended Mr. Reason, but she had never taken him up on his invitation, and she never mentioned the meeting to Anna. She had not gone to Brooklyn for church services because she could not, in good conscience, but neither could she explain to Mr. Reason that she was a nonbeliever. He would be surprised, she was sure, and almost certainly disapproving.

Why she had never mentioned the meeting to Anna was more difficult to explain even to herself. The simple truth was that she felt protective toward him, at least in part because she had recommended him to Dr. Garrison and had put him in danger's way. One thing was clear, however; it was ten o'clock on Sunday morning, and she had the day free.

Sophie got Mr. Reason's business card from her desk, checked the contents of her Gladstone bag—she could not make herself go anywhere without it—called into the kitchen that she was going out without providing details, and walked to the Second Avenue elevated train. By el and ferry and taxi it would take her at least an hour to get to Brooklyn; she could only hope that it would be time enough to think of a way to explain herself to Mr. Reason.

◆　◆　◆

CAP HAD BEEN born and lived still in a beautiful Murray Hill house built of marble and sandstone, exactly one and a half miles from Waverly Place. Anna had walked the distance so many times in her life that she could make the trip without thought or conscious effort. Certainly there was little to distract her on the first part of Fifth Avenue, each house almost as familiar to her as her own.

Fashionable neighborhoods shifted north as the city grew, with the result that the lower portion of Fifth Avenue was now populated primarily by the elder generations of the most prominent families: Delanos, de Rahms, Lenoxes, Morgans, and Astors. As a very little girl she had come to call in these houses with her aunt and uncle Quinlan. She remembered marble floors, statues far taller than herself, butlers with long-suffering expressions and silver trays, the smells of camphor and rubbing alcohol and dried lavender. Now a few very old but still very rich people lived in twenty or thirty shuttered rooms with their staffs as company.

But this bright Sunday morning was also the first of April and the weather had drawn the people outside, bringing the neighborhood back to life. A breeze tugged at her hat and buffeted the hem of her coat and infused her with energy, and Anna let herself be propelled, first to buy an iced bun from a vendor and then to stop and do business with a flower seller who wore a kerchief folded like a veil over her head and shoulders. Anna pointed to what she wanted and the woman wrapped the violet stems in moss and newspaper and tied it all together with a bit of string.

She stopped again to watch children chasing each other through a courtyard, howling with laughter. As she had once played, with such abandon. In that moment it occurred to her that she was procrastinating, and why.

All week she had been avoiding the discussion of the clinic in Switzerland for the simplest of reasons. It might be pure selfishness on her part but she did not want to give Cap up, to send him away and never see him again.

It came to her then as if she heard the words spoken out loud: Sophie wanted him to go, because she wanted to go with him. To Switzerland.

◆　◆　◆

FROM THE OTHER end of the room Cap said, "Aunt Q was here this week. I suppose you know. We discussed Dr. Zängerle's letter."

He was sitting in his desk chair, his posture rigid and his complexion the color of skimmed milk. All the windows were open, bringing the early spring breeze into the room to play with the papers on the desk. If she asked him if he was cold, he would offer to close the windows, for her. It had never been easy to get an answer from him about himself, and now it seemed impossible.

Anna let the question hang in the air for a while. "I did hear, yes."

"You think this is a creditable idea?"

"The doctor in question is creditable. His reputation is very good. If you're asking about the protocol, I haven't heard enough about it to say."

"But Sophie thinks it's promising."

Anna inclined her head. "Yes."

"And you'll go along with her." It wasn't a question, and Anna didn't answer.

After a moment she cleared her throat and said what she could not keep to herself. "Cap. If you talked to her about this, if you were to ask her—"

His gaze was direct. "You think I should go."

"That's beside the point."

"Really?" he huffed softly. "I thought that was exactly the point."

"She would go with you, if you asked her."

"As what?" He turned away to cough into his handkerchief, his shoulders jerking with the effort. When he could breathe again he repeated himself. "As what?"

"I don't understand."

"As what? My physician? Nurse? Caretaker? Jailer?"

"As your friend," Anna said. "As someone who loves you. And as a physician, of course."

"To study from afar," he said, a tinge of bitterness in his voice. "To sit across the room from me and observe."

"Cap," Anna said. "Four years ago we sat right in this room—at that table." She pointed with her chin. "And you told me that you would leave Manhattan and live in Paris or anywhere else if Sophie would be there with you. You were willing to give up everything you hold dear to win her and keep her."

"Yes. But she declined. She wouldn't give up everything she holds dear."

Anna drew in a sharp breath. "Do you really believe that?"

"Yes," he said fiercely. And then, deflated: "No. She thought I would regret the things I gave up for her, eventually. I couldn't make her understand."

"She understands now. Now she is willing to give up everything."

She wondered if he had heard her, and then she realized he was struggling to breathe. When she was about to reach for her bag he quieted. He was trembling, she could see, but not solely out of physical duress. Her own throat tightened in understanding and frustration, that she could do so little for him.

"You need to rest," she said, getting to her feet.

He looked out the window still, as if she had not spoken at all. "Cap?"

Without turning he said, "Tell her I will think about it, will you? Tell Aunt Quinlan how much her visit meant to me, and that I'll think about Switzerland. Will you do that for me?"

Anna nodded, encouraged and disturbed at the same time.

♦   ♦   ♦

Sophie had been to Brooklyn on occasion, to attend a lecture or observe a procedure at one of the hospitals, with Anna or colleagues. Today she was traveling alone in a crowd on the open deck of the ferry. All around her people stood, heads canted and gaze fixed upward, to get a closer look at the new bridge as they passed underneath. The newspapers said it was close to completion and would open in May. Sophie could see with her own eyes that this was the case, but it still seemed unreal.

There was something in the papers every day about the East River Bridge: construction, engineering, the sheer magnitude of the undertaking, the men who designed it and built it. Day by day all of New York had watched and wondered at it. Many doubted that it would ever be finished; others were convinced that once it did open it would collapse as soon as it was put to a real test.

"This must be what a bug feels like." A woman talking to a companion raised her voice to be heard over the combined noises of wind and water and steam engines.

Sophie's attention was focused on the network of cables that were part of the magic that held the bridge suspended over the river. Workmen were climbing all over it, like spiders on a web. The simplest misstep could cost—had claimed—more than one life. Sudden death was not unusual in the city, but few people looked the possibility directly in the face minute by minute. It took a certain kind of courage. Or desperation.

She shivered, and was embarrassed to realize that she was underdressed for the ferry crossing. Anna would laugh at her failure to realize that there would be a cold wind on the East River. But then she still had the gloves Anna had given her in the courtroom not so very long ago.

Sophie crouched to undo the straps of her bag and then dig down under carefully ordered tins and jars of medicines and ointments and instruments, fitted boxes of scalpels and forceps, glass bottles tightly corked and strapped down.

A shadow fell over the open bag and she looked up to see a little boy watching her.

"It looks heavy," he said.

"It is heavy," Sophie agreed. "But I'm used to it."

His eyes fixed on her stethoscope.

"What's that?"

Sophie found the gloves and pulled them out while she considered how to answer. "It's an instrument that lets me listen to a person's heart beating."

He put a hand over his chest as if she had suggested he submit his own heart for this purpose. While Sophie secured the straps on her bag his expression shifted from curiosity to doubt and, finally, distrust. As the ferry bumped against the dock he skittered away to yank on a woman's sleeve and point in Sophie's direction.

Very deliberately Sophie pulled on her gloves and joined the line to disembark, irritated to be reminded that she could not be herself in public. She must be the person white people saw when they looked at her: a woman of mixed race, respectably dressed, polite, retiring. They would assume her to be a governess, a housekeeper, a teacher at one of the colored schools, the wife of a minister or business owner. Someone who might be able to read, but a word like *stethoscope*— much less the use of the thing—that was reaching beyond herself.

She felt the boy's eyes on her back. Prideful as ever, she lifted her head and held it high.

◆　◆　◆

THE WHARF WAS crowded with people waiting to make the trip back to Manhattan, with flower sellers and postcard vendors, with omnibuses, carriages, and cabs to take the new arrivals where they wanted to go. Sophie walked along the line of drivers waiting for fares until she found one who would not turn her away. He sat hunched forward, the reins folded over enormous hands, and looked at her from under the brim of a spotless black top hat. When he nodded she climbed into the cab without his assistance.

"Where we going, miss?" Abrupt, but not disrespectful.

"To a printer's shop. Mr. Reason, by name. Do you know him?"

That got her a laugh. "I know everybody in Weeksville and they know me."

"Weeksville," Sophie echoed, looking at Mr. Reason's business card.

"It's what we call the neighborhood." His brow folded in on itself as he studied her. "How you come to know Sam Reason?"

"We met in Manhattan about a year and a half ago."

When she was seated, her bag on the floor at her feet, he chirruped to his horse and the cab took off with a jerk. The driver was still studying her over his shoulder, leaving the horse to find the way.

"You the one who fixed him up that time the cab he was in got run over?"

Sophie's mouth fell open and then shut with a click.

"Yes. But how do you know—"

He waved a hand as if to shoo away a fly. "Everybody know that story. And you are carrying a doctor's bag. I heard your name once but I can't recall."

Sophie introduced herself and in return was given his name: John Horatio Alger, Johnny to his friends.

"Now one thing," he said to her, still ignoring the horse and the road entirely. "Sunday morning Sam won't be in the shop. I'll find him for you, though. Sure enough."

Sophie sat back and watched Brooklyn pass her by. Spring was here, too, in every breath she took and the warmth of the sun on her face, in the new grass and the budding trees and the birds wheeling overhead.

A half hour later they turned onto an unpaved street and into a neighborhood like many Sophie visited in the course of her day. A large dog slept stretched out in the middle of the road; the horse went around him without breaking stride.

"You, Helmut!" the driver called to him. "I'ma run you over one day, you don't watch out." One long speckled ear cocked itself in feigned interest and then fell again.

The houses were small for the most part, some needing paint or repair but most so neat and cared for that the windows sparkled in the sunlight. Gardens were being dug everywhere, dark earth turned up to warm in the sun. A very old woman sat in the shade of a porch, knitting while she rocked a cradle with her knee. She looked up as the cab passed and raised a hand. The driver nodded in return, touching the brim of his hat.

The neighborhood was oddly empty. Sophie had just begun to wonder if she had gone wrong after all when they turned onto Dean Street and stopped in front of a small whitewashed building with the high arched windows of a church.

Before she could ask, Mr. Weeks said, "This here Bethel Tabernacle AME. The Reasons should be out any minute now."

The doors opened as if commanded, and two young men in dark suits stepped aside to let the churchgoers come pouring out.

"Just in time," the driver said.

Sophie understood that Weeksville was a colored neighborhood, but still it was a surprise to see such a sea of faces and not find one white person among them. Odder still, it seemed that every pair of eyes was looking at her. It made her both less and more anxious, and heightened her irritation with herself. Of course people must look at her. She was a stranger, no matter the color of her skin.

People called out to Johnny Alger, but their eyes focused on her and stayed there. There were smiles and polite nods and curious looks and a few, it seemed, who wanted to stop but then moved on anyway, too uncertain to approach her.

Ten minutes must have passed and the crowd began to thin out, but Sophie saw no sign of Mr. Reason. Then Mr. Alger stood up so that the carriage rocked, and called to a boy who was coming down the church steps. "George! George Reason!"

He was about sixteen, just coming into his full height and still awkward, knobby joints as limber as a puppet's. He stopped short of the cab, looked more closely at Sophie, and pulled his cap from his head to knead it.

The driver was saying, "Where's your folks this morning?"

"Home," George said. "Mary baby come along about sunrise. The women all too tired to listen to a sermon—"

"And the men too wound up," the driver finished for him.

Clearing her throat, Sophie said, "It sounds as though this isn't a good day for a visit—"

But George had already climbed up to sit next to the driver and they were off again, the conversation moving along without her.

◆   ◆   ◆

THE HOUSE WAS white clapboard with ivy-green shutters and a screened front porch. On one side was a garden in neat rows marked and sectioned off by string, and on the other a fenced yard was overrun with children.

The driver spoke a few words to his horse as they came to a stop.

"Are those all your—" Sophie stopped, and the boy grinned broadly at her uncertainty.

"Cousins, mostly," he said. "My two little sisters are there if you look, up high in the climbing tree. There's only about a half of us here today."

"Enough ,Reasons to populate all of Brooklyn, one end to the other. Yes sir, reasons enough." Mr. Alger grinned at his own wit.

From the other side of the house came the sound of a bell, and a woman's voice calling the family to table. George swung down from the driver's box, turned to offer a hand to Sophie, and waited while she paid Mr. Alger.

Sophie stood for a moment brushing at her skirt, adjusting her hat, and trying to calm her nerves. She thought of Aunt Quinlan, as she often did when courage failed her in such situations. Aunt Quinlan could go into any assembly, small or large, without hesitation or embarrassment, and talk to anyone. It was a skill Sophie had yet to acquire.

When she looked up, a familiar figure had appeared on the porch. Mr. Reason came toward her with a hand outstretched, smiling at her so openly that her breath caught in her throat.

"Dr. Savard," he said, when she met him halfway. "I was wondering if you'd ever come. Welcome. Come on now and meet the family. I hope you're hungry, because we got a ham the size of a small bear."

"I *am* hungry," Sophie said, as her stomach rumbled in agreement.

"Then come on. The whole family is looking forward to meeting you."

◆   ◆   ◆

FROM THE MOMENT she stepped through Mr. Reason's front door it was clear to Sophie that a quiet conversation would not be easy to achieve. Nobody could have a discussion in the middle of a gathering like this, people celebrating a new baby and—as she learned shortly—a wedding-to-be. Mr. Reason's grandson Michael had brought his girl home with him to announce their engagement.

So Sophie let herself be propelled to the table that stretched from one room into another, given a place of honor next to Mrs. Reason, and plied with food and iced tea until she began to worry about belching in public. Through all that she was introduced, again and again, answering questions and asking her own, telling the story of Mr. Reason's sprained ankle.

The Reasons had so many children and grandchildren and they were all so full of energy and curiosity that Sophie's excellent memory was quickly overtaxed. She could only be glad that half the family was missing. More unusual than the size of the Reason family was the fact that so far she had counted two sets of twins and one set of triplets. When she remarked on this, everyone looked at Mr. Reason.

"I stuttered as a boy." It clearly was a set piece, because the whole room erupted into a chiding laughter.

When the table had been cleared and the younger family members were bringing in pies and coffee, Mrs. Reason leaned closer to Sophie. "I'm so glad you finally found your way over here to see us," she said. "But am I right in thinking you have some business to discuss with my husband?"

Sophie nodded.

"Are you in a hurry to get back to the city?"

"Not a hurry," Sophie said. "But before dusk."

"Well, then," Mrs. Reason said. "We'll have us some pie, and then I'd like you to come meet my newest grandbaby and her mama, my youngest daughter."

The invitation was not for Sophie as a physician or a midwife, but because Mrs. Reason considered her a family friend. It was such an unusual turn of events that Sophie was confused for a single instant, and then she smiled. She said, "I like pie and I would love to meet your daughter."

As if Mrs. Reason had snapped her fingers to make it so, the men disappeared and Sophie spent the rest of the afternoon with daughters, daughters-in-law, granddaughters, and small children of both sexes, all of them talking to each other and to Sophie. The littlest were too shy to approach her but sent coy looks and grins. When the little girls got carried away, a look from their grandmother was enough to calm them down, but Mrs. Reason's daughters-in-law were not so easily subdued. They teased each other to the point of helpless laughter and stamping feet and mock outrage.

Althea was the second youngest of Mrs. Reason's children. "I about gave up hope for a girl," Mrs. Reason said. "Already had my first grandbabies when Althea and Mary came along, the last set of twins. After that I was done."

"She saved the best for last." Althea snagged one of her sons to wipe his face, holding on to the squirming five-year-old with one arm and wielding her handkerchief with the other.

A knock at the door brought the news that the new mother was awake. Every one of the women would have stampeded to get to her first, but Mrs. Reason had seen that coming and forestalled it by putting herself in the doorway. "All y'all have to wait your turn," she said. "I'm taking Miss Sophie in now."

"And me," Althea said, giving her mother a look that dared her to disagree.

•   •   •

IN A SUNNY bedroom that looked out over the fallow garden, Althea leaned over her sister to examine the sleeping baby's face.

"Ten grandsons," Althea said to Mary, "and you had to break stride."

"About time, too," Mrs. Reason said, coming around the other side of the bed to get closer. "Girl babies do dawdle along in this family." With sure hands she scooped the bundled newborn up to cradle her against a substantial bosom. "Come look at what Mary made," she said to Sophie. "Look at this beautiful child."

Sophie observed closely, both new mother and baby, and saw no signs of distress or trouble. Mrs. Reason's youngest daughter was a healthy woman, exhausted but satisfied with herself and her place in this world.

"What are you going to name her?" Sophie asked.

"Mason and me, we're still talking about that," Mary said. She tore her gaze away from the child in her mother's arms and smiled at Sophie. "You're a doctor. You catch a lot of babies?"

"At least a couple times a week," Sophie said. "But I also treat women and children more generally."

"Didn't even know there was colored woman doctors."

"More of us every year," Sophie said. "Maybe your daughter will be one too."

Mary looked directly startled at the idea, and then amused. "Could be," she said. "No children of your own yet?"

"I'm not married."

"You got to find a man with character enough to take pride in an educated wife," Althea said. "That's what Mama always told me." She looked at her mother and grinned. "And that's what I did."

"Althea taught school before her boys come along," Mrs. Reason told Sophie.

The baby began to fuss and Mary sat up against the pillows and gestured for her.

"You have a beautiful daughter," Sophie said. And to Mrs. Reason: "I need to think about getting back to the ferry."

"Come look at my garden first," she said. "The weather is just too beautiful to stay inside all day. While we're doing that I'll ask Mr. Reason to bring the carriage around."

◆   ◆   ◆

"THERE'S NOT MUCH to see yet." Mrs. Reason opened the gate into a large kitchen garden and then closed it behind them. "But I wanted a few minutes alone with you."

Sophie said, "I so much appreciate your hospitality and warm welcome." She spoke the truth, but the words sounded overly formal to her own ear. Mrs. Reason seemed not to notice, her attention turned inward. Sophie wondered if she had something more serious and personal to ask and began to compose her face into the expression that was meant to tell a woman that she was listening closely, and hearing.

"Have you ever thought about leaving Manhattan?"

Before Sophie could even begin to answer, she went on. "I realize it's been your home since the war and you have a practice there, but just imagine. Imagine what you could do for Weeksville. And I can promise you this, nobody will ever begrudge you your title or the respect you're owed."

In her surprise Sophie startled. "How did you know that?" And then, more quietly, "Of course you know."

Mrs. Reason was a woman of color who had lived in the north since before the War between the States. She had been here during the draft riots, and that was likely not the worst she had seen.

She said, "Is that why you and Mr. Reason settled here? To be among your own people?"

"That was a good part of it," Mrs. Reason said. "Weeksville is a little bit like home, like New Orleans. We are left mostly to ourselves and there's not much need to trade with white folk. We've got pretty much everything we need: lawyers, music teachers, tailors, a cobbler, carpenters and masons, nurses and midwives, too. It's our place. It could be your place."

She stood abruptly at the sound of a carriage. "I know I've given you a lot to think about. Will you do that?"

Sophie thought of home, of Aunt Quinlan's sweet face and of Anna's, curious and laughing and fierce by turns. She thought of the garden there and of Cap, the summer day he had caught her up against the pergola trellis, heavy with sweet jasmine, sugar in the air itself, and kissed her. The surprise of it. The soft touch of his mouth and the rough prickle of his cheek, the tripling pulse at the base of his throat, and how right and good it had been.

"I love my family," she told Mrs. Reason. "That's where I belong. For the time being, at least."

◆ ◆ ◆

THE JOURNEY BACK to the ferry was far too short for Sophie to hesitate about what she had to say, and so she told Mr. Reason about Comstock's determination to prosecute female physicians associated with Dr. Garrison.

"By extension this is a threat to you," she said. "Because I recommended your services to Dr. Garrison. He is not above entrapment and spying to lay his hands on a target. You must be alert."

When he glanced at her Mr. Reason's expression was calm, without even a hint of surprise.

"It's good of you to come so far to tell me about this. But do you really think there's a threat?"

"Yes," Sophie said. "I'm sorry to say, I think there's a threat. He has ruined businessmen for the challenge of it, and sent good doctors to prison. He takes satisfaction in such things. I had to come tell you in person because he monitors the mails."

After a moment he said, "There's no way you would know this, but I retired shortly after we met, the day of my accident. My eldest grandson took over the business. You didn't meet Sam today; he spent this last week in Savannah. Should be home tomorrow."

"Well," Sophie said, oddly deflated. "Could you possibly tell him about all this?"

"Or you could come out to dinner next Sunday, tell him yourself."

She grinned at him. "I can try to do that. But in the meantime—"

"Of course," Mr. Reason said. "And let me promise you one more thing. If you need help of any kind, send word. You can send a message to the law offices of Levi Jackson; he'll see it gets to me. There's a whole world of help over here in Weeksville. Will you remember that?"

Sophie wondered how such a thing could be forgotten.

• • •

IN THE CAB that took her from the ferry to Waverly Place, Sophie dozed, slipping in and out of quicksilver dreams. She was in Brooklyn and New Orleans, in Mrs. Campbell's austere kitchen, in the lecture hall where she had realized that yes, she wanted to be, she would be a doctor. She was a doctor. Tomorrow she would spend most of her day at the Foundling Hospital, where the nursing sisters took in infants who were too sick to save, and others that Sophie would treat. Some she would send on, to orphan asylums or back to their families. She could close her eyes and see many of those faces. They came to her in all colors. They came to her for help.

7

JACK MEZZANOTTE FOUND a bench in Washington Square Park and sat down to wait until three o'clock, when he could knock on Anna Savard's door without looking like a smitten schoolboy. The sun was warm on his face and he was bone tired, but he was not so short on sleep that he would shock the neighborhood by dozing in public. A patrolman was sure to pass by and then he'd never hear the end of it.

Two nursery maids came to a stop to talk, both of them rocking their carriages to keep their charges quiet while they sent quick side-long glances in his direction. Jack picked up his newspaper and hid behind it. There was a surplus of spinsters in the city, the long-term effects of the war still in evidence. So many young women without hope of families of their own. They made him think of his sisters, which in turn made him sad.

Thinking about Anna Savard, by comparison, didn't make him sad. He certainly spent too much time thinking about her. An edu-cated woman of strong opinions, self-sufficient. The nursemaids—pretty, educated to the point that they could read and write, keep track of household accounts, do needlework and mending, with fam-ilies and reputations good enough to gain employment looking after the children of the wealthiest families—they were more likely to marry than Anna or Sophie Savard. Or than his own sisters.

With that thought he caught sight of Anna headed his way. She had turned into the park from Fifth Avenue, walking quickly so that her skirts swirled around the toes of her boots and the edge of her cape—a deep evergreen color—kicked up with every step. Jack won-dered if she was wearing split skirts today, as she had the first time he saw her in that church basement, locking horns with Sister Ignatia.

He wondered if the hair she had coiled at the back of her head would curl once released from its pins.

She didn't see him sitting there and would have passed without taking any note.

"Pardon me, Dr. Savard."

She turned on point, alert, her frown shifting to surprise. "Detective Sergeant Mezzanotte. What are you doing here?"

He gestured to the bench. "Sitting. In the sunshine."

She looked up at the clock in the university tower. Her walk had put high color into her cheeks and at the very tip of her nose.

Jack said, "It's about half past two. You aren't late." And at her puzzled expression, "We have an appointment at three; did you forget?"

He waited until she took a seat on the very edge of the bench and folded her hands in her lap. She wore gloves embroidered with ivy.

"Is that your work?" He gestured to her gloves.

She frowned, not understanding him.

"The embroidery."

"No. You're interested in embroidery?"

"Only because I see so much of it. Both my sisters embroider, for various churches and for some well-to-do ladies who have less time or inclination."

She lifted a shoulder, almost apologetically. "The only kind of sewing I do is very different. You have two sisters?"

"And five brothers. And you?"

"I had an older brother, but he died when I was young. Now I have Sophie. And Cap."

She looked away into the depths of the park. Her eyes were the color of tarnished copper, tawny browns shot through with green.

"I'm sorry about your friend Mr. Verhoeven," Jack said.

There was a small silence. "Thank you," she said finally. And: "You have news about the Russo boys?"

"No," Jack said. "But there is someone to interview who might be of help. If you care to join me."

Her eyebrows lifted ever so slightly. "Today? Now?"

"Unless you have other appointments."

She seemed to bristle a little, as though she disliked the idea of being waited for. "Close enough to walk?"

"A half hour, at a reasonable pace."

She got up, and so did he.

"I'll take your bag," he said, but she swung it away from him.

"Peremptory of you, wouldn't you say?"

She was in a prickly mood. He looked forward to this walk.

• • •

THEY MADE THEIR way along the park to Greenwich Lane and then north, through neighborhoods of small houses and tenements. On this warm spring afternoon people had come out to sit in the sun on their stoops, grandmothers and children just walking, invalids and cripples, war veterans too numerous to count. A toddler lurched up and down the sidewalk with an older sister close behind.

A group of young girls were playing skully, stopping just long enough for Jack and Anna to pass by. As they approached a vacant lot, a whole pack of young boys came racing onto the sidewalk. In the middle of the group a grinning boy held a bloody pocketknife up, waving it like a trophy. He was limping, but his expression was pure victory.

Anna took in the details automatically: he was filthy from playing in the dirt, but he looked well nourished, and more important, he looked like a boy with no worries beyond the next challenge to his status as victor. No doubt he didn't even feel the wound on his foot.

"Oh dear," Anna said. "Mumblety-peg."

Jack laughed. "You don't approve."

"Do you know of any woman who does? There's something wrong with a game that you can win by pinning your foot to the ground with a dirty pocketknife."

"That's not the only way to win."

She looked at him sharply. "Did you play mumblety-peg with your brothers?"

"We still do, now and then."

She stopped, her mouth falling open.

"Boys bloody themselves," he said. "One way or the other."

"Yes," Anna said grumpily. "And they lose toes on occasion, too. I've sewn up more than a few lacerated feet over the last few years."

They walked in silence for a long minute. Jack had decided that discretion was the better part of valor and was declining to argue the merits of this particular game.

"The world is a dangerous place for children," she said finally. "As we both know too well. Those boys were just Tonino Russo's age."

Jack said, "Let's hope Tonino has nothing more dangerous than a game of mumblety-peg to deal with."

Another longer silence, in which they both remembered that they might never know what became of Tonino or his brother.

"You know," Anna said, "Rosa cries herself to sleep, but she's very careful to present a calm face to the world. She doesn't even ask about the letters Sophie and I have written, or the list of places we're putting together to visit. The only thing that's keeping her from breaking down is Lia. For Lia she puts on a brave show."

"And you?"

"I'm not much of an actress, but then I don't spend very much time with them. Margaret and Mrs. Lee and Aunt Quinlan deal with the day by day, and all of them have vast experience with orphaned children. Sophie and I are prime examples."

He was studying the sidewalk, it seemed to Anna. Trying to find something to say. She hoped he would realize that she would not want or need sympathy.

"Rosa said something to you about your brother, back in Hoboken. I've been thinking about it ever since."

Anna kept her silence, and he took this as permission to go on. "She said that your brother failed you, and you agreed."

"Did I," Anna said. Her voice caught a little, but he seemed determined to go on.

"What I was wondering was, has anyone else ever said as much to you? That your brother failed you?"

"No," Anna said. "Of course not. My brother was a West Point graduate. He was an army officer, and he did his duty. He was proud to do his duty. For that he deserves respect."

After a moment she glanced at Jack and saw an expression she didn't really understand. Not pity, she was fairly certain. Uncertainty, reservation, confusion. She was struck quite suddenly with an almost overwhelming fear: he would ask questions now, questions she didn't want to think about, much less answer.

An ambulance came rattling past them, pulling up to the portico at St. Vincent's, just ahead. Anna picked up her pace a little.

Just that simply the conversation slipped away.

•   •   •

JACK SAID, "DOES it make you curious, the ambulance?"

She seemed surprised by the question. "You mean professional curiosity, I suppose. Is that how you feel when you see an arrest being made?" And without waiting for his answer she went on.

"I wouldn't call it curiosity, but a kind of awareness, a tensing. After a while you can gauge the situation by the way the ambulance drivers move and by their voices. My guess is that this isn't a very serious case, so no. I'm not interested enough to interfere."

She had been easy with him, until they started talking about the Russo boys and then, by extension, her brother. He wished now that he had waited for another time to ask questions. She intrigued him, she surprised him. She went on surprising him while very little seemed to surprise her. But she was not without scars, ones she had no intention of showing or even, he realized now, acknowledging, even to herself.

She said, "Do you think that a woman wouldn't be able to cope with the realities of the work you do?"

This tone he understood; she was irritated and willing to let him know that.

"Your sensibilities don't strike me as fragile," he said. "So let me tell you about yesterday morning. A cobbler with a business on Taylor Street killed his wife. He is more than seventy, she was less than thirty."

She seemed to be interested. "Jealousy?"

"Italians make an art of it. So we got the call and went out, but the cobbler disappeared before we got there. We spent most of the day looking for him and were about to give up—it was just getting dark—when he walked past me. This was in the Italian colony in Brooklyn. It's not hard to disappear for a few days at a time over there."

Anna said, "You recognized the cobbler?"

"I had a description—short, bald, a gray mustache—"

"That must describe hundreds of men. You're smiling. Is there a joke here somewhere?"

Jack rubbed the corner of his mouth with a knuckle. "Not a joke, but maybe a bit of a secret weapon. I'll tell you how I caught him: I asked him a question."

She made a gesture with her hand, impatient for him to go on.

"I was standing on the corner when he walked past me. He fit the description so I said, 'Hey, Giacalone!' and he stopped and turned. Then I said, 'So why did you kill your wife?' He told me, and I arrested him. End of story."

She had stopped and was looking at him the same way he might look at a pickpocket with a dodgy alibi. "Why would he do that? Just because you used his name?"

"Don't you turn when somebody calls your name?"

"Yes, probably. But I wouldn't confess to a crime on that basis. There must be something more to it."

She liked puzzles, clearly, and would ask questions until she got to the bottom of things.

"Yes, there was more to it. I said it in his language."

"You spoke Italian."

"Sicilian."

"They don't speak Italian in Sicily?"

"The Italians in Sicily do. The Sicilians do not. I can see you don't believe me, but it's true."

"Say it for me. First in Italian and then Sicilian."

"A command performance," Jack said, giving her an exaggerated bow from the shoulders. "'*Perchè hai ammazzato la tua donna?*' would be a colloquial, friendly Italian. '*Picchì a ttò mugghieri l'ammazzasti?*' is Sicilian. Or one kind of Sicilian."

They walked on, and he could almost hear her thinking, looking for flaws in his story.

"There is more than one Sicilian language?"

"Dozens of dialects of Sicilian. Hundreds of dialects of Italian."

"How is it you speak Sicilian?"

"I don't, really. I just have a collection of sentences at the ready."

Her mouth contorted as if she were repressing a smile. "Do tell."

"'Why did you kill your wife—or friend, or neighbor?' 'What did you do with the money you took?'—that kind of thing."

"Are Sicilians responsible for most of the crime?"

"Oh, no," Jack said. "Which is why I know how to say those crucial sentences in more than one kind of Italian."

She was quiet for a full minute. "Detective Sergeant Mezzanotte," she said a little huffily, "I think you're pulling my leg."

"Test me, then, if you don't believe me."

"All right. Florence." She said it as if she knew for a fact that the men of Florence would never kill their wives.

He smiled openly at that. "*O perché tu ha'ammazzaho la tu' moglie?*"

She pressed her lips together while she thought. "Of course I have no way of knowing if that's right. You could be making it up out of whole cloth."

He laughed, and very deftly took her hand and hooked it through his crooked arm.

"Your claim," she began after a long pause, "is that this man was so taken by surprise to find a countryman that he let his guard down."

"Something like that."

"I find it hard to imagine."

"If you found yourself on the other side of the world in a country where you were disliked and distrusted on sight and you didn't speak the language—"

"I would learn the language."

He glanced at her. "You would learn the language. But you would miss your own language, your people. In a crowd you hear nothing but this other language that has been so much work for you, it gives you a headache sometimes trying to follow. The people you talk to make fun of your accent, the way you turn sentences around. They insult you to your face. Then all of a sudden you hear somebody speaking your language. The language of your town and family, the language you heard around the dinner table as a little girl, or playing with other little girls like yourself. It's like being handed a wonderful present with no warning. Suddenly you're not alone in the world."

She was listening closely, her head canted. "When you put it like that, yes. I can see it. To put it bluntly, you took advantage of his loneliness."

"He killed his wife," Jack said. "His feelings are not my concern."

"So you only pursue Italian-speaking criminals." Her tone was vaguely disbelieving and he wondered what she had up her sleeve.

"I never said that. I arrest all kinds of people, young and old, rich and poor. This week I arrested a banker, an associate of the Astors whose family has been here for two hundred years. For embezzlement, a rich man's crime."

"But your secret weapon works only with Italians."

"Dr. Savard, do you begrudge me my professional tools?"

"No," she said, and bit her lip. "Maybe a little. I am glad that the rest of the world is safe from your tricks."

He lifted a brow, and saw her expression shift.

"Now you are boasting. How many languages do you speak?"

"I don't know," Jack lied, just to see her expression. "I've never counted."

◆ ◆ ◆

WHAT HAD BEEN a neighborhood of factory workers and store clerks and wagon drivers gave way suddenly, and they found themselves surrounded by the tenements that housed the workers from the turpentine distilleries and the Manhattan Gas Works. Even on a Sunday the air was heavy with the smell of coal oil, of pine sap and resin, all together a soup that made Anna think of young men with drawn faces and lungs the color of ash.

She heard herself say, "I did some of my training at St. Vincent's. I've made calls in this neighborhood."

"I wasn't aware that surgeons make house calls."

"I was a physician first," she said. "My education was quite broad and thorough." She took firmer hold of his arm and yanked, stepping sideways to draw him away from the corner where an old man was coughing so hard that a mist of droplets shimmered in the air.

"Contagion," she said, a little embarrassed now at her temerity.

She wondered if he would take offense or find her way of expressing herself distasteful. The kind of thinking she thought she had conquered, finally, but here it was again. She reminded herself that people who shied away from her because she had a brain and a profession weren't worth her time. A friend was someone you didn't have to make excuses to. Someone who took you as you were. And another realization: she liked the man, and wanted him. As a friend.

She found it almost impossible to raise her head and look at him; she needed another minute to remind herself that he would have expectations that she would not be able to, would not want to, meet. But he made her laugh, and try as she might, Anna couldn't think of another person outside her family and Cap who could make her really laugh.

They passed Twentieth Street and the neighborhood changed again. There were trees here, small parks, and children shrieking as they played. Brownstone respectability, and then the open campus of the Theological Seminary, as staid and somber as the inside of a church.

Jack stopped in front of a small property just across from the seminary. He pulled a rope and the sound of the bell echoed from deep in the house.

After a full minute he said, "This is a home for elderly nuns. They are not quick."

"Nuns?"

"It's called St. Jerome's, a residence for retired religious."

Before she could ask him what help such people might be in helping them find two little boys, the heavy wooden door swung open. The nun wore rough homespun robes far too big for a tiny frame, cinched together by a rope at her waist. Beneath her wimple her eyes were a vivid, watery blue.

As she closed the door behind them Jack said, "Sister—"

She turned her back and left them there without bothering to hear or answer his question. Anna thought she must be deaf, but then a quavering voice rose over the departing shoulder.

"He's waiting for you."

"Where?"

That made her stop and turn to display a frown that consumed her lower face. "Where else? The kitchen."

8

THE MAN JACK was looking for sat at a long table reading a newspaper while he ate from a dish of olives and pickles and slices of raw onion. He held the paper so close to his eyes that when he looked up at them, the first thing Anna noticed was the newsprint on the end of a long, straight nose over an honest smile made up of teeth the color of old ivory.

"Jack," he said, folding his paper to set it aside. "So here you are." He looked at Anna. "Who is this young lady you've brought to see me?"

Anna felt Jack's hand touch her lower back very lightly, as if to urge her closer. "Brother Anselm, may I introduce Dr. Anna Savard. Anna, Brother Anselm knows everyone who has anything to do with orphaned or abandoned children in the city."

"I was once an orphaned boy myself," Brother Anselm said to Anna, gesturing to a chair. He was of middle size, a little bowed with age but still strong. She wondered what it meant that the detective sergeant called him Brother, if he was something less than or more than a priest.

He was watching her as she watched him, with an open curiosity. "You lost your parents very young, I think."

Anna paused, alarmed for no good reason.

"No need to worry, Jack hasn't been telling stories. It was just an intuition. Children who experience that kind of loss at a very young age sometimes develop a brittleness, for want of a better word."

"I strike you as fragile?"

"Christ save us, no."

Before Anna could pursue this odd conversation, he turned to Jack and pointed him to the other end of the kitchen. "Tea would be welcome." And then his attention was back with Anna. Jack went to carry out this command as if it were the most natural thing in the world, a detective sergeant of the New York Police Department making himself busy in the kitchen.

Brother Anselm said, "I was ten when we left France. Typhoid struck six days out of Marseilles and took my mother and father and three brothers. I arrived with nothing, not even English."

Anna could hear the French in his English now, the rhythm that gave him away.

"And when was that?"

"In the year 1805. When this"—he gestured widely, to take in the whole neighborhood—"was all farmland. I'm here on Sundays to say mass for the sisters. In return for a meal."

"You are in very good health for a man of eighty-eight years. Were you taken in by the sisters as a boy?"

"Eventually," he said. "But enough of my history. Tell me about these children you've taken on, and the ones you're looking for."

She began to tell the story, trying very hard to summarize facts without investing too much of her own opinion or emotions. As though she were telling another doctor a patient's case history, making sure she had all the information that could possibly be relevant.

Jack put a tea tray on the table with its stout teapot and cups, a small jug of milk, and a chipped sugar bowl. Without instruction he poured for all of them, holding up the milk for Anna's approval or rejection.

"Well trained, isn't he?" Brother Anselm said with an indulgent smile. There was clearly a long-standing friendship between these two that could tolerate such teasing. All his comment got from Jack was a lopsided smile.

When Anna had taken a sip of her milky tea, she folded her hands in her lap to continue with the story. Brother Anselm watched her while she talked, his gaze never wavering even when Jack added a comment.

"So the girls are with you and your aunt," he summarized.

"And my cousins," Anna finished.

"Tell me again what Sister Mary Augustin said to you about the boys."

Anna gathered her thoughts. "She said that the paperwork had gone missing. A Sister Perpetua was still searching for it that afternoon without success. She said that paperwork sometimes does go missing with so many children passing through."

"That's true," Brother Anselm said. "It's hard to imagine the number of children on the street, and yet only a portion of them ever are taken into an orphanage. I worked with them for sixty years and nothing we did ever seemed to make a dent. Paperwork and children both disappear without a trace."

"That sounds very ominous," Anna said.

"Sometimes it is ominous," Brother Anselm said. "There are people who look for every opportunity to take advantage of children. Slave labor, or worse. Surely you know of these cases, as a physician."

"My cousin Sophie sees more cases of that kind than I do."

He raised both eyebrows at once. "And who do you treat?"

"I'm a surgeon," Anna said. "My patients are usually women of childbearing age or older. Do you think that the Russo boys were—" She sought a word that she could say out loud. "Taken? Abducted?"

He shook his head. "There's no reason to assume the worst. If I had to guess—" But he paused.

"I won't hold you to it, whatever it is," Anna said. "Please just tell me what you're thinking."

"First I want you to tell me what you fear most. That they are dead? That you may never know what became of them?"

Anna met the detective sergeant's eyes. She wondered if he would think less of her. "Neither of those things," she said. "What I fear most is having to tell Rosa that I've failed."

The sounds of an argument in the street spiraled to a fever pitch and fell away while she waited for some comment.

"You worry that she will blame you. But you aren't at fault. She knows that in her heart, even if she forgets it in her sorrow. And that will temper, over time."

"Are you saying that I should simply tell her that there's no possibility of finding them?" Anna didn't know how she felt about such an idea, whether she should be relieved or resigned or outraged.

"Oh, no," said Brother Anselm. "It's not time to give up yet. But that time may come. You have to be prepared for that. And so must Rosa."

When she was calmer Anna said, "Where do we start?" She cleared her throat to hide her embarrassment. "Where do I start?"

"With Jack," said the older man. "Jack can ask questions where you can't. As you can, where he cannot." To Jack he said, "What does Mrs. Webb say?"

"We're going to see her when we leave you."

Anna had to physically stop herself from turning to look at him. He hadn't told her—hadn't asked her—about another call, and while she knew she should be irritated at his high-handed assumptions, she could only feel thankful that he had taken the lead.

Brother Anselm was saying, "The younger boy was about three months, you said. I would think that as long as he is healthy he will already have been adopted. What was his condition when you examined him?"

She lifted a shoulder. "An infant of normal size. A little underweight, certainly, but not extremely so. Very alert, with blue eyes like his sisters and brother. A handsome little boy, with a head full of dark hair."

"A healthy, good-looking, alert three-month-old boy with blue eyes—I doubt he spent more than a few nights under a convent roof. So many children on the street, invisible to everyone, but there is always a demand for healthy infants as long as the adoptive parents can convince themselves that the mother was of good character."

"But how—" she began.

"They can't know," Brother Anselm said. "But if the child is healthy and pretty enough, they convince themselves that it is so."

He got up from the table and went to a cabinet, where he rumbled in a small box. Then he returned to the table and put paper and pencil in front of Anna, and lowered himself back into his chair.

"May I assume the older boy is healthy, and looks much like his brother?"

"Yes," Anna said. "He's average size but very strong, with a mop of dark curly hair and blue eyes. Very shy, but so would any child be in such a situation."

"Seven years old," Brother Anselm said. "Strong. He might have wandered away and got lost. Jack, you're looking into the possibility he was picked up by one of the padroni?"

Anna felt herself startle. She had been very young when the padroni scandal had erupted, but she did remember the details quite well. An Italian would go to the small mountain villages in Italy and recruit young boys who showed even the slightest musical talent. He promised their families that they would be back in a couple of years with a substantial nest egg. The travel, clothes, food, lodging, training would be provided. All the boy had to give in return was good behavior and a willingness to make music.

And then the boy would be gone into the maw of the Crosby Street tenements, sleeping on filthy floors, insufficiently clothed and fed, and sent out to play the violin on street corners. Any boy who did not come back with the amount demanded would be beaten. More than one had died that way.

"I thought a law was passed—" Anna began, and stopped herself. Passing a law and enforcing it were entirely different matters, as anyone who lived in Manhattan knew.

"It's not as bad as it was ten years ago," Jack said. "But there are still a few of the padroni going about their business. I'll make some inquiries."

Brother Anselm seemed satisfied with that. "He could also have been taken in by any one of two dozen charitable organizations."

"And if he wasn't taken in?" Anna asked.

"We would hope that he ended up as a guttersnipe with one of the Italian street arab gangs. There are enough of them who steer clear of the homes and orphanages, after all. They'd train him in the fine art of picking pockets and minor larceny until he gets big enough to be considered an arab himself." He had been watching Anna closely, and so she said what she couldn't hold back.

"If you think that being raised to be a street arab is nothing to hope for, there are worse possibilities to consider."

"But not to start with," Brother Anselm said. "So I'll give you the names of people to contact and places to visit, if you'll write. My hands won't hold a pen anymore."

•   •   •

THE CHURCH BELLS were ringing five o'clock when they left Brother Anselm, the light slanted now in that way particular to spring evenings. They stood for a moment on the doorstep, not talking.

"One more stop," Jack said. "Would you rather I take you home? I can call on the matron at headquarters alone; I've been doing it every day since I heard they were missing."

She looked up at him with a confused expression.

"There's a woman who works at headquarters on Mulberry, the matron of the foundlings. Patrol officers bring abandoned or lost infants to her first, and she makes sure they're fed and clean. And even if she hasn't seen either of the boys, she might have heard some gossip that will be useful."

He saw her straighten her shoulders and draw in a deep breath. "Well, then," she said. "I suppose we better go talk to her."

◆　◆　◆

ONCE HE HAD flagged down a cab Jack leaned back against the seat and closed his eyes, trying to gather his thoughts. He could almost feel her gaze on his face, but when he opened his eyes she was looking out the window to a corner where boys played stickball.

He said, "I think that was a useful interview."

"It was," she agreed. "Not exactly positive, but not absolutely discouraging, either. Just a great deal of work to be done."

"You don't have to do it alone."

She might take it as an offer or a challenge, or she might sidestep the issue. In polite society she would thank him and insist that he had already done enough, and the conversation would circle back on itself until he gave up or she gave in. But he had the idea that Anna Savard did not put a great deal of value in such rituals, and this time he was right.

"Thank you. I would appreciate your help."

He had accomplished the two things he set out for himself: Anna had the information she needed to proceed, and he had reason and permission to spend as much time as he could spare with her while she did it.

They set off east along Nineteenth Street. Warehouses, mills, and factories gave way to smaller and then larger businesses and shops until they turned onto Broadway. The cabby circled around Union Square and Jack turned automatically to catch a glimpse of the family shop on the corner of Thirteenth Street before he steered the cab onto the Bowery, a move that always made Jack think of crossing a border from one kind of city to another.

Then the finer shops began to give way to cobblers and hardware merchants to secondhand clothiers, restaurants to beer gardens, banks to pawnshops, theaters to saloons. Soon they were surrounded on all sides by music halls, flophouses, stale beer joints, and bordellos. The businesses were closed up tight on a Sunday, but the dives and disorderly houses never closed despite the law. None of it seemed to take Anna Savard by surprise.

•   •   •

POLICE HEADQUARTERS WAS as busy as Anna would have guessed it to be, had she ever given it any thought. As they passed through the reception area to a steep flight of stairs, she took note of an older couple leaning against each other, half-asleep; a mother with a young boy on her lap; and a group of heavily made-up women who seemed distinctly unconcerned about their fate. One of them looked at her with dull eyes empty of all emotion, then let her gaze drop.

She followed the detective sergeant down one hall and another, and finally up a short flight of stairs. He opened the door and the purpose of the room announced itself by means of a wailing infant and the ammonia smell of wet winding clothes.

It was a long, narrow room lined with cots. There was a desk at one end and a treatment table at the other where a short, sturdy woman wrapped in an apron that covered her from neck to toe was leaning over an infant. The child was flailing unhappily about being lowered into the bathwater.

"Wheest," she murmured to the baby. "Wheest. There's a good girl. We'll get you cleaned up proper first, and then you can fill your belly."

A rocking chair creaked and Anna saw that there was another woman sitting in a shadowy corner. She seemed to be sleeping while an infant fretted at her breast. So small and so ferocious in its hunger, struggling for more and more as though he knew with certainty that he would never be fed again.

The three infants in the cots were asleep, swaddled securely, eyelids as pale as moonstone etched with a tracery of blue veins. Newborns should be rounded and padded and pink, but all of these babies were angular, like bundles of sticks wrapped in paper.

"Mrs. Webb?"

The woman bathing the baby looked over her shoulder.

"Detective Sergeant Mezzanotte. Good evening. What have you brought me today?"

"No babies today," he said, and she turned back to her work. The infant had stopped wailing and was staring up at her with utter fascination.

"You see," she said. "Not so bad, is it? Lovely warm water."

To Jack she said, "Then what can I do to help? Still looking for the little Italian boy?"

"I'm afraid so. Can we have a look at your register?"

She gestured with her chin to a large book that lay open on the desk.

He crossed the room directly, but Anna hesitated and then went to watch Mrs. Webb, who had clearly bathed more than a few babies in her time. She rinsed the newborn quickly and carefully and, as Anna watched, wound her into a towel and rubbed her dry. The child was severely underweight, so that her head seemed far too large for her spindly neck and body; more troublesome still was the umbilical cord, which was ragged and tied with a dirty string.

"A young mother did that," said Mrs. Webb. She had followed the line of Anna's gaze. "In a hurry to be done with the business and away. She left this little one wrapped in rags in a doorway, not more than a few hours old when a patrolman found her and brought her in to me early today. Poor thing."

Generally people believed that an abandoned child was illegitimate and that the mother had put it away from her to hide an inexcusable moral lapse. Anna herself had never challenged this traditional wisdom until she went to medical school and was obliged to look more closely. Abandoned children were a miserable lot, born in poverty and most of them sickly, but their mothers were often married, and desperate in their own way.

Mrs. Webb was saying, "Tomorrow all of this lot will go down to the Public Charities Office and a doctor will examine her. Maybe he can do something about the cord."

Anna said, "Does she have a name?"

Mrs. Webb began to swaddle the child with quick, efficient motions. "Sometimes the mother leaves a note with a name, but not for this little one. Tomorrow she'll get a name and a number too, and depending on the luck of the draw they'll baptize her Catholic or Protestant. And off she'll go to the Infant Hospital or the Foundling or wherever else they find a cot for her."

Anna hoped it wouldn't be the Infant Hospital on Randall's Island, infamous in medical circles. Overwhelmed by an endless stream of abandoned infants, never enough wet nurses, and very little skilled care meant that three-quarters of the infants admitted to the hospital would be dead within three months, and most of the rest within a year. But it was one thing to hear the figures spoken in a lecture hall or read a report, and another to know that the children in this room would likely be dead before the summer had finished.

Jack Mezzanotte looked up from the register he had opened on the desk and gestured her over. He had put a finger on a line to keep his space.

"Here's the day the Russo children came over from Hoboken. Forty-two children were logged in over the next seven days. This is the only one that comes even partially close."

Anna followed the closely written entry:

Male infant, ca. three months, no distinguishing marks, no outward injuries. Warmly dressed. Alert. Found sleeping on the grass under a tree in Stuyvesant Square at 5 o'clock by a clerk walking past on her way home from work. Officer A. Riordan.

"Hard to know," Anna said. "Without more of a description."

Mrs. Webb came over, the newly bathed baby on her arm and read over Anna's shoulder. "Remind me, who is it you're after finding?"

"A boy, about three months. Healthy. Very dark hair, blue eyes. Went missing on March twenty-sixth."

The matron was shaking her head. "No child like that come through here. When I get one that big and healthy, usually a mother comes around looking for it sooner or later. Most all of mine arrive half-dead already." Her tone was unremarkable; a sailor talking about the tides. "But they leave clean and warm with a full belly. Every one of them. After that it's up to the good Lord."

◆   ◆   ◆

WITHOUT DISCUSSION THEY started for Washington Square, turning left onto Bleecker before either of them even thought of talking. Then Jack said something that took her by surprise.

"You know better than to be in this neighborhood at dusk." Not a question, not a command. A simple statement.

"Of course."

It was always odd to be reminded how close the very worst of the city was to the house where she had grown up, where she knew all the neighbors and never felt even the slightest discomfort, no matter the hour. The city was like a deck of cards well shuffled; any corner could reveal disaster or deliverance.

•   •   •

WALKING THROUGH LENGTHENING shadows in Washington Square Park was almost dreamlike. For those last ten minutes Jack thought of what he might say, and rejected everything that came to mind.

At the corner of Waverly Place and the park she stopped and turned to him.

"Sophie and I are writing to all the smaller homes and orphan asylums, but there are several I think I need to visit personally."

"We can do that this week."

Sometimes when she smiled in a certain way, a dimple fluttered to life in her left cheek. It was there now. "That's kind of you."

He was wondering if she was really oblivious to his interest in her when she said, "I don't mean to be rude, but it would be better if you don't come to the door with me. If Rosa sees you she'll pin you down with a million questions."

He might have said *I can answer questions*, or *I'm not ready to leave you yet*, but neither of those things would move him toward his goal. A goal he had somehow formulated without much conscious thought, but one that had already put down roots. He had to clear his throat to speak.

"I'll send word tomorrow, or the day after, unless work gets in the way, and then it might not be until later in the week."

"Generally I'm in surgery in the mornings," she said. "We both have schedules to work around."

He took her hand as if to shake it and ran his thumb over the cool silk of her glove to feel the warm skin beneath it, stroking the cleft where palm met wrist. She started but didn't pull away. He wondered if it was possible for her to stop herself from blushing, or if it was a battle she always lost.

After a moment he passed her leather satchel back to her, and she turned and walked away. Jack watched her go, her pace picking up. Then she stopped and turned back, as if she had forgotten something important.

She called, "If your man yesterday had been French, what would you have said to him then?"

He laughed.

"You don't know!"

"Maybe not," he called back. "What part of France?"

9

BY THE TIME they had spent four nights in the house on Waverly Place, the little girls had settled into a routine. "Give children a clock to live by," Mrs. Lee said. "So they know what's coming, when it's coming, how long it will last. They'll take comfort in that knowing."

To Anna's surprise it was a comfort to her, too. Wherever she was—in surgery, with students, in an exam room or a meeting—she could look at the clock and know where the girls were and what they were doing. She knew, for example, that when Margaret went in to wake the girls at eight, Lia would be confused and tearful. She would let Rosa comfort her, and then she would spend some time being comforted by Margaret while she was made ready for the day. By half past they were at the breakfast table.

Over the course of the day Lia sought out every adult on a rotating schedule to ask questions about Sophie and Anna and when they would be home.

"She's worried about people disappearing," Sophie said. "She wakes up missing her mother and father and brothers. It will take some time for her to realize that we won't disappear too."

An outsider would see a sunny little girl curious about everything; enthusiastic about the meals put before her, the toys brought out of storage in the attic, the chickens that roamed the garden; full to bursting with questions that poured out of her in a tangle of Italian and English. Lia listened closely to every conversation whether it included her or not, and fished out words she didn't recognize to present like small puzzles. *Butcher? Bustle? Weeds? Sneeze? Swallow? Slippery?* Between Rosa and Aunt Quinlan she got the answers she wanted and by the third day Anna thought she had gained at least a hundred new words in English.

Rosa's mood was far more subdued. She was thoughtful, observant, and quick to be helpful in the way of children who are unsure
of their place and desperate for acceptance. Lia knew how to ask for
and accept comfort; Rosa could do neither. In fact, Rosa seemed to
wake up for the first time on their second full day, when she realized
that Anna and Sophie were talking about finding her brothers. They
began to organize the search for the boys by writing a classified
advertisement to put in the papers. Rosa asked Sophie to read it to
her twice.

> *Anyone with accurate information about the location of two missing*
> *children will receive a generous reward once they have been*
> *returned safely to their family. A boy of seven years called Anthony*
> *and his brother, three months old, called Vittorio. They may still be*
> *together, or have been separated. Both boys have dark curly hair and*
> *very blue eyes. Both went missing on Monday afternoon, March 26,*
> *near the Christopher Street ferry. Please write with details to Mrs.*
> *Quinlan, P.O. Box 446, Jefferson Market Post Office. All letters will*
> *be answered.*

Rosa could not have asked, but she was relieved to find that there
would truly be a search for her brothers. The advertisement was the
first step, but it was the letter writing that fired her imagination.

From Brother Anselm and the city *Directory of Social and Health
Services* they had identified almost a hundred places that had to be
considered. A dozen or so Anna planned to visit personally, and the
rest had to be contacted by mail. Rosa sat and watched them write
letters as she might have watched a play on a stage, produced for her
alone to enjoy.

Now Sophie reached for an envelope, and looked up to see Rosa
watching her closely.

"Almost forgot," she said. Then she cleared her throat and read:

April 3, 1883

Reverend Thomas M. Peters, Rector
St. Michael's Church
West 100th Street
Manhattanville

Dear Reverend Peters,

At midday on Monday, March 26, Tonino Russo, age seven, and
Vittorio Russo, age three months, arrived at the Christopher Street
ferry terminal in a larger party of recently orphaned Italian
children. An accident on the dock caused great confusion, and
during this time the boys disappeared without a trace. I am writing
to you regarding the search for these two brothers.

Both boys have Italian complexions, dark curly hair, and very
blue eyes. There are no other distinguishing marks.

As the founder of the Sheltering Arms you see too many lost and
homeless children to remember them each; nevertheless, I write to
ask you to please keep these boys in mind. If you or anyone on your
staff have seen any children fitting this description, alone or
together, I would be thankful for word from you at your earliest
convenience.

I am a graduate of the Woman's Medical School and a physician
registered at Sanitary Headquarters, but my concern for the Russo
brothers is personal. At your request I am ready to provide further
information as well as professional and personal references.

> *Sincerely yours,*
> *Dr. Sophie Élodie Savard*

When a letter had been signed and the envelope addressed, it
went into the pile in front of Rosa, who was as attentive as a bird
watching over a nest. But with every completed letter came questions.

"Will he write back?"

"I would think so," Anna told her. "But maybe not right away."

"Unless he knows where my brothers are."

"Of course," Sophie said. "In that case he would write to us immediately."

"Or come to the house," Rosa suggested. "He might just bring them here."

Gently Sophie said, "We can hope for that, but you know it's not likely."

Rosa knew no such thing. She was making order out of chaos by pure force of will.

"I am certain we'll hear back," Anna said. Her tone was firmer than Sophie's, something that did not escape the girl.

There was a moment's hesitation. "But how do you know?"

And that was the issue, of course. They knew almost nothing and might never learn more. They could make no promises beyond the one Anna repeated now.

"We will keep trying until we succeed, or we all decide together that we've tried long enough."

Tonight they had written letters to the Sheltering Arms Home, the Eighth Ward Mission, the Ladies' Aid Society of the Emmanuel Baptist Church, the Society of St. Vincent de Paul, and the Home for Little Wanderers.

With every letter Anna wondered if they were helping or harming the little girl consumed by guilt and sorrow and an anger she couldn't put into words.

When they had finished for the evening, Rosa went off to Margaret, who would see that the girls were bathed and put to bed.

"I wish somebody would do the same for me," she said to Sophie as she reached for her own mail, still to be read and answered.

"No, you don't," Sophie said. "You'd break out in hives if somebody fussed over you."

Anna ran her eyes over a letter written in an educated hand on very fine linen paper. "A referral," she said. "From Dr. Tait."

Sophie sat up a little straighter, and Anna went on. "A Mr. Drexel wants me to take over treatment of his wife when they arrive here from England."

"That's good news," Sophie said.

"It might be," Anna said. "If Dr. Tait remembered to tell him I'm female. He forgets that kind of thing, even if nobody else does."

Sophie rested her cheek on a fist and struggled to contain a yawn. "If only they were all so unconcerned with gender."

Anna would answer the inquiry, but she knew from experience what would happen: Mr. Drexel would first talk to his wife's original physician at Women's Hospital. Dr. Manderston would steer him back to Women's Hospital and one of his male colleagues. Anna told herself it didn't matter; her income was sufficient to her needs; she didn't lack for patients, and never would. The male doctors at Women's Hospital had little use for her or for Sophie or any of the other women who had studied medicine and taken up its practice, but most of them were conscientious physicians. If not especially insightful and dismissive of advances they themselves could take no credit for.

"I'll never lack for work where I am," Anna said. "I see us shuffling up and down the halls forty years from now, snapping at student nurses and torturing medical students."

"What a lovely picture." Sophie laughed. "But I hope there will be more to life than the New Amsterdam Charity Hospital."

There was a small silence while they both thought of things that should be discussed. Cap, first and foremost, and what Sophie wanted for him. For them both. Anna shifted to look at her cousin more directly.

Sophie said, "Don't, please. I don't have any answers. I won't have any until Cap makes a decision."

"But your decision is made?"

"Of course," Sophie said, almost irritably. "If he allows it, I'll be with him until the end. Have you heard from the detective sergeant?"

"No," Anna said.

"Not yet," Sophie amended.

Anna didn't want to think about Jack Mezzanotte because in truth, she didn't know if she would see him again. On Sunday they had worked together toward a common goal, but the Russo children were her concern.

"He was helpful," Anna agreed. "But he isn't obligated to help. I'm not sure why he'd want to."

"Ah," said Sophie, and closed the subject with a grin she didn't try to hide.

• • •

ON FRIDAY AT breakfast it was Rosa who asked about the detective sergeants. The fact that she was comfortable enough to ask such a question was a good sign, and one Anna couldn't ignore.

"Do you think the detective sergeants forgot us?"

She said, "It's just been since Sunday. And no doubt they are very busy."

"I thought they were going to help."

Anna swallowed the last of her coffee and said, "If we don't hear something today, then we will write a note to them this evening."

Rosa gave a cautious and extremely doubtful nod.

• • •

OVER THE COURSE of the day Anna repeated to herself the things she had said to Rosa: the detective sergeant would be very busy. Jack Mezzanotte had already done them a great service by introducing her to Brother Anselm; it was foolish to wait for the man or even to think about him. So severe was she with herself that for a moment she thought she must be imagining him when she left the hospital to find him waiting for her in the lobby.

He stood there completely at ease as people came and went around him, late afternoon light falling in narrow stripes so that his face was half in sun and half in shadow. But his smile was open, and it transformed his face; he was not a police officer, in that brief moment, but a man who was pleased by something he saw. And he was looking at her.

Beyond that odd fact, he looked exhausted. Anna reminded herself that it was not her place to notice such things about the man, and even less her place to instruct him on his sleeping habits. She returned his smile with one of her own.

"This is a surprise." She saw some of the tension leave him, as if he hadn't been sure of his reception.

"I was on nights most of this week, and things were busy."

"Language lessons?"

He grinned at her. "Among other things. I found the father."

The abrupt announcement made no sense to her at first. "Father?"

"Carmine Russo. It occurred to me it would be easier to find and claim the boys if we found the father first."

It had never crossed her mind that one Italian immigrant among many thousands could be found. If it had, she wouldn't have known where to start looking for him. Beyond that she was unsure of how to feel about Carmine Russo, who had abandoned his children.

She said, "Where is he, exactly?"

"On the island."

She took a moment to think it through. Blackwell's Island could mean only a few things and none of them good: he had been sentenced to the New York City Penitentiary or the workhouse, admitted to one of the hospitals for incurables, or committed to the almshouse or the insane asylum. And there was the smallpox hospital. All of that encompassed by those two words: *the island.*

The detective sergeant was saying, "He's been sentenced to six months in the workhouse. For dissipation and disorderly conduct."

A habitual drunk, then. "You're sure?"

"The details fit, but I can't be sure until I go talk to the man. You aren't obliged, but I thought you might want to see for yourself. I have a prisoner to transport being held at the dock on the police boat, and a cab waiting."

Anna dreaded the very idea, but if she balked at this first real challenge, what part of her promise to Rosa could she keep? The detective was watching her, his expression giving away nothing at all. He wouldn't try to convince her, and that alone was enough to resolve the question in her own mind. The fact that her pulse had picked up was simply an inconvenient and regrettable biological response to a man, one she could resist. There were more important things at stake.

She turned and called to the porter, who had been watching the conversation from the other side of the room.

"Mr. Abernathy, would you be so kind as to send a message to Waverly Place? Tell them I went out on a call and may be a few hours at least."

Mr. Abernathy had a frown that would stop most troublemakers in their tracks, and now he turned it on Detective Sergeant Mezzanotte.

Again Anna tried to get his attention. "Mr. Abernathy?"

His voice came gruff and disapproving. "If you're sure, Dr. Savard."

"I am. Thank you."

But Jack walked across the foyer and said something to the porter. To her surprise, the older man's expression shifted immediately, and he accepted the hand Jack Mezzanotte offered. Anna had never seen Mr. Abernathy shake anyone's hand.

As soon as the cab had started off she asked, "Whatever did you say to the porter?"

"He's a retired patrol officer, so I introduced myself."

"But how could you know that he's a retired police officer?"

He shrugged. "That scowl of his is standard issue."

"I still don't understand," Anna said. "Why would he disapprove of you?"

One eyebrow peaked. "You've never had a man come calling for you at the hospital, have you, Dr. Savard."

This felt like more of a challenge than a question.

"You think he saw you as—" She stopped and fought hard to keep her expression neutral.

"As?"

"You tell me," she said. "Why should he be suspicious of you?"

"If you had a daughter your own age and a strange man called for her, you wouldn't wonder about his intentions? Or hers?"

Anna heard herself sputtering. "He is not my father, obviously."

"But you are a young woman in his care. He saw me as a potential threat."

"That's ridiculous."

"He can't know that. I'm a man who is showing interest in you."

There was a moment's awkward silence.

"Is that what you're doing?"

He shook his head at her, as though she had said something very silly. Then he leaned forward and lowered his voice.

"Do you really not know the answer to that question?"

"So you're saying that you didn't come by to talk to me about Carmine Russo."

"I'm not saying that at all. I did need to talk to you about Carmine Russo, but this was also an opportunity to see you away from the hospital."

"You're embarrassing me," Anna said. And at that very moment her stomach announced that she had not taken time for lunch.

Without hesitation he reached into the pocket of his overcoat and handed her something wrapped in brown paper, still warm. He said, "I should have thought about your dinner; I apologize. I didn't finish mine; please go ahead."

There were a dozen things a lady was supposed to say in a situation like this, all adding up to polite but firm refusal. It wouldn't do to eat in public, in front of a stranger, in a cab, without the most rudimentary implements. But Anna was hungry and he had passed her his linen handkerchief to serve as a napkin.

She unwrapped what turned out to be half of a very large sandwich. The smell was so rich that she gave up all pretense and simply bit into it, hot and salty and exploding with flavor. The meat had been marinated in some combination of oil and lemon and garlic, and all of that had soaked into the bread, grilled until it was crisp at the edges. The pork itself was thinly sliced and succulent and Anna heard herself make a capitulatory sound.

After she had swallowed and used the handkerchief to blot her mouth she said, "Detective Sergeant Mezzanotte, I have never tasted anything so delicious in my life. I hope you really did eat, because I think you'd have to arrest me to get this back."

• • •

JACK TRIED TO temper his smile, but it was hard work. Her willingness to admit both hunger and pleasure in her food was surprising and intriguing, both. The polite thing would have been to avert his gaze while she ate, but he seemed to be incapable of courtesy until she was almost finished. Then she folded the wrapping paper, blotted her mouth once more, and sighed.

"That was excellent," she said. "But don't tell Mrs. Lee; she thinks she's the only real cook in the city."

"I had that impression," Jack said. "I imagine she likes having the little girls to feed."

Anna thought of Mrs. Lee, who served plates piled high three times a day. "So far they've kept up." She went on to tell him about the changes in the household, the way their sedentary habits had been turned upside down, and how positive that seemed to be.

"Lia is interested in everything. Rosa is interested primarily in the *Directory of Social and Health Services*. Margaret is teaching her to read from it."

"Your cousin Margaret seems to have taken on their cause without hesitation."

"We all have," Anna said. "Margaret just has more time to spend with them. And since her sons went off to travel, all her maternal instincts have been frustrated. She's delighted to have the girls to look after."

Jack saw the corner of her mouth twitch.

"But?"

She looked at him. "Do you read minds?"

"I read faces," he said. "Is there a problem?"

"Not with the girls," Anna said. "Everyone in the house dotes on them. Mr. and Mrs. Lee compete for their time."

And then she fell silent. In the evening light he saw new color in her cheeks. Something she was embarrassed or just reluctant to talk about, then.

"Is there a medical issue?"

She hesitated. "Only indirectly."

"Now you'll have to satisfy my curiosity."

She looked him directly in the eye. "Not every whim has to be satisfied, Detective Sergeant. I can tell you this much. Sophie and I refer to the matter more generally as the Corset War."

He laughed, he couldn't help himself. "That's enough information, you're right. Let me ask you something else then," he said. "Do you think you could call me by my first name?"

"You want me to call you Giancarlo?"

"I like Jack better. You object?"

She tilted her head a little, considering. "It might be seen as inappropriate, if we were to use first names."

"According to—"

She gestured at the city around them. "Everyone. We are two professional people working together to solve a problem, a certain degree of formality is called for."

"I call Oscar by his first name."

"Really? I have heard you call him Oscar, but more often you seem to call him Maroney. And he calls you Mezzanotte for the most part, as I recall. I could call you Mezzanotte, I suppose, and you could call me by my last name. It's how we were addressed in medical school until we earned our degrees."

"That would be a step in the right direction. In the spirit of cooperation. And friendship."

The word seemed to give her pause. "I don't have many friends outside the women I went to medical school with and other doctors," she said. "I scare people off, I think."

She had said more than she meant to; he saw that in the way she averted her gaze.

"Then," he said, "it's high time you widened your circle of friends."

◆　◆　◆

THE POLICE DEPARTMENT ferry was small and used primarily, as far as Anna could guess, for transporting convicted criminals from the Tombs to the city penitentiary on Blackwell's Island. Jack's prisoner was a middle-aged man wearing a good suit; he might have been a shopkeeper or a schoolteacher. He sat inside the locked cabin, his head thrown back against the wall and snoring so loudly that the glass rattled in the windowpane.

Jack went to talk to the pilot as they moved into the middle of the East River, crowded with anything and everything that could float. Another hour until the end of the workday, but it would be light for a good while yet.

She liked being on the water, the chilly air against her heated skin. Anna watched the city and the traffic, as busy now as it had been at nine in the morning. As they got closer to the island the different buildings began to distinguish themselves, all of them facing Manhattan like a pack of squat, humorless bulldogs. As a student Anna had been assigned here twice, for short periods. It was one of the few places so desperate for doctors willing to donate their time that they allowed women medical students to attend. It had been a useful experience, but she could not recall one positive memory of the place.

Today, she reminded herself, she wasn't here to treat anyone, but to interview a man who might be Carmine Russo. She was glad to have Jack Mezzanotte with her, not just because he spoke Italian, but because without him she would have no idea where to start beyond the very obvious and blunt question *Why did you abandon your children?*

Anna wondered if this sentence was on Mezzanotte's list of things he needed to be able to say in multiple languages. In her experience police detectives did not bother with abandoned children, but Jack Mezzanotte seemed to be the exception.

He came back to stand beside her at the rail, his eyes scanning from the workhouses to the hospitals and on to the penitentiary and back again. Anna was very aware of his size, the width of his shoulders, the way he held himself. He was far bigger than other Italians she knew, and why, she asked herself, was she comparing him to anyone at all?

And that was a truly inane question. Not an hour ago he had leaned toward her and declared his interest; he had opened a door, and she stood on the threshold, considering.

• • •

A MATRON MET them in the waiting room of the men's workhouse, a bony, unusually tall woman wearing a starched white apron and an old-fashioned white dimity cap over thinning gray hair. She listened to Jack's request with eyes averted, then led them through corridors toward the back of the building.

They passed through rooms where tailors and cobblers and rope makers were bent over their work. From the windows Anna saw the larger shops for carpenters and blacksmiths and wheelwrights and tinsmiths, with fewer uniformed guards than she might have supposed. The noise that came to her was all mechanical: saws and hammers and shovels. She wondered if the workers were not allowed to speak, or if they simply had nothing to say to each other. A good many of them bore clear signs of the choices that had brought them to this place. Sunken cheeks, broken teeth, palsy, wasted muscles, missing fingers, skin mottled with bruises and the dark red flush of broken capillaries in the cheeks and nose.

The matron led them outside to a shed where older men were sorting through nests of leather goods in need of repair. Bridles and harnesses, stirrups and straps, horn bags and saddles in great piles. The air was thick with the smells of castile soap, wax, and the vinegar used to clean mold from leather. Not unpleasant, but the air in the shed was heavy and hot, even on a cool spring afternoon.

A guard came up and asked a question not of the matron, but of Jack.

The matron ignored them both and called out in a voice that carried through the shed, "Carmine Russo."

All the men looked up, but only one got up from the stool where he had been working, surrounded by buckets. In one hand he held a large brush and in the other what looked to be a leather cartridge box. Middle-aged, his hair shorn almost to the scalp to discourage lice, pure white at the temples. His arms were ropy with muscle; his belly was rounded in a way that spoke not of hunger or even of beer, but of ascites. Worse still, his eyes were a startling blue in whites that had taken on a yellow cast. His natural skin tone was a bronze made deeper by jaundice.

Jack touched her elbow and they walked into the shed. Russo waited for them, water and suds dripping from the brush he still held in his hand to puddle on the packed earth floor.

"Signore Russo." Jack spoke in Italian for some time. Anna heard names: Rosa and Vittorio and Tonino and other words that she thought might mean *children* and *wife*.

Russo's gaze flickered toward Anna and away again while he listened. When Jack had finished, he shrugged.

"Why?" Anna said. "Why did he leave them in Hoboken and come to the city?"

It took many more minutes for Jack to get a reaction from Russo that went beyond a shrug. When the man spoke his voice was strained and rough, as though his vocal cords had suffered an insult. He might have been drinking something caustic for its alcohol content. She feared that he had been looking for a relief from pain and found only more of it, because it was clear to her that he was very ill.

"He couldn't feed them, he couldn't look after them, he couldn't bear to look at them," Jack translated. "He left them to the nuns."

"Does he want to reclaim them?"

Carmine Russo looked at her directly as if he understood her, but he said nothing.

"Please ask him to put those things down," Anna said, making a sudden decision. "Tell him I'm a physician and I'd like to examine him, just very quickly."

Jack's hesitation was so brief that she might have missed it had she not been expecting exactly that reaction. But then he spoke to Russo in a firm tone, one that sounded more like an order than a request.

She would have expected a protest, but instead Russo did as he was asked and then stood, his arms at his sides while Anna approached. She took off her gloves and handed them to Jack, and then gently turned Russo's head so that the light from the open door fell on his face. Then she ran her fingers over his jaw and neck, hesitating over swollen lymph nodes, and finally palpating his abdomen through his overalls, very gently. Three touches that told her everything she needed to know.

To Carmine Russo she said, "Your daughters are well. Healthy and cared for. If we can find your sons, we will see to it that they have what they need to grow into good men."

He had understood some part of that, she was sure of it, but he still looked at Jack. For the first time Russo asked a question, and Jack spoke to him for a few moments. When Carmine Russo looked at Anna directly, his eyes were damp with tears.

On the way out Anna took the matron aside to talk to, and Jack followed along.

"Mr. Russo's liver has failed," Anna said. "There's one very large tumor and other smaller ones. I'm surprised he's still on his feet, to be honest. The pain must be overwhelming. He needs to be admitted to the hospital."

The matron said, "Is there anything they can do for him there?"

"No," Anna said. "There's no treatment. It will just be a matter of days."

"Well, then," she said. "I'd send him to the incurables hospital but there isn't a single free bed. Can't send him to the regular hospital if there's nothing they can do for him. I'll have to send him back to his cell."

Anna paused, wondering why she had expected anything else. Then she took her bag from Jack, crouched down to open it, and came out with a corked bottle that she pressed into the matron's hand.

"Will you see to it that he is given enough of this to handle the worst of the pain? A teaspoon in a glass of water when it's more than he can stand. He might need it every few hours or even every hour toward the end. Used carefully it should see him through."

◆ ◆ ◆

AS THEY WALKED back to the ferry Anna's expression was almost cold, her thoughts clearly very far away. Thinking of Rosa, no doubt, and how to tell the little girl about her father's situation. The gesture she had made—the bottle of laudanum she had pressed on the matron—was as much for Rosa as it was for Carmine Russo. Anna could say, now, that his death would be quiet and painless.

As they waited for the pilot she said, "He's not an alcoholic, or if he was, that's no longer his problem. He has an advanced cancer, at least a year gone. Could you arrange for me to bring the girls here, so they can see their father and say good-bye?"

The question took him by surprise. "Do you think that's a good idea?"

Her expression was as sharp as a slap.

He said, "You think it necessary."

She turned her head and for a long moment her gaze was fixed on the workhouse. Then she turned back, her expression set hard.

"We're less than a mile from Randall's Island here. Could we go to the Infant Hospital, or do you have to go back to the station house?"

◆ ◆ ◆

THEY STEPPED ONTO the Randall's Island dock as a church bell somewhere nearby struck six. Beneath his hand the muscles of Anna Savard's arm were tense, but she tried to smile when she looked at him.

"I'm being superstitious and nonsensical," she said. "But if the baby is here—"

She didn't finish, and didn't need to. In her mind the recovery of Rosa's younger brother would outweigh the news of her father's condition. Jack understood the impulse and said nothing discouraging; until she saw for herself that the boy wasn't at the Infant Hospital, nothing he could say would help.

As many times as he had been on Blackwell on police business, Jack had never had occasion to visit Randall's Island. There were no prisoners here, no jails or holding cells. It was an island of children. And graves, he reminded himself as they came to the front entrance. From here he could see the pauper's graveyard in the distance, rows and rows of unmarked graves, stark earth tones with a backdrop of ocean and forest in deep blues and greens deepening toward night.

Anna's whole posture changed when they entered the building, as if, Jack thought, she was preparing herself for disappointment, or battle.

It took no more than ten minutes to find the matron, and for the matron, barely concealing her irritation, to show them to the room where the infants from three to six months old were assigned, two to a cot barely large enough for one.

As he stood in the doorway, Jack's heart began to hammer in his chest. He had seen many things in service: the worst multiple-murder scenes, cruelty beyond imagination, despair and senseless death. He had seen all that and more, but he couldn't remember ever being more shocked, and before him was just a sea of young children. Row after row of them in the dim room that stank of soiled diapers and sour milk. Not the slightest breeze to bring relief, nothing to look at but walls painted the color of mud, water-stained and speckled with mold, and other children who couldn't do anything for themselves.

But worse still was the silence. This room should have been too loud for normal conversation; as Jack knew from personal experience, healthy infants of this age made their needs known at the top of their lungs. It was true that many of the babies did seem to be asleep, but at least three dozen were awake, sitting like so many dolls and staring through the bars of their cots at nothing at all.

If Anna was shocked, she hid it well. She moved into the room and began to go up and down the aisles, pausing only rarely to look more closely and then once, for a full minute, reaching into the crib to touch, her expression lost in the dim light. The matron stood at one end of the room studying her own hands while Anna continued on from one row to the next, her posture never changing. Then she turned and shook her head to make it clear that the Russo boy wasn't here.

Instead of crossing the room again, she gestured him closer.

She pointed to her bag, and Jack put it on the only flat surface, a long table against one wall interrupted by a single deep sink. Jack hesitated and then cleared a space by pushing dirty bowls encrusted with mush to one side so that roaches went skittering in a wave.

Anna was taking things out of her bag and looking around herself as if something was missing. Without looking toward the matron she called, "I need a basin. Two clean basins, one filled with hot water."

Jack saw the woman hesitate only as long as it took for Anna to give her a look that could not be misinterpreted.

While the matron did as instructed, Anna was arranging instruments on a cloth she had spread out. Then she uncorked a bottle and the piercing smell of carbolic struck Jack hard enough to make him step away, and then back again, lest she think him so easily put off.

The liquid went into the empty basin, along with a pair of scissors and an instrument with handles like a scissors, but that ended in small paddles. She caught his glance.

"Forceps," she said.

The sound of Anna's voice had given the matron courage to speak. "And what is all this for?"

Anna ignored her, took a towel from her bag, and, turning, walked along the row of cots until she came to one where one child was sleeping and the other sat, neither awake or asleep.

She handed Jack the towel. "To protect your clothes. Please hold him in the crook of your arm while I get a few things ready. Talk to him, your voice will help."

"Help what?" the matron asked, her tone much sharper. "What exactly do you think you're doing, miss?"

Jack had introduced her to the matron as Dr. Savard, but the woman seemed to have forgotten that or gave it no credit. Now Anna paused and turned toward the matron, every fiber of her being thrumming with barely contained anger.

"That child—" Anna pointed toward the cot where Jack still stood. "That little boy is starving to death."

The matron's mouth fell open and snapped shut. "He is fed, I assure you. He receives a full ration, three times a day, the wet nurses see to him like the others—"

Anna interrupted her. "But he takes almost nothing."

The matron drew up. "And how would you know that?"

"Because," Anna said, biting off each word. "He is starving to death."

"Do you see how many children we have in just this one room?"

the matron said. She looked over the room. "We don't have the time to force-feed picky children."

All the color blanched from Anna's face.

She turned away from the matron and looked at Jack directly. In an alarmingly calm tone she said, "Could you bring him here, please, and hold him firmly in the crook of your arm? I need to look in his mouth."

"His mouth?" the matron sputtered.

Jack hoped never to experience a look like the one Anna turned on the matron.

"Whoever examined this child when he was admitted failed to notice that he has ankyloglossia. The frenulum that anchors his tongue is abnormally short and tight, which makes it impossible for him to suck properly. And that," she said, enunciating every syllable, "would account for his *pickiness*."

The matron started to protest, but Jack had had enough.

"Leave," he told her. "Don't come back before Dr. Savard has finished here."

The matron looked at Anna and Jack and back to Anna again, and she fled the room.

"Thank you," Anna said. "Now if you could bring him to me."

The child weighed less than Anna's doctor's bag, a bundle of bones held together by tendons and skin. The belly was distended, and the eyes dull and sunken.

"Hold him gently, but don't let him move." She spoke to Jack, but all her attention was on the baby. With her left hand she pressed gently on the child's cheeks until the mouth opened. She had poured more carbolic over her hands, and it made his eyes water.

Very quickly she used two fingers to explore the open mouth, her head turned away, Jack thought, to concentrate on what touch told her.

"This will take just a moment," she murmured to Jack. To the boy she spoke more softly, a low crooning. "You haven't been able to eat, have you? But that's about to change. You're a very strong boy to have survived this place as long as you have."

The child blinked at her drowsily.

In a series of swift, tightly controlled movements, Anna used the forceps to grasp the boy's tongue and hold it away so that she had a clear view of its underside. With her free hand she took up the scissors, reached in and snipped, as cleanly as a seamstress cutting a wayward thread.

With that the boy finally roused, jerking in Jack's arms. He opened his mouth and wailed, full throated, insulted, alive, his lethargy banished.

Anna had dropped the bloody instruments back into the basin and picked up a square of damp gauze. When she turned back to Jack she gave him a small, tight smile. "Almost finished," she said. "Hold him still, please."

Inside the open mouth the small tongue flapped wildly, as if sudden freedom were more than it could manage. This time when Anna opened the boy's mouth he tried to turn away from her, but she held his face firmly and packed gauze under his tongue.

"It will stop bleeding quite quickly," she said. As if Jack had challenged her somehow.

Then she looked up and gestured to the matron, who stood in the shadows by the door. Reluctantly the woman came toward them, her arms crossed at her waist.

"I will report this," she began, and Anna cut her off with a motion of her hand.

"Not before I do," she said. "Now listen, because you need to remember and follow these directions I'm about to give you exactly."

Jack had never served in the army, but he had the idea that no general could sound more sure of himself as he sent men into battle. Anna rattled off instructions on how and when to change the dressings, what and when and how much to feed the boy, what trouble signs to watch for. The matron was to rinse out his mouth with salt water three times a day.

"The wet nurse must be patient with him when he's feeding," Anna said. "He will have forgotten how to suckle, and it will take a little time for the natural instinct to come back to him. You can be sure that his hunger will overcome the discomfort of the incision once he realizes his belly is filling up. It may take a half hour for him to get his fill, but that will improve quickly. If his malnutrition is not too far advanced, he may recover. His chances are not good, but they are better than they were ten minutes ago."

She had been wiping and packing her instruments while she talked, but now she turned to look the matron in the eye. "You must scrub your hands in very hot water and potash soap before you deal with the dressing. You should be scrubbing your hands before you handle any of these children and using carbolic acid in a five percent solution. Never go from one to the next without doing so. Your hands are the most likely source of infection."

Through all this the baby had been wailing, but Anna's concentration was fixed on the matron.

"You understand these instructions?"

Reluctantly, her anger plain on her face, the matron nodded.

"If you feel you can't follow these simple directions, I'll find the doctor on call—there is a doctor on call, I assume? And go over it with him. Never mind, I'll do that anyway."

"That won't be necessary," the matron said, her voice fairly dripping with dislike.

Anna looked at her for a long moment. "However you feel about me, you will not take it out on this child. Someone will be coming by tomorrow and again the day after to check on his progress. If he is not improving, I will report you to the Society for the Prevention of Cruelty to Children. You would not enjoy their examination, I assure you. Do we understand each other?"

Anna took the boy from Jack and held him to her shoulder, rocking him back and forth with her mouth pressed to his ear while she watched the matron struggle to speak.

"Yes," the woman said finally.

"I hope so," Anna said. "Primarily for his sake, but also for yours."

•   •   •

THE SUN WAS low on the horizon by the time the police ferry had moved away from Randall's Island. Anna was very quiet, and Jack left her to her thoughts while he coped with his own. He had never doubted her intelligence or her training, but now he had a real sense of who she was, as a woman and a doctor.

She roused him from his thoughts by touching his arm.

She said, "My mother died in childbed. I was just three but I remember some of that day. Ma was too old, really, and the pregnancy was a surprise. She herself was born when her mother was near fifty and she drew strength from that. But she went into labor too early and very suddenly while my father was out on a call. There was a—" She paused. "It's called a placental abruption, a tearing of the womb. I don't remember any of those details, of course. I learned about all that much later. What I remember is the look on my father's face when he came in the door and found he had lost my mother and the new baby both."

She paused to gather her thoughts.

"Not long after, he died in a carriage accident. It was his fault, he wasn't paying attention. I have always thought that if he had been with her when she died, he might have been less—devastated, I suppose is the word. He might have coped with his grief differently."

Her tone was very even, and when she raised her eyes to his they were clear.

She said, "I don't know if it would help or hurt Rosa to see her father. I really haven't known her long enough to anticipate her reaction." And then: "What are you thinking?"

The urge to move closer was one Jack resisted in that moment. He said, "I'm thinking that you weren't with either of your parents when they died."

She jerked as if he had struck her. "I'm aware of that. Obviously."

"I'm thinking that somehow, as logical as you are, you still blame yourself for their deaths because you weren't with them. I can see it in your face when you talk about it."

"I was a little girl," she said, her voice catching. "I was just a baby."

Jack put his arm around her and pulled her into his side. She came to him without hesitation, letting herself be held. They stood just like that at the rail and watched as a storm came in from the west, moving like a great wave in the sky to overpower the sunset and displace the night itself. In the distance the first flicker of lightning and the breeze that washed over them made her shiver. He felt it.

When she turned in the circle of his arm she had to put her head back to look at him, and so he kissed her. It was a gentle, almost-nothing kiss and still through all the clothes between them he felt her tremble, as aware, as alive as the light that forked through the sky. He kissed her again in just the same way, a question without words. In reply she raised a hand and cupped his cheek. Her palm was cold—he had forgotten to give her back her gloves, he realized now—but her touch was sure. This time she met him halfway, her free hand curled into his lapel, her kiss open and warm and welcoming. A strong woman, fragile in his arms.

•   •   •

AT HOME THE little girls had already been put to bed and Sophie had gone out on a call. There was no sign of Mrs. Lee or Margaret, either, but Aunt Quinlan was waiting for her in the parlor. There was a fire in the hearth, which was a welcome counterpoint to the rain on the roof. All the drapes had been drawn shut with the exception of one, where Aunt Quinlan sat to watch the storm.

She had an open book in her lap but no light except the fire and the occasional blue-white splash of lightning. Anna sat down beside her and watched the trees bending in the wind.

"Did Mr. Lee get things in the garden tied down in time?"

"He always does," her aunt said with a small smile. "I'm looking forward to the garden this summer. I might move out there entirely, dressing table and clothes closet included."

Aunt Quinlan had grown up in a small village on the very edge of the northern forests, a world different in every way from the one she inhabited now. Anna had been born in that same village but had only the vaguest memories of it.

Now she said, "Is it the spring that makes you more homesick than usual?"

"I suppose it must be. My da has been on my mind today. Now are you going to tell me why it is Detective Sergeant Mezzanotte just helped you out of a cab, or must I torture you to get that information?"

"No torture necessary," Anna said. "He came to the hospital to tell me that he found—" She glanced behind herself to be absolutely sure they were alone. "Mr. Russo. The girls' father."

She related the details as briefly as she could manage. The story of the Infant Hospital she kept to herself, and might never tell at all.

It was true that Aunt Quinlan was not easily surprised, but Anna had expected a little bit more of a reaction when she heard about Mr. Russo's condition.

Her aunt said, "I didn't think we'd ever know for sure. That will be a comfort to the girls. Not tomorrow or the day after, but in time. And Rosa has such an imagination, she might have gotten lost in all the things that could have happened to him."

"You think I should tell them right away?"

The lily-blue gaze met hers calmly. "You are the one to make that decision."

"I don't want to lie to them."

"You don't want to hurt them," Aunt Quinlan corrected her. "But it will hurt, there's no avoiding it. You know that."

"As a doctor, yes, I know that. But it's different—"

"When they are your own. Yes."

It was an odd thought, but one she couldn't deny. Somehow in the space of a week, Rosa and Lia had become one of them.

"Now tell me about the detective sergeant."

Even if she wanted to lie to her aunt, Anna knew from past experience that she would fail. Instead she said, "I'm not ready to talk about him yet."

"Ah." Aunt Quinlan smiled. "That's encouraging. When will you see him again?"

"On Sunday," Anna said, knowing that her color was rising. "The Society for the Protection of Endangered Children, I think that's what Jack said." She realized she had used his first name, and found that almost funny. She had yet to use it to his face, even after what had happened on the ferry.

What exactly had happened on the ferry was unclear to her, except that it felt right and good and utterly alarming. Before her thoughts could be read off her face, she leaned forward and took the mail from the table and began to look through it.

Aunt Quinlan went off to bed but Anna stayed just where she was, unopened mail in her lap. It was full dark now, but in the circle of light thrown by the streetlamp just opposite she could see the rain falling, buffeted by the winds so that it almost seemed to be dancing. A man ran past the house holding a newspaper over his head.

A cab pulled up, the door opened, and Sophie's umbrella emerged and opened all at once.

Anna listened as Sophie opened the door, hung up her things, and then came into the parlor, her color high and her face wet with rain. She fell onto the couch across from Anna, put her head back to look at the ceiling, and let out a long, whistling sigh.

"You know how slimy the cobblestones can be at the produce market," she began. "Like ice in January."

"Broken bones? Concussion?"

"Both, and worse," Sophie said. "She was six months pregnant. Four children under ten at home, and a clueless father."

"A familiar story," Anna said. "And a sad one."

Sophie lowered her gaze to send Anna a puzzled look. "Why do you do that?"

"Do what?"

"You always assume dire things for large families."

"I do no such thing."

"Anna, I can give you a dozen examples without trying."

As sleepy as Anna had been, she came awake at this unusual tone in her cousin's voice. For a long moment they studied each other, and then Anna put her head back and blew out a breath that made the loose hair at her temple jump.

"I am cynical, it's my nature. You've decided all of a sudden that you need to change me?"

Sophie leaned forward to take a peppermint drop from a candy dish. "I don't want to change you."

"What do you want to change?"

"Nothing. Everything."

"No word from Cap, I take it."

Sophie took her time unwrapping the peppermint. She tucked it into her cheek and then spread the small square of waxed paper out over her knee, smoothing the wrinkles.

"Something else then, if it isn't Cap. Spit it out, Sophie, would you?"

"I am worried about Cap, but I also have to tell you about Sunday."

"This coming Sunday?"

She shook her head. "Last Sunday. When you went to see Cap, I went to Brooklyn."

Sophie watched Anna think this through and saw when the realization hit her.

"I had to do something, Anna. And there haven't been any repercussions."

Anna closed her eyes. "Yet."

She could argue, but Sophie knew that nothing she could say would ease Anna's worries. Instead she told her about the Reason family, about Weeksville and the cab ride and the fact that no one had asked her for medical advice, not even the new mother.

"You liked it there."

"Yes," Sophie said. "I did like it there." This wasn't a conversation they had ever had, really, for the simple reason that Anna didn't see her as a woman of color. If she were to say *It was good being among people like me*, Anna would not take her meaning unless Sophie provided explicit detail, and then—what? Would she be surprised? Worried? Hurt? Anna's generosity was bred in the bone, but she lived a narrow life and was often unaware of many things in her immediate surroundings.

"You're not moving to Brooklyn."

"Is that an order?"

Anna opened her eyes.

Sophie saw now that her cousin was very tired, and she regretted raising this topic. "No," she said then. "This is my home. If I'm going anywhere it's to Switzerland."

"Let's go find something to eat while we talk," Anna said. "I have things to tell you too. I wish I didn't."

•   •   •

"OF COURSE WE have to take them to see him," Sophie said. Her tone was matter-of-fact, no doubt or hesitation. When Anna started to get caught up in ambiguities, Sophie could be trusted to lead her out of the wilderness.

"You have reservations," Sophie said.

Anna wrapped her hands around her teacup. "I do have some concerns. Thinking back now, would you have wanted someone to take you to see your father, at the end?"

Sophie didn't answer that question. Instead she said, "The choice is whether we cause them pain now, or later."

"I think knowing is better than not knowing," Anna said.

"Well, then, we're decided. Do we need special permission to take them to the island? Can the detective sergeant arrange it for us?"

"I mentioned the possibility to him. He said he could make arrangements. I think he'll come too, if he can manage it," Anna said. "Having someone there who speaks Italian is a good idea. If not Mezzanotte, then maybe Detective Sergeant Maroney might be willing."

Sophie laughed. "You call him Mezzanotte? Why?"

Anna grimaced into her empty teacup and tried to construct an honest answer. "I suppose I've been trying to keep some distance."

"And failing."

"Oh, yes. Miserably."

Sophie put a hand on Anna's shoulder and squeezed but said nothing more. It was a kindness, and Anna managed a smile.

10

EARLY SATURDAY A note came from Jack, written on the police headquarters stationery: he had had word from the island. Carmine Russo had died the previous evening and would be buried at noon. If she wanted to attend with the little girls, he would arrange it. Detective Sergeant Maroney would call for them, take them to the burial, and then see them home. The message boy would wait for her answer.

All through that difficult day she wondered about the least important issue of all: Jack Mezzanotte sent his partner to accompany them, instead of coming himself.

Standing at the graveside with a trembling Rosa pressed against her side, Anna tried to block out the dull monotone of the chaplain reading from a funeral service in order to focus on the girls. What she could do for them. If anything could be done for them. What to say, or not say. Over the years she had developed a way to tell an adult that a mother or sister or daughter was gone. She tried to answer the questions, and she listened patiently. She was empathetic, but calm. None of that seemed possible standing by this particular grave and a coffin of cheap pine.

Rosa's sorrow was palpable, but Lia seemed to be in a kind of waking dream. Her expression was almost blank, her eyes fever-bright, and she made no noise at all. Oscar Maroney was holding her for the simple reason that when he tried to put her down, her legs wouldn't support her. Even Sophie, who had the gentlest and most compassionate of touches, could not get Lia's attention. When she reached out to put her hand on Lia's back, the girl turned her face to press it against Oscar Maroney's shoulder.

It was Maroney who got through to Lia, on the ferry ride back to Manhattan. She sat on his lap with Rosa close beside him, and for the whole journey he told them what Anna took to be children's stories. He changed his voice and hunched his shoulders, opened his eyes in mock surprise and whispered.

And this, she told herself, was why Jack had sent Oscar. Because he knew that Oscar had a talent for dealing with children in distress.

If only he could do that much for lady doctors in distress, too. She was embarrassed by this thought but could not deny the underlying truth: she had hoped to see Jack Mezzanotte, had wanted his support and help. Such a short amount of time she had spent with him, and already she had unrealistic expectations simply because he had flirted with her a bit. It was good that he had stayed away, she told herself. She would go home and nurse her hurt pride and wounded ego, and tomorrow she would start over again. A highly educated physician and surgeon, with work that satisfied her, and a loving family that now included two little girls.

◆   ◆   ◆

SHE HAD ALMOST convinced herself of this when they got back to Waverly Place to find a letter waiting.

> *Savard: If you are free tomorrow I suggest we go together to talk to the people at the Society for the Protection of Endangered Children about the boys. Unless I hear from you I'll expect to see you at the Washington Monument in Union Square at one. We can walk from there.*
>
> *I'm sorry I couldn't come with you today to help with Rosa and Lia.*
>
> —*Mezzanotte*

◆   ◆   ◆

AS JACK CAME out of the front door of the shop on Sunday afternoon, he saw Anna. She walked right by him, lost in her thoughts. He called her name and she came to a sudden stop and turned toward him.

"Detective Sergeant Mezzanotte."

Back to the formal, then. He inclined his head. "Dr. Savard." Her gaze moved over the sign above the door: MEZZANOTTE BROTHERS FLORISTS.

"Oh," she said. "This is where you live. I don't know why I didn't realize; I pass this corner all the time."

She was nervous, and embarrassed about being nervous.

"I don't live in the shop," he said, and turned to point. "The house is farther down, behind the brick wall. If you'd like to see—"

She shook her head, flustered now. "Another time, maybe."

"Come on," he said. "Let's stop for coffee, and you can tell me how it went yesterday."

◆   ◆   ◆

IT WAS A reasonable idea and something concrete to do; a chore to focus on. As soon as they found a table in the coffee shop across the street, Anna started talking and she didn't stop until she had related the whole grim story.

"It would have been so much worse without Detective Sergeant Maroney," she said. "We owe him—and you—a great favor. The girls needed more help than we could provide."

"You don't owe me anything." He paused as the waitress put down their coffee cups. "But if you feel strongly about it, there is something you can do for me."

Anna drew in a deep breath. "If it's in my power, of course."

He leaned forward—something he did a lot, she was noticing—and smiled.

"I'd like you to relax. There's nothing to be anxious about."

She let out a small laugh. "I'm normally a very composed person," she told him. And in a fit of honesty: "You make me nervous."

"That much is obvious."

For a minute there was a silence between them while they tended to their coffee cups.

She said, "I didn't realize that there was more than greenhouses behind that wall. It must feel like an oasis in the busiest part of the city, living there."

"The house was part of the original farm," he said. "With a walled garden. My uncle Massimo bought it when he first came from Italy, thirty years ago. There were still orchards then."

He talked easily about the extended Mezzanotte families, the uncles who came from Italy, one by one, and were all involved in the florist business in one way or another, about the cousins who worked in the shop and greenhouses, and about his aunt Philomena, a benevolent dictator, her supremacy in the kitchen unchallenged.

"She made the sandwich you liked so much."

"I still think about that sandwich," Anna said, a little wistfully. "So you live with your aunt and uncle while you're here in the city."

"No, there are two houses. Massimo and his family live in one on the far end of the original property. In the other it's just my two sisters and me."

"The sisters who embroider."

"Yes."

He was easy to talk to and slow to take offense, and so she let her curiosity rise to the occasion. She said, "When did you come to the States?"

It was a question he had answered before, most probably many times, no doubt sometimes put to him by people who were unhappy about immigrants or Italians or both. But he answered her in what she imagined was more detail than was usual with nothing in his tone but friendly interest. He had been three, he told her, with one younger and one older brother. They came at the invitation of an uncle who had bought a large farm about fifteen miles outside Hoboken.

"Massimo, the one who manages the business?"

"A different uncle. I've got a crowd of them."

When they had left the coffee shop and had started uptown, she gave in to her curiosity and picked up the subject again.

"Then you don't really remember Italy."

"Sure I do. I spent two years at the University of Padua." And in response to her raised brow: "Reading law. But I wanted to be home. My parents weren't happy, but it was the right decision."

After a moment he said, "How much do you know about this organization we're going to?"

He was changing the subject, which might mean she had asked too many questions, or questions he didn't care to answer. And really, she told herself, she shouldn't be surprised if he did take offense.

She cleared her throat. "Almost nothing, I have to admit, but even Sophie couldn't tell me much about it. She said she thought it was fairly new. She knows most of the orphan asylums, some of them quite well."

He struck his brow softly with a half-curled fist. "That reminds me. We'll have to get a sister from St. Patrick's to come with us when we go to the Foundling Hospital, or we won't get very far. Preferably someone who had personal contact with the Russo children. Maybe Sister Ignatia, since you got along with her so well in Hoboken."

He was grinning at her.

"You're teasing me."

"And you like it when I tease you."

Anna quickened her pace in an effort to regain her equilibrium. "Tell me what I need to know about this organization and what help they might be to us."

"For right now," Jack said, "you should know that they take in children in order to place them out. Sometimes to local foster families, but over the last few years they've been sending boys west by train. Mostly I think they go to farms."

"But Tonino Russo is so young."

"As I understand it, they sometimes place children as young as four."

Anna was silent for a long minute.

"You disapprove?"

She almost laughed. "On what grounds could I judge them? I can see that things would go wrong sometimes, maybe even disastrously wrong, but somebody is trying, at least." And then she told him what she had really been thinking.

"I shouldn't have to ask you or Sophie about these things. It's a failing, I recognize that. I close myself off in my work. I don't even read the newspapers. In some ways it feels as if I'm just waking up, and that's Rosa's doing."

◆　◆　◆

JACK WATCHED HER color rise as she told him about something that she saw as a flaw in the way she lived her life.

"I'd be at the hospital right now," she was saying, "if not for Sister Mary Augustin showing up at the door on that Monday morning. There was something about Rosa when I first saw her in that church basement. My history is nothing like hers, but feels as though it is, to me." She raised her head suddenly to look at him, disquieted, embarrassed. As if he would judge her.

She changed the subject abruptly. "I haven't told you about my visit to St. Patrick's Orphan Asylum. I went to vaccinate the children—you remember that conversation I had with Sister Ignatia, I'm sure—and found that in the meantime the mother superior had seen to it that they were all vaccinated."

"They didn't let you know?"

She shook her head. "She let me come anyway, because she wanted me to examine some of the sisters. My guess is that she knew one of them needed surgery and they don't want to go to the Catholic hospitals where they don't allow female surgeons."

"And you examined them, of course."

"Of course. And in the next weeks sometime I'll be operating on one of them."

"For . . ."

"That's not information I can share, Mezzanotte."

Back to last names; some progress was being made. "Well then," he said. "Tell me about some other surgery, something you've done recently."

She gave him a frankly suspicious glance. "You're not interested in the fine points of suturing internal incisions."

"But I am. Really, I'm curious."

She started slowly. As she went on and saw that he was paying attention, that his curiosity was sincere, she spoke more freely. Jack listened closely, because he had the idea that later there might be a quiz. It was one he wanted to pass.

◆   ◆   ◆

UNLIKE THE DEEP quiet at the Catholic orphan asylum that had made such an impression on Anna, the offices of the Society for the Protection of Endangered Children were chaotic. The society occupied most of an older building on Thirty-first Street, three floors of offices and children. Anna's first impression was that the place was cramped and overextended, but then that had been true of most of the agencies she had seen thus far. There was no lack of orphaned and homeless children, but funding was always sparse.

They passed a large room where a group of a dozen boys had presented themselves for some kind of meeting, all of them subdued. Anna paused to scan the faces she saw there. Two of the boys were of

the right age, but neither of them was Tonino Russo. She knew it was
naïve to hope that this search would end so quickly and easily, but
then she realized that Jack Mezzanotte was studying the boys as
well. It seemed that the detective sergeant was less cynical than she
would have expected.

They found the door they were looking for, and Jack opened it for
Anna.

◆ ◆ ◆

ANNA STARTED BY relating the short history of the Russo children in as far as she knew it. Jack had added some details, watching
the superintendent and not liking what he saw. Mr. Johnson swiv-
eled his chair away to look over the street as Anna finished, running
a hand over his scalp. He had long, thin fingers that tapered like
candlesticks.

"Let me understand this correctly," he said when he turned back
to them. "These boys you're looking for are not any blood relation?"

"They are not," Anna said. "But my family has taken in the girls,
and we would do the same for the boys if we can find them."

"And why, may I ask, would an unmarried lady with such an advanced education want to take on the trouble of four Italian orphans?"

Jack didn't like the man's tone or the implications. Anna seemed
not to notice or care, because she answered him.

"I myself was orphaned very young," she said. "My cousin—who is
also a physician—was orphaned at ten. We were fortunate to be taken
in by a loving aunt who is agreed on this course of action. I am very
aware of the responsibilities, and our finances are in good order."

It didn't answer the question he had asked, but it told him what
she wanted him to know.

"The whole idea is very irregular," said Mr. Johnson.

"We're not asking for your permission," Jack said flatly. "Consider
this a police matter, if that suits you better. Two little boys have gone
missing from St. Patrick's Orphan Asylum. We want to know if one or
both of them might have come through here, and where they would be
if they had. Now, can you help us?"

Mr. Johnson was taking great pains not to look intimidated, but
Jack saw the flutter of an errant muscle at the corner of his eye. A man
who was easily insulted and slow to forget. His inclination was to deny

them help, but he also had a solid understanding of what trouble the law could be if he made an enemy of a detective.

"We wouldn't have taken the baby," he said. "But it's possible that the older boy went out with one of the groups that left last week. Before we go any further, Dr. Savard, you do realize that there are thousands of destitute and homeless children in this city."

"Tens of thousands," Anna said, her tone much cooler.

"And I hope you've already submitted queries to the Catholic Church?"

When she assured him that they had, he got up to leave. "I may be a half hour or more," he said, and closed the door behind himself.

◆   ◆   ◆

THE OFFICE WAS small and overheated, and Anna felt perspiration gathering beneath the weight of her hair and along her spine. She stood abruptly, but Jack was already at the door and holding it open for her.

She said, "That group of boys we saw when we first came in. Do you think they were being sent out for placement?"

Jack said, "That would be my guess. They looked a lot like these boys." He inclined his head to a row of a dozen framed photos that lined the walls. Groups of boys bracketed by adults, staring solemnly at the camera. Neatly dressed according to the season, faces and shoes both polished to a shine. Children as old as fifteen, by her estimation, but there was little of childhood even in the youngest faces.

The most recent one was dated just the previous week and was neatly labeled.

Placement agents Charles Tenant and Michael Bunker departing March 1883 for Kansas with their charges: Gustaf Lundström, Alfred Jacobs, Federico DeLuca, Harrison Anders, Colum Domhnaill, Lucas Holtzmann, Samuel Harris, Michael and Dylan Joyce, James Gallagher, Zachary Blackburn, Galdino Iadanza, Nicholas Hall, Erik Gottlieb, Marco Itri, John Federova, Alfred LeRoy, George Doyle, and Henry Twomey.

Anna wondered what had become of these boys, if they were well looked after and content in their new homes. Common sense said that they would be better off out of a city where children routinely froze to death for lack of a roof, but sending children off to be taken in by total strangers gave her a deep sense of misgiving.

Behind them Mr. Johnson said, "Our most recent group. You see Michael and Dylan Joyce—" He indicated two boys alike enough to be twins. They were no more than eight, fair hair sticking out from under their caps.

"These two are from a family of seven children living in one room in Rotten Row in such filth, you can't imagine. The mother didn't want to let them go, but in the end she made the right decision. Not a sound tooth in her head, a drunkard for a husband, and her still putting out brats like rabbits." He huffed. "There ought to be a law."

Anna's voice sounded rough to her own ears. "What kind of law do you mean? Against toothlessness?"

She felt Jack's surprise in the way he tensed. Surprise, but not disagreement or disapproval. At least not yet, but Anna was not done and would not be condescended to.

Mr. Johnson cleared his throat. "Overpopulation is not a joking matter, Dr. Savard. The underclasses are not capable of restraint and not willing to work hard enough to support so many children, so that we—you and I—must bear the financial burden. And what is the solution to that?"

"Why, birth control," Anna said, holding on to her temper with all her strength.

"Artificial contraceptives are illegal, as I hope you are aware."

Anna drew in a deep breath. "I am aware. So let me ask you, Mr. Johnson. Contraception is illegal and so is abortion. History makes it clear that human beings are not capable of abstinence. The poor—wait, what did you call them? The underclasses. How do you suggest their numbers be kept to levels you find acceptable?"

Mr. Johnson's gaze shifted away and then back, the muscles in his jaw pulsing and jumping. "Is that a serious question?"

"Oh, yes," Anna said. "I would like to know what measures you advocate."

He stood a little straighter. "The first problem is the influx of the worst of Europe. The moral and intellectual dregs must be turned away. If such a policy had been put in place at the right time, Michael and Dylan Joyce would have been born in Ireland, and feeding them would not fall to us."

"At the right time," Anna echoed. "So, after *your* forefathers arrived."

The muscles in his jaw were clenching again. "You misunderstand me."

"No, I don't think so. I think I understand you very well."

Very dryly Jack said, "Do you have any information for us?"

Mr. Johnson turned his attention to Jack with obvious relief. "Not yet. I came back because I forgot one important point. Does this boy"—he checked his notes—"Tonino Russo. Does he speak English?"

Anna couldn't remember Tonino talking at all, but she was angry now and willing to cause the man as much discomfort as possible.

"He is bilingual."

"So he speaks English?"

"He speaks Italian," Jack said. "And French. And some German too, so I think you'd have to say he's at the very least trilingual."

Anna took one step back and poked him with her elbow even as she smiled at Mr. Johnson. Her dimples stayed hidden. "A very bright boy."

"Dr. Savard," Mr. Johnson said. "We do not send children west for placement if they don't speak English. Now, does the boy speak English, or not?"

◆   ◆   ◆

THEY HAD BEEN walking a full block before Anna broke her silence. "You said that they place orphans with families. But that's not where they stop, is it? They take children from their parents."

Jack knew her well enough already to understand that any effort to calm or placate her would be received very badly, and so he gave her the truth, as he understood it.

"The majority of the cases are orphans, but they aren't above separating children from their parents. From immigrant families, especially Irish and Germans. And Italians."

She stopped and turned to look him directly in the face, as if she expected to see some hidden truth written on his brow.

"It seems I do disapprove of the Society for the Protection of Endangered Children. And most especially I do not approve of Mr. Johnson's Malthusian philosophy. But thank you for arranging this interview. It was instructive, if not productive. I think I'll look for a cab."

Jack said, "There's one more visit we could make today, if you have time. The lodging house on Duane Street run by the Children's Aid Society."

"As we're already under way," she said, and then pointed east. "We should be walking that way. To the elevated train."

"No cab?" Jack said, amused and irritated both.

"No need," Anna said. "The elevated will take us all the way downtown."

She started off again, then stopped when she realized she had left him behind.

"Are you coming?"

"I don't know," Jack said.

She had a very expressive face, so mobile that Jack could see her irritation giving way, slowly, to confusion and then a kind of abashed awareness. He kept his own expression neutral and waited. After a moment she let out a long breath and started back until she stood directly before him, her face tilted up.

"That was rude of me. I apologize for taking my irritation out on you."

"Hold on with the apology," Jack said, as somberly as he could manage. "Maybe I'm a Malthusian and don't even know it."

The corner of her mouth jerked. "Malthusians believe that overpopulation will cause economic disaster and the end of civilized society. They put the blame for overpopulation—for everything, really—on the immigrant poor. It's xenophobia disguised as economic theory."

"So you're on the side of the Catholic Church, then. The more children, the better."

Her mouth fell open and then shut with a small click. "I'm on the side of women," she said, her voice hoarse. "Those individuals who actually bear and raise children. The human beings whom Malthusians and priests see as no more than mindless breeding stock."

Jack said, "Now it's my turn to apologize. I shouldn't have made light."

For a span of three heartbeats she studied his face as though she could read his thoughts. Quite suddenly she nodded, and took his arm.

"Children's Aid," she said. "Let's go."

•   •   •

"I HATE THESE trains," Jack said with a vehemence that took Anna by surprise. Standing in an overcrowded car, she looked up at him and then dropped her gaze immediately.

"They turn the streets into dark tunnels, shower everything with dirt and cinders, and screech like banshees."

The wagon swayed so that Anna's nose almost touched the hand-kerchief pocket of Jack's suit coat. He smelled faintly of mothballs, of starch and tobacco. And of himself. People had very distinctive smells; it was one of the first things she had noticed as a medical student. Certain illnesses had distinct smells, too, and Anna attempted to list them for herself in an effort to stem the impulse to raise her head. Because if she did, it would look like she was wanting to be kissed. She had worked hard to put the memory of kissing Jack Mez-zanotte out of her head, and she had even managed to do that for as much as an hour at a time.

He shifted a little and, leaning down, spoke directly into her ear. "Maybe I have to rethink this elevated train business. There might be some advantages to it, after all."

Anna bit her lip in an effort not to laugh, and instead let out a small hiccup of sound.

"What was that?"

His breath warmed the shell of her ear and stirred the few loose hairs that curled against her temple.

"I didn't say anything." She was talking to his handkerchief, which was a brilliant white and beautifully embroidered, something she knew because she had its twin at home, the one he had given to her along with half his dinner in the taxi. The next morning she found it in her pocket, and now it sat on her dresser, laundered and ironed and folded to show the initials on one corner. *GLM*. She had been wonder-ing for days what the L stood for. Lorenzo. Lucian. Leonardo. Lance-lot. Lucifer. Lunatic.

"Am I embarrassing you?"

She studied the way his feet were braced against the sway of the train's motion. Her own two feet, much smaller, between them. Feet entwined. She felt him smiling against her hair.

"I'll take that as a yes," he said.

Jack could resist the swaying of the train because he was holding on to one of the overhead straps that were out of Anna's reach. She had nothing to hold on to—nothing she could, in good conscience, hold on to. She must brush up against him at every curve.

"What is it you want, Mezzanotte?" she said, putting some backbone into her voice. "Did you want to kiss me on a crowded train?"

"Is that an offer?" Now his lips actually touched her ear, and gooseflesh raced down her neck and her spine to spark in places best not considered just at this moment.

The train stopped and the passengers inched toward the doors, flowing out over the platform and spreading to the stairwell where they came together again, a river pulsing through a canyon. With the car half-empty there was enough room to step away, but somehow Anna found it almost impossible to move.

It made her angry, how easily he took her calm from her. She said, "You clearly have the wrong idea about me. I'm not a girl looking for an adventure. I'm not even a woman looking for an admirer."

"Too late," Jack said. "On both counts."

She drew in a sharp breath, took three steps back, and forced herself to count to twenty. Then she looked up at him just as the train began to slow again and she saw where they were.

"This is where we get off."

He caught her wrist as she passed him and drew her back. Jack's hand was large and warm and rough, the hand of someone accustomed to hard work. She set her jaw and refused to raise her head, but she heard him laugh anyway. A short, low laugh, a satisfied sound.

"This is where we interrupt the journey," he corrected her. "But not for long."

◆   ◆   ◆

THIS TIME THE passengers were in no hurry, lingering on the platform in a way that made no sense to Anna until the train pulled away and the new suspension bridge came into view. It was monstrous in size, a long neck arching out over the river like a predatory bird watching for prey. Along the metal flanks tenements cowered, saloons and dance halls and alleys all lost in shadow that would never go away.

And still it was beautiful. Anna couldn't remember the last time she had looked at the bridge closely, and she saw now what had once seemed unlikely: it was very near done. In just over a month it would open to traffic.

The bridge itself crawled with laborers, with drays and wagons and carts laden with building materials. As they watched, a wagon pulled out of the barn-like terminal that stood between the bridge itself and Park Place.

"They just started test runs," Jack told her.

There would be a huge celebration with bands and fireworks and speeches, a summer party of sorts. She planned to walk from one side of the bridge to the other along the promenade, but she would likely wait until the early crowds had had their fill. She turned to Jack, who was studying the men at work.

"Have you been on the bridge yet?"

He glanced down at her and grinned. "As often as I can find an excuse."

"What is it like?"

"Windy."

She raised a brow at him, impatient.

"I think you must be a hard taskmaster with your students," he said. And when her scowl deepened he said, "It's like being a bird, looking out over the world."

"I was just thinking that," Anna told him. "It's like a bird of prey."

"If you want to see it for yourself, I'll take you up."

"To the top of the tower?" Her voice broke, but she was too startled at the idea to pretend nonchalance.

"The tower is solid stone. It's not like a church steeple, you can't climb up from the inside."

"That can't be true," Anna said. "The towers didn't grow like beanstalks, after all. There must be ladders fixed to the stone. Look, there's a flag flying at the top. Unless they've got fairies working for them, a human being climbed up there to mount it. I could do that."

She had surprised him out of his composure.

"You're telling me that you want to climb the outside of the tower."

"I said so. Don't you? Or have you already?"

Jack glanced around himself. Most everyone had drifted away, but he lowered his voice. "A stunt like that could get me suspended, if not fired."

Anna had to bite her lip hard to maintain a serious expression. "I see. You have been up to the top of one of the towers, but you won't take me up. Because I'm female?"

"Because you could break your neck."

She fluttered her fingers. "I was climbing trees at four."

"Falling out of a tree is a different proposition than falling off a suspension bridge."

"So you won't take me up the tower."

"No. But I will take you to the highest point on the promontory. Just as soon as weather and my schedule—both our schedules—permit."

Anna considered, and decided to save the battle for another day.

•   •   •

THE INTERSECTION OF Duane and Chambers Streets was jammed with omnibuses, wagons, coaches, cabs, and every kind of dray, all competing for space with vendors hawking cookware, tools, knife sharpening, shoeshines, buttons and sewing needles, oysters on the half shell, pickles, nuts, sausage, cheese and curds, meat pies, and hard candy. Newsboys shouted for customers, bellowing the more exciting or salacious headlines from the three o'clock editions.

Anna saw a younger man lounging against the wall of a coffee-house, his eyes roaming the crowd and then stopping on Jack. He disappeared almost instantly, which was proof of what she had known in theory. Jack was known to more people in the city—good and bad—than she could ever count.

The lodging house constructed and run by the Children's Aid Society was an imposing four-story brick building that took up most of a city block. A clothier occupied the front of the ground floor, but the rest of it provided shelter and food for homeless boys. During the day they hawked papers and matches, shined shoes, played battered violins on busy corners, lifted and hauled in factories and on the docks and wharves. There were scullery and stable and errand boys, rat catchers and wharf rats who stole what they could not earn or beg.

Anna did not see them as hapless victims or as hardened criminals, but as children who simply refused to give up and die. An unprotected child who survived the streets of the city for even a month was a child who had learned to take advantage of any opportunity, or to create opportunity where none existed.

Though she was watchful and aware, Anna had had her pocket picked more than once; early in her career she had learned that poor children could not be left alone in an examination room or office. Even the youngest of them would take anything that might have value on the street, from a few inches of gauze to wooden tongue depressors and once in a while, scalpels and retractors.

Jack opened a door and they went up a staircase, the floorboards swept clean, the banisters polished, and not a single mark on the whitewashed walls. She wondered how the housekeeper managed it with so many boys under her roof.

The reception area was almost empty in the middle of the afternoon but for a high counter and off to one side, a smaller table where a single boy sat frowning at an exercise book. Behind the counter a middle-aged man in shirtsleeves was writing in a ledger while a woman sorted through the afternoon mail. Jack made a polite sound in his throat to get their attention, and succeeded.

"Jack Mezzanotte!" The woman held out both arms as if he were a favorite brother come home unexpectedly. She was red-cheeked and rounded, her hair piled up into a fuzzy topknot, but there was a sharp intelligence in her eyes and a stubborn set to her chin, and Anna had the sense that she was not to be trifled with.

She was saying, "It's been too long. Where have you been keeping yourself?" Her gaze moved to Anna and her smile broadened. This time there was a dimple.

Jack introduced her to Mr. and Mrs. Howell and presented Anna first just by name and then, quite formally, added on the fact that she was a physician and surgeon. He did this as though a lady surgeon were nothing out of the ordinary, and still the cheerful look on both faces before them went momentarily blank with confusion.

Then their enthusiasm and good manners reasserted themselves and they lost no time ushering Jack and Anna into the manager's apartment just off the reception area. Mrs. Howell called to someone in the kitchen for tea, and then they sat down on well-used couches in faded chintz. For the next few minutes they peppered Jack with questions about his well-being, his family, goings-on at police head-quarters, the activities of the Italian Benevolent Society, and the case of one of their charges who had been arrested for theft.

Once the tea had been set out by one of the Howells' daughters, Mrs. Howell's attention turned in another direction.

"And how do you know Dr. Savard, Jack?"

Jack leaned back and smiled at her. "I'll let Anna tell the story. It's why we're here."

It was beginning to feel like a set piece, but Anna told it all. Mr. and Mrs. Howell listened closely, stopping her once in a while to ask questions.

"You examined all four of the children?"

"Yes," Anna told Mrs. Howell. "They were all comparatively healthy. Tonino was very well grown for his age, quite strong. The baby was alert and not fearful." She described them in as much detail as she could give.

"Jenny?" said Mr. Howell, looking at his wife.

She shook her head. "The baby wouldn't come through our doors, and I haven't seen the older boy. It doesn't mean he hasn't been through here, but it's unlikely. I'll ask our Thomas when he gets home from his classes; he takes the desk every day for a few hours. And there's—"

She paused as a younger boy came into the parlor to lean against her chair and send longing glances to the plate of cookies that sat untouched on the table. Anna wondered how many children of their own they had raised in this very building.

"Timothy," said Mrs. Howell. "Go see if Baldy is in, please. Tell him I need to talk to him, right away." She turned back to Anna.

"And in the meantime, I'd like to hear more about you, Dr. Savard."

◆　◆　◆

JACK DIVIDED HIS attention between Hank's story of a boy who had been arrested for drawing a knife on another boy in the dormitory, and Jenny Howell's sure-handed solicitation of Anna's help in one more worthy cause. And he was listening at the same time for Baldy. It was no more than five minutes before he burst into the room as if the roundsmen were at his heels. The kid had enough energy to fuel all of New York's elevated train lines by himself.

"Did you want to see me, Ma Howell?" Then he caught sight of Jack and drew up sharply, his long, gangly body suddenly utterly still.

"No trouble," Jack said. "I'm not here for you." And he added something in Italian that made the boy both relax and smile.

"Sit yourself down," said Hank. "The detective sergeant and this lady are looking for a boy, and you might be able to help."

Baldy lowered himself onto a stool and nodded. While Jack talked he listened with an expression that made it clear that while he would cooperate, he would not be so foolish as to believe anything this Detective Sergeant Mezzanotte had to say. A completely understandable position to take, after all. Jack had arrested him more than once.

When Jack had finished, Baldy said, "This kid, a Neopolitán with blue eyes?"

"Blue eyes, black hair."

"Somebody like that would stick out. You're sure he's Neopolitán?"

Jack nodded, and Baldy shook his head. "Can't help you."

"You could ask around," Jack said. "See if Vince or Bogie or anybody in one of the gangs has seen him."

"I could," Baldy said. His gaze had come to rest with obvious interest and curiosity on Anna. "You took his sisters in, miss?"

"This is Dr. Savard," Jack corrected him.

"Dr. Savard, if you're in the market for homeless Italian kids, I could volunteer myself." He thumped his chest with a fist. "I'm better than Italian. I'm one-hundred-ten-percent-head-to-toes Siciliano."

"And you're not a child," Mrs. Howell said. "Though you seem to forget from time to time. Eighteen is a man grown. Or should be."

The young man had a head of dark hair so thick that it stood straight up from his scalp and beneath that, a clever mind. Jack had issued some kind of challenge that Anna didn't catch, but Baldy jumped right into a conversation that was half banter and half dispute and all in Italian. Anna leaned toward Mrs. Howell and lowered her voice. "Is there somewhere I could speak to Baldy alone for a half hour or so?"

• • •

ANNA CLOSED THE door to Mr. Howell's office behind herself and smiled at the boy's attempt to look both worldly and innocent.

"Baldy," she began, and then interrupted herself with a question.

"What is your real name, if I may ask? There must be something more dignified to call you."

He inclined his head. "I am Giustiniano Gianbattista Garibaldi Nediani."

"I see." She paused.

"You don't like Baldy?"

"I don't dislike it, but it doesn't really suit you."

"I have a very long name," he said. "And I am very tall. If they had thought to give you a longer name, maybe you would have grown to a full size."

At that Anna had to laugh out loud. "Maybe Anna isn't my full name," she said. "If you don't have a preference, I'll call you Nediani or Ned. Does that suit?"

The boy gave an almost regal nod. "What is it you want to know?"

Anna didn't have to prompt very hard to hear his very brief story. Orphaned at age eight, abandoned by an uncle, four years on the streets, three of those as a newsie. Since then he had been working at the lodging house as a jack-of-all-trades and pursuing other avenues of self-improvement, as he put it. He rattled off the facts with such ease that Anna didn't know what to think. It might be a well-rehearsed story, or a history that had to be handled like a live coal, cautiously, quickly, lest it do more damage.

"You are still active as a newsie?"

"I outgrew that years ago, except for looking out for some of the younger boys. Mostly I'm busy here."

"Are you content to continue here, or do you have plans?"

At this he looked somewhat affronted. "I have three hundred twenty-two dollars and fifty-five cents in savings. You can ask Ma Howell, she keeps the books. I'm thinking when I've got enough saved, I'll buy an interest in a shop."

"That's very enterprising of you," Anna said. "But it is slow going, saving for a better life."

"You got a job you want me to do, right? You want me to find this little kid for you."

"Yes. I realize that we are asking you to look for a little boy you don't know, and that it might put you in a difficult position, now and then, to ask questions in certain quarters. On the other hand, you know the streets. Your experience and understanding of the way things work gives you a great advantage."

He inclined his head. "True."

"I am asking you to act as a kind of unofficial—detective, I suppose the title would be. And as such, you should be compensated."

As if she had spoken Jack's name aloud the boy said, "I don't want no business with no cops."

"This arrangement is between you and me," Anna said. "No one else. With the understanding that you will not put yourself in danger, under any circumstances."

He broke out in a wide and amused smile, and rightly so: it was naïve to think he could avoid trouble, or even wanted to.

She said, "Now about compensation. I've been thinking about it. Do I understand that staying here costs ten cents a night?"

"For older boys. The little ones pay six cents. Another dime for two meals," he said. "Morning and evening. Ma Howell runs a good kitchen."

"Very well," Anna said, endeavoring not to smile. "Let's say one and a half dollars a week for your lodging and meals. Six dollars would cover four weeks. That will serve as a retainer. If you are successful tomorrow or if we are successful, if anyone finds Tonino or reliable word of where he's gone, you will still keep the fee I am paying today. If you find him or reliable word of where he is, I will pay you another ten dollars. If in four weeks there is still no word of him, we will reassess the situation and discuss whether to continue. Are these terms agreeable to you?"

"Yes," he said with great dignity. "I accept."

She took papers from her bag and placed them on a corner of the desk. She had asked permission to use the pen and ink, and so she got those ready, too. "Now, I believe that you've been attending classes since you first came here, and so you can read and write English. I'm going to write out our agreement here and we'll both sign it. If that's acceptable?"

"I'm always ready. Write on, Dr. Savard."

•   •   •

WHEN SHE RETURNED to the parlor, both the manager and his wife had gone to take up their duties. Jack sat alone reading a paper, his legs stretched out and his ankles crossed. Something changed in his face when he saw her, but there was no suspicion there. She wondered if he was ever surprised by anything. She wondered if he played poker.

"What?" Anna said, as he unfolded his long frame from the chair.

"What?" she said again, as he stopped right in front of her, not touching but so close she could smell the starch in his shirt collar.

He said, "Did you bribe that kid?"

She raised her head sharply and took a step back; Jack moved two steps forward.

"I paid him for his services," Anna said, refusing to step away again and trying to convince herself this had to do with calm self-assertion and nothing else. "That's not bribery. Why must you always put things in terms of criminal behavior?"

The corner of his mouth quirked. "Because I'm a cop," he said. "And Baldy is a criminal."

Anna felt her heart pick up a beat. "He may have broken the law—" she began.

"Laws," Jack said. "Multiple. Often, with great skill and enthusiasm."

"Well," Anna said, shifting in her irritation. "Of course he's no angel."

"How much money did you give him?"

"Six dollars with the promise of a bonus if he's successful. And before you say anything else, Mezzanotte, you should know that if he just takes the six dollars and never does anything to earn it, I will still consider the investment to have been worthwhile."

For a long moment he looked down at her, a crease in the fold between his eyebrows, and one corner of his mouth pulled up, as though she were a puzzle that resisted solving.

"Come on," he said. "We have a couple more stops to make."

Anna said, "I'm almost afraid to ask."

•   •   •

FOR THE NEXT two weeks, Anna was on high alert and agitated with herself about it. Some days there was a note from Jack Mezzanotte with news about the search, but more often when she left for the day the porter would have a note asking her to meet somewhere: the Protestant orphan asylum, the Our Lady of the Rosary convent, the Boys' Protectory on Broome Street, the Sheltering Arms Home, the Society for the Relief of Destitute Children, the Asylum of St. Vincent de Paul.

They would meet, talk to the head of the asylum or hospital, and go their separate ways. If it was dark when they finished, Jack insisted on seeing her home, and they talked of everything and nothing at all. Anna wondered if she had imagined his interest in her. But then he would come to call and sit down to talk to Rosa about what they had learned and where they would go next, and during those visits she was well aware of his regard.

He touched her often, in ways that a more strictly brought-up woman would not have allowed. She felt his hand on her shoulder, very briefly, or he touched her lower back when they made their way through one room to another, so lightly that she might have imagined it, if not for the satisfied look on Mrs. Lee's face.

He was playful with the little girls and could make even Rosa laugh, while Lia giggled so hard that she would dissolve into hiccups. He told tall tales in English and Italian, he produced butterscotch drops out of a seemingly bottomless pocket, and all the time his gaze returned, again and again, to Anna.

One early evening on an omnibus traveling down Broadway he had picked up her hand and examined it as if it were some strange object found on a park bench. He undid the three mother-of-pearl buttons at her wrist, and then, too late, looked to her for permission.

"May I?"

She wanted to say that he should not, but somehow his manner was so disarming that she just nodded.

"The only time I've ever seen you without gloves in public was on Randall's Island, when you treated that infant with—" He couldn't recall the name.

"Ankyloglossia," Anna supplied. "He died that same week." After a moment she said, "I only take off my gloves when I'm working, or when I'm at home without chance of company."

With a few quick tugs he slipped it off and cradled her hand like an injured bird. And it was pitiful, rough and red and swollen, the nails cut to the quick for the sake of antisepsis. There was no denying that her hands were terrible.

"I wash—I *scrub* my hands and forearms dozens of times every day."

"What exactly do you use?"

"We used to scrub nails, hands, and lower arms with potash soap and then rinse with a five percent carbolic acid solution."

"Used to?"

"It worked fairly well. You can tell by dipping your hands in nutritive gelatin just after finishing the process. If no microbes grow in that culture in three days, that's proof that the regimen is killing all infectious agents. Unfortunately it also was horrendously hard on our hands. So now we start with scrubbing, as before, but rinse first with eighty percent alcohol for a minute and then a three percent carbolic acid solution. It works as a sterile procedure and isn't quite so hard on the hands. Still, Mrs. Lee's hands are not nearly as bad, and she's been scrubbing floors for all of her life."

She was rambling, but it was hard to watch him studying her hand while her fingers twitched, ever so slightly. "The whole thing is made more complicated by the fact that I can't operate if there's even the slightest break in my skin. Then I put myself at risk. Someday they will come up with a better way to protect the patient and the surgeon both from infection." And then, more hesitantly, "Are you put off by my hands?"

She had startled him. He raised his head to frown at her. "That would be very narrow-minded of me."

Anna tried to draw her hand away, but he held on to it, his grip gentle but unyielding. For a moment she had the sense he might kiss her palm, and the idea of his tongue against her skin made her squirm.

"Don't," she said quietly, and, with fingers that were almost numb, put the glove back on.

"What you need," Jack said after a long moment, "is some kind of glove made out of thin material. Not cloth, that wouldn't work. Something like—"

His expression went momentarily blank, and then cleared. "Something like condoms, for the fingers and hands."

The image that came to mind was outrageously funny. And intriguing, somehow.

He said, "Condoms are made out of lamb intestines, I think. If they could be sterilized and sewn into a glove, wouldn't that work?"

Anna couldn't help smiling. "This must be the oddest conversation of all time."

"But wouldn't it work?"

She thought for a moment. "That particular material is permeable, so the surgeon would still have to scrub diligently. I don't think soap alone would be enough."

"But say for a minute that it's possible to sew a sterilized glove out of lamb's intestine or something similar. You could test it with your gelatin—what did you call it?"

"Nutritive."

"—to see if microbes grow. And if they did, you could experiment with different kinds of materials and sterilization and how you treat your hands, first. Until you got the right combination."

"That would likely take years," Anna said. "And someone willing to do the labor. The curing and sewing and sterilizing."

"But it might just work," Jack said. "It's worth thinking about, at the very least."

That evening when he walked her to her door, he paused in the shadow of the garden wall to kiss her.

"Savard," he said, against her mouth. "I spend a lot of time thinking about you. Night and day, I think about you. And it's not your hands that first come to mind."

He kissed her again, thoroughly, roughly, and then waited until she had opened the door.

"I'm thinking about those gloves," he called up to her. "Even if you aren't."

11

AT THE VERY beginning of her medical training Sophie had realized that the most difficult challenge she would face was not chemistry or pathology, but what Aunt Quinlan called her tenderhearted nature. Medicine demanded calm, rational, reasoned thinking and quick decisions. The ability—the willingness—to cause discomfort and even pain in pursuit of a cure. Sophie learned to think of her heart as something she had to put away, lock away while she worked.

Children died of diseases that were preventable. Women died in childbirth despite the very best medical care. They came to her with cancers of the breast and womb and mind, with hands crushed in factory accidents, with burns and broken bones, with their fears and their stories. She listened, and where she could, she helped. She sometimes—too often—failed.

As now she feared she was failing Rosa. Certainly she had had no real comfort to offer when they took the girls to Blackwell's Island to see their father buried.

Lia took comfort in being held and rocked and read to. Rosa, calm, efficient, ferocious Rosa had retreated into her sorrow and anger and would accept nothing from anyone. The only time she seemed to relax at all was when she was in the garden with Mr. Lee, and it was only with Lia that she allowed herself to bend when her little sister remembered, suddenly, that they had found and lost their father on the same day.

Rosa wanted nothing for herself and was almost impossible to engage in any conversation, unless it had to do with her brothers.

For almost three weeks now Anna and Jack had been visiting child welfare institutions, whenever they both had a few hours to spare.

Twice or three times a week he would come for supper and then afterward sit at the kitchen table with Rosa and go over where they had been and what they had discovered. It was an impressive list, and a disappointing one. They had interviewed staff and children at the Society for the Protection of Endangered Children, the Children's Aid Society office and lodging house, the Howard Mission, the Shepherd's Fold, the Leake and Watts Orphan Asylum, the Society for the Prevention of Cruelty to Children, and orphan asylums run by the Episcopal, Protestant, Baptist, and Methodist churches. Within the next few days they would start visiting Roman Catholic orphan asylums together.

They made other inquiries, too, that they did not tell Rosa about, and might not simply because they hoped it would never occur to her that her brothers could be someplace far worse than an orphan asylum.

Just now Jack and Anna were in the kitchen talking to Aunt Quinlan and Rosa. From the open door came the sound of voices rising and falling in a regular rhythm, and then Rosa's voice rose and wobbled and broke. She so seldom cried that Sophie wondered what news Jack had brought.

• • •

SOPHIE GOT UP from her spot in the garden and held out her hand to Lia. "Shall we go for a walk?"

The little girl had begun to show some of the roundness that was appropriate to her age, her hair had taken on a glossiness, and her coloring was high. Where her sister was weighed down by worry, Lia was relentlessly calm, cheerful, and affectionate. Mrs. Lee reported that the only time she had seen the girl cry was when Margaret and Aunt Quinlan had been arguing about the relative importance and value of corsets, a difference of opinion that was aired daily. Lia's unhappiness, Mrs. Lee believed, came from the inability to climb into both laps at once to offer comfort.

Now Lia skipped along at Sophie's side, singing to herself, a melody Sophie didn't recognize. She held one of the old dolls from the attic firmly by a leg, and seemed unaware of or unconcerned by the doll's head dragging along behind her. When they sat down on a bench in the early evening light, Lia began to undress the doll, holding a conversation with her that sounded very much like Margaret talking to Lia herself. Suddenly she stopped and looked up at Sophie.

"What's a corset?"

Sophie had been waiting for this question, but she had assumed it would come from Rosa, who was at the center of the disagreement between Margaret and Aunt Quinlan.

"A corset is a kind of chemise."

Lia's expression was puzzled. Sophie doubted that even Aunt Quinlan knew the Italian word for *chemise*, and so she touched the doll's old-fashioned undergarment, knee length and low in the bosom, with sleeves that came to the elbow. "This is a chemise. You wear one, shorter than this."

Lia still looked puzzled and then her face cleared as she made a decision. She grabbed her pinafore, skirts, and petticoats in both hands and hefted them to peer down at her own belly and the cotton chemise that covered it. Sophie gently disengaged her little hands and smoothed down the skirts.

"A corset is a kind of chemise," Sophie repeated. "But not soft. It's made out of very stiff material. Some ladies wear corsets because if they are tight enough, it pinches in to make their middles look very small. They do this to be fashionable." She made a motion in the air, the outline of a woman with a tightly cinched waist.

Lia squeezed the rag doll's lumpy middle, frowning in concentration. She said, "Aunt Margaret wants Rosa to wear a corset."

It didn't surprise Sophie to hear this from Lia. While Italian was her first language, the little girl had an acute ear and could parrot things exactly, even if she didn't entirely understand them.

Sophie said, "Aunt Margaret thinks that all young girls should start wearing corsets as soon as possible, because she did as a girl."

"But Aunt Quinlan doesn't like corsets."

"No, she doesn't. She didn't allow Anna or me to wear them, not ever, because she believes corsets—" She paused and rethought her approach. "Girls who wear tight corsets can't run and play or climb trees or do anything much except sit. Aunt Quinlan says that being free to move is more important than this." She made the same figure in the air.

She could have added her own medical opinion and Anna's, but Lia had heard enough. The little girl propelled herself from the bench and onto the lawn, where she stopped to spin in place with her arms extended, the half-dressed doll still firmly in hand. Then she loped off, yelling behind herself, "I am the wind!"

"Yes you are," Sophie said with a laugh. "And so you shall always be."

◆ ◆ ◆

BY THE TIME Sophie and Lia got back, Jack Mezzanotte had gone home and Anna off to bed in anticipation of an early and difficult surgery. But Margaret was waiting and she immediately grabbed up Lia.

"Past her bath time," she said to Sophie. At the stairs she paused. "Mail came for you while you were out."

Sophie waved good-bye to Lia, who still held the half-dressed doll in one grubby hand.

On the hall table were two letters and a small packet that took her breath away. She would have recognized it by shape in a dark room, so often had she held it in her hand. The last time more than a year ago. Cap had written the address himself. Very deliberately she put it aside and picked up the first letter, waiting for the frantic beat of her heart to settle.

The handwriting was unfamiliar, an awkward scrawl that was nothing like Cap's measured, angular hand.

Dear Dr. Savard,

I write with the news that I have no news. I have spoke to the Arabs who run gangs from the Battery to the Park and nobody remembers a Guinea boy with dark hair and blue eyes, about seven years old or any other age. I also had a look around certain establishments you wouldn't be familiar with, places Detective Sergeant Mezzanotte can tell you about if you ask. No trace of the boy at the Hurdy Gurdy, Billy McGlory's and the like, nor did I hear of him in worse places still. I've got business up Haymarket way this coming week and will see what there is to see. With any luck, nothing at all. Better a train

headed west than the Black and Tan or one of the Chinee opium
joints, that's my opinion. I'll write again as soon as I have something
to report, good or bad.

> *Your humble servant*
> *G. Gianbattista Garibaldi Nediani—Ned*

Despite the serious subject matter, Sophie had to smile. Anna's description of Ned had been almost as colorful as the letter. She put it aside for Anna's attention.

The second letter had been written by someone with a clean, nimble hand that was also unfamiliar to her.

Dear Dr. Sophie,

It is just a few weeks since we had the pleasure of welcoming you to
our home on a beautiful spring afternoon, and now I find myself
writing not—as I had hoped—to invite you for another visit, but
to share the news of my husband's sudden death. We laid Sam to
rest on what would have been our fifty-second anniversary, just four
days ago.

We are steadfast in our faith in our Lord Jesus Christ and take
comfort in His tender mercies. He has called Sam to His side and
one day He will call me to join him. Until then I have family to look
after and work to do.

Aside from this sad news, I am also writing to say that our eldest
grandson, also called Samuel Reason, has taken over the printing
shop. You didn't meet Sam when you were here because he was on
his way home from Savannah, where he was visiting his wife's
family. Now he asks for permission to call on you to discuss business
matters. If you could send word to him at the shop on Hunterfly
Road about when he might call, I would be thankful for your help
during this difficult time.

I hope you know that you are welcome here at any time, for any
reason, and that you will not wait long to visit.

With sincere good regards and many thanks for the care and kindness you showed my beloved husband, I remain your true friend.

Mrs. Delilah Reason

Sophie sat quietly for a long time, thinking about Sam Reason. Mrs. Reason had her children and grandchildren, sisters and brothers and friends to support her and give her purpose. More than that, she had fifty-two years of memories to sustain her, an abundance Sophie found hard to imagine as she weighed Cap's unopened package in her hand.

Very carefully she clipped the string and folded away the thick brown paper wrapping. Inside she found the familiar, much-loved pen case that had passed back and forth between Cap and herself for ten years, always with a letter enclosed and sometimes with more. She had thought never to see it again and so for a moment she only studied it, tracing the carving of a single tree beside a lake of inlaid pearl.

Finally she opened it to take out a letter of many pages, rolled into a tube and tied with a bit of string. She was terrified and exultant all at once.

Sophie, my love,

Nothing has ever felt more right than the act of breaking the long and painful silence that I created between us. I could make no accusations if you were to tear up this letter without reading another word, but I hope you will not. I have things I must say to you.

I have hurt you and disappointed you and told myself that I acted for your own good. You know that my fears for your health are founded in fact but I must now confess that while I could not admit it to myself at the time, my decision to cut you off was about more than your health. I was angry because I wanted you for my wife and you rejected me. And so, to my shame, I rejected you and convinced myself it was the right thing to do.

Then Aunt Q came to call and when she went away she took my delusions and pretenses with her. I have been cruel and unfeeling, and I can only ask your forgiveness. I hope you will be more generous than I have been, though I don't deserve it.

I have missed you. Every day, every hour, every minute I have missed you. You must know that I love you still and always, as I have loved you since that June we were sixteen, standing in the shade of the rose arbor, my senses filled up with the scent of the flowers and the low hum of the bees, and then with you and nothing else. Your taste, the texture of your skin at the corner of your mouth, the very sound of your breath catching in your throat. I loved you then as I will love you on the day I die. And I will die, Sophie, and my death will come too soon.

And so I come to the letter from Dr. Zängerle which your good aunt brought me. I have read it many times and in the end, I cannot believe that Dr. Zängerle's methods will provide a cure, but I do think that his treatment might give me more time than I would otherwise have. You want me to go to Switzerland and put myself in Dr. Zängerle's care at the Rosenau clinic. I will agree, with some conditions:

However much time I may have, you and I will spend it together. You must come with me to Switzerland and stay with me until the end, whether it comes in a week or six months or even, as unlikely as it seems, a year. I want you to be my wife and when my time is done, my widow. Before we depart for Europe, we must be married in a legal ceremony with your family and witnesses of my choosing in attendance. Our marriage must be announced in the papers both before and after the fact. Whatever the uproar and accusations and scandal, nothing will be done in secret.

We will not share a bed or any kind of physical intimacy beyond the care a physician provides for a patient. You and I will both take every measure to ensure that I do not infect you, or anyone else.

There must be no ambiguity about our status as man and wife and thus the platonic nature of our marriage must not be public knowledge. You will promise to present yourself to the world as my wife in all ways, even after I am gone. This has to do with the law, and only secondarily with my pride.

When you are my widow, you will accept all rights and properties that come to you in accordance with the terms of my last will and testament, in which you will be named as my sole heir with the exception of provisions for Mrs. Harrison and the staff in their old age. You can be sure of two things: the testament will be rock-solid and unbreakable, and one or more of my aunts or cousins will attempt to break it anyway, in order to deny you your inheritance. To protect your interests I will make arrangements for the very best legal counsel to represent you before the courts in this and any other matter. Uncle Conrad will be the executor of my will, and he will coordinate all aspects of my estate working with the other attorney I have engaged, but your word will be final.

What you do with the estate once it is released to you will be entirely and exclusively up to you. If you choose to build a hospital, to donate it all to a school, or simply to live in comfort for the rest of your life, no one will be able to interfere with you. I know you, Sophie, and you are thinking just now that you don't care about money or property. But I do care. This is what I want, and in this point I will not be denied.

Before I fell ill you told me again and again that you loved me but could not marry me. You imagined that in time I would come to resent you. Somehow you convinced yourself I would miss taking tea with old aunts and regret the lost opportunity to guide debutantes around the dance floor, that gossip and fashion and interminable talk of bloodlines would become more important to me over time. You were wrong. You are wrong, but none of that matters once we are married and away from this city. Distance and death will put an end to whatever disapproval my Aunt Eugenie or Mrs. Astor and her ilk can bestow. And you will be mine, and I will be yours, and that is all that matters to me. In the days and hours of my life, you are all and everything.

It is a fine thing for me to ask for mercy where I showed none, but please do not make me wait long for your answer.

I am ever yours.
Cap

12

SOPHIE STARTED OUT of sleep at the first crow of Lia's beloved rooster and realized that she was still wearing yesterday's clothes. She had drifted off rereading Cap's letter, which she still held pressed to herself. Cap, who loved her and wanted her for his widow.

She needed to talk to Anna before she sat down to write a single word. With a sudden burst of energy she went about getting ready for the day, washing without looking at her face in the mirror for fear of what she might see there. No more than fifteen minutes later she slipped into Anna's room.

"An early morning visit." Anna stretched luxuriously, arms extended over her head. "I thought it might be Lia; she has been coming in quite often recently to tell me her stories." Then she looked at Sophie more closely and sat up, fully awake.

Sophie found that she couldn't say anything at all, and so she held up the letter.

Anna smiled broadly, both dimples popping into view. "Finally."

"Read it."

She frowned. "Sophie, it's too personal."

"Please. I wouldn't know where to start to put it in my own words. And I need your advice."

That made Anna laugh out loud. "When is the last time you took my advice?" But she accepted the letter and began to read.

• • •

ANNA WAS A slow reader, and always had been. It was the judge in her, Aunt Quinlan always said. She had to weigh every word before she could go on to the next. When she put the letter down, finally, she looked up at Sophie with tears in her eyes.

"What are you going to do?"

Sophie came forward and sat beside her cousin, folded her hands in her lap, and felt the relief and joy blossom inside her. She would say the words now and make it true.

"I'm going to marry him. Of course." And then, because she needed to be honest with herself, "I'm going to marry him and then be with him when he dies."

Anna put her arms around Sophie's shoulders and pulled her close. "Are you happy?"

"It seems wrong, but I am."

Anna stroked Sophie's hair. "You're marrying Cap because you love him and you want to be with him for what time he has left."

There was something in Anna's tone that struck Sophie as odd. She studied her cousin's face, and was not comforted by what she saw there.

"Tell me," Sophie said.

Anna didn't pretend to be confused. Instead she picked up the letter and ran her eyes over it until she found a specific phrase. She cleared her throat and read out loud. "'You want me to go to Switzerland and put myself in Dr. Zängerle's care at the Rosenau clinic.'"

A small tingle began at the bottom of Sophie's spine. Something was off, but her thoughts were racing so frantically she couldn't catch the one she needed.

Very gently Anna said, "How did Cap know the name of the village? It wasn't mentioned in any of the materials, as far as I remember. Was it?"

Sophie knew Dr. Zängerle's letters almost word by word, and she didn't recall any mention of a village called Rosenau. For ten seconds she held herself completely still, and then she let out a barking laugh.

"This is too much, even for Cap." But even as she said it, Sophie knew that it was not. Cap was more than capable of planning complex, long-reaching schemes; he took huge satisfaction in them. She had refused him, but he had never given up, not really.

"This is an insane idea. Are we really thinking that Cap cut himself off from me as a—" She reached for a word that would not come.

"Strategy," Anna supplied. "Yes, I think maybe he did."

"So he was in contact with Zängerle more than a year ago. But why a year? Why set this up and wait a year?"

Anna spread her hands out over her lap and considered. "He was aiming for your tipping point. The day you would be lonely enough for him to say yes to this—" She touched the letter.

"But Zängerle's letter, how could he have timed that?"

"By holding off and then delivering it himself. It wasn't dated, if I remember correctly."

Sophie felt herself flushing with anger and amusement, frustration and resignation. "What a stupid chance he took. What cheek, the underhanded swindler. Could he have really been so desperate?"

"Hold on," Anna said. "We're just speculating. This might not be what it seems."

Sophie let out a sputtering laugh. "Oh please. Once you pointed it out, it's obvious that it's one of his schemes." She put her face in her hands. "He kept us apart for a whole year to force this marriage." Her shoulders shook, but she wasn't sure if she was on the brink of laughter or tears.

"He knows you too well," Anna said. "A year ago, would you have accepted him under the same circumstances?"

Sophie tried to imagine how she would have reacted to this particular proposal. She had been so sure of herself when she refused him. "I don't know. I doubt it."

Anna said, "I can't get over the fact that he drew Dr. Zängerle into this scheme."

"Really?" Sophie said, taking out her handkerchief to wipe her eyes. "Now that I think about it, I'm wondering why it took so long."

She rolled over and pressed her face into Anna's pillow so that she could scream without rousing the house.

◆ ◆ ◆

LATER, BUTTONING HER shoes, Anna watched Sophie put the last pins in her hair. There was another subject she wanted to raise. She just couldn't imagine holding her own news back for a whole day.

When she looked up again, her cousin was studying her.

Sophie said, "What is it? Jack?"

Anna drew in a deep breath and nodded.

"Has it come that far?"

She lifted a shoulder and held out a hand, palm up. "Let's just say that I need to speak frankly to him before things go any further."

Sophie's usual calm manner had returned, and Anna was glad of it. She said, "What are you going to tell him, exactly?"

"Everything," Anna said. "I have to tell him everything."

"Yes," Sophie said. "Do that, and leave no room for misunderstanding."

•　•　•

THEY WENT TO work as if it were any other day, Anna off to the New Amsterdam where she had three surgeries scheduled, students to meet with, and patients to see; Sophie took the el and then an omnibus all the way north to the Infant Hospital and made the rounds with medical students, examined incoming patients, signed three death certificates, and taught a nursing student how to care for a surgical incision that was still draining. She put everything into her work, and still when she allowed herself to look at the watch pinned to her bodice, the hands seemed not to have moved at all. At three, when she had finished with a difficult case she went to see Dr. Granqvist, who served as the hospital's administrator.

Pius Granqvist was a fifty-year-old native of Sweden, a man who had been working with sick children for all of his career. He was nondescript, fairly short and thin with a frizzle of dark hair on the very top of his head and bushy eyebrows that he twisted at the ends into kinked horns. On first meeting him she had wondered if children found him frightening, but then she saw how his smile transformed him. His whole face changed shape, his mouth too wide, his nose too small, and his eyes disappearing into a mass of wrinkles. He looked like a sprite or an elf, but he was as gentle as any mother when he examined a frightened child.

With his staff he was neither gentle nor amusing. He ran the hospital like a dictator; where he had no authority he took it anyway, and narrowed his eyes at anyone who would gainsay him. And he did not like Sophie's news at all.

"You can't leave," he said shortly. "You're the best we have."

"Thank you for the compliment," Sophie said. "But I am leaving to get married." Saying the words out loud made her swallow hard.

The director's mouth puckered as if he had taken a mouthful of vinegar. "Anybody can get married, Dr. Savard. Few people can do what you do. Your fellow can find someone else to marry, but I can't find another doctor like you."

Because Sophie had anticipated this reaction, she had taken the time to write out her resignation in very formal language. Now she put the document on his desk. He jerked away and wrinkled his nose as though she had put a decomposing rat in front of him.

"This is my official resignation letter. Three weeks from today will be my last day on the staff."

When she left his office her hands were shaking, but otherwise she felt great relief. She had wondered if she would feel regret or even resentment, and found instead a heady joy, a child let out of school for the summer. She so rarely took time away from work, she had forgotten what it felt like to put down the multitude of burdens, small and large, just to breathe. In another day—or even an hour—she would begin to feel guilty, that was inevitable, but she would put it off as long as possible.

In her office she sat down to finish her chart notes and then she took a piece of her own stationery and wrote out the note she had been composing in her head for a day.

Dearest,

Today I handed in my resignation at the Infant Hospital, and tomorrow I will do the same at the New Amsterdam and the Colored Infirmary. On Saturday I will come to call midmorning so that we can talk about Switzerland.

With all my love,
your Sophie

It was her intention to have everything organized and in order before she went to see him. She wouldn't give him any opportunity to change his mind, or the terms he had offered. Given all he had arranged to force her hand, it would be foolish to underestimate his propensity for forging and then taking advantage of the tiniest of loopholes.

She stopped at the New Amsterdam to check on a patient before heading home for the day, and had just gone into her office when there was a soft knock at door. The student nurse who came in bobbed her head in apology.

"A Mrs. Campbell is here to see you. She says she doesn't have an appointment."

It took a moment to place the name, and then it came to her. Mrs. Campbell, four little boys and a postal inspector husband, one of Comstock's henchmen. Dr. Heath's patient, but here and asking to see her.

"Thank you, Mrs. Henshaw. Just a postpartum exam. Please send her in."

Just recently there had been a rash of letters, sent to the house by strangers pleading for medical intervention and contraceptives, and now she wondered if this visit could be coincidence, or if it was just another one of Comstock's tricks. Those thoughts left her as soon as Mrs. Campbell came in; she was a physician first, and she recognized that this woman was in trouble.

She was very pale, the flesh around her eyes so dark that in the first moment Sophie thought of healing bruises, and then saw just what would be expected when a woman had three small children and a new infant, without household help. Sleeplessness was to be her lot for some time to come. Sleeplessness, and irritability, and perhaps full-blown depression. Mrs. Campbell was a woman taxed to the point of breakdown.

"Dr. Savard. May I speak to you?"

A month before Mrs. Campbell had been rounded, cheek and hip and thigh, and strong. Now her jaw and cheekbones were more prominent, and there was a brittleness to the way she held herself.

Sophie gestured to a chair. "Please."

The fewer questions she asked at this stage, the sooner a patient would come to the point. Mrs. Campbell started slowly, relating facts about the new baby and the older three, her hands clasped in her lap so hard that her knuckles went white.

"And how are you, how is your health?"

Mrs. Campbell drew in a breath and held it for three heartbeats. "I don't know," she said. "I don't know how I am."

"Have you seen Dr. Heath since the birth?"

She shook her head, quite sharply.

"Then what can I do for you today?"

The pale face came up suddenly, her gaze fixed on Sophie. "I want you to examine me."

Rather than ask questions, Sophie went to wash her hands while

Mrs. Campbell disrobed behind the privacy screen. Throughout the examination she was quiet and cooperative, staring at the ceiling overhead blankly, hands still wound together.

"You are healing well," Sophie said. "But you are losing weight, and too quickly. You need four or five small meals throughout the day. Nothing too heavy or spicy. A poached egg and a piece of bread would do, or oatmeal with cream. Meat or fish once a day, but in small amounts. Leeks, collards, spinach, any kind of bean will provide you with the iron you need as a nursing mother."

The thin mouth contorted and an arm came up to cover her eyes.

"I'm pregnant, aren't I."

Sophie had turned away to pick up an instrument, but she looked over her shoulder in surprise.

"Pardon?"

Mrs. Campbell sat up, rough patches of color rising in her cheeks. "I know I am, I can always tell."

"What makes you think that? Have you missed your menses?"

"I haven't had a period for four years," Mrs. Campbell said. "Doesn't seem to matter, I fall pregnant anyway."

"I saw no indication of pregnancy," Sophie said.

"But I could be," Mrs. Campbell said. "He's been at me morning and night. I could be. And if not now, then next week."

Sophie spread out a hand. "It's not likely, Mrs. Campbell, but it's possible. In any case, there isn't any way for me to diagnose a pregnancy at such an early stage."

"I know what I know." There were tears in her eyes.

Women often did know very early that they had conceived, but in this case it was hard to say. Mrs. Campbell might still be feeling the aftereffects of pregnancy and birth, or in her anxiety and fear—because she was terribly afraid, without doubt—she could convince herself of something that simply wasn't true.

But she could be pregnant. Children born ten months apart were not all that unusual.

"Would you like me to write a letter ordering no intimacies for health reasons, until further notice?"

"He wouldn't credit it," Mrs. Campbell said, bitterly.

And that was certainly true; Mr. Campbell would ignore what

she had to say. The situation was simple and familiar and heartrending, because Sophie had no solutions to offer. She could not even ask if Mrs. Campbell had received the pamphlet she had sent, because she still could not be absolutely sure of the woman's true purpose.

Mrs. Campbell spoke under her breath, as if giving Sophie permission to ignore her. "I cannot, I cannot have another baby so soon. It will kill me."

Sophie could simply send the woman on her way with a few carefully chosen platitudes; it would be the safest and soundest thing to do. But it would also be cowardly and worse, a violation of the oath she had taken. She must try, at least, to pass on information the woman could use to help herself.

For a moment she imagined Anthony Comstock standing out in the hall, a smirk on his face, and then she looked at her patient and all other concerns had to be set aside.

"You realize the importance of attention to hygiene while you are still healing?"

Mrs. Campbell's expression shifted, something of hope there now. "I have heard something about that, but I don't know where to start."

"Let me explain to you about the most effective ways to maintain personal hygiene. If you have time?"

"I do," Mrs. Campbell said. "For this I do have time."

◆　◆　◆

AN HOUR LATER as she was getting ready to leave, Janine Campbell paused as if she had something she needed to say but would leave unsaid without encouragement.

"Mrs. Campbell, I can't promise to have an answer to every question, but I will do what I can for you."

"If scrupulous attention to personal hygiene is not enough, if I am already pregnant—"

The silence drew out for a long moment.

"Mrs. Campbell," Sophie said quietly. "I have given you all the information I have to share."

She closed her eyes for a moment, then opened them, looking resigned.

"But I can come back to see you?"

"Normally I would be happy to have you as a patient," Sophie said. "But I am just about to leave on a longer journey. I may be gone a year, or possibly more." *Or far less,* she added to herself.

It often fell to Sophie to give a patient very bad news. An imminent stillbirth, malignant tumors that could not be excised, a child who would not survive the night. She had seen all manner of grief and sorrow and anger, raging and tears and those who fell away into unconsciousness rather than face tragedy. She was seeing many of those things on Mrs. Campbell's face along with a cold resignation, and the force of it struck her.

"I have a number of colleagues who would give you excellent care," Sophie said. "Shall I give you some names? Female physicians, women I went to school with?"

"No," Janine Campbell said, her voice low and soft and hoarse. "No. I'll figure something out. But thank you."

•   •   •

ANNA GOT TO the hospital at dawn just as a cab pulled up. The door flew open and Sister Mary Augustin jumped down before the cabby could even get off the box. She was so intent on helping Sister Francis Xavier step down safely that she didn't notice Anna, standing a few feet away.

What Anna saw was that the older nun and the cabby wore almost identical expressions. *Crankit,* Aunt Quinlan would have called it, a bit of Scots left over from her first marriage.

While Sister Xavier fussed at Mary Augustin, the cabdriver dumped their satchels on the ground and turned to stalk away. Anna called after him.

"Take those inside, please," she said. "And leave them with the porter."

He gave her a long and speculative look, which Anna took to mean that he had been paid but not tipped. *Nuns might not know about what a working man has coming,* his look seemed to say, *but you should.* Anna produced a quarter dollar from her pocket and held it up; the cabby retrieved the bags with a surly grunt.

"Dr. Savard." Sister Xavier's voice was hoarse and brimming with impatience. Anna didn't expect pleasantries from people in pain, but then again she was glad that Mary Augustin had been sent along as Xavier's private nurse.

Now she smiled at both of them. "Good morning," she said. "Come, I'll show you to your room and you can make yourself comfortable."

"Comfortable," sputtered Sister Xavier. "I'm too old for fairy tales, and so are you."

•   •   •

MARY AUGUSTIN DID what she could to put her very agitated patient at ease, but by the time Sister Xavier was settled in the bed, all color had drained from her face and her complexion was the texture of candle wax.

It was very wrong, Mary Augustin told herself, to be so happy under these circumstances. To take pleasure in an opportunity that existed only because of Sister Xavier's pain was something she would have to confess, but absolution required repentance, and that was something she could not manage. She had been hoping for this ever since the day in Hoboken when she learned that women could be doctors and surgeons. She had tried to put that idea—that outrageous, impossible, unattainable idea—out of her head, without success.

There was a soft knock at the door and things began to happen very quickly. Later she would have trouble sorting it all out: nurses and medical students came and went, sometimes, it seemed, with the sole purpose of irritating Sister Xavier, which wasn't very hard to do anyway. Then Dr. Savard came in pushing a cart full of equipment, trailing two assistants behind her.

Under other circumstances the look on Sister Xavier's face might have struck her as funny, but it was only later that she could smile about it to herself. Fortunately Dr. Savard didn't seem put out by the tone of the questions that came her way in such rapid fire. She introduced her assistants as medical students and explained the purpose of the different objects on the rolling cart: the stethoscope made it possible to listen to the heart beating and blood moving—Sister Xavier shot Mary a sharp and questioning look, and she nodded.

"And that?" she pointed to a contraption that was quite odd, with multiple arms and pads and bulbs of India rubber. "There's a needle in there somewhere, I know it."

"No needles," Dr. Savard said calmly. "This is a sphygmoma-nometer—"

"A what?"

"A sphygmomanometer." She pulled up the single stool in the room and sat on it. That simple act seemed to make Sister Xavier relax.

"Your heart beats to push blood through your arteries. The blood brings oxygen and nutrition to the cells," she said in a tone of voice that had nothing schoolmarmish about it. "The force of the pulsing of the blood puts pressure on the walls of those arteries. This machine"—she touched it almost gently—"measures that. Your blood pressure."

"And why do you need to know about my blood pressure?" Sister Xavier was trying to sound irritated, and failing. Dr. Savard had tapped her curiosity and disarmed her completely.

"It's useful information for a surgeon," Dr. Savard said. "It will influence the kind and duration of anesthesia we use."

"Anesthesia?" Sister Xavier grabbed onto the word. "Anesthesia?"

At that moment Dr. Savard seemed to realize the source of Sister Xavier's agitation.

"Did you think you would be awake for the procedure?" Dr. Savard said. "I should have made clear to you, and I apologize." She turned to her assistants.

"Bring in one of the gas-ether regulators, please," she said. "So I can explain the way it works to Sister Xavier."

13

"So," Maroney said, sliding into his desk chair and leaning back with his hands behind his head. "I see you got a private letter this morning."

Jack let out a whistling breath. "Here," he said, and tossed it onto Oscar's desk. "Read it yourself."

It was the path of least resistance, Jack told himself. Maybe he should have done this weeks ago, and saved himself the henpecking.

"Mezzanotte," Oscar read aloud, and paused to raise an eyebrow in Jack's direction before he went on.

> *Sister Mary Augustin will be here in the hospital for the next three or four days looking after a patient from the convent. Today between one and three would probably be best if you want to talk to her. Ask the porter to send for me, and I'll arrange it.*

"She signed it 'Savard.'" Oscar looked at the back of the sheet of paper as if he'd find some explanation for such oddness there. "From this it sounds like she doesn't like you much."

"She likes me just fine." Jack's tone said that he would entertain no more questions in that direction.

Which Maroney ignored. "Is that so? And what about you?"

Jack picked up the newspaper and snapped it open. "I like me fine too."

"Ass," Maroney said. "What's this about a nun?"

"She'll make it easier to get answers at the Foundling."

After a long moment Oscar said, "It's a damn odd way to court a woman, chasing around the city looking for orphans for what, almost a month. You don't think you'll find them, do you?"

Jack considered, and then lowered his paper. "It's unlikely," he said. "But it's important to her."

"Hmmm," Oscar said, and picked up his own paper. From behind it he said, "Tell me where you've been so far."

Jack pulled out his notes and slid them across the desk. It had taken long enough to get Oscar to ask for them.

•   •   •

A NURSE IN training who looked to be all of fifteen showed Jack up to the third floor of the New Amsterdam Charity Hospital, casting glances over her shoulder when she thought he might not notice and then dropping her gaze to study the floor. He might have asked some questions, but he had the idea that she would have been too nervous to answer. Because he was with the police or because he was male or both; it was impossible to know.

She stopped outside a room with wide double doors and spoke to him without meeting his gaze.

"Dr. Savard said that if you would come in and sit at the back of the classroom, she'll be with you as soon as possible."

"I'll do that. Thank you."

She hesitated as if she had something else to say, then fairly sprinted away down the hall.

For almost a month now Anna had been setting up little tests, as though she couldn't decide how to feel about him until she had put him through his paces. If she had grown up in an Italian family, her father would have gone after the same information in one fifteen-minute, sweat-soaked interview. Jack didn't know much about her own father, but maybe he would have let her handle things this way, feeling her way forward, step by step.

He knew already how her mind worked. She was sure that sooner or later she'd reveal something about herself that would scare him off; he would decide that she was too forward, too opinionated, too educated. She would never defer to his opinion in anything except the law; she had no interest in keeping house. She was tough and uncompromising when it was called for. While she had never said it openly, he understood that she had no use for religion.

She could be irritable, but she was usually willing to let herself be distracted. In the middle of a sharp commentary about the traffic or something in the paper he would sometimes kiss her without warning. She always seemed surprised at first and then, suddenly, pleased, and she always kissed him back. They never discussed any of this, what it meant that she came to him gladly when he pulled her into a doorway and kept her there until she was soft and warm and pliant in his arms.

Sometimes at night, hovering between sleep and waking, Jack asked himself the very question she seemed determined to force: What would it take to make him see that they were not, in the end, suited? Thus far he hadn't come up with an answer.

Now he slipped into the classroom and sat in the back row to observe Anna as she taught.

The room was not very large, three rows of chairs arranged in a semicircle around a center worktable crowded with books and papers, beakers and covered bowls, and three microscopes. Eight young women were standing at the table, bent forward to watch as Anna described something she saw on the slide. One of them was Sister Mary Augustin, whose white bonnet and habit stood out against the dark blackboard as though she were lit up from the inside.

Anna straightened and turned to the blackboard where she had already printed *necrosis*, *epithelial*, and something in Greek. And she teased him about Italian.

As she spoke she wrote out instructions. "I want you to spend at least an hour preparing slides and then examining and documenting the tumor under the microscope. Your drawings and notes should be very specific, from the gross anatomical to cellular. You must discuss the tissue types as a foundation for your diagnosis. For tomorrow I'd like you to write up a prognosis and treatment plan. You may work in pairs if you like. Questions?"

Sister Mary Augustin said something very soft and low, and Anna turned to her. "You certainly are welcome to participate. Your patient will sleep for a few hours more, and a nurse will be sitting beside her until she wakes. Now you'll have to excuse me while I speak to Detective Sergeant Mezzanotte."

The little nun's head came up suddenly and her gaze fixed on Jack. He nodded to them both and left to wait in the hall.

• • •

JACK SAID, "ARE you poaching souls from the Catholic Church?" And was surprised to see that she was a little embarrassed.

"If you like," she said finally. In her office she sat on the edge of the desk directly across from Jack, who was leaning against the door. "Though I'd characterize it more as responding to intellectual curiosity. She hasn't taken final vows yet, has she?"

"What makes you think that?"

"She's wearing white. Most of the other Catholic nuns I've seen wear black habits."

"She wears white because she's a nursing sister," Jack said. "At the Foundling all the nuns wear white. All the nursing nuns."

Anna's expression shifted, irritation drawing a line between her brows. Apparently she didn't like this particular fact about the Sisters of Charity.

"Why are you here, anyway?"

Jack took some pleasure in flustering her, there was no denying it.

"Because you sent for me." And before she could work up any more of a temper he said, "You are very good in the classroom. Very much in control but not overpowering or unaware. You had their interest and attention."

Now he had embarrassed her, but she was pleased, too. "Thank you," she said quietly. When she raised her head again she was smiling. "Do you still have time to go to the Foundling on Sunday?"

He nodded. "Sister Mary Augustin?"

"There's something going on there, but I have no idea what. She seems subdued. The only way to know if she's willing to help is to ask her."

They were silent for a long moment, just looking at each other. "Then Sunday at noon, if that suits. But tonight, if you're still interested—"

She was waiting, her eyes on his face, her expression a study in hard-won composure.

"We could go up on the new bridge. We need to do it today or tomorrow, as I'm leaving Monday and I'm going to be away for a week or ten days." Watching her expression closely, all he saw was a vague fluttering of her eyelids.

"I see," she said finally.

"I was hoping you'd be able to visit the Catholic agencies with Sister Mary Augustin while I'm gone."

"Of course," she said, quite stiffly. "I'm quite familiar now with the way things work. I'm sure I can handle further inquiries without you. You've spent too much time as it is—" She was pivoting to go around the desk and sit down, but Jack stepped forward to take her wrist. She turned back to him with a jerk and looked at his hand as if it were contaminated. He couldn't help it, he laughed.

"Mezzanotte, please let go of me."

Instead he pulled her closer and then, holding on to her upper arms, swung her around so that her back was against the door. He put his hands flat to either side of her head, but she was looking down, all her muscles tensed.

"Look at me."

She raised her head, her eyes flashing with anger and what he thought might be disappointment.

She said, "I see I amuse you. Do you want to let me in on the joke?" Her gaze fell to his mouth and then jerked away.

"I'm not leaving to get out of helping you."

"It's none of my business why you're—"

He leaned down and caught her mouth in midlie. After she gave in with a small sigh, he kissed her again.

"Do you remember I told you about the swindle the Deparacio brothers were running?"

Her expression cleared. "The train tickets. To—Chicago?"

"Yes. They sold somewhere around five hundred forged tickets from Grand Central to Chicago for ten bucks apiece."

She nodded, curious now.

"We put out a bulletin. Today we got a telegram from the Chicago police; all three brothers are sitting in their jail. You know how they caught them?"

"They spoke Italian to them."

"That's my trick. No, the mopes were hanging around the train station selling fake tickets to Grand Central."

"You have to go to Chicago to bring them back here." Her color was rising. "And it's still none of my business, but I wish you a good trip."

Jack gave her a narrow look and then, bending down, put his mouth to her ear. "It is your business, Savard. And I can prove it."

She stiffened. "I have a reputation to uphold here."

"Then stop lying to me or face the consequences." He pressed his mouth to the soft skin just beneath her ear.

"I forbid you to take advantage of me in this office."

He touched his tongue to her throat and felt her shiver.

"If kissing your neck is forbidden, how about—"

She grabbed his ears and pressed her forehead to his. "I have work to do. Let me go."

"Just as soon as you admit—"

"Yes, all right. It's my business too."

He kept waiting and after a good while, she relaxed against him.

"Now that you're listening I have a couple things to say. First, if you get word from Baldy—"

"Ned."

"Ned. If you get word from Ned, don't go anywhere with him alone. Wait for me to get back. Are you going to be stubborn about this?"

"Oh, no," she said. "I know better."

She did know better—she regularly saw hard proof of the damage done to vulnerable women. And yet he had needed to say it.

"Second, there's one advantage to this assignment. I'll have a couple extra days free over the summer. In June sometime I want you to come with me to Greenwood."

Her expression went blank as she tried to place the name.

"Greenwood is where I grew up. My father's farm is a few miles south of the village."

"You want me to come to Greenwood," she said, a hitch in her voice so that she swallowed visibly before she went on. "You want me to meet your family?"

"I've met yours, Savard. Seems only fair."

She was studying him. "Why?"

"Why do I want you to meet my family?" He gave her his best frown. "That's a question for a longer conversation."

Jack stepped away just as someone knocked on the door. He watched Anna gather her thoughts and remind herself who she was. Then she opened it to find the same student nurse standing there.

"Dr. Morris and Dr. Sweet need a surgical consult on a patient who just came in," she said, her eyes darting to Jack and then away. Anna looked at him over her shoulder as she left the room.

"I'll come by for you tomorrow at seven," he said. "As soon as I've finished my shift."

◆ ◆ ◆

"JUST GO AWAY," Sister Xavier said to Mary Augustin. "And leave me to my headache."

"A headache is quite common after surgery, but it can be treated." She added two more drops of laudanum to the glass of water she had ready, aware that her patient was watching every movement.

"I see now how it is with you," said the older nun, refusing to take the glass Mary Augustin offered. "Meek as a mouse until you've got the weak and vulnerable to bully."

Mary Augustin allowed herself a small smile. "Yes, you've figured me out. I'm here to bedevil you. You can suffer in silence, or you can take the medicine that will relieve some of your discomfort and let you sleep. Which do you think I'd prefer?"

"Insolent," Xavier snapped. "Give me the glass." When she had drained it she sat back against the pillows. "Disgusting."

Mary Augustin poured another glass of water from the pitcher.

"This too," she said. "It's important to keep your humors in balance."

When the second glass had been emptied, Mary Augustin checked her dressing and went about the small things she could do to make the older nun comfortable.

"You watched the whole operation, I suppose."

"I did."

"And?"

Mary Augustin sat down on the stool beside the bed. "What do you want to know?"

Sister Xavier flapped a hand impatiently. "Don't be dense. Tell me what she did. Your Dr. Savard."

It was difficult to know where to start, how much detail to provide, whether it was her place to offer conclusions or if she should simply refuse to talk about the surgery itself. But it seemed to her that Sister Xavier had a right to know.

"Dr. Savard made room for me to stand beside her and watch," she began. Every minute was fresh in her memory, but Mary Augustin had the sense that it didn't matter how much time passed, she would remember it all, detail by detail. It was a revelation to watch Dr. Savard's hands moving very quickly and surely while she explained exactly what she was doing in a calm, methodological way. She had pointed out different types of vessels and tissues and the tumor itself, an encapsulated mass the size of a lemon.

"A lemon!" Sister Xavier interrupted her. "It felt far bigger to me."

"It was easily removed, which is good news. No blood vessels involved." She used a fresh cloth to wipe the perspiration from Sister Xavier's forehead until her hand was batted away.

"Where is it?"

"Pardon?"

"Where's the tumor they took out of me?"

"It was dissected and is being studied under a microscope." And she hoped that this would be enough information, because as curious as Sister Xavier was, Mary Augustin doubted she wanted to know about the tumor that had broken open like a bad egg on the laboratory table.

When she turned to look, the pain lines between Sister Xavier's brows had lessened and she blinked.

"You are a good nurse," she said, in an almost pleasant tone of voice. "I hope you won't regret giving it up."

14

ON SATURDAY MORNING just before ten, Sophie turned onto Park Place and came to a stop. For more than a year she had been avoiding this corner for fear that she might see Cap, and for fear that she might not. Now she took a moment to catch her breath.

The house was as it had always been, classical in its lines and elegant, the counterpoint to new mansions springing up along Fifth Avenue, where excess had become a religion. Here nothing had changed, and nothing was the same.

For days she had been reminding herself that the Cap she knew so well was gone. This man she was going to marry would look nothing like the boy she had grown up with. Where her Cap had been strong and lithe and restless, this man would sit quietly. He would be gaunt and flushed and feverish, and he would cough until he was bloody with it. What she could do for him medically was limited, but she could give him some peace of mind. She would look at him and not see the illness; she would put that aside, and concentrate on the man held hostage by the disease.

The familiar gave her some comfort: the gardens that framed the front of the house, perfectly kept, backed with blossoming magnolia trees. Each flower stood proudly upright like a fat pink candle on a leafless branch. Mrs. Harrison's beloved pansies overflowed the pots standing sentry to either side of the door, as old-fashioned and sweet as the housekeeper herself.

As soon as Sophie set foot on the walkway, before she could think about knocking, the front door opened and gave her the day's first surprise. Cap's uncle Conrad stood beaming at her, and just behind him were Bram and Baltus Decker, Cap's cousins and best friends.

The Decker twins, who had been as unruly as wild ponies as children and had not changed much with age.

"Here she is, Uncle." Bram touched Conrad's elbow as Sophie approached.

The older man's mouth quirked in a familiar expression. "I'm blind, Bram," he said with his usual great dignity. "Not deaf. I hear her." He held out both hands, and Sophie took them.

"Sophie, my dear," he said softly. "High time. High time indeed."

"You look surprised to see us," Baltus said, kissing Sophie's cheek. "Did you imagine we'd miss the fun?"

"Cap wanted us here at seven in case you came to breakfast," his brother added. "But you didn't, and so we had to do right by Mrs. Mack's pancakes without you."

Conrad said, "You see these two are as measured and mature as ever, Sophie. You should go ahead, Cap is waiting for you.

"Give a shout when you're ready," Bram said. "And we'll bring the photographer up. If he ever gets here."

Sophie stopped short. "Photographer?"

"For the engagement announcement. Got to have a picture, says Cap. Quite insistent."

Sophie looked from Bram and Baltus to Conrad.

"The family hasn't been told yet," Conrad said, as if she had put a question into words. "But that's not something to worry you. Go on now, he's waiting for you."

Sophie got no farther than the first landing, where Mrs. Harrison was waiting, her eyes red-rimmed and damp. At the sight of Sophie two teardrops rolled down her cheeks. "Miss Sophie," she said. "It's so good to see you, so good I could just cry."

"You are crying, Mrs. Harrison." Sophie took her handkerchief from her cuff and blotted the old woman's cheeks. "How is your lumbago?"

"Never mind about me," said Mrs. Harrison, waving a hand as if to discourage a fly. She picked up a small silver tray from the table beside her and held it out to Sophie. There was a mask of fine mesh and a pair of gloves. Both smelled vaguely of carbolic acid. Sophie was not surprised that Cap would have made such arrangements, but Mrs. Harrison looked embarrassed.

"It's perfectly all right," Sophie said. "I don't mind at all."

It was a lie; she hated the fact that such things were necessary, but she would not make a fuss over something that could not be changed.

"Miss Sophie," Mrs. Harrison's voice trembled.

Sophie reminded herself that Mrs. Harrison had raised Cap; she had been in the household when he was born and when his parents died, and all throughout his aunt May's tenure. When Cap left this house for Europe she would never see him again.

"Yes?"

"He's weak," she said. "But he's settled. I couldn't say comfortable, but he's so much more settled since—well, now that you're here. He's content."

Content was a word Sophie disliked intensely. *Content* was constrained and devoid of hope for more or better. *Content* would not do for Cap. But she nodded and thanked the housekeeper for her help, and then she went up to him.

• • •

WITHOUT HESITATION SOPHIE opened the door, walked into Cap's room, and then, quietly, closed the door behind herself.

It was a gesture more telling than any other, that they should close themselves off alone in a room. She took a moment to contemplate the significance of this simple thing, and then she turned to the windows.

He sat in a high-backed armchair, a folded blanket over his lap. He was smiling at her as she smiled at him behind her mask. The idea came to her just then that he would never see her face again, and that was simply unacceptable. Sophie let the mask drop to hang around her neck and walked toward him. She saw his expression shift from confusion to wariness to distress and stop just short of anger because by then she had knelt beside his chair and put her hands on his shoulders, leaned forward, and touched her cheek to his.

"Oh, no," he said, his voice just a whisper. "No, Sophie. You shouldn't have come if you can't keep yourself safe from me."

But he held on to her with all the meager strength of his arms, and Sophie was glad. She was glad to hold him like this, as little as it was.

She got up and went back to sit on the chair that had been made ready for her on the other side of the room; when she had mastered her voice she raised her face and looked at him.

"You have to promise not to do that again," he said.

"I can't make that promise."

There was a small silence between them. Sophie waited, and then she said, "Did you think I would have no conditions of my own?"

He rested his cheek on the wing of the chair, his gaze unwavering. "Tell me," he said finally. "What measures you are willing to take to protect your health."

Sophie took a sheet of paper from her reticule and, walking across the room once again, put it on the table where he could reach it, turned, and went back to her chair.

Cap took the paper and read, his brow creased and disapproving. There was a familiar tick at the corner of his mouth; she was trying his patience, which was exactly her intention.

"I can't agree to this first point. We cannot eat at the same table," he said.

"We can," Sophie corrected him. "But not from the same serving dishes or plates."

"Then you will wear a mask or I will."

"That will make eating quite a challenge."

He glared at her and turned back to her list. As he read, the corner of his mouth jerked in something that went beyond irritation, all the way, Sophie was beginning to hope, to a resigned amusement.

"I will concede points one through eight," he said. "But we cannot sleep in the same room. It's just too dangerous."

Sophie turned away for a moment, her eyes moving over the familiar four walls of this room he had had for all his life. Nothing changed here: books and paintings, the fossils and seashells and minerals brought back from his travels, carvings and small sculptures. She touched the chunk of raw amazonite brought back from a trip to the west, he said, because it was exactly the same blue-green color of her eyes.

She was making him wait for an answer, and found that it suited her to take her time. She stopped in front of a portrait of his mother at age nineteen, in 1854. Newly married against her father's express wishes, already carrying Cap. In this photograph Clarinda Belmont always struck Sophie as somber or even mournful, as if she knew that the time left to her was short; she would lose her husband before their son was born, and then succumb to influenza in the first year of the war. It had occurred to Sophie that Cap was following her example in marrying against his family's wishes. She wondered if the comparison would irritate or please him.

"I will take all precautions," Sophie said finally, going back to her chair. "But I am talking only about sharing a room, not a bed. Think very carefully before you respond, because I am prepared, I will go away." She folded her hands in her lap and watched him thinking.

I will go away, she repeated to herself. She couldn't pretend to be a lawyer, but she was proud of this flexible turn of phrase.

He said, "There's a box on the table beside you."

"So I see."

"Aren't you going to open it?"

"You haven't finished reading my list."

There was something in the way he turned his head, something off. "You're taking laudanum."

A spark of irritation moved across his face and then was banished. "I didn't want to cough during this—interview."

"Paregoric or tincture?"

He gave her a crooked grin. "I thought you might ask. It tastes of saffron and cloves. From Mr. Cunningham. A reputable apothecary, you told me once."

This was the Cap she knew, good natured even when he had been found out in a scheme. He wouldn't lie; he considered it beneath his dignity. As a boy of twelve he had once explained himself to Mrs. Lee. A good lawyer, he said, can achieve his end without resorting to a lie. Mrs. Lee had laughed, but Aunt Quinlan had frowned and later took Cap aside to discuss the ways that manipulation made a mockery of honesty.

"From now on I will oversee the compounding of whatever medication you need. Without interference. So where do we stand?"

"I will concede on the medication—"

"As if I'd allow anything else."

He raised a brow. "And I will concede on sharing a bedroom. But the arrangement of the room and the beds is mine."

"The rest of it?"

He glanced at her list. "I agree to the other points."

"Without reservation?"

"Of course I have reservations," he said. "But I am willing to compromise."

"You will concede to my decisions in medical matters."

"Yes, I said I would."

She allowed herself a smile. "You have the same scowl now you do when you're losing at cards."

Cap's glare was both affronted and amused. He said, "Another condition occurs to me. We must see each other every day until we leave for Europe."

It would be difficult to manage, but Sophie nodded.

"Now will you open the box?"

She knew what he was offering her. There was a portrait of his mother in the parlor in her wedding gown. She wore pearls and emeralds at her ears and around her neck, and a wedding ring that had at its center a diamond that had come down through the Belmont line. That very ring was in the small box he wanted her to open and then to put on her hand. When the photographer came to take their portrait, Cap would want it in plain sight, because the ring made all things clear in ways words could not.

Sophie said, "I am so angry at you."

He inclined his head, but there was no confession forthcoming.

"When did you first write to Dr. Zängerle?"

He waved a hand, as if the question could be shooed away like a fly. "A year ago."

"What a lot of time to waste when every minute is so precious." She made her voice firm.

His gaze was sharper now. "Last year at this time would you have agreed to go to Switzerland as my wife?" And then: "You know you wouldn't have. So will you wear the damn ring, or not?"

Sophie opened the box and looked at this ring she had never thought to wear.

"I know," Cap said. "It's truly hideous."

The ring his mother and grandmother had worn had a yellow diamond as its centerpiece. The stone was set against foil on a wrought silver band, with sapphires to either side that only made the stone look more yellow.

Sophie bit her lip and then laughed out loud.

"I could have the stone reset," he said.

"Do you think it would make a difference, really?"

He lifted a shoulder in agreement.

Any number of women would put this ring on without hesitation and declare it the prettiest thing ever made by man, but tomorrow their fathers would look up from the morning paper and say, *Cap Verhoeven is going to marry that mulatto woman.*

She slipped the ring onto her finger, her hands chapped and a little swollen, as they always were. Like gilding a wooden nickel, as Mrs. Lee would put it.

Cap's ring pinched, just slightly.

• • •

WHEN ANNA CAME into the dining room on Saturday evening Aunt Quinlan had already taken her place at the head of the table, with Margaret and Sophie to either side. The little girls, Margaret told her in a subdued tone, had had their supper and baths, and were already settled for the night. From the looks of things, there was an argument going on.

Anna said, "You know how I dislike coming in on the middle, so start again please. At the beginning. What are we arguing about?"

"We aren't arguing," Aunt Quinlan said in a tone that said just the opposite.

"This isn't about a corset for Rosa, is it?"

Somehow it was the right thing to say, because Aunt Quinlan and Sophie both gave a startled laugh. Margaret continued to frown into her soup bowl.

"No," Sophie said. "It's not about that at all." She drew in a deep breath. "I saw Cap today. We're going to Switzerland."

Anna got up, went to Sophie, and hugged her hard enough to make her protest. She picked up her cousin's hand and looked at the ring.

"You must really love the man if you're willing to wear this ring. It's awful."

"I know," Sophie said, grinning.

"Agreement on all points?"

"With some very small concessions, on both sides. Anna, you'll break my ribs."

"Does his family know?"

"The announcement will be in tomorrow's paper, but Cap's aunts and cousins will already have received word by messenger before that point."

"This is no surprise to you," Margaret said to Anna, her brow pulled down in displeasure.

"Of course not." Anna hugged Sophie again and returned to her place, where she fell into her chair with an unladylike plop. She couldn't stop smiling. She smiled through the kisses and hugs and tears; she smiled especially when Mr. Lee came into the dining room—something he almost never did, despite many invitations—and took Sophie's hand between his own two hands and wished her every good thing.

"We must have wine to toast the happy couple," said her aunt. "All of us."

"This is hardly something to celebrate without reservation," Margaret said irritably.

"Margaret," Aunt Quinlan said. "Two young people who love each other are getting married. That is something to celebrate."

Margaret waited until Mr. Lee had left the room, shifting uneasily. Anna thought of suggesting to her that her corset was too tightly cinched, a childish impulse that made her want to laugh anyway.

Before Margaret could get started with her questions, Anna asked what seemed to her the crucial question. "Margaret, why should you object?"

Aunt Quinlan answered for her stepdaughter. "Margaret is upset because Sophie is the only Catholic among us, and she thinks the Catholic Church won't let the little girls stay if she leaves."

"Margaret is upset," Margaret said, "because it is unfair. We should never have allowed the girls to stay if we weren't all prepared to stay with them. Just last week the Catholic Church took a baby away from a Protestant couple. It was in the paper, if you don't believe me."

"There's more to that story," Aunt Quinlan said. "The mother left a note with the boy asking that he be raised Catholic."

"According to the nuns," Margaret muttered.

"Are you suggesting that Sophie send Cap off to Switzerland alone?" Anna was careful not to inject anything dismissive in her tone, but Margaret was determined to be insulted.

"Cap is a grown man, able to fend for himself," she said.

There was a small but fraught silence while Anna tried to reconcile what she was hearing with the Margaret she had always known. Not the most effective or consistent of mothers to her two boys but deeply devoted. Stubborn, yes. A martyr to social convention, but not willfully cruel. Anna looked closely at Aunt Quinlan's stepdaughter and wondered if she was unwell.

"Mr. and Mrs. Lee are members of this household," Aunt Quinlan was saying. "They are Catholic, and in case you've misremembered, they've taken the girls to church with them every Sunday."

"Yes. And they are also—" Margaret lowered her voice and then was unable to go on.

"Colored," Sophie finished for her.

"Well, yes," Margaret said.

"And so am I."

"But you're different," Margaret said, growing more flustered.

Aunt Quinlan closed her eyes for the span of three heartbeats. It was a rare thing to see her lose her temper, but Margaret had managed to bring her to that point.

"Margaret," she said with misleading calm. "I believe you had a letter from your sons today."

Margaret started. "I did. But—"

"I take it they've decided to stay in Europe for another year. You miss them very much, I understand. Maybe it's time you joined them."

The color drained from Margaret's face. "But the girls—"

"You needn't worry about the girls."

"But—"

"I raised five daughters," Aunt Quinlan said, more sharply. "And a granddaughter, and two nieces. I think I can be trusted with two more." She turned to Sophie. "Have you and Cap decided on a date?"

Hesitantly Sophie said, "Cap has legal matters to settle first. We would hope to sail at the end of May, and marry that same morning. Cap's uncle Conrad has offered to give me away."

Conrad Belmont approved then, which was a relief. Some part of the family would be opposed and vocal, but the support of the eldest living Belmont would go a long way.

"Just a small ceremony," Sophie said. "For my side, just family and Mary and Abraham Jacobi. If they will come."

"Of course they will," Anna said. "They have always been your champions."

"Anna. For someone so relentlessly logical and clear-thinking you can be oblivious," Margaret said, pushing back her chair to stand up. "It doesn't matter if every physician in the city attends or if the president himself gives Sophie away, it is still the color of her skin that will be the sticking point."

"For whom, exactly?" Aunt Quinlan asked, her voice very low and calm. "Who exactly are you worried about? Do you think you'll be cut in public because a niece of mine has married a Belmont?"

Margaret did an admirable job of gathering her emotions and calming her voice. She folded her napkin and stood.

"My mother was born in this house. I was born here and so was my brother. The law may say that the house belongs to you as my father's widow, but in your heart you know that it's wrong to put me out because I insist on speaking truths you would rather ignore."

"This is getting out of hand," Anna said. "Margaret, this is your home if you're away for a day or a year. No one is putting you out. No one is sending you away. Aunt Quinlan was making a suggestion. Badly timed—" She glanced at her aunt and frowned. "But nothing more than a suggestion for you to take or leave."

Margaret's throat worked, but she said nothing.

After a moment Aunt Quinlan said, "I spoke more sharply than I should have, Margaret. I apologize. You must decide what you want to do for yourself, but you can't decide anything for Sophie. And as a family we will support her in her marriage and we will find a way to keep the girls with us without sacrificing Cap's medical treatment."

The silence drew out for a long moment, and then Margaret turned and left them.

• • •

THE TRAFFIC LANES that fed onto the bridge from either side were still blocked off, and more than that, the terminal doors were closed. A sour-faced patrolman stood at the top of the stairs scanning the street as if he expected an invasion, but Jack never hesitated; he tipped his chin up at the patrolman—it seemed that this was the way police officers of all kinds acknowledged each other—and then he opened the door for Anna and they walked past him and into the terminal to the sound of hammers and saws.

Even on a Saturday after seven in the evening there were carpenters and painters and electricians working in the waning light. None of them took note of two strangers walking through the terminal, but two roundsmen called out to Jack, gesturing him over. Anna supposed it was inevitable; he couldn't simply walk past a colleague without at least a short conversation. But she was so eager to be on the bridge that she found herself bouncing on the balls of her feet like a schoolgirl.

The conversation had to do with boxing. She tried to fix her face in a politely uninterested way, and realized that she was failing when Jack took her hand and tucked it into his coat pocket, where he squeezed it twice. *Be patient*, was the message. She pinched him, hard.

One of the roundsmen was looking at her. A grandfatherly type with a great waterfall of gray mustache and a complexion so weather-roughened it looked more like tweed than skin. But he had a kind smile.

"You are looking forward to the bridge?"

He had a German accent which followed from the fact that Jack had called him Franz, but his shield bore the name Hannigan. It was not out of the ordinary in New York to have one Irish and one German parent or two parents from opposite sides of the world, for that matter.

Anna smiled back at him. "Very much."

"*Lua*," murmured his partner. "*Wie die Grüable kriagt wenns lachat. Was globst, Franz, git's da n Ehering undr a Handshua?*" And he winked at Jack, who spoke no German. Or better said, Swiss, because that was what they were speaking, oddly enough. She looked at Jack and was relieved to see him looking back at her, waiting for a translation.

Before Anna could tell the man that there was not, in fact, a wedding ring under her glove, Officer Hannigan put the question to Jack in a more subtle way.

"And is this young lady a relative?"

Jack raised a brow and shot her a grin. "Not yet."

After a startled silence that seemed to last an hour, Anna pulled away from him. "*Na ja,*" she said to the roundsmen in a voice nothing like her own. "*Das werden wir mal sehen.*" We'll just see about that.

· · ·

A SHORT FLIGHT of stairs led down to the pedestrian walkway that stretched out before them, still cluttered with machinery, piles of wooden planks, wheels of wiring, and a dozen other things Anna couldn't put a name to. The first lampposts had been installed, but Anna could see that it would be a good while before the bridge could be lit at night.

Below them laborers were still busy on the train and omnibus tracks, but on the promenade they were alone in a cathedral of cables aligned with such precision that Anna was reminded of the inner workings of a piano. She looked up at the pointed arches of the nearer tower and thought again of climbing it. She could see the ladder bolted to the stonework from where they stood.

"So," Jack said. "What did they say?"

"Who?"

He made a face at her.

Irritated, she sidestepped again. "Said about what?"

"They said something about you in German."

"No, they didn't. They were speaking Swiss."

"So you didn't understand."

"They liked my dimples," Anna said.

Jack made a sound in his throat. "I'm sure there was something more to it than that. And what did you say to make them laugh like that?"

Anna shrugged, both unable and unwilling to open up the conversation. Instead she ran ahead, pulling off her hat to feel the breeze on her face and neck. And she needed a moment to think.

Not yet.

Jack teased; it was his nature. He enjoyed seeing her flustered, but he was never cruel or thoughtless. Or had never been. *Not yet.*

She stopped suddenly and turned to watch him walking toward her in long strides. He had left his hat in the terminal and the wind ruffled his hair. For that moment he looked more like a boy of twenty than a man of thirty-five.

As he got closer she said, "I don't want to talk about what you said to them. Not until I've told you some things you should know. You might well change your mind about me. And," she added briskly, "I haven't made up my mind about you."

He stopped so close to her that their shoes touched, and smiled down at her. "Liar."

But she would persist, and this accusation delivered with a grin could not make her forget what was at stake.

The river was teeming with paddleboats and ferries, colliers, canal boats, barges and steamers and sailboats, all against the backdrop of the town of Brooklyn. She had never thought of Brooklyn as a particularly pretty place, its shoreline crowded with factories and warehouses and wharves. But from here the highlands were a small sea of oak and maple and cedar trees interspersed with blossoming cherry and crab apple, all punctuated by steeples and chimneys.

She said, "I don't know what I'm looking at," and Jack came up behind her. He ducked down to follow her line of sight and with his hands on her shoulders, turned her a bit.

"Wallabout Bay and the Navy Yard." As they turned steadily and he put names to ferry landings and landmarks, one arm dropped to circle her waist. "Fort Columbus. Governor's Island." He pointed and said, "You can just see Bedloe, where they're going to put up that statue from France, once they've got the money together. Meant to welcome immigrants to the city." This was the cynic in Jack talking, a tone that she didn't often hear from him.

A large steam liner was just passing the fort, headed for England or Greece or on its way to round the horn. Anna hesitated and then said what was on her mind.

"Sophie and Cap will be getting married next month and then they're going to Switzerland, to the clinic I told you about."

He didn't seem surprised. "Is that what she really wants?"

Anna thought for a long moment. "What she really wants is a cure, but this is as much as she can ask for." She shook her head, determined to put Margaret out of her mind for the moment at least. Instead she put her cheek against Jack's shoulder and, leaning into him, turned to follow the Manhattan shoreline.

It was disquieting to realize that beyond Castle Garden and the spire of Trinity Church there was almost nothing she recognized, as if she were looking at a city she had never visited before. Behind docks and wharves and warehouses there were buildings of all sizes crowded together like grubby blocks a child had poured out of a bag for no other reason than to see how they fell. All along the river shore to the right the seventh district tenements leaned together like so many rotting teeth, but even there poles were going up as electricity wove its way through the city streets, wires crisscrossing over every intersection. Smokestacks belched far above the buildings they topped. In the distance the gas works looked like a cluster of tin cans. There were patches of green here and there, but for the most part it was a city of redbrick and cast iron and warped wood held together by grime and persistence.

She said, "You can just see the Hudson from here."

"From the top of the tower—" He paused.

"Yes?" She elbowed him less than gently.

He used a hand to immobilize her arm. "Looking up there now, you still want to climb to the top?"

She tipped her head back to consider. "I've climbed a couple of mountains," she said. "I don't suppose there are any bad-mannered goats on the way up that ladder, are there?"

His face was so close she could count his eyelashes. When he spoke his breath was warm on her face. "Do you dislike it that I am protective of you? Because that's bred in the bone."

She straightened and patted his cheek. "I don't mind. As long as you'll take my 'Yes, I will' as an answer to your 'No, you won't.'"

Jack gave a low laugh that she decided to read as surrender.

They sat down on a bench that was so new the hardware shone, and Anna turned her attention back to the skyline. Dusk was dropping down, casting the kindest of lights over the worst of the city, a sugar glaze that might fool the eye for the few minutes it lasted. But it was her city, the only home she remembered. She had left once to test herself and come back again.

She said, "Sometimes I work twelve- or fourteen-hour days. I am called out I would say on average two nights a week. And I will always be a doctor. I will never give up practicing medicine."

"Yes," he said. "I recognize that about you. I see it."

She hoped he was being honest with himself. "Aunt Quinlan calls me a freethinker, but in fact I'm an agnostic. I don't care what you believe, if it gives you comfort. But I will not convert."

Jack nodded as if this were no surprise. "Go on."

"I'm not—I have—" She was irritated with herself now. He was being his usual calm, rational self; she could be no less. She said, "I'm not a virgin. My experience is narrow, but I'm not a virgin. I'll answer questions if you have them."

He shook his head, the muscle in his jaw rolling in a way she couldn't read.

"Is there more?"

"Yes," Anna said. "I'm working up to it."

She thought of Sophie, who had encouraged her to say these things, to be clear. Sophie, who would be Cap's widow though she could be his wife only in name. She would bear the loss, and so could Anna.

She said, "I break the law on a regular basis, and without remorse. And I will continue to break the law as long as I am able."

"Contraceptives."

She let out a small sigh of relief at his matter-of-fact tone.

"Yes. I make information available in certain very strict circumstances and I also provide . . . recommendations, where possible. We—I am uncompromising about my patients' privacy and my own safety because I can't help anyone if I'm sitting in prison."

He was watching her. "You've just confessed a crime to me. You trust me."

"I do," Anna said, her voice catching. She waited until he nodded for her to go on. "I do trust you. Am I wrong?"

"No." No hesitation, no doubt.

She went on. "So you must know that whatever situation I find myself in eventually—with you or anyone else—I will use contraceptives. Until." She stopped herself.

"Until."

"Until the time is right."

He drew in a deep breath. "I see." And after a moment he said, "It's better than the alternatives."

"Do you think so?" Anna wanted to touch his face but stopped herself. "Do you mean it's better than bringing an unwanted child into the world, or it's better than abortion?"

She had finally unsettled him.

"Both."

He was still talking to her, which gave her the courage to tell him the rest.

"I agree with you that it's better than the alternatives. But again, you should know—" Her voice was suddenly hoarse. "You should know that under certain circumstances I would perform an abortion. I haven't yet, but I might someday. I don't know if you realize, but I would guess that at least a hundred successful abortions are performed every month, in this city alone. Poorer women care for themselves, but hundreds of procedures are done by doctors and midwives, and done safely. You only hear about the cases that have gone wrong."

"Is that something you see a lot?"

"All the time. Usually when a woman comes to the hospital after a badly done abortion it's already too late. But I have never reported the few who survived. And I never will."

"And their doctors?"

"I ask, but so far no one has ever given me a name. I'm not sure what I would do in that case. It depends on the circumstances."

Jack looked away over the river to the west. He was breathing deeply and evenly, and his arm stayed where it was, around her shoulders. As a minute passed and then another, a deep sadness began to gather in the corners of what Sophie would call her heart. Her vulnerable heart.

He started to say something, paused. "Would you—" he began. "Would you yourself—"

Anna interrupted him. "I can't imagine a situation where I would want an abortion for myself." She heard Sophie saying, *Leave no room for misunderstanding*, and she went on, reaching for the right words. "But that is at least in part because I have reliable access to contraceptives and understand how they work."

She held herself very still against him, aware of the pulse in his throat and wrists, the beat of his heart. In the next minutes she might have to walk away or watch him walk away, but until then she could be glad of his strength and warmth and the solid fact of him.

The breeze turned cool as the sun slid over the edge of the world.

Anna recited to herself the simplest truth: there was nothing more for her to say; she would not argue or reason or persuade.

◆   ◆   ◆

NOT YET. JACK had heard himself say those two words. They were nothing but the truth, and still he hadn't meant to speak them aloud. Not yet. And now she sat beside him, waiting for him to admit that she had been right. He had aunts who lived their lives in cloistered convents, a first cousin who was a Jesuit. He was a police officer sworn to uphold the law. She was not wrong to worry; if there were no more to him than those two facts he would have no choice but to wish her well and go. Touch her face one last time, trace the line of her brow and jaw, the curve of her cheek.

She was looking at him with such solemn purpose. If he left her now he would never be able to cross this bridge without seeing her sitting on this bench, her hair undone by the wind and loose curls falling across a cheek burnished red in the cool evening air. But he wouldn't leave her. He didn't want to.

"Well," she said, shifting as if to move away from him and stand up. But he held her firmly and shook his head when she glanced at him.

"Don't run off," he said. "There are things you should hear about me before you abandon ship."

That got him a smile. Tentative, dimple-less, but a smile nonetheless, and she let herself be coaxed back to sit beside him, tucked into his side.

"This is a very serious conversation for such a beautiful evening," he said after a while. She hummed her agreement but didn't throw him the lifeline he was almost hoping for. So he took a deep breath.

"You read in the paper how corrupt the police department is," he began. "And for the most part, the rumors are true."

He told her about the storekeepers who pressed things into a cop's hands to gain his attention and good graces. He took his share of free meals, cab rides, cigars, bottles of whiskey. Once in a while he studiously overlooked the sale of lottery tickets and went home with a few folded bills in his pocket. There were times he was rougher than he needed to be with criminals, and was responsible for a cracked rib or a bloody nose now and then. On occasion he had let somebody stew in the Tombs for an extra couple of days until he could make a case that would stick in front of a judge.

He had some rules that he didn't break: he never arrested a hungry child for stealing; he'd settle things with the grocer or baker or tavernkeeper and then send the kid on his way with a warning. He wasn't rough with women or cripples or the feebleminded, though he had had cause on more than one occasion.

Jack looked down at her and waited until she raised her head to meet his gaze.

"Unless there's a felony or children are involved, I don't arrest prostitutes," he said. "Male or female. And I never take bribes from them or the people they work for.

"There are other things, most of them pretty small. Right now what you really need to know is, I paid more than one bribe to get on the police force, and then again to get promoted."

"Ah," she said. "Because you're Italian?"

He shook his head. "Everybody pays. It helped that they needed another detective who speaks Italian, but sure. I still paid more than I would have if I had an Irish last name. The plain fact is, nothing happens without money changing hands. There are more than a few cops out there who would make good detectives, but they'll walk a beat until they drop dead, because they don't have money or the right connections. And there are crooks and worse in the city who have never spent a day in jail and never will. Every saloonkeeper pays, every week. The same is true for dance halls and gambling joints and opium dens and disorderly houses. The ones you read about in the paper, the ones who do end up in jail are almost always there because they couldn't or wouldn't pay the bribe."

She was watching him calmly, waiting. "Are you a part of that?"

Jack shook his head. "I'm not a beat cop."

"But you like it, your job. What you do."

"Most of the time, yes."

"That's something to be thankful for."

She surprised him, again.

• • •

JACK FLAGGED DOWN a cab and helped her in, gave directions to the cabby and took the moment to gather his thoughts. His heart was racing, and he had broken out in a sweat despite the cool night air. But he could wait. He would have to wait until she was ready to talk.

As they set off down Prince Street he said, "Are we still going to the Foundling tomorrow?"

She gave him a curious half smile. "Why wouldn't we?"

The cab went around the park before stopping at the corner where Fifth Avenue South met Washington Square. Jack helped her out without a word of explanation. He wanted to walk with her here, because he had more to say. The very idea made her throat go dry.

He stood there, his hand extended, and she took it.

•   •   •

"You don't walk here at night alone."

He wasn't asking her a question, but voicing a command, of sorts. She might take exception to commands, but she understood his concerns.

"The streetlights make a great difference, and there's nothing to fear from prostitutes."

"It's not the women you need to be wary of," Jack said.

She let out a sigh. "I'm very aware of that. I don't go through the park in the dark of night alone, but I do know every square inch of it. It was our playground when we were little, and later we—" She couldn't help grinning at the memory.

He raised a brow. "Go on."

"You saw that Margaret reads the *Police Gazette*, almost obsessively, I would say. She would talk about some of the crimes at the dinner table. Nothing violent, not when we were children. But she'd say, 'Colonel Maxwell was burgled yesterday, every piece of silver in the house.' And then she'd voice her opinion. Usually she'd say, 'I suspect the help.' Or she'd be specific. 'They hired that Irish cook.' Aunt Quinlan would take exception, and there would be a pointed discussion. Aunt never shielded us from this kind of thing, and eventually we were curious about the bits of the *Police Gazette* Margaret wasn't reading to us."

"Cap?"

She laughed. "It was his idea to wait until she had finished with one, and then he'd snap up the castoff before it could be burned. We read to each other in a corner somewhere about people who had been robbed on the street, corners where a fight broke out.

"Eventually we got up the courage and when we came across something that happened anywhere near us, we went to investigate. It didn't take long to notice that the police spent a lot of time just a few blocks away."

"French Town," Jack supplied, and she nodded.

"We didn't know the neighborhood had a name. We knew the cafés and the bakery and the fact that everyone speaks French—Sophie was our ambassador when we went exploring there. But it wasn't until we started studying the *Gazette* that we heard about the Taverne Alsacienne being raided and the disorderly houses."

The memory made her laugh.

"Tell me you didn't stop by the Alsacienne to sample their absinthe," Jack said.

"No, I was thinking about a terrific argument we had about a raid on a disorderly house on Greene Street. We didn't know what a disorderly house was at first, and Sophie got into a laughing fit imagining housekeepers being arrested because of dust bunnies under their beds. Cap did know what a disorderly house was, but he wouldn't tell us. So we went to Aunt Quinlan."

"She told you?" Jack looked both surprised and unsettled at this idea.

"Aunt Quinlan always answered our questions, no matter how odd or difficult." *Or painful,* Anna thought. "As I remember, it wasn't a long conversation. She didn't condone or condemn, but she talked about the way poor women live. I thought I understood what she was saying, but I didn't. I couldn't, really, at that age. But I do now."

Jack made a low humming sound as if he were thinking this through, and then he pulled her closer.

"I'm wondering what made you think of dust bunnies and the *Police Gazette* just now."

Anna felt herself flush with irritation, at herself and Jack both. He had figured out what she was thinking before she realized it herself, and she felt the sting of that. This was what came of raising the subject of sex, she told herself.

Her rational mind knew that a healthy man of thirty-five did not live like a monk, and further, that she had no right to judge him on that basis. But the idea of Jack Mezzanotte visiting prostitutes sat badly with her, and she couldn't pretend otherwise. And so she asked.

"Do you have allegiances I should know about?"

He was trying to look serious, and really, Anna thought, he could be insufferable at times. Standing in a pool of light from a lamppost, a curl of dark hair falling over his brow, he grinned at her and then, leaning down, kissed her forehead.

She batted at him. "What was that for?"

Jack caught her hand and pressed it to his chest, holding it there and pulling her in. Then he kissed her properly, the kind of kiss she had been expecting on the bridge, the kind of kiss that made everything else go away. Slow and soft and deep, his tongue stroked hers. She made a noise of surrender.

"We'll get arrested," she said against his mouth.

"Not a chance."

She cursed the lamplight but went to him with an enthusiasm she couldn't begin to hide. When his hand began to trace the curve of her hip, she tried again.

"We'll be charged with indecent behavior."

That made him laugh. "I'll show you what counts as indecent behavior—"

This time she managed to pull herself away and they stood a few feet apart, both breathing as though they had run a mile uphill.

She said, "Are you going to answer my question?"

Jack rubbed a hand over his face like a man trying to rouse himself out of sleep. "About my allegiances? I don't have any."

She raised a brow, crossed her arms. Waited.

"At the moment." He was trying not to smile, but the corner of his mouth jerked. "My last . . . allegiance ended at the new year."

"Because?"

"She was a widow; she moved away to keep house for her widowed brother-in-law in St. Louis, with the intention of marrying him. We separated on good terms. Satisfied?"

"Not really. That seems insufficient for a man of your age and vitality."

"I play handball," he said. "That settles things down for a while."

Handball was played all over the city, a hard game involving nothing more than the ball itself and walls. Watching teenage boys playing handball when she herself was a teenager had been unsettling in ways she didn't understand at the time. Now the idea of Jack playing handball, sweat-soaked, his muscles working, made her swallow.

He mistook her silence for something else. Jack put his hands on her face and lifted it into the lamplight. "I don't frequent disorderly houses. Even if I were tempted, the possibility of syphilis would stop me."

She put her forehead to his shoulder and nodded. "That's a relief."

After a long moment he said, "What are you thinking?"

"About you playing handball."

That made him laugh. "When I get back from Chicago you can come watch."

"I'll miss you. You'll be too busy to miss anybody, I'd guess."

"Hard to imagine."

From deeper in the park came the sound of a woman's laugh, high-pitched and less than sober. It roused them both out of their thoughts.

"So tomorrow we'll go to the Foundling, and then while I'm away you'll figure out what you want." He pressed his thumb to her mouth before she could say anything. "I already know what I want, Savard. I'm just waiting for you to catch up."

15

THE ENGAGEMENT ANNOUNCEMENT in Sunday morning's paper took up a full third of the Society News column, ten copies of which were on the breakfast table, arranged by Mrs. Lee before anyone had gotten out of bed. Breakfast itself was delayed for a half hour while each of them studied what Cap had written. Lia sat on Margaret's lap, and Rosa sat between Anna and Sophie, her concentration drifting away, her face creased with worry. If Margaret was right about nothing else, Anna knew, it was important that the girls had no doubt about their place in the household.

Aunt Quinlan and Margaret agreed that the whole piece was well done. Margaret was more settled this morning, a fact that followed, Anna believed, from the invitation that had arrived by messenger at nine o'clock exactly. The family was invited to take dinner and spend the afternoon and evening on Park Place to celebrate the engagement.

Anna did not doubt for a moment that Cap had anticipated Margaret's objections, and that this was his countermeasure.

Margaret was going over the announcement again. "The wording is perfect," she admitted. "But then I'd expect nothing less from a lawyer of Cap's standing."

> *Peter Belmont Verhoeven, Esq., son of the deceased Anton Verhoeven*
> *and Clarinda Belmont Verhoeven, is pleased to announce his*
> *engagement to be married to Dr. Sophie Élodie Savard, a graduate*
> *of the Woman's Medical School of the New York Infirmary for*
> *Women and Children and a native of New Orleans. The wedding*
> *will take place in the later part of May. Because Mr. Verhoeven has*
> *been in ill health, he and his affianced request that no parties or*
> *receptions be planned or proposed.*

"This won't keep people from calling," Aunt Quinlan said. "This afternoon there will be a steady river of people to present their cards. But we won't be here to be bothered. Very clever of Cap to arrange things this way."

"He is entirely too clever," Sophie agreed with a grim smile.

"Some of his old spirit is resurfacing," Anna observed.

Sophie said, "Oh, yes. The dry humor he uses to such devastating effect is already showing itself. I think he will have more than one surprise waiting for us this afternoon, but I have an appointment at the New Amsterdam at eleven that I can't miss."

It was decided that Sophie would meet with the younger Sam Reason as arranged and join them at Cap's at noon, while Anna would stay for dinner and then leave straightaway for her appointment at the Foundling with Jack Mezzanotte. As soon as the words were said Anna wished she had not spoken at all, because Rosa was suddenly brimming with tension.

She looked at Anna with a question written so plainly on her face, it was impossible to pretend not to see it.

"We hope for the best," she told Rosa. "But even if there's no word at the Foundling, we are far from exhausting all possibilities."

Margaret was frowning at her; Anna was quite aware of that without looking up. Lia had taken note of the change in the mood around the table, and she climbed down from Margaret's lap to stand beside her sister.

Aunt Quinlan said, "Come girls, come to me. We have some things to talk about before you get ready for the party. I need to know if you are willing to help me with the wedding preparations. And there's the matter of wedding cake to discuss."

• • •

AT TEN SOPHIE knocked on Sister Xavier's door and was summoned in with a gruff "Ave."

The charge nurse warned her that the older nun was recovering quickly both physically and mentally. The return of her taciturn disposition was a solid indication of improvement.

Sister Xavier sat propped up in bed surrounded by newspapers, spectacles perched on the end of her nose. With her full cheeks flushed red and the white cap tied so firmly under her chin, she reminded

Sophie of Old Mother Hubbard. Then Xavier made a sound much like the honk of an angry goose and the image of the kindly grandmother was gone.

She caught sight of Sophie with a stethoscope around her neck and her expression shifted to confusion.

"I'm Dr. Sophie Savard, looking after Anna Savard's patients today. May I examine you, Sister?"

The nun flushed and fumbled her newspaper in a way Sophie thought must be out of character. From all reports, this was not a shy or easily intimidated woman.

"You're the cousin?"

"Yes."

"She's as pale as milk," Sister Xavier said, as if this were news to Sophie. "And you're colored."

Sophie didn't often explain, but there was something disarming about the unabashed way in which the obvious had been laid out.

"Yes," she said. "My grandmother and Anna's mother were half sisters. They had the same father but different mothers. Technically I believe we are half cousins. Would you rather I didn't examine you?"

The heavy jaw worked for a moment. "I'm not sure."

Sophie sat beside the bed. "You don't appear to have a fever, which means that postsurgical infection is unlikely. Any pain?"

"A twinge now and then, when I lift my arm. Nothing really."

She might be lying, as most patients lied when they wanted something—or did not want something—specific from a doctor. But Sophie couldn't force Sister Xavier's confidence, and it would be a waste of time to try. "As there's no sign of a fever, it can wait until the other Dr. Savard sees you tomorrow, if you would be more comfortable."

There was a drawn-out moment while Sister Xavier struggled with her scruples. Finally she said, "You really are a doctor?"

"Fully trained and qualified," Sophie assured her. "If you're wondering about your tumor, I can tell you that it looked to be benign. Not malignant, though sometimes it is hard to know for sure. I would say that it is unlikely to reoccur."

"Then why do I sit here?"

"Until the incision is fully closed, infection is still a possibility. Well." She stood, and then sat again because Sister Xavier was pointing at the chair. Simply pointing. As if she were a student who had dared to rise without permission.

"Sister Mary Augustin is off somewhere," she said. "I think you should spend at least a little while here in compensation." She thrust a pile of newspaper at Sophie. "Read to me. My eyes can't cope with the fine print anymore, even with spectacles."

Sophie took the paper. "What kind of news do you want to hear?"

A hand rose and fell. "Anything," she said.

"Here's a story about the mayor."

"Anything but the mayor."

Sophie's suggestions were dismissed one by one until she gave up. "You don't want to hear me reading the paper," she said.

"I do," Sister Xavier insisted. "Just find something interesting."

Sophie said a small, quiet word of thanks that the sister wasn't interested in the society column. She did want to hear a story about a fight between Irish and Italians that had sent four men to the hospital. She listened closely to stories about a robbery, a murder on a train, and a police raid on an opium den.

A knock at the door brought Sophie's reading to a close.

"That will be my appointment. If I have time I'll come back later to read this story about a knifing on the White Line dock. Or this one, about the body of an unidentified woman in Battery Park."

"Thank you," Sister Xavier said with a sniff. "I would like that."

◆ ◆ ◆

SOPHIE WAS STILL laughing a little to herself when she got to her office and found the younger Sam Reason sitting on a chair in the hall. He stood when he saw her. A tall man, as straight as a rifle and lean, wiry in the way of men who worked hard and were abstemious in their habits. He was no more than thirty, and he bore no resemblance to his grandparents.

As Sophie remembered New Orleans, most people of color were some shade of brown, from her own pale caramel to the dark brown of rich earth, and New York was much the same. But Sam Reason was far darker, a deep black that stood out all the more for the crisp white of his shirt collar. She wondered if he might be adopted and then put the idea aside as irrelevant and more important, none of her business.

He had a good if somewhat somber smile, and he shook her hand without hesitation, firmly, as her father had taught her was proper. His voice was much like his skin color: very deep and rich in tone. There was a rasp that might mean nothing more than a stubborn cold but sounded to Sophie like an older injury to his vocal cords.

"Thank you for seeing me." He followed her into the office and took the chair she indicated, with his hat in his lap and the heels of his hands on his knees. "I don't mean to interrupt your work."

"I'm not even on duty," Sophie told him. "And your time is as important as mine." She brought the desk chair out so that she could sit across from him without a barrier. "I'm just sorry to meet you under these circumstances. My sincere condolences on your grandfather's death. I didn't know him well, but I liked him very much."

"The feeling was mutual, Dr. Savard."

"Please, call me Sophie."

"It's an honor. Thank you. I'm Sam."

Now that she had a chance to study him more closely Sophie noted that the beds of his fingernails were ink stained, and that reminded her why he had come.

"I expect you heard the basics about the trouble that Dr. Garrison was in."

"From my grandfather, yes. That's all settled now?"

"Yes and no," Sophie said. She told him a little about Comstock and his crusade, and the most recent attempt to send Dr. Garrison to the penitentiary. "And I doubt he's given up. He'll do his best to entrap her, and that's where your business comes in. The pamphlets Comstock brought into the courtroom as evidence were your grandfather's work. The only reason he wasn't arrested was that he didn't put his name or the company name on the materials he printed for us."

She paused, and he nodded for her to go on.

"My first question for you is, whether you would prefer us to find a different printer."

He studied his hands for a moment longer. "There's no reason you should know this, but I just recently took over the business when I moved back home from Savannah. I'm not even sure what my grandfather was printing for you."

Sophie went to her desk, unlocked a drawer, and took out a slim stack of pamphlets. "Personal Hygiene," "The Well-Considered Family," "A Woman's Health," "The Human Reproductive Cycle."

When he had looked over them briefly he said, "Dr. Garrison wrote these?"

"In part. A number of different physicians have had a hand in putting them together, including me. What you need to understand is that if you continue printing these pamphlets, you will place yourself in harm's way." She wondered if she would have to be more explicit.

He put the pamphlets on her desk. "According to the account books, Dr. Garrison is an excellent customer. My grandfather had no complaints about her or the work she brought to him. I think we can continue on in the same way. Do I have to introduce myself to her?"

"No," Sophie said. "Given the close attention Comstock is paying to her, the committee has decided to have her step back for the present. I had planned on taking over for her, but I've had a change in circumstance quite suddenly and will be away for as much"—her voice roughened—"as a year."

She could see that he was curious, but Sophie didn't want to open the discussion of where she would be, or with whom. She took a deep breath and continued. "Early next week we'll have decided who will take over the business end of things, and I will send you word if you decide you want to continue. But I think it's important you understand the seriousness of the situation before you decide."

He inclined his head in what might have been reluctant agreement.

"Comstock has made an art out of entrapment by mail," Sophie began. "He writes a letter to a doctor and pretends to be a young woman who has gotten in trouble without the benefit of marriage, pleading for help."

Sam Reason was frowning. "He signs someone else's name?"

"He makes up a story about someone who doesn't exist, and signs that person's name."

"Always a young woman?"

Sophie paused. "For the most part. There's the possibility that he sometimes writes as a man needing help for his wife. He does send both men and women to try to entrap physicians in their offices. Whoever he sends always has a convincing story about a desperate need for contraceptives or abortion. We've been approached more than once."

"We?"

"Pardon me, I haven't explained clearly. I live with an aunt and a cousin. My cousin Anna is also a physician. Comstock seems to be interested in both of us."

"There are two of you?" He seemed amused by this idea. "Two black women practicing medicine in the city?"

"She is my half cousin," Sophie explained. "And she is white. There are other women of color practicing medicine, here and elsewhere. A few of us, and more every year."

He started to say something and then stopped to listen, though he was clearly disturbed by what she was telling him. She went on to relate a cautionary tale that happened to be true. It was Dr. Newlight's history that kept physicians awake at night. He had received one of Comstock's entrapment letters and responded by sending a prescription for bismuth and gentian powder, a mild treatment for digestive ailments.

"For that he was convicted under the Comstock Act. He spent almost two years in the penitentiary."

Almost reluctantly he asked, "What this doctor sent wasn't illegal?"

"Nothing illegal about it. But the judge ruled that by responding to the decoy letter he had committed a crime. He wouldn't allow Dr. Newlight's attorney to call any witnesses, he simply instructed the jury to find the doctor guilty, and that's what they did."

She watched him think this through. "You know," he said, and there was a good dose of cynicism in his voice, "stories like that are not all that unusual, at least when the man standing trial is black. I assume this Dr. Newlight is a white man, and that's why it strikes you as unjust."

She drew up, surprised. "Are you suggesting that the jail sentence was appropriate because Dr. Newlight is white?"

"I'm just reminding you that black men are sent to jail or worse, every day, for far less reason." He met her gaze unapologetically.

Sophie's training had deprived her of the ability to be embarrassed, but she understood when her intelligence and morals had been insulted. She felt her temper slip out of her grasp.

"You don't need to educate me about what it means to be black," she told Sam Reason. "I spent my first ten years in New Orleans. As soon as I learned how to write my name I also learned that I could never sign anything without identifying myself as a free woman of color. It's not required in New York, but I still pause sometimes and feel a moment of panic because I forgot to write *FWC* after my signature.

"My father and my grandmother—neither of them white—were doctors who looked after the poor. As I do. I see dozens of patients every week, and almost all of them are some shade of brown or black or yellow, and poor. So yes, I am aware. In some ways more aware than you will ever be. I doubt you have ever had to treat a woman who has had a baby beaten out of her by a drunk husband. That happens far too often, to women of every color and age."

She saw little reaction in his expression beyond a steady and unwavering regard. He asked, "Why do you defend this Dr. Newlight?"

"I was not defending him. The story was meant to make clear to you how dangerous this business really is. What is bothering you? That I am sympathetic to a colleague who happens to be white, or that I have white relations?"

He said, "You want me to understand that this Comstock will do just about anything to send somebody to jail, and the truth don't much matter, one way or the other, as long as he gets his few minutes of glory."

"Yes," Sophie said. "Exactly. He has no respect for freedom of speech or freedom of the press or even basic civil liberties."

"And you're thinking maybe I won't want your business anymore because of that."

"I wanted you to have a full understanding of the dangers before you made any kind of commitment," she said.

"You want to absolve yourself of responsibility before the fact."

Sophie stood suddenly, pushing her chair back so abruptly that it tipped over and fell. Sam stood too, more slowly.

"I believe you've answered my question," she said, her voice shaking with anger. "I will find another printer. Thank you for your time, and please give your grandmother and family my condolences and best wishes."

She walked to the door and opened it, standing back to let him pass. But he stayed where he was, turning his hat in his hands.

"I apologize," he said, his accent softening and taking on more of a southern rhythm. "I was rude and unfair. Can we start again?"

Sophie closed the door and returned to the chair he had straightened for her, but she had to fold her hands together in her lap to keep them from trembling.

"I accept your apology." Sophie forced herself to meet his gaze. "But I don't think I can work with someone who holds me in such low regard."

"I don't hold you in low regard. Just the opposite."

"Then I'm at a loss to understand your animosity. Have I offended you somehow?" And suddenly, she understood. "You saw the announcement about my engagement in the paper today."

She saw the answer in the way his jaw tightened, very slightly. He nodded. "I did see that. Please accept my best wishes."

Sophie couldn't help herself; she let out a soft laugh. "Very convincing, Sam."

He turned his head away for a moment. "To start over at the beginning, I understand the dangers and I'd like to continue the business relationship."

Sophie studied the material of her dress, following the dark blue scrollwork pattern she had worn because she would leave here to go to a party in celebration of her engagement. She thought of the Reason family and the hour she had spent sitting with them at their table, the kindness and open affection they showed each other. Somehow she believed—she wanted to believe—that Delilah Reason and her daughters would not be so condemning as the man who sat opposite her.

She wanted to end the meeting and get away, but she reminded herself that her feelings were secondary to the business that needed to be conducted.

"If you have the time I'd like to send you back home with a new order."

"Yes," he said. "I have the time."

For a half hour they talked about paper and binding and printing costs, and during that whole time Sophie had the strong impression that Sam Reason was forbidding himself to look at her, for fear that doing so would turn him to a pillar of salt.

• • •

THE FOUNDLING HOSPITAL run by the Sisters of Charity was well beyond the city proper, and so Jack rented a surrey. He stopped first at the hospital to pick up Sister Mary Augustin, who was coming along to provide an introduction, and then on Waverly Place for Anna, only to be told she wasn't in. Instead, Mrs. Lee handed him a note:

Mezzanotte—

Please call for me at Cap's, the house at the northwest corner of 36th Street and Park Place. I will be ready to leave when you arrive.

Savard

He asked Mrs. Lee straight out. "Is Cap poorly?"

She frowned so completely that it seemed as though the corners of her mouth might meet on her chin. "Why would you say something like that? It's just an engagement party for Sophie and Cap."

Now she was craning her head around him and smiling, waving at Sister Mary Augustin, who waved back cheerfully.

She put the frown back on for him. "Go on now, she'll be waiting for you. Young people, stumbling over their own feet." She was laughing to herself as she closed the door.

• • •

CAP LIVED ON Park Place, a wide avenue divided down the middle by islands of greenery and trees. Old money, for the most part, and families far longer established than the magnates who built their mansions on upper Fifth Avenue. The house itself was very large, a formidable limestone and marble square with tall windows on all three floors. Elegant, almost regal in its lines.

As Jack brought the surrey to a stop the door opened and Anna came out, flew down the short flight of stairs, and almost leapt up without waiting for assistance, settling beside Sister Mary Augustin when the spot next to Jack was just as empty.

He was too busy threading his way back into traffic to ask her for explanations, and he was irritated, too, because she would know that and was making him wait anyway.

It took five full blocks for the traffic to thin out and the team to settle down, and then he turned to look at her. She was looking at him too and smiling. It was the kind of smile he didn't see very often from her, wide and open and unreserved.

"What?"

She shook her head and shrugged her shoulders all at once. "Cap and Sophie announced their engagement, and at least some of his family sent notes to wish them well."

"And why wouldn't they?" Sister Mary Augustin wanted to know.

Anna's expression shifted into something more familiar: thoughtful concern, calculation. Jack turned his attention back to the team, but he was listening.

"It's a complicated story," Anna said to Mary Augustin. "And really it's too fine a day to bother with unhappy details."

•   •   •

IT STRUCK JACK that two women could hardly look less alike. Sister Mary Augustin in her white bonnet and habit, so pale that he could see a network of veins in her temples, and Anna dressed as she always was for work, very proper and severe.

She wore a dark skirt and jacket and under that, a white shirt-waist with a short standing collar that accentuated the line of her jaw. There was a cameo pinned at the throat, but otherwise she wore no jewelry at all. And still, if he closed his eyes he could still see Anna turning to catch a silk scarf in the light of a dozen lanterns; long-necked and bare-armed, smiling at the footman. A pearl comb in her coiled dark hair.

Until he met Anna Jack had never given much thought to fashion, beyond the awareness that it was a ruling force in the lives of many women and enslaved some of them as surely as chains. Anna cared about her appearance, but that was evident only if a man looked closely and saw the details. He only knew what to look for because of his sisters, who talked of little else—not in the way of young girls wishing for finery, but as women who had made a profession out of producing beautiful things.

Anna's kidskin gloves were embroidered at the cuff, the buttons on her jacket were finely carved mother-of-pearl and jet, and every pleat or fold was pressed to a sharp edge. Today she had forsaken her usual bonnet for a simple felt hat with a rim that rolled up over one ear. Its only decoration was a small bunch of silk flowers—a few fat white rosebuds, a twig of deep red berries, and a spray of ivy.

Jack tried to imagine a third woman there as well, some well-bred lady in Sunday finery, blue or pink or yellow, with flounces and lace and ruffles and a bustle like a giant melon. To put a hand on that woman's waist would be to grasp something inanimate and inflexible and cold. Nothing like Anna at all. He had given up trying to put the idea of touching Anna out of his mind—mostly, he could admit to himself, because he didn't want to and saw no reason for it, not after their discussion the evening before. There was a hollow feeling in his gut when he thought of her, unfamiliar nerves sparking to life the closer she was.

They were traveling north on Lexington, leaving paving stones behind for a well-traveled dirt road at Fiftieth Street. A block to the west mansions were springing up along Fifth, their broad cold faces turned to the vast expanse of Central Park.

"So many different greens," he heard Sister Mary Augustin say. "A world of greens."

Anna said, "The park in spring always makes me think about my aunt Quinlan. She's an artist, or she was until arthritis put an end to it. When she was still working she spent every morning in her studio; at noon she'd come downstairs and scrub her hands at the kitchen sink, and she'd talk to me about the colors she was washing away. The names for all the kinds of green and yellow made sense to me. Jade. Celadon. Verdigris, Malachite. Moss and myrtle and chartreuse, aureolin and jasmine."

Jack glanced at her over his shoulder and she ducked her head, as if he had overheard an embarrassing revelation.

They passed an abandoned shanty, fields dotted with sheep and new lambs and dairy cows. At an intersection signs were nailed to a post: milk and eggs for sale, yearling colts, pigs, a plow. Small clusters of houses sprang up, some of them close to collapse, but others with whitewashed fences and bright clean window glass. The city was pushing north, as unstoppable as the tide.

Sister Mary Augustin was very far away in her thoughts, all her attention on the countryside. A man mending a fence, a young woman at work in a garden with a shallow basket balanced between hip and an extended arm, a grove of apple trees where children sat in the branches and pelted each other with hard green fruit no bigger than walnuts.

Anna asked Mary Augustin a question Jack would not have thought to ask of a nun. "I think you must have grown up on a farm."

"What makes you say that?"

Anna shrugged. "Just the way you're watching things. Do you miss it?"

"I didn't think I would, when I first left home, but I suppose I do. The smell of newly turned earth in the spring air makes me homesick. The new lambs and foals were always my favorite thing."

After a few moments of silence she went on. "I have six brothers. They were always falling out of trees and cutting themselves and dropping spades on their feet or beating each other bloody. I had a talent for patching them up. Mama wanted me to be a nun, and I wanted to be a nurse."

"I'm surprised she could let you go at all with so many children to look after."

Mary Augustin smiled. "She's got two sisters, and neither of them ever married. The three of them keep the house while my father runs the farm with the boys."

"And they sent you off to the convent."

"It wasn't meant to be a punishment. Mama said she wanted a quieter life for me. The Sisters of Charity are a nursing order, so we were both satisfied. But." She paused and looked at Anna. "It didn't even occur to me that they might send me into the city. I'm learning a great deal and it's sometimes very exciting, but I thought I'd be at the Foundling out here in the countryside."

"Maybe you can be transferred to the Foundling one day soon."

Mary Augustin gave a brief shake of the head. "I've been assigned other duties. It's unlikely now."

"Other duties—" Anna prompted.

"Sister Perpetua is retiring, and they are training me to take her place."

Jack heard the deep unhappiness in this simple statement. Anna seemed to hear it too because her tone changed.

She said, "I haven't said anything to you about the work you did in my class."

He sensed rather than saw the girl leaning forward, an eagerness there that had been missing.

"Your assignment was first-rate," Anna said. "You are very observant, very methodological. No hasty conclusions, but thoughtful questions and suggestions. You have a natural talent."

Jack raised one brow in a way that asked the question, *What exactly are you up to?* She ignored him, as he thought she would, her attention fixed on a problem that needed solving.

◆ ◆ ◆

ANNA CONSIDERED MARY Augustin, who had turned away to watch the scenery or, she thought more likely, to hide her expression. A hundred questions were going through her mind but she would limit herself to one.

"Are you being punished for something? Is that why you're not nursing anymore?"

The small face came around quickly, color rising to flood her cheeks.

"No," she said. "Not at all. Mother Superior says that the order encourages talent and potential where they find it."

"And they need to take you out of nursing to do that? You have nothing to say about it?"

"Cheerful obedience is a daily struggle," Mary Augustin said, her tone less steady now.

Anna bit back the response that came to mind. There was no need to distress the girl any further, but neither could she simply forget the look on her face, the deep sadness she saw there.

"The change in my duties will make it easier for me to help look for the Russo brothers," Mary Augustin offered, as if she needed to console Anna.

As a girl, Anna had often been told that she didn't know when to retreat. Uncle Quinlan had likened her to his terrier called Bull, who weighed no more than ten pounds but stood up to other dogs as though he were three times the size.

"It's not really a fault," he had explained to her in his patient way.

"Or it's not a fault in his nature, I should say. It's built into him, like the shape of his ears. But it is my responsibility to make him understand that it is often better to retreat and live to fight another day."

Many years later Anna often thought of that conversation, which had taken place on a sunny winter morning when she had been deeply frustrated by a math problem. It had taken time for her to fully learn the lesson he meant to teach, one that she drew on now: it would do no good to badger Mary Augustin about something so clearly distressing to her. She would put it aside for the moment, then. For the moment.

Once Jack had turned his attention back to the road she took the opportunity to look at him more closely. He had taken off his coat and folded his shirtsleeves up to just below the elbows. This was shockingly informal of him, and completely reasonable given the heat. He teased her about the fact that she attended meetings of the Rational Dress Society, but he was a member himself, whether he wanted to acknowledge it or not.

And still she had to admit that it was a distraction to have him sitting there in the bright sunshine, his wrists and forearms in plain sight. The human body was no mystery to her, after all, and should not demand so much of her attention. Just a few days ago she had spent hours operating on the hand and forearm of a brawny sixteen-year-old with an arm shot full of splinters, pulling them out of muscles and tendons. She knew how a man's wrists and arms were put together, and there was nothing unusual about Jack Mezzanotte. His wrists, broad as they were, twisted and flexed in exactly the same way as her own.

Which only sidestepped the fact that she was attracted to him in every way a woman could be attracted to a man, and he was leaving tomorrow for Chicago. A week or ten days, no amount of time at all. He would be back before she even began to miss him. But she hated the idea of his being gone, which made her realize, once and for all, that Jack Mezzanotte was nothing like Karl Levine, or more exactly: that she had been one person with Karl, and was becoming someone else with Jack.

She had liked and admired Karl for many reasons. He had a slow, thoughtful manner that masked a hot intelligence. He made her laugh. He was kind. He was unattached and not interested in a permanent relationship because his primary interest in life was medicine, and it demanded all his energy and attention. He knew that she would be in Vienna only a short time.

Before she had known him a week Anna had decided that he was her opportunity to experience that act which was at the center of so much of a woman's life.

Most important, she realized now, was the fact that they were both utterly consumed by work, which meant they had something else in common: ignorance. Two people who knew everything about the anatomy and physiology of the human body, about procreation and sex except, as it turned out, how to make it work. To mean something. She came away mystified and confounded both, with more questions than answers. Just looking at Jack gave her ideas about those unanswered questions.

She had left Karl to go on to Berlin without hesitation or qualms, and he seemed to have recovered just as easily. At the New Year she had had a card from him, all collegial politeness, and she had felt only a moment's guilt that she had not thought to write.

"Dr. Savard?" Sister Mary Augustin touched her shoulder, and Anna saw that the Foundling and its hospitals had come into view. It was an impressive sight, a central large brick building of some eight stories with two connected wings, and on either side of those wings, separate brick buildings, each four stories high.

"On the far right is St. Luke's, the new children's hospital." Mary Augustin pointed with her chin. She seemed to think Anna had never been here before, but the girl took such enjoyment in sharing information that it would have been mean-spirited to stop her.

"St. Anne's—the lying-in hospital—is on the far left nearest us, and in the center the offices and classrooms and the orphan asylum itself. The convent and the new chapel are behind the main building; you can't see them from here. This is where I trained."

Anna hadn't thought to ask about her training, but clearly Mary Augustin wanted to talk about it.

"Two full years," Mary Augustin said. "And then I was assigned to the orphan asylum at St. Patrick's, just before this new hospital opened. I haven't been back since."

Anna told her, "It's been a while since I've been here too. I'm looking forward to touring the hospital."

Over his shoulder Jack said, "Where do we start?"

Mary Augustin looked surprised at this question. "Everything at the Foundling begins and ends with Sister Mary Irene," she said. "Nothing happens without her approval."

◆　◆　◆

THERE WAS A cradle in the vestibule of the main building, one Jack had heard about but never seen. A cradle like any other, at first glance, but for as long as the Foundling Hospital had existed—first on Twelfth Street and eventually in this out-of-the-way spot—there had been a cradle like this one where anyone could leave an infant, for any reason. Young girls without husbands, women with too many children to feed or no place to sleep, distraught husbands and fathers, anyone of any faith could leave an infant here to be taken in by the Sisters of Charity. Most of them didn't identify themselves, and few ever returned to reclaim their children.

There were other orphanages for those who didn't want their children raised Catholic, but it was Jack's guess that for many, baptism was not too high a price for what they got in return: a place to leave a child and know it would be well taken care of.

They followed Sister Mary Augustin through a set of doors and down a hallway to an office where a young nun sat at a desk, copying out a passage from a book with medical illustrations. The conversation between the sisters was so quiet and brief that he had no idea what was happening, beyond the fact that they both left the office without a word of explanation.

Anna immediately bent over the book on the desk to look at it more closely. "Earlham and Jones," she said. "*Childhood Diseases.*"

"You sound doubtful."

She tore her gaze away from the book to look at Jack in surprise. "Not at all. This is a standard text, though the edition is quite out of date. She's reading about damage to the inner ear and causes of deafness. Many children are written off as idiots because nobody thinks to check their hearing."

"I'm familiar with that," Jack told her. "My sister Bambina—the youngest—didn't speak until she was three. Everybody thought she might be deaf, but then one day when we were eating she turned to me and said that if my fork touched her plate even one more time, she would stab me in the hand. And she said it so clearly and with such passion, there was no doubt she meant it. We all sat there with our mouths hanging open."

Anna liked this story, he could tell by her smile.

"I think Bambina and I would get along," she said. "But her name doesn't suit her, does it. Baby?"

"Baby Girl," Jack corrected. "It's not all that unusual a name in Italy."

She was trying not to pull a face. "But it doesn't suit an assertive woman who stands up for herself."

"You'd rename everyone if you had the power," Jack said.

"No I wouldn't. Your name suits you."

"And your name?"

She gave him a half grin. "It is a solid, no-nonsense, appropriate name for a physician who happens to be a woman."

Then Mary Augustin was back. Jack noted how animated the little sister was, as if this were a long wished-for homecoming. Which, he supposed, it must be, for her.

"Sister Mary Irene can see us in an hour. I'm supposed to give you a tour in the meantime. If you'd like?"

To turn down this offer would have wiped the smile from Mary Augustin's face, and so Jack followed the two women out into the hall.

•   •   •

AT THE DOOR of the new children's hospital Anna paused to gather her thoughts. Small infirmaries like this one were sometimes well run, but most she had come across failed the most basic test: strict adherence to antisepsis procedures as developed by Pasteur and Lister. The sisters were excellent housekeepers, but the first outbreak of measles or diphtheria would make the difference between a thorough dusting and maintaining a sterile environment painfully obvious.

At the opening of the door they were met with the familiar smells of carbolic acid, rubbing alcohol, vinegar, and potash soap. It made Jack wince, but to Anna it was familiar and comforting both.

The hall was wide and high-ceilinged, and the large windows

were fitted with screens. All in all, a pleasant, bright, airy setting superior to most hospitals, including the New Amsterdam.

Sister Mary Augustin said, "There's a separate department for the contagious and two small surgical suites. I need to find the charge nurse."

Then she went off once again, and they were left waiting outside a ward. Jack turned to Anna.

"What illnesses would they treat here?"

She listed the most common for him: ear, eye, and sinus infections; birth defects from cleft palates to spina bifida; breathing difficulties; influenza and the contagious diseases from measles to typhoid that killed so many children.

He was looking through glass panes set in the double doors to a small ward where Anna counted seven cots arranged in a semicircle around a nursing station.

She said, "The standards here are very high. It's a relief."

"Not always the case?"

She could feel her cheek muscles give an involuntary twitch. "I've gotten myself into more than one difficult situation because I pointed out what should have been obvious. A Dr.—well, call him Jones at— a hospital that will remain nameless—shouted names at me when I said that his shirt cuffs would contaminate any bedside he visited."

"He called you names?"

"He was outraged and especially inventive. He called me a trouble-monger and a devil-dealer."

Anna wore such insults as a badge of honor. As if she were made stronger by such run-ins and must give herself credit.

"What are these children here for?" he asked her.

"They do some surgery, children born with umbilical hernias and the like. Most are here because they were born too small and frail and have breathing difficulties or seizures, heart irregularities. And infections, of course. Most of them will die of infections because they have no natural immunity."

She said *Most of them will die* with perfect calm. Jack supposed that someone who worked with children like this had to build a wall in order to survive at all.

"But every once in a while," she went on, "one of them will surprise you and fight like the devil."

"Do you see that more often in boys or girls?"

She looked away as if she had to sort through data before she could answer. "Both, I think. All races, too. There's no predicting where the spark will show itself. It's what keeps me going, knowing that sometimes the least likely will pull through."

"I wonder," he said, feeling his way carefully, "why you chose to work with sick children when you could have been treating old ladies with gout."

She laughed outright. "Really?" she said. "You really wonder about that? Because I thought you knew me better. I would die of boredom or frustration or both."

He said, "I do know you that well. I just wanted to hear you put it into words."

Sister Mary Augustin came back with a man in a surgeon's tunic, but even without it Jack would have recognized him by his hands, which were much like Anna's: scrubbed so often and so hard that they struck other people as overused.

Mary Augustin introduced them to Dr. Reynolds, who had just come out of an emergency surgery.

Jack supposed it was inevitable that they get into a discussion of a six-month-old infant with something called an intussusception. It had to do with the abdomen and intestines. He picked out words like *ileo-ileac* and *tumor* and *linea semilunaris* and then, oddly enough, *telescope*. Anna had forgotten all about him, but Jack understood what it was to get caught up in the details of an interesting case. More than that, he considered jealousy one of the great flaws of his countrymen. And it didn't hurt at all that Dr. Reynolds was short and bald with a paunch like a small melon.

They were on to a discussion of another case, all three of them walking into the ward toward one of the nursing sisters who was leaning over a cot. The infant in question might be ill but it was not weak, Jack thought, given the power of its lungs.

He wandered off to explore and found a ward where a small group of children were very mobile. All of them had some kind of dressing—

he saw some plaster casts and slings—but otherwise they could be his own nieces and nephews. One of the nursing sisters came to the door, asked some questions, and then invited him to come in.

"The run-arounds always like company, but be aware, they will climb you like a mountain and wiggle their way into every pocket." *Run-arounds* was a good name for these small bumbling dynamos. She was right; every child in the room was headed in his direction, all of them as eager and indiscriminately affectionate as puppies.

◆ ◆ ◆

SISTER IRENE WAS the kind of woman you would pass on the street and not notice at all, unless you met her gaze, which was keen and directly unsettling. Jack doubted that children ever found the courage to lie to her, not with that gaze focused on them. There was nothing cruel or insensitive in her, Jack thought, but she would not tolerate much nonsense, which was why she reminded him of his mother. And with a place like this to manage, that was understandable.

Nor was she willing to sit quietly to talk. As soon as they arrived at her office she was off again with the three of them in tow, asking and answering questions as she left the building to cut across a soggy lawn and continue on around the north side. There she stopped, where they could talk while she watched the construction workers fitting windows and laying roof tiles to what looked like a new chapel.

This time it was Sister Mary Augustin who told the story of the Russo children, so concisely that Jack suspected she had written it out beforehand and memorized it.

"You're looking for two boys who went missing a little over a month ago, on the Hoboken ferry docks, do I have that right?" Sister Irene was looking at Anna.

"Yes," Anna said. "I realize that the chance of finding them is slim, but I made a promise."

"Promises made to children are rarely taken so seriously."

"Nevertheless," Anna said. "I will persist."

"For how long?" asked the nun.

"Until every reasonable avenue and most less reasonable avenues are exhausted." Her tone was matter-of-fact, without any defensive edge. Jack had the idea that she respected Sister Mary Irene and that her admiration was founded at least in part in their similarities. They recognized something in each other, much in the same way he had understood Oscar from the day they had been introduced.

"Come along, then," she said. "And we'll see."

•   •   •

ANNA WAS SO accustomed to disappointment that at first she didn't really take Sister Mary Irene's meaning, and had to ask her to repeat herself.

"I believe the younger boy was here." She stood over a ledger that lay open on a lectern. "He was brought in by a patrol officer on Easter Monday, no identifying papers of any kind. Abandoned, it seemed at the time. I expect somebody picked him up in the confusion on the dock."

"Is the patrolman's name in the record?" Jack asked.

"Officer Markham," she told him, her gaze still running over the written page. "There's no mention of his precinct here, and I haven't come across his name before. But I assume you will be able to track him down."

Sister Mary Augustin spoke up. "You say he was here?"

"Yes." She spared a smile for the younger sister. "We had him for just two days before he was transferred to Father McKinnawae's care. I remember the case now. A pretty child, very robust compared to the babies we see every day."

Anna said, "Who is this Father McKinnawae?"

"His name is on the list Brother Anselm gave us," Jack reminded her. "He built that newer home for newsboys on Lafayette, we went there in mid-April, I think."

She did remember. The Mission of the Immaculate Virgin was a new building, larger even than the newsboys' lodging on Duane. All ten stories were overrun with boys without families or homes. They hadn't met Father McKinnawae but one of his assistants, who had been polite but less than welcoming. It was then that Jack had told her that they would have to postpone visiting Catholic institutions until they had credentials that would open the right doors, which it seemed they did, now. Just before he was to leave for Chicago.

"The Mission of the Immaculate Virgin," Anna said. "Yes, they were helpful. But there was no sign or record of the Russos."

Mary Irene said, "If Father McKinnawae took responsibility for the boy, it was because he had a family in mind to adopt. That's something you'll have to ask him directly. I have to warn you, though, that he's unlikely to be helpful if that's the case."

"Would we find him at the mission on Lafayette today, do you think?" Anna asked.

"Unlikely," said Sister Mary Irene. "He bought a farm on Staten Island and he's building dormitories, getting it ready for the orphans. I suggest that you write to him first and explain your situation. Make sure he understands that the children were lost during the confusion on the ferry dock. And I have to remind you, it's possible that this is not the boy you're looking for. We took in fifteen abandoned infants that week alone, and we are only one institution."

She looked at Anna over the rim of her glasses. "I believe that's as much as I can do for you, Dr. Savard." To Sister Mary Augustin she said, "I am glad to hear that you are doing so well at St. Patrick's, but we felt your loss and still do."

Anna saw Sister Mary Augustin swallow and then nod, unable to respond in words.

◆ ◆ ◆

MOST OF THE way back to the city they debated whether to share this new information with Rosa. Jack thought it would be better to wait until they had confirmation; Anna swayed back and forth between agreeing and disagreeing. Many people withheld information from children out of a misguided understanding of what they most needed. She knew this from personal experience.

Mary Augustin said, "Are you going to write to Father McKinnawae, or go to see him?"

"I'll write first."

She was confused by this; Anna could see it, and felt compelled to explain.

"I will go straightaway if Father McKinnawae answers my letter with real information about the boys. Otherwise it must wait. I'm on night duty most of this week, and a trip to Staten Island requires at least one full day." She was oddly relieved to realize that this was all perfectly true: unless Father McKinnawae had more news to share than any of the other dozens of people she had written to or visited, Staten Island could safely wait until Jack was back and could go with her.

◆   ◆   ◆

WHEN THEY HAD dropped Mary Augustin off at the New Amsterdam to return to Sister Xavier's room, Jack motioned for her to come sit next to him on the front bench. Anna hesitated for just a moment. Under other circumstances she would have gone inside to check on her patients, but it was her day off, after all, and Jack was leaving.

Even on Sunday afternoon there was a good amount of traffic, and they were quiet as Jack negotiated the way south on Broadway. He would have to return the borrowed surrey to the police stables, and then what? She hated the nervous fluttering in her stomach, the wondering what he had in mind. Most likely he would take her home and then go home himself to get ready for his trip.

With that thought still in her head she put her hand on the bench between them and then shivered when he covered it with his own.

◆   ◆   ◆

IT WAS FIVE by the time they were free of the surrey, and then they stood for a moment in the tumult that was the corner of Mulberry and Prince Streets. Across from the police headquarters was an unbroken line of taverns and dance halls and theaters, cheek and jowl with oyster saloons and stale beer joints. She had once wondered how they could stay in business under the nose of the law, but from Jack she understood that this was nothing out of the usual. The beer would cost a penny more, and all those accumulated pennies would end up in the pocket of a roundsman and the superiors who had perfected the art of looking the other way, so long as they got appropriate recompense.

They had walked back to Waverly Place from this very spot more than once, but now Jack hailed a cab. Anna kept her confusion to herself; he never did anything without a well-thought-out reason that he was willing to talk about, if she asked. And this time she was afraid to ask because she suspected that they weren't going to Waverly Place at all.

Jack helped her up and then went to talk to the cabby. In the span of ten seconds or so it took to give the man directions, Anna reminded herself of her age, education, sensible disposition, and ability to make responsible decisions, and the fact that she wanted to go with Jack, wherever it was he was taking her. To his home, was her guess. She had never even seen the house, but not for lack of trying. The first time she had found a reason to walk past Mezzanotte Brothers Florists after he had explained to her exactly where he lived, she realized that only the very front, the shop itself, could be seen from the street. Everything else was hidden behind a high brick wall interrupted by recessed doors painted a deep glossy green.

Anna wondered if the power of speech had left her permanently, then realized that Jack was just as quiet. He held her hand in the cab, one finger tracing back and forth across her wrist very gently. The nerves of the wrist, Anna reminded herself. She could name them all and still she had had no idea that such a simple touch could be so engrossing. Even while this thought came to her, Jack opened the buttons on her jacket cuff with a shocking nimbleness.

She heard herself make a low sound, a clicking in the back of her throat while his fingers moved over wrist and forearm with a fine rasping touch. When he let her go Anna was breathing fast and the pulse at the base of her throat echoed like a drumroll.

Jack said, "We're here. I can ask the cabby to take us back to Waverly Place, if you're uncertain."

"Don't you dare." Her voice was a little creaky, but she managed a small smile.

◆　◆　◆

THE SHOP WAS closed on a late Sunday afternoon, but he used a key to open the door and took her through to the greenhouses, stopping to name plants and flowers, bending down to examine a leaf or break off a bud to show her. Anna breathed as deeply as she could to slow her pulse. She tried to ask intelligent questions and sometimes succeeded. A rose that originated in France in 1820, how exactly did they know that? He answered, and she immediately forgot.

Jack was in no hurry. He held her hand, never giving up the soft stroking of her wrist and palm that made her fingers jerk. Anna forced herself to concentrate.

"It's very quiet here, considering how close we are to Union Square. Peaceful."

Somehow it was the right thing to say, or maybe the wrong thing.

He was studying her face now, and his expression was not hard to interpret.

She said, "You're the one who isn't sure."

"Oh, I'm sure." He used both hands to cup her face and tilt it up so that he could kiss her. His hands and his mouth and nothing else, at this moment, and that was enough. For a long minute they were satisfied with the soft warm suckling and then Jack dropped one hand to press it to the small of her back.

Against the corner of her mouth he said, "Would you like to see the workrooms too? Or I can show you the house right now. If you like."

They left the greenhouses by a back exit that opened onto a narrow path paved with flagstones. An overarching arbor was dense with deep green foliage and flowers as white and round and flat as a plate. Another time she might have asked for a name to pass on to Mr. Lee, but the capacity for speech had left her.

Jack started to say something and then stopped, his head canting sharply toward the far end of the passageway and the green door in the perimeter wall, small with a rounded top. As it swung open a conversation came to them. Two women, speaking Italian. Jack closed his eyes and shook his head in obvious disbelief and frustration.

The women stopped where they were, as surprised to see Jack as he was to see them.

"Anna," he said. "Let me introduce you to my sisters. Just returned from New Jersey. Without notice."

16

ANNA HAD HEARD enough about Jack's sisters to be able to tell Bambina from Celestina. Bambina was the youngest, but her gaze was sharp and unflinching, while Celestina was confused and struggled to make sense of the unexpected sight of her brother with a woman.

The introductions were short and to the point, and then Jack disappeared to carry luggage into the house while his sisters made soft exclamations of pleasure: *Such an honor, please join us, coffee, cake?*

Celestina showed her into the parlor, excused herself, and disappeared down the hall to what Anna assumed was the kitchen, leaving her alone for the moment. By rights she should have found someplace to sit and stayed there with her hands folded in her lap, but curiosity was a powerful thing. She was calmer now than she had been a half hour ago when she thought the evening would end very differently. More than that, she was enjoying herself, as long as she didn't think too hard about what Jack Mezzanotte might be telling his sisters. *That's Anna,* she imagined him saying. *A heathen. Unsuited to housework, clever with only one kind of needle. Overeducated, stubborn, an advocate for rational dress, women's education, birth control, orphans, and the poor.*

She got up to explore after all.

•   •   •

WHILE HIS SISTERS made coffee and cut up the cake they had brought with them from home and lamented the lack of anything more substantial to offer their guest, Jack did his best to hide his irritation and answer their questions—very reasonable questions—with calm certainty. It was Bambina—it was always Bambina—who spoke the question he had been waiting for.

"Who is this Miss Savard to you?"

Jack considered. He would let Anna tell them that she was not a *Miss*, but the crux of the question was his to answer. On the promenade of the new bridge he had been glib, a mistake he would not make here. Nor would he be coy or dismissive or anything but honest. Anything else would be disrespectful to Anna and to his sisters and by extension, his parents as well.

They had paused their work to wait for his answer. Bambina studied him as she would a dropped stitch, weighing alternative approaches to get the solution she desired. Round faced, full in the chest and hips, she struck most people as the matronly type, which was a serious miscalculation. Many shopkeepers who had thought she was too dull to notice a miscalculation in cost had learned differently. And now she wanted to know about Anna.

They had gotten the tea cart ready, and he opened the door so it could be pushed into the hall.

"I'm going to marry her." It was the easiest, truest thing he could think to say.

❖   ❖   ❖

ANNA WALKED THE perimeter of the parlor, a large, square room with a Dutch oven tiled in blue and white in one corner, and what looked to be an embroidery frame beside it, the same dimensions as a baby's cradle. Wainscoting ran all the way around the room, the ledge crowded with cabinet cards and small watercolor paintings, bits of very old lace and pressed flowers preserved behind glass, china birds with gilt-edged wings and a trio of dogs carved from yellowing ivory. On the low table in the middle of the room topped with a lace tablecloth was a huge earthenware crock that was bursting with flowers, exuberant and unconstrained by the current fashions.

At the center were a half-dozen white roses with the vaguest hint of pink along the edge of the petals. The sight of La Dame Dorée gave her a jolt, though she should have remembered that they would be grown here. At home she had a small spray of the same rose pressed between the pages of an anatomy text where no one was likely to come across it. Except she herself. Every few days she opened it, and the lingering scent brought those few minutes in the courtyard outside Alva Vanderbilt's kitchen back in bright detail.

She forced herself to concentrate on her study of the parlor where nothing made of fabric—the draperies, the tablecloths, the bolsters and pillows and the deep armchair by the fire—had evaded the embroiderer's needle. Margaret would be able to tell her about the stitching, but to Anna's eye much of it looked like silk laid down, thread by thread, with precision.

She heard the sisters talking in the hall in a quick, vaguely agitated Italian, pausing to listen to Jack's calm, slow answers only to interrupt with more questions, all of this undercut by the squeak of a tea cart's wheels. Anna sat down abruptly on a horsehair sofa heaped with pillows, each embroidered with—she had to look twice to be sure—some kind of barn animal. She pulled a sheep with a stalk of lavender in its jaws into her lap. She had the sudden urge to march into the hall and announce that she could cook. Not that she had any interest in cooking, she might have to admit. But she had been trained because Aunt Quinlan was adamant: everyone, man and woman, should be able to feed themselves when necessary.

Celestina came through first with Bambina close behind and then Jack pushing the tea cart. There was a plate of cake and cups and saucers, sugar and cream and a coffee carafe.

"Brought from home," Celestina told her when she saw Anna looking.

It was comforting to realize that they were as nervous as she was. She stood up to greet them again, and together they came to stand in front of Anna as if this were a complex dance they had been studying for years, waiting for the opportunity to demonstrate their graceful mastery of the footwork.

Celestina put her hands on Anna's upper arms and then leaned forward to kiss her on one cheek and then the other. "You are going to be our sister. We are so pleased."

•   •   •

JACK KNEW IT would be very bad form to laugh out loud, but he couldn't help smiling. Anna looked in that moment like a girl. Her color was high and her eyes darted from Celestina to Bambina to Jack, where they stayed. He saw her draw in a deep breath and compose herself, draw all the dignity she could muster around herself like armor, and then she smiled at Celestina and Bambina in turn.

"Yes," she said. "It seems that I am."

• • •

ANNA CONTEMPLATED THE best way to kill Jack, or at least to make him sorry that he had called all this down on her head with no warning. While his sisters asked questions without pause and she answered the ones she could, she tried to convince herself that she had no grounds for anger. He knew how best to handle his own sisters. She hoped he did. The fact that he had never uttered the word *marriage* to her was irrelevant; it was marriage that they had been talking about, and it would be silly to claim otherwise.

The things she admitted to not knowing were many: they had no specific date in mind, they hadn't discussed a ceremony, she doubted that they would want a large wedding but it was something still to be decided; she did not, in fact, have a chest of wedding linen.

This seemed to surprise and unsettle them more than anything else.

"Is that a custom in Italy?" Anna asked.

"It is a custom everywhere," Bambina said. "We often embroider linen for young women even before they know if they will ever marry."

Anna managed a small smile. "I haven't had much experience with weddings, but my cousin will be getting married next month and it will be good practice for me, watching the preparations."

Jack was giving her a doubtful look. He knew her too well to buy what she was selling; she would never take time away from her work to make wedding arrangements. Before he could challenge her—in front of his sisters, no less—she sidestepped his objection.

"I hope I can count on you," she said to his sisters. "To guide me in this. I have so little experience, and I am very busy with my work."

That she had work at all was another surprise to Bambina and Celestina, one that struck them so forcefully that even Bambina sat speechless for a moment when Anna had explained her work.

"A surgeon?" Celestina said finally. "How unusual."

Jack stood up. "Bambina, do you want to show Anna your linen chest, since she's unfamiliar with the custom?"

He was up to something, but Anna saw no option and so she let herself be shown upstairs. She cast Jack a baleful glance, and got nothing more than a grin and a shrug in return.

• • •

IT WAS ALMOST eight before Anna could convince Jack's sisters that she had to get home. Celestina extracted a half-dozen promises before Anna reached the door. As soon as they were out of sight Anna stopped and turned to him.

"Don't yell at me," he said. "I had no idea they were on the way back."

She tapped her foot and waited.

"I would have handled it better with more warning," he went on. "Just how mad are you?"

"Not so much mad," she admitted.

"Really?" He was studying her face.

Very odd, Anna thought. He looked almost guilty.

"Maybe I should be mad. You're up to something," she said. "You asked Bambina to show me her linen chest to get us all out of the parlor. Admit it."

Instead of answering, he pulled her into one of the recessed doorways and produced a very large, old-fashioned key from his pocket.

She said, "Ah, that was why you needed to distract them. You stole the key to your own greenhouse."

"It's mine as much as theirs," Jack said as he unlocked the door and pushed it open. "No thievery required."

"Then why not just say—"

He took her wrist and pulled her after him, shut the door behind them, and locked it.

Then he smiled down at her. "You told my sisters you were going to marry me."

Anna commanded herself not to blush. "As you heard."

"I think that's something we need to talk about."

"Certainly. As soon as you get back from Chicago."

She saw now that they were standing in a workroom in a narrow corridor that ran between long wooden tables all laid out with gardening tools, trays of terra-cotta pots, neatly labeled bins and barrels, and stacks of buckets.

"I can't wait that long," Jack said. He stepped over a coiled canvas hose and Anna followed him, let herself be drawn along through the dim workroom, laughing at the absurdity of it all.

He looked at her over his shoulder. "Something funny?"

Anna said, "Did you realize that the minute they got me upstairs they started undressing me—"

He jerked around to look at her.

"They wanted to look at the construction of my skirts. My split skirts? You did realize—"

Jack laughed. "I realized. I have given your skirts quite a lot of thought."

They came to a sudden stop in front of another door, this one so low that Jack had to duck to get through it.

On the other side was a small room such as a groundskeeper would have for his own use. A standing desk in one corner, two chairs and a small table in the other, a bookcase filled with ledgers and manuals and catalogs, and under a single window where a white curtain rose and fell in the evening breeze a bed, neatly made. The pillowcases were edged with lace and embroidered; more of his sisters' work.

"Whose room is this?"

"Nobody's, now. My cousin Umberto lived here before he married."

Anna crossed the room. "The house is right there. And why is this window open?"

"You would make a good detective," Jack said dryly. "It was musty, so I opened it earlier today."

"You had this planned."

"I didn't plan on my sisters. This room was in case you were uncomfortable in the house."

"Your sisters would be shocked. I should be shocked." But she wasn't, and couldn't hide the fact.

"You don't need to worry, their rooms are on the other side of the house from here."

"Hmmm," Anna said. "Can I trust you on that?"

"You can trust me on everything. Anything." He paused. "Almost anything." He backed her up against the closed door and leaned in, his hands to either side of her head.

"But—"

He interrupted her. "Do you really want to be talking about my sisters just now?"

•   •   •

A FEW MINUTES later when he let her go Anna realized she had been robbed. Her mind was blank, emptied of common sense and reason both. And they were sitting on the edge of the bed.

"Mezzanotte."

"Hmmm?" He hummed it against her ear and sent a tidal wave of gooseflesh down her back.

"You are—" Her train of thought slipped away from her.

"What?" He sat back to look at her. "I'm what? Irresistible?"

"Single-minded," she said. "And irresistible."

He gave a short laugh and closed his hands around her forearms. No doubt he would feel her pulse racing, just as she felt his.

"And persistent," she added.

"Desperate," he agreed.

And now she had to laugh. "You are just caught up—"

He put his hand over her mouth and brought his forehead to hers. "I am in love."

The words blossomed in the very center of her being, sparked their way up her spine and along every nerve, closing her throat so that even breath was impossible for that moment while he watched her face.

He said, "Are you struck speechless?"

"Not quite," Anna said.

"Then I still have work to do."

•   •   •

ANNA REMEMBERED THAT just the night before she had found his kisses almost too much, as consuming as fire. He was showing her now how little she knew, leading her down and down into an embrace as bottomless and wide as the sea. The part of her mind that was still aware of the world asked her questions: about the sisters who were hopefully in their rooms on the other side of the house, about the way her sense of propriety had disappeared without a whimper, about Jack himself. She wondered at the simple beauty of him, at heavily muscled arms and shoulders and a chest so hard beneath his clothes that he might have been wearing a leather chestplate. She wondered at the strength he held in abeyance and how his hands—broad, callused, big-knuckled—could be so gentle. She lay back on the narrow bed and pulled him down with her.

Then she sat up again. "Wait—"

Jack reached into a pocket and pulled out a square of brown paper, no larger than a silver dollar. *One male capote*, the labeling read. *Finest sheep gut. Twenty-five cents.*

He said, "You look surprised."

"Um," Anna said. "Because I am surprised. Where did you get this?"

"Schmidt's on the Bowery, near Canal."

"The druggist?" She sat up and turned the wrapped condom over to study it from all angles, and then she handed it back to him. "With Comstock on the prowl lately, I'm surprised he hasn't been arrested."

"He doesn't advertise," Jack said. "And he has a very small customer base for such things. None of whom want to see him go to jail."

"How many druggists are there who sell these?"

"This type?"

"Any type."

He shrugged. "Pretty much every druggist has some kind of condom to sell. This particular brand is harder to find."

What a strange conversation, Anna thought, but then asked the next question anyway. "What's unusual about that brand?"

Jack thought for a minute. "This is Jacob Goldfarb's work. He runs the business out of his apartment on Forsyth. The whole family works together. They use lamb intestines. Before you ask, they don't keep sheep in a two-room apartment, and I have no idea where they get the raw material. I would guess from butchers."

"A family business that produces lambskin condoms," Anna said again. She heard the disbelief and irritation in her own voice, and shook herself. "Well, good for him, and for you too. But we don't need it. I have a cervical cap."

It was Jack's turn to look surprised. "A what?"

"Sit down," Anna said. "And I'll explain it to you."

He looked as frustrated as a man could be, which Anna understood, because she felt much the same. "Just a short explanation," she said, and took one of his hands between both of her own, traced the long strong fingers, and began to talk.

◆ ◆ ◆

FIVE MINUTES LATER Jack said, "I'm not the only one who planned ahead, am I?"

Anna grabbed him by the ears and kissed him until he stopped laughing.

Between kisses he unbuttoned and untied and unveiled, layer after layer, only to stop, transfixed by nothing more than the hollow at the base of her throat. He lay his head on her breast and drew in her scent and held it, as an opium eater held smoke until he stood on the brink of nothingness. Jack ran a hand over her chemise, his knuckles brushing against her breastbone as he opened the first button. By the time he reached the fifth she was distinctly light-headed.

"You smell of lavender." He nuzzled under her arm and inhaled deeply. "And oranges and cinnamon."

"You have a poetic nose," she said, her voice catching. "I couldn't smell like very much other than sweat and talcum powder and soap. And," she added, shifting under him, "your clothes may be very comfortable for you, but they are quite itchy on the outside."

He said, "Paying attention to the wrong things, Savard."

She knew a challenge when she heard it. He wanted evidence of the history she had related to him while they sat on the new bridge. Anna ran her palm down his chest over a tightly muscled abdomen to his groin and traced the shape of him.

"Oh," she said. And then: "I have seen many penises, you realize."

He gave her an elaborate frown. "A very technical term."

"I'm a doctor," Anna said. "I don't have use for anything but technical terms. I suppose you think of it as a cock."

He pressed his face to her shoulder and laughed.

"Or do you prefer dick? Or wait, what would it be in Italian?"

He was laughing so hard that he shook. Irritated and charmed in equal measure, Anna used the blunt edge of a fingernail to skim over the bulge of his erection. He drew in a sharp breath and stopped laughing.

"So," he said, catching his breath. "Since you've seen so many examples, how do I compare?"

Anna said, "We'll never know, will we, unless you take your pants off."

• • •

SOMETIME LATER WHEN they were glued together by sweat from knee to belly to breast, Jack said, "You look like you just spent a whole day in the desert sun." And realized that as unusual a woman as Anna might be, she was unlikely to take this as a compliment, though he meant it as one. He had never seen anything more beautiful than Anna flushed and breathless and undone, her hair rioting around her face.

She had to make an effort to focus her gaze on him. "What?"

"Nothing important." Jack rolled to his side but kept his face right next to hers, feathering small kisses over her jaw and her neck until she shuddered.

"So," she said. "That's what all the fuss is about."

He hummed agreement, wondering if there was anything he might say here that wouldn't get him in one kind of trouble or another. She hadn't been a virgin, but her surprise had been genuine. Then it occurred to him that this was a question he could ask Anna, just as long as it didn't sound like a question.

"That wasn't your first climax."

"Um, well. It was the first one I didn't arrange on my own. Oh look, now you're blushing. Many women masturbate, you know. It's exactly that fact that has the Comstocks of the world up in arms. They think we'll do away with men entirely and let the undesirables do all the reproducing."

"But this was different. I hope." He rubbed his face against her breast to give himself time to digest this new, oddly intriguing idea and his voice came muffled.

"Oh, yes." She slid down too, so they were face-to-face once again. "We don't have to talk about this if it makes you uneasy."

"That would be a shame," Jack said, pulling her closer. "Because I have a lot of questions I never thought I'd be able to ask."

She gave him her widest, most brilliant smile. "I've got a few of my own. And—" She hesitated, but then pushed on. "I've never been able to really study a male body. Or rather, I've only been able to study the very old and the very young. And the dead."

Jack wondered if there had ever been such an odd conversation between two people in this particular situation. Most men would be shocked, and many of them would run in the other direction. Anna knew that, which meant she trusted him. He lay back and put his hands behind his head, stretched out to his full length despite the undeniable proof that the conversation had only reawakened his interest.

"I'm yours to command," he said. "Until it's my turn."

•   •   •

THEY WALKED BACK to Waverly Place but talked hardly at all. Anna's thoughts were humming through her, taking her further and further away. She was feeling guilty, but if she said so to Jack he would think it was about what had happened between them, and that wasn't the case at all.

"Regrets?"

"Oh, no, not a single regret." She took his arm.

"But you are arguing with yourself, I can almost hear it."

"I am, I suppose."

"Are you going to tell me about it?"

She thought she must. It was another test, and a necessary one.

"There are some things I should know better than to joke about," Anna told him. "I'm unsure whether to tell you why, if it might be more than you want to hear. In technical, medical terms," she added.

"I like hearing about your surgeries, and I've got a strong stomach."

"Well, then. Listen. A few months ago I had a patient, a fifteen-year-old with abdominal pain. Her mother brought her in."

She paused, but he didn't give the least sign of hesitation or boredom. And so she told him about Kathleen O'Brien, who had brought her fifteen-year-old daughter to Anna's office to be examined. Mrs. O'Brien was embarrassed but determined, and after some close questioning, Anna realized what she was asking. Her daughter was very ill and needed surgery, but they didn't have the money to go to one of the bigger hospitals. She was worried not just for her daughter's health and well-being, but for her immortal soul. The girl had fallen into the sin of self-gratification.

She felt Jack start in surprise, and so she slowed down a little as she sought the right words to talk about a sincere, religious woman who believed that her daughter's trouble could be cut away. *You can make the trouble go away,* Mrs. O'Brien had said to her. *Just take it all away, and she won't be plagued by temptation.*

While Anna told him about that meeting with Mrs. O'Brien and her daughter, she watched Jack's expression go flat and thoughtful.

"She wanted you to operate and—"

"Yes. She wanted me to operate and remove everything external that made her daughter female. Not the internal organs; she wanted her to be able to have children. But everything else genital."

Jack looked dumbfounded. "Where would she get an idea like that, that such a thing was even possible?"

Anna was glad, even relieved, to see him struggling to grasp what she was telling him. She felt the old anger flaring up and had to force herself to provide the facts without emotion. There were physicians, she told him, who subscribed to a theory that women who are overly sexual in nature—who show interest in sex, or who turn to what they call self-gratification—are prone to develop sexual mania. "The worst part is, they convince a woman that she is at fault, that there's something wrong about her essential self that needs to be—that must be cut away."

Jack said, "There's a lot of talk about masturbation ruining a boy's health in religious circles, I've heard it spoken of myself. But as far as I know, nobody cuts boys to cure them of the inclination. And there are surgeons who do this to women? Reputable surgeons."

"If you want the details I'll give you the journals to read the articles."

"I think I've heard enough of the details. But do they achieve the end they're hoping for?"

"What do you think they hope for?"

He lifted a shoulder. "Biddable wives."

"That's the least of it. They want obedient, cheerful women who know their place and never ask questions and never, ever complain and above all are ladylike, which means, it seems, that they have no interest or pleasure in sex. They keep performing these surgeries, so maybe they think they are achieving something. The alternative is even worse, that they know that the operations are the equivalent of vivisection—" She stopped herself and swallowed. "—and carry on regardless. I ask myself how much these men who call themselves healers must truly dislike and even hate women."

"Mostly I would guess that women frighten them."

"That a mother would want such a thing for her daughter, that is what shocked me into paying more attention to the medical journals on this subject."

"It can't be very widespread," Jack said.

"It's not common," Anna said. "But it's done with some regularity."

"If you can think of it dispassionately, and forget you're dealing with human beings, it might seem reasonable. A doctor who is developing a new treatment or surgical instrument has to run tests as he fine-tunes his invention. The charity wards in big private hospitals are often where you'll find women who are part of some experimental protocol. Once the surgeon has perfected the procedure, then he presents it to other specialists at meetings or writes it up for a journal, and he starts offering the same services to the wives of rich men, and charge the world for it.

"Sophie says it is my cynical side, but I truly believe that gynecology has become popular as a specialty because rich men have wives, and doctors have anesthesia."

After a long moment Jack said, "Cynical or not, it makes some sense. Men of science want fine shirts custom-made from England and expensive carriages and ponies for their children. I can see how it would come about," he said. "I wish I couldn't."

Anna felt some of the tension running away from her. "To be clear," she said. "It's only a small number of surgeons who do this kind of thing."

"Not small enough," Jack said. "And I do understand what you mean about not making light of the subject. But you know that you can tell me anything. I like that you like—what happens between us. I wouldn't want it any other way. So do we understand each other?"

"Yes," she said, able to smile now. "On that point, yes. But I still don't understand where you came from. If there are more men like you out in the world, they are hiding themselves very well."

"My background is unconventional," he said. "And I haven't even told you all of it. That's what we have in common. It's worth—"

"Everything," Anna murmured.

"Yes," he said. "Everything."

They walked the rest of the way in silence.

17

By Wednesday Anna had all but convinced herself that it would be premature to make any announcements to her family. She couldn't say the words *I am going to marry Jack* because she had no foundation on which to base such a claim. Try as she might, she couldn't remember Jack actually asking her to marry him. His sisters acted as if he had, but they could have misunderstood him.

By Friday, when she still hadn't had any word from him, she was sure that she had created the whole idea of marriage out of her imagination and nothing more. Except the sex. That she knew she hadn't imagined. That she remembered in such detail that it was all she could do not to blush when it came to mind, something that seemed to happen a lot, despite her best intentions. The conversation that followed was almost as clear in her mind.

She hadn't realized how much she needed to talk to a man about Mrs. O'Brien and her daughter. How desperate she had been for reassurance that there were men in the world who would object and object strongly, if they knew.

When Jack had been gone for almost a week Anna came home from the hospital to find his sisters in the parlor. Apparently they had sent a note in the morning, to which Aunt Quinlan responded with an invitation for the evening. And why, Anna wanted to know, hadn't her aunt sent word to her at the hospital?

To this question—whispered as she kissed Aunt Quinlan hello—she got the answer she expected: "You would have found a reason to stay away." Anna didn't believe it was true, but it might have been even a month ago. She greeted Bambina and Celestina with hugs and kisses and apologies for her weeklong silence thinking, *If Jack can disappear from the face of the earth, well, then so can I.*

If only Sophie were there, she wouldn't have been quite so nervous. But Sophie was out on a call. Anna steeled her resolve; she could do this without Sophie at her back, and if not, she had no business even thinking about marriage. And so Anna let herself be steered to a chair, accepted a cup of milky sweet tea, and listened as everyone talked at once in an attempt to relay what had been happening in her absence.

Rosa sat between Bambina and Celestina with a small tooled leather case in her lap, laid open to reveal a sewing kit complete with scissors, an ivory thimble, a paper of pins and another of needles, a measuring tape, and a whole rainbow of cotton threads and fine woolen yarns.

"I'm going to learn to sew." She was smiling, a full and open smile, a rarity. Somehow the Mezzanotte sisters had managed to jolt her out of a steadily darkening mood, and Anna was truly thankful to them.

There were gifts for everyone, an embarrassment of riches: Lia had a sewing box too but was far more interested in a doll made, it seemed, of boiled wool; Mrs. Lee was busy arranging a double armful of roses—the sinfully expensive roses Anna had made such a fuss about—and peonies and lilac in three of the largest vases; on the table peeking out of a storm of tissue Anna could make out hand-hemmed and embroidered handkerchiefs, a beautiful wool shawl, several folded lengths of knitted lace, and a half-dozen other bits of finery.

"We have things for you too," Bambina said. "But I think you'll be more interested in this." She pressed a letter into Anna's hands, the plain brown envelope nothing out of the ordinary, but for the outline of a small box, barely one inch square.

"It arrived this morning with instructions to deliver it to you today," Celestina said.

Anna found herself unable to look away from the letter and her name written across it in Jack's strong hand. She wondered if she could find the patience to wait through the rest of the visit. When she looked up again she realized that everyone was watching her study the letter.

Aunt Quinlan gave her a sweet and almost melancholy smile. "Anna," she said. "You'll want to change for supper and I'd like to show our guests the garden. We'll sit in the pergola and enjoy the weather for a bit."

It was difficult, but Anna managed to leave the room without jumping for joy. She went straight to her room and closed the door behind herself.

◆   ◆   ◆

SOPHIE GOT HOME and was sent straight upstairs by Mrs. Lee, who announced that Detective Sergeant Mezzanotte's sisters had come and brought Anna a letter from Chicago. Right now the guests were sitting in the pergola with tea, but Sophie had a job to do. Before Mrs. Lee's curiosity got the better of her, Sophie had to find out what was in that letter from Chicago.

She found Anna sitting at her desk, the letter open on her lap. On her palm she held a package smaller than a matchbox, tied with a thin silk ribbon the color of buttercream. She smiled when Sophie came in, a rueful smile that said Mrs. Lee's curiosity was not unfounded.

"I'm glad you're here," Anna said. "I'm almost afraid to open this."

"A ring?"

"I think so."

"I take it you knew it was coming."

Anna made a humming noise, one that Sophie recognized as a plea for understanding.

"Why didn't you tell me?"

She shrugged. "I thought it would be better to wait until he gets home from Chicago. In case things changed."

Sophie sat down with a sigh. "Your cynicism costs you dearly sometimes, doesn't it? Take heart, Anna. Your ring can't be any worse than mine."

She held out her hand to display the evidence. "Or are you unsure you want to accept it at all?"

For a moment they studied Sophie's ring. Diamonds the color of tobacco in a setting that jutted up like the prow of a ship.

"You could put out an eye with that," Anna observed. "What was Cap's mother thinking?"

"It came from her mother-in-law," Sophie said. "He's apologized more than once, but if I don't wear it—"

Anna rolled her eyes. "He's terribly traditional for all his wickedness."

Sophie said, "Will you open that, please?"

"I don't see why I need to wear a ring at all," Anna grumbled as she loosened the ribbon. "Men don't wear engagement rings. And I'll have to leave it off for most of the day while I'm at the hospital." She unfolded the tissue, her whole face creased in a combination of irritation and worry.

"Well," she said after a moment. "It's not so bad as I feared."

◆   ◆   ◆

WHEN THE MEZZANOTTE sisters had gone and everyone else had retired, Sophie knocked on the door of the little parlor and went in without waiting. Aunt Quinlan slept very little—she claimed it was one of the few advantages of old age—and Sophie often sought her out like this when the house was quiet. Now she sat beside her aunt and for a moment took comfort in the familiar.

Sophie's memories of her earliest days in the house were very clear. In the beginning this spot had been the only place where she felt truly at ease. Desperately homesick and grieving for her family, Sophie was at first surprised and then relieved to find that Aunt Quinlan understood: silence was sometimes what was needed.

Within weeks Anna and Cap had won her over, but she continued to visit Aunt Quinlan to hear her stories, which were Sophie's stories too, of her grandmother Hannah, who had been Aunt Quinlan's half sister, and of other aunts and grandmothers from Montreal to New Orleans. One underlying idea repeated itself in all the stories: Sophie's grandmothers had been great healers, brave women who dealt with the worst fate had to offer and never became bitter.

The women who went before her—the dark-skinned women—had lived on the very edge of the white world, in places and times where survival was not guaranteed, even to women with paler skin. The stories Aunt Quinlan told were something Sophie needed in a city where she was reminded that she was not white, day in and day out. As she had been reminded by Sam Reason, who thought her not black enough, and by Jack Mezzanotte's sisters, who had seen her as too black.

Now Aunt Quinlan rocked quietly and waited for Sophie to find the words she needed.

"Everything is changing at once," she said.

A low hum of agreement was all the reply she got.

"And I'm worried about Anna."

"You don't approve of her choice?"

"His sisters are the issue."

"Not really," Aunt Quinlan said. "Not unless you allow them to be a problem."

But Sophie would never forget the look on Bambina Mezzanotte's face when she realized that the black woman being introduced to her was Anna's cousin.

"Do you think Anna saw?"

Aunt Quinlan didn't seem to have an opinion. It was true that Anna was unlikely to stand quietly by while someone was being treated badly, but whether or not she had witnessed the exchange, the issue remained.

"If his sisters disapprove, then his parents—"

Aunt Quinlan's hand pressed Sophie's shoulder firmly, cutting her off. "If Jack Mezzanotte is the man I think he is, he won't let himself be derailed so quickly. Do you want to talk to Anna about this?"

Sophie tried to imagine the conversation, and could not begin to put what needed to be said into words. She shook her head.

"Better to wait, I think," Aunt Quinlan agreed. "It might never be necessary. Now tell me about Cap's cousins."

It wasn't so much Cap's cousins as his aunts on behalf of his cousins. When it became clear that Cap would not live long enough to have children, they had begun a tug-of-war for his worldly goods. Cap thought the primary battle would be over the house on Park Place, which had come down to him through the female line when his mother died without a daughter. There were other properties, some more valuable, but the house on Park Place held special meaning in the family.

"Then let them have it," Sophie had said. They sat with Conrad going over the complicated provisions of a last will, something she had neither heart nor patience for. But Cap insisted because, he said, she needed to know what battles would come.

"I don't want the house if it means a battle," she told him. It was a sore subject between them, the house he loved so much and wanted her to love. If he had had his way, they would have married and raised a family in the house where he had been born and raised, and damn the disapproval that greeted them every time they went out onto the street. The things he took for granted—the things he loved about his life—would be gone, and not be available to their children.

Aunt Quinlan wanted to know how the question had been resolved.

"Cap thinks I can turn the house into a school or infirmary. At any rate, he refuses to change the provision in the will. Once we are married it will come to me. Along with all the rest of the property and all his holdings. I never realized how much work money could be."

Then her aunt said something that had shocked Sophie to the bone.

"Take advantage. Take the resources he is giving you, and start again. You can go anywhere. Back to New Orleans, if you like, to buy back the building where your father's infirmary was so that you can reopen it."

Her expression must have been transparent, because Aunt Quinlan squeezed her shoulder gently. "I'm not telling you to go, far from it. I want you as near as I can have you. But you should be thinking about a larger life, Sophie. You stand on a precipice with the world spread out before you."

"After Switzerland," Sophie said, her voice catching.

"It's a terrible price to pay," her aunt said. "I know."

✒ LETTERS ✑

SHERMAN HOUSE HOTEL
RANDOLF AND CLARK STREETS
CHICAGO, ILL.

May 2nd, 1883

Dearest Anna,

Here I am in a hotel room half asleep but I'm too busy missing you to go to bed. You're not here and yet you manage to follow me everywhere. You'll have to explain to me how you do it.

So now for the bad news first (and it's not about you or me, or you and me, I know how your mind works, so just put that aside). We should be leaving here on Saturday at the latest but it's going to be another week or ten days before we can escape the clutches of the CPD. Two of the three Deparacio brothers we are here to extradite are in the hospital nursing broken bones and other injuries, and it will be at least that long until they can travel. The head of detectives tells us that an unfortunate tumble down a set of stairs is to blame, and what a shame, isn't it, that we'll have to stay longer than planned. Oscar wondered out loud if this had something to do with the fact that Chicago has a sizable Italian immigrant population but not one detective who speaks Italian. Bjick's smirk was answer enough. My impulse is to put him into a room alone with the Deparacio boys for a half hour or so.

Oscar sends his best regards and bids me tell you that I am in the sourest of moods, but that he is enjoying the city and has decided that the lakefront in spring almost makes up for the stink of the stockyards.

I miss your bright face and clever mind and the feel of you, but more than missing you I am worried that you will have already talked yourself out of trusting me. You are thinking that we haven't known each other long enough, when the plain fact is, we knew each other immediately. You must admit it to yourself at least, you looked at me on the Hoboken ferry that morning in March and you saw me. As I saw you.

So I know you, and I would wager good money that you haven't told even Sophie that you are going to marry me. What you need is a token to remind you, and here you have it, from a Milanese jeweler on Wabash who talked my ear off, but then sold me what he says is the prettiest ring he has ever made. And I think he may be right.

You are stuck with me now, Savard, well and truly. As I am with you, and count myself a fortunate man.

Yours without doubt
Jack

• • •

DR. L. M. SAVARD
18 WAVERLY PLACE
NEW YORK, NEW YORK

Sunday, 6 May, evening

Mezzanotte—

A strange confession to start: I cannot address you as dearest. *Though I have not written the word, you should imagine it there before your name, because it is appropriate: you are very dear, and your letter was a strategic masterpiece.*

It made me realize a number of things. First, that you do understand me very well; second, that you like me because of (rather than despite) my faults; and third, that you know when to appeal to reason, and when reason will hold no sway. And most important, you are able to put into words the things that I find so hard to say, and write.

The ring is lovely, very pretty and elegant in its simplicity. Sophie asks me to congratulate you on your good taste, and Aunt Quinlan says you did very well. I didn't wear it at the hospital today, which I think you will understand as a practical and professional decision. I admit I did hesitate to put it on once I was home again. People will ask the most intrusive personal questions on the basis of a piece of jewelry, and I'm not sure yet how politely I can handle such inquisitions. Which reminds me. I am sorry that your return will be delayed, but I can be patient, especially given the amount of work to be done both at the hospital, and for Sophie's wedding.

When your sisters came yesterday they were laden with a cask of honey and buckets of rare roses and peonies, lace and shawls and embroidered handkerchiefs and presents for the little girls. Rosa took a special liking to Celestina, who has promised to teach her how to sew and embroider. I will write more about their visit in my next letter.

On other matters, I wrote some days ago to Father McKinnawae, who is spending the summer on Staten Island preparing the new orphan asylum, asking about the youngest of the Russo children, but have no reply as yet. From Ned I have had no word in a while, and I plan to write him a note as soon as I have a moment. I had hoped to visit a few of the Catholic orphanages with Mary Augustin during your absence, but she hasn't responded to my notes, quite oddly, I think. I don't feel confident enough to confront nuns on my own.

One last, happier subject. You will remember that the opening ceremonies for the new bridge on the East River are scheduled for the twenty-fourth of May and will include a grand display of fireworks after nightfall. Aunt Q has had an inordinate—even excessive—love of fireworks since childhood. Some time ago she talked her grandson Simon (he is a captain in the Navy) into finding and securing a small ferry and crew to hire for the entire day. Aunt has also been writing to family members as far away as Albany, and thus far has extracted promises from many of them to join us for the celebration by spending the afternoon and evening on the ferry. Mrs. Lee is in her element, planning a picnic with food enough to provision an army.

Added to this excitement is the fact that the next day—that very Friday morning—Sophie and Cap will be married and then sail in the afternoon for Europe. Family who come for the bridge opening and fireworks will stay for the wedding and the wedding luncheon. I expect you will be on duty on Thursday and Friday, but hope you will be able to spend a few hours with us in the evenings at least. And then there are trips to Staten Island and to Greenwood to plan.

So far this week I have had a great number of badly broken bones to deal with, a half dozen fistulas and tears. I corrected a bowel obstruction and two hernias, and amputated a hand, a leg to the knee, and the toes of a little boy who stuck his foot under a dray cart on a dare. We have had an unusual number of losses in the children's ward. I don't like to think of myself as superstitious, but I have had more difficult cases than usual since you left, and signed more death certificates than I like to remember, certainly more than is usual for this time of year. For the sake of the good citizens of New York but mostly

*because I do miss you, you should come home sooner rather
than later.*

*Your
Anna*

*Postscript. I decided to wait a day and think before telling you
the whole story of your sisters' visit. I have not talked to Sophie or
Aunt Quinlan about it and will not until I have had your thoughts on
how best to proceed.*

*Your sisters were very welcome guests, I think you will know
that. They were friendly and open and very polite. Everyone liked
them. I liked them. I would like to say that I still like them without
reservation, but this is where the trouble begins.*

*Sophie came in late, about an hour after I got home. I was
standing just outside the parlor when Aunt Quinlan introduced
Bambina and Celestina to her as Dr. Sophie Savard, Anna's cousin.
There was a short, shocked silence. Bambina especially could not
hide her surprise and disquiet. She stammered and withdrew,
making an excuse about finding her reticule. Celestina was
composed and less abrupt, but very quiet.*

*I am guessing that you didn't mention to them that not all
Savard family members are white, and that this news will not be well
received by your family. It occurred to me that I could take your
sisters aside and explain that Sophie is my half cousin, but I was
immediately ashamed by this impulse. I will not repudiate Sophie,
and I will not make excuses or provide explanations to quiet bigotry.
If indeed this is bigotry. I cannot imagine any other reason for what
happened, but if you can provide one, I will be both thankful and
relieved.*

*I saw not the slightest hint of prejudice in you; you treat Sophie
and Mr. and Mrs. Lee with respect and kindness, and I want to
believe you will not allow anyone to treat them in any other way.
Jack, I do not intend to alarm you, but neither could I pretend this
hadn't happened and I can't put aside the worry that others in your
family will feel as Bambina does, or worse.*

Now I need to hear your thoughts on how best to proceed. I would like to call on your sisters and raise the subject directly, but if you feel that will do more harm than good, I am willing to take your advice. I will also ask you not to threaten or browbeat them, if that is your impulse. I imagine that they will not change their minds. It will just teach them to hide their true feelings, for fear of angering you. In both our professions we see what can happen when anger is tamped down and never let vent.

Anna

◆　◆　◆

SHERMAN HOUSE HOTEL
RANDOLF AND CLARK STREETS
CHICAGO, ILL.

May 9th, 1883

Dearest Anna,

My heart leapt in my chest when the desk clerk handed me your letter. Oscar mocked the smile on my face until I came away to write to you, but I was not—am not—even a little embarrassed and I only raised an eyebrow at his more colorful turns of phrase. When he puts his mind to it Oscar can fluster anybody, but today he failed with me. I think he was truly shocked.

It is a great relief to know that you like the ring. It wasn't until I had sent it off that I realized that I was putting you in a difficult position, so let me say this clearly: never pretend with me. If I misstep, you must tell me, and I will do the same. It is one of the things I value most about you, your ability to speak plain where others hold back out of fear or manners or habit.

Assuming for a moment that the ring does please you and that you want it and me: I am happy to know that Sophie and your aunt approve of it. And of the man, as an aside.

We are scheduled to testify on the morning of the 17th in Superior Court, and by noon Oscar and I will be on the way home. If

I have to push the train myself I will arrive at Grand Central on Saturday the 19th late in the day. I will come to you as soon as we are free of our prisoners.

Now about my sisters. You are right, I didn't think to describe Sophie to them, though in retrospect it is clear that I should have. I am very sorry that Bambina handled herself so badly. I can apologize for my sisters, but the only promise I can make is that they will never again treat Sophie or Mr. and Mrs. Lee or anyone else with anything less than the respect they deserve. There is no excuse for Bambina's behavior and I would not try to manufacture one, even to quiet your fears. But I do have thoughts about where these opinions originate.

Bambina considers herself ugly and undesirable, a belief that goes so deep that I doubt even a sincere marriage proposal from someone she liked would make a difference. And Sophie is beautiful, and accomplished, and wears a ring which, to Bambina at least, is anything but ugly. I would guess that she sees the color of Sophie's skin as insult added to injury. I hope and trust she is clearheaded enough to admit fault and change her ways, though it may not happen as quickly as it should.

Now I'll surprise you: I do think you should pay Bambina a visit. At some point when it feels right, ask her why we left Italy. This is a subject I have been meaning to raise with you, but it may be a way to start a conversation with Bambina.

As to the rest of the family, I wrote to my parents about you and mailed the letter on my way to Grand Central on Monday morning. It will give my mother time to think, so that when she meets you she will be ready to love you.

When I come I expect to find you with a ring on your finger. I imagine you wearing nothing else, but that falls soundly into the realm of wishful thinking.

> *you and no other*
> *Jack*

PS: I was promised time off in compensation for what was to be a short trip, remember. Now I have grounds to request a couple

*additional days, and I will see to it that I am available to be
inspected by your extended family on the 24th and 25th, on board a
ferry, at a wedding breakfast, or anywhere else as long as you are
there. I am yours to command.*

◆   ◆   ◆

11th May, 1883

Dear Dr. Anna,

*I write to say that I have inquired with my friends who live in a
district you will not know, the one the coppers call the Tenderloin,
asking about the two boys you are looking for. Nobody knows
anything about a Dago kid with blue eyes. Now it could be that
somebody does know something but is waiting for more
encouragement to speak up. This is something I should have
talked to you about the day we signed our Contract, that
information usually comes at a price. If you are willing to put
up some kind of reward please let me know. It might make a
difference.*

*Also on another matter there is a rumor going around that you
are going to marry D.S. Mezzanotte. I have declared this to be a
falsehood. Why would someone like Dr. Anna who has money and
position and everything she needs want a copper for a husband? So
now, if this rumor is true, then of course I must offer you my best
wishes but I will also offer you an observation: even those convicted
to the penitentiary can look forward to the day they will be free of
the law, but you won't have that comfort. You will have a Life
Sentence with no possibility of parole.*

I will wait for your instructions on how to proceed.

Yours Most Sincerely,
Ned

◆   ◆   ◆

11 May 1883

Dr. Savard
New Amsterdam Charity Hospital
New York, N.Y.

Dear Dr. Savard,

My name is Ambrose Leach. I am a tailor with my own small shop on Broadway. I am a respectable, God-fearing Christian, born and raised in this city. I have as wife a good woman who works hard to make a comfortable home. We have six children, the eldest twelve years and the youngest six months. The doctor tells us that another child would ruin my wife's health and might well kill her, leaving me with six young children to raise on my own and a business to run and operate at the same time. And so I write to you. I need information on how to limit the size of my family, and without delay. Please, Dr. Savard, may I call on you for this purpose? I enclose a five-dollar note as a sign of my sincerity and hope to hear from you soonest.

Ambrose Leach
Post Office Box 1567
New York, NY

◆　◆　◆

CONRAD BELMONT, ESQ.
BELMONT AND VERHOEVEN
ATTORNEYS AT LAW

May 13, 1883

Mr. Anthony Comstock
Secretary
New York Society for the Suppression of Vice
150 Nassau Street
New York N.Y.

Dear Mr. Comstock,

I am writing on behalf of Drs. Liliane and Sophie Savard in re the matter of the enclosed reproduction of a letter, addressed to the Drs. Savard at their place of employ, New Amsterdam Charity Hospital, and signed Mr. Ambrose Leach. This letter, seeking reliable information on contraception, as well as the purchase of whatever implements necessary, was mailed to "Dr. Savard" and arrived May 11, with five (5) U.S. dollars enclosed. The five-dollar bill is described as a consultation fee.

According to the city directory there is no tailor named Leach on Broadway or anywhere else in the city, and the tax assessor's office has no record of such a person or business. I am forced to conclude that the letter constitutes an attempt on your part to entrap my clients for violation of the Comstock Act, as you have publicly admitted to doing with other physicians in the recent past.

A federal district judge has already thrown out one such case on the grounds that the authorities entrapped the accused (U.S. v. Whittier, 28 Fed. Cas. 591 (1878)), but if you are eager to see such practices condemned more emphatically, by a court closer to home, then by all means, proceed on your present course.

The Drs. Savard are members in good standing of the New York Society of Physicians and Surgeons, the American Medical Association, the New York Obstetrical Society, and the Association for the Advancement of the Medical Education of Women. Detailed information about this incident will be shared with these and similar organizations, and with the attorneys representing their interests.

In the unlikely event I am mistaken as to the provenance of this letter, please accept my humblest apologies.

Sincerely yours,
Conrad Belmont, Esq.

copies to: Peter Verhoeven, Esq., John Mayo, District Attorney.

◆ ◆ ◆

MOUNT LORETTO
STATEN ISLAND, N.Y.

May 15 1883

Dear Dr. Savard,

In receipt of your letter regarding an orphaned male infant about three months old, blue eyes, dark hair. Madam, we have no shortage of such orphans and every one of them is in dire need of a good Catholic family to adopt them. If you would like to pursue this matter you may find me at Mount Loretto on Staten Island.

Yours in Christ and in his Holy Mother
Father John McKinnawae

◆ ◆ ◆

THE FOUNDLING ASYLUM
SISTERS OF CHARITY
175 E. 68TH STREET
NEW YORK, NEW YORK

May 15 1883

Dear Dr. Savard,

I am in receipt of your letter requesting Sister Mary Augustin's assistance when you call on Father McKinnawae at the Mission of the Immaculate Virgin in the coming week.

Sister Mary Augustin has been reassigned to the Mother House where she can better contemplate devotion to duty and detachment from self. While she will not be joining you, please be assured that we Sisters of Charity pray for you and ask God to guide your heart and hand as you continue your search for the missing Russo children.

Diriget Deus
Sr. Mary Irene

◆ ◆ ◆

CITY OF CHICAGO
POLICE DEPARTMENT
SEVENTH DISTRICT
943 W. MAXWELL ST.
CHICAGO, ILL.

Wed., May 16 1883

Dearest Anna,

Tomorrow at noon we will be boarding the train and on our way home, the Deparacio brothers in tow. Look for me on Saturday evening. I will be polite for a half hour, and after that I will not want to share you with anyone, so be prepared to go out.

Some thoughts about the news in your last letter: I think that Baldy Ned is probably right. A reward might well be helpful but the amount is important. Too much will send the wrong message and could cause complications. Do you really need me to tell you your instincts are sound, or is there something else that has got you worried?

As for his suggestions regarding our plans, he is as cheeky as ever, but he is also absolutely right. It is a life sentence for both of us.

I was quite surprised by the Comstock business. This is something you haven't told me much about, and I think it is a conversation we need to have as soon as I am home. In the meantime, I think you won't have to worry about him now that you've handed the matter over to Conrad Belmont. Belmont's reputation should be enough to scare off the self-proclaimed Weeder in the Garden of the Lord for good. A rich, well-connected man who cannot be won over to Comstock's cause is one he avoids at all costs.

Finally, I am wondering if you paid Bambina a visit and are keeping that to yourself, or if you are still trying to work up the courage.

I fall asleep every night thinking of that last evening we spent together. I once believed that smells could not be recalled in isolation, but the scent of your skin at the nape of your neck is as real to me as the texture of your hair and the shape of your hands. Your beautiful, clever hands. I feel them on my face.

Evermore
Jack

18

ANNA SAT WITH Jack's letter open in front of her, calculating times and distances yet again, just to be sure of her conclusion: he would be home sometime in the late afternoon or evening of the next day. This was very good news, and at the same time, difficult; she really had been putting off the visit to his sisters. Something she would have to do this evening.

The day had been particularly long: two surgeries of her own, assisting at another, a particularly difficult patient who showed up every week because she would not follow instructions on how to care for an ulcerated cheek and would only accept Anna as a doctor, a committee meeting about the usual budget shortfall and plans for raising funds—of all the duties that came with a position on the hospital staff, fund-raising was the worst, without competition.

And at the end of the workday, there was the bimonthly meeting of the Rational Dress Society. It was a commitment she had made long ago but one that she might have let go, if not for the ongoing debate about corsets around the breakfast table, which had renewed her interest and resolve.

All that she had survived, to find herself in the Mezzanotte parlor, watching Celestina fuss with bone china coffee cups as transparent as paper held up to the sun. The rims and handles were decorated with green and gold tracery, the kind of detail that would normally escape Anna, but the china was so delicate and beautiful, it drew attention to itself as surely as a single painting on a stark white wall.

That thought was still in her head when Bambina came in with a plate of long, narrow biscuits dusted with sugar crystals. They were also as hard as rock, as Anna soon discovered when she tried to bite down on one. She watched Bambina dipping a biscuit directly into her coffee cup and followed her example. It was almost magical, the way it crumbled on her tongue to a buttery mass of crumbs that tasted of sweet coffee and vanilla and anise.

"These are very good," she said, quite sincerely. "The little experience I've had with Italian cooking gives me the sense that I will like it all."

"Experience?" Celestine smiled at her, inviting but not demanding more information.

"Jack once shared a sandwich of roasted pork; it may have been the best thing I have ever eaten. I still think of it sometimes, but I always forget to ask him where it came from."

Both sisters were smiling. "That must have been Aunt Philomena," said Celestina. "She's a wonderful cook. Jack eats with them once or twice a week when we are away at home. Though I suppose—" She broke off, embarrassed.

Anna did not consider herself insensitive, but she saw now that she had been oblivious to one crucially important aspect of their plans, one that would explain much of the nervous agitation in the room. When their brother married, the sisters would find themselves without a male protector. These two were raised to run a household, to care for others and to make beautiful things with their hands; they would never see themselves as independent, even if their needlework brought them sufficient income to make that claim. Unless Anna were to come here to live with all three of the Mezzanottes, Celestina and Bambina faced an uncertain future.

But she could make them no promises, not at this moment. Maybe never. Someone would have to move, and any move would disrupt this household in ways that could only be imagined.

"Um," she said, tongue-tied for once in her life. "I think I'll need a map of some kind to sort through all the Mezzanotte relatives. I haven't even met your uncle Massimo yet."

Celestina smiled as though she had been handed a gift and shot up from her seat. "What was I thinking? I'll go get him now, he's still in the shop. And you haven't met the cousins—"

"Wait," said Bambina, but the door was already closing behind her sister.

Bambina looked almost panicked and Anna wondered if Jack had written to express his disappointment with her after all. Anna wondered what subject she could raise that would put both of them at ease.

She said, "This china is very beautiful."

"Yes, isn't it? It was my grandmother's. My mother's mother."

"You brought it from Italy?"

"I was born here," Bambina said. "But it came over with my parents, yes. It came to my mother when her mother died. She was the only daughter."

And there it was, the opening she needed to ask the question Jack had suggested. But the truth was, after such a difficult and drawn-out day, she had little stomach for what would certainly be an awkward conversation. If not for the memory of Sophie's expression, the stillness that had come over her when Anna raised the subject of Jack's sisters, she might have let this go. But she did remember.

"Why did your parents decide to leave Italy?"

Bambina drew in a deep breath. "My brother didn't tell you?"

"He suggested I ask you to tell me the story."

Bambina's fingers began to trace the pattern of chevrons on her jacket sleeve. For a moment Anna wondered if she would simply ignore the question, but then she nodded to herself.

"The families—both of them—disapproved of the marriage," she said. "My father's brothers and Grandmother Bassani were the only members who didn't disown them, and when she died my parents decided to start new in the United States. My uncles Massimo and Alfonso were already here, and that gave them a place to land."

"But why did the families object?" Anna asked, curious now.

"You are not Roman Catholic," Bambina said, an odd turn in the conversation. She waited for Anna's nod. "Neither is my mother. She is from Livorno, the granddaughter of Reb Yaron Bassani. He was one of the city's most respected rabbis." She fell silent, her eyes fixed not on Anna, but on the wall behind her.

"Your mother is Jewish," Anna said in an even tone, one she didn't have to manufacture. Bambina was expecting her to be shocked and disturbed by this news, as many people disliked Jews on principle. Anna was not one of them, for reasons that she couldn't list without sounding as though she were pandering.

But this single fact explained so much about Jack and the man he was; it felt almost like the missing piece of a puzzle.

"Did your mother convert when she married your father?"

A muscle fluttered in the girl's jaw. "No. Which made my father's family very unhappy."

"That must have been very hard for her as a young mother. Do you consider yourself Roman Catholic or Jewish?"

Her gaze was steady and cool. "I claim neither. Why is that important?"

"It's not unusual, I would think," Anna said. "I'd guess it is even quite common for the children of a mixed marriage to avoid or even reject both sides."

Bambina frowned elaborately, her brows drawing down to an angle as defined as an arrowhead. "You would call this a mixed marriage, between a Jew and a Catholic?"

"It would be considered mixed by most people," Anna said. "But my family has been flouting expectations and traditions for a hundred years. My grandfather Bonner's first wife was Mohawk, and the daughter of that marriage—my aunt Hannah—married a man from New Orleans who had African, Seminole, and French grandparents. We are a complicated and colorful family. We avoid labels."

The younger woman closed her hands around her cup as if they needed warming and sipped, slowly. Anna took the opportunity to study her. It was true that Bambina was not especially pretty, but neither was she ugly. She had a round face, full cheeks, and a strong nose, but she also had beautiful eyes with thick dark lashes, and a full mouth. And she was intelligent. Just now her expression was much like Jack's when he was working through a problem.

"You must know," Anna went on, more slowly, "that after the war New York was overwhelmed with people like your parents, who left one place to start again in another. Sophie was just ten when she lost her family and home and left everything familiar behind to come here. From that time we have been as close as any sisters."

"My mother is Jewish," Bambina said. "She is not colored. You can't compare the two." Her tone was confrontational and also resentful; she was surprised that Anna would pursue the subject.

Anna met Bambina's gaze and reached carefully for the right

tone. "People descended from African slaves and the Indian tribes have some things in common with Jews. All three have survived despite open hostility and violence and even banishment. The Jews were driven out of Italy at one time, isn't that so?"

Bambina's gaze snapped toward her. "Why would you know that?"

"I had a broad and liberal education, and beyond that, we have family friends who are Jewish. I have students and colleagues who are Jewish. Sophie's mentor is Jewish."

"I still don't see the comparison." Her expression was chilly.

"Have you ever seen your mother being cut or openly insulted because of her religion?"

"No. Should I have?"

"And that's why your parents decided to leave Italy, so you wouldn't experience what it's like to have someone you love insulted or demeaned openly," Anna said. "But I would hope you could imagine a thing even if you haven't experienced it personally."

There was a moment of fraught silence, and then Celestina came into the room, breathless.

"They all want to meet you," she said. "But they don't want to come into the house in their work clothes. Aunt Philomena wants us to walk down to their house, at the end of the block."

Anna stood and smoothed her skirts. "Well, then, that's easy enough." She smiled at Bambina. "Will you come along?"

But Bambina disappeared down the hall toward the kitchen, without another word.

19

THE NEXT DAY Anna explained it to Sophie in simple terms. The daughter of a well-to-do and prominent Jewish family and the son of Livorno's biggest landowner fell in love, defied their parents, and married.

"Bambina made an excuse to get away from me and disappeared upstairs," Anna said. "But Celestina told me the whole story. The key point is, Rachel Bassani became Rachel Mezzanotte, and her father disowned her. But her mother didn't.

"Her mother refused to be cut off from Rachel. She was their best ally and support. On Ercole's side things were a little better. He had five brothers and they all supported the marriage. The two oldest of the brothers were already here and the other three followed. The Mezzanottes have been busy populating New York and New Jersey ever since."

"And how did this subject come up?" Sophie wanted to know. Her expression said she had certain ideas, but she wanted Anna to confirm them.

"Jack thought I should talk to her."

"Ah. Do you think it did any good?"

"It gave her something to think about."

"It gave you a lot to think about too," Sophie observed.

"It does make sense," Anna said. "If he had grown up in a traditional Italian family with strong ties to the Catholic Church—"

"We wouldn't be sitting here talking about him."

There were a dozen other issues that hung in the air, unvoiced, unanswered. But Sophie was yawning in the helpless way of the truly exhausted, and she was still planning on going to see Cap today, though she had been out most of the previous night treating a seven-year-old with meningitis. When Anna asked her about it she woke up a little, as if it was something she needed to share.

"On the Bend," she said.

Mulberry Bend was the very worst of the tenements. Hundreds of rooms, airless, lightless, no larger than closets, overrun with vermin, where whole families slept in shifts. The place where the most desperate and violent kept each other warm.

"Seven children in the same room. The hardest part was convincing the parents that the boy was contagious and had to be isolated. I finally sent for an ambulance and admitted him to Women and Children's. Jenny Fairclough agreed to put him on her patient list, though I would guess he has already died."

It was on Anna's tongue to ask Sophie why she was still taking calls. She had already resigned from the hospitals and dispensaries where she saw patients, precisely because all her time was taken up with the preparations for a wedding and a long journey. And with Cap, who didn't want to let her out of his sight, now that he finally had his way.

"You have done so much, Sophie. You have nothing to feel guilty about."

Sophie made a low humming sound, one that said very clearly that she did not agree and did not care to argue this subject they had gone over so many times.

From out in the hall came the sound of Lia climbing the stairs, singing to herself in time to the thump of her doll's head as it met each step. Then a small face appeared around the edge of the door frame, eyes wide with anticipation.

Anna got up. "Lia, is it time to go?"

"To Lilliput," Lia told Sophie. "To eat ice cream."

"Errands first," Anna said. "And then if you are not too tired after errands, Lilliput. And ice cream." She reached toward Lia, who jumped away, giggling.

"Cap's sent the carriage," Sophie said. "And I'm running late, but I can take you as far as Madison Square."

•   •   •

AT THE LAST minute Margaret decided that Anna could not be trusted with decisions about petticoats and footwear and hats, and so three women and two little girls climbed into Cap's fine carriage with the help of taciturn Mr. Vale for the trip north to Madison Square. For a moment Anna considered retiring and leaving the whole endeavor to Margaret, who liked visiting shops, after all. But the little girls were so excited to have her along. Anna realized with something like guilt that she had rarely been out of the house with them.

And of course, at home in the quiet of an almost-empty house she would have nothing to distract her from thinking about Jack, who was on a train headed this way. Rather than watching the clock she would concern herself with little girls and the Lilliput Children's Emporium.

◆　◆　◆

ANOTHER SET OF doubts rose up for Anna when they waved goodbye to Sophie, as the carriage bore her away to Park Place. On her way to spend the afternoon with Cap and whatever visitors came to call, overflowing with curiosity and, in some cases, malice. Even if no one called, Cap would take joy in arguing about every detail of the events to come.

"Because he can't touch me," Sophie said. "The next best thing is to make me mad."

It was entirely possible, Anna thought, that the joy of having Sophie nearby would be eclipsed by the reality of not having her close enough. Even illness could not banish sexual desire completely, though she had doubts that Cap would find the strength even if the possibility presented itself. And thus the anger, which must have an outlet. It had been terrible to see them both so unhappy in the year of Cap's self-imposed separation, but in some ways this resolution—together but not together—was just as hard.

◆　◆　◆

ONCE THE ENGAGEMENT had been publicly announced, Cap put his plans into action in anticipation of visitors—the curious, the gossip mavens, the disgruntled relatives—who would come to call. The Astors and De Peysters and the rest of the old Knickerbocker families would not come; Cap had effectively removed himself from their understanding of the world, and they would not see him if he were to meet one of them face-to-face on the street. Cap didn't care, of that Sophie was sure. She herself had no interest in formal visits with the commodore's widow, but she did resent the rejection of Cap, who was going away and would not be back again.

The parlor had been transformed since the formal announcement of the engagement. Most of the furniture had disappeared, leaving just two seating areas: one for Cap on the farthest wall between two windows, and the other twenty feet away. The heavy draperies had gone the way of the missing furniture and all the windows stood open, so that the parlor was filled with soft spring light and a tripling breeze. It was unorthodox and alarming and utterly pleasing to Sophie, not in the smallest part because it reminded her of New Orleans, where houses were built to welcome fresh air rather than keep it out. She thought of all that heavy, valuable fabric and at the same time of Jack Mezzanotte's sisters, who would know how to put it to good use. She wondered what the gossips would say if she were to make a gift of Mrs. Verhoeven's silk and brocade drapery to Italian needleworkers.

"Something for them to focus on other than your pretty face," Cap had said when she asked about the missing furniture and finery.

"Something more to be outraged about," she came back.

"Don't begrudge Aunt Undine her only source of entertainment." He said it with a grin, but Sophie knew he was worried about his mother's sisters, or at least, two of them. The less difficult of the two was Eugenie, who believed that because she had married a first cousin and retained the family name, her son Andrew should be Cap's heir. Undine was more difficult. She objected to everything, it seemed, on principle. And she never conceded.

Sophie might have simply forbidden visitors and given the importance of rest as her reason, but she was choosing her battles carefully.

"And it's hard to censure him when his spirits are so much improved," Anna pointed out, voicing that exact thought Sophie had not wanted to contemplate. The fact was that Cap overflowed with renewed energy at least in part because of overindulging in laudanum. When she confronted him he assured her that all would be well as soon as they were married and on their way; he would put himself in his wife's care, and follow every direction.

At that she snorted a laugh, and he returned a lopsided grin.

And so sitting apart they received visitors: his Belmont aunts and uncles and some cousins, many old enough to be his parents. With the exception of Bram and Baltus and Cap's uncle Conrad, most of the family members who visited were ill at ease or suspicious or both. None of them had the nerve to come out and say what they were thinking, or even why they had come. There were no congratulations to Cap, though most of them managed to greet Sophie politely.

Undine had not yet called, but Conrad had predicted that the day had come; he had suggested that Sophie find something else to do. Undine would not hesitate to say what she believed must be said, and she would not spare anyone's feelings. When her fiancé fell at Spotsylvania some twenty years before, Undine Belmont had put on mourning and had yet to give it up. She held on to her memories, her pennies, and every slight, real or imagined, with grim intensity. The twins called her Aunt Costive behind her back.

As Sophie reached the front door, Undine's carriage pulled up. So, Conrad had been right. She slipped in with a nod to Mrs. Harrison and made straight for the parlor, where Cap had settled for the afternoon.

"She's on the doorstep," Sophie said.

"Oh good," said Bram. "I was afraid we were going to miss the fun."

Cap said, "A half hour and you need never again deal with Undine Belmont."

When Undine came into the parlor, Bram and Baltus leapt to their feet and offered their aunt every comfort with exaggerated proper manners and good cheer, which only made her shiver with annoyance. Then she turned her gaze first to Cap, and then to Sophie, who she regarded as she would a serpent curled on a silk pillow, a calculated insult, dangerous and odd at the same time. It was true that she would have objected to Sophie if her skin were white, Sophie being overeducated, overopinionated, and unworthy on general principles.

The twins finally retreated to the card table in the corner and Conrad shifted so that he was facing the sofa where his sister had taken a seat. She maintained a chilly composure in Conrad's presence, even when he set out to provoke her. And he was so very good at it, in part, Sophie was sure, because he had been blinded in the war and did not hesitate to use that fact to his advantage. And these two had grown up together and knew each other's secrets.

"Sophie," Conrad said, holding out his hand until she came to sit beside him. "Cap's aunt Undine has come to welcome you into the family."

To Sophie it was obvious that Undine feared and resented her eldest brother, just as she disliked the twins and disapproved of Cap and was horrified by Sophie. She wondered if anyone met with the older woman's approval, and thought not. It was sad, but it wasn't enough to make her put down her guard.

To her brother Undine said, "Conrad. This is a serious matter."

"It is indeed," said Cap from across the room. His voice was reedy with effort, but he produced his grimmest smile. "We're about to travel halfway around the world."

"Undine has never been to Europe," Conrad supplied smoothly, cutting his sister off before she could reply to Cap's willful misunderstanding.

Sophie, tired of being ignored, stepped in. "Neither have I. But I'm looking forward to it." Truly, she was mostly looking forward to the end of the turmoil that would dog them to the altar.

Undine said, "Conrad, I hold you responsible for this entire debacle."

Surprised, Sophie raised a brow at Cap. He gave a curt shake of the head that told her it would be best to stay out of the discussion.

"If you had done your duty and married and produced a son, we would not be sitting here facing social ruin. As the head of the family you should know this without being told."

Conrad pursed his mouth thoughtfully. "Cap is my dearest sister's only child, the first of his generation, and as much as a son to me. In my opinion—and that is all he need take into account—he has chosen well."

"It is not just your concern." Her voice began to wobble with anger and her tongue darted to touch her thin upper lip. "It is family business. It is this family's shame."

"Undine," Conrad said with a chilly edge that Sophie thought was more at home in a courtroom. "If you cannot be civil and ladylike, you must leave."

"I am the only lady in this room, and I'm not finished," she said stiffly. "I have more to say."

"Pardon me," Sophie said. "While I see what's holding up our tea."

As she closed the parlor door behind herself, Sophie heard Undine Belmont say, "What kind of lawyers are the two of you; have you never heard of miscegenation laws? I quote: 'If any white person intermarry with a colored person he shall be guilty of a felony and shall be punished by confinement in the penitentiary—'"

"Congratulations," Cap interrupted. "You can read, but you should always start with the title. That is the law in Virginia, I believe. We find ourselves in New York State. Is your mind wandering of late, Aunt Undine?"

Sophie knew very well what was coming; Cap would twist his aunt into knots challenging her understanding of history, geography, law, ethics, and medicine until she got up and stormed out of the house. None of it was new and so she took her time visiting with Cook, went outside to talk to the gardener about the health of his rosebushes, and then went to the room that had been set aside for her use.

She washed her face and considered herself in the mirror. Her family history was there to read, in her bones and skin and hair, in the blue-green eyes that identified her as redbone in the south, a term some thought as offensive as anything Undine Belmont could come up with. But Cap didn't care about any of that, and Cap was the only thing that mattered.

Sophie took her time, and still managed to cross paths with Undine as she came into the hall, righting the veil over her face. She stopped and turned.

"Miss Savard," she said.

Sophie inclined her head, acknowledging both the greeting and the denial of her medical degree. "Miss Belmont."

"Very cleverly done," Undine said.

Sophie smiled at her, her best manners on display. "Yes," she said solemnly. "Cap has done very well for himself."

Then she ducked around Undine and into the parlor, where Conrad was laughing silently, his whole long thin shape contorted with pleasure. Cap's smile was quieter, but he looked at her with all the love and affection he had to offer. And that would be more than enough to put all the Undines of the world out of her mind.

◆ ◆ ◆

ANNA HAD SET out on this expedition determined to hold on to her sense of humor and patience both, and found it easier than she had imagined. It was the little girls who made the difference, in part because they were amazed by everything and in part because shop-keepers seemed to be drawn to them, and in equal part because their presence kept Margaret from starting conversations sure to cause a disagreement.

They picked out lace and bonnets and summer-weight stockings, stopped by the seamstress to have pinafores and skirts pinned up for alteration, retrieved purchases Aunt Quinlan had ordered from a jeweler. At four they had come as far as the Lilliput Children's Empo-rium, where the girls were allowed to look at toys and dolls as long as they did not touch. They finished up in the shoe department, where both of them were fitted with buff-colored leather half boots suitable for both summer outings and a small wedding.

Lia was beside herself with joy; Rosa, still somber, expressed her thanks and appreciation and fell back into silence. Anna fought still with the impulse to tell her about the upcoming trip to Staten Island and the hope that they would find her little brother, wanting so much to see some hope in that small serious face. But Jack and Sophie and Aunt Quinlan were united in the belief that it would be worse to raise her hopes only to dash them yet again, and so she had to content her-self with small gestures instead of fragile promises.

As a last stop they went to the confectioner's just two doors down, a place that smelled of caramelized sugar and yeast and cinnamon, French pastries filled with cream and drizzled with chocolate, layer cakes and tortes and little petit fours crowned with fruit as bright as jewels. They were shown to a table while Lia expressed her wishes in very concrete terms, waving the menu as if it were personal standard.

"Chocolate ice cream," she said. "With wafers and cherries and whipped cream."

"After something more substantial," Anna said. "Sandwiches and a pot of peppermint tea, I think."

A hint of rebellion showed itself on Lia's face, but her sister's sharp look was enough to nip insurrection in the bud.

"You'll like these sandwiches," Margaret promised the girls.

And they did. A plate of small triangles, white and brown bread trimmed of all crust and filled with delicate slices of cucumber, pot-ted cheese, and slivers of pink ham. The little girls hesitated at first and then ate up the whole platter under Margaret's watchful eye and constant small corrections.

Anna was just starting to long for home when she saw Rosa's face transform itself, her worries falling away to reveal a little girl whose fondest wish had just been granted. Even as Anna turned to follow Rosa's gaze, she knew that Jack was coming toward them, bold and dark and strong in this pastel-colored place designed for ladies and children. She twisted around and met his gaze, and knew that she could not hide from him or anyone at all what she was feeling.

His fingers brushed her shoulder as he passed by her chair and to the other side of the table to stand behind Rosa, who was chattering at him in Italian. He put his hands on her shoulders and leaned down to talk to her, just a few words in Italian, but the tears that had been welling in her eyes subsided as she nodded and smiled and swallowed. Then Lia had hooked her hands around his forearm and demanded her share of his attention.

Anna watched all this and felt her own throat swell so that even when Jack came to her and leaned over to kiss her cheek, she had not a word to offer him.

The waiter brought another chair and there was a good five minutes of adjusting and moving and ordering of more sandwiches and ice cream, during all of which Anna had nothing to say. Finally Jack turned to her, pressing her shoulder with his own. Under the table he caught her hand and put it on the long hard plane of his thigh to trace her ring. Her fingers twitched, and he folded his hand around hers.

He said, "I've robbed you of speech."

Anna nodded, and the little girls giggled, so delighted that they bounced on the red leather cushions of their chairs. Even Margaret was flushed with excitement. She wanted to know how Jack had found them.

"I stopped by Waverly Place," he said. "Mrs. Lee told me where I might find you. And here you are. Though Anna still won't talk to me." Jack, who remembered the shape of her hands, and the texture of her skin, and the smell of her hair at the nape of her neck. Under the table he squeezed her hand. "Maybe she's changed her mind about marrying me. Have you, Anna? Changed your mind?"

Lia chirped, "*Allora io ti sposerò.*"

"Ah," Jack said, leaning across the table to stroke the little girl's cheek. "That's a relief. Lia will marry me if you've changed your mind, Anna."

"Lia," Anna said. "It's a very kind offer, but you will have to find someone else to marry. Detective Sergeant Mezzanotte is spoken for."

• • •

JACK TRACED A pattern over Anna's palm, just to feel her tremble. This wasn't exactly the way he had hoped to find her but there were some advantages; he had never seen her so reticent or flustered. She vibrated with the need to be kissed, and he wanted nothing so much as to oblige her.

Then the food and ice cream arrived, and there was a moment's quiet while they turned their attention to their plates and bowls, all except Margaret, who wanted to know about the prisoners he had brought back from Chicago and where they had ended up.

"I don't know," Jack said, which was not exactly the truth, but close enough. "A couple patrolmen took charge of them in the station. You don't need to worry, you know. Even if they were out on the street, you wouldn't need to worry. They are very polite, gentlemen of the first order unless you're getting on a train, in which case they'll take your money, give you a worthless piece of paper in return, and bend over backward thanking you for your patronage."

"Forgers." Margaret sounded almost disappointed. "Not even money, but train tickets."

"Oh, a train ticket," Lia announced. "I love a train ticket. I got one of those at home."

"You wouldn't know a train ticket if it bit you on the nose," said her sister.

Lia was unconcerned by this accusation, her mouth too full of ice cream.

"Lia," Jack said. "Your English is almost as good as your sister's. Did you swallow a dictionary?"

She waved her spoon like a queen with a scepter. "Oh, a dictionary," she said agreeably. "I love a dictionary."

"She's got one of those at home," Rosa finished for her, and Jack couldn't help himself, he laughed out loud. For this moment he was content to sit with Anna beside him and talk to the little girls and even to Margaret, who had the makings of a police officer, if such things were possible, or a nun, if she were Roman Catholic. She spoke up as if she had read his mind.

"These girls need to get home, Anna. Shall I go on with them?" She managed to offer both help and disapproval in those few words, a skill that Jack had observed before in mature women who were worn to the bone by loneliness and loss.

"We'll all go," he said. "I'd like to say hello to your aunt Quinlan, and then Anna and I have an appointment to keep."

In an awkward scramble they managed to get two cabs, only to be held up by the girls, who both wanted to ride with Jack. The long afternoon had begun to wear on them, and tears and tempers were ready to erupt. In the end Jack took the girls in one cab, and left Anna and Margaret to the other.

Anna was damp with perspiration and her heart was thundering in her ears, but she worked hard to maintain a placid expression that would give Margaret nothing to grab onto.

Margaret said, "It's good to see you happy."

Surprised, Anna had to gather her thoughts before she could reply. "But I haven't been unhappy." She heard the defensive tone in her own voice and wondered what she was protecting: her understanding of herself, or Margaret's? The truth was, her life before Jack was a good life. She had fulfilling work and a family she loved. There were new things for her to discover every day. And that was the key, Anna realized. Margaret thought of her own life as a thing of the past, and anticipated nothing beyond more of the same.

"You could change things," Anna said. "You really could start out on a different life for yourself. You are not nearly so old as you feel."

Margaret smiled at her. "I was brought up to be a wife and a mother. I never wanted any other occupation and I still don't. Really all I want—" She stopped.

"Go on," Anna said.

"All I want is a household of my own," Margaret said. "With my own people, who look to me first instead of last."

Anna thought of Bambina and Celestina Mezzanotte and of all the other women she knew who considered themselves less than women because they had no households or husbands or children to care for. And she thought of Jack, the kind of man she had never even dared imagine.

She said, "If you had broken bones or a punctured lung I could help you. I wish there were more I could do."

The two of them sat quietly side by side swaying with the movement of the cab as it dodged one way and then another through traffic around Union Square and turned toward Waverly Place.

◆   ◆   ◆

SOPHIE WAS STILL at Cap's, but everyone else was in the garden when Anna and Margaret got home, Jack and the little girls included. There was a great deal of talk and laughter and then a spirited discussion about supper. Jack wanted to take Anna away to an appointment—she was still unclear on exactly what he meant with that word, but she had her suspicions—and promised to come back for Sunday dinner the very next day; there was a lot to discuss, after all.

Aunt Quinlan took his face in her hands when he bent down to kiss her cheek and studied his eyes for a long moment.

"Endeavor to deserve her," she said, and let him go.

"It's what her father said to her first husband when they married," Anna explained as they went back through the house. "Her husband said it to all her daughters' husbands."

Jack caught her wrist and drew her up against him while pressing her to the wall in the cool shadows of the front hall. When he had kissed her—less kiss than she had anticipated, but sweet nonetheless— he rubbed his cheek against hers.

"Did she say the same to Cap?"

"Multiple times, I'm sure."

He kissed her again, more seriously now and with all his attention.

"Wait." It was the only word she could get out between one kiss and the next, and in response she got only the curve of his smile pressed to her cheek.

She pulled away to say, "You can't smile and kiss at the same time."

"Watch me," Jack said.

"What about this mysterious appointment?"

He let her go, nodding. "There is that. Come on, let's get it over with."

•   •   •

THEY CROSSED WASHINGTON Square Park at a sharp angle, Jack only slowing when he realized she was almost running to keep up. Her expression was one he couldn't quite place, but the tone of her voice gave her irritation away.

"Where exactly are we going?"

He gestured with his chin to the southern border of the park. "Mazzini's Hotel."

She pulled up short and he stopped, too.

"Hotel?"

"Mazzini's, yes."

A line appeared between her brows. "For what purpose?"

And now he understood. He hadn't been clear and her mind had gone off in the wrong direction. An intriguing direction, but wrong. She stood in front of him in the late afternoon sunshine, framed all around by dogwood and crab apple trees in blossom with her own color rising in her cheeks. The most sexually open woman he had ever known, but inexperienced, too, confused and affronted and aroused, on top of all that.

He could not resist. "You're asking about my purpose?"

She crossed her arms and scowled at him, then stepped back when he stepped toward her. Jack advanced at a leisurely pace and she retreated, step for step.

"What purpose do you imagine I have?"

The next step brought her back up against a dogwood tree, and a flurry of petals fell, catching on her hair and shoulders. She was beautiful and irritated and confused.

"Did you think I meant to seduce you in a hotel room?" He propped a forearm against the tree trunk just over her head and leaned in to smell her hair. "Is that what you imagined?"

She pushed at him, half laughing now. "Get away."

"But I just got back." He nuzzled her temple as she pushed and pushed at his chest, and then, relaxing, slipped her arms around his waist and turned her face up to his.

"Did you really think I was taking you to a hotel room?"

She bit the lining of her cheek. "If you had just told me—"

"You did think I was taking you to a hotel room."

Anna ducked as if to slip away, but he caught her up again. There were people on the paths, people who could see them and at this moment, he didn't care and more than that, he didn't want Anna to care, either. So he kissed her until she forgot about the tree at her back and the park all around and the people in the park and everything in the world but the two of them.

Then he took her hand and pulled her away, to run with him through the park, breathless and flushed with a youth he had thought long past.

• • •

THERE WAS A chalkboard just outside the hotel lobby bracketed by the American flag on one side and the Italian flag on the other. An announcement had been written out carefully in English and Italian both: *Monthly Meeting of the Italian Benevolent Society Today at 6 p.m.*

"Wait," Jack said, holding her back a moment. "I have to confess. This meeting is being held in a room. In a hotel."

Anna pinched him with her hard surgeon's fingers and was satisfied with the yelp he produced. Then they were in the lobby and surrounded by a crowd of men who came toward Jack as if he were a long-lost son, stopping in an almost comic way, all at once, when they saw Anna. Jack put his arm around her waist in an overtly possessive gesture that should have irritated her. But she could not be agitated about his willingness to claim her publicly, nor could she even deplore that inability in herself. Because Jack was home and he had brought her here to show her off. She was vain enough to be pleased, and embarrassed too.

They were shopkeepers, carpenters, restaurant owners, cigar makers, laborers, masons, stable owners, grooms, manufacturers of pianos and pipe and hairbrushes. And they all held Jack in high esteem, and extended the same to her.

There was a meeting during dinner, all of the discussion in Italian. Anna recognized some words now, thanks to the Russo sisters and Jack: *orphan, family, money, school*. While she picked at her food—small square noodle packets filled with spiced meat, all in a combination of soft cheese and cooked tomatoes—Jack was asked a question and he answered in a tripling Italian that made Anna realize how slowly he had spoken otherwise.

Finally the liquor and cigars came out and Jack squeezed her hand and gestured with his chin toward the door. Anna felt like a child let out of school, but she resisted the urge to hurry. She was a highly educated, mature woman who did not have to give in to every impulse. But the urge to skip stayed with her all the way home.

All the way home they talked. About Chicago and the taciturn chief of detectives, about Anna's cases over the last week, about Bambina and Sophie and the wedding. Not once did Jack stop to kiss her. She wondered why, and then explained it to herself in a half-dozen reasonable ways. He was exhausted after such a long and difficult trip; his sisters were waiting at home and would begin to worry; he still had to go into the station to make a report, and so on and so on until they turned onto Waverly Place and her disappointment got the upper hand.

"You're just taking me home?"

His brow quirked. "You have an early surgery tomorrow, didn't you say?"

She found herself staring at him, dropped her gaze, and lifted it again, unsure of herself suddenly.

He was saying, "Tomorrow will be busy for me, too. It may be late evening by the time I'm finished. Should I come by then?"

"Yes." Her voice sounded a little hoarse. "I would be glad to see you." She tugged on his hand and he looked down at her. "I'm glad to see you now, Mezzanotte."

But all she got for her trouble was a chaste kiss at the door and a promise about the next day. He was truly tired, or he was making the point that he could be patient. Something Anna had not asked him to do or be, because it was a skill she lacked herself.

◆　◆　◆

OVER THE NEXT few days Anna saw Jack often, but never for more than a half hour at a time and always in the middle of a crowd of people who wanted to see him almost as much as Anna did.

She realized that the inability to keep Jack to herself for any amount of time at all was making her cranky, but there was no easy solution. His cousin Umberto's lodgings at the greenhouse had been claimed by a different cousin whose rooms had been damaged in a fire, news Bambina shared with Anna when they met for dinner on Monday. Bambina's tone was entirely too satisfied.

Out of his sisters' hearing Anna told Jack about this. "She knows about—you know."

He raised an eyebrow in mock confusion. "About?"

The rotter.

"About the night before you left for Chicago."

And when he still pretended ignorance, she poked him so hard that he captured her hand and held it still in self-defense. He was trying not to laugh.

"They don't know anything. And if they suspect, does it really matter?"

It didn't matter, but it felt as though it did. And that irritated. She was a seething mass of irritations.

Bending low to speak directly into her ear, Jack said, "Are you feeling deprived? Because—" He tightened his hold ever so slightly. "I am."

Somehow that made it all better, and Anna went back to the dinner table with Jack right behind her, so close that she could feel the heat of his body all along her spine.

Celestina, always the peacemaker, asked Anna about the search for the Russo brothers, a subject that made both girls put aside their gifts and turn toward her.

"I'm afraid there's not anything of substance to report. We've written to forty-six—"

"Fifty-one," Rosa corrected her. "As of last night, fifty-one."

Anna smiled at her. "—different places, asylums and child welfare agencies, individuals who might have some information. I hired a young man who was once a newsboy and is very well connected to ask questions. But we've had no positive responses."

"Sixteen letters weren't answered at all," Rosa said in a low voice.

"Rosa keeps track of the correspondence," Anna explained.

"You can read English?" Celestina asked, and Rosa sat up very straight. "I'm practicing every day. Auntie Margaret says I'm making excellent progress."

"That she is," Anna said.

Lia took hold of the conversation by telling Jack's sisters about the stories they were hearing at bedtime. She got off her chair to act out part of The Boy Who Cried Wolf, so delighted with this opportunity to pass the story on that they had to laugh with her.

The little girl had managed something that had seemed to Anna too much to hope for: the tense expectation that radiated from Bambina let up and then disappeared. And another thing for which Anna was very thankful: the impromptu storytelling crowded out any questions that might have been coming her way about wedding plans.

◆　◆　◆

LATER WHEN JACK walked her home, he said, "They are trying not to be impatient, but it's hard to hold back the questions. My mother is just as bad; I get a letter almost every day."

Anna's life had always been busy. She could spend every waking hour at the hospital and never run out of things to do, and now there were two little girls, two missing brothers, Sophie's wedding, Cap's farewell, and the entire Mezzanotte clan, and the idea of her own wedding to juggle. And Jack.

"Do you belong to a lot of associations like the Italian Benevolent Society?"

He shrugged. "Two or three. When there are legal matters to deal with I'm often called in. There aren't many lawyers in the city who speak Italian."

Anna considered. The obvious question was, did he want to be that lawyer? He was not too old to read law, after all. But as forward thinking as Jack Mezzanotte might be, few men liked having their career choices challenged. Instead she said, "I should learn Italian."

"It would be helpful."

"If I can find the time."

"You have a willing tutor right beside you."

"We'll never have a moment's quiet time."

Jack squeezed her hand. "Italian lessons can happen any time. Spontaneously."

Anna was glad of a cool evening breeze on her cheeks. "On demand?"

"If there's a room available, certainly. Or a suitable hotel."

And here they were back at the original problem. Not for the first time she wondered what other people who had no place to be alone together did. The birthrate was evidence that such things happened constantly and everywhere, and not just between married people who shared a bed.

"What are you thinking?" he wanted to know.

Anna started out of her thoughts. "About privacy," she said. "And the reason people rush into marriage."

20

THREE DAYS LATER Jack said, "There's something I wanted to tell you about."

Anna looked up from the medical journal article she was reading. They were sitting in the garden while the girls played hide-and-seek. For once there were no other adults nearby.

She said, "I'm listening."

"Where's your aunt?"

Anna's brows slanted down into a V shape. "Why?"

"Because I want to tell her about it too."

"Staten Island?"

"No," he said, vaguely irritated.

"We're not going?"

"We will go, but that's not what I want to talk to you about."

"And when will that happen, the trip to Staten Island?"

He realized she was winding him up, and let out what he hoped would sound like a long-suffering sigh.

"Saturday, if you like."

"It's a long journey. At least a half day if the ferries are running on time." She paused to study the binding of her journal. "I doubt we can get back at a reasonable hour. Are there hotels on Staten Island?"

Jack bit back a laugh. "We'd shock Sister Mary Augustin right out of her shoes."

Anna's face went slack with surprise.

"What?"

She sat up straighter. "I forgot to tell you about the letter I had from Mary Irene." She recited it to the best of her memory. "There was an odd phrase," she finished. "Something like she was reassigned to the

Mother House *where she can contemplate devotion to duty and detachment from self.* What does it mean? Is she being punished?"

Jack said, "I don't think they would see it that way. They are being protective."

"Ah." Anna sat back. "They are protecting her from her own curiosity and her talent—because she is talented, Jack. She has a natural affinity for medicine."

He waited for her to come to some conclusion, and hoped she wouldn't decide to rescue Mary Augustin. He could see her doing just that, and looking to him for help.

She was saying, "I don't understand it, but I don't see what I can do, either. If she wants a different life, she'll have to walk away on her own." She glanced at him and her frown deepened. "It's a terrible waste of a good mind."

"I agree."

"Do you really, or are you trying to appease me?"

"Savard," Jack said. "Listen to me now. I'm not the kind of man who will say anything to avoid an argument. In fact, I like arguing with you. In this case I do agree."

"You agree that her mind is being wasted?"

Jack shifted uneasily in his seat. "I agree that she's in a place where her gifts are not put to good use, yes."

"Could I write to her?"

"To what end?"

She shrugged. "I could offer her a position as a nurse; she'd have room and board and a small salary. And she could apply for medical school and a scholarship, if she wants to do that. Can I write to her?"

"Believe it or not, I've never been inside a convent and I don't have any idea what's allowed and what isn't. I wasn't raised a Catholic, you know that."

"There must be a way to get a letter to her. She's not a prisoner, is she?"

"No," Jack said. "Or better said, she's not being physically restrained. But there are other ways to tie people down."

Other women liked nothing better than a compliment, but his Anna was inordinately pleased when he offered her a way of looking at something she hadn't considered. Her smile said this was one of those moments.

"It will have to wait until after the wedding," she said. "But this weekend—"

"It will have to wait until Monday," Jack said firmly. "This weekend—" It was his turn to lift a brow.

"Staten Island?"

"Have you ever been?"

"No, I've never even thought of it."

"It's a wonderful place to visit, the beaches especially. Do you have a bathing costume?"

She shook her head.

"We'll have to remedy that. I'd like to see your hair down with the sun shining on it." She looked away, but he went on. "You are beautiful, you know."

Anna was up in a flash, too embarrassed to sit still, unwilling to be admired.

"I'm going to keep telling you things you don't like to hear," he called after her. "Until you believe them."

She threw up her hands in disgust and disappeared into the house.

◆　◆　◆

ANNA DROPPED ONTO the sofa across from her aunt, who sat contemplating a swatch of watered silk, the tender blue-green of Sophie's eyes.

"Did the fitting go well?"

"She will be a stunning bride." Aunt Quinlan smiled at Anna, something of wistfulness in her expression. "It's a good thing you're here, I might have turned maudlin without you to distract me. Where's Jack?"

"In the garden hatching plans. We're going to eat with his sisters this evening, to sort through some practical matters."

Aunt Quinlan's eyes were damp, and she blinked hard.

"Are you all right, Auntie?"

"I was just thinking that the house will be very empty when you go away. And I'm wondering about the little girls, if you'll want to take them with you."

Anna drew in a deep breath and held it for a moment. "I don't want to disrupt the girls now that they are settled, and I also can't imagine leaving you to handle this all on your own. Especially if we manage to find the boys."

"You're so sure the younger one is on Staten Island, but why?"

"We know Father McKinnawae took him from the Foundling, that's the one solid piece of information we have. So I think we need to have a plan in case we do bring him home. I know you and Mrs. Lee and Margaret like having children here, but it is too much to ask. We need to talk about hiring a nurse and a maid, too, I think."

Her aunt nodded. "You've decided to move in with the sisters, then."

Anna bit back a laugh. "God, no. I really don't want to leave here. I can't imagine living anywhere else but here."

"Then stay," her aunt said. "Jack is welcome, you know that."

Anna wrapped her arms around herself and offered a small and regretful smile. "He's too much of a bull for this china shop, Auntie."

Aunt Quinlan looked beyond Anna to the parlor door. "Come in, Jack," she said. "We were just talking about your plans."

He sat down next to Anna, not quite touching. "Bull in a china shop?"

A ripple of awareness ran down Anna's spine and along every nerve. She wondered if his voice would always elicit such a physical reaction from her.

"Listening at doors, Mezzanotte?"

He flashed a smile at her but spoke to Aunt Quinlan. "I came in to see if you two would take a very short walk with me."

Aunt Quinlan reached for her cane before the words were out of Jack's mouth.

Anna got up too. "Is this what you were wanting to tell me? Where are we going?"

"Mrs. Greber's." And in response to a blank look: "Your neighbor?"

Aunt Quinlan sat down again. "Katharina Greber?"

Mrs. Greber was one of the few people Aunt Quinlan truly disliked, and her tone gave that away. Anna was glad to see that Jack had it figured out.

"I see there's some history I don't know about. You aren't the best of friends?"

Anna scrambled for the shortest possible explanation. "Aunt Quinlan believes that Mrs. Greber took—"

"—stole."

"That Mrs. Greber is responsible for the disappearance of one of Mr. Lee's prize roses. Roots and all. There used to be a door in the wall between her garden and ours—"

"Anna," said Aunt Quinlan. "You know she took that rose."

Jack said, "So you won't miss her, now that she's moved away."

Aunt Quinlan's expression stilled, and then she produced a huge and unapologetic smile. "Moved?"

"To live with a son, I think."

"And the house is empty?"

Jack's gaze settled on Anna. "For the moment. I was thinking we might want to buy it."

"Anna," Aunt Quinlan said. "If you don't kiss that man, I'll have to do it for you."

◆ ◆ ◆

THE HOUSE WAS far smaller than the Quinlan residence, but similar in style and solidly built, most likely by the same architect. Buff-colored limestone walls and a tile roof, the rooms not especially large but more than sufficient. Inside it was in desperate need of renovation and repairs, but Jack had known immediately that it would suit. The expression on Anna's face told him he was right.

She went from room to room and then outside into the garden, almost as large as her aunt's, but terribly overgrown. The symmetry made it clear that this property must have once belonged to the Quinlan parcel, and according to Jack the plat book confirmed that. Both buildings constructed in 1840 by Jonathan Quinlan, Harrison Quinlan's grandfather. In her second marriage Lily Bonner Ballentyne had married into a family with a shipping fortune and, more rare still, an appreciation for beauty.

"Mr. Lee will need help to bring this garden back to order," Anna's aunt murmured.

"There are Mezzanotte cousins and nephews enough to help," Jack said to her, but he kept his gaze on Anna. "Mr. Lee can have his pick of an army of gardeners."

Anna walked away from them into waist-high weeds, scanning the brick wall and then pointing. "There's where the garden door was taken out and bricked over. Could that be restored, do you think?"

"It could," Jack said. "I would put it at the top of the list so you can come and go easily. It will be safer for the girls too."

She swept around, her eyes so bright that he thought for a moment that she might be on the verge of tears.

"How soon can it be brought into order, do you think?"

"I'll talk to the attorney tomorrow. We can start renovations next week, after we make plans and talk about a budget. If that's what you want to do."

She strode toward him. "Of course it is," she said. "It's exactly what I want. You're exactly what I want."

Jack heard Aunt Quinlan moving away and the door closing behind her just as Anna walked into his arms.

She said, "First on that list of things to do is to get a room together where a person can take a nap." And then she sneezed, three times in a row.

"Good idea," Jack said. "Unless we want these weeds mowed down first."

She sneezed once more, a triplet of high quick spasms that made him laugh out loud.

◆ ◆ ◆

ON THE WAY uptown later in the afternoon, Anna asked the question she could hold back no longer. "How long have you had that house up your sleeve?"

He shrugged. "Just since yesterday. I saw a mover's wagon pulling away from the curb and I asked some questions. This morning I talked to the attorney and made an offer. What?"

"Before you asked me?"

"It would have sold to someone else before the day ended. Did I misstep?"

"No," she said, quite truthfully. "You stepped perfectly." And after a long moment: "This will be difficult for your sisters."

Jack touched the small of her back to steer her around a group of girls playing with a jump rope. "There may be a way to lessen the sting."

She glanced up at him. "You are full of surprises today. What are you thinking?"

"Ask for their help. Unless you want to handle the furnishing and decorating yourself, of course."

That made her laugh out loud. "Do you think they're so easily distracted?"

"Ask them and find out. But be prepared, the first question they are going to ask you—"

"A date for the wedding." She sighed.

"Such enthusiasm," Jack said dryly.

She pressed his arm. "If the house can be ready, I would say late summer. Will that serve?"

"No," Jack muttered. "But it will have to do."

21

THURSDAY MORNING ANNA woke at dawn, full of energy, and left the house without eating anything at all; to step into the kitchen would mean being caught up in the frenzied preparations for the party on the East River or the wedding. All the way to the New Amsterdam, Anna kept tripping over the idea that Sophie and Cap would be getting married in just one day's time.

Anna had avoided dwelling on what it would mean to be without her cousin for months or even years, but now she could think of little else. There was a lot of letter writing in her future, but she had discovered that she liked writing letters to Jack, and she thought writing to Sophie and Cap might be a good thing, a way to sort through all the changes ahead.

She reminded herself that she had patients to see. She tried to remember the last time she had been unhappy to have to work, and could not remember a single instance. She wondered what it said about her that at almost twenty-eight years old she had never even imagined staying away from work. There were, in fact, more interesting and even more important things in her world.

There was Cap, who would board a ship tomorrow and never come home again. Anna imagined him wrapped in blankets and looking out into a world of winter blues and whites, the cold clear air and perfect silence of the high Alps.

The urge to turn around and go spend the day with Cap and Sophie came over her and had to be dismissed; she would see her patients and then spend the afternoon and evening on the East River. The party would be a great deal of fun, everyone talking and laughing, and the noise of the celebration on the bridge would overwhelm all else. Sophie would not be there, but Jack would.

At one he would fetch her and they would go to meet the rest of the family at the ferry dock and then she would be free for an unheard-of three and a half days: not on duty or on call until Monday. After the wedding her time was her own, to spend dozing in the garden or more likely, in the new house answering questions about window hangings and linen closets while Jack and his cousins began putting bigger things to rights and his sisters went to work on the sewing machine they had already determined must be installed before everything else.

By the time Anna reached the New Amsterdam she had reconciled herself to the day ahead and could turn her mind to rounds with her students, to a scheduled surgery and a meeting, and to seeing three patients who were in decline.

She left her most difficult case for the end of the workday, so that she didn't have to feel rushed. The patient was a fifty-nine-year-old woman, unmarried and without family, who would die sometime in the next day or two because she had ignored a cut on the sole of her foot too long. Anna had amputated, knowing that it was almost certainly too late, and so it had turned out to be. Rachel Branson had led a quiet, even peaceful life, but her death would be neither of those things.

◆ ◆ ◆

ANNA FOUND HER patient sitting quietly, her hands folded over the newspaper in her lap while she looked out the window. Her bed was at the very end of the surgical ward, which provided her with a little more privacy and a view.

Miss Branson was flushed with fever, her brow and throat damp with sweat. Pain had taken up permanent residence in her face, drawing creases down her cheeks and along her mouth. Anna reached for the chart that hung at the foot of the bed and made a note for an increase in her pain medication. She hoped that Miss Branson would slip into a coma before the pain outstripped every relief medicine had to offer.

Then she sat down on the single chair, holding the chart against herself.

"I've been watching the bit of the new bridge I can see," Miss Branson told her. "Such a lot of excitement, rushing back and forth.

The president is there, according to the newspaper. It's a wondrous thing." She raised her face to look at Anna. "Are you going to the celebration?"

"Yes," Anna said. "Later this afternoon."

"With friends?"

Over the time she had been practicing Anna had learned how to deflect personal questions without giving offense, but she found herself wanting to talk to Miss Branson.

"With my family. It's a busy time for us. Tomorrow my cousin is getting married and she'll be sailing for Europe with her new husband right away."

"Oh, that sounds lovely," Miss Branson said. "Fireworks and a spring wedding. I wouldn't know what to do with my excitement."

"It is exciting," Anna agreed.

After a long moment Miss Branson said, "I would have liked to see the fireworks."

"You have a good view of the sky from this window," Anna said. "You should be able to see them."

A thoughtful look passed over the older woman's face. "Maybe," she said finally. She seemed to rouse herself purposefully. "I have a little savings," she said. "I've written out instructions for the bank, to release those funds to the hospital to pay for my care and—afterward."

Some people needed to talk about practical matters, unwilling or unable to let go of details. Miss Branson outlined her arrangements for her small apartment and what would become of her things, and Anna listened without interrupting her.

"But really what I wanted to tell you is that I have some lovely hats," she was saying. "Do you think you might like to have them?"

Startled, Anna marshaled her thoughts, but Miss Branson held up a hand to forestall Anna's answer. "They are my own work, the best of my work. I started in a milliner's shop when I was just eight years old. Six days a week, from seven in the morning to seven in the evening. At first I swept floors and at thirty I was the designer. I trained under old Mr. Malcolm and then I worked for his son and finally his grandson. My whole life in that one place. Fifty years in the same shop on the same street."

"That is a very long time."

"He's still alive," Miss Branson said. Her gaze was far away, but her tone was matter-of-fact. "The first Mr. Malcolm. Ninety-four years old but still spry, the kind of elderly gentleman who seems just as dry and tough as gristle." She glanced at Anna, who nodded that she understood.

"But terribly absentminded about everything outside his business. Even when I first knew him, Mr. Malcolm could never remember birthdays—not even his own—or anniversaries or invitations, and he mixed up his children, running through all the names until he hit the right one. Jacob-Hans-Jeb or Amity-Ruth-Josie, just like that. They laughed it off, though I think when the children were little there were some hurt feelings, now and then. I didn't see it at first but as I got older I realized that it wasn't really comical, how much passed him by. How many small good things in his life went unnoticed."

She turned her head to watch the activity on the bridge for a moment, and then she picked up her story again. "He was a strict taskmaster, but not mean. Never mean. Gruff but good-hearted, is how I think of him. My own father died young and I felt the lack, so I sometimes pretended that Mr. Malcolm was my father. I think the idea came to me because he always remembered my name, you see. His daughters he couldn't keep straight, but he knew my name. And that made me think I was a little special."

Anna was fairly sure that Miss Branson had had no visitors, though she had been admitted to the hospital the previous Saturday.

"I sent word, Monday morning. Paid a messenger to take a note to say that I was here and couldn't come in. Didn't hear back but after—after you told me my situation I thought I should write again, but maybe not. They might be closed up for the celebration. They might."

Anna drew in a deep breath and held it. The simplest of stories, and her heart was beating so fiercely she could feel the pulse in her wrists. A physician had to keep some distance, but once in a while a simple story would catch her unawares, sliding like a needle through a crack in a thimble to embed itself deeply, without warning, in tender flesh.

Miss Branson was looking at Anna with an expression that couldn't be identified. Not pain or sorrow or regret, and nothing of anger. Anna could not rail against an insensitive and cruel employer in the face of such placid acceptance. She certainly could not disturb the woman's peaceful state of mind, not now or ever.

"Things never quite turn out the way you imagine, do they," Miss Branson said, her voice low and almost amused in tone. "You have to pay attention to the moment in your hands, before it's gone.

"Now, would you have any use for my hats? I don't like to leave my bills unpaid, and you have looked after me very well."

◆　◆　◆

ANNA CHANGED INTO the summer-weight frock she had brought with her, brushed out her hair and put it up again in a loose chignon on the back of her head, changed her shoes, and picked up the straw boater that would protect her from the sun on the river. She regarded herself in the mirror. Margaret was fond of pointing out that Jack had done wonders for Anna's complexion, making it more of a subtle accusation than a compliment. Anna saw that it was true, her color was high and her skin clear. She wondered if sexual frustration could be as invigorating as sex itself, wondered what Margaret would say to this question. The idea put a smile on her face. She hadn't been alone with Jack for a very long time, but that would change soon.

It was just after one and he would be waiting downstairs. She was suddenly very impatient to see him, and had to remind herself that it would not fill patients or staff with confidence to see a doctor skipping down the hall. She thought in passing of Maura Kingsolver, the surgeon coming on shift. Fortunately there were no pending surgeries that she had to be informed about. It seemed as if Anna might really get out of the hospital on time.

Jack was talking to Mr. Abernathy in the lobby. He stood with his hands in his pockets, rocking back on his heels, his chin lowered to his chest. A powerfully built man at ease in his own skin, listening closely to an old man's story. He had been raised in a household that valued stories and the people who told them. It was one part of what made him good at his work.

He was wearing a beautifully cut suit that fit him perfectly. A summer-weight wool of a deep buff color, his jacket was open to reveal a checked vest buttoned over a soft white shirt and a copper-colored silk tie in a loose bow around a standing collar. His sisters' influence, and one way in which Anna could never compete; she paid little attention to fashion and was satisfied to let her aunt and cousin choose for her. As they had today, because it wouldn't have occurred to her that the clothes she wore at the hospital were not right for an afternoon on the river. Or not until it was too late to go home and change.

Jack looked up and caught her eye. His whole face came alive as he broke into a smile. He was here for her. That odd and wondrous thought was in her mind still when the wide front doors flew open with a tremendous crash that made Anna jump in place.

An ambulance driver appeared holding up one end of a stretcher, backing through the door carefully. Jack and Mr. Abernathy were there before Anna even realized they were moving, blocking her view while they helped maneuver the stretcher all the way in and then carrying it through to the examination room.

A young woman wrapped in bloody sheets was struggling and writhing to free herself while the ambulance doctor tried to put three fingers to her throat to time her pulse. The driver stood back, arms crossed over his chest, looking studiously bored. To Anna he said, "This one's asking for a Dr. Savard." Ambulance drivers were notoriously hard to shock and often simply rude, but Anna had no time to teach him manners.

"You're in the way," Anna said. "Step outside."

♦ ♦ ♦

AMBULANCE DOCTORS WERE employees of the police department, generally men newly out of medical college and in need of practical experience. Jack knew most of them at least by sight, but this one he had never met before.

"I'm an intern at Bellevue, Neill Graham. You're Dr. Savard?"

"I'm one of two Dr. Savards at this hospital. This lady is a stranger to me. She must be my cousin's patient."

"You'll have to do," said Graham. "She can't wait."

Anna's expression cleared, all her questions and confusion leaving her face to be replaced by a focused calm. She looked over her shoulder at Mr. Abernathy. "Is Dr. Kingsolver available?"

"Already in surgery," he said. "Room two is free."

Orderlies appeared out of a side door to scoop up the stretcher.

To Neill Graham Anna said, "It's the first operating room on the right. Please stay with her until I get there, I'll just be a moment."

Then she turned to Jack.

"I'm sorry."

He nodded, adding a half shrug. He understood very well the regret, and knew too that it would last only until she stood in front of her patient. The woman's condition would drive all other thoughts out of her mind. He said, "I'll go to the ferry dock to explain."

"I'm sorry about your day too."

She was already moving away, but she changed direction and dashed toward him, stopping short to go up on tiptoe and press a kiss to his mouth, a fleeting touch he might have imagined if not for the scent of her skin. Then she was gone, flying down the hall to the operating rooms.

Jack had almost reached the cab waiting for him when another pulled up and a man leapt down before the horses came to a halt. He wore a black wool suit despite the warm weather and a matching bowler pulled down over frizzled red hair.

"Hold on!" the cabby bellowed. "Hold on there, what about my fare?"

The man yelled over his shoulder. "Archer Campbell, postal inspector. You'll get your fare."

"I'll get double my fare if you make me chase you down for it," the cabby shouted even as the man disappeared into the hospital. "Or I'll get the police after you, postal inspector or not!"

◆ ◆ ◆

WHEN ANNA CAME in, three nurses were already going about the business of preparing the operating room and the patient, who was still struggling despite firm hands and calm words. The nurses talked to her in a studiously attentive but calm tone as they had been taught to do. As Anna herself had once learned when she was a medical student and new to this world that was now her own.

They provided Anna with information without prompting: pulse 150 and thready, temperature 104. Anna was still trying to attach the name Mrs. Campbell to a memory, a patient of Sophie's she had been worried about—when the woman shouted.

"Dr. Savard!" And again: "Please, Dr. Savard!"

Time was of the essence but a terrified patient could not be ignored. She went to stand beside the operating table.

"I am Dr. Anna Savard. I think you must be a patient of my cousin

Sophie's. I will do my best for you, Mrs. Campbell. Can you tell me about your condition? What exactly was done?" She put a hand on the woman's abdomen and flinched as she shrieked in pain, curling away from Anna's touch.

In a whisper she said, "Where is Dr. Savard?"

"She has left the hospital staff and is moving to Europe. Can you tell me what you've done?"

The woman shook her head fiercely and turned her face away.

"Mrs. Campbell," Anna said. "Your situation is dire. You must realize that. I will do everything in my power to help you, but you must prepare yourself. Do you have a message for me to pass on?"

Again the violent shake of the head. Her voice was broken and hoarse, but Anna heard her clearly.

"I want nothing now but an end to it all."

Anna said, "Nurse Mitchard, please put the patient under as quickly as possible. There is not one second to waste."

•   •   •

NO TIME TO waste, and still hygiene could not be forgotten. Anna stood at the sink scrubbing her hands and lower arms furiously, counting out the seconds to herself. Beside her the ambulance doctor held his hands and shirtsleeves both under running water and was watching the blood wash away.

He introduced himself as Neill Graham, an intern from Bellevue.

"What can you tell me?" she asked him.

"She admitted nothing. Profuse hemorrhaging, guarding, pain on rebound, in and out of delirium. I couldn't examine her properly in the ambulance but by the smell, she's septic."

"The husband?"

"Neighbor sent word, I'm guessing he's on his way."

"Dr. Savard," one of the nurses called, a note of panic in her voice. "We've got a prolapsed umbilical cord already presenting."

To Neill Graham Anna said, "Anything else?"

"Just that she wanted to see Dr. Savard."

"Thank you," Anna said. "I'll take it from here."

"Could I observe?"

Anna paused. He was young, but his demeanor was professional and his interest seemed sincere. "I may need another pair of hands," she said. "But you'll have to get rid of that shirt and scrub in properly, nails especially. Don't spare on the carbolic. Nurse Walker is circulating, she'll find you a tunic."

•   •   •

When Anna came to the operating table, her hands still damp and stinging from the carbolic acid, Mrs. Campbell had already been calmed by the ether. She was strapped to the extended stirrups in the lithotomy position, her knees flexed and canted outward, her legs and torso draped. Instruments newly out of the autoclave were arranged neatly on sterile trays. The nursing staff stood waiting for Anna to begin.

Helen Mitchard sat at Mrs. Campbell's head monitoring anesthesia. She had already started to give the patient saline injections by means of a cannula, which might make some small difference.

"Status?"

She gave a sharp shake of her head, reaffirming what Anna already knew: it would take a miracle to turn this around.

Anna folded back the draping to reveal fresh dressings that were already soaked with blood and discharge. The effluvia was enough to make her head snap back. Septicemia had an unmistakable smell, but there was also a strong odor of feces. Whoever had operated on this woman had perforated her bowel.

Anna glanced at the nurse beside her. "Nurse—"

"Hawkins," the young woman supplied.

"I'm going to need a good three gallons of saline to irrigate. And when we're done here today, I'll want to talk to you about your grasp of human anatomy." She picked up a uterine sound that would give her an idea of the extent of the damage. "This is not an umbilical cord, Nurse Hawkins. It's a loop of lower intestine."

•   •   •

Jack stopped by Verhoeven's house to tell Sophie and Cap that the family party had boarded the ferry and departed as scheduled to cruise the East River. Without Anna.

"Or you," said Sophie. "There will be some very disappointed cousins."

They sat him down to eat lunch and talk through changes to the day's plans.

Cap said, "Bring her back here when she's free. We're planning on eating on the terrace in the evening. We have a good view of the new bridge from there."

Sophie walked Jack to the door. She put her hand on his lower arm, lowering her voice.

"Cap's been pushing himself far too hard," Sophie said. "But I really would like you to bring Anna and we'll eat together. Cap and I will both retire quite early given—"

"Tomorrow."

She nodded, a little flustered. "So you two will have the terrace to yourselves." Her expression was completely innocent, but Jack had begun to figure Sophie out, and he saw something like quiet amusement in her eyes. He leaned over and kissed her cheek, felt her start and then relax.

"It's good that you and Anna found each other," she said. "I would worry about her while I'm gone, if she didn't have you."

•   •   •

IT WAS PAST three by the time Jack got back to the New Amsterdam, where he found Anna waiting for him in her office. To his gently raised brow she said, "Her blood loss was too severe and the infection too far advanced. She began to convulse and I lost her. Someday when blood transfusions are safe, cases like this one will take a better end."

Jack sat down across from her, rested his elbow on the arm of the chair and his chin on his palm, and regarded Anna. Her demeanor was resigned, as it must be, he understood, for anyone who practiced medicine.

He said, "Her husband passed me on my way out, earlier."

Anna closed her eyes. "Yes, I know."

"Very distraught?"

"Angry, I would say. Confrontational. When I told him she had asked for Dr. Savard by name, he looked at me as if I had been caught in a lie. He said, 'She has a proper doctor at Women's Hospital, she has no business in a place like this.' As if the New Amsterdam were a brothel. I was glad he didn't ask me about a cause of death. I don't think he would have liked hearing about an abortion."

"Has the coroner been notified?"

She stood and stretched. "Yes, Mr. Abernathy took care of it. There will be an autopsy and an inquest, and I'll have to testify. But not until Monday. Shall we go?"

·   ·   ·

IN THE END Anna was glad to have missed the family party on the river. Once Cap and Sophie had sailed, they would spend the afternoon together in the garden with the visitors; for now it suited her to sit on Cap's terrace in the late afternoon sun with the people she loved best in the world.

Then Sophie surprised her. As soon as Anna started to describe the emergency surgery that had caused the change in plans, her cousin went very still.

"Don't you remember, Anna? I told you about Mrs. Campbell, you must remember. It was the day you went to Hoboken in my place."

Jack sat forward, his attention suddenly focused.

Sophie was saying, "Her fourth boy, the oldest barely five, and she was terribly afraid of another pregnancy."

Anna did recall. "The woman married to the postal inspector."

"Ah," Jack said. "I crossed paths with the man when he got to the New Amsterdam."

There was a small, fraught silence in which Anna knew she and Sophie were thinking the same thing: Mrs. Campbell had asked about contraceptives, and Sophie had sent her a pamphlet, anonymously.

Sophie asked, "How was he with you?"

Anna would have liked to forget Archer Campbell, who had raged at her like a man dressing down a groom responsible for the loss of a valuable mare. She had held on to her temper and swallowed her irritation, and most of all she had subdued her own feelings about losing a patient. Campbell was condescending and insulting, but he was also newly bereaved and must be shown both patience and compassion. Nothing she said had satisfied him, and in the end he went off to see what was keeping the coroner.

"He didn't know she was pregnant," Anna said to Sophie.

Sophie inclined her head to one side as if she had something to say, but then thought better of it. Instead she hummed, a low rough sound.

"He'll never accept that she had an abortion. I can only imagine what he's telling the coroner."

Jack rubbed her shoulder. "They'll do an autopsy, won't they?"

Anna made that same soft sound, neither yes or no.

"Get used to that sound," Cap told Jack. He sat a little apart from them, wrapped in blankets even in the warmth of the sun. To Anna he seemed content and agitated all at once, as though he had just come back from a long and strenuous hike and was determined to leave on another in short order.

"Used to what sound?" Jack asked.

"That rough humming in the back of the throat. They both do it. Ask any medical question that has to do with an actual human being and their voices drop a register and all you get is that noncommittal throat clearing. I think they're taught how to do it in medical school, like a secret handshake."

Sophie gave him a half smile. "Oh dear. Who told you about the secret handshake?"

Cap turned to Anna. "How many vertebrae in the human spine?"

She considered not answering, and then gave in. "Five fused together that make up the sacrum, the four coccygeal bones that form the tailbone, then seven cervical, twelve thoracic, and five lumbar vertebrae."

"Thank you," Cap said. "I'll get out my abacus to add that all together later. Now I've been meaning to say that I've had a stitch in my side all day. Does that mean something?"

Anna and Sophie turned toward him, heads canted at the same angle, and hummed in exactly the same key. Then they exchanged a glance and laughed.

"You've figured us out," Sophie said to Cap. "Now I will have to show you the secret handshake."

"So he's right," Jack said. "You do hum when you're asked a medical question."

"I suppose so." Anna rubbed a knuckle between her brows. "It's a way to encourage the patient to talk without interrupting or giving away findings."

"The patient doesn't want to know what you're thinking?"

Anna said, "Certainly. But it's a truism that patients lie without reservation, and anything I say will only add to the confusion."

"Patients often lie for no obvious reason," Sophie added. "Most don't even realize that they are lying."

"There's a trick to it. They tell you what's wrong," Anna went on, "and you have to try to sort out what's true, what's supposition, imagination, wishful thinking, and unadulterated prevarication. So you see, you can't give your thoughts away."

"I would guess it's a lot like police work," Cap said.

Sophie looked surprised. "In a way. People who are sick often feel guilty about work left undone or the people who need them. It's one of the things that get in the way of figuring out what's wrong."

"There is some similarity," Jack said. "There are people who will confess to any crime out of fear of the police."

Anna thought again of her patient's husband. "If Archer Campbell had been able to read my mind, he might well have shot me on the spot."

Jack frowned. "What were you accusing him of in your mind?"

With some vehemence Sophie said, "A man has to be both blind and heartless to not see that the person he sleeps beside every night lives in terror."

"That's a strong word," Cap said.

"Hardly strong enough. Look at what her desperation drove her to."

Anna clapped her hands suddenly. "Too dark a subject for a beautiful summer afternoon. I came hoping for Mrs. Harrison's wafer cake and coffee."

Sophie got up. "I'll tell her we're ready."

Halfway to the French doors that opened into the house proper, she turned back. "Cap, you'd tell me if you did have a stitch in your side, wouldn't you?" And smiled, embarrassed, when they all laughed.

◆　◆　◆

THEY PLAYED CARDS and talked, about the Greber house and Aunt Quinlan's delight at the turn of events that would install Anna and Jack if not in the same house, close enough to see every day.

"It needs a lot of work," Jack said. "The plumbing and gas lines and wall sconces have to be replaced, and none of the fittings in the bedrooms are sound. I wonder that the place didn't burn down long ago."

"It's a big house," Sophie said, the corner of her mouth curling upward. "It will take you some time to fill it up."

Anna wrinkled her nose at her cousin. "Don't start."

"I've been wondering if you might like to put in a suite of rooms for a private practice," Jack said to Anna.

Anna felt her mouth fall open before she could catch herself. She closed it on a click, trying to find something sensible to say in the flurry of thoughts that were racing by.

Jack raised a brow. "Not a good idea?"

"I don't know," Anna said. "I'll have to think about it."

"You are grimacing," Cap said.

"Am I?" Anna shook her head to clear her thoughts. "I suppose I am. It's just that there are so many decisions to make. Jack's sisters have been bombarding me already about drapery fabrics and table linen and bedding."

"Poor Anna," Cap said. "Forced to choose between periwinkle and primrose, silk and brocade and linen."

"It's worse than that," Anna said. "I have to talk about prices."

"There you have it," Cap said to Jack. "Our Anna's biggest secret. Any merchant can overcharge her without fear of accusation. I think she'd break out in a rash before she challenged a price."

"I'll have to pay attention now," Anna said. "Or I'll bankrupt us before we get started, and send Jack's sisters to the poorhouse while I'm at it. He says I can't pay them or even reimburse them for materials."

"They would be insulted," Jack agreed. "And you won't put them in the poorhouse. My mother has everything well in hand."

"You see," Anna said. "I'm doomed."

"But you like the house," Sophie prompted.

"Oh, I love the house and I especially love the garden. Weeds and all."

"Then everything will work out in the end." Sophie leaned over and kissed Anna's cheek. "You must tell yourself that every morning and every evening. And Jack must remind you when you forget."

•   •   •

THEY TOLD STORIES, Jack about his family and his time studying in Italy, Cap and Sophie and Anna about their childhood misadventures, most of which put Anna in a central and less than angelic spotlight. As the sun was setting they ate a light supper of lamb, new potatoes, and peas braised in cream and dressed with mint. All Cap's favorites, which reminded Anna that it was also the last time he would sit down to Mrs. Harrison's cooking. Her appetite left her just that suddenly, and it was hard work to get down even half of what she had been served.

When Jack went to sit closer to Cap to talk about the journey, Sophie's mind turned back to Janine Campbell.

"She came to see me weeks ago, asking questions I couldn't answer for fear that Comstock was behind it. She was distraught but I didn't think she was in such despair that she would risk—what she risked. You think she aborted herself?"

Anna said, "From the angle of the puncture wounds, yes. But in the end I don't think it's possible to know unless whoever did it comes forward to confess, and you know that won't happen. The coroner will have an opinion." Anna took her cousin's hand. "It's a terrible thing, Sophie. But you have to put it out of your mind now. You have nothing to feel guilty about."

"I don't feel guilty," Sophie said quietly. "I am just terribly sorry and sad. For her and for those little boys. And I'm frustrated, that I have to admit. I may as well have been bound and gagged when she came to see me, for all the good I did her."

• • •

IT WAS HARDLY seven when Cap excused himself to retire for the night. The fireworks were still an hour off but he was wan, his hair and face damp with perspiration. They all knew what these things meant and it would do no good to point out the obvious, and still Anna found it difficult to stand back when he was so clearly in distress. If by some miracle he lived another thirty years with tuberculosis, she knew she would never be able to accept the necessity of distance between them.

She heard herself say, "Do you remember when we were little, how we napped together in Uncle Quinlan's hammock between the apricot trees?"

"I remember you turning over so suddenly that I ended up on the ground." Cap's smile was faraway and sad and still Anna was glad to have raised this image, this picture of themselves as children with no worries on a summer afternoon, able to sleep in the shade of trees heavy with fruit, simply because it pleased them.

To Jack Cap said, "You'll have to watch out for her, she's a turbulent sleeper."

"It will be my privilege to watch out for her," Jack said. "Always."

•   •   •

WHEN THEY WERE alone they sat in companionable silence for a good while.

"Sophie has always been the soul of calm in any storm," Anna said. "She is fearless when it comes to her patients; she'll confront anyone even against her own best interests. But after tomorrow her natural inclination to protect Cap will be underwritten by law. And I'm glad of it, for both of them."

"You find it hard to let him go," Jack said. "To say good-bye."

She nodded, not trusting her voice. When she had control of it again she said, "I've always wondered if what Sophie experienced in New Orleans during the war took the ability to be frightened from her."

"She had a difficult time of it, I take it."

Anna gave him a grim smile. "I don't know exactly. She has never spoken of it to any of us. I'm sure Cap knows, but I have never pressed her for the details. Someday maybe she will talk to me about it. I've been short with everyone this last week, but I'm especially sorry to have been short with her."

Jack leaned forward, took her by the wrist, and pulled her out of her chair and onto his lap.

"They'll be gone at this time tomorrow," Anna said, pressing her cheek to his shoulder. "I know that, but it still doesn't feel real."

The urge to tease her was more than he could withstand. "Just now you feel pretty real to me." He slid his hand from her waist down over her hip, and she shivered and turned her face to hide her smile.

"You make me blush like a little girl."

"You are anything but a little girl to me, Savard."

Anna began to yawn and then caught herself.

"You have a busy day tomorrow too," Jack said. "Do you want to skip the fireworks for a good night's sleep?"

After a very long pause she said, "It will be hours before anyone comes home." Her voice had gone low and a little rough. "I can't remember the last time I was in the house by myself."

The sound of band music came to them on the breeze, drums and trumpets and horns too faint to make out a melody. "Such a fine summer evening," Jack said against her hair. "It would be a shame to spend it alone."

◆　◆　◆

THEY WALKED TO Waverly Place at a comfortable pace, holding hands and talking very little. The city streets were far emptier than usual but as it turned out, the citizens of Manhattan had only migrated upward onto roofs. It seemed that everyone who had not gone to the new bridge had found a high place to perch, and voices drifted down to them now and then. Fretting children, young people excited by the novelty and the day's festivities. There were rooster calls back and forth followed by laughter.

"What is that about?" Anna wondered.

"Mrs. Roebling had the honor of crossing the bridge first, since she did all the work after her husband was injured," Jack told her. "Apparently with a rooster in her lap for good luck."

Good luck. Anna had never taken comfort in such ideas, but she wished, just now, that she could. If there was any good luck to be had in the world, Sophie and Cap should have it all.

"Where has your mind gone?" Jack's voice, low and a little gruff, set something off in her, a prickling that raced down her back to spread out and out. She pressed his hand and leaned against his arm, as if she meant to push him off the sidewalk. Jack Mezzanotte, as solid as a wall.

"I'm just where I want to be," Anna said. "Except for one odd thing. I've walked this way home too many times to count, but tonight it seems to have stretched to double the normal distance."

"You're impatient." He pulled her closer. "And that puts me in a good mood."

He kissed her, full-mouthed, intent, his hands framing her face. When he lifted his head he said, "You make the most intriguing sounds. Little squeaks and a soft clicking at the back of your throat. As if you were drinking me in."

"That's a backhanded compliment," Anna said, laughing. "If it's a compliment at all."

She tried to pull away, but he wouldn't let her. He spread his hands to span the full width of her back. "Take me to your bed, Savard, and I'll come up with compliments to make you blush for days."

They ran the rest of the way, breathless, laughing.

• • •

INSTEAD OF USING the front door they circled around to the passageway that led to the carriage house, passing the small stable and the garden sheds, the chicken coop closed up tight, an icehouse. The air smelled of newly cut grass and hay, ripening compost and flowering lilac bushes, taller even than Jack, that divided the working parts of the garden from the rest.

Anna went ahead, gesturing for him to wait where he was.

He wandered through the garden, lit by the moon and the reflected glow of the streetlamps. It surprised him still, this quiet island behind brick walls. There were fruit and specimen trees and flower beds that even his father could not have found fault with, a rose arbor overhung with vines weighed down with buds, the neat rows where vegetables had been planted.

The pergola reminded him of home, where the family ate out of doors in the warm months at a long table under a grape arbor. Someone familiar with the way things were done in Italy and southern France had designed this place, for privacy and comfort. Jack sat down on a wide chaise longue upholstered in dark velvet and piled with cushions. Shadows moved with the breeze, every leaf and shoot, blossom and vine dancing.

Jack thought, *It seems I am turning into a poet.*

Now he realized that Anna wasn't going to take him to her bed after all, but she would come to him here. They would lie down together in a bower of blossoming lilac and wait for the fireworks to arch across the sky. And he would have her here. It had been too long, and he wasn't willing to wait even one more hour.

Things hadn't gone as planned today, but it occurred to him that a doctor was the right wife for him; she really would understand when work kept him out late or took him away unexpectedly. He knew more than a few detectives with unhappy wives and sour views on marriage, something that had kept him from thinking too much about the institution for himself. Until Anna.

And now she came around the corner carrying an old-fashioned hurricane lamp, as round and bright as a sun in the new dark. It covered her in light and lifted her face out of the night, and Jack heard himself catch his breath. She had changed into a loose white gown of some fine fabric and let her hair out of its pleats and tucks so that the breeze sent it twisting and twirling around her like a dark lacy shawl.

The words that came to mind were ones he could not say. To tell Anna Savard that she looked like an angel would embarrass them both with such triteness. To say she was the most beautiful thing he had ever seen in his life would diminish the truth of it. And so he got up and went to her. He took the lamp from her and put it on the table. The pergola came to life, the crockery vase filled with white lilac and deep red Rose de Rescht he had sent from the greenhouse, the blue leather binding of a book that had been left out, the jumble of cushions, yellows and greens and pinks, that lined the chaise longue with its velvet upholstery worn thin and silky as a woman's skin.

She was looking over her shoulder into the dark garden, as if she did not trust herself to look at him. He caught her wrist, threaded his fingers through hers, long and strong and tough with constant scrubbing and still gentle enough to remind him that she was female, and fragile in ways she would never admit to him or herself.

"Look," she said, her voice hoarse as he drew her into his arms. "Look, Jack. The first fireflies."

He took his time with her, exploring skin that never saw the light of day: the backs of her knees, the soft crease between thigh and buttock, the small of her back. He pressed his face to her belly and slid up to nuzzle her breasts, suckling with a wet and greedy mouth until she gasped and tried to twist away. He would have none of it. He held her down to take what she wanted to give him, and here was another shock: she liked being at his mercy.

With some small part of her mind she realized that the fireworks had begun. Colors fell like rain in the whispering dark.

22

NEW YORK SUN

Friday, May 25, 1883

BELMONT HEIR TO MARRY CREOLE

There is great agitation among the upper classes of this city about a wedding to take place this morning at Trinity Chapel. The groom is Peter Verhoeven, Esq., son of Anton Verhoeven, a prominent Belgian architect, deceased, and Clarinda Belmont of this city, also deceased. Through his mother Mr. Verhoeven, an attorney, inherited a large portion of the Belmont fortune as well as a fine home on Park Place.

The bride is Sophie Élodie Savard, a beautiful mulatto lady, highly educated and refined in person and habit. The couple have known each other from childhood.

According to the city clerk, a marriage license has been issued. In light of this fact, members of the Belmont and related families declared the intention to disown Mr. Verhoeven should the scandalous and unnatural union go forward.

Both bride and groom have declined to be interviewed, but the *Sun* has learned that they plan to leave for Europe after the wedding ceremony and luncheon. They will travel to Switzerland, where Mr. Verhoeven will be admitted to a private sanatorium for treatment of advanced consumption. His new wife, who is a qualified physician, will attend him there.

NEW YORK SUN

Friday, May 25, 1883

MOTHER'S TRAGIC DEATH

FOUR LITTLE BOYS LEFT BEHIND

MALPRACTICE SUSPECTED

Mrs. Janine Lavoie Campbell, aged 26 years, of 19 Charles Street, died yesterday afternoon at the New Amsterdam Charity Hospital as a result of possible medical malpractice.

Originally from Maine, Mrs. Campbell was employed by the Bangor post office until her marriage to Mr. Archer Campbell of this city. The marriage was a fruitful one, producing four boys in five years.

Yesterday morning a neighbor called on Mrs. Campbell and found her to be very unwell. A police ambulance was summoned, and Dr. Neill Graham of that service examined Mrs. Campbell and declared her to be in danger of her life.

In accordance with her wishes, Mrs. Campbell was transported to the New Amsterdam Charity Hospital to be delivered into the care of Dr. Sophie Savard, who was not present. Instead Mrs. Campbell was seen and operated on by Dr. Anna Savard. She did not survive the surgery.

The coroner was notified by the hospital, and an autopsy was arranged with all speed. The report of the postmortem examination carried out yesterday evening has not yet been made public.

Confusion in this case stems from the fact that two female physicians with the surname Savard were involved in treating Mrs. Campbell. Dr. Anna Savard and Dr. Sophie Savard are reportedly distant cousins who studied together at Woman's Medical School. Dr. Sophie Savard is a mulatto. How she came to have a white lady of good family as a patient is a matter still under investigation.

Mr. Archer Campbell, a senior postal inspector and husband of the deceased, directed that his wife's body be taken to his home. This young mother of four was by all accounts a virtuous woman beyond reproach.

◆ ◆ ◆

JACK STOOD OUTSIDE Trinity Chapel watching a couple dozen people, Bonners and Ballentynes, Scotts and Quinlans and Savards greeting each other. Small groups would drift together and then apart, but nobody ever strayed very far from Anna's aunt Quinlan. The old lady stood holding the Russo girls by the hand, both of them too excited to do anything but bounce in place while she talked to daughters and grandchildren, cousins and nieces.

As he left Waverly Place the evening before he had been introduced to most of them, returning from the excursion on the river. He made excuses for Anna, who had slipped away upstairs to put herself to rights. Jack wondered what she could have possibly done to chase the flush from her neck and face, and grinned to himself.

All of the family members he had met so far were friendly, but seven-year-old Martha Bonner had assigned herself as his companion and inquisitor. She had come to the city from Albany with her grandfather Adam. Adam Bonner, as he had introduced himself, was lean and straight, with pure white hair cut unfashionably close to the scalp. It set off the warm brown of his complexion and eyes of an unusual shade that could be called golden. Jack was reminded of the glow of Sophie's skin and realized that the connection must be through the New Orleans branch of the family, though he could not think of a way to ask that would not be rude. He might have come up with something if not for Martha, who demanded his attention.

Like her grandfather the little girl had a complexion that seemed to draw in sunlight. Her eyes were a milder and deeper brown, in stark contrast to the energy that bubbled out of every pore. She wanted to know his whole name, if he had sisters and brothers, how tall he was (too tall, she announced, when he told her), if he liked eggs, and whether he had dogs. Now, it seemed, she had come to a matter of greatest importance just as he realized he had lost the thread of her conversation.

"You're not listening," she told him with a touch of impatience.

"Sorry," Jack said. "Pardon me. My attention wandered, but you have it now. What did you need to know?"

"Who is the flower girl?" And in response to his blank face: "A bride needs a flower girl. Who is Sophie's flower girl?"

Jack thought back to the chaos at the house on Waverly Place when he had stopped by just an hour ago.

"I don't think she has one."

"But she has to," Martha Bonner said. "Are you sure?"

Jack said, "Fairly sure, yes."

"Well," she said, straightening narrow shoulders. "I am Sophie's second cousin once removed. Her great-grandfather Nathaniel is my great-great-grandfather, and she has no flower girl and really, that's not the way things are done."

To his own surprise, Jack followed this reasoning. "They must be very distracted to have forgot something so important."

She nodded her approval and smiled, showing off the gap where her front teeth were coming in. "Anna says you have lots and lots of flowers at your house."

"That is true," Jack acknowledged. "But my house is far away from here."

"You could take a cab," she suggested. "I could help you find one."

"Martha," said her grandfather as he came up to hear this part of the conversation. "What devilment are you up to now?"

The elderly woman on his arm gestured to her. "Martha, child, come here to me. Nobody has introduced me to this young man, so you'll have to do it."

The girl didn't hesitate. "This is Auntie Martha Bonner. Martha Bonner like me, except old. This is Detective Sergeant Mezza—" She paused.

"Mezzanotte," Jack finished for her, "Jack Mezzanotte," and he gently shook the hand the old lady offered, aware of the swollen joints. She looked nothing like any other member of the family; there was still a touch of red in her hair, and her skin was so fair he could see a tracery of veins just below the surface.

"Aunt Martha," Adam said. "Excuse me, please. Your namesake and I are off in search of flowers." He winked at her. "So you can conduct your interview in private."

•   •   •

"YOU INTEND TO marry our Anna," Martha Bonner said, cutting right to the heart of the matter.

"As soon as she'll have me," Jack agreed. "But I may need a little time to learn all your names and faces. Especially the names. How many Martha Bonners are there?"

"Four at last count, but only two of us here today. We are a confusing family," she said, taking his arm. "So now, pay attention."

What followed was a rapid-fire sketch of the descendants of Nathaniel Bonner by three different women, one a youthful indiscretion followed by two marriages.

"But not at the same time," she clarified. "So think of the family as divided into three branches for the three women, Somerville, Wolf, and Middleton."

"And you are?"

"I married into the Middleton line," she said. "My husband was Lily's twin brother. Their little sister Birdie—your Anna's ma—was a favorite of mine."

"Lily is—"

"They call her Aunt Quinlan these days, but you'll have to ask Anna why. Now, Birdie was the youngest of the Middleton line and the twins the oldest, born some twenty years apart, mind you. Adam—" She looked over her shoulder, but he had disappeared with the younger Martha. "Is the Somerville line."

"And Sophie?"

"Sophie is Hannah's granddaughter, Wolf line. It would take paper and pencil to draw it all out for you, and that will have to wait. The bride is here." A kind of sorrowful quiet came over the old woman's face as she watched Sophie being helped down from the carriage with Anna just behind her. "She doesn't look anything like her grandmother Hannah, but she has her spirit and her mind. I hate to think of her so far away from family when she'll most need support."

After a moment Jack said, "I've come to know Sophie fairly well. I don't think anything could change her mind."

"Hannah's granddaughter," she repeated. "And Curiosity Freeman's great-great-granddaughter. Strong women with excellent minds, loving hearts, loyal unto death. It's bred in the bone."

• • •

TOGETHER CONRAD AND Cap had planned the ceremony with two things in mind: Cap was not strong enough to be in public for very long, and he needed to keep his distance from everyone, including the woman he was marrying. Somehow Conrad had convinced the rector and the vicar to go along with these requirements.

Anna was less sanguine about his decision to allow a small group of newspaper reporters into the back of the church, but she was certain that there was some strategy there. The papers couldn't be controlled, but they could be manipulated by means of favors granted. The rest of the reporters from the cheaper papers waited outside the gate that surrounded the church. Uninterested in the facts, they would write the stories that sold the most newspapers. Only so much could be handled, even by Conrad Belmont.

There would be stories about the fact that none of Cap's five aunts were present, about Cap's finances and Sophie's childhood, and worst, the public would be reminded that Cap Verhoeven was ill unto death. One more titillating fact to add to the mess of innuendo, rumor, and half truths that would be spun into headlines, which she imagined, unable to stop herself.

MULATTO LADY DOCTOR SNAGS DYING KNICKERBOCKER SCION

HE MARRIED IN SHAME AND FLED THE COUNTRY

OLD GUARD SHAKEN BY SCANDAL ON PARK PLACE

With the exception of Conrad, Bram, and Baltus, and a few of Cap's household staff, the groom's side of the church was empty until Adam noticed and migrated, taking his granddaughter and a pew full of Bonners and Ballentynes with him. Anna was glad of her family, sensible, observant, kind people who had long ago embraced Cap without hesitation or reservation and never wavered. Doubts they would have, she knew that, but doubts would not be voiced unless Sophie asked specifically about them.

Anna wanted to listen as Sophie recited her vows but found it almost impossible to concentrate. Her attention kept creeping away to roam through the church pew by pew, taking note of family members she had not seen for too long, and landing always on Jack.

He was watching her, too, and sent one of his most sincere and comforting smiles, which reminded her: whatever the newspapers printed, whatever scandal occupied the city because a white man of means had married an educated woman of mixed race, Cap and Sophie would not have to deal with any of it, and Anna would not have to deal with it alone.

As soon as the vicar had declared the couple married, Cap and Sophie started down the aisle, Cap walking with the assistance of two canes when he might have managed with none at all. He had taken them up to provide an excuse and explanation to curious strangers who would certainly note that the bride and groom never touched as they left the church. But Sophie was smiling, and there was nothing artificial or staged about the simple joy on Cap's face, now that there was a ring on Sophie's hand.

◆   ◆   ◆

THE WEDDING LUNCHEON was exactly as perfect as Anna knew it would be, because Mrs. Lee and Mrs. Harrison had had the planning of it.

The party gathered in the large formal dining room around a table that was set for two dozen people, laid out with what had once been Clarinda Belmont's wedding china and crystal and silver. Serving staff stood at attention next to a sideboard, waiting for the signal to start. Anna's stomach growled quite reasonably, she reminded herself, as she hadn't had breakfast.

She felt some of the anxious tension flow away as she sat down beside Jack; she had no work to do here, and no strangers to worry about. While the waiters served a first course of clear soup, Bram and Baltus entertained everyone with their usual irreverent observations, amusing chatter, awful puns, and worse doggerel. Most of their observations had to do with Cap, and all of them ended in the same place, with the conclusion that he had done very well for himself by marrying Sophie before anyone else could get to her. There was no talk of illness or the coming farewells.

Cap was trying, but to Anna he looked to be in pain. She watched him stifle a cough, which meant that the laudanum he took to see him through the ceremony was wearing off. Through one course and two more Anna talked to Jack and the trio of little girls—Martha had joined forces with Lia and Rosa—who came to her with one scheme after the other, and she watched Cap, comforting herself with the knowledge that in just a few hours he would be away to the docks and what she hoped would be a peaceful Atlantic crossing.

The knowledge that time was so short also made her terribly sad, and so she left Jack to his conversations with curious relatives and little girls and went to the head of the table to crouch down beside Sophie. Her cousin leaned over and pressed her cheek to Anna's but said nothing, though her throat worked.

"So, Mrs. Verhoeven." Anna put a hand on Sophie's shoulder and squeezed gently.

Sophie's smile was a little weary but there was also a deep content in her expression. She said, "I will miss you so."

"Well, of course." Then Anna pressed her mouth together to keep silent, because anything she might have been able to say would have made all three of them lose what was left of their composure. Instead she went around Sophie to Cap. He held up a hand in warning and she laughed at him, violating the perimeter he had set around himself to hug him, this bonier, slighter version of the boy and man she thought of as a brother.

"Provocative as ever," he said, grumpily.

Anna made a face. "You can't begrudge me a single hug on the day you marry. And I need another one, as you'll be gone tomorrow on my birthday."

But he turned away to cough into his handkerchief. When he began breathing again, he said, "I hope you have something better to do on your birthday than sit in a sickroom looking at me. Even if I were here to look at."

Sophie shook her head at Anna. He was at the very end of his energy and irritated with himself.

"Look," Sophie said. "Adam is about to start the toasts. It won't be long now."

The double doors at the far end of the room opened a crack, enough to let Mrs. Harrison slip in. She stood there, one fist pressed to her diaphragm in a way that spoke of distress. With her free hand she crooked a finger at Jack, who looked puzzled but not particularly concerned.

He shrugged at Anna and slipped away just as Adam began his toast with a story about Sophie and Cap. As the door opened wider to let him out, Anna saw that Oscar Maroney was waiting in the hall, and that another man, a stranger, stood beside him.

"This is about a prank that turned into a love story," Adam was saying. Later Anna couldn't recall a single sentence of what followed.

•   •   •

"OSCAR. CAPTAIN BAKER."

The captain had appeared at Sophie Savard's wedding luncheon for no reason Jack could imagine until the older man held up a distinctive roll of paper. Jack shot an alarmed look at Oscar, who closed his eyes briefly and then held up one palm. *Wait*, that palm said. But Jack could not.

"What is that?"

"Damn coroner," Baker huffed. "Useless bugger. It's a summons, as you know damn well."

He looked apologetic and even embarrassed. The captain embarrassed was something new to Jack, and far more unsettling than one of his rages.

"What's this about?"

Oscar cleared his throat. "A Mrs. Campbell, deceased yesterday," he said. "Postmortem came back this morning suggesting malpractice. Coroner Hawthorn wants to see both the lady doctors today," he added. "Seems they both treated her."

If he hadn't been so distracted, Jack told himself, he might have anticipated that the emergency surgery of the previous afternoon was likely to have quick repercussions.

"Does the coroner realize that Sophie Savard—I should say, Mr. and Mrs. Verhoeven—that they are supposed to board a ship for Europe this afternoon?"

Captain Baker cleared his throat. "He does know, yes."

Oscar gave a brief jerk of the head, a silent warning to Jack to hold back his commentary. Right now they had the captain on their side, and it was important to keep it that way.

Jack said, "Give me five minutes," and slipped back into the dining room without waiting for permission.

•   •   •

ADAM WAS COMING to the end of his toast with the attention of every person in the room firmly in hand. Every person except Anna, who was looking right at Jack. He gave her a grim smile—he would put off disrupting things as long as possible—and, turning, gestured to one of the servants who stood at the rear of the room. A man of forty or more, blank faced, not likely to make a fuss.

"I need to get a message to Conrad Belmont."

Getting a quiet message to a blind man in the middle of a boisterous party would be a challenge, but the servant inclined his head and spread out a hand, waiting.

Once Conrad had left the room to meet the two unexpected visitors, it didn't take long to explain the situation. While Jack read the summons out loud he canted his head to listen.

Dr. Anna Savard and Dr. Sophie Savard are hereby summoned to appear before Lorenzo Hawthorn, Coroner of the City of New York, on the 28th day of May, 1883, at two o'clock, in his office then and there to answer questions in the matter of the death of Mrs. Janine Campbell.

"Do you know this Hawthorn?" Jack asked Conrad.

"I've heard the name, but I've never dealt with the man. Damn me if I'm going to break up this wedding luncheon. Hawthorn will have to wait. Will one of you talk to him? Captain Baker? Tell him we'll be there by four." He turned toward Oscar and said, "Would you be so kind as to send a telegram to Cunard and let them know that Mr. and Mrs. Verhoeven won't be sailing today? Mrs. Harrison will have to do something about the luggage that's gone ahead."

Just that easily Belmont had gotten both men out of the house, and then he turned on Jack. He let out a deep sigh and pressed three fingers to his brow as if to locate a headache. "You're not on duty."

Jack said, "No. My allegiance here is to Anna and Sophie, and Cap."

"Good. Good." He was silent for another long moment. Jack could almost hear him thinking, his mind sorting through hundreds of questions and options. Jack had more than a few of his own, but he could bide his time.

"Go back to the luncheon, please, and tell them it's a business matter that wouldn't wait. You'll have to convince Anna to stay where she is, then come find me in Cap's study. There's a lot to do before four o'clock."

Conrad Belmont was a first-class litigator and brilliant attorney, but he didn't know the Savard women, not really. He seemed to think they could be kept in the dark while the men acted on their behalf.

"You'll want Anna," Jack said. "She'd be unhappy—more than unhappy—to be excluded from this business. Sophie, too, under other circumstances."

"I mean to protect them," Belmont said, clearly surprised.

"They won't thank you for it."

He lifted a hand in surrender. "Tell Anna to come along to the study, but I want to keep Sophie and Cap out of this for as long as possible."

•   •   •

THE COMING AND going did not escape Sophie, who kept her place beside Cap at the head of the table while her uncle Adam talked. First Jack, then Conrad, and finally Anna had disappeared into the hall. She watched the door but none of them came back.

Cap didn't seem to have noticed, which was proof of what she had known for the last hour: he could take no more. She herself was so weary that she could not formulate even the vaguest plan on how to put a polite end to the celebration.

Aunt Quinlan was saying, "On behalf of my beloved niece Sophie and her new husband, I thank you all for your good wishes and welcome company today. It's time that the newlyweds withdraw. They need to get ready for the adventure just ahead of them, and then I invite you all to a garden party on Waverly Place."

Aunt Quinlan had seen and understood and acted. Sophie commanded herself not to weep with relief and thankfulness.

•   •   •

WHEN THE ROOM was empty—even the servants had withdrawn to leave Cap and Sophie alone for as long as they wanted privacy—Cap let out a long, hoarse sigh. He was trying to smile, and Sophie was trying not to cry. They made an excellent couple.

The only time he had touched her today had been the moment he put the ring on her finger, but now as they rose he took her elbow. His grip was firmer than she would have expected.

"My body is failing me," he told her. "But my mind is still as it ever was. Tell me what's going on that took Conrad, Jack, and Anna out of the room."

She grimaced. "I don't know. Really, I don't."

"Then we have a mystery to solve. I suspect my study is the place to start."

• • •

ANNA SAT AT the long worktable in Cap's study and ran her hands over the polished oak. Once the whole surface had been covered with a riot of papers and pens and books; now a single sheet of paper had been laid in the middle. A summons, with her own name on it.

The men sitting at the table with her showed nothing of concern or worry, each of them so relaxed that they might have settled here to drink brandy and play poker. Anna took little comfort in this, because, as she had told Jack just yesterday evening, that aura of utter calm was a kind of camouflage that doctors had to employ too, lest they alarm patients and make things worse. Now she was learning what it felt like to want answers and get only a pleasantly blank expression.

The coroner wanted to see her and Sophie both. The idea kept surfacing like a cork in a stormy sea. Clearly the autopsy report had raised questions, and the coroner wasn't satisfied with the cause of death. Mrs. Campbell had died on her operating table, but Anna knew without doubt that she had not caused the death or even contributed to it. Any competent doctor performing the postmortem would see that, too. The coroner was a very different matter.

In Albany and Boston and every city of any size, coroners were the source of countless stories. Anna had heard many over the years, sometimes troubling, sometimes amusing, but most often just irritating for the depth of incompetence of the work done. She said something like this aloud.

"That's what happens," Jack pointed out, "when you ask a man who manufactures boilers or runs a silk factory to gather twelve of his friends to interpret medical evidence."

"Nothing they say or do is binding by law," Conrad reminded her.

"But we still have to appear when summoned," Anna said dryly.

At that moment the door opened and Sophie came in, followed by Cap.

He said, "Uncle Conrad, I hope you don't mind if we join the party. Tell me, what is that official-looking paper on the table?"

•   •   •

CAP HAD COVERED his lower face with a gauze mask and now he settled far back from the table, listening intently as Jack first read the summons out loud. Anna studied him, but she could make out little of what he was thinking.

Sophie said, "I imagined a dozen things that might have disrupted this day, from old ladies throwing themselves across the church door to"—she hesitated—"to medical emergencies. I never imagined a summons. And I still don't know what we're being accused of. Malpractice?"

"No reason to jump to that conclusion," Conrad said. "The inquiry is a nuisance and an inconvenience, but nothing more than that."

Cap said, "Comstock is behind this, I just know it."

"That may be," Conrad said. "But more likely it's the family who is agitating, in my experience."

"They are looking for someone to blame," Anna said.

Conrad inclined his head in agreement.

Today was meant to be a happy one for Sophie and Cap, but when Anna looked at them she saw exhaustion and weariness and worry. She was overcome by anger she could not give voice to, and so she leaned over and covered Sophie's hand with her own. "This is nothing more than a delay. Do you hear me, Sophie? A delay."

Sophie forced a small smile. "I have to ask again, what kind of charges might we see?"

"Nobody is being charged with anything yet," Jack said. "The coroner can only send the case to the grand jury if he finds sufficient cause to suspect something other than natural causes. At that point the grand jury may issue indictments, for anything from—"

"It won't get that far," Cap interrupted.

"It will not," his uncle echoed. "But until we know what the autopsy says, it's difficult to know how best to approach the matter."

He turned toward Anna. "We have to start somewhere. Can you tell me about the case?"

It was a question Jack would have asked before all others, had he had the chance to talk to Anna alone. She seemed to have been expecting it, because she sat up straighter and folded her hands in her lap.

"She was brought to the New Amsterdam by ambulance, near death. I took her straight into surgery but as soon as I began I knew there was nothing to be done. If you're asking me for an exact cause of death, I'm sorry to say it's not a straightforward matter. Cryptogenic pyaemia was certainly the immediate cause, and that was the result of damage to the uterus and intestines."

Conrad started visibly, and Anna realized that he really knew nothing at all about what had transpired. The idea of being charged with malpractice had not evoked for him what it did for every practicing physician: abortion.

He said, "This Mrs. Campbell died of complications of an illegal operation?"

So he was familiar with the euphemisms.

"Yes," Anna said. "An attempted abortion. Under the law it would be seen as a criminal abortion."

"If she was with child at all," Sophie volunteered.

"That's a valid point," Anna said. "So to be more exact, she died of a massive infection following from an attempted abortion. Some kind of probe or instrument was introduced through the vagina that punctured the cervix and uterus and the adjoining internal organs, most notably the descending colon. Something with a curved or oval head, with a keen but not an especially sharp edge. I am sorry to speak so bluntly, Conrad, but there's no delicate way to describe these things."

• • •

JACK WATCHED CONRAD Belmont shift in his seat, and he understood the man's discomfort. In the privacy of a shared bed he could listen to Anna talk about anything, but in company it was quite a different matter to hear her use terminology only she and Sophie would consider technical and benign.

"A curette?" Sophie asked.

"Possibly," Anna said. "Or a long-handled metal scraper or spoon of some kind."

"Do I understand correctly that Mrs. Campbell may have undergone the operation to end a pregnancy that didn't exist in the first place? And this was her own work? Self-induced?"

"I think it must have been," Anna said. "But I can't be sure; I was working as fast as possible. The doctors who did the postmortem will have more to say on that count."

"Was she unbalanced, to have done this?" Conrad asked.

Anna said, "Desperate, certainly. Unbalanced is a different matter entirely."

Conrad folded his hands on the table and was silent while he gathered his thoughts.

"I'm going to assume for a minute that neither of you has ever been questioned by the coroner before," he began. "First, you will not be under oath and you don't have to answer any question put to you. I'll speak up if I don't want you to answer. The other thing to remember—and it's something most people don't realize at all: the coroner himself and the lawyers who question you—during this hearing or at trial—are not under oath."

Jack's face was set in a grim smile, and Anna took note. She would have questions for him later, when they could speak freely.

23

ON THE WAY to the coroner's office, alone in a cab with Anna, it seemed to Jack that she had regained her calm, or at least to have gotten the upper hand over her anger.

Sophie had changed her clothes before they left for the coroner's office, but there hadn't been time for Anna to go home, and so she still wore the pretty gown she had put on this morning for the wedding. It was pale yellow with a raised pattern woven in; there was a name for it that he couldn't recall just now, and really, he asked himself, why was he worried about fashions at this moment? He wasn't, of course. His worries were elsewhere.

He covered her hand with his own and could feel how cold it was, even through her glove.

"Are you worried?"

The question surprised him. He said, "I wish we were married already."

She smiled at him. "You want some kind of legal grounding to stand beside me?"

"Married or not, nothing less than a bullet would move me from where I am right now."

She drew in a short, startled breath and pressed her forehead to his shoulder. He had robbed her of words and made her forget her question, which was exactly what he hoped to do. The simple truth was, he wasn't sure he could lie convincingly, and he was glad not to have to admit to her that he was very worried indeed.

◆ ◆ ◆

FOR SOPHIE THE first surprise came before she had even gotten out of the carriage in front of the coroner's office. Newspaper reporters—too many of them to count—were jostling for position like boys at a baseball game. They shouted questions before the horses came to a full stop, their voices clashing, tossing up random words impossible to overhear: *Dr. Savard* and *Cap Verhoeven* and *coroner* and *malpractice* and *marriage.* She wondered if the day's scandals might even warrant an extra edition.

"Don't," Cap said. "Don't engage them in any way."

"Try to keep your face neutral," Conrad said. He sat across from her, his hat resting on his lap. "Don't respond to even the simplest question. Don't scowl, but don't smile, either."

Sophie swallowed hard to make sure her voice wouldn't wobble. "I will do my best."

Cap was sitting tucked back into the corner of the leather cushions, his lower face still masked. Sophie saw now that it was flecked with a fine spray of blood.

"You should be at home," she said. "Right now, turn the carriage around and go home."

"Nonsense." The gauze mask puckered when he smiled. "I am perfectly comfortable right here. We'll drive off a ways and come back to wait around the corner. Then I'll nap while we wait. Anna and Jack are here. Best to get inside as soon as possible."

The second surprise was the coroner's clerk, who was polite and even deferential. Mr. Horner greeted them in a deep, damaged voice and bowed to Sophie and Anna solemnly, without a trace of condescension or mockery. He was a tall, cadaverously thin man, dressed in an ancient black suit carefully pressed and brushed. The knotted wide linen tie at his neck didn't quite cover a winding scar, as thick and pale as a slug, reaching almost from one ear to the other. A veteran of the war, as were most men of his age.

Anna was studying Mr. Horner too, and Sophie knew her cousin was trying to work out for herself what injury the clerk had suffered, what the surgeon had done, and whether she could have done a better job and left less of a scar. This small evidence that Anna was, as always, more interested in practicing medicine than talking about it gave Sophie a way to focus her thoughts.

The issue before them was medical in nature, and medicine was her field.

They were shown into a meeting room that smelled of stale tobacco and sweat: damp walls, peeling paint, windows grimy with soot, the floorboards warped. City Hall always seemed to be rotting from the inside out.

Conrad's clerk was already in place, arranging papers and notepads, ink bottles and pens.

Mr. Horner withdrew, closing the door behind himself, and their small party took seats around the industrious Mr. York, Conrad's law clerk, who had managed to gather a great deal of information in very little time.

"The autopsy report," he said, pushing a closely written sheet of paper into the middle of the table. "It might be best if one of the physicians read it out loud, sir."

Anna took it up, to Sophie's great relief. She thought her own voice would waver, and she didn't want to give away her fear, not even to her own people.

As soon as Anna began to read, Mr. York turned to the business of making notes, his head lowered over the paper before him.

"It's dated seven this morning," Anna said, and read on quickly, stopping to summarize. "He notes normal signs of multiple pregnancies and a recent birth. This is a very blunt, technical document, I should warn you."

"Read on," Conrad said. "You needn't worry about offending anyone here."

Anna cleared her throat and did as she was asked.

The abdomen shows a standard laparoscopic incision neatly closed which I reopen. I find a puncture wound that passed through the cervix to tear the uterine wall from horn to horn made by an instrument similar in shape to a curette or probe. After sectioning and removal of the reproductive organs, intestinal and mesenteric injuries corresponding to the uterine perforation are visible. A four-inch-long piece of the ileum is torn from the mesentery. Visceral and parietal peritoneum is filled with yellow exudate, fecal matter, serum, albumin, and approximately two quarts of pus. A displaced intestinal loop was covered by fibrino-purulent deposits.

The other abdominal organs showed no irregularities, and beyond these, none other were examined, sufficient injuries being found in the reproductive organs to reach a conclusion.

Cause of death: Shock, septic peritonitis, and blood loss due to an illegal, negligent, and incompetent operation carried out by person or persons unknown between twenty-four and forty-eight hours previous to death.

◆　◆　◆

"IT'S SIGNED DR. Donald Manderston," she finished. "I don't know the man. Sophie?"

She shook her head. "The name sounds familiar, but no."

"At least now we know why we're here," Conrad said. "The sticking point is *person or persons unknown*. Mrs. Campbell's injuries were not of her own making, in other words. They're looking for her abortionist."

"Only if you accept Manderston's premise," Sophie said, irritation blooming in her voice in a way she couldn't temper. "Will this Dr. Manderston be here to answer questions?"

"Oh, yes," Conrad said. "Here they come now. But Sophie, my dear. Leave the asking of questions to me."

◆　◆　◆

OSCAR WAS THE last man through the door, winded and windblown, a welcome face for all its ill humor. Somehow or another he had managed to insert himself into this matter, which was a stroke of luck. Another detective might not be quite so forthcoming as Oscar would be when Jack hit him with some difficult questions.

First and foremost, he wanted to know why it was that an assistant district attorney had taken a seat right next to the coroner. A district attorney meant that this wasn't a simple meeting to clear up a few questions. A district attorney meant blood in the water. In the company of police and prosecutors, the words *person or persons unknown* were as much as a red flag to a bull. The coroner's mind-set would be pivotal, and the coroner was an unknown.

Jack studied the man. He had very little to distinguish him beyond a mane of gray hair and an unruly beard. Together they hid almost every inch of skin, while pince-nez spectacles wedged between two lowering brows caught the sun and made it difficult to see the man's eyes. Jack imagined, very briefly, a barber advancing on that wealth of hair with weapons at the ready.

Hawthorn introduced everyone in the room, starting with two stout, expensively dressed men, the physician Manderston, who had done the postmortem, and someone called Frank Heath, apparently Mrs. Campbell's physician prior to Sophie. Manderston seemed half-asleep, while Heath was agitated and jumpy. He had nodded at Anna and Sophie with obvious reluctance and something far short of the courtesy professionals owed each other.

Then Hawthorn turned to his left. "And District Attorney Mayo has joined us."

Conrad Belmont sat up straighter. "This is a simple inquiry, as I understood it. Why is the district attorney here, if I may inquire?"

"I asked him to join us," the coroner said shortly. "And now I'd like to get started. This is a sad business before us, one that requires some examination before it can be settled. We'll work backward, I think. Dr. Anna Savard, you were the last physician to treat the deceased. Can you provide some information on your background and training?"

Some of the nervous energy that Anna had been unable to completely govern seemed to disappear, now that the questioning had begun. She simply provided information: what and where and with whom she had studied, her exams and qualifications, hospitals and clinics where she had seen patients, her experiences as a surgeon, organizations that she belonged to, and finally she mentioned her time studying in Vienna, Berlin, and Birmingham, England.

Jack had heard all of this before, and so he concentrated on the faces of the men around the table. There was little to make out about the coroner's mind-set, hidden as he was behind his beard. The clerks—three of them, Jack counted—wore identical blank expressions as they scratched away. John Mayo gave away only slightly more, but Heath's and Manderston's feelings about what they were hearing were plain to see. When Anna mentioned working in England with a Dr. Tait, Manderston sat up straight and pointed at her.

"Your name was familiar to me, and now I realize why. You tried to poach one of my patients. A Mrs. Drexel. You tried to get her to leave my care."

Jack saw Anna's brow crease in confusion, and then just as suddenly, clear. "You are mistaken," she said calmly, but two red spots had appeared on her cheeks. "Dr. Tait referred Mr. Drexel to me, and he wrote asking me to consult on his wife's case. I replied. I never heard from him again, and I never approached him or his wife. In fact, I suspected that letter to be one of Mr. Comstock's falsifications designed to entrap doctors."

Jack wondered if Anna and Sophie would be relieved to know for sure that the referral had not been one of Comstock's tricks. Instead it had just been a man's reluctance to let a woman physician treat his wife.

Manderston sat back, arms crossed on his chest. "So you say."

Hawthorn rapped on the table with his fist. "Dr. Manderston, please remember why we are here. Whatever issues you have to discuss with Dr. Savard must wait. Now Dr. Savard Verhoeven, may we hear from you?"

Sophie's description of her training and experience met with even less approval from Manderston and Heath, who had begun to shift in their chairs. A question from the coroner changed all that.

"Dr. Heath, you were Mrs. Campbell's physician of record until recently. How long had you been treating her?"

"She was my patient from the time of her marriage when she first came to this city. I last saw her in February, when she was near to term on her last pregnancy."

"But you didn't attend that birth."

"No," Heath said. "I had to be out of town. Miss Savard—Mrs. Verhoeven agreed to go in my place."

"Dr. Verhoeven," Conrad corrected, his voice carrying sharply.

"Dr. Verhoeven," Heath echoed with a sour twist of his mouth. "Dr. Verhoeven attended the birth. That was all it was supposed to be. I didn't think she'd have the gall to steal my patient."

Belmont said, "Dr. Heath is making unsubstantiated accusations. Unless he has evidence that Mrs. Campbell was somehow coerced into seeing Dr. Verhoeven?"

Heath frowned, but had nothing to say.

"As I thought," Belmont said. "If I may ask a question, Dr. Heath. How did you find Mrs. Campbell when you last saw her?"

He seemed ready for this question. "She was healthy, no sign or indication of trouble."

"And her state of mind?"

Now he did look surprised, as if he had never heard such a question before. "What does that have to do with anything?"

"It's not an unreasonable question," the coroner said.

"She seemed herself. Nothing out of the ordinary."

Jack sat back and folded his hands across his midsection, ready to sit through what promised to be one of Belmont's infamous wandering explorations, designed, it seemed to Jack, to extract information by artful prodding. Within a half hour he had Heath tripping over his own tongue, admitting that he didn't know about Mrs. Campbell's state of mind because he hadn't asked her, and he hadn't asked her because, well, he said, turning a hand, palm up, what difference did it make?

After a short silence the coroner turned to Sophie. "Dr. Verhoeven, you delivered Mrs. Campbell in March, as I understand it."

Sophie agreed that she had.

"Did you see her after she gave birth in March?"

"Yes, I called on her two days later to make sure she was healing, and then she came to see me in my office some weeks ago."

All heads came up abruptly.

"I don't think I had that information," said Hawthorn. "She came to see you in your office, for what reason?"

"She asked me to examine her."

"Aha. And what were your findings?"

"She was a healthy young woman about a month postpartum. That is, she was physically healthy, but very melancholy and even despairing."

"As is common after any birth," Heath interjected.

"Not to this degree," Sophie contradicted him.

Heath gave a dismissive wave of the hand.

The coroner said, "Did she give a reason for her state of mind?"

Sophie didn't hesitate. "She believed herself to be with child, and she was terrified about another pregnancy so soon."

"She said that exactly?"

"No," Sophie said. "As I remember her words, she said, 'I just can't have another baby so soon, it will be the end of me.'"

Jack saw no surprise or even concern on the faces around the table, and for the first time got a sense of what Anna and Sophie meant when they talked about men's willful blindness.

"Mrs. Campbell was with child." The coroner was asking for confirmation of what he believed to be true, but Sophie was not so easily led.

"She may have been," she said. "But it was too early to tell by examination."

"She had an active imagination." Heath ignored the sharp look that Sophie sent him, and Hawthorn seemed not to notice.

He said, "Did you operate on Mrs. Campbell, Dr. Savard?"

Conrad cleared his throat.

"Pardon me," the coroner said. "Dr. Verhoeven."

"I did not," Sophie said.

"Did she ask you for the name of someone who would perform an abortion?"

"She did not."

"Did you volunteer names of such persons?"

"That is a leading question," Conrad said. "Please rephrase, or I will instruct my client not to answer."

"I'll let it go for the moment. Dr. Savard, you did operate on Mrs. Campbell."

"Yesterday," Anna said. "Yes."

"And previous to that?"

"I never saw Mrs. Campbell previous to her arrival at the New Amsterdam yesterday."

"You've read Dr. Manderston's report. Do you agree with his finding on the cause of death?"

Jack was glad that they had finally come to the heart of the matter. It seemed Anna was glad too, because she spoke in the calm, matter-of-fact voice she had used in her laboratory classroom. "I found Dr. Manderston's observations to be similar to my own, but I don't agree with his conclusion that an operation was carried out by person or persons unknown."

Mayo leaned forward, his long nose twitching as if he had caught the scent of something interesting. "The operation was legal?"

"Don't answer that until and unless District Attorney Mayo clarifies what he means by 'operation,'" Belmont said.

Mayo inclined his head. "Would you say that Mrs. Campbell underwent an abortion?"

"I couldn't say that with certainty," Anna said. "It's unclear to me whether she was pregnant in the first place."

"You wouldn't recognize pregnancy at this early stage upon opening the reproductive organs?"

"If the uterus had been intact, certainly. But the damage was extensive, and at least a day old."

"Then let's say it this way. Did she undergo an attempted abortion?"

Anna looked the man directly in the eye. "In my professional opinion, the procedure in question was meant to interrupt a pregnancy. If there was a pregnancy. When undertaken for that specific purpose, such operations are illegal. As you well know."

Mayo was running a finger back and forth over the tabletop as if he had found something etched into the wood that he needed to understand. To Jack it looked like a mannerism developed to distract and disorient a witness, but he had misread Anna if he thought she was so easily unsettled.

Mayo said, "You have never performed this operation yourself?"

"Do not answer that," Belmont said, sourly. "It's not relevant to the case at hand."

"I agree," Hawthorn said. And: "Dr. Savard, on what point exactly do you disagree with Dr. Manderston's findings?"

"I believe Dr. Manderston was incorrect when he wrote 'person or persons unknown.'"

Mayo widened his eyes in mock distress. "You know who operated on Mrs. Campbell? If you had said so to start with, we wouldn't be sitting here."

Anna looked at Manderston for a long moment, then spoke to him directly. "In my opinion, Mrs. Campbell's injuries were self-inflicted."

Heath gave a startled laugh. "That is utterly ridiculous."

"I would say patently impossible," Manderston volunteered.

The coroner raised a brow in Manderston's direction. "As I understand it, many women perform such operations on themselves, and often with success."

"Not in this case," said Manderston. "This was no simple scraping gone bad. The damage was considerable and the pain would have stopped her."

The coroner looked at Anna. "Dr. Savard?"

"The pain might well stop a man," Anna agreed.

Sophie said, "Desperate women are capable of even worse."

Heath snorted openly. "In your extensive experience, I suppose you've seen worse?"

"I have," Sophie said. "But then I work mostly with the poorest women, and desperation is the rule rather than the exception." She looked from Manderston to Heath and back again. "You would have less experience of this kind at your hospital."

"I was practicing medicine before you were born," Heath said, his lip curling.

"Of course," Sophie said. "But in the homes of the rich or in your own clinic."

"Mrs. Campbell was my patient, if I may remind you."

"And she left your care."

"Because she knew I wouldn't perform the operation she wanted."

"Because she was terrified, and knew you didn't care."

"Coroner Hawthorn," Heath barked. "I will not be spoken to this way by a—by a—" He coughed and sputtered as he pushed himself out of his chair.

"Sit down, Dr. Heath," Hawthorn said. "We are almost finished here. I see no option but to convene a coroner's jury to decide if this was an accidental suicide or a death following from malpractice."

"Or both," Manderston muttered loud enough to be heard throughout the room.

"We'll meet on Monday," Hawthorn went on, ignoring him.

Sophie rose immediately and leaned over to Anna, putting a hand on Jack's shoulder to draw him into the conversation. "I must go down to Cap," she said. "And get him home and into bed. Will you call later?"

"Not this evening," Anna said. "You are in desperate need of rest, too, Sophie. Let's let Conrad do his work, and we can talk over the weekend. We have until Monday to work out a strategy."

They turned to look to the front of the room, where the attorneys and clerks and coroner were deep in conversation.

"What is that about, do you think?" Anna asked.

Jack said, "Belmont will be insisting on a second autopsy, and no doubt he's arguing about the jurors. In other cases like these he would want as many doctors as he could get—"

He broke off, and Anna took up what he had been reluctant to say. "But not in our case. Not male physicians, at any rate, to sit in judgment of us."

"Then who?" Sophie asked. "May we suggest names?"

"I think that you should," Jack said. "Give them to Conrad as soon as possible, and let him steer things in that direction."

"I'll do that," Anna said to Sophie. "You go on to Cap, and give him my love. Tell him Conrad has things well in hand."

"I will," Sophie said. "Though I don't quite believe it myself."

24

NEW YORK TIMES

Friday, May 25, 1883

EVENING EDITION

CORONER'S JURY TO EXAMINE TWO WOMEN PHYSICIANS IN CONNECTION WITH THE DEATH OF JANINE CAMPBELL

Just one day ago, while the rest of the city enjoyed the fireworks display that closed the ceremonies for the new East River Bridge, an autopsy was performed at the New Amsterdam Charity Hospital. The deceased, Mrs. Janine Campbell, a married lady of respectable family and mother of four small boys, died earlier yesterday. The postmortem examination revealed evidence of malpractice.

The physicians subpoenaed for questioning in connection with this case were Dr. Sophie Verhoeven, who attended Mrs. Campbell at the birth of her fourth son in March, and Dr. Anna Savard, the surgeon on duty when Mrs. Campbell arrived at the New Amsterdam yesterday.

The two lady physicians are distant cousins who grew up together on Waverly Place. Sophie Savard Verhoeven, a mulatto, was born in New Orleans and came to New York as an orphan in 1865. Both women are graduates of Woman's Medical School and properly registered at Sanitary Headquarters.

Drs. Savard and Verhoeven met with Coroner Lorenzo Hawthorn at his offices this afternoon, accompanied by their attorney, Conrad Belmont, Esq., to answer questions arising from an autopsy performed by Dr. Donald Manderston of Women's Hospital. Subsequent to that meeting Coroner Hawthorn announced he will convene a jury. Jurors will decide if Mrs. Campbell's death can be attributed to criminal malpractice on the part of one of the doctors who treated her. Such a finding would cause the doctors to be bound over to the grand jury to determine whether indictments are called for.

NEW YORK WORLD

Friday, May 25, 1883

EVENING EDITION

MULATTO BRIDE TO FACE CORONER'S JURY

As reported in the early morning edition of the *Post*, Sophie E. Savard, married this morning to Peter Verhoeven, Esq., the wealthy son of one of the city's most noble families, has been instructed to appear before a coroner's jury on Monday. The deceased is Mrs. Janine Campbell, a young woman who was in Dr. Savard Verhoeven's care at the time of her death by malpractice. Also being questioned is Dr. Anna Savard, the last physician to treat the victim on the day of her death.

Accordingly Mr. and Mrs. Verhoeven have postponed their departure for Marseilles.

•   •   •

ANNA TOOK A cab to the Staten Island Ferry at the foot of Whitehall Street early Saturday morning, where Jack was waiting. He kissed her cheek and took her Gladstone bag and valise, bought tickets, and found seats quickly and without fuss. Anna, ill at ease and out of sorts after a poor night's sleep, took exception. He seemed untouched by the events of the previous day, good and bad both. It set her teeth on edge.

When they had settled in for the journey Anna thought that he would raise the subject of the inquest, and was both relieved and irritated when he did not. Instead he talked of a letter from his mother

and an ongoing rivalry between two sisters-in-law that had to do with
what he called tomato gravy, Uncle Alfonso's complaints about the
utter lack of logic in the way English was spelled, and Oscar's landlady's dog who had produced six puppies in the middle of the night
without uttering a sound. Or maybe, Jack suggested, Oscar's consumption of beer had had something to do with his undisturbed sleep.
Comforting, easy conversation that had nothing to do with death or
postmortems or the Comstock Act. There was no talk of Sophie or
Cap, and really, she reminded herself, hadn't she just this morning
wished to have a day she could spend with Jack alone?

When there was a pause in his storytelling Anna pointed something out. "You're trying to rob me of my mood."

Jack stretched out his legs and crossed his ankles, put his hands
behind his head, and tilted his face to the salt breeze. He grinned
without looking at her.

"How am I doing?"

Anna bit back her own smile but conceded defeat; it was too fine
a summer morning to fret over things that could not be changed or
even prepared for. It all had to be left to Conrad Belmont, for the
moment at least.

"Surprisingly well."

"That's a relief. It's bad luck to scowl on your birthday."

Anna closed her eyes and put her head back. "Sophie has been
telling tales."

"It's not your birthday?"

Anna hummed.

"You don't want any presents, she told me. You dislike birthdays."

"True."

"I like presents," Jack said.

"Is it your birthday?"

"It is not, but if you're not using yours—"

Anna turned toward him. "So what is it you want for your not-
birthday?"

"I'll think of something," he said. Then he roused himself to take a
wrapped package from his valise while he talked about progress he had
made arranging repairs to the old Greber house. Except he didn't call it
the old Greber house or *my new house* or even *our new house*, but *Weeds.*

The Russo girls had given the new house that very odd name to distinguish it from Aunt Quinlan's, now renamed Roses, as in *We're going over to Weeds to play*, or *They'll be wondering about us at Roses*. Without comment or discussion, everyone had taken up the new names. Anna feared that even after Mr. Lee had transformed the neglected garden into a showpiece the name would stick. In fifty years, quite likely, few people would remember why.

He handed her the package wrapped in brown paper.

"Not a birthday present," he said. "Wallpaper samples. My sisters want to know what appeals to you."

Anna unfolded the samples and spread them out on her lap. Huge fussy sunflowers against a background of maroon and brown, scrolling agapanthus in olive greens and grays, cabbage roses in pink and red rioting over a trellis interrupted here and there with blue globules that were meant, she thought, to be songbirds. She folded the samples and retied the bundle while she thought.

She said, "Do we have to have wallpaper?"

He let out a relieved sigh. "Maybe together we can convince my sisters that we don't. I'd get a headache looking at any of those every day."

"Tell them—never mind, you shouldn't have to speak for me. I'll take them to a friend's house that I admire. Maybe that will be enough."

"Friend?"

She looked at him closely. "You sound surprised."

"Not in the least," he said. "I'm just remembering you told me once that you didn't have many friends."

"It's very rude of you to remember everything I say." She made an effort to sound severe and produced only an indigent huff. "And I do have a few friends. This one's name is Lisped; her daughter went to school with us at the Cooper Union. Annika married a Swede and moved back there, but her mother is still here."

"Wait, you and Sophie went to the Cooper Union? I thought they only taught classes for adults."

"The institute has a class for the children of faculty members. Aunt Quinlan taught drawing and painting, Cap's uncle Vantroyen taught engineering, and Annika's father taught mathematics. That's how I met Cap, at a lecture the grown-ups went to hear, before we even started school."

"You've never told me much about any of this."

"Haven't I?" Anna considered. "I don't think the stories are anything out of the ordinary. We were overindulged, I suppose, when it came to school. Any curiosity was to be encouraged, and everything was a game, from mathematics to Latin. We took every opportunity to go off on our own to explore. Annika and her brother Nils sometimes joined us.

"But my point was, I very much like her mother's house. Lisped is someone I admire greatly. If there's time to go visit, I wonder if your sisters would be shocked."

"They might surprise you."

Anna thought, *That would be nice.*

For a long time they didn't talk at all, and Anna was free to take in the ocean air and the sun on the water, and the promise of what just might turn out to be a perfect day. Little by little she was aware of her mood floating away from her to disappear without a trace. She let out a breath she hadn't realized she had been holding, put her head on Jack's shoulder, and fell asleep. It was such a deep sleep that she was disoriented when he woke her an hour later, his breath on her ear sending a shiver running up and down her spine.

He said, "Vanderbilt's Landing, Savard. Rise and shine."

• • •

"You know, you could call me Anna at this point," she told him as they made their way from the ferry landing to the Stapleton train station. As they walked she was scanning the shoreline and all the mansions that overlooked the sound, the homes of men who traveled to Brooklyn or Manhattan by ferry, mornings and evenings.

He said, "You still call me Mezzanotte for the most part."

"Because I like the sound of it. If your last name were Düsediekerbäumer or Gooch or Quisenberry—" She shrugged.

"You would never have talked to me at all?"

"Well," she said, stepping neatly away. "Of course I would have talked to you. But I couldn't marry someone with the name Düsediekerbäumer. In fact, it's odd that I'm marrying anybody at all. I didn't think I ever would."

She was in a lighter mood, even playful, but not far beneath the surface she was still exhausted. Standing next to him on the platform she almost swayed in the breeze, blinking owlishly in the bright sun.

"What about Anna Mezzanotte, do you like the sound of that?"

She jerked and came fully awake. "Um," she said.

Jack had wondered if this would be an issue, if she would resist taking his name. He hoped he wouldn't have to convince her, because this was one point on which his parents—his father, most especially—would balk.

"I have a suggestion," he said before she could think how to respond. "But let's wait until we've found our seats."

As soon as the train jerked its way out of the station she said, "Your suggestion?"

"As a doctor, you will want to remain Dr. Savard, I understand that. But at home, and when children come along—"

"They would have your last name, of course." Relief flooded her expression. "I thought you would be unhappy about—my professional name."

He shook his head, thinking, *Pick your battles.* He said, "At home you're one woman and at the hospital, another."

She collapsed, boneless, against her seat back, and yawned again. "I don't seem to be able to keep my eyes open."

"Then sleep," he said, leaning a shoulder toward her in invitation. "Anything exciting happens, I'll wake you up."

She laughed, rubbing her cheek against his jacket as if to find the right spot. "I wonder what would count as exciting on Staten Island. A deer on the tracks?" She had other questions about the route—if the train line ran close along Raritan Bay, whether there might be time to walk on the beaches later—and then she was asleep again without waiting for comment or answers.

He put his arm around her to hold her steady against the sway and lurch of the train and looked up to see that they were being observed by two old women—farmers' wives, almost certainly, by their faded sunbonnets and aprons. Watching Anna sleep as attentively as they might have watched a play on the stage. Sleep robbed her face of its fierce intelligence and turned her into nothing more or less than a woman in the full blush of her youth at rest, innocent, almost otherworldly. Then the women turned to look out the window, and the moment passed.

For a moment Jack weighed the idea of getting the *Times* out of his valise, and then remembered the article just under the fold on the front page, where Anna's name figured so prominently. She might not have seen it. He hoped she had not. Even more, he hoped she hadn't seen the *Post* or any of the other rags that were having such a good time dissecting the Savard women. Tomorrow would be soon enough for all that, or the day after. For today they were free of everything and everyone.

They traveled along Raritan Bay for a while, slow enough to take in long stretches of dunes that revealed and then hid the shore where oystermen were hauling nets. On the horizon he could just make out boats like smudges of paint shimmering in the sun.

According to the train schedule the journey would take an hour, which Jack soon realized was more a fanciful guess than a statement of fact. He watched passengers amble along to get on and off as if they had never heard the word *timetable*. At one stop the conductor sat himself down on a convenient pile of luggage and launched into what looked like a serious conversation with the stationmaster, pausing only to light his pipe. So close to Manhattan, and a different world altogether, different from Greenwood, too, in ways he couldn't quite pinpoint except that Greenwood was home.

Stapleton was a proper town, but the rest of the interior of Staten Island would be like this: farms, forest, wilderness. The next stop was in a village spread out around the train station like an apron: pretty, slightly tattered, and very quiet but for the huff of the train engine. A stand of tulip trees cast shade over the road where a leggy girl in wooden clogs was herding a couple of goats along the road. The baby balanced on her hip had one small fist knotted in the sleeve of her dress.

On the other side of the train tracks orchards spread out, apricot and plum and cherry in bloom, swaths of white and pink and red as far as he could see.

The stops were ten or twenty minutes apart, interrupted for long stretches for no apparent reason. Every station was simpler and smaller than the one before, with less of a village around it. The stretches of forest got longer, crab apples scattered between cedar and gum trees, their petals floating on the breeze. Passengers came and went, greeted each other, and talked in the way of people who knew each other's parents and grandparents, secrets and foibles. Anna slept through all of it, unaware.

He had been told that Pleasant Plains was the stop closest to the new mission at Mount Loretto, but Jack bought tickets for Tottenville, two stops on, a more substantial village and the final train stop on the southernmost shore with another ferry station, this one with service to Perth Amboy in Jersey. In Tottenville he hoped they would be able to find lunch and directions and a livery stable to rent a horse and trap and then, finally, a hotel, if fate was kind.

When the conductor came through calling out *Tottenville, end of the line, Tottenville!* Jack got some basic information: the name of a restaurant where they could get a good lunch, and, when Jack mentioned they would be going to Mount Loretto, the news that Father McKinnawae had gone to the city just this morning, traveling north to the ferry on this very train. He wouldn't be back for a couple of days, some kind of emergency at his Mission of the Immaculate Virgin, but then wasn't that always the way with those street arabs. McKinnawae was a saint, papist or not, and you couldn't convince Tom Bottoms any different.

"There's nobody at Mount Loretto at all?" Jack asked.

"Didn't say that, did I. The place is overrun with monkish types, you know, brown robes and bald spots"—he took off his hat to point to his own pate, shiny with perspiration—"they give themselves, on purpose. Like a hive of worker bees," said the conductor. "Work till they drop."

•   •   •

WALKING TO THE inn for lunch, Anna wondered why she wasn't more upset. All this way for no good reason. Of course they would still go to Mount Loretto and ask questions, but the chance of real progress seemed unlikely. They might just as well turn around and go back to the city, but neither of them raised the subject, and Anna was glad. The very idea made her head ache.

The restaurant was more of a café, just a few tables and a lunch counter where older men hunched over coffee cups and slabs of pie. They got the last free table, one that overlooked the ferry terminal. Through windows polished to a high shine Anna watched seagulls wheeling overhead calling to each other in voices that had always struck her as forlorn, even in such bright weather.

"We can go to Mount Loretto this afternoon," Jack said. "And find a beach to walk on, after. Take a nap somewhere in the shade. Maybe I should write a thank-you note to McKinnawae for not being here."

Anna thought of saying what came to mind: maybe it was time to give up. The Russo boys were gone, they could only hope to good families. But instead the waitress came, and they ordered oyster stew—the freshest on the island, they were told—thick with potatoes and carrots all jumbled together in a silky broth, served over great rounds of delicate buttery pastry.

"I can't eat all this," Anna said, and then proved herself wrong. She stopped just short of the last spoonful, which Jack was glad to finish off. And he was still hungry; that was obvious by the way he was sizing up the row of pies kept under glass domes. He ordered lemon meringue and offered her a taste on his fork, smooth and tart and sweet all at once.

What an oddly intimate thing, to eat from the same fork. Anna let the pie rest on her tongue, enjoying the flavors and textures, and enjoying too the way Jack's eyes were fixed on her mouth and then her throat as she swallowed. There was no sheen of perspiration on his skin but still she thought there was a scent, maybe one that she alone could perceive. She was aware of the beat of her own pulse at her wrists and at the base of her throat and low in the very core of her being.

They were almost finished when a cranky toddler sitting with his parents at the next table let out an impatient bellow and launched himself out of his chair, so abruptly that neither mother nor father had any chance of catching him. He hit the floor chin first, and bounced to his feet like the three-year-old rubber ball he was.

For one second there was silence all around and then he realized that a sheet of blood was pouring off his chin. To Anna's ear it was clear that he wasn't howling in pain, but outrage, to have been so thwarted. His parents, on the other hand, looked as though they might swoon.

Anna got up.

"May I have a look? I'm a doctor." And at their confused expressions: "A physician."

At first she thought they would send her away, outraged at such an obvious lie. Then common sense won out, and the young man with a face almost as smooth as his son's picked the boy up and thrust him into her arms. Anna sat down with the boy on her lap, angled so that he would bleed on his already ruined clothes rather than her own.

"His name is Ernst," the mother offered, her hands fisted together as if she had to fight the urge to snatch him up and away.

Jack had already brought her bag over and opened it for her, crouching beside it and waiting to hear what she might need.

"My goodness," she said to the little boy called Ernst, and pointed to an invisible spot on the floorboards. "Look at the hole you made in the floor. You must have a very hard head."

Startled, he stopped his wailing and considered the floor. While Anna blotted away the blood with a square of gauze, she talked to him in a calm voice, offering observations that made him forget how insulted he was supposed to be.

"There," she said, gesturing to his parents to come closer. "He's sprung a leak, but just a small one. No need for stitches. It just needs disinfecting and a plaster to keep it clean."

Anna looked up and caught sight of Jack watching her, his expression open and frank and unmistakable: he really did love her. She had wanted to believe it, she had set herself the task of believing it, but now she saw it as clearly as she saw the face of the little boy in her arms, round cheeks and sea-green eyes still full of tears.

Ernst looked at her solemnly and said, "I made a hole in the floor?"

◆　◆　◆

IT WAS THE waitress who warned them about Mr. Malone at the livery: he liked a nap in the early afternoon, and never in the same place.

"Calling his name will do you no good," she said. "On a good day he's mostly deaf, and he hasn't had a good day in a year or more."

"Now, Nell," called someone from the other side of the room. "Don't be telling tales. Your old dad always shows up by two bells."

She laughed. "Me dad can't hear the bells. But," she admitted, Jack thought with some affection, "he shouldn't be too long now."

◆　◆　◆

MR. MALONE DID appear in fairly short order, with wisps of hay in his sparse gray hair. Shouting, they managed well enough to rent a horse and trap, but by that time it was already half past two, and they still didn't know exactly where they were going.

"We'll have to go someplace else to ask directions," Jack said.

But Anna had other ideas. She produced a pencil and a piece of paper and put them on the counter in front of the old man. On it she printed in clear letters: *Please draw a map to Mount Loretto.*

You would have thought she had handed him a hundred-dollar bill, he was so pleased to be able to help. In five minutes they had a decent map, with roads marked. Anna gave the man a fifty-cent piece, and he winked at her.

"I was starting to think this whole undertaking was doomed," Anna said, once they set off.

Jack bumped her with his shoulder. "Got to have more faith than that, Savard."

For a few minutes the chestnut—young and up to tricks in the fine weather—demanded his full attention, and by the time he could look at Anna, she was focused on the view. He wondered what he had missed, because it seemed, just then, that she was holding back something she could not quite bring herself to say. But he wouldn't press, not on such a fine afternoon. They passed a small farmstead surrounded by dogwood and mountain laurel in trembling first blossom. Geese were busy looking for worms and slugs in a newly turned garden plot, stark white against the dark soil.

Jack pointed out a stand of shrubby persimmon trees covered in waxy white blossoms, Pinxterbloom azaleas, violas and violets.

"I couldn't name more than three of the hundreds of plants I'm seeing," Anna said. "But to you they all have personalities."

"I suppose that's true," Jack said. "My mother talks about plants that way, as if they had minds of their own."

"Do you think she'll approve of me?" She asked the question lightly, but she was anxious. As Jack knew he would be anxious if her father were alive and unknown to him.

"Yes," he said. "I really think she will."

"Even if I'm the cause of your sisters going home?"

"She'll love you all the more for that," Jack said. "She'd like to have them home."

Anna hummed. He looked at her and saw an expression that was doubtful and suspicious both.

"What if your sisters don't want to go back to Greenwood?"

He said, "Unmarried young women do not live alone. It's an unwritten but sacrosanct law in Italian families. If something should happen to one of them, it's the men in the family who are seen as having failed."

After a long and almost tense pause she said, "We would have room for them in the new house."

He heard himself draw in a sharp breath. "You're not serious."

"No," Anna admitted. "But the possibility should be discussed, at least."

"They will make you crazy."

"Maybe," Anna conceded. "But I am at work all day, and I don't have time to cook and clean. If they are willing to keep the house—"

"I don't want to share you with my sisters," Jack said. "And we can afford a housekeeper."

They had had a frank discussion about money: earnings and savings and property. In return for surrendering his interest in the family farm Jack had a share in the commercial end of the business in the city, which bolstered the modest salary he drew as a detective sergeant. Anna's father had liquidated his property in New Orleans long before the war; the estate had gone to her brother, and then it had come to her. If not for the 1873 panic and the depression that followed they would be moderately wealthy; as it was, they were far better off than most of their generation. They wouldn't be building mansions on Fifth Avenue, but that would be true if they had as much money as the Astor and Vanderbilt families combined. They could afford a housekeeper, and they would need one, of that there was no question.

She nodded in reluctant agreement. "The thing is, if they are forced back to Greenwood because of me, I'll never have a chance to win them over. What?" she said. "You look surprised."

"I didn't think you ever worried about things like that. What people think of you."

"Of course I do," Anna said. And then, when he held her gaze for a moment: "Well, all right. I might not worry about what a store clerk thinks about my boots or what the district attorney thinks about my education, but this is your family we're talking about. Your mother, above all. I would like her to be happy for you. Which reminds me—"

Jack tensed.

"—You must have had some pressure to marry before this point. Did they pick you out a wife?"

"As a matter of fact," Jack said, and it was Anna's turn to tense.

"You can't be serious."

"Let's just say that I've been introduced to a number of young women my mother took a liking to. All Italian, of course."

"And Jewish?"

He lowered his brow in thought. "Two of them were, if I remember correctly."

"And you declined?"

"Of course I declined," Jack said. "Did you think I had a wife squirreled away somewhere?"

"You didn't like any of them?"

"I liked them well enough."

"Pretty?"

"Oh, no," Jack said. "We're not going down that road."

"Ha," Anna said. "You opened the door, and I'm not going to let you shut it so quickly. So your mother—"

"Not just my mother. Aunts, cousins."

"I see. So they found you a good Italian daughter, a pretty girl brought up to keep house and produce babies. So why do you think they'll approve of me?"

"Because they are my people," Jack said. "Because they want me to be happy, and you make me happy. It's that simple."

She didn't want to smile, but couldn't help herself. Anna wondered, in one part of her mind, why she was pursuing such a difficult subject today, of all days. As a little girl she had often provoked even gentle people to outbursts of frustration. Over the years Aunt Quinlan had curbed this impulse, so that as an adult she could resist, in most situations.

"I'm being difficult," she said to Jack now. "And I'm not sure why. I apologize for needling you."

Jack took this in with his usual calm expression. "You're nervous about the Russo boy. If he is here, we could be taking him back to the city. Of course you're nervous."

"That might be true, if Father McKinnawae were here, but he's not." And Anna was thankful, but kept that to herself.

They came over a rise to see Mount Loretto—or what would one day soon be Mount Loretto—spread out before them.

There were a half-dozen buildings, some barely begun, others almost finished, set around a large square with the foundations of a brick building, most likely a church by its shape and size. Some dozen men were at work, all of them wearing rough brown robes. On the far side of the main development, more men were at work on a barn while still more drove oxen as they turned under meadow. Great piles of lumber and brick and shingles separated the clearing from a wood.

"Monks," Jack said, before she could ask the question. "Franciscan; I think there's a monastery not too far away. Look, it's right on the bay."

He pointed and Anna saw the glint of sun on water through a stand of trees.

"This is a huge undertaking. It's overwhelming," Anna said.

"The Catholic Church," Jack agreed. "They move mountains when it suits them. Should we ask for a tour?"

"We've come this far," Anna said.

$$\bullet \quad \bullet \quad \bullet$$

THEY WERE DIRECTED to one of the buildings that was almost finished, with a makeshift office on the ground floor. One wall of shelves was already filled with overstuffed binders, all neatly labeled. Under a single window a desk was heaped with file folders and correspondence boxes. A thick wad of receipts and bills of lading and orders had been threaded onto a long nail driven through a block of wood. A small jug held pencil stubs and a few pens, the nibs in clear need of attention.

In the middle of the room a monk leaned over a table where a set of architectural drawings had been rolled out and secured with bricks. He was making notations with a pencil, working with his nose almost pressed to the paper.

He looked up at the sound of Jack's knock, his expression friendly and welcoming. Anna let Jack handle the introductions because she was never sure of the proper protocol in such circumstances, but she was sure that the protocol was important to getting the discussion off on the right foot.

"You aren't the first callers to go away disappointed today," he was saying to Jack. "I'm very sorry that you've come so far for no good reason."

Brother Jeremy struck her as a no-nonsense, well-intentioned sort, and she was inclined to believe that he meant what he said. He was well over fifty, with short iron-gray hair and a sunburned nose, wide in the shoulder with great square hands that were stained with ink and paint both. He reminded her of Uncle Quinlan, she realized suddenly, but could not put her finger on why that might be.

Jack pulled out their single ace: "It was Sister Irene at the Foundling who suggested we talk to Father McKinnawae."

"Ah, Sister Irene," said Brother Jeremy. "You've left no stone unturned. I can only wish you better luck with your next visit. Now, may I give you a short tour?"

It was not unexpected, but Anna still struggled with disappointment as they walked the property with Brother Jeremy. They saw buildings that would serve as dormitories, looked at classrooms and workrooms and washrooms and offices. There was a very large kitchen where ten people could work side by side, and an attached dining hall. There was an infirmary, as yet nothing more than walls, with plumbing in place.

It seemed to Anna that any boy who had been living on the streets of the city unsure of even the next day's meal must be content here. At the very least he would be warm and fed, and he would learn to read and write and a trade, too, Brother Jeremy assured them. "Carpentry, toolmaking, sailmaking, farming. Any boy who shows a calling will be sent on to a seminary when he's old enough."

Anna swallowed that fact without comment and felt Jack relax beside her.

Brother Jeremy said, "You might like to walk along the bay, while you're here. We'll water and graze your horse while you're gone if you like."

Jack offered Anna his arm, and they set off through a small wood full of birdsong and trees in new leaf. A flickering of yellow caught Anna's eye; had Jack seen it? A warbler, he thought from the song.

High in a tree was a pure white owl, and nearby, a woodpecker hard at work.

They were quiet, and Anna wondered if things would be awkward now that they had only each other to deal with. That thought was still in her mind when they came out on a narrow footpath that wound through brush and shrubs. It struck her like a drawing out of a children's adventure story, and the idea made her pick up her pace.

Jack let out a small laugh, one that told her he was just as intrigued. Together they followed the path until it brought them to a narrow marsh where someone had put a wide board down to serve as a bridge, and beyond that point the grasses began to fall away, showing up spottily on the swells of sand that blocked their view of the beach.

Birds were everywhere, but Jack was almost as clueless as Anna about their names. Long-legged, knobby-kneed birds with narrow arched beaks like scimitars stood in the marsh waters where ducks with different markings and colors were busy among the reeds. The sound of great wings beating the air made Anna look up to see a bird as big as a man—or so it seemed—heading away from the bay with a fish in its talons. A falcon? An eagle? She had no idea, and felt the lack. She could name every bone and muscle in the human body, but she had no idea what to call the small brown birds with white bellies that strutted along like little old men.

They climbed the ridge of sand and found the ocean spread out before them. The water was deep blue and choppy, tumbling white-combed waves catching sunlight so bright that tears sprang to Anna's eyes despite her broad-brimmed straw hat. There were boats on the horizon, too small to make out, and a little ways down the beach a small group of people were gathered around a picnic basket.

"Over there." Jack inclined his head toward a protected spot overhung by a stand of tall bushes.

They made themselves comfortable despite the fact that they were both dressed to pay a call on a priest. Jack took off his jacket and spread it over a bush, but there was nothing Anna could shed. She was wearing her favorite summer walking dress with a shirtwaist of fine batiste, pleated from the shoulders and embroidered along the neckline, and most important, completely out of fashion because the sleeves were cut wide to give her freedom of movement. She spread the skirts around herself, layers of silk charmeuse and dimity that caught the breeze and lifted up to reveal her stockings and shoes. Her half boots were kid leather and practical for walking, but Rosa had insisted on lacing them with pale green ribbons to match her stockings.

"When we were little, Aunt Quinlan would take us to visit a friend who lives on Long Island, and we ran half-naked on the beaches, all day long. It was heaven."

Jack looked over his shoulder at the family with the picnic basket. "That I would like to see."

"Unlikely," Anna said. "Unless you can find a beach like Robinson Crusoe's."

"You were happy here, as a child."

Anna considered. "After my parents died, Aunt Quinlan dedicated herself to me—and to Sophie, when she came. She would have nothing less than our happiness." She stopped herself. "Tell me about when you were young; did you swim?"

Greenwood, he told her, was a good place to raise children. There had been a lot of hard work in the fields and greenhouses and among the beehives, but they were free to roam when their chores were done. There was a stream overhung by trees and a small lake, and they swam in high summer at every opportunity.

While he talked they watched the small family, and in particular the antics of a little girl who capered around them. The sound of her voice came to them in snatches on the wind, high and laughing.

All at once she let out a screech of delight and hightailed it for the water, a man—her father, Anna guessed—chasing after her roaring in mock pursuit. They were both wearing bathing costumes of bright red fabric, and they stood out against the sand like candle flames. He picked the little girl up and held her over his head, straight-armed, while he stalked into the water, where he threatened and she cajoled, and then, finally, where he dropped her. Sputtering, she jumped out of the shallow water and ran for her mother and a towel.

"That's a good lesson for a girl her age," Anna said. "Be prepared to reap what you sow. I always detested girls who screamed no when they really meant yes."

But Jack seemed not to hear her. He was still studying the little family, something odd in his expression.

Anna said, "What is it? Do you know them?"

"No, I don't think so." He stood up, retrieved his coat, and hung it over his shoulder by one crooked finger. "We should probably get back to town. The last train is at four, or we will have to find a hotel room."

This decision had been hanging over her head for days, even weeks, and now it could be avoided no longer. She could do the simplest and most conventional thing and go back to the city to sleep in her own room. Or they could stay here, together. In a single hotel room, with no one to interrupt or distract them.

Anna believed that she was free of most of the restrictions society put on young women. Here was the real test.

"Will we register as husband and wife?"

"If we want one room, yes. They are likely to refuse us, otherwise. What part of it makes you uncomfortable?"

"I should be able to rent a hotel room without lying," Anna said. "It's no one's business but my own."

"Ah, well," Jack said. "There the good citizens of New York disagree with you. There are all kinds of laws on the books about what goes on behind closed doors."

"And you enforce them?"

"Not if I can help it. Not unless someone is being harmed."

"I would like to stay here," Anna said. "So we can present ourselves as a married couple, if we must. If you're sure."

That got her a half smile. "I'm more than sure."

"Then why the serious face?"

He hesitated, then shook his head. "I had an odd idea, but I don't want to go into it right now."

Anna was brushing the sand from her skirts but noticed that Jack had turned his attention away again.

"Let's go this way," he said, and held out his hand.

•　•　•

THE FATHER AND daughter had wrapped themselves in towels and settled down with the rest of the family when Anna and Jack approached. A family like a million others, father, mother, an elderly woman who would be a grandmother, the little girl, and a babe in arms, swaddled in layers of linen and cotton, with a white lace cap on its head.

"Good afternoon!" the father called over the noise of the waves and the gulls.

Anna turned to return the greeting and stopped. The little girl was crouching in front of her mother, kissing the baby's cheek with all the affection a very young girl could bring to the task. Anna was reminded of Lia, though this girl was blond and fair skinned.

She must have felt Anna's gaze, because she looked up and then launched herself toward them, bouncing with every step.

"I am Theresa Ann Mullen and I have a baby brother," she said, pronouncing each word carefully. "His name is Timothy Seamus Mullen. Do you want to see him?"

Somehow Anna knew, even before the young mother turned the baby in her arms to show him off. She knew what she would see: a child of about five months, with very dark hair that curled, and eyes the color of the cloudless sky overhead.

For a moment she could make no sound at all, and finally her voice came rough.

"Hello," she said. "What beautiful children you have, Mrs. Mullen. Truly beautiful."

The young woman smiled shyly and murmured her thanks.

"Will you sit and take something to drink?" her husband asked. He had a deep, almost melodious voice, as purely Irish as Anna had ever heard.

"You're very kind to ask." Jack took her elbow. "But we do need to get back to town."

⋅   ⋅   ⋅

THEY WALKED IN an arc back toward Mount Loretto. As they crested the low sand dunes, a cottage came into sight. It was surrounded by trees and a pasture where cows and a few horses grazed.

"Do you think?" Anna asked. "Is this where they live?"

"Very likely," Jack said. "They couldn't have walked very far with everything they had with them."

They didn't talk again until they had gotten back to the building site, reclaimed the horse and trap, and set out for the town.

"I wasn't sure," Jack said. "I just caught a glimpse of his head. You think it's him?"

"Yes."

She had known him almost immediately. When she first saw Vittorio in Hoboken he had been in Rosa's arms. A strong child, who held up his head and turned toward the sound of his sister's voice, kicked vigorously and produced a wide, toothless smile—all signs of timely development.

"Two months is an eternity in the life of an infant," she said. "Vittorio Russo is almost twice the age he was when I examined him in Hoboken. But yes, I think it is him. The coloring is distinctive, and it's hard to overlook the fact that this family lives so near Mount Loretto."

"The father had blue eyes," Jack said.

"Did he?"

"And he was fair-haired. They all were."

"It's unlikely that they would produce a dark-haired child, then."

Jack said, "Is there a way to find out for sure—beyond asking Father McKinnawae?"

They were silent for a few minutes as the horse picked up its pace. Horses wanted to get home as much as people did, Mr. Lee had told her once.

"We could talk to the parents," Anna said, finally.

"No, we can't," Jack said, easily.

And he was right; approaching the family was to be avoided at all costs. They would take offense or feel threatened or both, and not without cause.

Anna said, "I wonder who delivers children here. If there's a midwife or a doctor."

"I think Nell is probably the better prospect," Jack said.

"Nell?" And then Anna remembered, the waitress at the café. "You're right, I think. She spends all day watching people come and go, but the café isn't open in the evening."

If they stayed overnight, they could talk to Nell over breakfast. Anna found she didn't have the courage to make such a suggestion.

◆   ◆   ◆

THEY RETURNED THE horse and trap to a cheerful Mr. James Malone, who had been joined by a Michael Malone, the very image of his father and far more talkative.

While the men discussed horses and the weather—Jack was working his way around to asking about a hotel, she was sure—Anna wandered away to read notices nailed to the wall of the livery. Livestock for sale, someone hoping to buy a secondhand plow, a lost dog, a boatswain open for business, a respectable lady who did laundry at a very reasonable rate. There were notices of church services in Perth Amboy: First Presbyterian, United Methodist, St. Peter's Episcopal, Second Baptist, and St. Mary's Catholic. She wondered if Mount Loretto's church would serve the community too. There seemed to be a large Irish population. On the notices she saw a scattering of German names, but many more like Ryan, McCarthy, O'Neill, Daly, Duffy, and O'Shea.

Jack came up behind her. "Let's go for a walk."

Tottenville was more a village than a town, but a growing one and well kept, the sidewalks swept, gutters cleaned, and display windows free of grime. They passed a dry goods store, a grocer, a barbershop, all doing a lot of business late on a Saturday afternoon.

"Here's the doctor you were wondering about." Jack inclined his head to a shingle that hung on the gate of a substantial house. Dr. Nelson Drake was responsible for the health and well-being of this pretty town at the southernmost point of New York State, and he seemed to be prospering. Just across from the doctor was the town court and post office, still open for business and beyond that, the Tottenville Hotel.

A block farther on they found a smithy with a sign nailed to the outside wall:

EAMON MULLEN
GENERAL BLACKSMITHING, HORSESHOEING,
PLOW AND WOODWORK

The wide doors were shut and the window shuttered, no sign of life anywhere.

They had come to the end of the little street, where they found a bench that looked out over a small wilderness and beyond that, the sea.

"We don't even know if it's the same Mullen," Anna said.

Jack covered her hand with his own. "It's harder now, isn't it. Seeing him with a family. He looked healthy."

"Yes," Anna agreed. "He looked healthy and well loved. And the older sister, too. No lack of nourishment or attention."

"Why would they have adopted?" Jack asked.

Anna thought back over all the women she had cared for, the ones who were desperate to have children, and those who were terrified by the idea. Almost every woman she knew had a story of a mother or sister or aunt who had died giving birth or shortly thereafter, or who had lost one child after another. There were women who grew shells that allowed them to survive such losses, and others who broke under the weight.

"She might have lost a child," Anna said. "Or she can't conceive. That's not uncommon."

"Was the daughter adopted too, do you think?"

Anna was surprised by the question, which hadn't occurred to her. "She could be, I suppose. There's no way really to know, and if she is, it's likely she hasn't been told and never will be told. Most people who adopt seem to want it that way."

Jack pushed out his legs and crossed them at the ankle. "Italians don't think like that," he said. "We pass children around like pieces on a chessboard."

Anna hiccupped a laugh. "What does that mean?"

He shrugged. "One family has too many kids, the sister-in-law has none, they share the wealth, so to speak, send over some kids to be raised in that household. But it's never kept a secret. In small villages that would be impossible, and even in a city, I can't imagine it."

"Your parents never thought to send one of you back to Italy to be raised by an aunt or uncle?" Too late, Anna remembered the reason the Mezzanottes had left Italy, but Jack wasn't disturbed.

"They did send me back," he said. "They just waited until I was old enough to stand up for myself to do it."

Anna shifted to look at him directly. "Do you mean in regard to religion, because of the way the families reacted to your parents' marriage?"

"In part. When I left for Italy they both warned me not to let the older relatives play tug-of-war with me."

"Did they do that? Try to win you over to one side or the other?"

He gave her a solemn look. "You can't imagine the things Italian women will compete for. But I made my position clear right at the start, and after that they kind of lost heart, I suppose. I took the fun out of the battle for my soul."

"You know," Anna said. "You've never told me where you stand. Do you consider yourself Jewish?"

"Judaism is matrilineal. So whatever I consider myself, my mother's family sees me as Jewish. But here's how it worked, when I was a kid. Our parents sat us down and told us the whole story, and then they stood back. It was up to each of us to decide for ourselves. Two of my brothers married Jewish women, and the others married Roman Catholics. Some of them observe the Sabbath, some of them go to church. I can never remember who does what."

"You are still evading the question," Anna said.

"I thought it would be clear by now. I haven't taken a side, and I don't plan to. I'm happy floating in uncharted waters. I'm the odd one out in the family, not cut out for the farm, too smart for my own good. So they sent me to Italy to study law."

"We may need a lawyer before this is all resolved," Anna said after a long moment. "What do you think we should do about the baby?"

"Would you want to claim him?"

Anna tried to gather her thoughts, but they refused to order themselves. It wasn't the boy she was thinking about, but his mother—the woman who had become his mother—holding him up for the world to admire. Her expression had been serene and utterly calm, as if she had no other purpose but to care for the children gathered to her.

"They haven't done anything wrong," Jack said.

Anna glanced at him sharply. "I never said they had. If it is him, they took in an orphan to raise as their own."

"Not wanting to give him up wouldn't be wrong, either," Jack said. "He's been with that family for two months. Would he have any memory of his real mother, of Rosa or Lia or Tonino?"

"No," Anna said. "Or at least, I've never seen any evidence of that. He's well cared for by kind and loving people, and that's his universe. The only life he knows. Would we have to approach Father McKinnawae as a first step?"

"I think that would be the best way," Jack said. "If we want to go that route."

"So not this weekend, then."

"No."

"We can take a few days to think it all through, and talk to Aunt Quinlan. But not to the girls."

Jack said, "That's a sensible plan."

"Not talk to the girls yet," Anna amended.

Jack put a hand on the nape of her neck and rocked her head gently back and forth. For a few long minutes they just sat, and then Jack cleared his throat.

It was a sound Anna knew. He had something to suggest he thought she might not like. Something important. She was trying to remember the last time she had heard him make this sound and it had just come to her—the afternoon he broke the news about buying the old Greber place—when he took her hand.

He said, "I think we should get married."

Surprised, Anna looked at him. "Haven't we already agreed to do that?"

He gave a small shake of the head. "I think we should get married today. Right now. By the justice of the peace at the courthouse we just passed."

"Is this about the hotel room?" Anna said. "Because if we want to stay overnight I'm not so very uncomfortable about registering—"

"No," Jack said. "It's not about that. Did you want a big wedding?"

Anna had to clear her own throat. "No. Really, no."

"Well," Jack said, smiling. "It's one way to celebrate your birthday. Why not?"

She studied his expression. "Is this about the Russo baby, about talking to Father McKinnawae?"

That made him laugh. He cupped her face in both hands and kissed her. A simple, chaste kiss.

"Father McKinnawae is about the furthest thing from my mind. This isn't about Sophie and Cap or the inquest or anything but me, wanting to marry you. Today. I'm tired of waiting. I want to go to sleep with you and wake up with you. Starting today."

"It's a little more complicated than that, Jack. Where would we live? I can't move out of the house just when Sophie's going; it would be terribly disruptive to the girls and Aunt Quinlan, all of them."

"I see that. But I could move in, just until Weeds is ready."

Anna knew that her mouth was hanging open, and more than that, she could see that Jack was pleased with her. Because she hadn't refused, out of hand? Because she was thinking about it?

Because she was thinking about it. Then something occurred to her.

"Your sisters? Your mother? They won't be offended at being left out?"

"My mother, no. She's practical. As far as my sisters are concerned, they are so wound up in transforming Weeds that they won't much care. Really, think about it, Anna. It's the best part. With my sisters so busy with the house, they'll point-blank refuse to go home to Greenwood, and Mama will see the logic in letting them finish. Maybe by the time Weeds is ready, everybody will be comfortable with the idea of them staying in the city."

Anna put a hand over her mouth to keep herself from laughing out loud.

"Can you come up with any real objections?"

Slowly, she shook her head.

Jack peeled her hand away from her face, kissed the palm, and held on to it.

"Savard, if you're not ready, all you have to do is say those three words. 'I'm not ready.'"

Anna's voice cracked. "What about—Monday? The inquest? Will it complicate things?"

"Just the opposite," Jack said. "Nobody will be able to challenge my place next to you."

"In theory I could end up in prison," Anna said. "If Comstock has his way, that's exactly what will happen."

Jack studied their linked hands for a moment, and then he gave her an even, calculating look.

"There are people working on your behalf this weekend."

"That's an oddly momentous statement. I do trust Conrad, but—"

"Oscar is hard at work, too."

That gave her pause. "Oscar?"

"If they want to send somebody to prison, it's going to be the person who did Janine Campbell harm."

"Jack," Anna said. "I appreciate Oscar's help, but it's entirely possible that she acted alone, without any assistance."

"Maybe so," Jack said. "But Oscar is tracking her movements for the days before she died, I can pretty much guarantee that. If she saw no one out of the ordinary and no one out of the ordinary came to see her—if Oscar can account for all of your time in the last week—that will be the end of the matter. As far as your connection, of course."

Anna drew in a very deep breath and held it. She could see a half-dozen ways this plan might fail, but then again, it might succeed.

"So can you put that worry out of your mind for the rest of the weekend?"

"I suppose I must," Anna said. She stood, but he stayed where he was, looking up at her.

"Are you coming?" she said. "They may have already closed the town hall for the day, and then what?"

• • •

IN FACT, THE justice of the peace was almost out the door when they found him. He had already put an old-fashioned stovepipe hat on his perfectly bald head and was standing in the doorway. He looked at them over the top of his spectacles with what could only be called suspicion.

Before Jack had said five words, the man turned his back on them and went back into his office, leaving the door open.

Jack ushered her inside, following closely.

The man who had taken a seat behind the desk was Theodore Baugh, Esq., according to the placard on his desk. He gestured to two chairs, and they sat. Anna wondered if the man would ever speak, and whether she should be nervous about the way he was studying her. Before she could think of something to say that wouldn't sound silly or inappropriate, the man put both hands on his desk and leaned forward a little.

"Witnesses?"

Jack said, "I'll go ask the clerk down the hall."

"The clerk down the hall. In a hurry, I see."

He didn't ask why they were in a hurry, and Jack didn't volunteer any information. Anna was starting to enjoy herself, though she wasn't sure why.

Justice Baugh pursed his lips thoughtfully, then pointed to something on the wall behind them. Anna and Jack both turned to see a carefully lettered proverb in a simple black frame: *Marry in Haste, Repent at Leisure.*

A full minute passed while they sat silently, being studied. Anna thought of oral exams in front of a row of professors, grim or bored or encouraging, but she was willing to leave all this to Jack. Somehow she knew that he would not speak first, that he had taken the justice of the peace at face value and accepted a challenge of sorts. She was really quite curious about how the impasse would end.

Another minute passed. With a sigh Justice Baugh got up from his chair, walked around the desk to the door, and opened it. His voice boomed down the hall.

"Mr. Macklin, Mr. Reynolds, I need you down here right away."

Anna whispered to Jack, "Is he sending for the constables to arrest us, do you think?"

Jack's mouth quirked at the corner.

When Justice Baugh returned to his desk chair he drew a piece of paper toward himself, took the cork from a bottle of ink, and picked up his pen. He looked at Jack.

"Name?"

By the time he had finished making a record of Jack's name, profession, age, place of birth and residence, and the names and birthplaces of his parents, two young men had come into the office. Baugh ignored them as he turned to Anna.

"My name is Liliane Mathilde Savard. I am a physician and surgeon, and today is my twenty-eighth birthday. I was born in Paradise, Hamilton County, New York, and I live at number eighteen Waverly Place in the city. My father was Dr. Henry de Guise Savard, born in New Orleans. My mother was also a physician, Curiosity Bonner Savard, born in Paradise, Hamilton County, New York."

Justice Baugh's eyebrows had climbed his forehead while she talked, but he didn't challenge her. Anna decided that she liked him.

"Either of you have any legal impediments to this marriage?"

When they assured him they did not, he scribbled something on his paper and without looking up said, "Five dollars for the marriage license. Five for the civil ceremony."

It seemed that Jack had anticipated this much, because he put the money on the desk without looking for his wallet. The bills disappeared into Justice Baugh's desk drawer with amazing speed.

Then he looked at them over his spectacles one more time, and his whole face split into a smile.

◆ ◆ ◆

FIFTEEN MINUTES LATER they left Justice Baugh's office. In his hand Jack held the marriage license and certificate, ink just barely dry, and regarded them as if he had never seen paper before in his life.

"Here," Anna said, gesturing for them. "I have a folio in my bag."

Her hands were trembling a little as she tucked the documents away, but the sight of her own signature, strong and clear, gave her back her equilibrium. They had married in haste, it was true, but they had also married out of affection and common interests and love. Even if she had yet to say the word, it was true.

When she straightened again, he was smiling down at her.

"Here we are," he said. "Married."

"So it seems. Now what?"

"Now we check into the hotel and find some dinner."

The first raindrops fell as they started down the street and so they ran the rest of the way, and stopped under the portico just as the sky opened up in earnest. The smell of rain hitting earth and cobblestones warm from the sun rose around them, the sweetest of perfumes.

Jack opened the door and looked at her quizzically. "What are you thinking?"

"I hope it rains all night," she said. "I love this. I love—" She swallowed. "I love summer rain."

He bent down and kissed the corner of her mouth. Against her ear he said, "I love you too, Anna Savard."

◆ ◆ ◆

THEY ATE AN early supper in the hotel restaurant: a thick broth full of wide noodles, roasted lamb and buttery mashed turnips, the first salad greens of the season and marinated mushrooms. In between courses they talked about the practical matters they had so studiously avoided before stepping into Justice Baugh's office.

"I should send a telegram to Aunt Quinlan, and one to Cap and Sophie, too. Do you want to send one to your sisters?"

The corner of his mouth jerked. "Now that would offend my mother, if she heard the news after my sisters."

"We could go to Greenwood tomorrow," Anna said. "If we took the ferry to Perth Amboy, we could find transportation from there, no? That would be better than a telegram."

As soon as the words left her mouth Anna wished she could call them back. The idea of adding a trip to Greenwood had come to her out of a sense of propriety, but it also filled her with dread. Jack saw all that on her face, and in that moment Anna forgave him for his frustrating talent for reading her mind.

"Anna," he said. "We've got a one-day honeymoon, and I'll be damned if we'll spend it anywhere but in bed."

The blossoming of heat on her throat and cheeks made him laugh, and Anna decided she could forgive him for that, too.

◆   ◆   ◆

ANNA WATCHED FOR a while as Jack worked on the telegrams for his parents and sisters, his usually confident hand pausing over each word. Just at this moment she was glad she didn't speak Italian, though at some point she would want to know what he had written. She had never heard him speaking to his parents and had no idea if he would be deferential or self-assertive. Italians, she had come to understand, could be terribly formal in certain situations.

He had written a telegram for Oscar, too, but it was tucked under the others and Anna had the idea that she should leave well enough alone. Better not to hover. She made another tour of the room and stopped to watch the storm. The rain was moving across the bay in long sinuous strokes that shimmered in the half-light. She shivered a little but didn't bother to dig the shawl out of her valise. This kind of shivering was not about the chill in the air, but her nerves.

The room was well kept and comfortable with a dresser, a divan, a desk, and a good wide bed with a thick comforter that would be welcome in the cool night salt air. The innkeeper himself had come to bring them a pitcher of fresh water for the washstand and to lay a fire in the grate, nodding toward the window and the rain in explanation. When he had gone and Jack was still bent over the telegram form on the desk, Anna found herself yawning. She stretched out on the divan and let herself be seduced by the falling rain, drifting into sleep only to wake with a start sometime later when lightning streaked across the sky. A blanket had been draped over her, light and warm.

The room was lit only by the trembling touch of lightning and the fire in the hearth. Jack was nowhere to be seen. Most likely he had gone off to arrange for the telegrams to be sent first thing in the morning. Maybe he had even told her he was going to do that, thinking she was awake, and in fact there had been some vague dream in which she was sitting in front of the coroner with a telegram in her hand. She read it out loud, just five words: *Janine Campbell stop. Stop. Stop.*

All day she had been successfully forbidding herself to dwell on Monday's inquest, but it had found a back door into her waking mind. The Russo boy had been in the dream too, sleeping in the arms of a faceless woman.

She got up now and used the water closet and washbasin, and in short order she unpacked her valise and set out the few things she required. The day had been too long and too full of surprises, and she was exhausted. And where had Jack gotten to, anyway?

She cleaned her teeth and let her hair down, forgoing her usual braid because Jack liked her hair unbound. When she was changed and ready for bed she got out the medical journal she had brought along in case she had time to read, and made herself comfortable.

•　•　•

JACK MEANT TO be away for just a few minutes, but the hotel clerk was in no hurry at all; just the opposite, he counted and recounted every word on all five Western Union telegram forms, frowning deeply at the Italian.

"I'm sorry," he said. "I don't speak this language, whatever it is."

"It's Italian, and you don't need to speak it," Jack said. "Count the words as you would English. I've printed very carefully. The telegraph clerk shouldn't have any problem."

"Aubrey doesn't speak anything but English either," the young man said.

"He doesn't need to," Jack said, again. "Any competent telegraph clerk could handle this. Is this Aubrey around? Maybe I should talk to him directly."

Aubrey wasn't available, but he could be fetched if Jack would like to come back in an hour—

Jack would not.

The conscientious, fastidious, and frustrating clerk turned back to his study of the telegrams. He pointed with his stub of pencil.

"If you take out this word and these, and this one, you'll save—"

"I want to send them exactly as they are," Jack said.

The young man mumbled to himself as he labored over the short column of figures, adding them three times while Jack fumed silently to himself. Then it turned out that there wasn't enough change in the cash drawer. If the detective sergeant would wait—

Jack would not. He assured the clerk that morning would be soon enough to collect his change, and left before the young man could find something else that needed counting.

Every once in a while he came across a person who was determined to demonstrate how seriously they regarded the law, as if Jack were watching closely for an excuse to make an arrest. He took the stairs two at a time, stopped to say good evening to a startled older couple with a teenage daughter, and arrived at the door of the room some fifteen minutes later than he had hoped. *Mezzanotte,* he told himself. *You are behaving like a sixteen-year-old. Snap to.*

With a deep breath he opened the door.

By the light of the fire he made out her shape in the bed, a small form under the blankets. She was asleep, with a journal open under her hands. Her color was high, from scrubbing or the day's exercise or the breeze from the window she had cracked open. A heart-shaped face with strong dark brows and deep-set eyes and a wide mouth the color of raspberries just coming into full ripeness.

He saw all this and more, but he must keep it to himself. She could simply not tolerate praise and always found a reason to walk away or change the subject.

Jack took a moment to consider. There was a nightshirt at the very bottom of his valise, along with a facecloth and toothbrush. He didn't want to wake her, not just yet. He made some tactical decisions.

◆   ◆   ◆

ANNA WOKE WHEN Jack slipped into bed, six feet four inches of naked male radiating heat like a giant and very prickly hot-water bottle. His head propped on one hand, he was leaning over her to study the open journal page.

"You know, I'm sure that clinical observations on tracheal tubes by mouth instead of—"

"Tracheostomy," she supplied.

"Tracheostomy," Jack echoed, drawing the journal away and dropping it behind him so it fluttered to the floor. "Exactly that interesting topic can wait—"

"Forever," she finished, grinning so broadly that her cheeks began to ache. She rolled onto her side to face him. "Where have you been?"

"Did you think I hopped a ferry?"

She pressed her forehead under his chin and against his throat, shaking her head because she knew her voice would wobble. And how could she be expected to put together a single sentence while his fingers hooked into her nightdress and skimmed up her leg. He tugged, and she lifted and turned and shivered as the fabric dragged over her skin inch by inch, until it snagged.

"There's a button caught in your hair. Hold still."

His arms came around her head as his fingers threaded through individual strands of hair, pulling gently one by one so that gooseflesh ran up and down her spine. His breath was warm on her scalp, and she shivered and shivered and shivered.

"You're not cold." His tone was almost accusatory.

"Not cold," she agreed.

He pulled the nightdress up and off, and it disappeared behind him to join the medical journal on the floor.

"So now that we're finally here," he said, his arms slipping around her waist to pull her close, "what should we do with ourselves?"

◆   ◆   ◆

THEY LAY FACE-TO-FACE in the shadowy cave of white sheets, damp skinned, swathed in each other's heat. Quiet but alert, both of them. Anna had the idea that she could hear his heart beating, just as she saw it in the throbbing pulse at his throat and temples. She leaned forward to draw in his scent just there, burrowing into his hair.

She said, "The smell of you puts me in a trance."

When she pulled away he raised a hand to touch her face. His fingers were long and thick and strong, big knuckled, with blunt, square fingertips, clean nails cut to the quick. She would never have thought that a man's hands could arouse so much feeling, but nerves fired all along her spine at the simple sight of him holding a news-paper or a fork, lifting a valise. Unbuttoning a shirt.

He cupped her face with one palm, threaded his fingers into her hair, and pulled her close, lingering for a heartbeat, their mouths almost touching. Anna felt him draw in a deeper breath, as if his lungs were suddenly too small. She closed the distance between them, opened her mouth against his, and let herself be drawn down and down into a kiss that rendered her limp, soft and open and welcoming, pressed against him from knee to belly to breast to mouth, where he stroked her tongue with his own and called up her response, small murmurs and gasps.

He took over. She found herself on her back with his weight sus-pended over her so that she still felt every tensed muscle, the hard planes of his thighs and belly and between them the evidence that he wanted her. He was turgid, arching, weeping, the broad head of his erection seeking blindly, tapping against her belly.

"Come," she said. "Come to me."

He made a clucking noise, mock surprise and male satisfaction rolled into one. "So impatient." And he slipped down to press his face to the curve of her breast. "We have all night," he mumbled against her skin. "What's the hurry?"

She shook her head and laughed and gave in, arching up to rub against him, running a heel down his thigh through rough hair and then stopping when he drew her nipple deep into his mouth and suckled.

The hot pull distracted her so that she didn't realize they were moving until they sat, face-to-face, Jack on his knees, her legs spread wide over his hips, his hands tangled in the hair that cascaded down her back, holding her just so while he drew hard at her breast, suckled and suckled until she groaned, flexing against him, stretched open and wet.

She reached for him but he blocked one hand and then the other, gathering them behind her to keep them at the small of her back as efficiently as handcuffs. It went against the grain and he knew it, knew she'd struggle and resist, and that she'd stop, as she did, as he used his free hand to fit himself to her.

Anna dropped her head to watch it happen. She wanted to rock against him in welcome, to drag him in and then retreat so that he must follow, but he knew her game. He held her and moved her exactly as he wanted, entering her with excruciating, exacting intention: he penetrated mind and heart and body, insisting that she give in and take all of him, everything he had to offer. When she thought there was no more to surrender he still inched forward, crooning at her, *come and come and come to me.* Finally he released his grip on her wrists and cupped her buttocks in his hands to lift her, just so.

His mouth grazed her jaw, suckled at her earlobe. He whispered to her.

"I fill you up."

She pulsed and strained against him, took his mouth and the kiss she wanted as he began to rock into her, deep and deeper still. She began to shudder, coming undone by the simple fact of him. Joined at the quick, for once and always.

25

WESTERN UNION

TOTTENVILLE S.I. N.Y. DIST TELEGRAPH OFFICE XUS23 S902JD

SUN MAY 27 1883 7 A.M.

MRS LILY QUINLAN, MRS MARGARET COOPER, MR AND MRS LEE,

ROSA AND LIA RUSSO

    18 WAVERLY PLACE NY NY

DEAREST ALL. WE WERE MARRIED SATURDAY AFTERNOON IN TOTTENVILLE S.I.
SHOCKINGLY SPONTANEOUS BEHAVIOR BUT WE ARE VERY PLEASED WITH OURSELVES.
HOPE THERE IS ROOM FOR US BOTH AT ROSES UNTIL WEEDS IS READY. WILL BE
BACK LATER TODAY AFTER SEEING SOPHIE AND CAP AND JACK'S SISTERS. HOPE TO
BE THERE BY SIX. PLEASE NO PARTY UNTIL RESOLUTION OF INQUEST. LOVE TO YOU
ALL. ANNA AND JACK

WESTERN UNION

TOTTENVILLE S.I. N.Y. DIST TELEGRAPH OFFICE XUS23 S902JD

SUN MAY 27 1883 7:10 A.M.

MR PETER VERHOEVEN ESQ AND DR SOPHIE SAVARD VERHOEVEN

    40 PARK PLACE NY NY

DEAREST SOPHIE AND CAP. WE TRIED TO WAIT OUT THE IMPULSE BUT HAVE HAPPILY
SUCCUMBED TO A REVOLUTIONARY MINDSET AND FOLLOWED YOU INTO MATRIMONY
HERE IN TOTTENVILLE S.I. PLAN TO RETURN ON THE THREE O'CLOCK FERRY AND
WILL COME STRAIGHT TO PARK PLACE TO TALK. WITH ALL OUR LOVE. ANNA AND
JACK

WESTERN UNION

TOTTENVILLE S.I. N.Y. DIST TELEGRAPH OFFICE XUS23 S902JD

SUN MAY 27 1883 7:15 A.M.

DET SERGEANT OSCAR MARONEY

   86 GROVE ST NY NY

WILL BE BACK LATE TONIGHT AND AT HEADQUARTERS FOR FIRST SHIFT TOMORROW.
ANY NEWS THAT CANNOT WAIT LEAVE WORD FOR ME ON WAVERLY PLACE WHERE I'LL
BE LIVING FOR THE NEXT WHILE AS I FINALLY TALKED ANNA INTO MARRYING ME.
JACK

◆ ◆ ◆

NEW YORK POST

Sunday, May 27, 1883

MORNING EDITION

WHERE ARE ARCHER CAMPBELL'S LITTLE BOYS?

*FOUR SONS LAST SEEN THE DAY BEFORE THEIR
MOTHER'S SUSPICIOUS DEATH*

POLICE DEPARTMENT REQUESTING INFORMATION
FROM THE PUBLIC

FOUL PLAY FEARED

Readers following the story of the tragic death of Mrs. Janine Campbell last Thursday will be shocked to learn that her four young sons are missing. Archer Campbell, husband of the deceased, a postal inspector and senior detective for the New York Society for the Suppression of Vice last saw his sons (Archer, Jr., 5 years old, Steven, 4 years old, Gregory, 2 years old, and Michael, 2 months old) just the morning before their mother's death.

In a statement made to the police, Mr. Campbell related the following facts: Last Tuesday evening his wife announced that she was taking the children to spend a week on the Connecticut farm of his brother Harold Campbell, a common occurrence that raised no suspicion. However, when Mr. Campbell came home on Wednesday he found his wife had collapsed upon return from Connecticut and retired to her bed. She assured him she would be better after a good night's sleep, and took laudanum to that end. She was still abed when he left the next morning for work and could not be roused, which he attributed to the effects of the laudanum.

By one o'clock that afternoon Mrs. Campbell was dead, the victim of suspected malpractice and criminal abortion gone wrong. Mr. Campbell spent Thursday afternoon and all of Friday much occupied with the investigation into his wife's death and the arrangements for her burial. Late Friday evening he sent a telegram to his brother Harold in Connecticut, announcing the death of his wife, plans for the funeral to take place the next afternoon, and a request that the boys be brought home in order to attend.

Early Saturday morning he received an express telegram from his brother in which he learned that his boys were not in Connecticut. It had been many months since Janine Campbell or her sons had last visited the Connecticut farm, and even longer since they had had a letter. Harold Campbell knew nothing of the whereabouts of his nephews.

Mr. Campbell went immediately to police headquarters to report that his sons were missing. Telegrams to family members as far away as Maine have provided no information or help. All that is known with certainty is that Mrs. Campbell left the city with them last Wednesday morning by train, and returned without them later the same day. Police inquiries began on Saturday, and will continue until the boys are found and returned to their grieving father.

The mayor has directed the police department to spare no effort to locate the Campbell boys. In turn, the police and family ask that any person or persons with information about the boys or about Mrs. Campbell's movements in the days before her death come forward without delay. Information leading to the safe return of the boys will be amply rewarded.

NEW YORK TIMES

Sunday, May 27, 1883

CORONER ASSEMBLES A JURY FOR THE MRS. JANINE CAMPBELL INQUEST

DISTINGUISHED PHYSICIANS AGREE TO SERVE

Coroner Hawthorn has called on some of this city's most respected physicians to hear testimony and examine evidence in the case of Janine Campbell's death by criminal abortion.

A postmortem found the cause of death to be infection and blood poisoning following from an illegal operation. The coroner's jury will meet to determine if an unknown party or parties performed the procedure or if Mrs. Campbell operated on herself. If that is so, there will be an inquiry into who provided her with the information and instruments she used.

The last two physicians to treat Mrs. Campbell, Dr. Anna Savard and Dr. Sophie Savard, will be present at the inquest with their attorney, Conrad Belmont, Esq., and must be prepared to give testimony to a jury of six more experienced experts, as well as an officer of the New York Society for the Suppression of Vice.

In an unusual twist, Mr. Belmont, attorney for the two lady doctors, approached the coroner to request that the jury include at least two female physicians, who by their sex, experience, and training would be best able to understand and judge the evidence. This request was denied for reasons of law, custom, and propriety, but the coroner will allow female physicians to be present in Judge Benedict's courtroom, where the inquest will begin at 1 p.m. tomorrow. As is customary, anyone admitted to the gallery may question witnesses.

Whether the disappearance of the four Campbell sons will be addressed in the inquest is unclear, though insiders believe that it will be necessary to take the facts of the case into account.

◆   ◆   ◆

THEY GOT TO the Tottenville train station and onto the train at the very last second. Jack jumped onboard with both valises and then hauled Anna and her Gladstone bag up behind him, just as they jerked into motion.

The train was crowded, overheated, and awash in tobacco smoke. Anna fell into a seat with a great heaving sigh, lifting her hair off her damp neck. By the time Jack had stowed away the bags and joined her, she was coughing into her handkerchief.

They escaped to the covered vestibule between the two cars, where the window had been left open. It meant standing for the entire hour and swaying hard with every jolt, but it was worth any amount of jostling to stand in the cool rush of air.

"We're not the only ones with a bright idea." Jack inclined his head to the two women who had appeared at the vestibule door in search of clean air. They squeezed together to make room.

They were mother and daughter; nothing could be more obvious unless it was the fact that the younger woman was close to giving birth. Mrs. Stillwater and Mrs. Reynolds, as they introduced themselves, on their way to visit friends. Mrs. Reynolds rubbed her great belly with the palm of one hand and could not hide her curiosity.

She said, "I think you must be the newlyweds."

Her mother's face lit up with interest.

"My husband is Joe Reynolds; he's a law clerk. He was one of your witnesses?"

Anna had no real memory of the witnesses whom the justice of the peace had called into his office, but she nodded.

Mrs. Reynolds was saying, "Joe described you. You don't have any way to know this, but Judge Baugh refuses to marry almost everybody. He says he won't be a party to a disaster."

"You impressed him," added her mother. "It bodes well for your future. Are you really a doctor?"

Anna agreed that she was. She knew where the conversation would go, and so she started it on her own.

"You are very close to your time, I think."

The younger woman shrugged. "Everybody says so, but I don't feel so uncomfortable the way most women talk about. Except maybe at night when the kicking and thumping keeps me from getting to sleep."

"It's a good time of year to have a baby," Anna offered, because it was true. "Will you stay here on the island?"

She felt Jack's attention focus as he realized what she was up to. Anna elbowed him gently to let him know he was not to jump in or offer any comments and heard him huff his resignation all too clear. In her experience mothers and daughters had a set way of telling their maternal histories, and she must let it run its course.

The mother, born and raised herself on Staten Island, had had all of her children right at home with the help of Meg Quinn, the midwife who had delivered almost everybody on the south end of Staten Island.

"She's only ever lost two children and one mother," the daughter said. "In thirty years of catching babies."

"That's an excellent record," Anna said, and saw them both relax a little. "We've seen quite a few babies this weekend," Anna went on. "Twins, about three months old—"

"The Dorsey girls," the mother suggested.

"I wouldn't care for twins," her daughter said, but her nervous smile said she wasn't so sure. Most young women her age did like the idea of twins but found the reality more than they had imagined or wanted to deal with.

"I heard a very young baby crying when we passed a house on the main street this morning—"

"Mrs. Caruthers's first, poor thing's got the colic something terrible."

"—and, then yesterday—" She paused to look at Jack.

"Yes?" the mother prompted, also turning to Jack and smiling in a way that made her look more her daughter's age.

"We were on the beach very near Mount Loretto," he said. "We met a family with a friendly little girl who introduced us to her parents and grandmother and her new baby brother."

"That would be Eamon and Helen Mullen, don't you think, Allie? Helen is a good friend of both my daughters. She married the same week as my older girl, my Jess."

"They looked very happy," Anna said.

"Oh, yes," said Allie Reynolds, her hand returning to rub her belly in gentle circles. "But they have had some heartache." She lowered her voice. "Helen lost her own little boy to a fever when he was just three months old. He was gone so quick, they couldn't even send for the doctor."

The story went on for a while, mother and daughter reconstructing the death of the Mullens' son.

"Then she couldn't catch again," said the daughter. "Three years, they tried. It was hard to see her so unhappy."

"She seems very satisfied now," Anna said.

"That little boy was a blessing, it's true. They adopted him, you know. There's no lack of little Irish orphans in the city, is what we hear. So the new priest arranged for them to get one and it's made all the difference to the Mullens. Brought them all back to life, you might even say."

◆   ◆   ◆

THE PASSENGERS WERE coming off the ferry just as Jack and Anna left the train station, a small crowd of people on their way to Tottenville. The last person they passed was a priest in a Roman collar, a man in his fifties or more, rotund, with blazing red cheeks and sharp blue eyes. This would be the evasive Father McKinnawae, Jack was fairly sure. But there was no time to stop and introduce themselves. It was a conversation that would need careful planning.

"Maybe I should write to him again," Anna said when the ferry had begun its trip north on Raritan Bay.

"It would be better if I approached him," Jack said. "If you can leave that to me once the inquest is over. At least we know the baby is healthy and in good hands."

"Yes," Anna said. "That's one less thing to worry about. I don't mind admitting, my head is spinning."

"I'll take that as a compliment," Jack said, slipping an arm around her shoulders.

She gave him a half smile. "It will be a very strange honeymoon. I have surgery all tomorrow morning and then in the afternoon—"

Her expression was almost blank when she was thinking about the inquest. Out of self-preservation, Jack thought. Distancing herself in any way she could in order to better see and understand and analyze.

"We'll have to be inventive," he whispered against her ear, and she smiled and shivered a little.

Then he saw her attention shift to the empty seat beside her where an abandoned newspaper fluttered in the breeze. She leaned over to pick it up, and Jack saw the headline, each word like a slash:

FOUR CAMPBELL SONS MISSING

INQUEST INTO MOTHER'S DEATH STARTS TOMORROW

◆ ◆ ◆

CAP SAID, "YOU must have that telegram by heart now. How many times have you read it?"

"I'll keep reading it until they show up at the door and I know it's really true."

In fact Sophie didn't doubt the news at all, but studying the telegram gave her a few moments to think of other things without being observed too closely. A necessary deception, she told herself. Cap was still recovering from Friday, and she had gone to some lengths to see that nothing new was laid before him for as long as humanly possible. If their places were reversed she would not thank him for such interference, but she was his physician as well as his wife, and as such it was her responsibility. And more than that, she could not bring herself to open up the discussion of the Campbell boys; she could barely stand to think about them at all.

And still the image of Janine Campbell as she had last seen her would not be banished. All over the city people were convincing themselves that she had killed her sons, but Sophie hadn't seen any evidence of psychosis when she saw her, just weeks ago. Depression, yes. Anger, too, and despair. But to deliberately set out with the boys to kill them and return home alone, that required a coldhearted forethought or a complete break with reality, neither of which she could see.

When the door chime came to them Cap said, "Go on, I know you can't wait."

She flew across the room and smiled at him from the door as she took off her protective mask. "I'll bring them straight up."

• • •

ANNA LOOKED ALMOST burnished, as if she had been buffeted by hard winds off a cold sea and then polished by sunlight. And she was smiling, a sincere smile without artifice. Sophie folded her cousin into her arms and hugged her as hard as she could.

"Ouch." Anna laughed, pulling away. "You never will learn your own strength."

Sophie turned to Jack and hugged him, too, and got no complaints.

"You two," Sophie said. "Always up to tricks." She had tears in her eyes, but she didn't care and for once Anna didn't seem to mind at all. Her calm, resolute, generally impenetrable expression was gone. For today, at least.

"How's Cap?" Jack wanted to know.

"Fairly calm. Recovering." It was close enough to the truth. "He met with Conrad for two hours this afternoon and then I put an end to it. But we can talk about that later."

They started up the stairs and Sophie noticed the paper tucked under Jack's arm.

He caught her gaze and nodded.

Sophie said, "Let's leave that sorry business aside for now too, can we do that? He hasn't seen the paper yet."

Anna raised a brow in surprise. "Cap without the Sunday news-papers—"

"It took some finagling," Sophie admitted. "And now I'm going to insist that we leave everything else aside, to celebrate—"

"Anna's capitulation," Jack supplied.

Anna paused on the stair to look over her shoulder and raise her brow at him. "I'll argue with you about that word later."

"And I'll look forward to the argument."

It was good to see them bantering and at ease with each other. Sophie wished she could say the same of herself and Cap. He was distant and worried and in pain, and she wanted very badly to get him on the next ship that left New York harbor. Anna would know all this without being told in explicit terms. No doubt she had spoken to Jack about it. For the moment, though, Anna's attention was focused in a different direction.

"Have you had word from Roses today?" she asked.

From his room Cap called out, "An avalanche of words. One note after the other."

Anna stopped in the doorway to look at him. "Not about a party, I hope."

Sophie nudged her into the room and took Jack's arm to get him moving, too. Then she closed the door behind them.

"Of course," Cap said. "You didn't really think you could talk them out of one, I hope."

Jack said, "Cap, you look a sight better than the last time I saw you. Marriage agrees with you."

Cap's lopsided grin came and went. "You have dark circles under your eyes, so I'll assume the same for you."

Sophie let out a squawk of surprised laughter, but Anna just frowned at Cap. "Marriage hasn't done anything for your manners. But I am glad to see you, nonetheless."

Jack said, "So you're saying we need to be prepared for a surprise party when we get to Roses?"

Sophie shot Cap an irritated frown, but she should have known he couldn't keep the news to himself.

"You might as well tell us," Anna said. "What is Auntie up to?"

"Never mind about Auntie for the moment," Sophie said. "Let's sit down. I want to hear about this sudden launch into marriage. Every detail. Right from the beginning."

The conversation stretched from one side of the room to the other, where Cap sat in strict isolation. Sophie thought she might someday get used to this, this being close and far at once. If fate was kind she would have the chance.

Cap said, "If you wanted to get married in a hurry you didn't need to go off to Staten Island. You could have done it at City Hall with less fuss."

"We didn't go to Staten Island thinking we'd get married," Jack said. "That was just fortunate timing and my good luck."

"They went to talk to the priest about the littlest Russo boy," Sophie reminded Cap. She turned to Anna. "No success?"

"We didn't find Father McKinnawae," Anna said, and then hesitated, her face turned toward the closed door. "What are those voices I'm hearing downstairs?"

Sophie shrugged at her apologetically. "You knew Auntie couldn't help herself."

"Everybody? The whole household is here?"

"Your people too," Cap said to Jack. "You never said your father was a giant."

Jack's expression had been calm, almost sleepy, Sophie thought, but his head came around with a jerk.

"My people?"

"Your sisters, and your parents," Sophie said. "Aunts, uncles, a couple brothers. I didn't catch all the names."

Anna gave a small shake of the head, and then she laughed.

"We thought we were so clever," she said. "That will show us."

Jack put a hand on her neck and kissed the top of her head. "Between my sisters and your aunt it was inevitable. None of them has any self-control when it comes to a party."

"They love you," Sophie said. "We love you. And we're all happy for you."

Cap said, "You'd better go down before they storm the castle, but tell us first about what happened on Staten Island. You didn't find your Father McKinnawae, but something happened, I can tell from Anna's expression."

Anna said, "We can't talk about this with the Russo girls in the house. Not a word about Father McKinnawae or Staten Island. Not today. Maybe not ever."

"You found him," Sophie said. "You found Vittorio?"

Anna nodded and Jack studied his shoes. Another set of complications, something Sophie hadn't anticipated.

"You're right," Cap said. "This is a discussion for another day. Go on now, there's a party waiting to get started in the garden. Come back up here when you can," he added. "That will be time enough to talk about the inquest and the Campbell boys."

Sophie froze where she stood.

From the door Anna looked back at her. "Of course he's read the papers. You know how he is."

"She did her best to keep them from me," Cap said. "But all she had was Mrs. Harrison helping her, while I had Mr. Vine on my side, and Mr. Vine has a checkered but quite useful past when it comes to smuggling."

◆   ◆   ◆

IN THE HALL outside Cap's room Sophie said, "I did try to hide the news from him. Or I suppose I was trying to hide it from myself. I can't bear to think about those boys."

Anna put an arm around her shoulder and kissed her cheek. "Sophie, I don't mean to be unfeeling, really. I am terribly worried about the Campbell boys, but I'm asking you to put all that aside for just a little while. I'm about to meet my parents-in-law and I can't think of much else."

"Come on then," Jack said with a resigned smile. "Let's put you out of your misery."

"I don't even have time to change into better clothes," Anna mumbled, but she let herself be led downstairs.

"We've been outmaneuvered," Jack said, squeezing her hand. "Let's surrender with our dignity intact."

◆   ◆   ◆

THE FIRST THING Anna noticed as they walked into the garden was Rosa and Lia, each of them hopping in excitement, their arms full of flowers. They hurtled themselves toward her, and she crouched down, arms spread, to catch them up. She thought, *Your brother is healthy and well and I'm sorry I can't say even that much to you.* Instead she hugged them and kissed their cheeks and took the bouquets they thrust at her, fat pink and white peonies so full of scent that she sneezed, and set the whole party to laughing.

When she looked up Aunt Quinlan was there, leaning on her cane. Anna went to her, this small woman as fragile as an iron rod, unflinching and absolute in her love and devotion. She pressed her face to her aunt's and drew in a deep breath. There was nothing to say, because she couldn't put what she was feeling into words.

"Come now," her aunt said. "Let me have a look at this husband of yours, and then we'll sit down with your new family."

◆   ◆   ◆

FROM THE HALL windows Sophie and Cap watched as Anna was drawn into the circle of Jack's family, with his mother at the center and his father as tall and solid as a tree trunk beside her. Jack was very tall, but his father was a half head taller still. Mrs. Mezzanotte was straight and strong too, a woman sure of herself, with a gaze that was not stern, exactly, but missed nothing. Very much like Anna herself. Her two daughters were with her, the quiet and gentle Celestina and Bambina, younger and harder of heart, and two aunts. All of the women stepped forward to draw Anna in while the men of the family looked on.

"At least this way she doesn't have to meet the whole family at once," Sophie said. Most of Anna's new family had stayed behind at Greenwood. Mrs. Mezzanotte had explained the reasoning to Sophie in her excellent English, almost as if she were apologizing for failing to produce every Mezzanotte on the continent.

She had said, "They are all of them unhappy with me, because they wanted to be here to welcome Anna into the family. But my daughters-in-law are a force to be reckoned with, and I put down my foot. I wanted her to myself for this afternoon, at least."

For Sophie it had been an awkward introduction, because Bambina was standing next to her mother and she had heard more about Bambina than she really cared to know. But the younger Mezzanotte sister had smiled and spoken to Sophie with all good manners. Either she had undergone a change of heart, or she had been threatened with dire consequences. Sophie knew it was most likely the latter, but Mrs. Mezzanotte's kind smile gave her some reason to think that the situation might turn out well.

*   *   *

IN THE GARDEN Jack's father took Anna by the shoulders, eyes narrowed as if he were examining a botanical specimen, and then kissed her on each cheek, breaking into a smile so much like Jack's that Sophie found herself laughing.

"I've never seen Anna so nervous," Sophie said, still at the window. "And all for naught. They love her."

"Italians are supposed to be shouting at each other all the time," Cap said. "I thought there would at least be some sparks."

Anna, who was uncomfortable with strangers and never overly demonstrative even with those she loved best, her cousin Anna was being passed from stranger to stranger like a precious but unbreakable treasure. They turned her one way and another to examine her from all sides, touched her face, ran hands over her hair. And she was smiling, answering questions and asking them, too, sometimes looking to Jack and sometimes not.

"That man is besotted," Cap said. "And damned lucky, too." His voice wavered, as Sophie knew her own voice might.

"Let's go sit together," she said. "Side by side. Can we do that, just for a little while?"

His hand came to rest lightly on her shoulder, a gentle brushing. Such sadness and resignation in his face. Sophie followed him, listening to the sounds of the party in the garden that would go on, as was right and necessary, without them.

◆　◆　◆

ANNA PLEADED EXHAUSTION and an early start to her Monday, promised long visits and dinners and talks, tours of Roses and Weeds and the New Amsterdam, and finally with Jack's help she was able to extricate herself from the crowd of Mezzanottes in Cap's garden. She corrected herself: in Cap and Sophie's garden.

Rosa and Lia made impassioned pleas to go back with them to Waverly Place but were distracted very easily by Mrs. Mezzanotte. Anna listened to a very serious discussion in Italian, and remembered what Jack had said about the comfort of hearing your own language in a strange land.

In the end they climbed into a taxi alone. They had never managed to talk to Sophie and Cap about the inquest or about the Campbell boys. Like so many things, it would have to wait.

Jack put an arm around her and she leaned into him and hummed. "I like your parents."

"I hoped you would. It wasn't the way I planned it happening, but there were some advantages to the spontaneous."

"Aunt Quinlan," Anna agreed. "She got hold of them first and paved the way. She does that a lot. She would have made an excellent ambassador."

"Did you notice Lia?" Jack said. "She wouldn't let go of my father. Margaret didn't seem to mind, she was off in a corner talking to Aunt Philomena."

"Everybody was on their best behavior," Anna agreed. "But I still feel as if I was run over by an omnibus."

• • •

MR. LEE WAS waiting for them at the house. The minute he took her hands in his, the calm and dignity that Anna had held on to so tightly all afternoon just melted away.

"Miss Anna," he said. "I wish you and your new husband the very best."

Her voice suddenly hoarse, Anna said, "Why thank you, Mr. Lee. And I almost got through the whole day without tears."

"We missed you at the party," Jack said, shaking the hand Mr. Lee extended to him.

"I wanted to stay behind, be the first one to welcome you both home." With his free hand he squeezed Jack's forearm, a fatherly gesture that wasn't lost on Anna. "I expect you've had a long day and would like to retire."

Before Jack turned away, Mr. Lee held up a letter. "For you. Came just an hour ago."

Anna raised an eyebrow.

"From Oscar," Jack said. "It will wait."

• • •

JACK HAD NEVER seen Anna's room before, though he had hinted and sometimes came right out and asked. She had always put him off with a smile.

It was a large room, the windows looking out over the garden, where the day still burned bright though it was after seven. Wallpaper too faded to make out a pattern above wainscoting painted white, a gleaming wooden floor covered with small rugs, a bookcase over a desk piled with books and files and papers.

Anna stood in the doorway for a long moment, looking nonplussed.

"Something wrong?"

"That's a new bed," she said. "And the dresser is new too, twice the height of my old one."

"That's my dresser," Jack said. "They must have commandeered the delivery wagons."

"I can't believe they managed all this in such a short time." She walked across the room to open a closet door and glanced at him over her shoulder. "It's all here. Your suits and shirts and your shoes—everything put away tidily. They must have started as soon as they got the telegrams this morning."

There were two chairs facing each other in front of a small fireplace with a low table between them. A vase of roses sat there on an embroidered cloth that Jack recognized as the work of one of his sisters. Nothing elaborate, but still too much, it seemed.

"Are you put out about the changes?"

She turned toward him suddenly. "Surprised, but not put out. I'm—happy that you're here. I am, really."

But she stood on the opposite side of the room, on the opposite side of the bed, her hands clasped together at her waist.

Jack said, "Come and tell me about these pictures."

Having something to do seemed to relax her. She joined him, but stood a little apart and fixed her attention on the neatly framed photographs and paintings and drawings that were staggered across the full width of the wall over a dressing table. They seemed to be arranged chronologically, the oldest and simplest nearest the door: a drawing of a couple in their fifties, sitting together on a porch. Along the bottom was printed *Uphill House 1823*, and then a signature, *L. Ballentyne*. For a few minutes Jack just studied one picture after another, so many faces, all Anna's people and Sophie's too, because there was a watercolor of a woman who was clearly Indian, standing with a strongly built man who was Indian and African both, by his features. Again the work of L. Ballentyne: *Hannah and Ben, Downhill House 1840*.

Anna stepped closer to the wall to touch a frame that had been carved with vines and flowers. The portrait was a simple charcoal drawing of another couple, very young and full of life. They sat shoulder to shoulder with a young boy no more than two between them. Before reading the words written along the bottom he knew that these were Anna's parents and the brother she never spoke of.

"Your aunt did all of these drawings and paintings."

She nodded, clearing her throat. "Aunt Quinlan's first husband was a Ballentyne." She inclined her head toward a small painting, no larger than a hand. The man pictured there was real enough to talk to.

Anna nodded to the painting of her parents and brother. "There are other pictures of them, but this is my favorite of all. They seem so alive, sometimes it's hard to look at them."

"You look something like your mother, but I think this"—he nodded to the first frame—"must be your grandmother, because you are
her image exactly."

"So they tell me. She was a schoolteacher and even so she had
great adventures. I never met her."

Jack thought for a moment, wondering if he should have left the
portraits for another time. Asking her to talk about the family she
had lost when so many other things were pressing on her.

She said, "I have an idea. Every night before we go to sleep I can
tell you about the people in one of these portraits. I think that way it
will come to me more easily. And you could tell me one of your stories. But now I want to go to bed. I have to leave for the hospital at
half past five in the morning."

"Is it too strange—"

"I want you here," she interrupted him. "I really do want you
here."

And it seemed she did. She was more herself as she went about
unpacking her valise and putting out clothes for the next day, talking
to him about everything and nothing. When she went off to have a
bath Jack pulled Oscar's letter out of his pocket.

Jack—

Since Friday:

> *Item. We managed to nail down all Janine Campbell's
> movements from Sunday until she arrived at the New Amsterdam,
> and both Anna and Sophie have solid alibis and witnesses to swear
> to their whereabouts. If somebody besides the deceased had a hand
> in the operation, it wasn't either of the Drs. Savard.*

> *Item. Don't have much to say about the Campbell boys yet, what
> there is to tell I'll do that face-to-face.*

> *Item. Comstock's men went through the Campbells' place before
> I could get there and came away with pamphlets that have got him
> yelling in the D.A.'s ear. Haven't been able to get close enough to
> know what exactly he found but I'm working on it.*

> *Item. I've had a tail on Campbell since Friday 3 pm, nothing to
> report there.*

Item. Belmont thinks that if we can shake loose from Comstock and the damn pamphlets that will put an end to the whole mess by Tuesday and the Verhoevens can get on the next ship.

Item. Comstock is one of the jurors. Belmont did his best to get him thrown off but no luck so far. I should know more before the hearing starts on Monday.

O.M.

◆ ◆ ◆

WHEN IT WAS his turn, Jack took his time in the bathroom, thinking about Oscar's letter, trying to draw from the words the things he would have read otherwise from the man's face. He gave up finally with the realization that the morning would bring a long and difficult day, and they both needed their sleep. And still, the idea of Anna waiting for him in bed made him want her.

There was a lock on the bedroom door and Jack was glad of it, because he didn't intend to sleep in anything but bare skin, as he always had. He stripped down while she watched him, stretched out on her side, trying to stay awake.

When he got under the covers she smiled at him sleepily and held out her arms for his kiss, gentle as it was. By the time he had made himself comfortable the dusk had filled the room, and Anna was asleep.

He lay awake for a long time, thinking of the Campbell boys and of Oscar's letter. In the morning he'd walk with Anna to the New Amsterdam and they would talk. With that idea in his head he fell asleep and dreamed of the sailboats on Raritan Bay, moving farther and farther out of sight.

26

NEW YORK SUN

Monday, May 28, 1883

NO TRACE OF MISSING CAMPBELL BOYS

DID JANINE CAMPBELL SUFFER FROM PUERPERAL INSANITY?

On Tuesday of last week, Mrs. Janine Campbell calmly lied to her husband about her plans for the next day. She told him she was taking their four sons to spend a week with their cousins in the countryside.

"Those boys loved it here," Mrs. Harold Campbell, sister-in-law to the deceased, told the *Sun.* "They never wanted to go home. All the fresh air and good food, and the freedom to play. It breaks my heart to think of them lost, out there in the world wondering where their mother is, and why she left them. Janine can't have been in her right mind."

An autopsy determined that Mrs. Campbell underwent an illegal operation sometime on Tuesday or Wednesday, a fact her husband will not credit.

Nevertheless, physicians are agreed that she did indeed have an abortion. How she managed to travel out of town is less certain. "She must have been fevered and in terrible pain," said Dr. Hannibal Morgan of Bellevue. "I can only imagine that she dosed herself with opiates."

Thus far detectives have been unable to find anyone who saw Janine Campbell traveling with her boys that Wednesday, but inquiries are still being conducted.

By all accounts Mrs. Campbell was a virtuous woman who kept a spotless home and showered her sons with maternal affection. None of her neighbors have a bad word to say about her.

"She was just three months out of childbed," noted Dr. Morgan. "This has all the hallmarks of puerperal insanity. In extreme cases even murder cannot be ruled out."

NEW YORK TIMES

Monday, May 28, 1883

INQUEST BEGINS TODAY

*JURY OF EMINENT PHYSICIANS TO
RULE ON CAMPBELL DEATH*

Coroner Lorenzo Hawthorn has released the names of the jurors who will hear evidence in the inquest into the death of Mrs. Janine Campbell. They are Dr. Morgan Hancock of Women's Hospital; Dr. Manuel Thalberg, lead physician at the German Dispensary; Dr. Nicholas Lambert, a forensics specialist at Bellevue; Dr. Abraham Jacobi of Children's Hospital and president of the New York Medical Association; Dr. Josiah Stanton of Women's Hospital; and Dr. Benjamin Quinn, surgeon on the faculty at both Bellevue's School of Medicine and the Woman's Medical School. In addition, Anthony Comstock will serve on the jury as a representative of the New York Society for the Suppression of Vice.

◆   ◆   ◆

THE CORONER INSTRUCTED his clerk to call the inquest to order, and the murmuring in the courtroom trailed off. Sophie took a last look at the notes laid out before her, shuffled them into a pile, and folded her hands in her lap. Beside her Anna was scribbling already, all her attention on the first of many blank pages she would fill before day's end. The jury would think her inordinately attentive, but Sophie had gone to school with Anna and she knew better. Her cousin scribbled as she listened, writing down odd words that taken together made little sense; when she got home, she would hand all the closely written pages to Mrs. Lee to use as tinder for the fire.

What Anna needed to know, she retained without writing down; she took notes for another reason altogether. As a girl she had disliked being called on in class and found that most teachers would leave her be if she looked busy. It wasn't that she couldn't answer questions, only that she wanted to decide which ones to answer. Some teachers left her this small vanity, and others did not, but nothing kept her from her scribbling.

Cap had often stolen her notebook away to read those random words out loud, like an actor on a stage. But they weren't children anymore, and Cap was at home where he belonged, fighting for every breath.

She made herself focus on the proceedings.

Judge Benedict's courtroom had been made available for the inquest, given the number of witnesses, the size of the jury, and the overwhelming public interest. Sophie had hoped that Judge Benedict himself would be absent, and was relieved to see that he was. Benedict and Comstock together were a disaster for any woman who came to their combined attention.

Because it was an inquest and not a trial, Hawthorn had some latitude in how he ran things. He handpicked the reporters—just three of them—to sit in the back of the courtroom—and he had spent some part of the morning considering case by case people who applied for permission to sit in the gallery. The ones he turned away were the ones who were there hoping for scandal and in particular, news of the missing Campbell boys. The whole city seethed with rumors and supposition about those little boys. They rarely left Sophie's mind.

The coroner was saying, "This is an inquest into the death of Mrs. Janine Campbell, nothing more or less. We are here to decide whether her death was the result of malpractice and criminal abortion, and if so, the police will then be responsible for locating the responsible individuals and bringing them into a court of law to be tried. The jury may also rule that Mrs. Campbell died of self-inflicted injuries amounting to suicide. Given the complexities of the case, I have asked physicians to hear the evidence. They are free to ask questions at any time. Persons admitted to the gallery may also ask questions but should first apply to me."

There were different kinds of evidence, he went on to explain. They would be considering the autopsy and physical items found at the Campbell home, and also they would discuss the deceased's state of mind.

He said, "This is not an inquiry into the whereabouts and fate of the Campbell sons. The subject will come up but will be kept within bounds. I also want to remind both the jury and those sitting in the gallery that the question of pregnancy is irrelevant. Under the law, it doesn't matter if the deceased was actually with child. The operation itself is illegal, in any case.

"This final point. The chief of police has submitted the results of a preliminary investigation, and on that basis both Dr. Savard and Dr. Savard Verhoeven have been cleared of any direct involvement in the illegal operation. They are here because they were the last physicians to treat the deceased and their testimony will be relevant.

"However, it has been pointed out to me that one or both of them may or may not be guilty of a different but related crime, that of supplying information and instruments to the deceased that made it possible for her to carry out the operation on herself."

Sophie didn't look at the jury box. She had sworn to herself that she would not, because there was nothing to be gained by it. She knew exactly who had reminded the coroner that dispensing medical advice of certain kinds was illegal, and he was sitting just fifteen feet away.

Comstock was just a single vote of seven. Of the six physicians, three could be counted as allies: Abraham Jacobi of Children's Hospital, Manuel Thalberg of the German Dispensary, and Dr. Quinn, a Bellevue surgeon who also taught surgery at the Women's Hospital and had been something of a surly but effective mentor to Anna. The other physicians were known to her only by name and reputation. Dr. Stanton, because he had published article after article attacking women physicians and the New Amsterdam in particular, and Dr. Hancock because he was one of the surgeons from Women's Hospital, where women physicians were not welcome or even tolerated. The last physician she knew only as a Dr. Lambert, a specialist in forensics, one with an excellent reputation.

With the exception of Thalberg, who worked exclusively among the poor German immigrants, all of the physicians had thriving practices. Some of them—Jacobi in particular—also did a large amount of charity work, but they all lived well. In this group Comstock looked out of place. The physicians were all carefully groomed and expensively clothed, while Comstock, ponderous and pompous, wore his poorly fitting black wool suit and standard grim expression. But for the whiskers he always reminded Sophie of an overgrown infant. It was his round face with its flawless complexion and high spots of color where the cheekbones would be, below the layer of fat. She had no intention of studying the man, but it was impossible to ignore the habit he had of sucking his front teeth.

Sophie and Anna sat in the foremost row of the gallery, behind the table where the defense would be situated in a real trial. Behind them in the second row were Conrad and his clerk, and beyond them, about two dozen faces scattered in a room that would have seated many more. Hawthorn might be a businessman with little knowledge of medicine, but in Sophie's view of things, he had done very well in arranging the inquest.

She smiled a greeting at five classmates from Woman's Medical School, and then got up to greet the three professors who had come as a powerful gesture of support: Mary Putnam Jacobi, Clara Garrison, and Maude Clarke. Sophie was especially surprised to see Dr. Garrison, who had so recently been on trial herself, another one of Comstock's favored targets. She was especially glad to see Mary Putnam, who had a mind sharper than any of the men in the room, including her husband, Abraham Jacobi, who sat on the jury.

"Steady on," Mary said, and left everything else unsaid.

• • •

JUST AS SOPHIE returned to her seat the coroner asked the jury to put forward any questions they might have.

"I'd like a clarification."

"Dr. Hancock, please go ahead."

"You've mentioned the possibility that the deceased may have operated on herself in a frame of mind that amounted to suicide. I agree, it's something to consider, but if we're going to look at suicide, we are talking about a woman who was suffering from severe mental illness. That discussion will necessarily lead to consideration of the Campbell sons, and what happened to them."

Anna stopped scribbling and her gaze fixed on the jury box. Then she wrote something down and turned the writing pad toward Sophie. She was writing with pencil, in sharp, straight strokes that pressed through many layers of paper. In her bag she'd have another dozen sharpened pencils to replace the one in hand when it got too dull. She had written, *Morgan Hancock, Women's Hospital?*

Sophie nodded.

Studied with Czerny?

Sophie nodded again.

"I didn't forbid the subject," the coroner was saying. "But I would like to keep in mind that our primary purpose is something else entirely."

The coroner said, "We'll start with Dr. Graham of the ambulance service."

•   •   •

ANNA WAS AWARE of Jack at the back of the room. He stood there with Oscar Maroney and another detective, his arms crossed and his chin lowered to his chest as he listened to Neill Graham recount what had happened the previous Thursday.

Graham was a good witness, clear and focused. The jurors asked questions—some of them very pointed—but Neill Graham didn't fluster.

"How many abdominal surgeries have you observed?" Abraham Jacobi's tone was neither kind nor confrontational.

"Mrs. Campbell's case was the thirty-third."

"And your impressions of Dr. Savard's performance?"

He faltered then and glanced in Anna's direction. She focused on her writing pad, where she wrote *thirty-third* and *impressions of.* Abraham Jacobi was asking questions he knew the answers to, to reestablish her credentials. He was subtle, as ever, in his support and therefore very effective.

"I'm not asking you for a detailed critique," said Jacobi. "Just your impression."

Graham didn't hesitate any further. "She was confident. She moved quickly but not hastily. And she told me what she was doing and pointed out what she was seeing. I learned quite a bit in that short period of time."

Benjamin Quinn cleared his throat. "And what was it you learned?"

"I thought I was pretty good at thinking on my feet, but I have a long way to go."

Anna wrote: *a long way to go.*

Conrad Belmont leaned forward and put a hand on her shoulder to whisper. "He said not one thing to contradict your testimony."

"Of course he didn't," Anna whispered back, irritably.

Conrad patted her as if she needed encouragement, and she resisted the urge to pull away.

*   *   *

NEW YORK POST

Monday, May 28, 1883

CAMPBELL INQUEST BEGINS

A NEIGHBOR'S CONCERNS FOR THE MISSING BOYS

SUICIDE MENTIONED FOR THE FIRST TIME

THE DECEASED'S HUSBAND TO TESTIFY TOMORROW

Coroner Lorenzo Hawthorn began the inquest into the death of Mrs. Janine Campbell today by presenting seven prominent and educated men with a long list of admonishments about their responsibilities as jurors. A short discussion of the possibility of suicide, insanity, and the relevance of the Campbell sons' disappearance was left unresolved, but it was the coroner himself who first raised the subject with one of the witnesses.

The first witness was Dr. Neill Graham, an intern at Bellevue who works part-time for the police ambulance service. Despite pointed questions from the jury, Dr. Graham had only praise for Dr. Anna Savard, the surgeon who tried to save Mrs. Campbell's life.

The day's second witness provided compelling testimony and insight into the life and death of Mrs. Campbell. We provide it here in fulfillment of our pledge to bring all the facts of this disturbing case to our readers.

Inquest Testimony

Mrs. Mabel Stone, housewife, resident at 24 Charles Street, appears before Coroner Hawthorn's jury and makes the following statement.

Coroner: Please start by explaining how you knew the deceased.

Mrs. Stone: The Campbells are our neighbors and have been since they were first married, seven years this summer.

Coroner: You considered her a friend?

Mrs. Stone: I did. Janine Campbell was a no-nonsense kind of person, which I am myself. We saw eye to eye.

Coroner: Did you see her often?

Mrs. Stone: Janine had her hands full from dawn till dark with those little boys and the house. I myself have no children but have always felt the lack, and so I lent a hand wherever I could. I saw her every day, just about. Except Sundays.

Coroner: And now if you could tell us about last week.

Mrs. Stone: Early last Wednesday I went by train to visit my sister in Albany. I was back Thursday morning, and I noticed how quiet it was at the Campbells' and so I went over to say hello. There was no answer when I knocked so I went around back to see was she hanging out laundry, but she wasn't. So I looked in the kitchen window.

Coroner: Is this common practice in the neighborhood?

Mrs. Stone: It's common enough between friendly families. So as I was saying, I looked in the kitchen window, and there she was.

Coroner: This is difficult, I understand, Mrs. Stone. But please be specific. Exactly what did you see?

Mrs. Stone: I saw Janine—Mrs. Campbell—lying on the floor, in a pool of blood.

Coroner: And then?

Mrs. Stone: Well, I went in, of course like anybody would. At first I thought she was dead she was so pale, but when I lifted up her head she opened her eyes. "Easy now," says I to her. "I'll send for a doctor." But she said no, she didn't want me to.

Coroner: Was she in pain?

Mrs. Stone: Yes sir, in terrible pain, curled up tight with her knees to her chest. Hardly able to talk, but she didn't want a doctor and she said so. Asked me to help her into bed so she could sleep. And I says to her, "Janine, you are bleeding to beat the band. You're having a miscarriage and you need a doctor."

Coroner: How did you know she was having a miscarriage?

Mrs. Stone: Only a man would ask such a question. You don't get to be my age without seeing miscarriages and worse. Why, I'd seen Janine herself miscarry twice before. Near bled to death the second time, but Mr. Campbell was home. He got the doctor to come and late the next day she was out of bed and back to work. She didn't have much choice.

Coroner: These are things you witnessed yourself?

Mrs. Stone: Yes. And I saw the doctor come. That gentleman, right there.

Coroner: Let the record reflect that the witness is pointing to Dr. Heath in the gallery. Go on, Mrs. Stone.

Mrs. Stone: As I say, I seen Mrs. Campbell in such a state before, so I knew why she was bleeding. But this time was far worse than the other two, so I says to her again, "I have to send for an ambulance." And she says, "No, just leave me here. Archer will find me when he gets home."

Coroner: Those were her exact words?

Mrs. Stone: Exact. But I ran outside and saw the baker's boy and I told him to run as fast as he could to the Jefferson Market police station—just three blocks away—and tell them we needed an ambulance. And he did.

Coroner: Where were the Campbell children while all this was going on?

Mrs. Stone: I don't know. I just don't know. At the time I barely noticed they were gone except to think to myself—I do remember this—thank the Lord they don't have to see their mam in such a state. But I didn't ask her. That was my mistake.

Coroner: It wasn't unusual for the boys to be away from home?

Mrs. Stone: It happened maybe three times a year that she sent them off to stay with relatives. Usually it was to Mr. Campbell's brother, the one with the farm in Connecticut, but sometimes to another brother in New Haven. She sent them away when it was time to do the spring cleaning, usually, because they were too little to help and slowed her down. One thing she never had enough of was time.

Coroner: Mrs. Campbell didn't mention her sons to you while you waited for the ambulance?

Mrs. Stone: Not a word. She fell away into a faint and didn't rouse again until the young doctor—Dr. Graham, who spoke before me just now—came, not a quarter hour after I sent the boy running. He made me go out while he examined her but I heard her scream—scream loud—and then she was saying she didn't want an ambulance. But he called for the stretcher anyway, as was proper. When they took her out of the house she grabbed my hand and said, "Send word to Mr. Campbell now, Mabel, would you? Tell him he'll find me at the New Amsterdam." And those are the last words I heard her say. Out she went into the ambulance and then she was gone. I hardly knew what to do with myself, I was that agitated. So I cleaned the floors, there was a terrible lot of blood, you see, and I took the bedding away to soak. Next I knew Mr. Campbell was at my door, telling me his wife was dead.

Clerk: There is a question from the gallery.

Coroner: So I see. Dr. Heath was once Mrs. Campbell's physician of record. Please go ahead, Doctor.

Dr. Heath: I am Dr. Heath. Did Mrs. Campbell ever mention me to you?

Mrs. Stone: No.

Dr. Heath: She never said she had gone to see Dr. Heath at Women's Hospital?

Mrs. Stone: No, she did not.

Dr. Heath: Did she mention any other doctor or nurse or midwife?

Mrs. Stone: No.

Dr. Heath: Never said a word about her health?

Mrs. Stone: That's a different question altogether. We talked from time to time about such things, as women do.

Dr. Heath: And in all those conversations she never mentioned a doctor's name?

Mrs. Stone: Doctor, you'll forgive me for my blunt nature, but I doubt Mrs. Campbell ever gave you a thought. She was up to her ears in work, dawn till dark and beyond. When she took ten minutes for herself, to sit down with a neighbor to have a cup of tea, you were the last thing on her mind.

Coroner: We're off the subject. Mrs. Stone, just two more questions. When we spoke to Dr. Graham of the ambulance service he told us that Mrs. Campbell specifically requested she be delivered into Dr. Savard's care at the New Amsterdam. Did she mention Dr. Savard to you before the ambulance arrived?

Mrs. Stone: She did not.

Coroner: This is the last matter we need to raise. Mrs. Stone, did Mrs. Campbell ever talk to you about abortion?

Mrs. Stone: Janine Campbell was a good Christian woman, sir. Mr. Campbell wasn't the easiest of husbands but she persevered as a woman must. She obeyed and kept house and raised those boys to be polite and helpful and made sure that dinner wasn't a single minute late and her husband's coffee was exactly the way he liked it, and when her health failed her, she bore up under that too. She wasn't a complainer. She never spent a day in bed except when she was new delivered.

Coroner: We have another question from someone in the gallery. Dr. Garrison, is it?

Dr. Clara Garrison: Mrs. Stone, I'm a physician and a professor at Woman's Medical School. May I ask, did you ever notice any signs of instability in Mrs. Campbell? Some of the questions before the coroner's jury have to do with her state of mind and her sanity. You saw her almost every day, as I understand it. Would you have an opinion on this?

Mrs. Stone: Hard work never killed anybody, that's what my mam used to say, but it can grind a woman down to dust. Janine was tired and her spirits were low but I never heard her talk crazy or do anything but what she always did, housework and tending to the boys. She was a good mother, too, and her boys adored her. Some women take things out on their children, but Janine handled them different. She could get what she wanted with a soft word. And that's the way she was, she worked hard, day in and day out and she looked after those boys—

Coroner: This is very difficult, I understand. Take a moment to gather your thoughts.

Mrs. Stone: She said to me once that her own father was too eager with the rod, and that she wanted something else for her boys. She didn't have an easy life and she swallowed down more than her fair share of bile, but was no more insane than I am or you are, Dr. Garrison.

Coroner: Thank you, Mrs. Stone; you're excused.

•　•　•

ON THE WAY home from the inquest Monday evening Anna went over the long list of things she needed to do, all of which involved other people. Aunt Quinlan and Mrs. Lee would want to hear about Staten Island and about the inquest, Jack's parents would be expecting them to call after supper, and once there, his sisters would raise the subject of the new house. Anna was curious, she could admit to herself, about Jack's mother. It was odd to look forward to and dread something at the same time, but what she found oddest of all was this idea of herself as a daughter-in-law. As someone with parents, when for all these years she had been without. Anna realized that she had always assumed she wouldn't marry, specifically because she had trouble imagining herself with a family that included parents and brothers and sisters. And now she had all of that.

But what she wanted to do was slip between cool sheets and fall asleep in a breeze from an open window. She wanted to sleep for days on end, and to wake up when the whole sorry business of the inquest and the missing boys had been resolved. She wanted sleep in order to put Mrs. Stone's testimony out of her head, and at the same time she wanted to bind all those words together into a club and hit every man in the room over the head with it. Because they hadn't really understood the story behind the story, and what Mrs. Stone was trying to tell them about Janine Campbell's life. Mrs. Stone had called herself plain-speaking and blunt, but she had wrapped every observation in the language of well-brought-up women, with the result that none of the men had any real sense of the anger and frustration that drove Janine Campbell.

She wanted to sleep, and she wanted Jack sleeping beside her. Instead she had to resign herself to an evening of talking, one that started over supper. Then Sophie joined them, and Anna felt much better. She had come especially to hear about Vittorio Russo, something Jack's parents made possible when they took the little girls off to be fed by his aunt Philomena and coddled by a house full of Mezzanottes.

"And to speak Italian," Mrs. Mezzanotte had explained. "They miss the language."

For once Margaret didn't seem to mind letting them go off without her, but then she wanted to hear about the youngest Mezzanotte boy as well.

Jack told the story in a very ordered, very complete manner that struck Anna as unlike him, until she realized that this was how he presented a case to his superiors, the men who judged his performance and made decisions about his career. It was a change from the way stories were usually told around Aunt Quinlan's table, but then it was a serious subject.

"He's a beautiful child," Anna said when he had finished. "Dearly loved. The picture of rude good health."

At the startled look on Jack's face aunt Quinlan laughed. "A family turn of phrase," she said. "Sophie's great-grandmother used it for children who were thriving and content."

"Then it fits in his case," Jack said.

He turned to Margaret, who had been silent throughout the story.

"You've spent more time with the girls than anybody. Do you have any thoughts on how to proceed?"

She took a moment to pat her mouth dry with her napkin, and then she cleared her throat. Margaret appreciated good manners and respectful gestures, and Jack gave her both. In return she answered with more candor than Anna would have anticipated.

"I do have an opinion," she said. "But I'm afraid I'll offend you, as a Catholic."

Jack said, "I'm not Catholic. I was never baptized, but that's a longer story for another time. Go on and say what you're thinking."

Margaret studied him for a moment. Anna could read her expression very easily: she was fighting the urge to ask him for details. Margaret needed to put him in a box marked Lutheran or Protestant or Baptist; it would never occur to her that he might be something other than Christian. But Jack respected her opinion in the matter of the Russo children, and so she restrained her curiosity.

"From everything I've read about the Church of Rome, I can't imagine that they'd allow a child to be taken away from a good Catholic home to be brought up in such an unconventional household as this one. It could take months or years and might even go to court, and that without much hope of success. Worst of all, the girls will have to live through it all. They are just starting to really come into their own, but this—this would set them back. The knowledge that their brother is nearby but cut off from them would be more than Rosa could cope with."

Sophie said, "There's also the boy himself, and the family to think about. We might well do more harm than good, in the greater scheme of things."

This morning, getting ready for the day on one side of the room while Jack dressed on the other, Anna had hoped that going back to work would be distraction enough to keep her mind off Vittorio, but the image of him in his adoptive mother's arms stayed with her while she saw patients and met with her assistants and students and answered mail.

Even in Judge Benedict's courtroom her thoughts kept wandering back to Staten Island. And not to the good things—the excellent things—that had transpired, but to the little boy who was no longer lost, and still, not yet found.

She said, "I promised Rosa I would try."

"You have tried," her aunt said. "Are you feeling guilty?"

Anna felt Jack's gaze on her, waiting, patient. "Not guilty exactly, but to make myself feel better I would have to cause a lot of other people great distress. I'm not so self-centered as that."

Aunt Quinlan nodded, pleased with her.

Jack said, "I'll approach Father McKinnawae. Just to be sure of what we think we know. And in the meantime—" He paused, and Anna could almost see the question hovering there, unspoken: *What will you do with the boy if you get him?*

"I won't be here to deal with the results of your decision," Sophie said, as if Jack had spoken out loud. "But I will be back, and I will do whatever needs to be done. I would gladly take on all three children, if it comes to that."

"You'd give up your profession?" Margaret's tone was unapologetically doubtful.

"I don't know," Sophie said. "But it's a possibility."

Anna didn't like that idea at all, but she understood, too, that Sophie would want something to come home to, when Cap was gone. She wondered if her cousin was even aware of this herself.

When Jack announced that he would see Sophie home and then spend a little time with his parents, Anna was so happy to go off to bed that she could barely contain herself. She kissed him good-bye in the front hall, and tried to think of something to say. *Be quick. Be careful. Hurry home. Must you go?* None of those things would come out of her mouth.

"Married barely two days and you're eager to get rid of me."

She was relieved and surprised both by the way he was smiling at her.

"Savard, you need a little time to yourself. I'm not offended. I'll try not to wake you when I come in."

Anna went to bed, and slept.

• ◆ •

AS THEY GOT into Cap's carriage—Sophie's carriage, now, Jack reminded himself—a police runner dashed up and handed him an envelope. He put it away in his pocket without looking at it, but she had not missed the exchange.

"From Oscar," he explained. "It can wait." Which wasn't exactly true, but he would act as if it were.

Sophie looked distracted, and he was fairly sure he knew why. Still he waited for her to ask.

"Do you know anything about the Campbell boys that isn't in the newspapers?"

He shook his head. She didn't believe him, he could see it, but why should she? Men lied to women all the time, and called it protection or concern for their sensibilities when really what they wanted was an end to the questioning.

"I would like to hear the truth," she said. "No matter what it is."

He inclined his head. "That's good to know. The truth is, I don't have any information that isn't in the papers, at this moment. If and when I do, I will share that information with you. No matter how distressing."

Satisfied, Sophie sat back. She said, "What do you think should happen with Vittorio?"

This was a question Jack could answer without hesitation. "I think he should stay where he is."

"Does Anna know you feel that way?"

"No, but then she hasn't asked me directly. If she does, I won't lie to her."

"She isn't sure herself what would be best."

"Yes, she is," Jack said. "But she's not ready to acknowledge it."

"You do understand her," Sophie said. "I'm glad."

"Don't congratulate me yet," Jack said. "I'm sure to fall on my face sooner or later."

"You'll pick yourself back up, and let me tell you a secret about Anna. She doesn't hold a grudge. At least not with people she loves."

• • •

AT HOME—AT what used to be home—Jack spent a half hour being peppered with questions, some of which he answered, many of which he ignored. It was a familiar dance with his mother; he ignored a question, she stepped away and then swung around to approach it from another direction.

"I like her," his mother said. "You know that I like her."

"I know that you wouldn't hesitate to tell me if you didn't," Jack said. "Married or not."

His father barked a short laugh, then went back to his newspaper. In the kitchen there was sudden silence, because his sisters were listening. Which meant that the little girls were listening, too, something his mother was well aware of.

"But we are married," he went on. "For better or worse."

Some of the tension in her face retreated.

"Mama," he said then. "She'll never be a housewife. Not even when we have a family."

That got him a smile. "She wants a family."

"Yes," Jack said. "Though I don't know why you would mind if she didn't. You've got too many grandchildren to keep track of as it is."

"Never too many grandchildren," his father said from behind the pages of il *Giornale.*

"Never," his mother echoed.

Jack stood up. "My work here is done."

"We still have things to discuss," his mother said. "But go back to your bride."

◆　◆　◆

INSTEAD HE WENT to the station house and took the time at the duty desk to write a note and arranged for it to be delivered to Anna at home.

Called into the station house, may be very late but I'll be there to
walk you to work in the morning. Ever yours, JM

◆　◆　◆

UPSTAIRS OSCAR WAS leaning back in his chair, his feet crossed at the ankle and one heel propped on the edge of the desk. It was how he did his best thinking, but it was also how he napped. Sometimes it was hard to tell the difference. In either case Jack didn't see the need to disturb him straightaway, so he sat down to the pile of paperwork that had appeared on his own desk.

Arrest reports, most of it. He had been reading for a few minutes when Oscar said, "You leave for three days and I get stuck with two homicides, three assaults, and pulling Baldy out of trouble. Yet again."

"Anna has rechristened him Ned," Jack said. "He's in the Tombs, I take it."

"I'll let him go tomorrow. No real evidence, but I thought he needed a night to cool off."

"Your note said he pulled a knife."

"Which disappeared."

Jack whistled under his breath. "Where was this?"

"Outside the Black and Tan. He went looking for one of the younger boys and found him exactly where he didn't want to find him. It got ugly."

"As it always does."

Oscar nodded and pulled his hat back down over his eyes.

He was an excellent detective, but not overly hampered by the letter of the law. Jack wondered if he should tell Anna about this newest situation with Baldy, and decided that the matter could wait. He needed to talk to Oscar about the Campbell boys, but instead Jack turned his attention to the paperwork and waited for his partner to rouse himself for the next conversation.

If he submitted the arrest reports as they stood, the whole pile would end up back here on Jack's desk because nobody else could make out Maroney's handwriting. He picked up a pen and uncorked an ink bottle.

Oscar's feet hit the floor with a thump. "So what happened with McKinnawae?"

Jack put the cork back in the ink bottle and told him about Mount Loretto and Vittorio Russo. He watched as Oscar's expression shifted from weariness to surprise.

"I'll be damned," he said. "You did it. You found the baby."

"I'm just as surprised as you are. But it's far from settled, and there's still the older boy. Now, are you going to tell me about the Campbell case?"

Oscar said, "I'm hungry." He got up and walked out of the office, fitting his hat to his head as he went. Jack followed him, raising a hand in greeting to a couple of other detectives bent over paperwork on the other side of the room. He wasn't sure if his getting married was general knowledge yet, but he didn't want to find out at the moment.

By the time he got downstairs Oscar had already disappeared down the hallway that led to the rear exit. Jack found his partner in the corner booth at MacNeil's, with a cup of coffee in front of him.

The only door into the diner was in the alley behind police headquarters, which was why every man he'd ever seen in the place either had a badge now or had had one in the past. MacNeil himself had been a cop about a hundred years ago, before he lost a leg at Spotsylvania. Now he stumped around the diner's kitchen shouting at everybody, good mood or bad. He worked the night shift alone and his sons took the day shift.

Jack paused at the counter to get the cup of coffee the old man poured for him, took a couple of minutes to be shouted at about the follies of marriage, and then slid into a booth across from Oscar.

"Any luck tracing Mrs. Campbell's movements?"

MacNeil thumped a plate of eggs and bacon down, so Jack sat back to wait while Oscar ate. At the halfway mark he wiped his mouth and started to talk.

"You know what Grand Central's like. I talked to every ticket seller, flower girl, bootblack, and baggage man that I could find who was working the depot that day. A few think they saw her with the boys, but nobody's sure. I'm thinking now they traveled some other road."

"A steamer?"

"I looked into that. Don't seem likely, not for somebody watching her pennies."

They were quiet while Oscar finished his plate. He had a dainty way of going about it for a big man with an appetite, something Jack hadn't figured out until he had known the man a good six months: Maroney was vain about his mustache and lived in fear of getting food caught up in it.

He ate the last of his bacon, crossed his knife and fork over the plate, and leaned back in the booth, trying to look casual as he ran one knuckle over the brush on his upper lip.

Jack hid his face in his coffee cup for as long as it took to get rid of a smile.

"What are you thinking?" he asked, finally.

"Well, I don't think she drowned them. That's the rumor, you know. She went to the shore to toss those boys in the drink."

Jack hadn't been around long enough to catch up on the gossip, but it made sense that people would be anticipating the worst. A rumor was like an army on the march, no stopping it.

"But the timing just doesn't work out," Oscar went on. "She was home when Campbell came in from work on Wednesday. Don't see how you could drown four boys and come away looking like nothing fails you. And then there's what the Stone woman had to say, that business about her husband finding her when he got home."

"Hawthorn didn't seem to take any note of that," Jack said.

"That's because he owns a string of lumber mills and doesn't know what he's doing, questioning somebody on the stand. Boston went ahead and got rid of the coroner system, you'd think we could do the same."

Jack had had the exact same thought, listening to Hawthorn question Mrs. Stone. He might be well-meaning and thoughtful, but he was also uninformed and untrained. If Janine Campbell had said *Archer will find me when he gets home*, then that was as good as a confession: she knew she was dying, and she wanted her husband to find her dead. A lawyer would have homed in on that and asked Mrs. Stone a dozen more questions, trying to get her to clarify the deceased's state of mind.

Oscar said, "She figured it was less trouble killing herself than it would have been to kill him. So I'm wondering, if she was that angry, maybe she did find a way to kill the boys."

"I don't think so," Jack said. "She knew she was dying, sure. What she wanted was not to leave the boys to their father's tender mercies. He looks like a hard case to me."

Oscar nodded. "Worse, he looks like a closet hard case. One who uses his fists behind closed doors. They didn't say anything about bruises on the autopsy, though."

"Wouldn't be the first time a body turned up dead with no marks to show how it got that way."

Oscar swallowed the rest of his coffee. "So she stowed the boys away somewhere, is that what you're thinking?"

Jack lifted a shoulder. "They could be anywhere, by now. Canada comes to mind."

"She was from Maine."

Jack nodded. "I suppose we could get in touch with the Bangor coppers, but it's a big state."

"Well." Oscar reached for his hat. "Tomorrow's another day, as they say so clever and all. And there's other things to be thinking about. First and most important, you've got to be back here at six thirty to start your shift and you've left your new bride all alone, just three days married."

"Two days," Jack said. "And five hours." He rarely flushed, but now color ran up his throat to his face.

Oscar laughed, and slapped him on the back.

• • •

HE SLIPPED INTO bed quietly, drawn into the nest of often-washed linen sheets that smelled of sunshine and lavender and Anna. His Anna, her cheeks flushed with sleep, on her side so that he could study her face in the vague soft light of the lamp before he put it out.

One part of him wanted to wake her, but she had earned her rest. There would be more nights and mornings and middays, too, when they'd have privacy and time enough. He'd made sure of it.

27

Tuesday morning near the end of May might have been July, by the weather. Later in the summer Anna would keep an extra set of clothes in her office, but today she was faced with a choice. She could take the noon hour to try to catch up with her paperwork—in which case she'd show up at the inquest wilted and damp with sweat, or she could go home and change.

She went home and found Aunt Quinlan alone in the parlor, smiling as if Anna's arrival were the only thing in the world she had ever wished for. In return Anna might have started to cry. Things had happened so quickly, and she had let herself be drawn along without taking time for her aunt.

"Get changed quickly," Auntie said. "And I'll arrange things down here."

By the time she got back Mrs. Lee had put out a plate of sandwiches and a pot of tea and disappeared back into the kitchen. Anna sat just beside her aunt and gently picked up one of her hands. They were very delicate, as if the bones had gone as hollow as a bird's. The skin was soft and shiny and speckled with age spots.

"You've been using the wax bath for your joints," Anna said. "I hope it helps with the pain."

"It does," her aunt said. "The heat is wonderful. And the teas, they help too."

But not enough, Anna knew. This woman who had spent all her life doing things with her hands would sit just as she was, for whatever time was left to her.

"I can remember you painting," Anna said. "You handled the paintbrush like I handle a scalpel. I was little, but I remember."

"You were seven when I stopped."

Anna nodded. "When you were working I had the idea that you were painting a window I could walk through if I tried."

Her aunt smiled. "Very fanciful, for such a serious young mind. You were so quiet, sitting in the corner. I often forgot you were there. Of course that was before Sophie."

Anna remembered what it had felt like to be alone. "I love Sophie and Cap," Anna said. "And wouldn't change a thing, but sometimes it's nice to have you to myself."

"So," Aunt Quinlan said. "Here we are, by ourselves. You married Jack Mezzanotte."

Anna laughed. "Yes, I did. Although sometimes it all feels unreal. Was it like that when you got married?"

Her aunt's expression was thoughtful. After a moment she said, "You know that your aunt Hannah's people believe that the dead are never far away. She told me once—and this was before she met Ben—that her first husband and little boy sometimes came from the Shadowlands to talk to her. Some people dislike that idea because it frightens them. But when Simon died, I waited and waited. I wanted him to come back to talk to me, in my dreams at least. I wanted to scold him for being so reckless on the ice floes, the day he died. And he did come, finally, but by that time I wasn't angry at him anymore. I just missed him.

"He still comes now and then, and when he does he looks as he did when we were young. Sometimes he has our littlest three girls with him, the ones we lost too soon."

"And Nathaniel?"

Aunt Quinlan talked sometimes about her son, the last of six and the only boy. Nathaniel Ballentyne had died at Shiloh, on his twenty-fifth birthday, unmarried, childless.

"Nathaniel most of all," her aunt said. "He knew how angry I was about him going off to fight. He's been trying to make it up to me ever since. Sometimes he is as real to me as you are, sitting there."

She shook herself a little. "Enough of that. There was something I wanted to tell you, and you let me wander off."

Anna tried to prepare her mind, but Aunt Quinlan's stories were never predictable.

"As a little girl you already knew what it meant to lose the people you love, and that made you shy. Then the war came along and we lost Paul and Harrison, and made it ten times worse. When you and Cap got to be friends I thought, *Maybe he'll pull her out of it*, and he did. A good ways, he brought you back to being brave enough to face the world. Sophie brought you along even further. But it's there in you still, the need to hide away."

Anna had heard this before and she knew that it was at least in part true.

"So you're saying Jack is going to change my view of things?"

Aunt Quinlan looked at her with an expression that was pure surprise. "That would be a silly thing to say, Anna. You know as well as I do that people rarely change once they reach a certain age. What I'm saying is, you're a turned-inward soul; it's the way you cope with the hard things in life. You hide away."

"You think Jack doesn't realize that about me."

"Maybe he does," her aunt said. "But if he does it's only in his mind; he doesn't know what it will feel like. I'm taking a long time to get to my point, so here it is. Hard things come along; they always have and they always will. When that time comes, you have to turn toward Jack and not away from him. And that's not in your nature. You love the man—don't bother blushing, I know you love him even if you can't say the word in your own mind—but your first instinct will be still to shut him out. So be aware of that, and do what you can to stop yourself."

Anna tried to smile. It made sense that Aunt Quinlan would worry about such things, simply because she had suffered so many losses herself. Nathaniel was gone, but she had also lost three girls before age ten, one to childbirth, and her second youngest to a cancer of the breast when she was just fifty. Only her oldest was left. There were grandchildren and great-grandchildren; she had her brother Gabriel, though she hadn't seen him in a long time for the simple reason that she would not go home to the village where she was born, and he wouldn't leave it. She was closest to her sister-in-law Martha, who wrote every week and did sometimes come to the city. And there were nieces and nephews and their families. But she felt the losses, and how could she not?

She said, "Auntie, I was right here, beside you, when the worst news came. I'd like to think that I learned something from you. That I have some of your strength."

"That's just it," her aunt said. "That's the hardest part, being strong enough to let the hurt in, and deal with it, and then let it settle in time, as it will."

"Yes," Anna said. "I see that. I can make one promise at least. I will think of you and this conversation when things are hard, and try not to turn away from it."

"That's all I'm asking," said her aunt. "Now eat before you have to go off to the courthouse, or Mrs. Lee will scold me without mercy."

"I have a few more minutes." Anna bit into a sandwich, thinking. When she swallowed she said, "You've been following the news about Janine Campbell in the paper?"

"I have."

"The rumors going around are that she killed her boys."

Aunt Quinlan had a particular look, one that said she was at the end of her patience, and it was there now. "That's pure foolishness."

Anna swallowed another bite. "What do you think happened to them?"

"I can't say, but I do know that nobody is asking the real question, the important one. *Ubi est morbus?*"

Anna laughed out loud to hear her aunt quoting the great physician Morgagni. *Where is the disease?*

"Where did that old chestnut come from?" she asked.

"This family is chock-full of doctors," her aunt said. "You know when your ma and pa came to Paradise to take over Hannah's practice, they lived with us at first. And did they love to talk medicine. They did it over every meal. Sometimes your aunt Hannah would be there too and they'd get into arguments and drag out books to prove each other wrong or themselves right. Nothing mean-spirited about it, mind. They were laughing half the time. And when they couldn't get anywhere with a case, one of them would put that question on the table, *Ubi est morbus?*, and they'd start looking at the evidence again, from the very beginning. And most of the time, they figured out what was going on, and more than that, why they had been looking in the wrong place."

"You're not asking me what disease Mrs. Campbell had."

"No, I'm saying that you have got to look and think symptom, not disease. If she's a symptom, then ask, where is the disease?"

And Anna knew two things: her aunt was right, and she wouldn't be able to get it out of her head until she could talk it through with Jack.

◆ ◆ ◆

THE COURTROOM WAS crowded and hot, and Sophie wished herself away, someplace where she wouldn't have to sit and listen to men talk about Janine Campbell. A woman they had never known and would never understand, not if her ghost came forward to answer their questions.

When the coroner announced that Archer Campbell was delayed, there was a great sigh from the reporters at the back of the room. Then he called Anna to the stand and Sophie thought that they would have enough to write about, once Anna started to testify.

She took her seat across from the jury of men who were, supposedly, her peers. With the exception of Comstock, all of them dressed in somber colors and expensively tailored suits. Most of them had been reading journals or newspapers, but as she approached, Abraham Jacobi and Manuel Thalberg met her gaze and nodded, as colleagues greeted each other across a room. Dr. Lambert even raised a hand, which was a bit of a surprise. She couldn't remember ever speaking to the man, but apparently he knew Anna.

The coroner left most of the questions to the physicians, and there were many of them, but Anna was a good teacher and that carried over to her testimony. Even when Josiah Stanton asked the same question three times like a particularly dull student, she stayed calm. She described her education, talked about medical school and work at dispensaries and clinics when she was an intern, about postgraduate work and the professors she had studied with in New York and abroad.

Stanton wore an expression of unapologetic surprise that a woman physician should have such credentials. For a moment Sophie thought he was going to challenge Anna, but then he thought better of it. And good for him.

The coroner had only one real question for her.

"In your professional opinion, Dr. Savard, how did Mrs. Campbell die?"

Sophie appreciated the man's clarity and lack of melodrama, and so did Anna, because she answered in kind.

"Sometime late on Tuesday or early Wednesday Mrs. Campbell attempted to induce an abortion on herself by means of an instrument as much as ten inches long, with a keen edge. In the process she punctured her uterus and caused damage to other abdominal organs. Infection will have set in immediately and once that happened, her death was inevitable."

"Why would you assume that?" Hawthorn asked.

Anna blinked at him, and really, it was a question that should need no answer.

She said, "Dr. Lister's and Dr. Pasteur's findings on antisepsis have been accepted by doctors and surgeons—" Anna paused to look at the jury, her expression almost inviting someone to disagree. Morgan Hancock of Women's Hospital stared back at her, his mouth in a hard line. If he was going to challenge the very idea of bacteriology, they would be here a very long time. There was a pause, and he looked away.

"It is accepted," Anna repeated, "that bacteria, which are too small to be observed by the human eye, are the cause of infection. Some types of bacteria are harmless or even beneficial, but there are also pathogenic bacteria that cause infection and illness. Bacteria are everywhere, but an infection starts, or can start, I should say, when pathogenic bacteria enter the body through a wound. Surely you're aware of the way President Garfield died."

She stopped herself, because James Garfield's death was still a very controversial subject among doctors. If the coroner asked for clarification, there might be an extended debate. But he did not, and she went on.

"In Mrs. Campbell's case, she used an instrument that was not sterilized—in a well-run operating room, every object that comes in contact with a patient is sterilized, made free of bacteria by means of heat. Mrs. Campbell inadvertently introduced pathogenic bacteria of many different kinds into puncture wounds in the uterus and intestines. If she had come into any good hospital at that point there's a chance she might have been saved if all the septic matter had been evacuated, but only a very small chance. Would any of the jury care to disagree with me? Dr. Hancock?"

"No," Hancock said, his voice gruff.

Anna allowed herself a small smile. "As it was, the infection ran riot, so to speak. There was so much damage and so many different kinds of bacteria, the natural defenses of the body were simply overwhelmed. The result was a systemic infection, and the huge amount of pus and purulent matter found in her abdomen. When she was brought to the New Amsterdam she was near death following from cryptogenic pyaemia, blood loss, and shock."

"But you operated anyway."

"I didn't know the extent of the damage until I had her on the operating table. She died not five minutes after I made the first incision."

"To be clear, you agree with the postmortem report on the cause of death?"

"I agree on the cause, but I do not agree about the agent. The postmortem reads 'person or persons unknown' performed the operation. I am fairly certain that it was Mrs. Campbell who operated on herself."

"What makes you so sure of that?" Stanton asked. "For my part I am not convinced."

Anna sat up straighter and looked at him directly. "I have treated many women who came to the New Amsterdam after a poorly done abortion. Some of them will say, in the vaguest way, that they went to someone for help. No one has ever volunteered the name of a practitioner—"

"An abortionist," Anthony Comstock interrupted.

"As you like," Anna said, without looking at him. "You may condemn those people who perform operations, but they are generally technically skilled. Some are less particular about hygiene, which is the cause of most complications in such cases. There was nothing skilled about the operation performed on Mrs. Campbell. It was clumsy, even violent."

For a full ten minutes she answered very specific questions about the surgery and Mrs. Campbell's condition. When the jurors began to argue among themselves about definitions, Hawthorn interrupted.

"Dr. Savard, it is your opinion that Mrs. Campbell operated on herself in such a violent way that she caused fatal injury. You believe that she could have done such a thing on her own though she was not a very large woman."

"Mr. Hawthorn," she said. "Mrs. Campbell ran a household, did the scrubbing and cleaning and laundry. Have you ever lifted a tub of wet linen? She didn't lead a pampered life. She gave birth four times and miscarried twice. She was not frail. Whatever thoughts or emotions motivated her to such an extreme act, she was determined and capable, and she persevered through the pain. As women do, every day. In your place I would want to know what drove her to such a point that she saw no other option than this drastic procedure she performed on herself."

"Well, I can think of another question." Comstock's voice rose over the steady murmuring in the gallery. He looked out, Sophie thought, to make sure he had everyone's attention.

"How would a simple, uneducated woman know what to do? Where did she get the knowledge and the surgical instruments she used? Did she have some text or instructions to follow? Maybe something like the pamphlet that was found in her dresser drawer, 'Female Health and Hygiene.' Are you familiar with it?"

"I'm willing to answer your questions, Mr. Comstock, but one by one. Could you start again?"

"I am Inspector Comstock," he said stiffly. "And I'll start again, but at the end. Are you familiar with the pamphlet that was found in her dresser drawer?"

"I was never in her home, and I know nothing about the contents of her dresser drawers."

"Come now, Dr. Savard. Are you familiar with the pamphlet we found, or not?"

"I don't recognize the title," Anna said.

"No? Well, if the coroner will permit me to show it to you—"

Anna didn't wait for the coroner's opinion. She just held out a hand, looking Comstock directly in the eye. His mouth worked, puckering and jerking with pleasure he didn't try to conceal. He stood up to approach her, but the coroner's clerk stopped him.

"I'll take it, sir."

Anna could not let herself smirk at Comstock, and so she smiled at the clerk and thanked him.

She turned the pages of the pamphlet deliberately, slowly, and then handed it back to the clerk.

"I have seen pamphlets on hygiene, of course. Not this exact pamphlet, but others like it."

"Isn't it true that the hygienic measures described in that pamphlet are also used to induce abortion?"

"If there is a discussion of abortion in that pamphlet, I didn't see it."

"That doesn't answer my question."

Anna decided to give him the information he so clearly wanted. She said, "I have treated women who flooded themselves with lye soap, carbolic acid, rubbing alcohol, gin, quinine, bleach—the list is very long and the results are often ugly. Women with a little more money sometimes take medicines. Most of them are nothing more than weak tea; others are as bad as arsenic. Many women try three or four times with such medicines and then seek help elsewhere. The very poor care for themselves. They use straws or wires or bougies, almost any kind of spoon or slender, long instrument. Rubber tubing, metal probes, whalebone stays from old corsets. Your pamphlet addresses none of these things. And as far as I could see, it provided no instructions on terminating a pregnancy. Does that answer your question?"

Comstock met her gaze with sputtering animosity. He said, "I have no further questions at this time."

"Then let's move on," the coroner said.

Anna turned toward him. "If I may suggest a solution to the question on the table?" Without waiting, she went on. "Dr. Lambert could speak to the question of how capable women are of injuring themselves. Dr. Lambert?"

Lambert's whole face contorted with surprise, but he spoke to Anna directly. "I think this point won't be settled without a second postmortem. The remains?"

"The Bellevue dead house," said the clerk.

Anna sat back, clearly satisfied to have achieved exactly this outcome. The coroner seemed less pleased, but he didn't try to object. The jury would go to the morgue and the inquest would reconvene at four.

Conrad leaned forward and touched Sophie's shoulder. "Go with them," he said. "Your testimony will be compromised if you don't."

Sophie inhaled a sharp breath. The idea of a second autopsy in the damp recesses of the Bellevue dead house was unwelcome. It wasn't so much the smells of putrification and mold, or the water that leached into the walls from the East River; those things were never pleasant but could be coped with. It was the idea of the men in the jury gathered around Janine Campbell, poking and prodding when she had been through so much already. But she would have to be there. With a female physician present the others would be utterly professional and focused on procedure. She only wished she could ask Anna to come along, but it was too much of an imposition.

Then help came from another quarter. Mary Putnam waved her closer, took Sophie's hand, and shook it firmly. Small and wiry, a plain woman who could be transformed and animated into something more when she had a medical issue to debate. Mary Putnam had also been one of their professors at medical school. Her expertise as a physician and a scientist was unquestioned, even by the most unapproachable male doctors. She was without a doubt the most exacting instructor Sophie had ever encountered. Together with her husband they made a formidable team. And they were both here.

Sophie reminded herself that she could reveal every facet of the Campbell case to Abraham and Mary Putnam Jacobi without hesitation or fear, because she had given the best treatment there was to offer.

"I'm coming too," Mary Putnam said. "The more female practitioners present, the better."

"Will it be possible to keep Comstock out of the room?" Sophie asked.

"It will be possible," she said. "I will see to it."

• • •

SOPHIE AND MARY Putnam left with the jurors and the coroner to make the trip to Bellevue while Anna stayed just where she was. She said good-bye to Conrad and his law clerk and spoke to the friends who had come to lend support, but she never moved from her seat.

Finally the reporters approached her, but she sent them off with a sharp shake of the head. She had no answers for them, but she did have an unanswered question of her own, one that had been growing in her mind since her aunt put it there: *Ubi est morbus?*

It was the right question to put to the jury, and she had come very close to saying as much. Then Comstock had interrupted her with his outrage over that pamphlet, one he claimed to have found in Mrs. Campbell's dresser. Nothing Comstock had to say was a surprise, but the pamphlet had been something of a shock, because she really had never seen it before.

From that fact followed two questions: what happened to the pamphlet Sophie had sent to Mrs. Campbell, and where had the one Comstock showed her come from? Which made Anna wonder what else she had gotten wrong from the start. It should have occurred to her that Mrs. Campbell would visit other doctors and midwives in the hope that someone would give her the help that Sophie would not provide.

Contrary to what Comstock and the physicians on the jury seemed to believe, women in distress could find a way to end an unwanted pregnancy, so long as they could pay for it. For every case that came to public view because something went terribly wrong, there were a hundred or more that remained a private matter. Though she had not said as much to Jack, Anna knew of three midwives and two male physicians who performed the procedure as a matter of course, and without ever having lost a mother. She knew another, who was retired, very well: her own cousin Amelie had cared for women in the city for forty years.

It occurred to her now that she didn't know who had delivered Mrs. Campbell's first three children. More than that, it was possible, she admitted to herself, that in her desperation Janine Campbell had put herself into the hands of a charlatan, one of the men and women who worked the darker corners of worst neighborhoods. Someone who took her money and promised results but had not the slightest training or interest in anything but the coin to be had.

Ubi est morbus?

Janine Campbell's social standing and income made it unlikely that she had ventured into the tenements to find the help she needed. And so Anna found herself back at square one.

By the courtroom clock she saw that she had an hour and a half until the inquest reconvened. A lot could be done in that amount of time, and so she left, slipping through one of the side entrances onto the street, where she hailed a cab to take her back to the New Amsterdam. If she thought about something else hard and long enough, often the answer to a difficult question that evaded her would present itself.

◆ ◆ ◆

WHEN JACK FINALLY got to the New Amsterdam he found he had missed Anna by a quarter hour. She had gone back to the Tombs, where the inquest was about to reconvene.

Oscar hailed a cab and they reached Judge Benedict's courtroom just as the jury took their seats. From their expressions it seemed to Jack that they had not come to any kind of concord, which might mean another hour or more before the coroner closed deliberations for the day.

Anna sat in her usual spot beside Sophie, both of them in conversation with another woman Jack didn't know. Conrad was listening closely while his clerk took notes.

Jack followed Oscar to the back of the room to stand against the wall, the usual spot for any police officers who had an interest in a trial or inquest. He watched Hawthorn, who stood behind the bench, thumbs tucked into his vest pockets while he stared at the floor. His complexion had gone the color of old cheese, and even from the back of the room the perspiration on his brow was obvious. Jack had the idea that he wouldn't be eager to watch another autopsy anytime soon.

Hawthorn cleared his throat a number of times before he could be heard. "I am going to poll the jury on a single question, before we proceed. Gentlemen of the jury, on the basis of the evidence you have just seen, do you concur with the testimony of Dr. Savard, in which she stated her opinion that it was Mrs. Campbell herself who performed the operation to end a pregnancy?"

There was silence for a long moment, and then Abraham Jacobi spoke, his tone modulated and professional. He was not a big man, but his voice was deep and had a rasp, as was sometimes the case with men who were too free with tobacco. His German accent was strong, but there was nothing in the least inarticulate about the way he expressed himself.

He said, "I agree with Dr. Savard that the operation was done in a violent way, and I find it hard to imagine any practitioner, even a new or poorly trained one, could have done such damage. For those reasons, I am satisfied with a ruling that identifies Mrs. Campbell as the cause of her own death."

Three of the physicians followed this lead, but the rest of the jury—Comstock the most vocal—did not. They wanted to hear the rest of the testimony, especially that of Mr. Campbell himself.

"Given the missing Campbell boys," Stanton said, "it seems sensible to interview the father, especially."

"Very well," said Hawthorn. "As Mr. Campbell is still out of the city looking for his sons, we will continue with Dr. Sophie Savard Verhoeven."

The whole room seemed to lean forward as Sophie left her seat and approached the dock. Even when she had taken her place, there was an expectant hush. Jack had the idea that they would be disappointed, if they were looking for drama. Sophie was utterly calm, her expression neutral. She wore a gown of leaf green, some kind of figured brocade, Jack thought, cut loose in the style his sisters called *rational*, for some reason he had never been able to pinpoint. The only jewelry she wore was a brooch at her throat and most probably a ring or two, but like Anna she hid her hands with gloves.

Her manner was polite and professional as she answered questions. There were a lot of them, far more than Anna had gotten from the jurors. And they were more personal, about her childhood and the reasons she came to New York, her experiences of the war.

Abraham Jacobi changed direction and asked her very specific questions about her training as a doctor, and she answered those questions with more warmth.

"You are in private practice," Stanton said to her. Not a question, by his tone.

"I am attached to the New Amsterdam and the Colored Hospital as well as a number of clinics and infirmaries," she corrected him. "And I am sometimes called to consult on difficult cases."

Stanton gave her a doubtful look. "Oh really? And who calls on you for your"—he paused—"expertise?"

Just a flicker of anger on Sophie's face, but before she could answer, the doctor who ran the German Dispensary spoke up.

"She has consulted on a number of cases for me," he said. "And with great success."

Stanton made a muffled, disbelieving sound, and Thalberg took the chance to say more.

"Dr. Savard Verhoeven is especially skilled when it comes to problematic presentations. I have seen her manage deliveries I thought impossible. She is also an excellent diagnostician and professional in all her dealings."

Before the conversation could be taken any further, Hawthorn interrupted.

"In that case," he said. "I would like to hear Dr. Savard Verhoeven's diagnosis of Mrs. Campbell's condition."

The room was very silent while Sophie considered, her gaze on her own folded hands.

Finally she looked directly at Hawthorn and spoke to him alone. "She gave birth to a healthy boy when I attended her on Easter Monday. Her labor was long but not particularly difficult. It was her fourth full-term delivery and she coped quite well. The word *diagnosis* is used when there is some kind of disease or injury. A woman who is pregnant and gives birth without trouble is not ill or injured in any way. What I can say is that I noted symptoms of extreme melancholy and even depression in Mrs. Campbell after the birth of her son."

"And that is unusual?"

"Not in and of itself," Sophie said. "Women react in different ways to giving birth. But Mrs. Campbell was very forthright about her feelings."

"She told you she was unhappy."

"Yes."

"In what way?"

Sophie paused. "She talked about her husband's insistence that they have six boys. The idea frightened her, because she believed he would not—" She cleared her throat. "He would not desist in his attentions until he had reached that goal. She said it was a competition he had going with his brothers."

"Which brothers?" asked Comstock, as if to catch her up in a lie.

"She didn't say," Sophie answered him. "She only said 'his brothers.'"

"Did she tell you she was frightened?" asked another juror, the one with the beard the color of tobacco juice.

"She said that it would kill her to have another baby too soon, that she couldn't bear the thought."

"She was asking you for contraceptives," Comstock announced to the room.

"Yes," Sophie said. "She was."

"And you gave her—?"

"Nothing," Sophie said, quietly. "Because of the laws that forbid me to provide her with the help she needed, I gave her nothing, and now she is dead."

"She is dead because she violated the laws of God and man," Comstock shot back at her. "She reaped the terrible harvest of her sins. And somebody helped her, at least as far as providing the information she needed. Was it you?"

Conrad stood to speak, his voice projecting easily through the room. "My client has rights under the law, and I am here to see that they are protected."

Hawthorn said, "Mr. Belmont, I assure you, we see eye to eye on this matter. Now, Mr. Comstock. Dr. Savard Verhoeven has not been accused of any crime, nor is there any evidence to indicate that such an accusation is forthcoming. Mind your manners, sir."

"I will mind the word of the Lord my God," thundered Comstock. "I will mind the laws of this great country. You, sir, are in no way equal to either of those authorities."

"But I have been appointed coroner and this is my inquest," said Hawthorn mildly. "If you will not desist, I will remove you from my jury. And that I swear to God."

Comstock's whole body was shaking in anger. For a moment Jack wondered if he would lose his infamous temper and be thrown out, but then he took his seat and crossed his arms over his chest.

Sophie said, "I am happy to answer the question. I did not give Mrs. Campbell contraceptives of any kind, nor did I give her information on how to end a pregnancy. I did remind her that the law would not allow it."

Abraham Jacobi said, "And when she came to your office a month ago?"

"Yes. At that visit she was convinced that she had already fallen pregnant. She may have been right, but it was far too early for any clinical signs."

The man from Bellevue leaned toward her. "You did a thorough manual examination? What were your findings, exactly?"

"I observed no changes to the cervix or the uterus. Changes to the breasts would be difficult to determine, as she was still nursing. But there was ample evidence of recent sexual activity, in line with the history she gave me."

Hawthorn wanted clarification, which made all the doctors in the jury shift uneasily. Sophie didn't seem to notice.

"Mrs. Campbell told me that her husband resumed sexual activity almost immediately after she gave birth. She used the phrase 'morning and night' to describe his attentions."

"Coroner Hawthorn!" A man in the gallery struggled to his feet with the help of a cane.

"There's a question in the gallery," said the clerk. "Your name, sir?"

"I am a retired physician. Cameron. James McGrath Cameron, and I do have something to say. I cannot believe that a woman is allowed to speak of such private matters in a public court of law. What a man does with his wife in the privacy of his home is no one else's concern or business, and certainly not a matter for discussion here, by a—a—woman, no less. Shame on you, sir, for allowing it." With a triple thump of his cane, he sat down again.

Hawthorn cleared his throat. "Dr. Cameron. The witness is a fully trained and qualified physician, and she was answering a question put to her by another physician. That is why we are here, to look at the evidence—all the evidence. That is why the general public has not been allowed admission. If you find it disturbs your sense of propriety, I suggest you leave this courtroom now."

Cameron jumped up again and began to make his way up the aisle toward the exit, stabbing down with his cane with each step. "I will do just that," he said, his voice rising. "But I want it on the record that I protest. Such things are not discussed in public. I am going home to my supper."

"I wish you a good evening."

The door closed behind Dr. Cameron before the sentence was out of Hawthorn's mouth. He let out a deep sigh. "Dr. Savard Verhoeven," he said. "I assume you are familiar with the concept of puerperal insanity?"

Sophie agreed that she was.

"Have you ever seen a case in your own practice?"

"I have seen women lose touch with themselves and the world after a difficult birth. Sometimes a woman will exhibit behaviors that would generally be regarded as insanity. While in training I observed a patient who was so disoriented after the birth of her third child that she was confined to an asylum, primarily because she imagined that God was speaking to her so loudly and insistently that she couldn't sleep."

"And what became of that patient?" asked Hawthorn.

"She is still in the private asylum, to the best of my knowledge."

"And tell us now, did you see any such symptoms in Mrs. Campbell? Please take your time in answering if necessary."

"I don't need time to consider," Sophie said. "I can tell you that Mrs. Campbell was greatly distressed, desperately unhappy, and that she was consumed with anger. But she was in her right mind."

"Consumed with anger?" asked Stanton, a queer half smile on his face. "Consumed with anger at whom? Her husband? The father of her children?"

"Yes," Sophie said simply. "Mrs. Campbell was very angry at her husband. I saw no evidence that she was a danger to herself or her sons, but I would not have been surprised to learn that she hurt her husband. In her mind, he was the source of all her troubles. And to be truthful, Dr. Stanton, I see a good deal of logic in her view of things."

"What a remarkably opinionated young woman you are," said Stanton. "Truly remarkable, for someone of your sex and station and—origins."

"I concur," said Comstock. "You should be glad that this jury does not sit in judgment of you, Mrs. Verhoeven. All right, all right, Hawthorn. Dr. Verhoeven. Now I've got one last question."

* * *

OSCAR WAS MUTTERING under his breath. "I'll knock his little rat teeth down his throat if he insults her again."

"You'd have to beat me to it," Jack said. "Look, he's got that damn pamphlet out. He's like a dog with a bone."

Sophie looked up from the pamphlet the clerk had handed to her. She said, "No, I am not familiar with this pamphlet."

"But you are familiar with other pamphlets of this kind?"

Sophie looked at Comstock for a long moment, her expression thoughtful. "Certainly," she said finally. "I can show you an example, if you like. This pamphlet—" She drew some folded pages out of her reticule. "This pamphlet was written specifically about methods to inhibit conception."

Comstock's mouth fell open in surprise, and so Sophie turned to Hawthorn. "Shall I go on?"

"Um," said Hawthorn. "Well."

"Please do," said Jacobi. "I'd like to hear."

Sophie smiled broadly, and while Jack could not see Anna's face, the way she held her head made him think she must be smiling too. As a number of the women in the gallery were smiling.

"It's a very professionally produced piece, as you can see. Twelve pages, with illustrations. The very kind of pamphlet that Mr. Comstock works so hard to keep out of the hands of the innocent. Right here it opens with the proclamation that 'prevention is better than cure,' and it goes on: 'Vaseline charged with four to five grains of salicylic acid will destroy spermatozoa, without injury to the uterus or vagina.'"

She looked at Comstock, her expression utterly grim. "This pamphlet has been in circulation for a few years, I believe. Has your office been successful in bringing the company—" She looked at the cover of the pamphlet, as if she were searching for something elusive. "Yes, here. Colgate is the company that makes Vaseline and printed this pamphlet on contraception. Have you brought Samuel Colgate to court and charged him with violation of your Comstock laws? But wait, isn't Samuel Colgate the president of your New York Society for the Suppression of Vice? That must put you in a difficult position, Mr. Comstock."

The reporters were scribbling as fast as they could while the murmur of voices in the gallery grew louder. In the jury box the physicians were waiting, brows raised, for Comstock's reply. But there was none forthcoming; for once Anthony Comstock had been struck dumb. He sat utterly still except for the tic that appeared at the corner of his mouth, fluttering and jerking.

"Mr. Comstock?" Hawthorn asked. And then, after a long moment. "If this line of questioning is finished, I have an announcement. The officer of the court has brought a note that says Mr. Campbell is returned to the city and will be available to testify here tomorrow afternoon. I hope that his testimony will be enough to allow the jury to reach a conclusion in this matter. And now we will adjourn. It's already six."

Jack lost sight of Comstock as people began to leave the courtroom.

Oscar said, "I can't believe she had the courage to ask him that question. I'd like to buy her a drink. She sat up there with a straight face and asked Comstock whether he had arrested one of the richest men in the city. Samuel Colgate marched into court by Comstock, can you see it? She's got guts," he said again, and pulled out a handkerchief to wipe his eyes.

"She has guts," Jack agreed. "But at this point she also has nothing to lose."

• • •

ANNA TOOK SOPHIE by the elbow and pulled her in for a hug. It was very unlike Anna, and Sophie was both surprised and pleased.

"I thought you'd decided not to do it," she said. "But you timed it perfectly."

"It was harder than I imagined it would be," Sophie said. "Once he was looking at me. But it needed to be done. Maybe it will have some positive effects, if the newspapers dare print it." She looked up to see Oscar Maroney beaming at her, with Jack just behind.

"Well done," said Detective Sergeant Maroney. "I thought Comstock would have a stroke right there in front of God and man. Well done."

Jack was smiling too, but with less obvious enthusiasm. Anna poked him.

"You don't approve?"

"Oh, I approve," he said, catching her poking finger and folding his hand around hers. "I just hope he lets it go and doesn't cook up some scheme to pay you back."

"That's why I wouldn't let Anna do it," Sophie said. "There's not much he can do to me now, is there?"

Anna was looking around herself. "For once I would happily talk to a reporter, and they are all gone."

"Off to file a story about Samuel Colgate, the contraceptives peddler," said Oscar. "By God, I can't wait to see that."

• • •

SOPHIE HAD THE Verhoeven carriage waiting; Jack wanted to hail a cab, but Anna wanted to walk. She sent Sophie home and considered Jack's unhappy expression.

"Are you so tired?" she teased him. "That you can't manage a half hour's walk?"

He narrowed his eyes at her. "And if I weren't here? You'd walk home on your own?"

Anna studied the street for a moment. There was a dead horse in the gutter at the corner of Franklin, the carcass at least a week old. A crowd of boys were busy wrenching out ribs to be used as swords. One of them already had his and used this advantage to poke a playmate in the belly. They fell into the gutter beside the horse, fists flying. Anna would guess them no more than eight.

She said, "I could lie to you."

One brow went up, which was disagreement enough.

"In the early evening when it's still light, Broadway is safe enough. I might have walked home alone."

He took her bag from her and offered his free arm. "You're lucky you still have your skin," Jack said.

They walked along quietly for a moment. Anna kept one eye on the brawl, which was attracting little boys from every hidey-hole, all of them battering wildly at one another, crashing into the carcass of the horse and climbing out again.

"Do you want to volunteer to clean up their battle wounds?"

"No," Anna said. "That would be a mistake. I learned that lesson soon after I qualified. Stay out of arguments."

He wanted to know more, and Anna didn't mind telling stories that showed her to disadvantage. At least, not with family and friends. And Jack, she reminded herself, was both.

"A girl of about seventeen, I think. She came into the New Amsterdam with some cracked ribs and a broken nose and two black eyes. I guessed it might have been her father or husband, and I was trying to think how to ask—"

Jack hummed under his breath.

"When her sister came rushing in, looking almost as bad. She had stripes on both cheeks." Anna held up one hand, the fingers bent into a claw shape. "There was a clump of hair missing from her head above her left ear, too. Do you know the strength it takes to rip out hair like that?"

"I've never tried it," Jack said dryly. "But I've seen it done."

"She was screaming, and spraying blood from a split lip with every movement of her head. The sister on the examination table almost levitated. She just launched herself, or she tried to, but I put my hands on her shoulders to hold her down."

Jack was listening, but she couldn't read his expression.

"She might have put a rib through a lung, that's what was going through my head," she went on. "And I just acted on that basis. And I said to the sister who had come in, 'Stop this nonsense, immediately.' It didn't have quite the impact I thought it would."

"Yes?"

Anna shrugged. "They both started screaming at me. The one on the table for speaking to her sister rudely, and the other one for treating her sister roughly. If an orderly hadn't come in I think they might have joined forces to teach me a lesson."

She let out a small laugh. "And from that I learned not to put myself in the middle of a fight. I call for the orderlies instead."

"Sensible," Jack said. "Do you know what they were fighting about?"

"Money," said Anna. "It's almost always money, unless the patient comes in drunk. Then it can be about anything. The color of the sky, the name of the president, the month of the year."

Broadway was crowded with street vendors and delivery wagons, newsboys and clerks on their way home for the day. An elderly woman with a back so crooked that it forced her to stare at the ground had turned her head sideways to barter for a measure of dried beans. Her voice was cheerful and she was grinning at the man who scowled down at her, because, Anna could see, she was about to get the best of him. It was the end of the day and he wouldn't want to drag unsold wares home.

"Really, though, it's always about money," Anna repeated. "Even when it seems not to be."

Jack's eyes were scanning the street, as if he were expecting to be confronted and didn't know from what direction it would come.

Anna said, "You deal with the worst of humankind, day in and day out. It makes you doubt everybody."

"I don't doubt you," he said. "The first minute I saw you, I knew you for a good person."

"Because I was treating orphaned children?"

"Because you stood up to that nun. Sister—"

"Ignatia. She made me angry."

"That was obvious."

"It was about the children who weren't vaccinated. Vaccination is free at dispensaries all over the city. She made a decision based on her own fears and superstitions, and put children at danger. There's no excuse for such ignorance."

"I got that, too."

She drew a deep breath and waited for her pulse to stop racing. "So you were attracted to me because I stood up to a nun."

"I was impressed. Attraction had to do with other things."

Anna waited, wondering what she was hoping to hear.

He said, "Your hair is hard to overlook. The deep color of it, and the way it curls even when it's rolled up on the back of your head. It's always fighting to be free. While you were leaning over one of the children I saw a curl escape from the pins and fall behind your ear along the line of your throat. You have a beautiful neck, Anna. And I had an almost uncontrollable urge to tuck that curl back into place."

Embarrassed, she said, "I thought I'd never see you again, when I left the ferry."

"Really?" Jack looked down at her. "I was busy trying to figure out how to make sure you did."

"You were not."

"I was. And then there you were, not twelve hours later, going into Alva Vanderbilt's monstrosity of a new house. You took my breath away."

All along her spine, nerves jumped. She was afraid to raise her head to look at him.

"This damn city," Jack said. "No place for a man to kiss his wife without an audience."

"Jack Mezzanotte," Anna said, her voice catching. "I never took you for a coward."

♦ ♦ ♦

"Maybe that wasn't such a good idea," Anna said when they had walked another block. "My knees have gone all wobbly. And my pulse won't slow down."

Her hand was trembling a little, but then so was Jack's. He rubbed a thumb over the juncture of wrist and palm, the silk of her glove whispering.

He said, "Take this off."

"No." She pulled her hand away with a jerk.

"Now who's the coward?"

Her brows pulled down in irritation, but she stripped the glove from her hand and looked at it and then at him, as if she had never seen such a creature before.

Jack held his jacket open. "Put it here, in the inside pocket."

He wondered why he felt the need to provoke her on South Broadway, of all places. But her jaw was set now, and she was not going to back down. Standing very close, she tucked the glove into his pocket, the one that rested just over his heart.

She was looking him in the eye as she stepped back and let her hand trail down his vest front. Like a blade of grass being drawn over his skin. Her hand continued downward, and he grabbed her wrist to stop her.

"Very funny."

Both dimples came to the fore. "I thought so."

"Just wait," Jack said. "Until I get you home."

♦ ♦ ♦

Anna felt fevered, though the evening breeze was cool. When the house came into view her heart was beating so hard that she could feel it in her eardrums. She thought of the people—the people she loved and cared for—who would want to talk to her and feed her and hear about her day, and she wondered if she could just be honest. Say something like, *Jack and I will be back in an hour. Don't hold dinner for us.* But the very idea made her throat go dry with anticipated embarrassment, because of course they would know why and what and even how. But it could not be avoided, and so she turned toward the garden, where everyone would be on a beautiful afternoon like this. Then Jack stopped her by pulling her closer. He pointed with his chin in the other direction.

"What?"

"Something to show you."

"Now?"

"Right now."

They climbed the front stairs to the new house—*Weeds*, Anna reminded herself, *everyone is calling it Weeds*—and she waited while he fished a key out of his pocket and opened the door. In the hall he put her Gladstone bag down while Anna peered around, feeling oddly shy about exploring.

Even from where she stood she could see that someone had been hard at work. Everything from the ceiling to the floors had been scrubbed clean, the old paper scraped from the walls, and the floors sanded and polished. The air smelled of lye soap and wax and something else familiar. "What is that—"

"Lemon," said Jack. "My mother believes in the cleansing power of lemon."

Then he was tugging her up the stairs.

"They'll be waiting dinner for us," she said, holding back.

"They can wait a while longer."

"Jack."

He raised a brow.

"I don't have my—"

With a sigh he picked her up and carried her, taking the stairs two at a time. He walked straight to the largest room, the one that would be theirs when they finally moved in, and opened the door by leaning into it.

"Oh," Anna said.

The walls had been cleaned and painted, the floors polished, and new curtains hung at the windows, simple cream-colored linen over white lace panels. There was a large four-poster bed, neatly made with plump pillows and a beautiful white-on-white quilt; there were two dressers and a table. An earthenware jug filled with white roses and lilac was the only decoration placed on the mantelpiece over the small fireplace, and two chairs angled toward each other in front of it. It was all very simple but pleasing.

Jack dropped her onto the bed.

"When did you manage all this?"

"I don't think that's what you mean to say." He let his jacket fall to the floor and started unbuttoning his vest. "What you mean to say is, 'Oh, well done.'"

Anna reached up and pulled him down to her by tugging on a suspender.

"Well done," she said against his mouth. "But I still need my cervical cap."

He kissed her so thoroughly that she lost her train of thought. Jack reminded her by leaning over to open a drawer on the bedside stand. He brought out a familiar box.

"You are farsighted," she said. "Very resourceful. Now, do you know what to do with it?"

•　•　•

"AND A QUICK study, too," she said as he pulled her underneath him ten minutes later. She was already flushed, damp with perspiration, and a little embarrassed, Jack thought.

She arched against him, gasping. He leaned down to suckle the curve of her throat and tasted soap and salt and Anna. She was wriggling, undulating around him, pinned down by the simple fact of his possession, wet and hot and very tight, and Jack thought he would lose his mind if he didn't start moving in her immediately, but he held off nonetheless.

The heel of her hand struck him above the ear and he laughed, pleased with her and himself.

"Jack," she said, struggling, lifting against him. "Jack."

"So impatient." His mouth moved up her neck to her ear and the flesh underneath it, pulsing warm. He pressed the flat of his tongue there and felt her whole body tensing around him: a clenched fist, dragging at him.

"What are you waiting for?"

She was irritated with him, and he found, just now, he liked that. He kissed her mouth, soft and wet and greedy.

"You don't like this?"

"You rotter." Her feet slid up his legs, pressed his thighs. She dug her heels into the small of his back, arching to the exact angle he had been waiting for, the one that gave him the last inch he needed so that he could settle, finally, where he needed to be.

"Too much?" He rocked against her and she put her head back and groaned, a hoarse sound that made gooseflesh rise all along his back.

"Anna. Too much?"

"Jack. Don't coddle me."

She could still shock him, a kind of seduction all its own. He set out to test her resolve, and his own limits.

◆　◆　◆

JACK'S PARENTS WERE at the dinner table, and Anna was stuck between them, caught in the web of their curiosity and ready affection. She desperately wanted to at least change her shirtwaist, but they had come in late. It would be rude to ask people to wait any longer. She just wished she could be sure she didn't smell too much like, well, what she must smell like.

She had little appetite, but filling her plate was something to do while she talked to Mrs. Mezzanotte, who wanted to know about Weeds, which she had seen earlier in the afternoon. Anna didn't look at Jack, but she knew he was grinning.

"It's a fine house," his mother said. "And it will be beautiful when it's finished." She had some furniture she thought would suit, and would send it to town the next time there was a greenhouse delivery. "Nothing elaborate," she said. From her tone Anna got the idea that Celestina and Bambina had explained to their mother that Jack's new wife had austere tastes.

She thought of linen curtains fluttering in the breeze and hoped her blush wasn't too obvious.

"You will have to come to Greenwood before much longer," Mrs. Mezzanotte said. "Or your new sisters-in-law will hunt you down."

In her surprise, Anna let out an awkward laugh. "That sounds ominous."

"Strong-minded women," said Mr. Mezzanotte. "I married one, and so did all our sons. The noise sometimes." He put down his fork and placed his hands over his ears to rock his head from side to side. "Incredible." He winked at the little girls and said, "*Come di cento scimmie.*"

"Stop," said Mrs. Mezzanotte. "They aren't as bad as monkeys."

"Yes they are," said Jack. "But we love them anyway. All except Benedetta."

"Jack!" his mother gasped.

"She's so bossy," Jack said. "Of course, so is Mariangela. I'm not sure which one would win a bossy cow contest."

"First monkeys and now cows," said Mrs. Mezzanotte. "Stop." But she was smiling.

"Neither of them would win that contest," said his father. "The prize would go to Susanna."

Mrs. Mezzanotte's mouth made a perfect O for three heartbeats, and then she shrugged, conceding the point. "Susanna," she said. "No doubt about it."

She turned to Anna. "We'll scare you off."

Aunt Quinlan laughed. "Not our Anna," she said. "She's made of sterner stuff than that. And she likes strong-minded women."

"Because I was raised by them," Anna agreed.

While Mrs. Mezzanotte talked at more length about her daughters-in-law—each of whom she clearly liked and loved—Anna was listening with half an ear to Lia as she told Jack a story, waving her fork in the air like a baton. Italian spilled out of her in a rush.

Rosa grabbed the fork out of Lia's hand, her mouth pursed in disapproval. *"Non parla inglese al tavolo, è maleducato."*

Lia blinked, her face solemn. *"Com' si dice maleducato in inglese?"*

Aunt Quinlan said, "Rude. The word in English is 'rude.'"

Lia grabbed her fork back from her sister with a wrenching motion and thumped it on the table, tears brimming and ready to fall.

"It's not rude. Italian is not rude. Everybody should speak Italian! If I have to speak Italian and English, then everybody else should speak English and Italian!"

She put out her lower lip in a thunderous gesture of rebellion and cast an accusatory look around the table, daring someone to disagree.

Before Rosa could stop sputtering long enough to answer, Anna said, "You know, Lia, you're right. Aunt Quinlan speaks Italian, and you speak Italian, and everybody here speaks Italian. Except me, and Margaret."

"Margaret is learning Italian," Rosa said, almost under her breath.

"Then I had better catch up," Anna said.

That got her one of Margaret's rare wide smiles.

"In the meantime, I don't want you to have to keep a story to yourself if you only know it in Italian. So go right ahead."

Aunt Quinlan reached over to put a hand on Lia's head. "And listen now, my henny. The next time you have a point to make, you can do it without shouting and people will still listen to you."

Lia wrinkled her nose as if she doubted this bit of wisdom, but she also nodded. Reluctant acceptance, Anna thought. She wondered how long it would last.

"So I'll need an Italian tutor," Anna said.

Both girls raised their hands, and so did Jack. She elbowed him, not too gently. "I was hoping you'd volunteer," she said to the girls. "But I'm going to need more help still. I've got somebody in mind. I'll bring him by for you to approve."

Jack looked at her doubtfully, and Anna kept her smile to herself.

• • •

THAT NIGHT WHEN they went to bed, Anna told Jack the story of how her parents met.

"My mother went to New Orleans to study medicine with Uncle Ben's brothers, because they ran a clinic there and took on students. This was long before Dr. Blackwell—the one who founded Woman's Medical School?—long before she fought the battle to be the first woman admitted to medical school. Women who wanted to study medicine had to apprentice."

"Have you told me about your uncle Ben?"

Anna pointed to a particular portrait. "Ben Savard. He met Aunt Hannah when she was in New Orleans during the war of 1812, and they settled in Paradise. Ben's half brother Paul was the head of the clinic, and my mother studied under him. Aunt Hannah thought he would be the best teacher for her because he wouldn't put up with her nonsense, but he also wouldn't take offense when she turned out to be smarter than everybody else."

"Was she?"

"Smarter than most, I think. So Ben's brother Paul had a son who went to France to study medicine; that was Henry Savard, my father. My mother was two years into her studies in New Orleans when Henry came back from Paris, qualified in medicine and surgery too. He wasn't happy to find that my mother had taken his place and had won everybody over. My mother took exception to him, too. At first."

"And they fell in love and got married," Jack prompted.

"It was a stormy romance, or so the story goes. But yes, they fell in love and got married. By that time my aunt Hannah said there were more people in Paradise than she could doctor, and so my parents decided that they'd move north and practice medicine with her. Which is what they did."

The tree frogs were making music outside the window. For a long time they lay listening and then Anna roused. She said, "What about your parents?"

He stifled a yawn. "That's a story they tell every year on their anniversary. I think you should wait to hear it from them."

"Is that an Italian custom?"

"A family custom, I'd say. You might want to think about the story you'll tell, when the time comes."

And then he fell asleep, as if he hadn't just handed her an assignment to worry over for the next eleven months.

28

NEW YORK POST

Wednesday, May 30, 1883

ARCHER CAMPBELL RETURNS
WITHOUT HIS SONS

TESTIMONY GOES ON TWO HOURS

Mr. Archer Campbell, whose wife died under mysterious circumstances last week, has returned home after a fruitless search for his four missing sons, ages two months to five years. He last saw the boys the day before their mother's death, when she took them away from home and out of the city to a destination and fate as yet undetermined.

The complete and unexplained disappearance of four young boys has occasioned considerable speculation from all quarters. The suggestion that Mrs. Campbell might have harmed her sons was addressed in Tuesday's testimony taken during the inquiry into her death.

Dr. Sophie Savard Verhoeven, the last physician to treat Mrs. Campbell, contends that her patient did not suffer from puerperal insanity. The medical men on the jury were not all in accordance with this view. In an interview, Dr. Stanton expressed his doubts to the *Post*.

"Well-brought-up women who become good wives do not break with the habits of a lifetime for no reason. Mrs. Campbell had an excellent husband and a fine home. She was a caring and attentive mother. It is possible that her physicians did not look closely enough to see the evidence of puerperal insanity before it was

too late, or that she was unduly influenced in a way not yet discovered."

NEW YORK TRIBUNE

Wednesday, May 30, 1883

LETTERS TO THE EDITOR

Sirs: The coroner's inquest currently under way in the matter of
Mrs. Janine Campbell's death reveals the true nature of those who
campaign for "women's rights," and it can be summarized in a few
words: they think they know better. In this inquest female doctors
have given testimony. They speak in rough terms about unladylike, lewd topics, naysaying their betters simply because they are
female and they know better. Nature has decreed a certain divi-
sion of labor, but they know better. The founders of this great
nation set out rights and responsibilities for its citizens, but, the
women tell us, they know better. The truth is that gentle, worthy
ladies brought up in Christian households have their rights already. Good women have the right to influence the race in the
nursery, in the family, in the school, and thus through all the race
of life. They have the right to be respected by all the respectable.
They have the right to be tenderly loved by all whose love is worth
enjoying. They have the right to be protected and provided for by
men. Healthy, God-fearing women take pleasure and joy from the
rights accorded them by the Almighty. If you doubt the dangers of
women's rights, you have only to observe the way female doctors
behave when they are called to give testimony. It is a scandal and
a tragedy, for them and for the nation.

A Concerned Physician

• • •

ANNA SAID, "OF course you should sail, Sophie. If the district attorney says you are free to go—"

"Wait," Sophie said. She paced from one side of Anna's office to the other. "There was something in the paper this morning that has me worried. Did you see Clara's letter?"

"I haven't had much time to read the paper these last few days." She took the clipping that Sophie handed her and looked at it. Another letter to the editor.

Sirs: In his tireless compulsion to rid the city and state of all material he personally finds distasteful, Anthony Comstock of the New York Society for the Suppression of Vice seems never to sleep. We note that in two days he has arrested four people for the sale of obscene literature as well as a printer he suspects of printing such materials, raided a reputable and well-respected art dealer, and impounded paintings by one of the greatest artists now living (again because in his superior opinion, they are inappropriate and immoral). In addition to all this, he serves on a coroner's jury in the tragic case of a young woman's untimely death, using that opportunity to insult and attempt—note, Sirs, I say attempt—to bully female physicians.

We find it outrageous that Anthony Comstock is permitted to use the justice system to harass people engaged in lawful business, and worse still, to pass judgment on the way qualified physicians treat patients in crisis. Note, too, that Comstock discreetly looks the other way when one of his colleagues on the board of the Society for the Suppression of Vice manufactures, advertises, and sells the contraceptives he—and the society—finds so personally and morally disgusting. It is high time Mr. Comstock's antics—in and out of the courtroom—be curtailed.

Dr. C. E. Garrison
Secretary
Association for the Advancement of the Medical Education of Women

Anna looked from the newspaper clipping to Sophie and back again. "I wondered if the papers would allow Samuel Colgate's name to be printed. Vaseline is the smallest part of what they manufacture, and the papers won't want to lose the advertising revenue. I realize it's disappointing—"

"Not that," Sophie said. "The part about the printer. Comstock has arrested a printer suspected of supplying immoral materials."

"Oh," Anna said. "I see."

"I went to Clara first to see if she had any more information, but she had inquired at the Tombs and couldn't get a name. Do you think Jack could find out?"

Anna said, "I should think so."

"I can't just walk away and leave the Reasons at the mercy of Anthony Comstock." Her voice wobbled in a way decidedly unlike Sophie's usual calm appraisal of even catastrophic events.

After a moment's thought Anna cleared her throat. "But you would trust the matter to us, I hope. With Jack and Oscar, I think we can certainly get to the bottom of this."

"And if it is Sam Reason who has been arrested, I'll ask Conrad to represent him. Them."

"The Reasons might have a lawyer of their own," Anna said.

"But they shouldn't have to bear the cost."

Anna sat down and pointed to the other chair. After a moment Sophie took it. She drew in a deep breath and let it go in a sigh.

"He was terribly rude to me," Sophie said. "But he was also painfully honest."

"Sam Reason's grandson?"

She nodded. "I realize that there is only so much that can be done—who knows what evidence Comstock has. Or thinks he has. But I want to be sure that Sam Reason gets the very best representation. And Anna, this is important."

Anna waited while Sophie tried to collect her thoughts.

"He is very proud. It's important to me that he not feel condescended to or patronized."

"I understand," Anna said, though she did not, completely.

"So this is what I'm going to do. I'm going to leave a bank draft for expenses. A large bank draft. Use all of it, and if you need more, send me a telegram and I'll arrange it."

She got up suddenly, looking at the watch pinned to her bodice. "I need to get home to Cap before the inquest."

"I think you could reasonably stay away from the Tombs," Anna said. "Tomorrow at this time you'll be boarding the *Cosimo* and there are more urgent things to be done."

"Absolutely not. I owe Janine Campbell that much. I will see the inquest through to the end."

Anna got to her feet and hugged her cousin. "And so will I."

•   •   •

JACK LISTENED TO the whole story attentively, his expression giving away nothing of his thoughts. The more Anna saw of him in his professional guise, the more she realized how very much like a doctor he had to conduct himself. He gave nothing away, just as she would give no indication of her findings if she were to examine his mother or one of his sisters.

They were standing on the steps of the Tombs. All around them reporters were trying to get Anna's attention, but Jack's posture, his protective stance, kept them from coming closer. The crowd was very large today, no doubt because Archer Campbell was actually here—Anna had caught sight of his red head going into the building—and would give testimony.

Whatever delay had been keeping the entryway blocked suddenly cleared, and Jack propelled her into the lobby. The uniformed officers nodded to him and touched their hats to Anna. She recognized one of the men from their visit to the Brooklyn Bridge, and was glad not to be able to stop, because she knew that questions would be asked, and what she would have to answer. So she let herself be guided down hallways and up the stairs to the courtroom.

Jack leaned over to speak to her without being overheard. "I'll find out what I can about the printer now. It may take a while, but I'll be back here as soon as possible."

He brushed a kiss across her ear and, turning away, disappeared into the crowd in the hall.

The inquest was already being called to order when Anna took her seat next to Sophie. She got out her lap desk and writing paper and pencil, and while the coroner went on about the purpose of the inquest, she wrote Sophie a note: *Cap?*

Sophie took the pencil and wrote: *Looking forward to sailing tomorrow.*

Anna could imagine that very well. Cap would be desperate to get away not so much for his own health, but for Sophie's well-being.

Sophie wrote: *The printer? Sam Reason?*

Anna thought for a moment and took back the paper to write: *Jack has gone to find out.*

Sophie gave her a relieved smile and then Archer Campbell was taking the witness seat. He looked drawn, with shadows in the hollows of his cheeks and under his eyes so dark they might have been bruises. His expression was grim and even angry.

"Mr. Campbell," the coroner began. "My deepest condolences on the sad loss of your wife. You've had no success in locating your sons, I take it."

"None," Campbell said.

"I am sorry to hear it."

"If that's the case, you'll call an end to this charade and let me get back to the search."

Hawthorn looked almost startled. Anna thought he was going to challenge Campbell's less-than-veiled insult, but saw him think better of it.

"We'll get right to it then. Tell us please about your wife and how you came to marry."

With obvious displeasure, Campbell told the story in as few words as possible: In Bangor on post office business, he had been introduced to a young lady who worked in the dead-letter office. Her family background was not ideal, but she was healthy, a good Christian, and a hard worker. After two weeks' courtship, when he had to return to New York, he had decided to marry her.

"She married with her family's blessing?"

A ghost of sour smile moved across Campbell's face. "Five unmarried daughters, they were glad to be shut of her."

"I see. Mr. Campbell, can you shed any light on the events that led to your wife's death?"

Campbell's jaw worked silently for a moment. Then he said, "I don't know anything about the particulars."

"Did you realize that she was with child?"

"No."

"She didn't speak to you of it?"

"She never talked about such things. Wouldn't be proper."

"When did you first notice something was off?"

Campbell seemed to relax a little. Maybe he had been expecting accusations, and realized now that there were none forthcoming.

"The house," he said. "It was out of order when I came home from work on Tuesday evening." Campbell shifted in his chair.

"That was unusual?"

"She knew nothing about keeping house when we married, but then from what I've seen of French Canadians, they don't put much value on cleanliness. I had to teach her what it means to keep a house, the way my mother had. A place for everything and everything in its place. No fingerprints on the windows or anywhere else, for that matter. Floors polished, stove blacked, laundry cleaned and pressed and mended, good plain food on the table when I came through the door. Waste not, want not. Children who know their place, and don't speak lest they're spoke to.

"But that day, as soon as I came in the door I knew there was trouble. The boys were sitting at the kitchen table like so many poppets. Big eyes, like they knew they had a hiding due. My oldest boy was holding the baby, trying to keep it quiet."

"If you'd just go on," said the coroner. "Tell the story as it comes to you."

Campbell frowned. "There's not much to tell. She had lost track of time, she said. She had a headache. She got headaches now and then, but my belief is, you work through the pain. Don't let it get the best of you. But she did. That Tuesday night, she did. Put cold meat and bread out, something I wouldn't tolerate normally. A man needs a hot meal. But I made do. She cleaned the kitchen, took care of the boys, and sat down with the mending."

"Did she say anything about arrangements for the next day?"

"She asked if she could take the boys to my brother's farm." A flush of color appeared on Campbell's cheeks. "So she could get the house cleaned proper. I almost said no and by God, I wish I had."

Anna could almost hear the unease around her in the gallery. Most of the onlookers had been disposed to feel sympathy for Campbell, but his brusque manner was making that difficult. Even Comstock looked unnerved.

"She seemed unwell, that Tuesday evening."

"As I said."

"You didn't call a doctor."

"Rich people call a doctor for every little thing," he said. "The rest of us make do. She said she'd be right in the morning, and I believed her. And so she was. Now I'm thinking nothing failed her at all. It was just her way of putting me off the scent, not asking about things being out of order."

Hawthorn gave a doubtful low hum. "Tell us about that Wednesday morning."

Campbell didn't try to hide his impatience. "She went about her business, as she always did. Breakfast and seeing to the boys and so forth. Getting them ready for the train."

"Did you see her off at the Grand Central Depot?"

"Look," Campbell said. "It was nothing out of the ordinary. I went to work; she got herself and the boys to Grand Central by omnibus. I don't hold with cosseting. My mother raised six boys to good men, and she did it with the Bible in one hand and a hickory switch in the other."

"All right," said Hawthorn. His tone was short. "Then we'd like to hear about Wednesday evening when you got home."

"She was in bed," Campbell said. "Vomiting into a basin, curled up under the covers. So I got my own dinner—cold meat, again— and read the paper like I always do. I heard her moving around some and so I went to check and she was trying to get a bottle of laudanum open. I opened it for her, and I went back to my paper and then to bed. That was at about nine."

"Did Mrs. Campbell wake in the night?"

"I slept in the boys' room. It was her idea, thinking I shouldn't catch the bug that had her so sick."

From the jury Dr. Stanton cleared his throat. "You didn't notice blood, I take it? There would have been a great deal of it."

Campbell looked distinctly uncomfortable. "She told me she had her monthlies, and I left it at that."

Abraham Jacobi said, "Were you disappointed to hear that Mrs. Campbell's menses had started?"

For the first time Campbell looked confused. "I don't follow you."

"We heard testimony that you were hoping to increase the size of your family as quickly as possible. Something about a wager with your brothers. The news that your wife wasn't with child, then, was that a disappointment?"

Beside Anna, Sophie went very still while Campbell's neck and face flooded with color.

"That's a private matter. Who told you that? Whose testimony?"

"Mr. Campbell," said Hawthorn. "Please answer the question."

Campbell's head was turning as he scanned the gallery, moving from face to face. Sophie sat quietly, composed, unwilling to let Campbell read anything from her expression, once he found her where she sat.

"Mr. Campbell."

He turned back to the coroner with clear reluctance. "I wanted a big family," he said. "She knew that before she married me. She wanted the same."

Dr. Thalberg said, "She never expressed doubts?"

"Doubts?" Campbell fairly spat the word out. "What do doubts have to do with anything? Man proposes, God disposes, so goes the saying. A woman raised right knows that, and accepts it as her duty."

"But the evidence indicates that Mrs. Campbell performed an abortion on herself," said Hawthorn.

"If that's so," Campbell said with great deliberation, "then she lied to my face and she's burning in hell, where she belongs."

There was a moment of shocked silence in the courtroom.

Jacobi said, "Where do you think your sons are? Do you have any sense of what's become of them?"

Campbell's whole face contorted. "If what you're telling me about my wife is true, then I'd put nothing past her. Maybe she stole away and killed them, to spite me."

Anna felt flushed with heat. Whatever they had imagined about Janine's home life, it had been far worse. Casual cruelty and callous indifference could destroy a woman as effectively as fists.

"Then let me ask one more question," Abraham Jacobi was saying. "Assuming for a moment that your sons will not be returned to you, did you have no idea that your wife held you in such contempt, that she was angry enough with you to do such unspeakable things?"

Campbell stood up suddenly, and so did Anthony Comstock. "The man is not on trial," Comstock said. "You are making grave accusations without the least bit of evidence."

"Your own tactics, Comstock. Come home to roost," noted Dr. Thalberg.

"I beg your pardon!" Comstock bellowed. "How dare you!"

"Sit down, Mr. Comstock, and remember the seriousness of this inquest," said Hawthorn. "Mr. Campbell, you too, sit down immediately." He paused to take a deep breath.

"You may find Dr. Jacobi's question insulting, Mr. Campbell, but it is a reasonable question. If your wife was so deeply unhappy and disturbed enough to do the things we're talking about, where did those feelings originate?"

Finally, Anna thought. *Finally.*

• • •

THE DEBATE WENT on and on, it seemed to Anna, but nobody in the gallery moved a muscle. It was as good as a theater production, one with an excellent director. Her opinion of Mr. Hawthorn grew to considerable proportions as she watched him play the jurors off each other and off Campbell, stepping in exactly when things began to escalate too quickly, providing small jolts when things began to lag.

On her pad she wrote, *no history of mental illness she admitted to* and *French Canadian* and *save the rod.*

Mrs. Campbell did not approve of harsh physical punishment, it seemed. Her husband offered this as evidence of her deceptive character; because, he suggested, there was nothing gentle about a woman who could wrong him the way she had.

Anna had had more than her fill of Archer Campbell when the coroner declared the inquest at an end and cleared the courtroom of everyone but the jury. The hallway, already crowded with reporters, doubled in density. In the tumult of the crowd Anna stayed very close to Sophie, her Gladstone bag bumping against her leg as people pressed forward around islands of reporters who stood scribbling madly on paper held open against a palm. Perspiration was running down her back and sides, and she had never wanted to see an open window as much in her life as she did at that moment.

"Sophie Verhoeven." A reporter pushed in front of them, his face lowered so that the brim of his hat would have touched Sophie's forehead, had she not shoved him away.

"Don't you want people to know—"

"What I want," Sophie said, "is for you to remove yourself immediately. Immediately."

Anna took her by the arm and pulled her aside. "Jack, there."

He was easy to spot in a crowd, a head taller than the tallest man. Anna gave a very solid push in his direction, and Sophie followed.

"Let's go," Jack said. He used his body to create a protective wall, a passageway that moved with them. He opened a door and gestured them into another hallway, this one empty and dim and cool.

Anna leaned against the wall for a moment to catch her breath. Sophie stood very stiffly, her mouth pressed hard shut and streaks on her cheeks that had only one origin.

"Oh, Sophie." Anna put a hand on her cousin's elbow, and Sophie turned to her, pressed her face to Anna's shoulder, and wept as though the world had ended.

To his credit, Jack stood back and let them be. Anna smiled wanly at him over Sophie's head.

"She should have killed him," Sophie said finally. "And saved herself."

Anna fumbled a handkerchief out of her sleeve and wiped Sophie's damp face. "In a just world, yes." She felt very close to tears herself, until she saw Jack's face.

"What?"

He said, "Sophie, Sam Reason and his grandmother are waiting in a room just down the hall to talk to you."

Sophie stiffened. "He was arrested?"

Jack nodded. "But he won't be charged. He's free to go home."

"What? How?"

"Comstock overplayed his hand. And he's not the only one who knows people in the district attorney's office. Sophie, be warned, Reason is—"

"Rude. I know," she said. "But he has cause."

• • •

DELILAH REASON WAS thinner than she had been, her cheekbones more prominent and the shoulders of her shirtwaist not quite so well filled out. But her smile was genuine, and Sophie was so glad to see that small sign of sincere welcome that her hands began to tremble.

"I'm so glad to see you," Sophie said. "Though I wish the circumstances weren't quite so grim."

"You look like you haven't got much sleep," Mrs. Reason said. "Are you taking care of yourself?"

"Dr. Verhoeven has staff to take care of her," Sam Reason said. He was standing near the door, very straight and tall and so tense he seemed to vibrate.

"Sam," said Mrs. Reason. "I did not raise you to be impolite. Dr. Savard—"

"Sophie. Please, call me Sophie. Sam has good cause to be angry with me."

They both looked at her as if she had suddenly started speaking Greek.

Sophie said, "I assumed that Comstock raided your offices because of our pamphlets, that he traced them somehow. That's not what happened?"

"The other way around," said Sam Reason. "He—or better said, one of his men—brought one of your pamphlets in to me and asked what it would cost to reprint it."

"But why were you arrested?" Sophie asked him directly.

"I was caught off guard and I did the first thing that came to mind. I handed him our price sheet. The one I use to calculate estimates, page count and paper stock, and so on. That's all it took. Next thing Comstock came in himself and arrested me."

"Because he didn't reject the job straight out," Mrs. Reason supplied.

"But it was one of the pamphlets I showed you?"

Sam nodded. "No doubt in my mind, it was my grandfather's work."

"It's none of your doing," said his grandmother to Sophie.

"I fear it is. I embarrassed Comstock in court yesterday," Sophie told them. "I can't help feeling there's a connection."

"Maybe so." Sam Reason turned his hat around and around in his hands. "But it's over and done now. Maybe you can thank the detective sergeant for speaking up for me. I'd be spending another night in a cell if he hadn't."

"I have already asked him to keep an eye out for Comstock on your behalf. You must be very careful from now on. He doesn't like being bested."

For the first time she saw a flicker of a smile on Sam Reason's face. "Nobody does."

Mrs. Reason picked up her reticule, and, taking a moment to gather her thoughts, she launched into what Sophie thought must have been a rehearsed speech.

"I saw in the newspaper that you married just a few days ago," she said. "And I'd like to wish you and Mr. Verhoeven every happiness."

"Thank you." Sophie resisted the urge to turn away. "I should explain—"

"You don't owe anybody an explanation," Sam said. "It's nobody's business but your own who you marry."

Sophie nodded. "Still, I wanted to say that I had hoped to come and visit again, but there have been so many complications. We leave tomorrow for Europe. Cap—my husband—Cap is going into treatment at a sanatorium, for tuberculosis. I don't know when I'll be back."

"Whenever that is, you are both very welcome at my home. Any time at all. I hope Mr. Verhoeven's health is restored to him quickly."

"That's very unlikely," Sophie said, and at the look on Mrs. Reason's face, she realized how heartless she must have sounded.

"He is very ill," she started again. "It is a matter of months, at the most."

Sam moved suddenly. "I'll wait outside." And just that quickly he was gone.

"Talk of illness makes him uneasy. He has a deep fear of it."

"Most people do," Sophie pointed out.

"Sam more than most. He lost his wife to cancer, you see. When you visited us that Sunday, he was gone to Savannah to tell her family in person. He's been very shut off since her death, but I expect you're familiar with that kind of thing, as a doctor."

"I thought he disapproved of my marriage."

Mrs. Reason lifted a shoulder, as if to shrug off the possibility. "But I do not, and you are welcome in Brooklyn when you come back. You will come back?"

"Oh, yes," Sophie said. "Of course I will. This is my home."

•   •   •

NEW YORK TRIBUNE

Wednesday, May 30, 1883

LATE EDITION

CONCLUSION OF THE CORONER'S INQUEST INTO JANINE CAMPBELL'S DEATH

VERDICT OF THE JURY

The jury impaneled to investigate the death of Mrs. Janine Campbell of 19 Charles Street on Thursday, May 24, met this evening at 5 o'clock pursuant to adjournment, in Judge Benedict's courtroom at the Tombs.

Coroner Hawthorn informed the jurors that Archer Campbell, husband of the deceased, was the final witness to be called. He instructed the jury to give the matter careful consideration and to render a verdict regardless of consequences or public opinion. The jury retired and two hours later rendered the following

Verdict

We, the jury, duly sworn and charged to inquire on behalf of the State and City of New York how and in what manner Janine Campbell came to her death, do upon their oaths and affirmations, say that the said Janine Campbell came to her death by septic peritonitis and blood loss due to an illegal and incompetent abortion performed late on Tuesday, May 22nd or early Wednesday, May 23rd. On the basis of the available evidence and sworn testimonies we are unable to reach a conclusion on the deceased's state of mind or sanity at the time of the operation.

Further, we entirely exculpate Dr. Sophie Savard Verhoeven and Dr. Anna Savard, who attended her, from all blame and responsibility.

After close scrutiny of the evidence, we find that the abortion that led to Mrs. Campbell's death may have been performed by the deceased herself, and otherwise was the

work of person or persons unknown. We refer this matter
to the police department for further investigation.

Dr. Morgan Hancock, Women's Hospital
Dr. Manuel Thalberg, German Dispensary
Dr. Nicholas Lambert, Bellevue
Dr. Abraham Jacobi, Children's Hospital
Dr. Josiah Stanton, Women's Hospital
Dr. Benjamin Quinn, Bellevue and the Woman's Medical School
Mr. Anthony Comstock, New York Society for the Suppression of Vice

NEW YORK TRIBUNE

Thursday, May 31, 1883

LETTERS TO THE EDITOR

Sirs: Yesterday the inquest into the matter of the death of Mrs. Janine
Campbell came to a close, but not before observers and reporters
were treated to the questioning and testimony of the deceased's husband, Archer Campbell, in the most disturbing and unnecessarily
crass manner.

Mr. Campbell, having lost his wife to an illegal operation, has
also lost his four young sons to an uncertain fate. Rather than
plead prostration he has been searching for them day and night
and only paused in his efforts in order to appear yesterday before
the coroner's jury to give testimony. For almost two hours Mr.
Campbell suffered bullying and browbeating, and to what end? He
was never a suspect. It was not he who performed the operation
that ended his wife's life; nor did he take his boys away from home
and leave them somewhere without parental care and protection.

He gave honest answers to often impertinent questions posed,
it seemed, for the titillation of the jury and gallery both. Mr.
Campbell is a man of upright character and Christian morals, a
man who took his responsibilities to his wife and children with all
seriousness and provided an excellent home for them. A loving
father, if a strict one, and yet Coroner Hawthorn and the jurors
seemed determined to paint him a cruel and uncaring husband, a

man of narrow sensibilities, as if that were enough to excuse the terrible crimes visited upon himself and his sons, by a wife who was not worthy of his trust, a wife who deceived him and must, as he put so honestly, suffer the fires of hell for her sins.

We may never know the details of the operation that led to Mrs. Campbell's death, but it is certain that she sought out and submitted to a vile procedure that violates the laws of God and man. She alone was culpable, and she has paid the price and will continue to pay it through all eternity. Mr. Campbell is free of blame; indeed, Coroner Hawthorn and the jurors are more worthy of disdain and correction than this good man who has suffered so much.

Dr. James McGrath Cameron

NEW YORK TRIBUNE
Thursday, May 31, 1883

SEARCH FOR THE MISSING CAMPBELL
SONS WILL CONTINUE

While there is no news to report on the fate of the four young sons of Archer Campbell, police departments from Philadelphia to Boston have stated their firm intention to carry on with the investigation and search. The Campbell family is offering a substantial reward for any information leading to the boys' recovery.

In related news, Mrs. Janine Campbell will be laid to rest tomorrow in a private ceremony at an undisclosed location.

29

ANNA DIDN'T LIKE to think of herself as a cowardly person, but the idea of having to say good-bye to Cap and Sophie a second time was more than she could face. Instead she went to the New Amsterdam and spent the day being short with her students and assistants and the staff, always with one eye on the door. If things went wrong again, sooner or later Jack would show up to tell her so.

The lunch hour she dedicated to paperwork, and at exactly one o'clock Kathleen Hawkins presented herself, as directed, at Anna's door for the discussion about her training and nursing skills. Anna got no satisfaction out of this kind of interview, but she also would not procrastinate. She thought Hawkins would be glad to postpone this meeting indefinitely.

She was very young, Anna reminded herself, just twenty. More training, hard work, and supervised experience would make a nurse of her in the end. The question was whether Hawkins was willing to do what was necessary.

While the girl waited for Anna to begin, she kept her eyes strictly on her own folded hands, her posture erect.

"You know why you're here, Nurse Hawkins?"

"Mrs. Campbell's surgery and my poor performance."

No excuses or rationalizations, which gave Anna some reason to think there was chance for improvement. She said, "There are two options. You can voluntarily repeat your last semester of training with additional course work in anatomy, or you can leave the New Amsterdam to find employment elsewhere. But without a letter of recommendation or referral."

The girl's shoulders sagged. For a moment she seemed to be on the brink of tears, but she pulled together her resolve.

"If I may remark—"

"You may not," Anna interrupted her. "There is no excuse for your performance during an emergency surgical procedure."

The girl stared at her, incredulous. "But the—"

"Yes, it was a terrible presentation," Anna said, taking care to keep emotion out of her voice. "Enough to make an experienced surgeon blanch. But the patient comes first, and no matter how bad the situation, you have to push through your inclinations and keep your head. Which you did not."

"The—smells disoriented me," Nurse Hawkins said in a small voice. "I do know anatomy."

Explanations and rationalizations. Anna had no patience with either, but she made an effort to soften her tone. "However well you think you know anatomy, that knowledge abandoned you at a crucial moment. It was your job to assist me, not to hinder me in my efforts. Do you think you met that very basic obligation?"

Mute, she gave a tight shake of the head.

"So, your decision?"

"You want me to decide between giving up nursing altogether and repeating a semester of training. But I can't afford to do that, Dr. Savard. I couldn't pay my rent."

"Of course not," Anna said. "You'll have to move back into the nursing residence."

The pale face flushed red.

"You have until tomorrow to reach a decision. If you want to continue at the New Amsterdam I will arrange for your reenrollment to begin on Monday. That should give you time to see to the practical matters. I realize this is difficult for you, but in the end I hope you'll understand why I find it necessary."

She watched the girl leave, and wondered whether she would see her again. She wondered too if she should have said something more encouraging. *I hope you decide to stay,* for example. But the truth was, she wasn't sure that it would be good for anyone if she did.

There was a murmuring in the hall, not unexpected. Hawkins's friends would have come with her to provide support, and no doubt they were now venting their outrage. One of them would be suggesting a letter of protest to be signed by all, while others argued that a

letter would only draw more attention and make things more difficult. She hoped the calmer heads would prevail, but she could and
would deal with whatever came her way.

For the next hour people streamed in and out. Clerks with questions and letters to be signed, students asking questions about assign-
ments, assistants with updates on the conditions of the patients they
were assigned. At four one of the boys who ran errands for the Mulberry Street police station popped in, dropped a note on her desk,
and backed out again, as if she were a regent and he a commoner.
Which might seem to him to be the case.

"Jimmy."

He paused, one brow raised.

"Have you had your lunch?"

The other brow joined the first while he contemplated the question. If he told her yes, he had eaten, he would never know what she
had been prepared to offer him. If he said no, she might cause trouble at the station house, where he was supposed to get his meals as
the only payment for his services.

"Never mind," she said, and reached down to take something out
of her bag. "I have a half sandwich that's going to waste. Can you find
someone who might want it? Roast beef."

He disappeared with the sandwich clamped tight in one dirty
hand. Anna made a note to herself to speak to the Mulberry Street
matron about providing water and soap for the messenger boys.

The note was in Jack's strong handwriting:

They are safe away, in calm good spirits. I'll be by to walk home
with you at six.

Anna let out the breath she had been holding for what seemed
like hours. It was done, then. Cap was gone, and she would never see
him again. What an odd idea, really, to know that someone so very
necessary in your life was lost to you and couldn't be called back. Of
all the people she had lost, Cap would be the first since she gained
adulthood. She reminded herself that there would be letters, but
then thought that it would almost be like communicating with someone from beyond the grave.

How Cap would laugh to know she was thinking like the spiritu-alists whose tappings and whispering she truly abhorred. She could almost hear him. In mock solemnity he would promise that when he passed on, his first project would be to learn Morse code so he could really communicate, none of this silly *one tap for yes, two for no*. He would provide a travelogue, of sorts, from the other side.

She would miss him for the rest of her life.

Tonight she would write a letter of her own, one that would be waiting when they got to Switzerland if she sent it express. It would be worth the cost to think of Sophie reading it out loud while they sat on a veranda overlooking the mountains that were glacier bound all through the year. That was the picture she would hold on to.

Another knock at the door jarred her out of her thoughts, this one almost timid. Irritated, she got up and went to open it, ready to speak her mind, and very plainly.

The young woman standing there was a stranger: she carried a valise in each hand and wore an old-fashioned skirt and jacket, much mended at the hems and far too large. Anna had little sense of fashions in color, but even she knew that a true redhead—as this young woman was, her mop of thick hair shorn short—could not wear a green and brown dress. Only the sharp angles of cheekbones and jaw saved her from looking like a tomato coming into full ripeness on the vine.

The young woman's expression, open and hopeful, gave way to something like sadness. She said, "You don't recognize me."

It was the voice that made the difference. Anna stepped back-ward in her surprise. "Sister Mary Augustin?"

"Elise Mercier," said the young woman who was, apparently, no longer a nun. "Might I please come in?"

•   •   •

ANNA TRIED NOT to stare and failed.

"To say I'm taken aback would be an understatement. I thought you had gone away for good. That's the impression I was given."

An honest smile replaced the uncertainty. "You asked about me?"

"Well, yes. Was that a mistake? Did my letter cause you problems of some kind?"

"Oh, no," said Elise Mercier. "I'm glad to hear it. I thought maybe you'd just turn me away."

"You have to start from the beginning and tell me about—this change in your circumstances."

"It's not very complicated," she began.

And it seemed she was right. Elise Mercier, was, after all, still the young woman Anna had liked for her simple ability to express herself, for her intelligence and curiosity. With no fanfare she explained she had come to question her calling to the religious life, primarily because she could not push away the bone-deep itch to study medicine. She went to her superiors with these doubts, and in response they had sent her back to the Mother House where she could contemplate in solitude. Not a punishment, she added quickly. Just the opposite; the sisters had encouraged her to consider all the consequences of her choice. She could be a servant of God, nun or layperson.

"I decided to leave the order," she ended. After a moment she added: "It was the right decision, I knew immediately. Like suddenly putting down a burden. The sisters gave me their blessing and these clothes—" She looked down at herself and grimaced.

Anna bit back a smile.

"I know, it's awful. But there wasn't much choice."

"If you have no clothes, what's in your bags?"

Elise blinked. "Some books and my notes."

"From your studies?"

"I've kept a journal or a daybook, I suppose you'd call it, since I began training as a nurse. There wasn't really anyone to talk to about the details of the cases I saw, so it seemed important to at least record my observations and the questions that couldn't be answered. It's very odd of me, I'm sure."

"Just the opposite," Anna said. "It bodes well for your education. So the sisters just—waved good-bye?"

"They gave me train fare and arranged a ride to the station. I'm embarrassed to say that they thought I was going to go home to my family and I didn't correct them. I took the first train into the city. I had just arrived when it occurred to me that I should have written to ask first. You might have changed your mind."

"About?"

She raised an eyebrow in surprise. "Well, I would like to study medicine. After I've served as a nurse for as long as necessary, of course. But I do want to be a doctor, if I can fulfill the requirements and be accepted into Woman's Medical School, on a scholarship—" Elise bit her lip. "Saying it out loud like that makes me sound either very conceited or unsophisticated or both. I don't expect it to be easy. But if you meant what you said, and you're willing to help me get started—or have I assumed too much?"

Anna said, "Not as far as I am concerned, but then I'm hardly an objective observer. Will you regret your decision, do you think?"

The question didn't surprise her. "Sometimes I'll regret the things I gave up," Elise said. "But isn't that always the way? Everyone makes choices and most people doubt themselves at one time or another. I may miss the solitude of the convent, but I know now that it wasn't right for me."

"Your family will object."

"I think my mother will understand. What she wanted for me was a life free from the drudgery of a household and family."

And this, Anna thought, was the time to say that her own thinking had changed on the subject, and that like Sister Mary Augustin— Elise Mercier, she corrected herself—like Elise, she had made some fundamental changes. But she couldn't think how to start.

Instead she said, "If you apply yourself and work hard, I don't doubt that you will be an excellent physician. Now we can go talk to the head of the nursing staff, and see how best to put you to work. Would that suit?"

So many things had been pressing on Anna, so many changes in such a short time, she hadn't realized how unsettled she had been. But somehow the ability to help this sincere young woman, to put something important within her reach, that helped. A success to hold on to in a world where good young men went and stayed away.

30

IN THE YEARS since Anna came to the New Amsterdam she had heard the emergency alarm go off just three times: once for a fire in the next building; once when a staircase collapsed, casting dozens of orphans to a cobblestone courtyard; and the last time when an omnibus and a delivery wagon collided right in front of their door. She was introducing Elise to the nursing matron when the alarm sounded again, the rough clanging of the bell being yanked, and hard, from the porter's desk in the entry hall.

There were rules for how staff conducted themselves when the alarm rang; first and foremost, the patients must not be unduly alarmed. Nurses and orderlies stayed in the wards until they got further instructions, and they kept the halls and stairways clear. Doctors and nurses not currently with patients walked as quickly as they could without breaking into a run.

Anna explained this to Elise as they made their way downstairs, voices raised around them as people wondered out loud what had happened.

They came into the lobby to find a total lack of chaos. There were a half-dozen children, and every one of them was surrounded by staff. Anna would have turned back and stayed out of the way—there was no obvious need for a surgeon, as of yet—but for the sight of Jack, his face bloody and his clothes torn. A nurse was taking a boy of about five years out of one crooked arm. The other hand he had fisted in the shirt of a wild-eyed boy about twelve.

She saw that he was not seriously hurt, but she went to him anyway. The matron grabbed Elise and took her off somewhere else, a baptism by fire.

He said, "There was a panic on the new bridge; somebody tripped on the stair and somebody else screamed and started a stampede. I saw it from the el platform. It was all over in a half hour, but what a mess. *Marron, che macello.* Maybe twenty dead, kids torn away from their parents. I stopped a wagon and piled these six in. Broken bones, but nothing life-threatening, I don't think."

While he talked she pulled his head down so she could look at his pupils and examine his scalp for lacerations.

"Not my blood," he said. "There was plenty to go around, but none of it is mine."

He drew in a deep breath and seemed to notice for the first time that he had a death grip on a boy who had all the markings of a street arab, from his bare feet and ragged clothes and hollow cheeks to an expression as black and hard as a frightened dog. But there was no sign of injury at all, save for a bruise on a cheekbone.

"And who is this?"

"Ah. This would be Jem O'Malley, also known as Trotter, grandson of Jem O'Malley, also known as Porker, of the Boodle gang. Porker masterminded the hijack of a two-hundred-pound pig from a butcher's shop—" He shook the boy. "When was it, Trotter?"

The boy bared a mouthful of rotten teeth in something approximating a grin. "Eighteen hundred and sixty-two, the first of September. We celebrate it every year."

Jack grimaced. "The industrious younger members of the Boodle gang decided to take advantage of hundreds of people crushed half to death by helping themselves to wallets and pocketbooks and watches and the like. Trotter here didn't trot away fast enough, so he's off to the Tombs."

"Fine by me," the boy said. "Could use a rest."

Jack's expression wasn't hard to read, disgust and exasperation layered on top of each other. He glanced around the lobby. "I'll let the patrolmen match up these little ones with their folks. Be back here in an hour to walk you home."

And then he was gone before Anna could say even one more word.

•   •   •

SHE EXPECTED HIM to come back in a dark mood, but there was no sign of that at all; beyond the torn clothes it might have been any normal day. More than that, Jack recognized the former Sister Mary

Augustin right away, which Anna found just a little irritating. His powers of observation were superior to her own in some very specific ways that had to do with his profession: he had an uncanny memory for faces, something she had never been very good at for reasons Aunt Quinlan would attribute to her introverted nature.

He gave them what news he had about the trouble at the new bridge. "Panic," he said. "One person falls, another person screams, 'The bridge is coming down!' And they're off like a herd of buffalo across the prairie."

There were twelve confirmed dead, and twice as many injured, many of those in hospitals, from St. Vincent's to Bellevue. To Elise he said, "An exciting day to move into the city, though I'm sure you could have done without it. I wonder what Mrs. Lee has got for dinner; I am starving."

Anna told Jack about Elise's plans, drawing her into the conversation wherever possible.

"Sophie's room is available," Anna said to her. "You are welcome to stay until you've gotten settled. You may want to live in the nurses' boardinghouse for convenience alone. But I can predict with some confidence that my aunt will ask you to stay on."

She paused. "Another thing is your clothes. You'll need new—"

"Everything," Elise supplied. "This dress is ugly, I know. But my funds are also extremely limited."

Jack said, "We'll cover your expenses until you get your first pay envelope. It would be our pleasure."

Elise dropped her eyes and looked away, apparently embarrassed by Jack's offer. Anna was trying to sort out the reason for it, but Jack got there first.

"Of course," he said. "You don't have any way of knowing. There's nothing improper about the offer. I managed to persuade Anna to marry me, just this past Saturday. So you see, you're not the only one with surprising news."

"Oh," Elise said, flustered. "May I—should I—wish you every happiness?"

"Thank you," Anna said, almost as embarrassed as Elise was herself.

"It's very good of you to wish Anna every happiness," Jack said with a grin. "But you're supposed to congratulate me. Apparently it's rude to do it the other way around, or so my sisters claim."

"She's confused enough as it is," Anna said. "Have mercy."

"No, it's all right. I have to learn. So I congratulate you, Detective Sergeant Mezzanotte, and wish Dr. Savard every happiness."

Elise Mercier was practical, intelligent, and eager to learn, and Anna sensed in her a steadfast dedication. Women who pursued medicine as a profession had to be stubborn, but most of all they had to have the courage of their convictions. It seemed to her that Elise did. She hoped she was right.

She was saying, "And I would be thankful if you would help me with a few dresses and a pair of shoes—" She looked at her feet with a slightly bemused expression. "And I will, of course, repay everything. Including room and board, for as long as I stay with you. If you are really sure."

Anna said, "I am really sure, and I know Aunt Quinlan and Mrs. Lee will both be very happy to have you. Mr. and Mrs. Lee are Catholic, so you won't be entirely out of familiar territory."

Some of the color left the girl's face. "They won't approve."

"They will approve," Anna said. "I can promise you that much. What I can't promise you is that Aunt Quinlan will take any money from you, no matter how long you stay. If anything is likely to put her in a sour mood, it would be you insisting on paying her for room and board. She won't have it."

Elise glanced at Jack as if looking for confirmation. Jack nodded, to the girl's obvious discomfort.

Whatever awkwardness Elise might have worried about, her concerns were put to rest by Aunt Quinlan's inability to be surprised or put out by the arrival of an unannounced houseguest. Of course Elise was welcome to stay, and how nice it would be to have her. Mrs. Lee went off straightaway to make sure Sophie's old room was ready, Mr. Lee took her valises up, and the little Russo girls did cartwheels of joy to see her again. The news that she wasn't going away again anytime soon had them hatching plans. They waited impatiently through an impromptu family meeting over tea where the adults discussed practicalities, and then they pounced. Elise must have the grand tour, without delay.

"Do not run that young lady off her feet," Mrs. Lee called after them. "She's had a long day."

But Anna was less worried. It seemed to her that Rosa and Lia would provide the perfect introduction to a usual household.

• • •

ELISE HAD NO objections to being dragged off by the Russo sisters. They dashed up to an attic filled with boxes and crates and trunks, each one full of treasure, Lia assured her, and worked their way down, floor by floor. She was firm in her unwillingness to be shown personal rooms other than the one they shared. They wanted her to admire the pretty quilt on the bed, the view out the window, the cushions on the window seat, the wardrobe filled with neat piles of little girls' clothes. She complimented Lia's dolls and Rosa's first attempts at needlework. Then they were off again to see the bathrooms and the wondrous plumbing—they still could not fathom the miracle of water, hot or cold, at the turn of a tap, and the toilet was to them a magical convenience. Elise admitted that she was almost as unfamiliar as they were with this invention, which won her a fierce smile from Rosa. She had passed some test without realizing how closely she was being examined.

Back downstairs she saw the little parlor, the dining room, the main parlor, the kitchen and pantry. They would have shown her the cellar, too, but Mrs. Lee put a stop to that plan. In the garden she admired the neat rows of beanpoles, the cabbage and carrot and turnip plantings, the apple and pear trees, the flower garden already full of color and bees hard at work. They were especially proud of the enclosed porch they called a pergola, with its reclining couch and chairs and table.

She was not spared the stable or the little cottage where Mr. and Mrs. Lee lived, or even the henhouse, where she was introduced to eight setting hens and a rooster who demanded respect and distance both, she was told. Elise might have explained that she had grown up on a farm and knew all about roosters, but it gave them such joy to instruct her, she kept her silence except to make encouraging sounds.

There was a short debate on whether they should take her to a place they called *Weeds*. Before Elise could ask for clarification she was hurried through a rounded wooden door set in the garden wall into another garden, this one bare except for ancient grapevines over a collapsing trellis, a small greenhouse engulfed in ivy, and a few apple and holly trees. The soil had been recently turned, and the smells of compost and manure were strong in the air. The girls pulled her into another house that was being made over for Dr. Savard and the detective sergeant, this one stripped down to its bones as the garden had been. They showed her every room, with colorful commentary about how many children would fit into the bedrooms; the new bathtub, as big as a pond; the lace at the windows; and neat stacks of sheets and towels in the linen closet.

By the time they got back to Roses—now Elise had caught on to the Weeds and Roses names—dinner was on the table, and her stomach gave a terrific growl that made the girls first startle and then laugh with delight. Even at the table they were full of life and talk and stories, very different little girls from the ones she had first met in Hoboken and cared for at the orphanage. They weren't scolded for their talkativeness, Elise thought, because their silence was inevitable, secured by the combination of healthy appetites and good food on the table.

There was a soup thick with dumplings and a roast of pork, pickled red cabbage and potatoes mashed with butter and milk which they were instructed to enjoy because, Mrs. Lee told them, there would be no more until the new crop of spuds came in late in the summer. The garden was the topic of conversation for a good time and Elise took her part in the discussion, but she also had the distinct idea that they were all holding back, waiting for her to catch her breath and volunteer the stories they hesitated to ask for.

The middle-aged woman Anna had introduced as her cousin Margaret stole looks at Elise every time she took a bite of food. And that was signal enough. She put down her napkin and said, "You are all very kind, but I know you are wondering about me."

"Well," Lia piped right up. "I was wondering about your dress and your shoes and if you lost your bonnet, the white one that made your eyes look so blue."

Mrs. Quinlan said, "All interesting questions. But I think we should take turns, and Elise will answer only some of them. We don't want to use up all her stories right away."

"That's all right, Mrs. Quinlan," Elise said.

"Oh, no," said Lia, as if Elise had committed some terrible breach of etiquette. "You have to call her Aunt Quinlan. Everybody does. But you don't get punished if you forget," Lia reassured her.

The girls thought of her not as a grown-up, not even as a woman, but as a creature out of her element, someone who was as new to this world as they were. And in that they weren't entirely wrong.

Anna said, "That rule doesn't apply to everyone. I'll bet Elise has aunts of her own."

"I do," Elise said. "I have two aunts who are always coming up with schemes. The stories I could tell—" She paused for effect. "And I will tell them, if you're interested."

Margaret said, "Where did you grow up, Elise?"

From the corner of her eye Elise saw a quick flash of irritation cross Anna's face, but she smiled at Margaret.

"In Vermont, on the Quebec border. My father has a farm outside Canaan, sheep and goats and dairy cattle and some crops. They make cheese, mostly, to sell."

It had been so long since she had been asked—even allowed—to speak about herself that it came to her slowly, the things that could and should be said.

"I have been through the area," said Mrs. Quinlan. "By sleigh, in the deep of winter."

Anna smiled at her great-aunt. "During the war?"

"Oh, the war—" Lia began, but Jack reached over and cupped the crown of her head in his head.

"Not the war you've heard about," he told her. "A war that happened a very long time ago. I am right, Aunt Quinlan?"

"It was 1812, and I was very young," Aunt Quinlan agreed. "And very much in love with my first husband, though I wouldn't admit it to anyone, not even myself. Elise, go on please and tell us about your family."

She told them about her younger brothers, her parents, her two maiden aunts who spoke only French but on occasion tried English, to everybody's amusement: Aunt Bijou's *Oh my cows!* when she was startled, Aunt Nini's *But why the cockroach?* when someone was making a sad face.

To her own surprise Elise found that she was still a good story-teller. Even the cautious and reserved Margaret was smiling.

She felt as if she had passed a test, one she had set herself. Leaving the convent, she had assured Mother Superior and everyone else that she would fit into the world again, but on some level she had doubted herself. Now she knew that it would take time, but that she could be Elise Mercier, and that the strangeness would go away, with time.

• • •

JACK HAD BEEN friendly and talkative on the way home, but he was unusually quiet during dinner. He smiled at the right moments and responded when somebody talked to him, and still some part of his mind was elsewhere. He might be thinking about the bridge disaster, or some other case, or his mother, or wondering how to say he disliked red cabbage. Anna resolved not to ask, out of common courtesy. She had always disliked being prodded to reveal what she was thinking about. He would tell her if and when he was ready. But what if he was waiting for her to ask?

Enough, she told herself, and fixed her attention on Elise, who had an unassuming way of answering personal questions, engaging and modest at the same time. When she talked about her family it seemed as if she were shaking the dust off parts of herself she had hidden away for safekeeping, small treasures to be studied and polished before she shared them, even in such a gathering of people who had welcomed her so warmly.

Elise looked very much like someone who needed a good night's sleep, but there was an energy in her that wasn't so easily subdued by weariness. Not a beautiful girl, but so alive and curious and filled with goodwill that few people would notice.

While the little girls helped Mrs. Lee with clearing the table and wiping dishes, Aunt Quinlan called for Mr. Lee and asked him to bring down certain boxes from the attic. Jack went along to help, which left the four women alone in the parlor where the windows were open to the evening breeze. Margaret picked up her sewing right away, but Aunt Quinlan sat studying Elise openly, as she might have studied an interesting painting.

"You have had a very long day," Aunt Quinlan said. "But I hope

another hour won't be too much to ask. I think some of the clothes I
have put away will suit you. They will need a good brushing and
some adjustments, but with any luck they'll hold you over until we
can manage something new."

With a nervous smile Elise said, "You are very kind, but I don't
want to be a burden."

Anna said, "Elise, Auntie doesn't like to be challenged in these matters. She gets a great deal of satisfaction out of imposing her goodwill,
and we humor her."

"Why you—" Aunt Quinlan began, and then gave in to laughter.
They all did, even Elise.

＊ ＊ ＊

AT NINE ELISE could not keep her eyes open any longer. Mrs. Quinlan sent her off to bed with a pile of borrowed nightclothes that
smelled of cedar shavings and lavender.

"I put out some things so you won't have to go searching, soap
and such," Mrs. Lee said. "Now if you said thank you this evening
five times you've said it fifty. Go to bed, girl."

"Then I'll say good night instead." But she stood there in the
doorway, feeling as if something important were hanging in the air
waiting to be made real.

Mrs. Lee had turned back to the sorting of the clothes from the
attic, putting aside the ones she would wash and press for Elise to
use. The urge to protest was strong, but Elise had the idea that Mrs.
Lee would not be amused.

"Really," said Mrs. Quinlan, kindly. "If you're going to start at the
hospital tomorrow, you will need your sleep."

＊ ＊ ＊

THE DOOR TO the room Elise was meant to use stood half open. She
hesitated, wondering why this particular moment was so difficult,
and why it felt more final than getting on the train headed for the
city. The room as her own for as long as she cared to stay, Mrs. Quinlan had told her. And how was a person to deal with such generosity?

To start with, she could appreciate the beautiful things around her.

There was a desk where she would do her work and study, below
a window that looked out over the garden. Beside it was a small
bookcase where she would line up her books—chemistry and anat-

omy, pharmacology and therapeutics. If that weren't enough, there was a deep upholstered armchair to read in.

The bed was covered with a red and white quilt. Four plump pillows butted up against a high headboard that looked very old, the dark wood carved into a mural of branches in leaf and birds. She took note of the wardrobe and washstand with a jug of water and a painted porcelain basin. Mrs. Lee had put out a cake soap still wrapped in paper, a toothbrush, and a can of toothpowder with an elaborate label: *Dr. Martin's Camphorated Dentifrice for Clean, Healthy Teeth.*

The whole house was full of pictures, and this room had its share. Elise especially liked the portraits of young children, most of them very simple, just touched with color. There were three in this room: two young girls with white-blond curls, a bald baby with fat red cheeks in a wheelbarrow, and four little boys standing in a row trying to look very fierce. The only portrait of an adult hung opposite the bed. An elderly black woman with deep-set, honey-brown eyes below a head cloth of sprigged muslin. She seemed to be watching over the bed itself, her expression patient. It was a very old face, quite possibly older than Sister Theresa, who was more than ninety.

It just occurred to Elise now that she would never see Sister Theresa again, and with that the tears she had expected when she walked away from the convent finally came.

With some resolve she opened her valises and unpacked the few personal items she had brought with her: underclothes, books and notebooks, a battered pen box, her missal and rosary, a comb. For a moment she considered the small bundle of letters from home, the first thing she had packed.

There weren't many letters—just one for every year since she left to start her novitiate—but they were all many pages long and close-written. Every Easter her mother and aunts wrote the annual letter together, reading passages out loud at the dinner table for comments and soliciting contributions. The letters were almost like a magical mirror that let Elise watch them as they sat around the kitchen table arguing about when exactly the old mule had died, and the lightning strike that had taken down two trees at once on the far edge of the property, or Aldonce the butcher's annual visit, when he came to call with such high hopes, and went home empty-handed because Aunt

Bijou had turned him down, as she always did. As soon as he was out of sight Bijou would start contemplating next year's excuse, because she liked Aldonce well enough and had no wish to injure him.

Elise had a letter of her own to write, but it must wait until she had slept. The things she needed to say would need careful wording.

She undressed and hung the awful dress on a hook in the wardrobe. The shoes she set neatly beneath. She washed and finally pulled the soft muslin nightdress over her head and let it drop, so that the hem whispered against her bare feet.

Now there was only the bed to conquer. It was the word that came to mind, as if she stood before a mountain.

This particular bed with its odd carvings was wide enough for three adults or six children, or even more, if they were turned sideways. She could imagine all of her brothers as she had last seen them, packed like a row of sardines in a can. And they would have thought themselves in heaven on such a thick mattress under layers of sheets and quilts.

She climbed in. The sheets were homespun, which surprised and pleased her both. She didn't know what she had been expecting, but the weave of the linen against her cheek was familiar and comforting. They had been washed so often that they felt as soft as silk; they smelled of fresh air and just a touch of carbolic because this was a household that observed Lister's antibacterial practices. But the pillow slips smelled of lilac.

In all her life she had never slept with even a single pillow, and now here she was confronted with four. It was like sharing a bed with a herd of overfed and indolent cats. Elise fell asleep with one of them clasped to her chest, like a doll.

◆   ◆   ◆

ANNA FINISHED THE letter to Cap and Sophie and climbed into bed, where Jack was reading the *Police Gazette* with a severe expression that was almost a scowl. Without looking up he transferred the folded newspaper to his right hand and lifted the other arm. Anna scooted closer to put her head on his shoulder and the arm dropped into place, as solid as a club.

She said, "Still thinking about the bridge?"

He hesitated for just a moment, then put the paper on the bedside table and turned toward her. The heavy shadow of his beard made him look like a ruffian of the first order. Somehow this big, very masculine being had found a way into her life and bed in just two months' time. She didn't know which one of them was more surprised. Or pleased.

"What are you grinning about?"

Anna rubbed her cheek against his shoulder. "Nothing in particular. What are you scowling about?"

"Was I scowling? I was reading the *Police Gazette*. I suppose Margaret gets more satisfaction out of it than I do."

"Jack."

He drew in a very deep breath and let it go, slowly. "Sometimes it's hard to leave work behind on Mulberry."

"I like hearing about your work."

The corner of his mouth jerked. "Even you might not have the stomach for some of it."

This reminded her of Hawkins, who had not been able to stomach what had happened to Janine Campbell. From there her thoughts went to the missing boys. The inquest into their mother's death had ended just a few days ago, and the boys had already slipped her mind. It made her angry and sad and unhappy. She was going to say as much to Jack when he spoke up.

"There was a fight in one of the tenements on Elizabeth Street," he said. "Have you ever been in any of them?"

"When I was an intern, yes." Dark halls barely wide enough for a man of normal size, damp walls, the smells of mildew and rats and cooking and human waste. And the noise. The noise was what Anna remembered mostly.

Jack said, "We arrested a stevedore for killing his son. Caved the boy's head in because he tried to protect his mother."

He was quiet for a long minute. Anna waited, wondering if he needed to tell the whole story, to shake the images out of his head. She could imagine a dozen different situations that ended just this way, because she had seen them herself. It was another thing they had in common.

She asked, "The mother?"

"She'll end up in the poorhouse. Maybe she'll be able to keep the oldest girl with her, but the other three will be parceled out to one of the Catholic asylums. The only thing I know for sure is this: the minute they're out of that room the greedy slob of a landlord will have another family in there."

They were quiet for a moment. The night was clear and cool, and the breeze from the window was comforting. Anna took Jack's hand and threaded her fingers through his.

"And to top it all off," he went on, "we were called out to Bellevue because they had an unidentified dead woman."

And now she was surprised. "They must have twenty mortalities without names every day. Do they call the detectives every time?"

"This woman was young, dressed in silks and brocades. If her hands are any indication she never worked a day in her life."

"So where did she come from?"

"A cabby dropped her off, but he was gone before anybody thought to question him. She had a purse on her, mostly empty. There were no obvious wounds I could see, no marks on her throat. They'll do a postmortem."

Anna traced along his knuckles with her thumb. "It is unusual. I wonder why a wealthy woman would ask to be taken to Bellevue."

"Somebody will come looking for her, and the autopsy will explain the rest. If you want to see the postmortem when we get it, I can do that."

"Oddly enough, I think I do want to see it," Anna said. "A young woman who drops dead for no apparent reason."

Jack turned on his side and lifted her hand to kiss her palm and then nipped the pad of flesh below the thumb. There was a look in his eyes she recognized, one that sent gooseflesh up her back and pooled in her breasts and everywhere else, every part of her that knew his touch.

"Enough talk."

She found herself grinning, and thought she should be appalled to be so easily distracted from such a sad story. But she wasn't. Not with the way Jack was looking at her.

She said, "What exactly have you got in mind?"

"You," he said, pulling her up to press all along him. "Exactly you are on my mind."

She said, "I thought you were going to play handball today."

Jack stilled. "I did play handball. And?"

"You said that when you were feeling—the need, you played handball to work off energy. Don't you remember telling me that?"

He buried his face in the crook of her neck and laughed. "Anna," he said finally. "Having you up against me like this would rouse me out of a coma. The smell of your hair alone could raise Lazarus. I could play handball twelve hours without a break and still want you after. Though I would be pretty ripe by that point."

Anna knew she was blushing, not out of embarrassment, but pleasure. Because he wanted her, because she pleased him. As inexperienced and clumsy as she might be, it didn't matter.

"That's good," she said. "Because suddenly sleep is the last thing on my mind."

31

BEFORE THEIR SHIFT started Jack found Oscar at MacNeil's, a cigar clamped between his teeth while he squinted at the newspaper, holding it right up to his face.

He said, "If you're done analyzing the news of the world, we should get a move on."

"Mezzanotte," Oscar said solemnly. "You'll be bleeding from the ears if you strain any harder for the wit. It's just not in you, man. Especially these days. Married—how long?"

"A week on Saturday."

"Nine days married and you're soft as soap already. And how is the bride?"

They left the diner and took a shortcut down the alley to the police stables, where they claimed a rig for the day. Jack took the reins and turned the horse north, debating with himself on the most direct route. It was the same debate, every time, and he never did seem to guess right. No matter which way he went, the traffic was better someplace else.

Oscar said, "You were telling me about Anna."

Jack grinned. "I wasn't, but I will. She's got more energy than a lightning strike. She worked Friday and Saturday nights, and yesterday when she should have been catching up on her sleep, the freight wagon from Greenwood shows up with a load of furniture, both my sisters, and a niece."

"Which one?"

"Chiara. She's going to be helping Margaret with the little girls. So there's this freight truck piled with furniture my mother sent. It was good luck that there were a half-dozen men from the nursery working in the garden or Anna would have carried every chair and table and bedpost into the house on her own. Or at least she would have tried."

They were cut off by an omnibus, which was why Jack had the reins. Oscar would have gone after the driver and might have ended up in a fistfight, but it took more than traffic to rouse Jack's temper. For a moment he thought Oscar might go after the wagon driver anyway, but then he settled down, grumbling.

"Sounds like you've got a circus going. How's the little nun?"

"She goes by Elise these days. Or Miss Mercier, to you. She's adjusting."

"Full house."

Jack wondered to himself if he could speak his whole mind, and decided that he could trust Oscar to listen without making judgments.

"Alfonso and Massimo send between eight and twelve men every day to work on the house or in the garden, and of course they all need feeding and watering. Mrs. Lee couldn't keep up with them, so Celestina and Bambina are around all day cooking and running things. Then the Lees brought in their granddaughter Laura to help with the laundry and cleaning. So there's a half-dozen men, Chiara, Celestina, Bambina, Margaret, Elise, Laura Lee, Rosa, and Lia around for most of the day."

"Surrounded by females, you poor sod." Oscar yawned.

Jack laughed as he encouraged the horse into the traffic on Broadway. When they were moving along at a decent clip, Oscar said, "You see the notice in the papers, about the unidentified woman at Bellevue?"

Jack had seen it; in fact, Margaret had drawn it to his attention. "No family's come forward?"

"It's been in four different city papers since Friday, and not one inquiry."

That was unusual. The poor often went unnamed to their graves, but a young woman from a well-to-do family, that was a different matter. "Where did they run the notice?"

"From Philadelphia to Boston."

"The postmortem?"

"Early tomorrow."

Jack said, "Her family might not even realize she's missing yet. Maybe she came in from some small town to stay with friends and isn't expected back for a while."

Oscar jerked a shoulder, as if he didn't especially like this reading but wouldn't argue. Just now.

"So then what were you thinking?"

"I thought maybe we could stop by a couple of the high-class hotels, see if they're missing anybody."

Jack thought about this as he threaded his way through traffic around Madison Square and then west into the Tenderloin. Every city had a neighborhood like this, but Jack had visited some of those places and nothing compared. Every night of the week the whole thing—some thirty blocks—was as loud and raucous as a carnival. Music from every door and window, the bellowing of the crowds watching prize-fights or cockfights or dancers or musicales, street and alley brawls where broken bottles were the weapon of choice, the constant flow of men in and out of gambling dens and saloons and disorderly houses, and the women who walked the street or leaned out of windows half-naked, calling out to likely customers. This Monday morning looked like every other: as if a battle had been fought and lost.

The streets were full of trash, the sewers clogged with debris. Adults and children alike sifted through the muck and mire for anything they could sell: a cuff link, scraps of paper, empty bottles, rags. Cigar butts were especially prized because they could be sold back to the cigar factories, a nickel for two dozen.

They had an errand to run at the precinct station, where the whole complement of cops and roundsmen would be busy sorting through the aftermath. Dozens of regulars slept in the drunk tank; cells were crowded with gamblers and shysters not sober or quick enough to get out of the way, with thieves and pickpockets and prostitutes.

A filthy man staggered out of a doorway, bent over double, and vomited into the gutter.

"Oh, the glory," Oscar said, and tucked a fresh cigar, whole and unblemished, into the corner of his mouth.

•   •   •

IN THE EARLY afternoon they went first to the Avalon, the most luxurious and expensive hotel on Fifth Avenue. Jack thought they might be overshooting—the dead woman had not been dripping with jewels, after all—but Oscar loved the Avalon almost as much as he disliked the Avalon's general manager, and he took any opportunity to visit the former and irritate the latter.

The closest Jack could get to an understanding was the fact that Oscar had grown up in the same Lower East Side tenement with Thomas Roth, who had clearly worked his way up and out. Oscar's lodgings were evidence that he didn't put much value on material possessions, but at the same time he resented Thomas Roth for having them. Now he pulled the concierge aside, flashed his badge, and insisted on an immediate meeting with Mr. Roth. They would be waiting in the lobby.

The carpets underfoot were Persian, the deep chairs and sofas of the softest leather, the mahogany tables inlaid with rosewood and pearl, spittoons of hammered copper with carved marble feet, porcelain vases three feet high, chiseled mirrors in carved and gilded frames. As a Christmas present Jack had brought his sisters here for tea on a particularly miserable December afternoon. He had never seen them more enchanted with anything than they were with the Avalon dining room: silver coffee urns, hand-painted china, pristine linen, perfect sandwiches and petit fours, and waiters as straight and exacting as soldiers.

Oscar deposited himself in a deep club chair and sighed, content.

The fuss made Jack antsy. He said, "I'm going to check in." If not for the perfect ring of smoke floating toward the ceiling, Jack might have thought Oscar had fallen asleep. Jack went back out onto the street and the call box on the corner. He was back not ten minutes later, just in time to see the general manager approaching. Thomas Roth was stalking toward them like a man on a suicide mission.

Jack picked up his pace to intercept and called out: "Oscar. Word from the Gilsey House at headquarters, they've got a missing guest who may be our Jane Doe. Jimmy Breslin is waiting for us."

Oscar waved an arm in the air as he sauntered away. "Never mind, Roth. I'll be back to deal with you another day."

◆　◆　◆

THE GILSEY HOUSE general manager was an old friend, the brother of Jack's first partner when he walked a beat.

"Jimmy," Jack said with real pleasure. "The last time I saw you was on the handball court, what, six months ago. You beat me soundly, if I remember correctly."

"Sure I did," Breslin said. "Right after you beat me twice in a row. I'll be back there someday soon to try my luck again."

"We hear you've misplaced one of your guests," Oscar said.

For a split second Jack thought Jimmy might take offense, which meant that he was on edge, which meant there really was something to talk about and in fact, he didn't waste words.

"We had a lady check in last Tuesday, someone we see now and then with her husband, but this time she was alone. She said she was waiting for her sister to join her, but no sister ever showed up."

Jack took out his notebook and let Oscar lead with the questions. Now and then he glanced up to gauge the look on Breslin's face, and saw nothing more than the professional demeanor of the general manager of one of Manhattan's most exclusive hotels. The guest—he identified the missing woman as Abigail Liljeström, the wife of a Buffalo industrialist—had gone out early on Wednesday and asked that no one disturb her room until she specifically requested service. She hadn't been seen in the dining hall or any other part of the hotel since.

"So that's five days that nobody's seen her," Oscar clarified.

Jimmy nodded. "This morning the matron came to mention it to me, with a copy of the newspaper article—" He dug it out of his pocket to show them. "That's when I called it in."

"The matron recognized the description in the article as Abigail Liljeström?"

"She did. So I came up here to see. There's no sign of trouble but she hasn't been here for days."

Jack thought for a moment. "We'll need to talk to the matron and to any of the maids who dealt with Mrs. Liljeström directly. The desk clerks too. We'll want one or two of them to come to the morgue to identify the body."

"Should I send a telegram to her family?"

"We'll do that," Jack said. "But not until we're sure what we have."

• • •

JACK STAYED BEHIND to go through the room while Oscar took two maids and the matron to the morgue. It wasn't something Jack especially liked doing, but he had a knack for the work, a way of piecing things together that he often didn't understand himself.

He went through the clothes hanging in the wardrobe: day dresses, carriage and walking dresses, a robe, a nightdress, a pelisse all in silks and velvets and fine wools. He checked the pocketbooks and came up with an unaddressed envelope, a few coins, a handkerchief, but no identification. The clothes were very fine, but it was the shoes that made him pause. They were custom made for someone with very small feet, leather dyed purple or green or red, some with mother-of-pearl buckles, others with silk flowers. There were three hatboxes, and a trunk with fitted drawers for handkerchiefs, stockings, garters, ribbons, and undergarments. It occurred to him that one of the maids must have helped her lace her stays, but none of the three they had interviewed mentioned that particular service.

There were a few books on the bedside table along with framed photos: an older couple, a balding man of thirty-five or forty who was probably the industrialist husband, and two children, a boy and a girl. Well fed, overdressed, looking solemnly into the camera.

He found nothing in the drawers of the desk or dresser and finished quickly, skipped the elevator and ran down six flights to talk to the desk clerk. Thinking to himself that the industrialist had gone wrong somewhere, to have let it come to this.

32

THE SISTERS OF Charity did not tolerate idleness. Thinking back, Elise couldn't ever remember having nothing to do; in the convent the novitiates scrubbed floors, peeled potatoes, carried slop buckets; later there was work in the infirmaries, learning how to clean and bind wounds, dispense medications, handle sick children. If she hadn't shown an affinity for the infirmary she might have ended up in the laundry, starching and ironing habits. The idea could still make her shudder.

She had never known what it was to be idle, but now with her third full day as Nurse Mercier at the New Amsterdam, she really understood what it meant to be busy. The children she had cared for at the orphanage had come into the infirmary with colds, infected scrapes, sore ears, lice, rickets, upset stomachs. Children with scarlet fever or broken bones or needing surgery had been transferred to St. Vincent's, where doctors took over. She rarely learned what had happened, and asking was discouraged.

At the New Amsterdam she had already assisted in the setting of a broken ankle; she had debrided and dressed lacerations and burns, recorded temperatures and pulse rates, sterilized surgical instruments, the variety of which was astounding. She gave shots and enemas and emptied her share of bedpans. She learned the names of instruments: bistouries, tenotomes, tenacula, curved and straight scalpels, forceps and bougies and probes. Twice already she had been allowed to assist the circulating nurse during surgeries: one to correct an umbilical hernia, and another to remove a tumor of the breast. Which reminded her, of course, of Sister Xavier, who had been her patient the first time she had come to the New Amsterdam. She wondered if she would ever miss Sister Xavier the way she missed some of the others, and decided that it was unlikely. In fact every time she asked a question—and she took every opportunity to do just that—she thought of Sister Xavier's scowl and she had to suppress a grin.

The freedom to ask questions was the best thing of all, better than the kind generosity on Waverly Place, better than the bed overrun by pillows, better than the simple uniform that let her move unrestricted, and the freedom from the bonnet she had never learned to like. She was careful not to overtax people; she portioned out questions, watching for signs of irritation or distraction, and withdrew.

Of course she also sterilized bedpans, folded sheets and towels, ran errands, fetched medicines from the pharmacist in his little warren of rooms, took care of charts, and filed endless amounts of paper, but none of those things bothered her. She wanted to be of help; she wanted to be indispensable, so that no one ever considered sending her away.

When her shift ended at three, she was going to walk to the Woman's Medical School and present herself to be interviewed as a prospective student. In her pocket she had a sealed letter of reference from Dr. Savard (Anna, as she was supposed to be called outside the hospital). Then she would walk back to Waverly Place and change out of her uniform while Lia and Rosa and Chiara—fourteen years old but just as impetuous and full of energy as the littler girls—interrogated her about her day, half in English and half in Italian. She would help wherever she was needed until dinnertime, and then she would be at the table with all the good people who had taken her in as if she were a treasured niece rather than a stranger who had come to their door without warning.

She wondered when things would start to go wrong.

•   •   •

DINNER AT AUNT Quinlan's table had never been quiet; she liked discussion and debate, gossip and news of the world, and most of all, she liked stories. Sometimes she told her own. If the table discussion was particularly loud Auntie Quinlan could bring about a magical silence by raising a single finger, which signaled her willingness to talk about her childhood or her years living abroad or her own children.

But this evening they were all lost in their own thoughts. Anna studied the faces around the table one by one, and her attention came to rest on Elise. The girl had been pushing herself at an inhuman pace since she arrived; Anna reasoned that she had finally exhausted her energy, something that would be fixed by an early night. Just then Elise looked up, saw Anna studying her, and dropped her gaze again, as if she had been caught doing something forbidden.

"All right, Elise," Jack said suddenly. He had been studying her too, it seemed. "What's wrong?"

"I am perfectly well." She produced a stiff smile.

"She's not," Lia said. "She's not well, but she wouldn't tell me."

"Folks have a right to their privacy," Aunt Quinlan said. "And we don't plague people we like and care about at the dinner table."

"I'm not plaguing her," Lia said, sniffing. "I'm worried."

Elise closed her eyes briefly and then, opening them, looked at Anna directly. She said, "I spoke to Dr. Montgomery at Woman's Medical School today."

Anna drew in a deep breath. "Well, that explains a lot. She told you that you'd never make a doctor and to put away foolish dreams."

Elise's mouth fell open. "How did you know?"

"Because," Aunt Quinlan answered for Anna. "Dr. Montgomery says the same thing to every young woman who comes asking about enrolling."

"She told me I was far too enamored of what little intellect I had." Anna could smile at the memory, these many years later. "And she was just getting started."

Elise looked both affronted and relieved. "But why would she say something like that to you?"

"Because I was too enamored of my intelligence," Anna said. "Small or large."

Jack said, "Surely not."

She elbowed him, and the girls giggled.

"If it's any comfort to you, Elise, the more insulting she is, the more she hopes you'll succeed and do well. But she's superstitious."

Chiara made very large eyes. In a whisper she said, "*Maloch, Zio Jack.*"

"We don't allow the evil eye at this dinner table," Aunt Quinlan said to her. "But if it makes you feel better"—and she tossed a bit of salt over her shoulder—"Dr. Montgomery is protective," she went on, speaking to Elise. "If she can scare you away, she thinks you didn't belong in the first place."

"Oh," said Rosa. "Like Billy Goat Gruff."

"Just like that," said Aunt Quinlan. "She's daring you to cross the bridge, Elise. Are you going to back away?"

Some color came back into her cheeks. "No," she said. "Not when I've come this far."

• • •

OSCAR MARONEY SHOWED up just as the girls were clearing the last of the dessert dishes and was more than happy to be talked into a serving of pie. For some reason Jack was always surprised at how easily Oscar won over women of all ages. Every face around the table lit up at the sight of him.

His partner understood women; he knew when to tease and when to pay a compliment and when neither would be a good idea, and then he listened, and focused all his attention. Jack watched him weave his usual magic, wondering in another part of his mind what trouble had brought him to their door. Because it was Oscar's habit to spend Monday nights playing cards, and only something very important would make him miss his chance to fleece his brothers-in-law.

Jack waited until he had finished pie and coffee, and suggested that if he wanted a cigar, they should step out into the garden.

"Why don't you show me this wonder of a house you bought for your new bride," Oscar countered. "Let's bring her along too. I'd like to get her opinion on something."

So whatever had brought Oscar to the door was something that couldn't be discussed in front of women and children. He wondered if Anna understood she had been paid a compliment when Oscar excluded her from that group.

• • •

AS FAR AS Anna was concerned, the furniture Jack's parents had sent from Greenwood rendered the house habitable, and she would have moved in immediately if the idea hadn't scandalized every other female within ten miles.

"Not until there are curtains on the windows," Mrs. Lee said, Bambina and Celestina nodding in agreement behind her.

"There are curtains in the bedroom," Anna said. "It's not like I'm planning on romping through the rest of the house in a state of undress."

Bambina's mouth quirked. "Maybe you aren't."

That made Anna draw up in surprise and then retreat until she could ask Jack some pointed questions.

Now she sat at the kitchen table with Jack and Oscar and tried not to fidget. To her own surprise it was difficult not to get up and start sorting through boxes of dishes that had yet to be unpacked. She would have to write to Sophie about the unanticipated streak of domesticity she had uncovered in herself. Cap would weep with laughter at the idea of Anna Savard's sudden urge to explore the complexities of bed linens and tea services.

Jack was saying, "Anna, Oscar is asking a question."

"Sorry." She made more of an effort to focus on Oscar, who had unfolded a piece of paper and smoothed it out on the table. "What's that?"

"You remember the unidentified woman from late last week," Jack said. "It turns out she's from Buffalo and was just in town for a few days."

Looking across the table, Anna realized she was familiar with the kind of document Oscar had brought.

"Is that the postmortem?"

Oscar slid it across the table toward her. "If you wouldn't mind having a look, your thoughts on it would be much appreciated."

"What happened?" Anna asked.

"Read it first," Jack said. "Then you tell us."

• • •

JACK WATCHED HER eyes moving back and forth, her expression calm, her hands spread flat on the table to either side of the report.

She looked up. "What is it you want to know?"

"Whatever strikes you as important."

She didn't like vague requests, but he saw she was trying. With a shift of the shoulders she turned her attention back to the report and scanned it again. "The postmortem was done by Nicholas Lambert. He was on the Campbell jury, did you realize? High coloring, dark hair and beard? He's a forensics specialist, and very good at what he does. This report is far better than the one written for Janine Campbell."

Her gaze shifted from Jack to Oscar and back again. "Is there some connection between the two women?"

"That's what we are wondering about," Oscar said. "Could you go through the report with us, and start from the beginning?"

"It's very straightforward," Anna said. "Healthy woman of about twenty-five, no external signs of violence. Evidence of at least one and probably more than one birth."

"Where does it say that?" Jack leaned toward her and she pointed to the relevant bit of writing.

"'Striae gravidarum' is Latin for stretch marks."

Oscar's expression made it clear he wasn't familiar with the phrase, and Jack assumed that his own face did the same.

"In pregnancy the skin of the abdomen is stretched beyond the point of normal elasticity," she offered. "So there are stress lines that appear purple at first, and eventually fade to white. This lady's abdomen showed stretch marks of two distinct shades, some almost white, others still pink." She waited, and got nods from both of them before she went on.

"In addition to stretch marks, there is scarring to the perineum. Wait," she said, in response to Jack's raised brow. "I'll explain. If the birth is difficult—say, the child is large and the mother is weak after a long labor—an attending doctor will often make an incision from the vagina toward the anus to increase the circumference of the birth canal. The idea is to avoid tearing, which can be difficult to stitch. Closing an incision is easier than stitching a tear; at least that's how the reasoning goes."

Anna could almost hear Oscar blushing, and Jack, she thought, wasn't much better, despite the frank discussions they had been having recently. She studied the report for a long minute. When she thought they had had enough time to compose themselves, she went on.

"The surgical procedure is called an episiotomy. It's done too often, in my opinion, usually by doctors who are in a hurry. In Mrs. Liljeström's case the person who delivered her made an unusually large incision that didn't heal well. She had granulomas along the suture line, nodules of scar tissue that indicate that her sutures weren't removed very carefully. Even tiny bits of suture can cause irritation and infection, and the body reacts by isolating the fragment and walling it off, so to speak."

Oscar cleared his throat. "That's in the past, though."

"Yes," Anna said. "But a thorough autopsy doesn't leave anything out."

Jack said, "The granulomas aren't relevant to the cause of death?"

Anna considered for a moment. "That would be conjecture on my part."

"Go on and conject," said Oscar. "We won't tattle on you."

She gave him a half smile. "The scarring indicates that she had at least one very difficult birth. Some women have such bad experiences that they simply can't face the prospect again. This woman had an abortion, that's undeniable, but there's no way to know if she was driven by fear of childbirth. But she had a hard time of it, that's a certainty."

"The operation itself," Oscar said. "Anything you find unusual?"

"It does happen sometimes, especially with less experienced practitioners. Too much pressure with the instrument in exactly the wrong spot, and it sliced through the wall of the uterus and severed the uterine artery. The blood loss would be catastrophic, and very fast."

"Like cutting a throat?" Jack asked.

"Something like that," Anna said.

Oscar said, "So no similarities to Janine Campbell's case."

"The outcome was the same, of course. But in Mrs. Campbell's case no major blood vessels were damaged, which is why she had such a long and painful death. She bled, yes, but it was the infection that killed her. This second case is different. Mrs. Liljeström suffered very little beyond the initial pain of dilating the cervix to introduce the instrument. It was, relatively speaking, a merciful death. Or at least, fairly quick."

"She arrived at Bellevue in a cab," Oscar reminded her. "Still alive, but just barely."

"That is odd. And another thing—" She paused, and forged ahead. "Dr. Lambert notes that she was fully clothed when she died, and she was very tightly laced."

"You're wondering why she wasn't undressed for the operation," Jack said. "And if she did undress, who got her dressed afterward and tightened her stays."

"Yes," Anna said. "She couldn't have done that on her own. I'm not sure how any of this could have happened."

"That's our job," said Oscar. "Figuring out the how and why of it."

• • •

LATER, ALONE IN their room, Anna was thoughtful. She said, "The most unusual thing about Mrs. Liljeström is her wealth. Women with money can get excellent care when they want an abortion without looking very far at all. But whoever she went to had very poor skills."

Jack thought, *Or very good ones.* He said, "There are odder deaths every day in this city, and a good number of them go unsolved."

She raised a brow, wanting the story but not sure if she could ask for it.

"A few years ago on a January morning we found a man of about seventy dressed in the uniform of a Confederate officer sitting upright on a bench in Union Square Park."

He could see her trying to imagine it. "Did he freeze to death?"

Jack shook his head. "Strangled. We never did identify him, though notices were put in papers all over the south. Never had a single viable suspect."

"But this shouldn't be one of those cases. When rich women like Mrs. Liljeström need this particular kind of help, they talk to other women like themselves. I imagine she didn't want to take the chance of being recognized in Buffalo, and so she came here prepared to pay for anonymity and excellent care. Mrs. Campbell didn't have the same kind of resources."

"You don't know what kind of resources she had," Jack pointed out.

Anna said, "Campbell didn't mention money at all, in his testimony."

"Do you think he would have admitted it, if she emptied out their savings?"

"Women generally can't just go to a bank and withdraw funds that are there in a husband's name," Anna said.

He shrugged, as if he didn't care to pursue the point.

Anna paused in her slow march back and forth across the room. Then she came to sit on the edge of the bed.

"You're still thinking that there's a connection between the two cases," she said. "But I don't see it. Hundreds of women die from complications of a badly done abortion every year."

"Poor women," Jack said. "Or very young. Have you ever read a newspaper article about a married woman with money who died as the result of an illegal operation?"

"You're saying that these two cases have something in common that distinguishes them from other failed abortions." That suggestion seemed to intrigue her. "I don't discredit it out of hand," she said. "Can you explain what it is you're seeing that I don't?"

Jack thought for a while. "Not clearly."

She said, "Is your hypothesis that the same person operated on both women?"

"I think it's possible. They look a lot alike, the two women. Janine Campbell and Abigail Liljeström were both in their midtwenties, slender, with a great deal of dark hair and brown eyes. About the same height. I know that there are hundreds of women in the city who fit that description, but think for a moment about this. Both of them already had children and homes. They both had husbands with very good jobs, and access to money. They both had reason to fear childbirth. They were both desperate."

Anna drew in a long breath and let it out slowly. "You are making a large logical leap about Mrs. Liljeström."

"It's a working hypothesis," Jack said. "Tomorrow I'm going to talk to her husband—he's coming in from Buffalo. She had a sister I want to talk to as well."

"I wonder why her sister didn't come with her to the appointment in the first place," Anna said.

"Because the sister lives here already," Jack said. "And that's another question not answered. Why did she come to New York and stay in a hotel when she could have stayed with her sister?"

"Because she didn't want her sister to know," Anna said. "Do you really think the sister will be willing to talk to you about this?"

Jack shrugged a shoulder. "I'll do my best to convince her. Unless you'd like to come along?"

At that she laughed, clearly pleased and embarrassed both. "I wouldn't know where to start."

"I think you would."

"Yes, well," she said. "Tomorrow I have surgery in the morning and at midday I have an appointment with Father McKinnawae on Lafayette Place, at his mission. Now I've surprised you."

"Maybe I was just hoping you'd let it go."

She pulled back to examine his expression. "Really? You really think we should just let Vittorio Russo go?"

He flopped back to lie on the bed, his feet still on the floor. "I guess I don't want to see you drawn into the situation. It won't be pleasant."

"I'm already drawn in. And if I only did pleasant things—"

"You wouldn't be you. So when did you make the appointment?"

"I sent a request in the morning mail and got a reply in the afternoon. I did plan to tell you about it, but then Oscar came and it slipped my mind."

Jack said, "I'd go with you if I could."

"I'm not going alone," Anna said. "I'm taking Elise with me. She might not be a nun anymore, but she still knows how to talk to priests, I should hope."

He made a sound in his throat he hoped she would take as mild disagreement.

She yawned and reclined against him, her head burrowing into the plane of his shoulder. Then she said, "If you think of the two dead women as the product of one diseased mind, how do you account for the difference in the way they were treated? Mrs. Campbell's death was very hard, and Mrs. Liljeström's was quick and relatively painless."

A hundred answers went through Jack's mind in a rush, but they all came down to the same thing. "The question is, was he more satisfied with his first attempt, or his second?"

Anna jerked in surprise, and for a long time Jack rubbed her back until he felt her give up the images he had put in her mind. He thought she was falling asleep and was thinking about how to rouse her to get under the covers when she spoke again.

"Why do you assume it was a man?"

33

As it turned out, Elise liked the idea of going to see Father Mc-
Kinnawae even less than Jack did. When Anna asked her to join her
for the interview, color rose in her cheeks, almost as if she had been
slapped.

"You have no reason to tell him your own history, you realize.
We're going there to ask about Vittorio Russo."

Elise looked doubtful. "But he's a priest," she said. "He'll know."

"Why would he? Do they send out a notice to all priests in the city
when someone leaves a convent?"

"Of course not."

"Then what are you afraid of? That he'll read your mind?"

"Priests have been known to do just that."

"Nonsense," Anna said. "You ascribe far too much power to the
man."

"Or maybe you ascribe too little."

That made Anna smile. "He can't drag you back to the convent by
the hair."

Elise shook her head. "He has a reputation," she said finally. "For
speaking his mind."

"And so do I," Anna said. "Now, shall we go?"

• • •

FATHER MCKINNAWAE HAD raised funds to build the asylum for
homeless boys that spanned a full block on Lafayette. It spoke to his
determination and drive, things that Anna did not underestimate. He
was a man who cared about the fate of the children he took in, and on
that basis she hoped he would be willing to discuss the Russo case.

The building was larger than the New Amsterdam, utilitarian in
design and materials, and while Anna imagined that every bed was

already filled, there was a deserted air about it. She wondered if most of the boys were out on the streets selling papers and blacking shoes, or if they had someplace else to be.

Elise said very little. She walked with her chin to her chest and her arms folded against her abdomen.

"If he realizes that you were once a nun, it will be because of your posture and the way you stare at the ground," Anna said. "Look at people directly when they talk to you. I know it's not easy after so many years of hiding away, but it's a crucial skill to learn."

"I've been trying," Elise said dryly. "It's a hard habit to break."

Anna felt a flush of embarrassment. "I apologize," she said. "For patronizing you."

Elise stopped, surprised. "You have nothing to apologize for. I owe you everything."

"No, you don't," she said firmly. "I am simply lending a hand to a promising student. All the work is yours. And while I'm lecturing you on your habits, I should at least be doing as much for myself."

One side of the wide mouth curled up in what Anna took for reluctant agreement.

"Let's face down the lion together," she said, and opened the door for Elise to pass through first.

• • •

"I AM DR. Anna Savard, and this is Nurse Elise Mercier. We have an appointment with Father McKinnawae."

The young man who sat at the reception desk sorting through papers glanced up at them. Anna felt herself judged, but whatever conclusions were reached, he hid them away well.

"Father McKinnawae's office is down the hall." He spoke English with an accent that could have been German or Danish, a young man of maybe twenty years. Not a priest or a monk, by his clothes. He gestured with his head to point them in the right direction. "It's clearly marked."

Before they had turned away he spoke to Elise. "Do I recognize your face?"

"I don't know," Elise said. "Do you?"

"I'm good with faces."

"But I'm not. I'm sorry, I don't remember you."

But he continued to study her, his curiosity overriding common good manners.

He said, "I'm Elmo Tschirner. From Holland."

A little color came into Elise's cheeks. "I'm sorry, I don't recognize your face or your name."

"Are you Irish? You have the coloring, that red hair."

"I'm not," Elise said. "Pardon me, we need to be going."

"Was it something I said?" he called after them, and Anna saw a spark of surprise and pleasure in the younger woman's face.

•　•　•

THE HALLS ECHOED with the sounds of boys' voices reciting lessons. Multiplication tables, primarily. From farther away there was the faint echo of hammers and saws. There was still the bite of fresh lumber in the air, and just below that, lye soap.

"It feels very familiar," Elise said. "Like every other orphan asylum and mission I've seen. It's good that they get lessons, don't you think?"

Anna did agree. Homeless children needed food and shelter and someone who cared about their welfare and their futures. Father McKinnawae certainly took those needs to heart, and, she told herself, that was reason enough to respect the man, sight unseen. Even given Elise's clear concerns.

The first door they came across had *Father John McKinnawae* stenciled in plain black on wood painted a dull green. It stood half open, but Anna knocked anyway, pushing the door open as she did.

The man standing at the window turned to them, iron-gray eyebrows jumping high on a shiny pink forehead. "Is it that time already?" He looked at a clock hanging over the door. "So it is. Come in. Come in. Did you find your way without difficulty?"

"Mr. Tschirner was helpful," Anna said.

"Yes, a fine lad, excellent manners. I was lucky to find him. Now, which one of you is Dr. Savard?"

It took a moment for them to satisfy the need for polite introductions, and then Anna and Elise sat down across a desk as broad as a boat. It was covered with papers and binders and books, but everything seemed to be carefully ordered.

"Now, how can I help you?"

Anna took in a deep breath and told the story of the Russo children, starting with the church basement in Hoboken. She had decided to say nothing of Staten Island in the hope that he would volunteer the information. As she talked she watched his face, broad and unremarkable and unreadable.

"You've gone to a lot of trouble for these children," he said when she had finished.

"We've done what we can. We'd like to do more."

"Why? Why these four children? Why not some other children?"

Anna hesitated. "I don't have a good answer for that, except that Rosa made an impression on me."

"You pitied her."

Anna wondered if this was a provocation. "I felt compassion for all the children, but her situation I found particularly difficult. May I ask why this is relevant?"

He made a tent of his hands, the fingers touching his chin. "The children in my care are vulnerable." His gaze pivoted to Elise.

"Miss Mercier," he said. "What's your interest in the fate of these children?"

At first Anna thought that Elise would simply not answer, but then she cleared her throat. "I was there when the two boys went missing. I'd like to help in any way I can."

"You feel responsible?"

She nodded. "Yes, I do."

"Father McKinnawae," Anna said. "We would like to talk to you about the youngest of the children, Vittorio Russo. We believe that he was taken to the Foundling on the twenty-sixth of March, and that you found him there and took him away with you the next day."

He blinked at her with what she thought was meant to be seen as mild surprise. "Why ever would you think that?"

"We went to the Foundling and looked at the records. Sister Mary Irene remembered the boy because of his unusual coloring. She was very helpful."

"More helpful than I can be. I'm afraid I have no information for you." His expression was stony, even hostile.

"You may not remember that you answered a letter of mine some weeks ago and suggested I come see you at Mount Loretto on Staten

Island. My husband and I did in fact go to Staten Island on the twenty-sixth of May, but you had been called away because of some emergency."

He had a polite but empty way of looking at her, as if he were humoring her need to tell a story.

"Brother Jerome gave us a tour, and then we went for a walk on the beach. That's when we happened to see Vittorio with his adoptive family. He was introduced as Timothy Mullen. We didn't intrude or ask questions, but I am certain that the boy called Timothy is in fact Vittorio."

The empty expression gave way to irritation. "Did this child you think is Vittorio Russo seem to be suffering in some way? Underfed? Abused? Uncared for?"

"No," Anna said. "He looked very content, and he is clearly much loved. Did you place him with the family, Father McKinnawae?"

"I know nothing about a child called Vittorio Russo," said the priest. "Let me clarify something for you, Dr. Savard. Adoptions are private and anonymous. They are not discussed. With anyone, for any reason. Once a child has been adopted into a family, there is no turning back. It would be terrible for the child and the adoptive parents both. I'm sure you would agree that a child in the situation you've described has been through enough, and shouldn't be wretched from a stable and loving family."

"So you are saying that Timothy Mullen is not in fact Vittorio Russo."

A line appeared between his brows, as if she were a dull student giving him a headache. "As I have said, I cannot help you."

"Let me understand," Anna said. "If a child were separated from his parents in an emergency—a fire, for example—and they came to you in the hope you might know something of their missing son, a child you had taken in, you would lie to them."

"That isn't the situation at hand."

"But if the child already has a family—"

"Does this boy you're asking about have parents?"

Anna pulled up. "They are both deceased. But he does have sisters, who love him and miss him."

"Dr. Savard," the priest said with great solemnity. "I will try again to make you understand. Where we can, we find good, stable Catholic families to adopt orphaned children, and then we step back and allow those families their privacy. I can't talk to you about any case, even in hypothetical terms. Do we understand each other now?"

"I understand that I have to tell two little girls who have lost everything that their brother is lost to them too, because the Church won't allow them to be reunited."

The smooth pink mouth puckered. "You are used to getting your way, Dr. Savard. But this time you will not."

"The girls are Catholic," Anna said. "As a priest, would you care to explain your position to them?"

He smiled at her. "Certainly. You may bring them to see me anytime. Now tell me, who has legal custody of these two Catholic children? Are they being raised in the Church?"

Anna gave him the same insincere smile as she got to her feet. "That is not a topic open to discussion. With anyone, for any reason. I want you to know that I may decide to talk to the Mullen family without your permission."

There had been some condescension in his manner, and now that disappeared entirely.

"Do not test me, Dr. Savard."

"But you are having such a grand time testing me, Father McKinnawae. And turnabout is fair play, even for Catholics."

◆ ◆ ◆

ELISE SAID, "I feared as much. I'm so sorry."

"I'm not finished yet."

They turned from Great Jones Street onto Fourth Avenue, walking briskly. Elise wondered if it would be best to leave the subject until Dr. Savard had time to gather her thoughts, but then decided it was best not to hesitate.

"He will do what he can to stop you," she said.

"And what would that be? Will he try to have me arrested, do you think?" She produced a sour smile.

"Would you really approach the family?"

Dr. Savard stopped and looked at her. "I might. Do you have objections?"

"Concerns." Elise didn't look away.

"Yes, there is no shortage of concerns." Her posture relaxed, quite suddenly. "Don't worry that I'm going to go marching off to Staten Island to confront the Mullen family. I have no interest in hurting them. We'll talk about it at home, when the girls are asleep, and decide how to proceed. Does that put your worries to rest?"

Elise said, "I don't know."

"Fair enough," said Dr. Savard. "Neither do I."

They walked back to the New Amsterdam in silence.

•　•　•

DETECTIVES LIKED TO think of themselves as foolproof, able to tell an honest man from one who played at being honest. In Jack's view of things this was true much of the time, but only because the first lesson learned on the job was not to trust anybody about anything. Something like Anna's work, where she had to assume that all patients lied, whether they meant to or not.

Harry Liljeström wasn't lying about anything. His wife's death had torn him in two; at the morgue he stood looking at her remains with tears streaming down his face. Jack stood back to leave the man his privacy, then took him to the Gilsey House, where he had arrangements to make and a bill to settle.

"I have questions," Jack said. "But if you'd like to wait until tomorrow—"

Liljeström was ashen, almost as if he were about to faint. "I have to get back home. Ask your questions now."

They sat in a quiet corner of the hotel's main lobby. Liljeström cleared his throat, wiped his face with a sodden handkerchief, straightened his shoulders, and looked Jack in the eye.

Jack decided that the direct approach would be best. He said, "There was a postmortem. Your wife died of blood loss following an operation." He waited, watching Liljeström's expression. He was a man like a thousand others in the city, someone Jack might have walked past every day and never noticed. But there was a dignity about him, and when he spoke his tone was even and unapologetic.

"We have two children," he said. "Healthy, beautiful children. A boy and a girl. But the first confinement was hard, and the second even worse. Our doctor said that she was unlikely to survive a third pregnancy."

"So you are aware of the operation she had."

The man had very pale blue eyes, almost colorless. "Yes. She missed twice, you see, and we decided together that it was the right thing to go to a doctor who could bring her courses on. I wanted to come with her but she refused. It wasn't the first time, and she thought she had nothing to fear."

Jack said, "She had the procedure done previously? By the same doctor?"

"She had it done once before, but that doctor died, and she decided she didn't want to approach anyone else near home. We've heard of women being blackmailed, you see."

Jack sat back. "Well, no, I haven't run into that before. Does it happen often?"

"I don't know," said Liljeström. "I only know of one case, a lady who goes to our church. Her daughter was in trouble and so they went to a doctor who could fix the problem. Afterward his nurse threatened the lady that she'd tell everybody about her daughter's shame if she didn't give her money."

"How do you know this?" Jack asked.

"Because the lady is a close friend of my wife's. Was a close friend."

His eyes filled with tears. Jack concentrated for a moment on his notebook, and then in an even tone he said, "Do you know the doctor's name, the one your wife came to see? Anything about him?"

"I only know that she was confident about his qualifications, and that his office is here in the city in a safe neighborhood."

"To be clear, we believe that what happened to your wife might have been done with malice aforethought. Any information you have could be helpful in bringing the responsible party to account," Jack said.

Color flooded the man's face, rising from his neck like mercury in a thermometer. "You mean to say this wasn't a simple error by the surgeon?"

"We have reason to believe that it may well have been premeditated. It's still under investigation. And so perhaps you'll understand why any information at all is important."

"I would tell you if I knew. All I can say with certainty is that he charged two hundred fifty dollars, and was supposed to provide nursing care for up to three days, or until she was ready to come home." He let out a harsh laugh, then pressed his handkerchief to his eyes. "He put her in a cab and sent her to a hospital. I know that I'd kill him with my own two hands, if he were standing here with me, and if it meant going to the gallows."

"Would your sister-in-law know more about your wife's arrangements?"

Liljeström's head came up quickly. "No. She had no idea that Abigail was here. She wouldn't have approved."

"So it wasn't Mrs. Liljeström's sister who gave her the name of the doctor. Did she have other close friends in the city?"

"No. I really don't know how she found him. Believe me, if I knew who was responsible, I wouldn't keep it to myself. Are we almost done? I have arrangements to make. I want to take her home. The children and her parents—" He closed his eyes briefly, and then let out a long sigh.

"Just one more question," Jack said. "They gave you her things at the morgue, and you've been through her room here. Is anything missing? Jewelry, anything of value?"

"She didn't bring jewelry with her when we traveled," Liljeström said. "It's still at home in the safe. Her wedding ring was on the bedside table in her room."

He stood abruptly. "You have my address if you have more questions."

Jack shook Liljeström's hand. "I'm very sorry for your loss. Would you like to be notified when we find the responsible party?"

"I want to know when he's dead," said Harry Liljeström. "I want to know that he's burning in hell."

◆ ◆ ◆

ANNA SOMETIMES WOKE suddenly in the middle of the night, her heart hammering, sure that something crucial had been forgotten and left undone. Most usually Jack went right on sleeping. She wondered if it should irritate her that he was so impervious to her sleeplessness, and decided that it did not. It would be unfair, and beyond that, these short episodes provided her with the rare opportunity to study his face without embarrassing either of them. He teased her about her inability to accept compliments, but he disliked being studied and would go to lengths to distract her when she did it. Extreme lengths, on occasion.

In the dimmest light she saw that his eyes were moving behind closed lids. Scanning for trouble, even in his dreams.

Almost a week had passed and they had made no progress with Mrs. Liljeström's case. There was still no indication of where she had gone the morning she died, or how she had found the person who operated on her. Apparently a case like this one became more difficult to solve with every passing day.

Oscar and Jack were still convinced that there was a connection between Janine Campbell and Abigail Liljeström, something they had missed. Anna wished—as she did every day—that Sophie were here to talk through this with her. Sophie had always been the better diagnostician, able to jump with dexterity from fact to fact, weaving them together until she had spun an answer.

Now Jack turned on his side and gave her his back, broad and high and hard as a wall. As if he had heard her thinking and was irritated with her inability to see something so obvious. She moved so her face almost touched the back of his head, better to draw in his smell, soap and shaving cream and something peppery, the very essence of Jack Mezzanotte himself. She drifted back to sleep, just exactly in that position.

With the first light she woke again. Jack was talking, but not to her. He sometimes had long conversations in his sleep, always in Italian. Another thing on her list as yet not even begun. Italian lessons. At least, Italian lessons that she could put to use in company. Everything Jack taught her was very much focused on the personal. It made her blush to think of it, and then she was irritated with herself for blushing. A trained physician familiar with every aspect of human anatomy and physiology, and he could make her blush. He delighted in making her blush.

She would learn Italian, if for no other reason than to scold him when he was being outrageous. Somehow she would make room in her day, one more difficult but not impossible task on a long list, with Vittorio Russo and Father McKinnawae at the top. For the sake of the little girls, but also for her own sake she needed to make a plan, come to some kind of resolution.

The problem was that she didn't really know what she wanted, what was best for Vittorio or Rosa and Lia, the Mullens, and everyone else. The subject was never very far from her mind. Just a few days ago Jack had made an observation that had struck her to her core, though he didn't seem to realize it.

For Rosa, he had said, losing a brother was like losing a part of herself. She had failed him in her own mind, if nobody else's, and would never forgive herself.

It wasn't often that Anna allowed herself to think about her own brother. Even after so much time it was almost too painful to bear. One day soon she would need to talk about Paul, pull out the few memories she had, and explain it all to Jack. The last person she had told about him was Rosa, standing in the basement of a Hoboken church with her youngest brother held protectively to her heart.

34

AT THE DINNER table on Saturday evening the little girls were more excited than usual. A long summer afternoon out of doors, running between Roses and Weeds, had not slowed them down at all. They fidgeted and giggled and whispered, waiting impatiently for Jack to come to the table. He came in late, almost twenty-four hours since he had been called out on a robbery.

He went around the table kissing cheeks, something he had done one evening not realizing he was initiating a routine he would never be allowed to forsake. He ended with Anna and slid into his place with a sigh.

Margaret said, "Go on, girls, or you'll burst with the news."

Lia jumped in place. *"Il palazzo delle erbacce è finito!"*

"No," Rosa corrected her sister. "We shouldn't call it Weeds anymore because there are no more weeds, not one."

"Too late," Jack said. "Once a name sticks, it's stuck for good. Ask Anna about that, she'll tell you."

Rosa wrinkled her whole face, trying to decide whether to argue. Then she set the subject aside.

"It is finished," she repeated. "Your sisters put up the last curtains and Georgio and—" She hesitated.

"Mario." Chiara supplied her with the name she was missing. Anna was continually surprised that Rosa remembered as much as she did, given all the Mezzanotte cousins who had been in and out during the renovation. She herself didn't remember exactly where Mario and Georgio fit into the family tree.

Rosa was saying, "And Mario finished with the gaslights and now it's ready."

Anna turned to Jack. "Really? It's ready?"

One eyebrow peaked. "I'm as surprised as you are."

Chiara said, "Just in time for the picnic."

Now Jack's look of surprise was more genuine. "That's tomorrow?"

Anna said, "Jack, we've been talking about it all week." And saw that he was grinning.

"We're all going," added Margaret.

"Unless you have to go chase robbers again," Rosa said to Jack.

"Or Auntie Anna needs to sew somebody back together," Lia added. Her small face took on a troubled look, as if she imagined that possibility for herself.

Anna tried not to smile as the girls related the plans for the next day in a manner that was worthy of a stage production. Every Italian in the whole United States, as Lia understood it, would be coming to their own park, just down the street, to eat and sing and dance and listen to music by the Seventh Regiment Band. Under the direction, Chiara added with considerable pride, of Uncle Cappa.

Margaret sat up straighter at this and directed an incredulous look directly at Jack. "Carlo Cappa is your uncle?"

"Not exactly," Jack said. "His daughter Susanna is married to my brother Matteo. He's my—I don't know. What do you call your sister-in-law's father?"

"Uncle," said Lia, in a decisive tone.

"You call everybody aunt or uncle," said Rosa.

Lia looked both furious and terribly affronted.

Anna said, "I'm happy to be called Aunt. Or Uncle, if you prefer, Lia."

The girls gaped, and then all of them, Elise included, burst into laughter.

Jack held up a hand as if he were directing traffic, and the laughter cut off. "I can't allow that," he said in his most serious tone. "No Uncle Anna here, unless I can be Aunt Jack."

Aunt Quinlan was smiling, but her eyes were damp. "Yes," she said. "That's the house rule. Aunts and uncles and grandmas and grandpas, all around. For anyone who needs one, at any time."

•   •   •

AFTER DINNER JACK wanted to go for a walk, Anna suspected because he had something to talk about that he didn't want others to hear. They started out in the direction of Washington Square, passing a group of young men coming out of New York University in high spirits, charwomen on their way home, and Mr. Pettigrew, a neighbor. He stopped right in front of them, all but demanding an introduction that was, strictly speaking, overdue. They should have gone to see all the neighbors as a newly married couple, but as they had done everything unconventionally, the visits had been put off.

Jack was attentive and friendly to Maynard Pettigrew, but his smile was a little strained. When they had finally extracted themselves and crossed the street to enter the park, Jack took her hand and pulled her arm through his so they were walking as close as they could without tripping over each other's feet.

He said, "Tell me about your day."

"It wasn't very good."

"Tell me anyway."

She thought for a long moment and told him about the fourteen-year-old girl with syphilis, a mouth full of suppurating ulcers, and ascites.

"Ascites is a condition where a lot of fluid builds up in the abdomen so that it looks bloated. It can be very uncomfortable."

"And what causes that?"

"Nothing very good. Possibly cancer, more likely liver failure, as she spends most of her time at the Grand Duke's Theater and lives off nothing but stale beer. Why is it the police keep closing that place down only to have it open again a few days later?"

With his free hand Jack rubbed his thumb against his fingers in the universal signal for hard cash.

Anna, expecting nothing less, shook her head. "I aspirated a half gallon of exudate to give her some relief, but she'll probably be back again before long. If she stops drinking immediately her liver could recover. I sent inquiries to some of the missions, see if anyone has room for her. If she comes back, of course."

"You're right," Jack said. "You didn't have a very good day."

"And I only gave you the highlights. But then neither did you, by the face you're making. No progress with the Liljeström case?"

"Just the opposite," he said. "Another case a lot like it."

They came to the bench where they had once sat together, when they had barely known each other. She tugged, and he sat down.

There was a lovely evening breeze, and from not very far off the sound of children romping with a very excited dog. From an open window came something that Anna thought was supposed to be music, an oboe being played, very badly but with real enthusiasm.

"I'm listening," she said.

"A woman called Eula Schmitt was found dead in her hotel room this morning."

"Not the Gilsey House again."

"The Windsor. A lot of valuable jewelry and a wardrobe full of expensive clothes. Better off than Mrs. Liljeström."

"What did the coroner have to say?"

"At first he thought it was"—he paused to take a notebook out of his jacket pocket—"an ectopic pregnancy, but they did a postmortem at Bellevue this afternoon."

"Abortion, then."

He inclined his head. "Maybe two days ago. She died of the same thing as Janine Campbell, peritonitis. Did I get that word right?"

Anna nodded.

He said, "But all we have on her is a name, and that may not even be real. No identification, not even a monogram on a handkerchief or a label on her luggage. A few dollars in her purse, no train or steamer tickets, nothing. I asked the doctor who did the autopsy—McNamara is his name—if there was any sign of previous pregnancies, and he said yes, ample evidence. The hotel staff doesn't know anything about her except that she paid for her room a week in advance, four days ago. She hasn't stayed there before, that anybody remembers."

Anna closed her eyes to think for a moment. It was getting harder to dismiss the idea that the cases were related. "What does your captain think?"

"He gave us a couple days to look into it. Oscar is already going through the newspaper ads; he's got a couple of the new patrol officers working with him."

"The newspaper advertisements? There must be hundreds of them."

"Try to stop him when he gets an idea in his head. Anyway, the man never sleeps."

Anna said, "I can't imagine why somebody would be doing this. There's no logic to it."

"No logic that you see, or I see. But whoever it is, he's settling in now for the longer haul."

Longer haul. The phrase struck her as particularly brutal, the idea that someone had set himself a lifelong task that involved condemning women to terribly painful deaths.

Jack was saying, "It's the worst kind of situation. He's dedicated. He doesn't rush."

He was still assuming the guilty party was a man, which was likely, after all. Women killed with poison; men made a science of inflicting pain.

"Do you know other cases like this one?"

He glanced at her. "It's not something the police are proud of, but there are at least a couple others, and not just here. There's an unsolved case in Texas with five dead over two years, and a couple in England; one of those has been going on for five years at least. Men who get a taste for a certain very specific kind of crime. The ones who can control themselves and stick to a plan are almost impossible to catch. Unless they get sloppy, most of them will live to a ripe old age and die in their beds. The scientists working on fingerprints seem to think they can come up with a way to identify and keep track of suspects, but nobody knows when that will be."

She rubbed her cheek against his shoulder. "So you'll be working tomorrow."

He read her thoughts, as he did so often, and leaned over to kiss the corner of her mouth. "Just in the morning. Couldn't miss the June picnic. Even if you didn't mind, Oscar would. So where do we sleep tonight, Mrs. Mezzanotte?"

"I don't mind," Anna said. "But we do have a lot to move, clothes and all the rest."

"Then not tonight." He kissed the other corner of her mouth, nibbling softly until she laughed and pushed him away.

"Also, there's the small matter of food. We need to talk about a housekeeper, Jack. I don't have the time for cooking or any of the rest of it."

He sat back. "I promised your aunt that we'd have supper with them, every evening."

There was nothing to do about that but laugh. "And she made me promise her that we'd eat breakfast with them."

"She's determined," Jack said.

Anna hummed. "I could think of a few other words that might serve better. And still, we will need someone for the laundry and cleaning and all the rest of it. Really, this is something we should have thought of to start with."

"Anna," Jack said, slipping his hand to the nape of her neck, threading his fingers into the twist of her hair and tugging, so that gooseflesh ran down her spine. "It won't take much effort to find a solution, and think what we're getting in return. A place of our own. Family close by, but real privacy, the kind we haven't had yet, not even on Staten Island, with maids coming and going and walls too thin for your—enthusiasm."

"Why, you—"

He caught her hands to protect himself, pulled her closer to put his arms around her shoulders and hold her still. Laughing like a boy very satisfied with a prank.

An older couple walked by, the lady making her disapproval known by clucking her tongue. A spasm of irritation passed over Jack's face and she felt him tense, and so Anna did the logical thing, damn the disapproval on a beautiful summer evening. She kissed him, and, getting up, she pulled him onto his feet.

"Let's go try out the privacy. See if it lives up to your expectations and my enthusiasms."

Jack said, "Did you notice the size of the bathtub?"

35

ELISE HAD A free day, though she had protested she needed no such indulgence. The matron had insisted, and so that morning she woke to the sound of church bells, thinking of mass. She should get up now, and dress, and go with Mr. and Mrs. Lee and the Russo girls. She had left the convent, but not the Church.

She rolled onto her stomach and buried her face in one of the fat pillows that she had so quickly come to appreciate.

They wouldn't badger her if she stayed behind. They wouldn't need to badger her, because she would be doing enough of that for all of them. With a groan she rolled out of bed and set about getting ready.

One thing at a time, she told herself. One change at a time. They would walk to church, the little girls skipping ahead with spring hats pinned firmly in place. She liked walking, and being out in the city when the weather was so fine. She liked Mr. and Mrs. Lee. What she dreaded was the sight of the confessionals in a row along one wall. She hadn't left the Church, but neither had she been to confession since she got on the train for the city, and that in itself was something to atone for.

Bless me, Father, for I have sinned . . . I miss nothing at all about the convent; I miss none of the sisters who taught me and cared for me; I love this world, and the place I have in it, the work I do and the things I'm learning, and I go all day without praying or even thinking of it.

She heard Rosa and Lia burst out of their room. Margaret called after them, a litany of manners to be remembered. They called back, agreeing cheerfully to anything and everything in the need to be moving. Elise followed them, smiling to herself.

. . .

ANNA WENT IN on Sunday morning to check on a patient who, as it turned out, had died in the night. It was not unexpected, but sad nonetheless. She spoke to the husband, an old man who shuddered with palsy and grief while she wrote out the death certificate, asking questions with the help of one of the nurses who spoke Italian. He answered in a wavering voice: Anna Maria Vega had been born on the first day of March in the year 1810 in Ragusa, Sicily, to Emilio and Anna Theresa Vega. To this Anna added the fact that she died in New York on a mild summer night of an abdominal aortic aneurysm, one that had been plain to diagnose, and inoperable.

Before Anna left the ward, another nurse stopped her and she wrote three more death certificates and then walked down to the clerk's office, where she would sign them in his presence so that he could file them with the coroner.

The office door stood open, but there was no sign of the clerk. Anna sat down to wait. If she went back to the wards she would be drawn into one case or another and might not get away in time for the picnic. She was actually looking forward to finally meeting the Mezzanottes she had been hearing about. It would be easier in this setting than any other; the picnic and all the rest of it would come to an end, and she could escape. It was the word that came to mind. She wondered if Jack realized how unsettled she was by the prospect of so many new relatives, all at once. She wondered too if he had engineered the previous evening, if he realized that her muscles would still be twitching, over-stimulated from a single hour in the bath. It was hard to worry about much at all when her mind kept wandering back to him, wrapped around her, hot water and soap and sliding skin.

She stood up to go to the window and noticed a newspaper on the desk, folded open to the advertisements. Thinking of Oscar Maroney, she picked it up and began to scan the small print, column after column of breathless announcements for cocoa, short pants, pianos, beer, seaside vacations, miracle cures, straw hats, Makassar oil, crocodile handbags, vaporizing inhalers, musicales, calligraphic pens, Brussels lace, cigars, felt tooth polishers, and hair renewers. When she came to the listing of physicians in private practice she sat down and glanced through the announcements: addresses, office hours, areas of expertise, educations. Interspersed with the legitimate offerings were the questionable ones:

MARRIED AND SINGLE LADIES in need of medical consultation of a private and personal nature can turn with confidence to Dr. Crane, who has had the finest medical education available. Twenty years in practice. Simple removal of all obstructions to nature's rhythms. Modern hygienic methods, safe, and discreet. Box 29, Broadway Post Office. All inquiries answered by mail within a day.

RESPECTABLE LADIES requiring specialized medical care and treatment should be aware that Dr. Weiss, a specialist in the very particular needs of the weaker sex, renowned for his kind, professional, and efficient methods, is seeing patients at his offices in the Hughes Building.

LADIES IN DISTRESS and without other recourse, married or maiden, may apply to Dr. Sanders, a physician and professor of women's indispositions with many years' experience. Inquiries to the Park Avenue Post Office, Box 4. By return mail you will receive a description of services offered. Specific details of your case will make a detailed response, including costs, possible.

She counted thirty ads of the same type, and estimated twice as many for pills and teas guaranteed to restore a lady's health and circulation, a euphemism that always set Anna's teeth on edge. As if a woman's menstrual cycle were an ailment that required a male's better understanding to bring under control. If she took the time to go through the dozens of daily newspapers she would find hundreds of ads that targeted the most desperate, and none of them could provide the help they claimed to offer. The reputable doctors and midwives who performed abortions didn't advertise at all and were by necessity extremely cautious in accepting patients.

She read on, skimming the more personal and for the most part, undecipherable ads: *A.Y.: all is prepared. Tomorrow at eight at the agreed place. W.G.G.* Were A.Y. and W.G.G. eloping, or committing adultery, or planning a robbery? It struck her as quite understandable that people might be caught up in the mystery and intrigue of what could be taken as very short stories, ripe for development. Mrs. Lee and Aunt Quinlan sometimes talked about them as if the parties were old acquaintances.

Anna wondered what Jack and Oscar thought they might gain by going through newspaper advertisements, and if they intended to investigate every one of the practitioners who made outlandish and irresponsible claims under false names. As she folded the paper to put it back on the desk, another ad caught her eye. While she was studying it the clerk came in.

Anna nodded impatiently at the long-winded excuse for his absence and held up the paper. "Is this yours, Mr. Andrews?"

He was tall and slender to the point of emaciation, his skin livid with inflamed eruptions that a luckier person would have outgrown years since. Anna imagined very well that he never looked at his reflection if he could help it. Now sweat broke out on his brow because she had looked at him. She turned her attention back to the paper.

"You're not in any trouble," she said in a kinder tone. "I came in with some death certificates, and noticed the paper. I was just wondering if I might take this page of advertisements, or if that would interrupt your reading?"

He raised both hands, palms out, as if he were surrendering to a greater military power.

"Please," he said. "Help yourself."

•　•　•

JACK AND OSCAR knocked on Archer Campbell's door at ten in the morning, and kept knocking until they heard him cursing as he marched through the house. He yanked the door open to glare at them, his eyes bloodshot and red-rimmed.

His sleeves were pushed up to the elbows, his hands and forearms scalded red and dripping with water and soapsuds. His trousers were wet from the knee to the ankle, and his shoes were scuffed and caked with dirt.

"What do you want?"

"A few questions," Oscar said. His tone was not so sharp as Jack would have anticipated.

"I've got a few of my own," said Campbell. "But I doubt you'll have any answers. Fuckin useless buggers, every one of youse."

They followed him into the house, through the small parlor and dining room to a kitchen that had been emptied of furniture, and the windows and rear door stood wide open. The room smelled of lye soap and carbolic. They stepped around a bucket and a scrub brush and followed him into the yard, where a washtub full of clothes waited.

"Get on with it," Campbell said. "Or were you expecting cake and coffee first?"

Oscar said, "How much money did your wife take with her when she left with the boys that Wednesday morning?"

Campbell's head jerked up. "What?"

"How much money—"

"Never mind. Why would you care?"

"We're trying to track down the doctor who treated her," Jack said. "Money is relevant."

"She never lacked a thing," Campbell said hotly. "Her or the boys."

Oscar glanced at Jack, but they kept their silence.

Campbell put back his head and looked up into the sky. After a long moment he said, "She took it all. One thousand two hundred twenty-two dollars, every penny I've saved since I started to work on the day I turned eleven."

"You kept it in the house."

"Show me a man who put his trust in a bank, and I'll show you a fool. It was well hidden, that you can believe, but not well enough. It never occurred to me she'd have the guts to rob her own husband, but then as it turns out, I didn't know her at all, did I?"

"Have you given up the search for your boys?"

Campbell's expression hardened. "With what money? Train fares and private detectives and all the rest cost plenty."

He glanced over his shoulder as if he were worried about being overheard.

"She planned it all out. Took the money so she could pay the doctor, the one who fixed her and did such a grand job of it. I think she already knew how things stood, that she was dying, so she paid some-body to take all four boys in. She stole my savings and used it to hide my boys from me, tied my hands so I couldn't go looking for them proper. Miserable bitch. I'll never get the stink of her out of my house."

•   •   •

ANNA LEFT THE New Amsterdam and hailed a cab, headed all the way uptown on Bloomingdale Road to a little farm that had been one of her favorite places as a child. It was a trip she and Sophie and Aunt Quinlan each made once a month, but Anna had last visited in March, the week before she went to Hoboken. Amelie would not make accusa-tions, but Anna was regretful, nonetheless.

When the cabdriver balked about going so far, she promised him an extra dollar on top of his normal fare if he would wait for her. He stopped in front of the garden gate, heavy with twining flower vines studded with blossoms as big as saucers, bright blue in the sunlight.

The farm belonged to Amelie, her cousin—her half cousin, really, who was just sixty-five but had given up her midwifery practice. These days she never left home; she hadn't come to Sophie's wedding, and wouldn't have come to Anna's, if there had been one. Amelie had withdrawn from the world, it was that simple, and more than that: she kept her reasons to herself.

At the garden gate Anna stopped a minute to look and take comfort in the fact that nothing changed here. A small barn in good repair, a pasture where sheep and a donkey and a very old horse grazed, and the small cottage surrounded by a garden where chickens scuffled and scoured the earth. The herbs that grew along the walkway—mint, comfrey, sage, thyme, tansy, pennyroyal, blue cohosh, mugwort, ver-bena, rue—rioted on the very edge of anarchy, which was true of the whole garden. *Abundance* was the word that came to mind.

"Beauregard," she said, surprised to see Amelie's old dog sleeping in his usual spot. She always went away thinking he'd be gone before she returned, but here he was. His eyes were milky with cataracts but his tail thumped at the sound of her voice. She crouched down to rub the crown of his head, and he flopped over onto his back to offer his belly instead.

"Doesn't matter how old he gets," said a familiar voice from the far side of the garden. "He demands his toll. Anna Savard, look at you."

Anna got up and wound her way through the garden beds—cabbage, squash, carrots, cucumbers, parsnips, beans, peas, turnips—until she reached Amelie, who got up from her weeding and held out both arms.

"Beauregard ain't the only one whose toll has to be paid. Come here and give me my due."

Her arms were thin but she hugged Anna with all her strength. Then she stepped back and caught up her hands to squeeze them. Her hazel eyes were damp with tears, but if Anna were to point this out, she would deny it.

"Don't you look more like Birdie every day, bless her sweet soul. Come on now, these weeds ain't going nowhere. They'll wait on me but I'll bet you're in a hurry."

At that moment Anna would have gladly forgotten everything and everyone else just to spend the afternoon working in the garden with Amelie. It was Amelie who had delivered her, far away from this tidy farm, on the very edge of the endless forest. Anna promised herself that before the summer was out she would come for a whole day, and bring Jack with her. Jack should hear Amelie's stories from Amelie herself.

"Sophie and Cap were here right before they sailed," Amelie was saying over her shoulder. "I hope you won't be mad that they told me your news. And don't start apologizing, I know how busy you are."

"I should apologize," Anna said.

"But don't. Come in the kitchen, I've got cake."

Anna followed the winding path to the back of the house, lined with bushes in flower and alive with bees and hummingbirds. As a little girl she had always thought of this house as she did of the cottages in fairy tales, full of secret cabinets and hidden stairs and most of all, stories. It was an odd structure, out of kilter at every corner, an old lady plagued by arthritis but cheerful, nonetheless. Front and kitchen doors and every window stood open to the breeze because as old-fashioned as the house and Amelie herself might seem, she was keen on new inventions and had screens installed everywhere, bought from a man in Chicago and shipped at great expense. And worth every penny, she said when people asked; she would have paid more for fresh air without the flies and mosquitoes that plagued man and beast on a farm.

While Amelie went about her business, Anna took the chance to study her cousin: the river of hair, iron and silver and black, in a long braid down her back, her clothes flowing and old-fashioned, worn soft and faded. In comparison her complexion was far younger than her years, supple and smooth, still unlined. She was the daughter and granddaughter of slaves and slave holders, of Mohawk and Seminole, and all those bloodlines had come together to a color that had entranced Anna as a very young child. It still reminded her of burning sugar, caramel on the verge of something even deeper. She remembered, vaguely, tasting the skin of Amelie's arm, and coming away with simple salt on the tongue where she had expected sugar.

Amelie disappeared into the pantry, raising her voice to be heard above the noise she was making, shifting through baskets and bins.

"Tell me about your Jack."

"First tell me your news."

Amelie always had news of her sister, who lived in Boston and had raised a family of ten children who had, in turn, produced eighteen children of their own, and of her brother Henry who was still working as an engineer on the railroads though he was almost seventy.

"Can't slow him down. Takes after Da that way."

Her head appeared around the corner of the pantry. "Stop stalling now and tell me."

So Anna put together the story of Jack Mezzanotte while Amelie gathered what she needed, mashed boiled ginger root, sorted through dried peppermint leaves, and put both to steep.

"Mezzanotte, you say. Do his people keep bees, in Jersey somewhere?"

"Yes," Anna said. "I should have realized you'd recognize the name."

"I do indeed. All right, I approve."

That made Anna laugh. "Because his parents keep bees?"

"Because you do nothing by halves," Amelie said. "And because it's clear to me that he did indeed sneak up on you, which means you let your guard down, and that tells me everything. Hand me that tin, would you?"

She put things on the table: a teapot with a mismatched lid, thick cups on chipped saucers, a jug of milk and a bowl of brown sugar lumps. Then she levered the lid off the cake tin so that the smells of browned butter and cardamom could slip out, like a genie released from a bottle.

Amelie said, "Do you have a case for me?"

"No," Anna said. "Not today. But I have cases I wanted to tell you about, to get your opinion on." She went to the sink to wash her hands, then dried them on the towel Amelie handed her.

Amelie leaned back in her chair. "Start at the beginning," she said. "And don't leave anything out."

◆　◆　◆

WHEN ANNA HAD finished recounting all she knew about Janine Campbell, Abigail Liljeström, and Eula Schmitt, Amelie went about cutting cake. Anna let the silence stretch out, patient with Amelie because patience and patience alone would bring rewards.

"I read about the Campbell inquest in the paper," Amelie said finally. "Tell me, why didn't Sophie send the woman to me?"

"You know why," Anna said. "We said we wouldn't send anybody until Comstock stops this campaign of his. Mrs. Campbell's husband actually works for Comstock. It was too dangerous, and in the end your safety was more important to us."

"You thought Comstock would follow her here," her cousin said.

"You know he does that kind of thing."

She rocked her head from side to side, considering. "So you think that the Campbell woman went to somebody who advertised himself as a reputable doctor, but wasn't. You know that happens every day."

"It's more than that," Anna said. "Whoever did Janine Campbell's procedure was angry. It was more like a stabbing than anything else. I didn't see the postmortem, but I did read the Liljeström autopsy report, and the similarities are hard to deny. Then this third case, and more of the same."

"What does your Jack think?"

Anna took a few moments to gather her thoughts. "He thinks there's a man, maybe a doctor, maybe not, who has a compulsion to do this to women. Somebody very intelligent, who plans ahead."

"Does Jack know about me?"

Anna had been waiting for this question, and she shook her head. "Not yet."

"He'll disapprove."

"I think he'll withhold judgment until he meets you, and then he'll be satisfied."

That got her a smile. "Now, that you'll have to explain."

"He's unusual, Amelie. Because of his family background, he doesn't jump to condemnation and he tries to see below the surface. It's the reason we were drawn to each other, I think."

"A perfect man."

"Hardly," Anna said, laughing. "And I still haven't met all his family, so there may be trouble waiting there. In fact, I know there is." This was not the time to talk about Bambina, though she would have liked to.

"If you want my opinion, Jack may well be right in his suspicions about the way these three women died," Amelie said.

Anna had been expecting something less definitive. "Can you explain to me how you come to that conclusion?"

"It just feels off to me, based on forty years of looking after women."

"Do you have any suggestions on where to start? Any names?"

Her cousin studied her teacup for a good while. "There was one doctor, thirty years ago or more. He wasn't young then, so he'll be long gone. But he was brutal with his patients, more bent on purifying their souls than saving their lives. I could imagine him letting a woman die. I think he probably did, and more than once. But that's a far cry from these cases of yours. Something like this takes a special kind of monster."

Anne retrieved the page of the newspaper she had brought with her from the city and, laying it in front of Amelie, pointed to the advertisement that had raised her suspicions.

To the refined, dignified but distraught lady departing Smithson's near the Jefferson Market yesterday morning: I believe I can provide the assistance you require. Write for particulars to Dr. dePaul, Station A, Union Square.

When Amelie finished reading and looked up, Anna asked her question.

"Isn't Smithson the druggist who takes messages for Sarah?"

"It is. Or it was. Sarah moved to Jersey to live with her son's family."

"She's unwell?"

"She's seventy-eight this past November."

Anna gave her an apologetic half smile. "I didn't realize. Did someone take over her practice?"

"I thought Nan did," Amelie said. "You remember Nan Gray."

"Vaguely. Is she one of yours?"

Over the years Amelie had trained or mentored a hundred mid-wives, and she tried to keep track of all of them.

"Not mine. She came up from Washington, maybe twenty years ago. But maybe she's not the one who stepped in for Sarah. You're thinking that this Dr. dePaul, whoever he is, watches for women coming out of Smithson's? That seems a very chancy way to set a trap. If that's what's going on."

Anna said, "But it's written in such vague terms, anyone might think themselves the target of his attention. If he only gets one response a month, that's probably more than he can deal with. I hope."

Amelie hummed to herself as she poured more tea. "Practicing medicine requires a cynical turn of mind, but this—" She shook her head. "Let me understand you correctly. You think there's a man who trolls for women in distress, offers them his services, and operates in a way that assures that they don't survive, and even that they die in terrible pain. That his purpose is what—to punish them? To make examples of them?"

"I don't know," Anna said. "But I have this sense that it would be a mistake to dismiss the possibility."

Amelie went quiet, her head turned away as if she were looking out into the garden, but in fact Anna knew she wasn't seeing anything at all. Her cousin had a way of climbing right inside a problem and sitting there until she found a way out. She had been trained by her own mother, Anna's aunt Hannah, a doctor of almost mythic fame on the New York frontier, and it seemed to Anna that Amelie understood the minds of doctors as well as she did the women they cared for.

She tapped the newspaper advertisement. "You know where to start."

"I was thinking the same thing, but it helped to talk it through with you. I'll send word if I make any progress. Now I have to go meet some fifty Mezzanottes, so please wish me luck."

"Luck is greatly overrated," said Amelie. "Your native good sense will serve you far better."

• • •

THE ANNUAL ITALIAN Benevolent Society picnic and band concert was a popular event, one that might even overflow the boundaries of Washington Square Park. Since early in the morning groups had been coming in on foot carrying baskets or pushing wheeled carts, by omnibus or streetcar, others driving their own rigs. There were families from as far away as Long Island and Jersey City, street urchins watching for unattended purses and free meals, and police and roundsmen who strolled at a leisurely pace, stopping to watch a game of horseshoes.

Elise sat with Chiara and Bambina on a bench on the corner opposite New York University, where the Mezzanotte family was busy getting ready. A familiar freight wagon stood at the curb, with *Mezzanotte Brothers, Greenwood, N.J.* painted on its side. Elise had first seen it waiting to cross an intersection not a block from where she sat now. Then it had been filled with flowers, but this time it carried benches and planks and barrels, boxes of linen and dishware, and baskets of food. The unloading was happening under the sharp eye of one of the Mezzanotte aunts, all in black, bent low by age. She ordered young men around with all the authority and finesse of Sister Xavier.

The three of them had been spared physical labor, assigned instead to supervision of the run-arounds, all the Mezzanotte children or the children of Mezzanotte cousins old enough to walk, but less than four. They tumbled and rolled around on the grass, and occasionally made a break for freedom, often for no other reason than the joy of being chased by Chiara or Elise. Bambina stayed where she was, knitting lace from fine white thread as quickly and evenly as a machine. Knitting didn't slow down her conversation, though. Together with Bambina they were giving Elise an education on all things Italian.

Bambina pointed out families: the barber Amadio, a widower with four married daughters who lived in the same building and competed for his favor by feeding him multiple times every day; Maria Bella, who was already twice a widow at age thirty; Signore Coniglio, who taught at the Italian school and talked all the time about becoming a priest, though he was more than forty; Joe Moretto, who had lost both legs fighting under Grant, but had managed to produce seven sons anyway. Elise paid attention but knew that most of the names and faces would blend together by the end of the day.

Just a little farther away, under trees in a pool of shade, the older ladies sat together gossiping and tending to the very youngest. Mrs. Quinlan and Margaret were there too, because the detective sergeant had made sure to find places for them next to his aunt Philomena. There seemed to be a law that dictated black clothing for Italian women over a certain age, but Mrs. Quinlan wore a simple day dress of sprigged cotton, white flowers against a turquoise background, and looked like an exotic bird among the crows.

The older men were playing a gentle game that reminded Elise of horseshoes, but with a ball. It looked interesting, but Italians were like everybody else, with strict ideas of where women belonged, and where they didn't. Her place was here looking after the little ones.

Beyond the very old and the very young, everyone had something to do. Every once in a while Elise got a glimpse of Rosa and Lia in the middle of a small group of girls who had been given rags and piles of dishes to wipe. They were completely absorbed in this work, chattering with the other kids as if they had all grown up together. Children survived, if they had half a chance. Children who could form attachments survived best.

"Look," said Chiara. "Cesare is going to fall off the ladder and break his head."

The band pavilion was crowded with people arranging chairs and music stands. Younger men stood on ladders, hanging red, white, and green bunting on a frame. One of them was reaching so far that it did seem as if the ladder would tip.

"Sicilian," Bambina said, frowning at her knitting. "Made of rubber. They bounce."

Her tone was not complimentary. Elise considered for a moment and then asked, "You don't like Sicilians?"

A pained expression crossed Bambina's face. "I've got nothing against them, as long as they stay away from me."

Elise decided that it would be better to ask Jack about this. Bambina seemed to want to change the subject, too, because she decided that Elise needed to be able to identify all the band instruments being taken out of cases. She pointed out a sousaphone, trumpets, bassoons, clarinets, and three kinds of drums, every bit of brass and copper polished so that it reflected in the sun.

At home in Vermont Elise had known only fiddles and penny-whistles and Mr. Esquibel's fipple flute, brought out at parties. Once she entered the convent she had heard no musical instruments beyond the organ. She knew that there were other kinds of instruments but had never given them much thought. Certainly she hadn't imagined anything like this, especially when the band began to tune their instruments. All the sounds wound together like a badly pieced quilt, wavering up and down and finally settling.

The bandleader was standing off to the side, all his attention taken up by an elegantly dressed older man. This, Chiara said in an almost reverent tone, was Mr. Moro, head of the Benevolent Society.

Then Anna appeared out of nowhere, sliding in neatly between Bambina and Chiara. She had changed out of the very plain suit she wore when she left for the hospital to a summery gown. There was a layer of pale sea green, another with a faint narrow stripe in the same color, and an overdress printed with twining vines and budding flowers. The bodice of the overdress was constructed of panels that flowed into a split skirt. The back was just as striking, pleats falling from a graceful curved yoke at the shoulders. The whole effect was simple and somehow misleading. You might not notice how pretty it was unless you took the time to look closely, and no doubt some wouldn't bother because it was completely out of fashion.

Most of the Mezzanotte women were dressed like country women everywhere, in comfortable sleeveless bodices worn over linen blouses, wide skirts and aprons. Only Bambina wore something that might have come out of an illustrated magazine, not flamboyant but very stylish, her skirts bunched at the sides to reveal a ruffled underskirt.

Elise couldn't stop herself from asking. "Dr. Savard—Anna. Is that the dress you wore when you got married?"

Chiara's whole posture changed, like a hunting dog coming across a promising scent. She was always wanting to know more about the quiet little wedding ceremony on Staten Island. Somehow she didn't believe it could have been as simple as both Anna and Jack claimed. Bambina was just as curious, Chiara knew that for a fact, but she wore a more studiously disinterested expression.

"No," Anna said. "Remind me later and I'll show you what dress I was wearing. It was nothing out of the ordinary, Chiara. We didn't set out that day with plans to marry."

Chiara's expression was resigned, but then she asked a question Elise would never have known how to put into an acceptable form.

"Why do you dress like you do? Don't you care about fashion?"

Anna didn't take offense easily, it seemed. She said, "Mostly it has to do with my work. Tight bodices and narrow skirts are the last thing you want in an operating room. You have to be able to move freely. When I'm not working I can't see the logic in being uncomfortable, either."

Bambina said, "Anna belongs to the Rational Dress Society. The one that is so radical about what women wear. They'd have us all in trousers if they ruled the world."

"And we'd be more comfortable," Anna said dryly. "But really the Rational Dress Society isn't so extreme as you think. You should come with me to a meeting, Bambina."

The look on Bambina's face was almost comical, but she was spared answering because the detective sergeant was walking toward them.

He had taken off his suit jacket and vest to reveal emerald-green suspenders over a white shirt, his sleeves folded up to reveal muscular forearms. Elise had little experience of men beyond her father and brothers and priests, but she could see why Jack Mezzanotte was considered handsome. It was more than his features; it had to do with the way he moved, the energy and purpose of him. Right now he was coming for Anna, and Elise wondered what that would be like, to have a man look at her with such obvious affection and pleasure.

He stopped right in front of Anna and, bending down, kissed her cheek.

This was nothing out of the ordinary for Italians, as Elise had observed. They hugged and kissed as a matter of course, men just as unself-consciously as women. Men kissed brothers and sons and nephews, clasping hands on both shoulders. Mothers and sisters, aunts and young children were kissed more gently, sometimes with an arm looped around the neck.

And still this kiss was different. Because she was sitting so close, Elise saw exactly how it fell, the touch of his mouth not to cheek or jaw or even to mouth, but high on Anna's neck, below her ear. It was simple and devastating, a gesture that spoke of possession and passion. She felt her own cheeks flushing with color, as Anna's did.

"Savard," Jack said with a smile. "Let's go." He stood back, pulling her up to walk with him. She went without protest and only the slightest hint of hesitation.

"Elise," Jack said. "Come and meet my family."

In her surprise she heard herself stutter. "I'm—I'm needed here."

"Go ahead," Chiara said. "We'll cope just fine."

• • •

BECAUSE THERE WAS no way to remember all the names and faces, Elise simply didn't try, and really, it didn't matter; the detective sergeant's family members were mostly interested in Anna, which was to be expected. What did surprise her was Anna's easy way of handling it all. She remained calm and friendly, concentrating completely on whoever was in front of her in the moment, answering questions with no trace of the impatience she would show if an orderly moved too slowly or a nurse was less than precise. Another surprise was that all of Jack's generation spoke English without any trace of accent, and none of them talked Italian among themselves, at least not when Anna and Elise were nearby. Out of courtesy or as a matter of course, that was hard to tell.

The one exception was Carmela, the wife of Jack's second oldest brother. Her English seemed hard-won, something she used because it was expected of her, a chore to be gotten out of the way.

Carmela had a baby on her hip, a little girl called Lolo who clung like a monkey. She had huge bright eyes and a shock of black hair, and she smiled toothlessly at everyone who stopped to admire her. Lolo first looked at Elise solemnly, her forehead creased. Then she leaned forward and launched herself as though she could fly. Elise caught her neatly, looking to her mother to see if she might be taking offense.

"She's never seen a redhead, I take it." And then, touching her own hair. "*Sono rossa.*"

"Yes," Carmela smiled. "She will pull your red hairs."

Elise tilted her head down for the baby's examination. "What's a little hair pulling between friends?"

• • •

JACK HAD WARNED Anna that the importance of food in Italian culture could not be underestimated, but Anna had managed somehow to do just that. The bowls and platters would have fed everyone in the park, but every now and then another rig would pull up and disgorge relatives who carried steaming pots and covered dishes.

All the adults had gathered around one long table, while children were seated at another, close enough to keep an eye on but not so close that they drowned out adult conversation. A few older nieces were stationed there to make sure high spirits didn't get in the way of eating. Babies had been put down for naps on blankets, with a couple of dogs on alert nearby.

"Jude's primarily a sheep farmer," Jack explained. "His dogs do double duty on days like this, keeping track of the kids and making sure they don't get too close to the fire pits."

A lamb and a young pig had been turning on spits since the early morning. The aroma would have caused poorly trained dogs to abandon their duties, but Jude's animals lay very still, only the twitching of noses giving away their interest. Anna had less control and was glad that the growling of her stomach could not be heard over the many voices. She passed her plate and watched as it was filled, determined not to make a fuss about the amount of food put down in front of her. She would try everything on her plate, take careful note of textures and tastes and ask questions. There would be a test later, she knew. Many tests to come, and she had no intention of failing even one of them.

So she ate, and talked, and ate. Between sips of red wine she ate a salad of tomatoes tossed with soft cheese and bread and olive oil, wild boar sausage and wide noodles cooked with artichokes and capers, white beans and marinated mushrooms, pork slathered with garlic and lemon and rosemary. They ate and talked, and ate, and talked. And ate. Small bites, long pauses to ask questions and answer more.

Jack said, "Look over there, do you see the boy sitting at the end of the table, next to Rosa?"

Anna did, and said so.

"You don't recognize him."

She didn't, and said that too. But then she looked more closely. Twelve years old, in her estimation, thin but properly nourished, his color high, the very picture of health.

"Hoboken. That's the boy who wanted to find work to save money for passage home."

"Santino Bacigalup, you're right. Looks like a different boy, doesn't he?"

Jack's mother leaned toward them. "Good food, sunshine, a safe place to sleep. He's a hard worker, that one. I wrote to his sister in Palermo for him, but we haven't had word back yet."

"It's been two months," Anna said. That day in Hoboken seemed even longer ago, and in some ways, not so long at all.

"No cause for worry," said her mother-in-law. "His sister probably had to take the letter to her priest so he could read it to her, and then she'll tell him what to say and he'll write back. It's the way things work."

"But if you don't hear back?"

"Then he stays with us," Jack's brother Leo said. "He's already like a brother to my boys, and he loves Carmela and Lolo. She follows him around with her eyes, wherever he goes."

"He's a fortunate boy," Anna said. "We still don't know what became of Rosa and Lia's brother Tonino. He could be anywhere, or nowhere. If he was sent west on one of the orphan trains we'll never know what happened to him. Jack," she said, as a thought occurred to her. "Have you told your mother about Vittorio?"

"I mentioned it."

"Do you have an opinion, Mrs. Mezzanotte?"

Her mother-in-law put down her fork with an unhappy little click. "You are uncomfortable calling me Mama?"

Anna felt a dozen eyes turning in her direction.

"Ma," Jack began, but Anna put a hand on his wrist.

"Let me answer. It has to do mostly with my own mother. I don't remember her very clearly. Just a sense of her face and her voice. But I hold on to those small things, and wouldn't want to lose them."

"It would feel disloyal to call someone else Mama."

"No, not exactly. It's like—" She tried to make her voice sound matter-of-fact. "It feels like admitting that she's gone, and if I do that, she will be. It makes no logical sense, I know."

"It makes every kind of sense," said Mrs. Mezzanotte. "My mother died thirty-five years ago, and every once in a while I still dream about her scolding me because I don't come visit often enough."

"Yes," Anna said. "Like that."

"I understand. But you can't call me Mrs. Mezzanotte, it's too formal. You will call me Rachel, to start."

"Rachel," Anna said. "Thank you. I was wondering if you have an opinion about Vittorio Russo."

"My opinion is, there is no easy solution to this problem. There are too many hearts to be broken and I'm not brave enough to recommend one over another."

•   •   •

"It's a good thing I don't wear a corset," Anna said under her breath a little later. "I'd be ready to pop just about now. I may do that anyway."

Jack rubbed her back. "Savard. You have to learn to say no."

She laughed at him outright. "That's the way to endear myself to your mother and aunts. I'll eventually say no, when necessary. But not today. A short walk would help."

Everybody close enough to hear this stopped eating and looked at her, concern writ clear on their faces. Anna wondered if the idea of a walk violated some unwritten law, but Jack climbed over the bench to stand, and held out a hand.

"I think a walk is a good idea."

The look he gave her said very clearly that he knew she was up to something, but that he had no intention of disappointing her or even asking questions that might be taken as less than supportive.

"*Ma chiaramente*," Anna heard Jack's father say softly. "*Sono sposini novelli.*"

When they were out of hearing, Anna looked at him expectantly.

"Newlyweds," Jack explained. "*Sposini novelli*, that's us. We can get away with a lot on that basis."

She found herself smiling. "You don't get away with much otherwise?"

"You did just spend time with my mother," Jack said. "What do you think?"

At the corner of Fifth Avenue and Washington Square Park they worked their way through a crowd of children watching a puppet show, past an organ grinder whose monkey held out a greasy old hat for coins, newsboys hawking their papers, and pushcarts displaying cans of tobacco, cigars, hard candy, handkerchiefs, small Italian and American flags, peanuts, inexpensive jewelry, and religious medals. When they were free of the worst of the crowds Jack took her hand and they walked north.

"Oscar is always uneasy on this part of Fifth Avenue," Jack said. "He got caught up in the draft riots around here, just a couple days after he joined the force. Do you remember anything about them?"

"I remember the noise, but that's all. We were a household of women and children and we locked ourselves in, you see. Uncle Quinlan was dead, Mr. Lee was in the army somewhere in the south, and Margaret had come to stay with her boys. We weren't allowed out of the house during the riots, not even in the garden. Auntie wouldn't even let us see the newspapers once it was all over."

Jack looked almost relieved to hear this.

"So, Savard," he said. "Where exactly are we going?"

"Patience. Just a couple more minutes."

She would have raised the subject of the suspicious ad in the paper, but Anna had begun to doubt her suspicions and could no longer see a connection between the newspaper clippings and the deaths of three women. She would only embarrass herself, like a child who came into the hospital with a scratch and demanded a plaster cast.

Then again, Jack wouldn't laugh at her, even if there was nothing of merit in what she wanted to show him. He would listen, and they would talk about it. Then, she was almost certain, he would put her suspicions to rest and they would go back to listen to the band and watch the children playing as the day slipped away to evening.

As they turned west on Ninth Street Jack said, "We talked to Archer Campbell this morning, Oscar and me."

Anna was glad of the distraction. "About the money question?"

"Mostly. She had over a thousand dollars with her when she left with the boys that morning, but there was no trace of it on her person or in the house when it was searched after her death. Campbell thinks she paid somebody to take the boys in."

Anna considered. "So you were correct, she had enough money to pay a reputable doctor. But how would she find someone to take four young boys she could trust? A thousand dollars is a great deal of money, but at the very minimum that would have to last fifteen years."

Jack said, "We don't know where the money went. The house was empty for a good while once the ambulance took her away, and then there's the ambulance ride itself. I've arrested more than one orderly with pockets full of cash and jewelry they took off their charges. Chances are slim we'll be able to pin anything down, but it's worth looking at."

Jefferson Market came into view, all the stalls empty and shuttered on a Sunday afternoon. In a few hours the aisles would be full of street arabs and the outdoor poor, who would fight to keep a spot under that leaky tin roof. A few were already standing nearby in the shadow of the Sixth Avenue elevated train tracks. At the sight of Jack they slipped away around corners.

Behind the market the redbrick bulk of the Jefferson Court House loomed, proud and fanciful both in an island of small houses and tenements, home mostly to skilled workers and small business owners.

"Now I'm even more curious," Jack said, teasing. "You can't mean to take me on a tour of the courthouse? The police station?"

Anna said, "No, look there."

She nodded toward the storefronts that faced the market. A tailor, a cobbler, a greengrocer, a steam laundry. Between the grocer and the cobbler one shop stood out, a little wider than the others, the awning newer, the show windows spotless. The weathered sign was the only thing that gave away the shop's age, old-fashioned script spelling out the name: *Geo. Smithson, Apothecary.*

There were dozens of druggist's shops like it in the city, but Smithson was one of the oldest and most respected. The shop was closed on a Sunday, of course. But she had counted on that.

Jack was watching her, curious but patient.

She took the newspaper cuttings from her reticule and handed him the one on the top.

"I came across that first advertisement by accident early today. I was a little later than I should have been to the picnic because I stopped to buy different newspapers to look through." She fanned out the other clippings for him to see.

"Of the five I bought, four had identical ads."

Jack studied the clippings briefly, then glanced across the street to the druggist.

"What you probably don't know," she went on, "is that neighborhood midwives almost always have a druggist they work with, where they consult and get whatever preparations they need. Druggists keep a list of midwives who work in the area, and take messages for them. Some druggists work with only one or two midwives they trust. My cousin Amelie—I haven't told you about her yet—worked with Smithson for more than thirty years before she gave up her practice. Another midwife took her place, her name was Sarah Conroy, but she's retired now too. I'm not sure who's working with Smithson now, but this—" She touched the newspaper advertisement. "This makes me wonder."

Jack was listening closely, keeping his thoughts to himself. Anna knew her voice had gone hoarse, but she would tell all of it. She had to tell all of it.

"Amelie was an excellent midwife. People still talk about her. Sarah was just as good. And both of them would help women who came to them in trouble."

She saw that he understood. For a long moment he considered the newspaper clipping, and then he took in a deep breath and let it go.

Jack asked, "Do you know who took Sarah's place? Who's working with Smithson now?"

"No, not with any certainty. But I could find out."

"Wait," Jack said. "Let me see if I follow your thinking. A woman comes to talk to this Smithson when she's looking for a midwife, either to deliver her when the time comes, or to regulate her courses—" He was using the euphemistic wording from the newspaper.

"To end the pregnancy," Anna clarified. "Yes."

"And it's always worked that way?"

"It's not the only way a woman finds a midwife, but it is one way, yes."

"And you're thinking that this Dr. dePaul is trying to get the attention of women who come to Smithson's for this purpose."

"When you say it like that, it sounds very far-fetched—"

"No," Jack said. "I see it that way too. But there are a couple of other possible explanations. First, it could be nothing more than a way to stand out from the other advertisements. This dePaul might be running the more usual kind of ad as well, he's just casting a wider net—"

Anna managed a shaky smile. "Of course. I should have thought of that."

"—hold on, I wasn't finished." He cradled the back of her neck in one hand and drew her in to him, put his mouth to her ear. "Sometimes a thing feels just a little bit off. Not quite right. That's probably what you picked up, that feeling, because I've got a whiff of it too. So let's talk to Oscar about this, put our heads together."

A train rattled by overhead, and they stayed just as they were until it was gone. Then Anna pulled back to look at him directly. "You're not just humoring me?"

"Hell, no," Jack said. He gave her a grim smile. "I've got my faults, but I'm not stupid. You'd never stand for that, and I wouldn't want you to."

• • •

THEY WERE CUTTING across the park and almost back to the family when Jack saw that Anna's aunt Quinlan was walking toward home, braced on either side by Elise and Margaret.

Just that quickly Anna's expression shifted to what Jack had come to think of as her professional mask. Without discussion they both broke into a jog. By the time they caught up, Anna had managed to produce an easier smile. She said, "You are more sensible than I am, Auntie. I should take a nap too."

Her aunt wasn't so easily taken in. "Don't fuss, I'm perfectly fine. Jack, take that girl back to the picnic, would you? She's going to try my patience."

The uncharacteristic peevish tone seemed not to alarm Anna, but to put her worries to rest. "You'll send word if you need me?"

"Of course I will. Give me a kiss and go on. You too, Elise. And don't argue with me, I won't have it. A short walk will do me good. I'll send Margaret back just as soon as I'm settled."

Jack said, "Don't I have any say in this?"

Four faces turned to him. He sighed in mock disappointment, leaned down, and, moving gently, lifted Anna's beloved aunt into the cradle of his arms.

"Don't fuss," he said to her. "I won't have it." And he started down the street at a brisk pace.

For a moment he thought she was going to box his ears, but suddenly she gave a squawk of a laugh and relaxed.

"You do remind me sometimes of my Simon. I had a difficult time when I was expecting Blue, and so he carried me everywhere." She looped an arm around his neck and patted his cheek. "I am so glad to know you'll be looking after my Anna."

•   •   •

IT WASN'T MORE than a quarter hour before he got back to the park, but Rosa and Lia were lying in wait and jumped out at him. He took one look at their expressions and crouched down.

"Aunt Quinlan is just fine," he said. "Nothing to worry about."

"We're not worried," Rosa said. "We're confused."

"About?"

Lia leaned against his arm and pointed. "See that man over there?"

Jack recognized Ned from the way he held himself, a young man neatly if plainly dressed, his posture erect but his shoulders bent forward toward Anna while she talked, the very picture of manly solicitude.

"I do. His name is Baldy. Or Ned. What about him?"

All the brimming energy left them just that simply, because this information only confused them further. They wanted to know why he would have two names, and which was the right one? When it turned out that Jack had no satisfactory explanation for this strange state of affairs, they went ahead with their story, which had to do with Anna, Bambina, and Baldy-Ned. Jack winced but didn't interrupt to correct them because they were off at a gallop.

It seemed that Baldy-Ned had walked right up to Anna, had smiled at her and called her Dr. Anna, and asked was it true she had gone ahead and married the Dago detective sergeant contrary to common good sense? Which had gotten Anna to laugh the way ladies laughed when they were being teased and liked it. The confusing part was Bambina, who, it seemed to them, had taken an instant dislike to Baldy-Ned. She didn't like what he said, or the way he said it, or the idea that Baldy-Ned was going to teach Anna Italian—something that had come out, and wasn't that good news, that Anna was learning Italian?—and then Baldy-Ned had just smiled at Bambina and called her *cara*.

"She didn't like that at all, that he called her *cara*," Rosa said. "But it's a nice thing to call somebody."

Lia, hopping in place, wanted to know what it meant that Bambina turned all red and her jaw got tight. Most important, what did it mean when Anna said that he, Jack, had introduced her, Anna, to Baldy-Ned with perfect manners, and that Bambina might want to follow her brother's example?

It was all very confusing and sad because they thought Baldy-Ned was nice and they would like him to come around the house to talk Italian, to Anna and to them, too.

"So," Rosa said. "Can you fix it?"

• • •

BEFORE HE COULD even get to Anna, the band started up and Baldy-Ned disappeared. There would be no fixing of anything or even any talking over the music, which would give Jack some time to think. He was glad of it.

Rosa and Lia plopped themselves down on the blanket where Anna had settled, and Jack followed their example. He leaned against Anna and bumped her shoulder with his own. She smiled at him and both dimples came to the fore, a welcome sight that put his worries to rest. Whatever trouble Bambina had stirred up, it hadn't robbed Anna of her mood.

He wondered if he should talk to his mother about her youngest and most troublesome daughter and decided that it would only make things worse. Instead he leaned into Anna and threaded his fingers through hers. Despite the brass and drums, he was half-asleep himself and would have dropped off when the band took a break, if Oscar hadn't come to crouch beside them.

"I'm going to talk to that Graham, the young ambulance doctor who testified in the Campbell case. I'll fill you in tomorrow."

Anna leaned across Jack to smile at Oscar. "Working on a Sunday evening in June?"

"Anna, my dear," he said with a puff of breath that might have been sixty proof. "I love my work. Why don't you two come along, Jack," Oscar said. "She speaks doctor, after all. And she might find it interesting."

"I would," Anna agreed, nudging this time with her elbow. "Take me along, Mezzanotte. I'm interested."

• • •

ANNA WONDERED AT herself, that she should find this so compelling. She would be quiet and observant, she promised herself, and hoped it was a promise she could keep.

Neill Graham had a room in a boardinghouse not five minutes from Bellevue, a rambling, threadbare place typical of the living quarters interns and medical students could afford. The carpet was worn, but there wasn't a stain or stray dust mote to be seen anywhere.

The landlady introduced herself as the Widow Jennings and blinked at them while Oscar talked. Then she cleared her throat and straightened her shoulders.

"I've been letting rooms to young men studying to be doctors for twenty years now," she said, leading them into the parlor. "Since the day Mr. Jennings did us all a favor and dropped down dead. Terrible mean, he was. Awful mean. There I was with this big house and no money—he was a drinker, you see, was Mr. Jennings, drank himself into an early grave. Just not quite early enough. So I said to myself, Hitty, young people would bring some joy into this vale of tears, and I've had every room occupied ever since I started. Because I'm fair, you see. I don't overcharge and I cook good plain food, but plenty of it. My boarders don't go hungry, and I don't stick my nose where it don't belong, I can promise you that.

"Now you have to tell me why you're wanting to talk to young Neill Graham. I can't say my boys never get in trouble, but I'm surprised to hear it's Neill you're fixed on. Can't hardly remember a nicer boy, hardworking, polite. His grandfather lives way downtown, which is why he boards with me. A responsible young man. I always wanted a son, but instead I just had Mr. Jennings, and he gave me nothing but heartache and moneylenders at the door and crabs, more than once."

Anna bit back a laugh, because really, it wasn't at all funny. Unexpected, but not funny. It was only a very small comfort to see that Oscar had gone red in the face, too. Jack was better at hiding things.

He was saying, "Could we speak to him here in your parlor, Mrs. Jennings?"

"Yes, of course. Just set, make yourselves comfortable. I'll fetch him."

When the sound of her climbing the stairs faded away, Oscar drew in a hiccuppy laugh, shook his head, and took out a handkerchief to wipe his eyes. His shoulders were still shaking when Neill Graham came through the parlor door, one side of his face pillowcreased and his hair standing up.

"Keeping odd hours, Dr. Graham." Oscar's tone was vaguely accusatory.

Anna's impulse was to explain that interns learned to sleep whenever the opportunity presented itself, but she stopped. Oscar might be provoking the young man on purpose.

Neill Graham gave a soft laugh. "You could say that." With thumb and forefinger he rubbed his eyes for a moment and then opened them to focus on Anna.

"Dr. Savard. Is this about the Campbell case?"

"It is," Jack said. "We want to hear about that day again, in as much detail as you can summon."

Mrs. Jennings appeared in the doorway with a tray laden down with a teapot and cups.

"But first a cup of tea," Anna said. "That will wake you up. Thank you, Mrs. Jennings. You are very thoughtful."

• • •

THE CUP OF tea did its work. Graham talked for ten minutes, telling them when he got up that morning and when he reported for his shift on the Bellevue ambulance service.

"And your first call, when did that come?"

"I'd have to check my notes to be sure, but it was about a quarter past seven. An omnibus clipped a boy on the Bowery near Clinton. We got there about half past the hour, and I worked on the boy about ten minutes before we got him loaded into the ambulance."

In Anna's experience, interns were often not at their best in a critical situation like the one he was describing, but in his memory, at least, he had followed a sensible course of action. He talked about the boy's death in the ambulance in the same measured tone, with some regret but without guilt, which said to Anna that he was competent and realistic, in control of his emotions when he was working. He talked about two more calls, about eating the lunch that Mrs. Jennings packed, the cost included in his room and board.

"And what time did you get the call about Mrs. Campbell?"

"I can tell you we got word from the Jefferson Market precinct desk sergeant at just before one. It was a baker's boy who brought word to the station, but I only know that because I heard the neighbor lady say so on the stand."

He took a swallow of cold tea, put down the cup very carefully, and placed his hands flat on his knees.

"The Campbell house is maybe three blocks from Jefferson Market, so we got there quick. The door was standing open and there were neighbors milling around, the way they do when there's trouble. You must see that happen all the time." He looked at Oscar, who gave him a curt nod.

Oscar was not exactly severe or disapproving, but he didn't give Graham much indication of how he was doing. Jack rarely looked up from his note taking. Anna was curious about what it all meant, if the two men were exchanging information in some way she didn't recognize.

Graham was saying, "I went in with my bag, through the parlor and a hall into the kitchen. The neighbor, I'm forgetting her name—"

"Mrs. Stone," Oscar said.

"Mrs. Stone was standing in the bedroom doorway, wringing her hands. There was a pool of blood on the kitchen floor and a trail into the bedroom. I didn't ask her direct, but I assumed that Mrs. Stone had helped Mrs. Campbell get from the kitchen into bed. I asked her to stay in the kitchen and I went in and examined Mrs. Campbell. Do I need to go over her condition again?"

When Oscar said yes, he did need to go over every detail, Graham looked uncomfortable for the first time. His manner changed and his gaze shifted to Anna, as if he preferred to talk to a male physician about such things. It had to do with his training, something Anna could mention later.

When he paused Oscar said, "Tell me what you said and what she said, to the best of your memory."

"I said who I was, and I asked her to lie flat on her back so I could examine her. She just turned her head, wouldn't say anything. I asked a lot of questions about the pain and when it had started. I asked if she had had an operation, but she didn't say one word. The only sound she made was crying out when I palpated her abdomen.

"So I opened the door and called to the driver he should bring the stretcher, and he did, and we got her off the bed and onto it. She didn't say a word to me."

Oscar's head turned toward him, quite sharply.

"Did she say a word to somebody else?"

Graham looked flustered. "Mrs. Stone was talking to her, the way people do in that kind of situation. She said, 'Oh no, oh no, Janine,' and 'My poor girl,' and 'It was too much,' and other things like that. And she touched her, her face, and stroked her hair. I think Mrs. Campbell might have said a few words back, then, but I couldn't say for sure. We were trying to maneuver the stretcher through the little hall, and the floor was slippery with blood. The last I remember of Mrs. Stone was her standing in the door, her hands clutched to herself—" He demonstrated. "She was weeping, quiet but weeping a waterfall. Then in the ambulance Mrs. Campbell spoke to me direct for the first time. She said she wanted to be taken to the New Amsterdam. She grabbed onto my sleeve hard, and said it twice, Dr. Savard at the New Amsterdam. And that's what we did."

"She didn't talk to you otherwise?"

"I was surprised she managed that much, in her condition. She didn't say anything more."

"And where was Mrs. Campbell's purse in all of this?"

Graham blinked, confused. "Her purse?"

"Was her purse on the stretcher with her?"

"I don't—"

"Mrs. Campbell had more than a thousand dollars in her purse that has never been recovered. What became of that money, do you think?"

Neill Graham's mouth fell open. People often described such things, but Anna couldn't remember ever seeing someone's jaw drop. The color left his face, and his gaze jerked from Oscar to Jack and then to Anna. She did her best to keep her expression neutral.

"Are you asking—" he said, and stopped. "Are you saying—"

"I think I was clear. Mrs. Campbell had a thousand dollars with her that day, and that money disappeared."

Now Graham's color came back in a rush. "I took nothing. There wasn't anything to take. She didn't have any purse or satchel with her. I didn't see a single coin, and I certainly didn't take anything. Are you charging me with a crime?"

Jack stood up. "If you allow us to search your room, that will go some way to clearing you." He shook his head when Graham got to his feet. "I'll ask Mrs. Jennings to show me to your room, and she can stand by and watch. But you need to stay here."

"I'll come along with you," Oscar said. He looked at Anna, as somber as she had ever experienced him. "Will you sit here with Dr. Graham?"

"Yes," Anna said. "Gladly."

When they were the only two left in the parlor Neill Graham buried his face in his hands and rocked forward, a man in shock. When he looked at her again his eyes were red-rimmed.

"This will be the end of my career," he said hoarsely. "It doesn't matter that I'm innocent; if word gets out, I'm finished."

Anna thought of many things she could say. First and foremost was the simple truth: he was correct. But it was also true that Jack and Oscar didn't really suspect Neill Graham of anything. Anna understood that they were staging a drama in the hope that unsettling the young man would jog his memory and he would remember exactly what Mrs. Campbell said to Mrs. Stone.

Finally she poured more tea into his cup, a gesture that he might take for sympathy or understanding.

He said, "Dr. Savard—"

Jack and Oscar were back, followed by Mrs. Jennings, whose hands were fluttering like birds.

"Clean as a whistle," Jack said. He looked at Anna and tilted his head to the door. She glanced at Graham, who had once again lost control over his jaw. He got to his feet, his knee knocking the side table so that the cups and saucers clattered.

"You're not charging me with anything?"

Oscar took his hat off the coatrack and turned to smile, as if the entire conversation had never happened. "Nothing to charge you with, Dr. Graham. You did your best with poor Mrs. Campbell. Thank you for your time. Wait. One more thing."

He gave a thoughtful pause. "When you last saw Mrs. Stone standing in front of the house with her hands folded on her breast, what was she holding?"

Graham blinked and blinked again. "A purse," he said. "A black purse."

"And where did the purse come from?"

A silent shake of the head. "I swear I don't know."

"Fair enough. Thank you, Dr. Graham."

Anna said, "Stop by and see me at the New Amsterdam, if you are interested in observing my surgeries. I think we can arrange something."

She wondered if that would be enough to soothe the sting and if he would be brave enough to take her up on her offer. Many of his colleagues at Bellevue would disapprove.

• • •

IN THE CAB she said, "Really, was that necessary?"

The men looked at her silently.

"All right," Anna said. "Maybe it was. But I didn't like it."

"Neither did I, believe it or not," said Oscar.

Anna hummed under her breath. After a moment she asked, "Did you get anything useful out of that?"

"A purse," Jack said. "That's something no one mentioned before. We'll go talk to Mrs. Stone. Should we drop you off at home first?"

"I think she wants to come along," said Oscar. "Don't you, Anna?"

It was the first time he had called her by her familiar name. It was cheeky, but it was also a compliment.

"You are right. I'd like to see what comes of this purse business. Do I understand correctly that you don't really suspect anyone of taking the money? This is more a way of getting your foot in the door."

Oscar elbowed Jack, who elbowed him back. Jack said, "You don't have to prove to me that she's got a brain. I knew that the first time I saw her."

Anna leaned back to watch the sky out of the cab's small window. Still full light at seven. She should be tired after such a long day, but there was a humming in her, a sense of the unanticipated. She was in the company of two good men who saw things she did not, and valued the things she saw.

• • •

THE CAMPBELL HOUSE was on one of the small, crooked lanes that seemed designed to confuse strangers. A few small houses, a couple of ancient cottages that had probably been built when the whole area was pasture or farmland, one newer tenement. Archer Campbell's house was one of the newer houses but locked up tight, no sign of life despite Oscar's hammering at doors both front and rear.

Anna sat on the edge of the porch while the men consulted. She was a little relieved about this sudden halt to their plans, and wondered at herself that she had been so eager to come along. Now that she was here, even the thought of the man was a challenge to her professional demeanor.

The truth was, Campbell wasn't going to be any different today or tomorrow or ten years down the road than he had been on the stand, full of righteous indignation, convinced that he was the best of husbands and fathers. No doubt he would marry again, and probably soon. Certainly he'd have no trouble finding a wife; there were hundreds of women in the city who would give anything for a home of their own. This modest house would look like paradise to an unmarried daughter in a poor household. As it had once looked to Janine, no doubt.

She caught movement from the corner of her eye and saw a woman peeking out from behind the curtains across the way.

"Is Mrs. Stone in the house across the street?"

Jack turned. "She is."

"I ask because somebody is watching you from the parlor windows."

She got up to follow Jack, with Oscar trailing behind. A shawl would have been a good idea; her prettiest summer dress was not quite the thing for a call like this one. Maybe she should have gone home, after all. With that thought she realized that she was dreading this conversation. What she remembered of Mrs. Stone on the stand was her willingness to speak her mind and what seemed like real sorrow about Janine Campbell's death, and they had nothing new to offer her, no information that might relieve her mind.

Then the door opened to Jack's knock and a man stood there, rotund, his face as pink as a ham, a great shock of white hair and white eyebrows so long that they fell over his eyes like curtains. He had a sweet but vacant smile, a little confused but welcoming.

Veterans of the last war were so common on the city streets that their scars and missing limbs were almost invisible, but this man's injuries could not be overlooked. His left arm had been amputated near the shoulder and the left side of his head was distorted, with a round indentation over the ear that Anna estimated to be an inch deep at its center.

"Mr. Stone?" Oscar's tone was friendly, unremarkable, respectful, perfectly gauged.

The smile widened to show shiny pink gums with no teeth at all on the left.

"*Guten Abend,*" he said. "*Ich bin Heinrich Steinmauer. Wer seid Ihr?*"

Then Mrs. Stone was there, her hand on his shoulder to guide him back into the house. She murmured to the old man in German, and he nodded, smiling at her with great affection.

"Mrs. Stone," Jack said. "We have a few questions regarding Janine Campbell's death. May we impose on you for a short while?"

She glanced over her shoulder, unsettled, and then back at them.

"He's worst in the evenings," she said. "My husband, Henry. The evening isn't a good time for him."

"He was very polite to us," Anna said.

"But his mind is wandering. He forgets. He imagines he's back home in Munich, where he grew up. We changed our name to Stone years ago, but he forgets even that."

Oscar said, "Would you like us to come back tomorrow?"

Anna was surprised at Oscar's solicitous tone, something she hadn't heard from him before.

She said, "No, no. Please come in. If we sit quietly with him in the parlor while we talk he will probably be fine. But he'll speak German to you, please be aware."

Anna might have told her that she spoke German, but she didn't want to draw more attention to herself. Instead she said, "He was wounded in the war?"

"July of sixty-one, at Bull Run."

"My brother died at Bull Run," Anna heard herself say.

Both Jack and Oscar turned to look at her. Maybe it was the tone of her voice, or the fact that she had yet to tell Jack anything about Paul.

In the parlor Jack lowered his head to speak softly into her ear. "Is this too much, then?"

Anna answered Jack by taking a seat on a sofa that creaked with age. The cushions were ancient but carefully mended at the corners and backed with embroidered antimacassars.

While Oscar tried to make himself comfortable with a chair far too small for his bulk, Anna watched Mr. Stone, who sat in a rocker by the window with a small dog in his lap. He was talking to the dog in a way he might have talked to an old friend or a brother who simply didn't talk very much. She heard him mentioning a carriage going down the street with a single piebald horse, a neighbor who seemed to have forgotten his hat, children chasing fireflies in the new dark.

The dog seemed to understand it all, looking obediently where his attention was directed. His tail gave a thump whenever a name was mentioned, as if to comment.

Oscar was saying, "Now, I believe you said that you left to visit your sister on the day before Mrs. Campbell's death. Is that right?"

"Yes, that's right. In Albany."

"That's a long way to go for a one-day visit. You'd almost have to turn around and come back within a few hours. You were home on Thursday morning?"

A little color had begun to creep into her face, but she nodded.

"Did you go to the train station with Mrs. Campbell and her sons that Wednesday?"

"Yes," she said. Her voice was hoarse now, and she cleared her throat. "To help with the boys. Why do you ask?"

"Mrs. Stone," Oscar said. "Where are the boys you helped Mrs. Campbell hide away?"

The room was completely silent but for the ticking of the mantel clock. Anna, as surprised as Mrs. Stone seemed to be, watched the older woman's face flush and then drain of all color. Her fingers were working in her skirts, gathering the fabric and then smoothing it, again and again. Jack and Oscar waited patiently, nothing to read from their faces, no judgment or disapproval.

Mrs. Stone cleared her throat again. "What do you mean?"

"I would like to know where the Campbell boys are. Archer, Steven—"

Mr. Stone turned toward them.

"*Kommen die Buben heut' abend?*" There was real excitement and pleasure in his expression. "*Kommen die Buben endlich?*"

"*Nein,*" said his wife. "*Noch nicht.*"

Below shaggy eyebrows the blue eyes lowered in disappointment. "*Schade,*" he said. "*Montgomery, die Buben kommen immer noch nicht.*"

"My husband loves those boys," Mrs. Stone said, a little stiffly. "He asks for them every day, many times. I can't explain to him."

"What can't you explain?" Oscar asked.

"That they are gone away. That they won't be back. I tell him but he doesn't believe me."

"Because he expects to see them again," Anna suggested.

Oscar asked again, quite gently. "Mrs. Stone. What happened to the boys?"

She gave a sharp shake of the head and lowered her chin to her chest. When she looked up again she said, "Which one? Which one do you want to know about? Let's start with Steven. Nobody at the inquest asked where the older boys were when the baby was coming into the world. If they had asked me I would have said. I would have told God and man about those poor boys.

"Because they were right here with us, with me and Henry. Junior and Gregory were playing with a puzzle in the kitchen and I was tending to Steven. He had bloody stripes on his legs and bottom and his back too, and it wasn't the first time, wasn't going to be the last, either. Their father used the buckle end of his belt to beat them with. The scars will last those boys a lifetime. And poor Junior—"

She sat back, breathless, her mouth pressed hard.

"What about Junior?" Oscar asked.

"He didn't beat that boy near as bad as the other two. But he'd say, Junior, which one of your brothers should wear your stripes today? And made him choose. If he hesitated, both boys got the belt. To remind them who was master of the house, and that disobedience has consequences. Oh, he loved teaching that lesson. So let me ask you, Detective Sergeant, what would you have done in my place?" She looked at Oscar with something like defiance in her gaze.

"I can answer that," Anna said. "I would have helped Mrs. Campbell get away with her boys. Far away, where he'd never find her. Is that what you did?"

"Yes," Mrs. Stone said, her voice breaking. "But it was all for naught, now. All for naught. And I promised her I'd get them away safe."

"Away to where?" Anna asked.

From a notebook that sat on the table beside her, Mrs. Stone took a newspaper advertisement. She read it to them in a wavering voice but Anna had the sense that she could have recited it by heart:

Rhode Island. Comfortable cottage for sale. Nicely furnished, 8 rooms besides pantry &c. with chicken house, stable & small barn all in good order. One acre land. Fruit trees, vegetable garden, strawberry bed, pasture. Good pure water & excellent well. Sakonnet Harbor. $2,000. Inquiries J. Barnes, Main St. Little Compton.

There was a long moment's silence while Mrs. Stone tried to gather her composure. She said, "Janine wrote to Mr. Barnes and I mailed the letter. He wrote back to this address and after a few letters back and forth they came to an agreement. She bought the place sight unseen and sent the money express. I said to her, Janine, you're taking an awful chance, but she was desperate to get the boys away to a safe place.

"The plan was that we would all live in that house together. She gave her name as Jane Steinmauer, a widow woman coming with the boys and us, her parents-in-law. Henry has never got used to the name Stone anyway, and the boys are young enough to learn to answer to new ones. We'd be like any other family, keeping chickens and a garden. But poor Janine, she never got as far as Rhode Island."

She stopped to get her handkerchief from her sleeve and wipe the tears from her cheeks.

"I went ahead with the boys. Janine came with us to the train station by omnibus and then I took the boys by cab to the steamer office. The plan was, she was supposed to come later in the day. It made me terrible nervous. I was so worried about that cottage, maybe it would turn out to be a hovel or maybe it didn't exist at all, but in the end she was right. It was just the way it's described here."

She touched the newspaper cutting. "You should have seen the boys, they could hardly have been happier if you set them down in heaven itself. The harbor and the boats and the garden and the house with a nice big kitchen." She pressed her mouth hard, as if she were telling herself to be quiet, she had spoken enough. But the question came out just the same: "Can I ask, did Campbell go to the police saying he'd been robbed?"

When Oscar said that no complaint had been filed, she nodded.

"Janine said he wouldn't. That he couldn't tell the police about the money because he didn't come by it honest."

Jack said, "Mrs. Stone, I'm confused. Campbell told us that he was missing just over twelve hundred dollars cash. Where was the money coming from to buy the house? From you?"

That almost got him a smile. "All we have is Henry's pension, the bit I make mending and sewing, and this little house I was born in, termites and leaky roof and all."

"Do you know how she paid for the Rhode Island house?" Oscar asked.

In fits and starts the story came together. Mrs. Campbell had indeed had something over a thousand dollars in cash, most of which she had passed to Mrs. Stone when she left with the boys for the cost of travel and provisions, and getting settled in the new house.

It was true that was the only cash, but it wasn't the only money.

"That's why she stayed behind when I left with the boys. Or at least, that's what she said. Here, it's easier to show you."

Mrs. Stone took up a large sewing basket, set the lid aside, and began to unpack it. There was a tray of threads and a pincushion, shears, a roll of muslin, patches, a darning egg, knitting needles, a man's shirt neatly folded, a chemise. When it seemed to be empty she turned it over and thumped the bottom with the heel of one hand. Two solid blows and a false bottom went clattering to the floor, followed by a black pocketbook.

With trembling hands she took out a thick roll of oversized bills. This she handed to Oscar, and he slid a binding string down and off so he could spread the roll flat on his lap.

"Bearer bonds," he said. "Issued by the State of Massachusetts."

The bills were elaborately engraved and printed in three colors. Anna had to look twice before she could convince herself that she was seeing correctly.

"Five hundred dollars," she said. "For each?"

"Forty-six of them," Mrs. Stone said. "Of the original fifty. That Thursday morning I found her near dead, she gave me the purse with the bonds before the ambulance came. But I'm not keeping it for myself," she added, new color flooding her face. "The money is to raise the boys, for food and clothes and school fees and the like, and—"

"No one suspects you of plotting to steal the bonds," Jack said.

Anna wondered if that was strictly true. She could see the Campbell house through the front windows, still dark. If Archer Campbell suspected that Mrs. Stone had the bearer bonds, she didn't doubt he was looking for a way to get them back.

"Bearer bonds." Oscar rubbed both hands over his face.

Mrs. Stone said, "All I know is, Janine said he hadn't come by them honest."

"It's not important right now," Jack said. "But it's still unclear to me why she didn't just leave with you and the boys that Wednesday morning."

Anna said, "She had a doctor's appointment, didn't she?"

Mrs. Stone's head dropped. "That was it. I didn't figure it out until later, but she went to that doctor who charged so much to fix things." She rocked a little in place. "She was so worried about another baby, sick, really, in her head and heart both. She went to that doctor right after she saw me off with the boys. She had a ticket for the noon steamer, that's in the purse still. But it didn't work out the way she planned.

"She told me when I found her Thursday morning, she knew as soon as she left the doctor's office that something was wrong. She was in so much pain and bleeding so bad she couldn't get on a steamer. She could hardly get back here."

A fresh welling of tears cascaded down her cheeks. "I get so mad at her when I think about it. What's another baby when there's hands enough to do the work and money to put food on the table? But she couldn't bear the idea, and so she went and had the operation and she never lived to see the place she bought, or her boys so happy."

"When did you decide to go back to the city to look for her?" Jack asked.

"Wednesday evening. She wasn't on the steamer when she was supposed to be, or the one after that. The plan we made was to meet back here if something went wrong, and it did go wrong. If you can imagine it, Janine had to spend another night with that man, knowing she was sick unto death, thinking she'd be dead within a day and what was going to happen to the boys?

"So I did come back, and thank God. Just before the ambulance came she gave me the purse with the bearer bonds. She said, 'Mabel, think how much worse it would be if Archer had realized what I took from him. I wouldn't have anything to give you for the boys. Now you can raise them up right and they'll be safe.'

"Then the doctor came in and examined her in the bedroom. Not ten minutes later they put her in the ambulance and I never saw her again. It's a sin and a shame the way she died, but she went easier, knowing I would go back to the boys. That's all I want, to go back to the boys, me and Henry, but we can't get away. And I don't know how much longer Mrs. Barnes can look after them."

Jack got up and paced the length of the parlor. "You think Campbell suspects?"

"I know he suspects," she said, almost sharply. "Didn't he say as much, right to my face? He said, 'Mabel Stone, remember one thing. I'll have what's mine.' And now he sits there watching us, day and night. Like a spider in a web he watches us. I know he didn't answer when you pounded on the door, but he's there. You can see his cigar, it's like an evil red eye in the dark. I think he's waiting for us both to be out of the house so he can come in and search."

She rocked forward and crossed her arms across her chest, weeping silently but for short indrawn breaths. Anna leaned close and put a hand on the bowed back. The kind of touch that might provide a grieving mother some small comfort. Because Mrs. Stone had lost a daughter in Janine Campbell.

They talked for a half hour more, asking questions that Mrs. Stone tried to answer. She didn't know where or how Archer Campbell had gotten some twenty-five thousand dollars in bearer bonds; she didn't know where Janine Campbell had gone for the abortion or who had performed it. All she could say for sure was that she had paid the doctor three hundred dollars.

"She thought it was the only way to get it done quick and safe. And truth be told, I think she got some satisfaction out of the idea that it was Archer's money that paid the doctor. Three hundred dollars, and for that he butchered our girl and now those boys have got nobody. Nobody who knows them and loves them. If we go to them, Campbell will follow. For the bonds, if not the boys."

Jack said, "Mrs. Stone, does anybody else know about this, the whole story?"

She shook her head. "The only person who knows anything at all is a neighbor from down the street. Mrs. Oglethorp. She stayed with my Henry while I was gone. She thinks I went to my sister, too."

Anna asked, "How can you be sure Henry didn't tell Mrs. Oglethorp anything, given his state of mind?"

"I can be sure because Mary doesn't speak German, and Henry lost every word he ever knew of English on the battlefield at Bull Run."

Oscar stood up, his expression thoughtful as he walked toward the window where Mr. Stone sat rocking. He crouched down and smiled at both man and dog, held out a hand to be sniffed, and scratched behind Montgomery's ear.

"Henry," he said.

Mr. Stone looked at him expectantly, a smile on his face that could almost be called hopeful.

"A fine dog you've got here. His name is bigger than he is, though. Why'd you name him Montgomery?"

An uncertain look was all the response he got.

"Henry, where are the little boys from across the street?"

The smile faded. He turned in his seat to look at his wife, his brows raised.

"*Schon recht,*" she said to him. "*Macht nichts.*" To Jack she said, "The boys and Henry, what's to become of them when you take me away?"

Anna had never seen a human being so terribly frightened. Not even the sickest patient with nothing but death to look forward to, not parents with a desperately ill child. Mabel Stone wasn't frightened for herself but for the people who depended on her. Anna was about to tell Jack and Oscar that some other solution had to be found when Jack spoke up.

"We're not here to arrest you," Jack said. "You went with Mrs. Campbell and her sons because you were asked to, and you took the money she gave you to look after the boys. Between us I think we can find a way to get you and Henry back to those boys. Safely."

"With the bonds," Oscar added. "Campbell will have stolen them somewhere, that's something we'll look into down the road, but you don't have to worry about it. He'll never be punished but it'll eat him alive, the idea that she got the better of him."

Mrs. Stone looked between them, studying their faces until she seemed satisfied.

"You'd think I'd run out of tears." She folded her damp handkerchief and pressed it to her eyes. "If you mean it, then God bless you."

"We mean it," Jack said.

Anna said, "Can I ask one more question?"

"Anything," Mrs. Stone said.

"Do you happen to know if Mrs. Campbell ever traded at Smithson's, the druggist across from the Jefferson Market?"

At Mrs. Stone's blank expression Anna said, "Never mind, it was just an idea."

"But I do know Smithson's," Mrs. Stone said. "It's where my mother traded and where I go. When Janine first moved down here from Maine I took her there too, to introduce her. It can't be Mr. Smithson who hurt her. He's as gentle as a lamb and just about as strong. And retired, too, since last year."

"I didn't mean to suggest that Mr. Smithson had anything to do with Mrs. Campbell. It's something else, that may be related."

"Is he in trouble?"

"Nobody is in trouble," Jack said. "Except the person who operated on Mrs. Campbell, and we don't have any idea yet who that is. But if you think of anything she might have said, no matter how small—"

"I will come see you. Or write to you, if we are already away. When do you think we could leave here? I do need to get back to the boys. And Henry misses them so."

Oscar said, "Could you leave now?"

Mrs. Stone's expression stilled. "We don't have much luggage, and it's been packed for weeks. Do you mean it?"

"I do. I can put you two and Montgomery somewhere safe tonight and tomorrow I'll see to it you get onto the first steamer headed in the direction of Sakonnet Harbor. I'll need a half hour or so, so sit tight. Jack, you'll want to stay."

Anna could almost hear the silent discussion that went back and forth between them. No doubt Campbell had seen them entering the Stones' house, and by now he would have suspicions. Anna was glad Jack was staying behind.

Oscar grinned. "I won't be long," he said. "You'll be free of Campbell before you know it."

·   ·   ·

A FEW MINUTES later when Mrs. Stone had gone to check over their luggage, Anna said, "Do I want to know what he's up to?"

Jack shrugged. "You never know with Oscar. He can be inventive, on both sides of the law. But he'll get them to Rhode Island and Campbell will be none the wiser, you can put money on that much."

"We set out to find an answer to one question and instead we found the answer to a different one altogether."

Mrs. Stone came back into the parlor, her agitation and excitement plain to read in the way she sat and then jumped up again.

Anna said, "Will your husband have trouble adjusting, do you think? You've been in the city for a long time."

The older lady sat down again. "He loves those boys so, I don't think he'll care where he is."

She looked at her husband, who had fallen asleep in his rocking chair. "All these years I have missed the Henry I married, but just now it's better this way. He hardly understands what's happening, but you should have seen him as a young man. He had a gift for numbers, he could add and multiply and divide in his head, big numbers, too. And he was so strong, it was a joy just to watch him working. When he first came from Germany he came to see my father—he was from Munich too—to ask about work. He came into the shop, and I was at the counter helping a customer. He smiled at me, and that was that.

"As a girl I hated that we spoke German at home, but Henry made me glad of it, that I could talk to him. I was the one who taught him English, and he made good progress. With other people it was harder sometimes." She smiled with such sweetness that she looked much as she must have the day Heinrich Steinmauer came into her father's shop so many years ago.

"Once he wanted to buy a fish for supper—" She stopped. "It's an old story, you won't want to hear it."

Jack said, "I'm always up for a good fish story."

"Yes," Anna said. "If you don't tell us I'll be wondering for days."

Mrs. Stone started again. "We were at the Fulton Street market because Henry wanted fish for his supper. There was a big trout he liked the look of, but the fishmonger wanted a dollar for it, and Henry thought it was too much. You see, the fishmonger was rude because of us being German; that used to be even worse than it is these days. So they got to arguing and they both dug in, like bulls. 'A dollar,' says the fishmonger. 'One American dollar.' Now back then when Henry lost his temper his English got lost too. So he's yelling in his big deep voice, 'That is a shame! A shame!'" She pushed out her chest and thumped it manfully.

"And everybody was looking at us and the fishmonger, but Henry was too mad to notice. He bellows, 'Behold your fish! I can become a fish myself for two bits, just around the corner!'"

Anna laughed, a great bark of laughter that would have embarrassed her in other company. Jack's expression was vaguely confused, a man who dearly wanted in on the joke and would have been glad of the reason to laugh. For some reason Anna couldn't explain, that made her laugh all the harder.

◆ ◆ ◆

THAT EVENING AS they got ready for bed, Jack expected Anna would talk, finally, about her brother. Some small thing that would be a start, the first crack in the dam that held back all the sorrow that ate away at her still, so many years later.

It was the last night they would sleep under her aunt's roof. Tomorrow night they would go to bed in their own place. He liked the idea of a fresh start, getting the worst and saddest memories out in the light of day.

But she went about getting ready for bed, talking about the surgery she would perform in the morning, the hiring of a housekeeper and cook, where she would find the time for Italian lessons, wanting to know if Jack would be in court this week, if he was scheduled for night duty. She didn't mention Mrs. Stone or Archer Campbell, and Jack had the idea that she needed to talk to her aunt before they took up the subject.

He loved watching her when she didn't realize she was being studied. There was economy in every movement and she managed still to be graceful, in the way she bent from the waist to sweep her long hair to one side, her fingers moving rapidly as she began to plait, working each twist with precision until a long rope fell down her back, and orderly as a rosary but for the stray hair that escaped to curl on her neck, another at her brow.

"Jack?"

He started, coming back to himself with a jerk.

"Sorry," he said. "My mind wandered."

One side of her mouth quirked so that a single dimple popped to the surface. She knelt on the edge of the bed and bowed down to kiss his cheek, his temple, the corner of his mouth.

"Let me guess where it wandered to," she said, and hiccupped with laughter when he grabbed her wrists and flipped her onto her back.

"Wait," she said. "Wait, there's something I need to ask."

He kissed her soundly until he felt her begin to forget what she had been wanting to say, and then he drew away and settled beside her.

She hated to surrender control, or had always hated it. He liked to think that she was coming to see that occasional surrender had its rewards. He watched her make a concerted effort to return her breathing to something more normal.

"Forgot already?"

She elbowed him, hard. Then she sat up again, cross-legged, and faced him.

"Bambina. She is so bad tempered at times, really terrible."

"So I hear."

"From the girls?"

He nodded. "They are very concerned. They like Baldy-Ned—"

"Oh, no." Anna put a hand over her mouth to smother a laugh.

"It's your fault," Jack said. "Baldy wasn't a good enough name, so you saddled him with another one. The results are already out of your control. So I was saying, they're afraid that Bambina scared Baldy-Ned away, and they like him."

"He's very personable with the girls."

"He's personable with girls of all ages."

That made her pause. "Bambina never met him before today."

"That doesn't seem to matter. He's got a way of looking at young women that turns their heads. In Bambina's case that means she's going to go on the attack."

"Something has to be done."

He turned toward her. "You're afraid that if he's around more she'll do what, exactly?"

Anna frowned.

"You don't need to worry about him. He's had a lifetime of standing up to far worse than Bambina."

"That's just it," Anna said. "She's too fragile for the kinds of games he plays."

"Bambina. Fragile?"

She shook her head. "Never mind. I see that the male mind is not nimble enough to deal with this situation."

"But yours is?"

"Of course. Wait," she said, as he reached for her.

"I completely forgot to say that there was a letter from Sophie and Cap yesterday. There were separate letters for everybody, and this one for you and me. I waited to read it with you." She leaned back to take an envelope from her bedside table. "Do you want to hear it?"

She was already opening the envelope.

Dear Anna and Jack,

We are arrived here in reasonable good health and are, I think, settled. Or as settled as we can be. I know Anna will want all the details about the clinic and treatment plan, but for the moment I will just say that I am very satisfied that Dr. Zängerle knows what he's doing and has some promising ideas.

The journey was almost more than Cap could bear, and for the first two days I feared the trip was a mistake that would take a quick and unhappy end. Then on the third day he rallied, as he has done so often in the past. Now he is distinctly cranky, and what a fine thing it is to have to listen to complaints about the rug on his lap and the sound of cowbells coming from higher pastures in the night. I said I found the cowbells oddly comforting, an alpine counterpoint to the screech of the omnibuses he slept through so easily at home. That made him smile. No one here is put off by his mood, and thus he has already given up on it.

This morning we sat on a wide balcony overlooking the mountains and valley below, the air cool and refreshing and the sun mild enough to be pleasant. I was reading aloud from a newspaper, when I realized that he had fallen asleep. He looked no older than seventeen, one arm thrown up over his head and his face turned away from me.

For one moment I thought he had gone. That he had slipped away without a word of farewell, and I sat struck dumb. I remember thinking I shouldn't begrudge him a peaceful end to such a terrible and drawn-out illness, but in my heart I was so angry at him for going without me. Then he stirred, and my heart began to beat again.

Now, many hours later, I realize that this trip is as much for me as it is for him. I am learning what it will be like, and when it does happen, I think I will be able to bear it.

This letter was meant to offer you the kind of comfort I took from the day's events. I hope I have succeeded.

Tomorrow or the next day I will write with more details. In the meantime ask the girls about their letter. They have a story about a cow in the garden and the very, very ugly dog who sits next to Cap at every opportunity, tail thumping hopefully for the tidbits Cap gives him.

We are together, and content to make the most of the time left to us in this beautiful place.

> With great affection and love from both of us.
> Your Sophie and Cap

Postscript. Cap instructs me to say that he wants news of the Campbell situation, gossip from Waverly Place, and a report on how you find marriage. I just want to know that you are happy.

36

ON FRIDAY MORNING Jack asked Anna over breakfast if there was a difficult case that was robbing her of sleep. It was true that she was sleeping badly, but she had made every effort to keep her restlessness to herself.

"Nothing so worthy," she told him. She thought for a moment and chose her words carefully. "Life is so full, it feels like a waste of time to be sleeping."

"What we need is a rainy Saturday," he said. "With no chance of being called out on an emergency. You might remember then how nice it can be to spend time in bed. I could remind you." He waggled both brows at her.

She made a face at him. "You're not talking about sleeping."

"I am. Maybe not exclusively, but sleeping—" He stopped and smiled widely. "In between."

"So then, Detective Sergeant. Order up a rainy Saturday, would you?"

Mrs. Cabot came to refill their coffee cups and Anna reminded herself to send Jack's aunt Philomena a thank-you note for finding them the housekeeper. She had sent three; Mrs. Lee had interviewed them one by one and hired Eve Cabot, a Yankee of the first order, born and raised in Maine, an excellent housekeeper and cook. She moved into the bedroom off the kitchen with one suitcase, a pot of violets she put on the windowsill above the kitchen sink, and Skidder, a genial Jack Russell terrier who hung on every word she said.

Anna liked Mrs. Cabot for her dry humor, her refusal to be taken aback by the oddities of the household, and the easy way she was with the girls.

"Anna," Jack said, and inclined his head toward the pocket watch he had put on the table.

She jumped up, kissed Jack's cheek, gathered up her things, and rushed out, but not before Ned came in the kitchen door. He had had his breakfast under Mrs. Lee's watchful eye, and now would allow Mrs. Cabot to feed him too. It made them happy, and he lived for nothing so much as pleasing the women who fed him.

Anna waved a hand over her head, meant for both hello and good-bye, and studiously ignored the question that followed her out the door. She was almost as far as the Cooper Union when Ned caught up with her, brushing bread crumbs from his shirt.

"I don't have time to stop," Anna said.

After a full minute of silence she realized why he was walking along with her, and what he was waiting for.

"You are a sincere and dedicated teacher," she said to him. "And I pay your fees happily. But sometimes Italian can't be the first thing on my list of priorities."

She had stopped in spite of herself, and now set off again.

He said, "What's going on with Staten Island?"

That made her pause again, but only momentarily. "What do you mean? Jack and I got married on Staten Island."

"There's something more," he said. "I heard Margaret talking about it to Mrs. Lee."

Anna had no intention of telling Ned about the Mullen family. They hadn't even decided on how, or whether, to tell the girls. The inability to come to an agreement was starting to fray the nerves on all sides, but Margaret was having the hardest time.

Ned said, "Does it have something to do with the Russo boys?"

That did bring her up short. "What exactly did you hear?"

"Not much." But he looked away.

"I will strangle Margaret," Anna said, without heat. "In the meantime we need to keep Rosa especially clear of such conversations."

"So it is about her brothers."

Late as she was, Anna stopped to consider this young man who was fast being drawn into both households on Waverly Place, simply by making himself indispensable. He spent his afternoons working for the Howells at the newsboys' lodging, but the rest of the day he was busy making himself welcome among the Savard and Mezzanotte clans. He was a favorite of Margaret, who loved having a young man to mother; of Aunt Quinlan, who liked his banter and quickness of mind; of Mr. Lee, because he was as tireless as a work-horse and would turn his hand to anything; of Mrs. Lee and Mrs. Cabot, who alternately fed and scolded, ordered around and spoiled him. He was polite but more formal with Chiara and Laura Lee when they were working in the house, probably, Anna thought, because he knew the danger of showing favoritism. Jack had had more than one private conversation with Ned to be sure he understood the boundaries, but Anna hadn't asked for details.

Bambina was the only person he hadn't won over. When she and Ned were in the same room she made a science of expressing her dislike and disapproval in such a way that it was hard to correct or admonish her. Even this didn't seem to worry Ned. Just the opposite.

Jack thought Bambina was jealous because the girls were so enamored of him, and Mrs. Lee agreed. "Things come so easy to him. He only has to snap his fingers and the little girls let everything else drop. We're going to have a talk, Mr. Baldy-Ned and me."

Everyone was talking to Ned. Anna was as sure as she could be that he would behave himself. Now it seemed like the time had come to take him into closer confidence.

"Can I trust you to do what you can to keep the girls safe and calm?"

He nodded. "Of course."

"Staten Island does have to do with one of the boys, but it's a very delicate situation. Telling Rosa at this point would make things much more difficult, but we do need a plan. We can talk about that tonight once the girls are asleep. I'm trusting you to keep an eye on things until then."

He gave a sharp bow from the shoulders, as neatly as a soldier. "I've got to get back. Bambina is coming over to hang some curtains, and you know how she looks forward to insulting me."

Anna watched him run off, switched her Gladstone bag to her other hand, and picked up her pace.

◆ ◆ ◆

ELISE GENERALLY SAW little of Anna during the workday, and when they did cross paths she made herself small. She had begun to make some friends among the nurses and medical students; she didn't want to draw attention to the fact that Dr. Savard—who frightened almost everyone—had taken Elise under her wing. They were likely to accuse her of getting special treatment, which was in fact the case.

But there was another truth, one she reinforced with all her energy and concentration, every day: She didn't take advantage. She worked very hard, asked no favors, and offered her help wherever she could, both at the hospital and on Waverly Place. And still today, just as she was finishing her shift Anna sent for her. Elise found her with her advanced medical students, all of them getting ready to leave the building.

"I thought you might want to come with us," Anna said. "To see a thyroidectomy. It's a very challenging operation. I myself have never done one. Not yet."

Ten minutes earlier Elise had been looking forward to the garden and putting her feet up for the twenty minutes she allotted herself; now she felt as though she could sprout wings and fly.

They set off for New-York Hospital on foot, matching Anna's quick pace. Elise was curious about the surgery, but she kept her silence and listened to the snatches of conversations that came to her about exams, a visit home, a lost notebook, a recent case they had been called on to write up as an assignment and how strictly Dr. Savard marked their efforts.

She wondered if these young women talked about Anna when she was out of earshot, and decided that they almost certainly did. About her classes and expectations, but also about her recent marriage. One of the nurses had approached her and asked straight out was it true, Dr. Savard had married an Italian? Because she couldn't indulge in irritation, Elise feigned confusion. Better to be thought a little dim than to gossip about the person who had made this new life possible.

Even when the subject wasn't forbidden, Elise often found herself at a loss, listening to the young women talk among themselves. They were hardworking, ambitious, and serious about their studies; they had made choices knowing full well that the goals they set for themselves would likely cut them off from the things most young women hoped for. Some of them would marry, according to Anna, but most would not. And still they admired men, and thought of them as potential mates, or at least bed partners.

Chiara had been the one to point out to Elise that men watched her.

"Watch me? Why?"

"Why not? You're pretty."

"I'm odd looking." She ruffled her short hair.

"You're pretty in an uncommon way, and you move like a ballerina."

Upon close questioning it turned out that Chiara had never seen a ballerina except on a poster, but she stuck stubbornly to her assessment.

"I am a dumpling in the making," Chiara insisted. "It's the family curse. Age fifty, I'll blow up." She puffed out her cheeks to demonstrate. "But you've got long legs and a long neck and skin like silk. Men watch you because you're nice to look at."

The whole subject made her uncomfortable, but Chiara had started something that Rosa picked up on. When they were out in public together they kept a constant vigil and pointed out every admirer, some of which Elise truly believed they manufactured solely to fluster her. On the omnibus, a fair-haired man with a stack of books on his lap. A clerk at the notions counter at Denning's Dry Goods with ears that stuck out from his head. The grooms standing outside Stewart's stables, cheeky monkeys, every one. They swore that there were three different young men living in the Jansen Apartments—just across the way—who had gotten into the sudden habit of walking past the house at least twice a day, morning and evening. Chiara made up names for each of them, and jobs too: Alto was the tallest one and an assistant manager at a bank, Bruno had a big dark brown beard and taught at the Academy of Music, and Bello, with a face like an angel, was a passenger agent on the White Star Line. And all of them lived for a glimpse of Elise.

"If you're right about this," she wanted to know, "why haven't any of them said a word to me?"

"Because you are pretty but distant. What's the word—"

"Uninterested."

"That's not it. *Distante*. Aloof!"

Elise wondered if it was true. Did strangers see her as arrogant?

Conceited? These were serious character flaws that were dealt with summarily in the convent. Had she learned them in the few weeks since she left?

This line of thought stayed with her until they reached the hospital, where they filed through the doors like so many schoolgirls. The smell of carbolic and lye soap stripped away all the trappings and just that easily they were physicians in training, sober, observant, somber.

It was a relief to be back in a familiar environment, where there were things to occupy her beyond the mysteries of men. There was, in fact, a delicate, dangerous procedure that involved wielding a scalpel to remove the thyroid, cocooned in veins, embedded in the platysma, sternothyroid, and sternohyoid muscles at the base of throat, without damaging carotid arteries, leaving the trachea and the larynx intact. She wondered if they might get a piece of the tissue to study under a microscope.

◆　◆　◆

ANNA SENT HER students back to the New Amsterdam and went in search of an orthopedic surgeon she knew, hoping he'd have a minute to discuss a case. His office door stood open and the office was empty, but she could hear a conversation going on farther down the hall and so she went to investigate.

Dr. Mayfair stood with two colleagues in a triangle, their heads bent together. She began to back away, but David Mayfair looked up and caught sight of her.

"Dr. Savard." He gestured for her to come closer. "Let me introduce you."

There were reasons for her to be on her way, but it was a rare opportunity to meet with male colleagues who saw her not as an upstart or a threat, but as an equal. It made her nervous, she could admit that, because she so much wanted to be accepted. Striking the right tone was far more tiring than surgery, this kind of interaction.

"We were just talking about one of Dr. Harrison's cases," Dr. Mayfair said. "A young mother, and a terrible loss. You do more gynecological surgery than anyone here, maybe you could make more sense of it."

All thoughts of the cuneiform osteotomy she had wanted to discuss disappeared. She cleared her throat. "What kind of case?"

Emil Harrison was a slight man of average height with a luxurious head of hair and the habit of picking at his beard. Anna couldn't recall ever hearing his name before, but there were so many physicians in the city, that was nothing unusual. He seemed to be hesitant, and Anna was ready to excuse herself when Albert Wesniewski spoke up.

"I'd like to hear her opinion."

"Fine, let's go have a look." Harrison didn't sound as though he relished the idea.

David Mayfair said, "It's too bad your students have gone already, Dr. Savard. This would have been an excellent experience."

• • •

THE PHRASE THAT kept coming back to Anna later was *excellent experience*. David Mayfair wasn't purposefully trivializing what had happened to the dead woman, and in fact he was more respectful than most. But it was an irritation, and one she could do nothing about, especially when he had gone out of his way to include her. Young women studying medicine would have to learn this lesson as well.

On the way to the morgue Emil Harrison gave her his patient's history. He had been treating Irina Dmitrievna Svetlova for five years, and knew her quite well: age twenty-eight, born in St. Petersburg, the wife of a professor of Russian language and literature at Columbia College. Two sons, both born in New York and delivered by a German midwife without incident. The boys were thriving, and neither had there been anything wrong with Irina Svetlova except the fact that she was pregnant and did not want to be.

Dr. Harrison didn't perform abortions, and did not refer her to any other doctor who might have done the procedure, for obvious reasons. But on Thursday morning he had been called to their home.

"The note said only that she was unwell," Harrison went on. The Svetlovs lived in an elegant French flat on Fifth Avenue, where he found her in danger of her life.

"My first inclination was to attend her there so that she could die at home with her family nearby, but her husband insisted on a lapa-rotomy."

Something in the back of Anna's mind suddenly became clear: they only knew about the deaths that came to the attention of the authorities. There could be many more, women who had gone home to die and been tended to by their own people. That idea so distracted her that she found it hard to shift her attention when they reached the morgue.

Anna steeled herself, but it was no good. No human being could look upon such devastation and remain unmoved. The postmortem would reduce what had happened to this woman to cold observations: tears and puncture wounds to the cervix, uterus, omentum, large intestine, and the body's frantic response to the invasion of bacteria: infection, exudate, and pus. What had been a well-formed, healthy human body laid waste.

"Have you ever seen such an extreme example of malpractice?" Mayfair asked her.

"I'm sorry to say I have," Anna answered. "Almost exactly like this. Do you know who did the procedure?"

"No," said Harrison. "By the time I saw her she was convulsing from the fever. She never regained consciousness."

"The husband?"

"He's in shock."

"I'd like to talk to him, if I may."

•   •   •

ANNA FOUND PROFESSOR Svetlov sitting in the main lobby, his hat clamped between his hands, his head lowered. At the sound of her voice a tremor ran through him.

"Professor Svetlov," Anna repeated. "May I speak with you? I'm Doctor Anna Savard."

Anna dealt with grieving husbands and fathers, brothers and sons every day. She strove for calm compassion without emotional attachment, but it was a battle that would never be completely won.

When she had introduced herself again and expressed her condolences, she forced herself to look him directly in the eye and ask her question.

"Professor, do you have any idea who she went to for this procedure?"

He shook his head, a single sharp jerk.

"Any information would be useful for the detectives. You don't know what part of the city she went to? How much money she paid? How she heard about his services?"

His voice came raw and rough. "I don't know any of that. She went out in the morning. She came back early afternoon, and went straight to bed. She wouldn't open the door to anybody. This morning when I finally got in to see her—" He pressed the heels of his hands to his eyes and shook his head. "Please, leave me in peace."

•   •   •

JACK WAS WORKING the night shift, but there was no end of things to keep Anna busy. She could spend the evening reading journals or marking papers, and she owed Sophie a long letter. She could go visit with Aunt Quinlan and Margaret or spend some time with the little girls. What she couldn't do was talk to anyone about Irina Svetlova.

Talking to the woman's husband—trying to talk to him—had been a mistake, and she hadn't even asked the most important question. It seemed unlikely that a wealthy Russian woman would ever have had occasion to frequent Smithson's, located as it was in the shadows beneath the elevated train, but she would leave that determination to the honorable detective sergeants. They never presumed to perform surgery, and from now on she would leave the police work to them. Unless, of course, they specifically asked for her help.

With that self-admonishment clear in mind, she finished changing into casual clothes and went downstairs to find mail on the hall table. A letter from her cousin Blue, Aunt Quinlan's oldest daughter who still lived in Paradise at Uphill House, where Anna had been born. Another from one of the Savard cousins in New Orleans. Sales offers from medical supply companies and publishers, a newsletter from the Women's Medical Society. And one rough envelope with handwriting that was unfamiliar, rather old-fashioned and stiff.

For a moment she contemplated not opening it at all. If it was another of Comstock's traps, it would ruin the rest of her evening. But she took it to a window to study it more closely and was able to make out the postmark, just barely. Mailed two days before in Rhode Island.

At the desk she slit the envelope open and found two close-written sheets.

Dear Dr. Savard,

I write to you because Det. Sarg. Maroney gave me your address and asked me to send word about how we are getting on.

Henry and Montgomery and me got here by steamer with no fuss at all, clear skies and calm seas, and found a Mr. Knowles who took us and our bags and boxes in his wagon to the house and wouldn't take a nickel for his trouble. The boys (Hannes, Markus, Wiese, Günther, as we call them now, and they call us Oma and Opa) were just sitting down to supper made for them by Mrs. Barnes, whose husband sold us the house. There was such a great excitement in the kitchen, Henry with tears rolling down his stubbly cheeks for joy, and Montgomery leaping into the air like a rubber ball, and the boys all pressing together against us like they'd never let go.

They were terrible upset to hear about their mam, which is why I took so long to write this letter. It hit Hannes the hardest, but he is slowly coming back to himself. Today he took the baby on his lap and played with him and made him laugh. It does a body good to hear a baby laugh like that, from deep in the belly.

Last night Markus and Wiese both slept through the night for the first time since we brought the sad news with us from home.

Henry is enjoying the fine weather and the sea just as much as the boys do. You will recall that he is fond of fish, and he has already got into the habit of walking down to the bay when the fishermen come in to buy something for supper. He takes a dollar with him, and is pleased to bring back change.

I count myself very lucky. We needn't fear sickness for there is a good doctor and an apothecary in town and we can pay them. Hannes will start at the little school in the village in the fall with new shoes and a primer and whatever else children need these days. The boys are my life's work, now, and I intend to do it proper. Good food and fresh air and a bit of work around the place for each of them (excepting the baby, of course). And a hug and kiss at bedtime, the way their mam would want.

If Henry was clear in his mind he would write himself to thank you and say how much we appreciate the kindness you all showed us

in our hour of need. There are good people in the world, after all. We
pray every day for our dearest girl, gone forever but never forgot.

Yours truly,
May Steinmauer

Anna tried to remember the last time there had been a mention in
the papers about the Campbell boys but could not. It was as if they had
used up their portion of the public's interest and concern and would
not get any more attention unless they earned it. In a city where thousands of children lived on the streets, that would be hard to do.

On the desk in front of her she had the draft of a letter she had
been meaning to finish and mail since the fruitless meeting with
Father McKinnawae. She had revised it multiple times, and had yet
to copy it in its final form on to her personal stationery.

Mr. and Mrs. Eamon Mullen
Tottenville, Staten Island, NY

Dear Mr. and Mrs. Mullen,

I am Anna Savard Mezzanotte, of New York city. On May 26th my
husband and I met your family very briefly on the beach near Mount
Loretto. Your daughter Theresa Ann introduced us to you and her
baby brother, you may recall.

We hope you might be willing to grant a favor. May we stop by
and visit with you one Saturday or Sunday afternoon, at your
convenience? This has to do with a family connection, one I would
prefer not to spell out in a letter. I realize this sounds very
mysterious, but let me assure you that our designs are friendly, and
we mean you only well. In all probability we will visit for less than
an hour.

Of course, you may well want to check references before you
reply this letter. I provide the following information to that end:

I am physician and surgeon, a graduate of the Woman's Medical
School here in New York, and registered at Sanitary Headquarters,

as required by law. I am on staff at the New Amsterdam Charity
Hospital. My husband, Detective Sergeant Giancarlo Mezzanotte, is
on the New York City police force and is stationed at Police
Headquarters on Mulberry Street. We live at No. 18 Waverly Place.
With very best wishes to you and your family.

> *I am most sincerely yours,*
> *Dr. Anna Savard*

She knew she needed to show the letter to Aunt Quinlan and Jack
and maybe even Conrad Belmont and take advice before sending
it. Anna asked herself what these people might say, if they would
disapprove.

With considerable effort she tried to clear her mind and read the
letter as Mrs. Mullen might read it. Would she be affronted, afraid,
insulted, or simply curious? The only thing Anna knew for certain
was that the situation had to be addressed soon.

She sat for a moment looking at a blank sheet of stationery. Engraved
across the top in an elegant typeface was her full name: Dr. Liliane
Mathilde Savard. A graduation present from Margaret. Anna had
thanked her and then put the box away, only to find that she did have
a use for stationery like this. It put a certain distance between herself
and the person she was writing to. A private individual requesting a
consultation, a colleague asking her to read the draft of a journal article, invitations to conferences and meetings, a request for a contribution to an educational fund: in each case she had to balance interest
and concern with the demands on her time and energy.

The house was dim and cool and very quiet. Before she could change
her mind, she got out a pen and ink and a fresh sheet of stationery. In a
fluid hand she copied out the final version of the letter to the Mullens.
While the ink dried she addressed an envelope. She folded the letter
neatly, went over the creases with the letter opener, put it in the envelope, and set it aside.

Then she started another, far more pleasant letter, one that would
cheer up both Sophie and Cap. This letter she wanted to write. A
letter with answers instead of questions. She thought of them sitting

on a terrace overlooking mountains and pastures, and she wrote down for them the rest of Janine Campbell's story.

⋄   ⋄   ⋄

SHE DIDN'T REALIZE it, Elise was sure, but with a simple statement Anna had handed her what felt like keys to a vast kingdom.

"There are books and journals enough in the house," she had said. "You're free to take any of them to your room. You can start studying now, and you'll be that much more prepared when classes start."

The idea of going to medical school still struck Elise as alternately ridiculous and overwhelming, but it was now a fact. She carried the acceptance letter with its offer of a scholarship on her person, folded small and tucked in the waistband of her uniform skirt. As if it were a ticket that once lost, could never be replaced.

She began writing longer passages in her daybook, listing questions that occurred to her while with one patient or another. And now she had the books that would make it possible to start.

Early Monday a surgery was scheduled that she was now determined to watch. As a nurse she had no claim on a spot in the gallery, but as a new medical student she could at least try. Along with every other doctor and medical student in the city, in this case. Dr. Shifra Rosenmeyer would begin with an orotracheal intubation, and then move on to resecting six-year-old Regina Sartore's retropharyngeal tumor. With surgery the little girl's chances of survival were poor; without surgery she would be dead in weeks, if not days. But she would have a chance.

Elise gathered a pile of books and sat down on the floor to begin sorting out everything there was to know about the operation to come.

⋄   ⋄   ⋄

AT NINE SHE got up to light the lamps and give her eyes a rest. The windows were open to the night breezes and city noises. Slowly she was learning to ignore the most common ones: iron wheels on steel tracks, hoofs on pavement, the huff of steam engines, the shouts of the boys playing stickball or craps in a nearby alley. She had wondered at first how children got any sleep at all, but Rosa and Lia rarely sat still, and by bedtime they never lasted long. When they begged for bedtime stories it was quite safe to agree to a chapter or three. To Elise's certain knowledge they had yet to get past the first chapter of *Little Women*.

She was almost alone in the house: the little girls asleep, the older ladies sitting in the garden pergola watching fireflies and slapping at mosquitoes. Chiara had gone to spend the night with Celestina to work on some embroidery project that was giving her fits, and Laura Lee went home every day once supper was on the table.

In the daytime the house was usually overrun with busy people. The exception was Mrs. Quinlan, who spent a good part of the morning in her little study. Mrs. Lee gladly played the dragon before the moat; Chiara swore that even the quietest footsteps passing Mrs. Quinlan's door would cause Mrs. Lee to appear with a wooden spoon that she tapped into an open palm. But then Chiara was very fond of a good story and believed that facts were there to be bent to the needs of the storyteller.

Elise decided she was thirsty enough to go in search of the cold mint tea Mrs. Lee made by the bucketful. Maybe she would sit in the garden for a little while, if the mosquitoes weren't too bloodthirsty. She opened her door and stepped into the hallway, where she found Rosa poised for flight, her face pale with shock.

She wore a clean pinafore over a muslin dress and her sturdiest shoes. There was a shawl folded over her arm, half hiding a small basket.

In such a situation Elise would have expected flustered excuses and a quick retreat back into her room, but Rosa stood there without flinching.

She said, "If you stop me now, I'll go another time. You can't watch me forever."

Confused, alarmed, Elise came closer and crouched down until their faces were on the same level. "But where is it you're going?"

Relief flowed through the little girl, as visible as a storm tide dying out on a beach.

"To Staten Island," she said with a note of impatience. "To get my little brother. Would you come with me?"

"Sit here with me a minute." Elise tugged her to the staircase where they sat side by side, speaking in low whispers.

"Why do you think your brother—"

"Vittorio," Rosa supplied. "The baby."

"Why do you think he's on Staten Island?"

From the basket Rosa took a single sheet of paper and held it out. Anna's handwriting, with much crossing out and many insertions. The letter had not come easily to her.

Rather than take it in hand, Elise said, "Tell me what it says."

Rosa bit her lip so hard that Elise expected to see blood.

"I have to go now before they come in from the garden. Won't you come with me?"

"Wait," Elise said.

"No," Rosa said, getting up. "I'm not going to wait anymore."

"Rosa—"

"You can't stop me. It's your fault that he got lost in the first place. You lost him, and now they know where he is but they aren't doing anything about it. Well, I'll do something."

She began to run down the stairs.

"Rosa," Elise said, trying to keep her voice calm. "There's no ferry at this time of night. You can't get to Staten Island until morning." Which might not be strictly true, but she had nothing else to offer.

The girl paused to look over her shoulder. Elise had never seen such an expression on a child's face, misery and anger and flint-hard determination.

"I'll hide until morning," she said. "I've done it before."

Elise saw Jack coming out of the hall from the kitchen. Rosa followed her shifting gaze and then she was dashing for the door.

Before she could even turn the lock, he was there.

Rosa screamed. A scream that would tear a hard man's heart in two, and Jack was not hard of heart. He picked up a kicking Rosa and held her while she screamed and thrashed. He simply kept her against his chest, in the circle of his arms.

Jack was talking to her, a low river of sound. When she tried to bite him, he adjusted his grip and kept talking. When Mrs. Quinlan and Mrs. Cooper came rushing into the hall, he kept talking. Rosa was still howling, her mouth a dark hole. She ripped the buttons from Jack's shirt collar and threw them, her other fist hitting him on the jaw, the cheek, the ear. He never flinched, and he never stopped murmuring to her.

Now she was shouting at him, directing all her anger and frustration into his face in a rushing, tumbling stream of Italian. By his expression it was clear Jack understood her. A kind of calm came over him and seemed to pass into Rosa, who slumped against his shoulder.

A door opened behind Elise. Lia came into the light, sleep-tousled, her thumb firmly in her mouth and tears pouring down her face in a sheet.

"Oh baby," Elise said. "Come here." She pulled the little girl close and folded her into her lap, smoothing her hair.

"Shall we go into my room and get into the big bed?"

Lia wound her free hand in Elise's shirtwaist so tightly that she felt the pull of it at her throat.

"Shall we?"

Her head jerked from side to side: no.

"It will be all right," Elise whispered to her. "I know this is scary, but it will be all right. We'll all sit down together and find a way to make Rosa feel better. We can do that, Lia."

She realized then that Mrs. Cooper had come up the stairs and stood motionless, her hands flat on her waist, arms akimbo. Lia's eyes, brimming with tears, blinked once, and then she held her arms out.

Elise had had more than one uncharitable thought about Margaret Cooper, and she was embarrassed to remember how quickly she had judged. Her whole person, body and mind, belonged to Lia, who had wrapped her arms and legs around Mrs. Cooper's neck and slender waist. She murmured to the little girl, soft sounds that might have been words but were meant for no one in the world but Lia. When the door to the girls' room closed behind them, Elise had to put her forehead down on her knees and let herself be swept away, just in that moment, home to her own mother.

Rosa was still talking in ragged bursts. Jack held her safely in his arms, listening. In small, easy steps he moved into the parlor.

Mrs. Quinlan gestured for Elise. She had an errand and didn't want to wake Mr. Lee. Would Elise be so good?

"Of course. Just tell me what I can do."

She pressed money into Elise's hand and closed her fingers over the bills. "Walk over to the New York Hotel front entrance, tell Mr. Manchester I've sent you. He'll get you a cab. Let him get the cab for you, do you hear me? Then go straight to the New Amsterdam and tell Anna what has happened here. Ask her to come home as soon as she's able."

All the questions tumbling through her head, but only one presented itself. "What now?"

Mrs. Quinlan was very old, but there was nothing frail about her. She was filled with calm determination that settled Elise's own jangling nerves. Some women had that strength hidden inside them, a light that flared to life when everyone else was overwhelmed.

She patted Elise's cheek and smiled at her, a weary but fond smile. "Tomorrow Anna and Jack will take the girls to Staten Island to see their brother Vittorio," she said. "Nothing else will do."

37

THE RAINY DAY that Anna had wished for came, and would not be wished away again. All the way to the ferry terminal she worried that their departure would be suspended due to rough waters. At the last moment the winds died back and they were allowed to board.

In the hurry not to miss the ferry she had forgotten things: she hadn't checked to see if the girls had handkerchiefs, or how much money she had in her pocketbook, or if her hat was pinned firmly in place. A gust of wind made her think of the pins, because it almost took the hat from her head. At the same time it took the only umbrella she had found in the rush and turned it inside out with a great pop.

But they got onto the ferry, and it left as scheduled to plow its way through the chop.

Anna held Lia's head while she was sick, both of them soaked by rain that was falling so hard that each drop bounced like a grasshopper off rail and deck. Lia's complexion went a sickly yellow green.

The only reasonable, sensible thing to do was to turn around and go home, but one look in Rosa's direction made it clear that she would fight such a suggestion with all the strength she could muster.

Anna carried Lia back into the cabin and settled with her on a wooden bench across from Jack, who had already accumulated a small pond around himself. On another day she would have had to laugh—he would have laughed at himself. But for Rosa, who sat a little apart, her body angled away from them. She answered Jack in monosyllables when he asked a question, but she would not even look in Anna's direction. She was in shock; Anna understood that and lectured herself: any attempt to explain or justify would only make things worse. She tried to work out what she might say:

A priest found Vittorio at the Foundling and gave him to a Catholic family to raise as their own. Now he's Timothy Mullen, and the law will do nothing to restore him to his sisters. Or she could leave the Church out of it: *He is a healthy, happy child, one who is very much loved, and who loves. Timothy Mullen clings to his adoptive mother because he remembers no other.*

Rosa was not interested in logic or reason or the law. All attempts to engage her met with a blank look; she was as brittle and unreachable as a stroke victim.

The rain fell all the way across Raritan Bay and was still falling when they left the ferry and walked the short distance to the railway station, where stranded travelers were packed, all wet and cold and not inclined to see the situation as anything but inexcusable. But a tree had fallen across the tracks and it would be at least an hour, probably two, until anybody went anywhere.

Lia was a sodden bundle of miserable little girl in her arms. She needed to be stripped out of the wet clothes and rubbed down, but for the moment any small distraction might help. Anna wiggled her way through muttering discontents to get to a window made opaque by condensation. With her gloved hand she wiped it clean, and began to point things out: a yellow dinghy tugging at its ropes like a restless dog, a runaway hat tumbling over and over in the gusting wind, a flash of lightning in the distance, a lady who stood in the doorway of the bakery, peeking out from under her umbrella, watching for someone who was clearly late.

"Who do you think she's waiting for?" Anna asked. It was a game Lia loved, the making up of stories, but there was nothing there today, not the least spark. Jack and Rosa had come to stand behind them—or Jack had come, leading Rosa by the hand. He was talking to Rosa, but Lia was listening.

On so little sleep Anna's mind would have nothing to do with Italian, and so she waited while Jack talked and the girls asked questions. When Rosa's shoulders slumped Anna knew that he had made the situation clear to her; the only way to Tottenville was by train, trains ran on tracks, tracks were sometimes made impassable by the weather, and the weather was out of everyone's control. They were all of them wet and hungry, Jack was telling them, but there was a hotel just down the street.

One small good thing struck Anna once they were out in the weather: Stapleton was a wealthy town, so that the roads were paved and the sidewalks raised. They would not have to slog through the mud.

The Stapleton Arms lobby smelled of wet wool and coal oil and sweat. Within a minute Anna decided that she would rather be wet outside than steaming hot in a crowded lobby.

Jack paid a premium for two rooms while Anna talked to the matron about towels, cocoa and buttered toast, tea and sandwiches. The matron went bustling off, and Anna hoped the rest of the staff was as sharp and quick.

Finally in the room, she decided she could forgive the hotel owner for overheating the lobby. It was a very pleasant room with an attached bath—Anna wondered briefly how much Jack had had to pay—a small table, a comfortable chair, and a good-sized bed with clean linen and a pretty quilt. As the first order of business she cracked both windows for fresh air.

She had barely taken off her hat when they were invaded by the matron, leading her maids like soldiers into battle. There were stacks of towels and loaded trays, dry socks and facecloths. Jack took a few towels for himself and disappeared into the next room while Anna began stripping wet clothes off Lia. The matron did the same for Rosa, who allowed this service without comment.

The food was set out on the table, and then the maids ducked their heads and withdrew. Lia, wrapped in towels, managed a smile for the matron, who brought her a cup of cocoa. Rosa accepted a cup too, and soon began to blink sleepily. They had another hour to wait, and a nap seemed the best use of that time.

The matron—Mrs. Singer, as it turned out—had brought a dressing gown for Anna to use. Old and frayed at the hem, but sweet smelling. Anna went behind the privacy screen to strip and handed her clothes over to Mrs. Singer.

"I'll hang all your things in the kitchen, where it's warmest."

"I don't know what you can do to make them dry in an hour," Anna said. "But thank you for trying."

Mrs. Singer raised one thin eyebrow. "If the next train leaves before three, I'll eat my own hat and yours for good measure. It always takes longer than they claim."

The matron went out as Jack came in.

Rosa said, "Where did you get that?"

"It's pink," Lia said, and giggled.

"These girls are mocking me, Anna. Mocking me."

"You're wearing a pink dressing gown," Lia pointed out. "You look silly." It was true, the old dressing gown the landlord had found for him was big enough, but it had faded over the years from what had probably been a somber maroon to a delicate pink.

"And you have cocoa all around your mouth, like a mustache and beard. Let's get you cleaned up and down for a nap."

Anna's stomach gave a terrific growl and so she sat down to eat while Jack folded back the covers. Both the girls were asleep before he had finished tucking them in. Anna, her hair still dripping, sat in the chair beside the bed and went about the business of putting herself in order, when she would have liked nothing more than to climb into bed with them.

Jack came up behind her with a fresh towel. "Here," he said. "Let me."

While he pressed water from her hair she closed her eyes and let herself be drawn down and down into the comfort of it. Then he ruined her lovely half sleep. "Listen now, while I talk. No arguments, just listen."

Anna drew in a deep breath and let it go in one long sigh. She got up from the chair and went to the window, but he followed her.

Jack said, "Nobody in this world could have done more for these girls than you have. Rosa doesn't see that now, but she will. You have to remember that and leave guilt and remorse behind, because while it seems as though she's ignoring you, she's watching every move you make."

Anna nodded and yawned, and, leaning forward to put her head on Jack's unyielding shoulder, she fell asleep.

• • •

THE SUN BROKE through the last of the clouds just as they reached the railroad office, and that, Jack decided, could be taken as a good omen. From there things moved quickly; tickets were bought, and all four of them settled on the crowded train while a faint rainbow appeared over Raritan Bay.

Anna sat across the aisle with Lia, who was taking in the scenery with something like astonishment. After Washington Square's walk-ways and benches and neatly manicured bushes and trees, Staten Island would be overwhelming.

Once or twice he had heard Aunt Quinlan telling stories of her childhood in the endless forests and mountains of northernmost New York state, and so it came as no surprise when Lia asked about bears and panthers, wolves and moose.

"Not here," Anna told her. "The endless forests are far away. It's a long journey."

"Beaver?" Lia asked hopefully. "There must be beaver."

Anna raised a shoulder. "I don't know. Maybe the conductor could tell you. See, he's coming now to take our tickets."

You had to admire Anna's way of dealing with the girls. Rather than try to convince them they should not be sad or angry or disap-pointed in something, she gave them something else to concentrate on. He had seen this strategy work dozens of times already, as it worked now. Lia tugged on the conductor's sleeve to ask a question, and for the rest of the journey she looked forward to his trips through the car, when he would stop and tell her about Staten Island when he was a boy, about plentiful beaver and deer, porcupines and foxes.

Rosa was listening, but she took no part in the conversation. Jack tried to imagine what she would be feeling, the relief of knowing her brother was alive and well, the fear that she would be turned away and not allowed to see him. She was angry at everyone and every-thing, but she focused most of that anger on Anna and Elise.

"It's understandable," Anna had said to him last night. "She trusts me not to reject her for being angry. If I could be dispassionate about any of it, I might say that she is thinking of me like a mother. Some-one who will take the worst she has to offer, and never turn away."

Drifting between consciousness and sleep, he had thought about this Anna, who had once lost a brother. She understood Rosa's sor-row and anger better than he ever could.

◆ ◆ ◆

IN TOTTENVILLE THEY wasted no time wandering through the vil-lage or finding a meal but went straight to Mr. Malone. The old man's face broke into a wide smile at the sight of them, but this time he didn't try to communicate. Instead he picked up a short rod and struck a bell that hung over his head. Before Jack could make sense of it, Mr. Malone's son stuck his head out of a workroom of some kind, his hands full of tack.

"On my way!"

Anna looked at Jack with something like bemused resignation, and she was right; because they had been here before, the Malones felt obliged to inquire about their journey, their health, their newly married state, their feelings on the weather as it had been in the city and what might be to come here, and then in great detail about the girls, who Jack introduced at their wards.

"Italian," said the younger Malone. "I never would have guessed it."

Jack bit back what he might have said: *Imagine our surprise to get Italian orphans who aren't filthy and diseased!* Because he saw the confusion on the man's face, his inability to reconcile the little girls he saw before him with what he had heard and read about Italian immigrant hordes ruining the country.

It was Anna's hand on his arm that made him pull himself together and end the conversation with a curt nod.

One thing the Malones didn't ask, to Jack's relief, was their destination. When they finally climbed into the little rig, with the four of them squeezed together in on one seat, he set the placid old piebald mare off at a quick trot. Anna, busy with the girls, didn't look up at him until they were on the road north toward Mount Loretto, and Jack was glad. She hadn't seen the odd pale rectangle on the side of a building where a sign had been taken down, but Jack remembered it.

EAMON MULLEN
GENERAL BLACKSMITHING, HORSESHOEING,
PLOW AND WOODWORK

Maybe the sign was being repainted, he told himself. Maybe Mullen had moved his business to a bigger space somewhere else in Tottenville. And maybe, he had to deal with the possibility, what he had interpreted as a turn in their luck was nothing more than the eye of the storm.

◆ ◆ ◆

SOMETHING WAS WRONG with Jack, something other than young Michael Malone's careless insult. Anna saw it in the set of his jaw, in the line of his back. The girls sensed it too, because they were quiet. They were hardly out of town when Lia climbed into Anna's lap, not looking forward but pressing her face to Anna's shoulder.

Then he pulled to the side of the road under a stand of oak trees and tried to smile.

"I need a minute." Jack secured the reins and jumped down, trotting back the way they had come to disappear behind a stand of bushes.

The girls seemed almost to relax, assuming, as most people would, that Jack's distracted mood and sudden leaving had to do with nature's call. But Anna knew somehow that it was something else entirely. He had walked off to gather his thoughts and his courage, because he knew something, had heard or seen something that she had not.

She wanted to go talk to him, but the girls would be terrified to be left alone even for a few moments in this strange landscape of fields and pastures and orchards with so much at stake just a few minutes away. For years she had trained to be able to make fast decisions in difficult situations. With a scalpel in her hand some part of her mind took over, made decisions and acted. But this was foreign to her, this kind of need, and she was at a loss.

Jack climbed back up onto the seat and took up the reins. He hesitated for a long moment and then he turned to the girls.

He said, "I have a feeling that the family we're going to see isn't going to be there. That they've gone away. I want you to be prepared for that possibility, both of you. Once we know whether I'm right, we can talk about what to do next."

It took considerable effort, but Anna held her questions back. When they turned onto the narrow lane that would take them to the little house near the beach, her stomach gave a lurch and climbed into her throat. The girls looked stunned, like children who have passed beyond fear to a protective numbness.

In the first few seconds it seemed that Jack had been wrong. The house wasn't deserted; the front door stood ajar, and the sound of someone chopping wood came from somewhere behind it.

Jack looked at Rosa and then at Lia, his expression not exactly grave, but solemn. He said, "Wait here. Mind me now, you need to wait here." Then he squeezed Anna's hand and was gone.

• ◆ •

WHEN JACK JOINED the police department one of the first and hardest lessons, one that he still struggled with, was something obvious. In his case, at least, anger was far harder to manage than a gun. As he walked toward the front door of the cottage, he reminded himself that he was not here as a police officer. He had no right to ask questions, much less demand answers. That thought was still in his mind when a woman came to the door.

Two facts presented themselves immediately. This small, dark-haired woman was close to giving birth—her hands were folded across the great expanse of her belly—and she was not Mrs. Mullen.

Jack took off his hat and inclined his head politely. "Ma'am," he said. "We're looking for the Mullen family. Have I got the right house?"

It was the right house, without question, but the Mullen family had moved away. In her uncertain English the lady of the house explained to him that her husband had bought the house and the business from Mr. Mullen, who had moved away a week ago with his family.

"I don't know where they went," she said, and seemed to be searching for words. "Would you like to come in, you and your family?" She stepped back and opened the door in a welcoming gesture. Behind him Jack heard a scuffle and Rosa's voice, raised in protest.

He did not want to bother these people, but he could see no other way to convince Rosa of the truth.

As she arrived at his side, breathless, trembling, he said, "Rosa, this lady has invited us in to talk for a few minutes." In Italian he added, "If you can't mind your manners, you'll have to wait outside."

The truculent look on her face did not escape him.

• ◆ •

MAGDA AND ISTVAN Szabó were Hungarian immigrants who had come to the States five years earlier and finally saved enough money to buy a place of their own.

With Lia on her lap Anna spoke to Mr. Szabó, who had come in to talk with them because his English was very good. His gaze kept shifting to Rosa, who stood stiffly by the door with Jack.

It was obvious that nothing but the truth would do in this situation. She said, "Mr. Szabó, I realize this is very odd, but if I could just explain—"

Drawing on all the skills honed in years of recounting patient histories during rounds, she told the story of the four Russo children, how they had come to Manhattan, and the loss of the boys. He held up a hand only when he wanted her to pause long enough so he could translate for his wife.

Anna fixed her gaze on Mrs. Szabó. She had a kind face and an open expression, where her husband was more reserved.

"We believe that the Mullens adopted Vittorio," Anna finished. "And his sisters want so much to see him, we couldn't keep the truth from them any longer."

The Szabós were talking, a hushed conversation that was impossible to interpret. Anna was paying such close attention that Lia had slipped from her lap before she realized what was happening. She walked toward Mrs. Szabó, her eyes as big as silver dollars.

"May I see my brother? He's so little"—a small sharp hiccup escaped her—"*deve avere molto paura*."

Rosa spoke up, her voice strained. "She says he must be very afraid."

The room was suddenly so still that Anna could hear the far-off crash of waves on the beach. In the quiet Rosa came forward and put an arm around her sister. They looked so much alike, and were so different in the way they saw the world. She wondered if Rosa might have been a child more like her sister if circumstance hadn't demanded the impossible of her.

Mrs. Szabó was clearly moved by the two girls. She looked very near to tears.

"I am very sorry, but I don't know your brother. I saw him once, a very beautiful boy. A happy boy. But he moved away with his—"

She looked to her husband. *"Az új családja?"*

"His new family," he supplied.

"Yes, his new family. We don't know where they went. I'm very sorry that we can't help you. But maybe—"

Rosa's head came up sharply.

"Maybe if you talk to the priest—"

"Father McKinnawae?" Jack asked.

"Yes. Father McKinnawae," she said. "At Mount Loretto. Maybe he can help you."

• • •

As THEY CAME over the hillside to see the mission spread out before them, it seemed to Anna that quite a lot of progress had been made since their last visit. On the day they got married, she reminded herself. Only one of the buildings looked to be finished, its chimney putting out a long dark streak of smoke. The two largest buildings were far from finished, but today there was no sign of monks or workmen of any kind. She wondered if they had run out of supplies or volunteers or both. It would be many months before any boys could be made at home here. And she really could not work up any interest. She would always associate this place with Vittorio's loss. Because he was lost. They went to see the priest because Rosa must see this through, but in Anna's mind there was no doubt: Vittorio would live his life as Timothy Mullen. She wished him happy and well.

Anna met Jack's eye over the girls' heads and understood that he had most probably reached the same conclusions she had come to. There would be time enough to talk about it, once they were back home again. What she had to do now was prepare herself for Father McKinnawae.

She had to keep her thoughts to herself, but the girls put question after question to Jack. He answered each question honestly: no, he didn't know when the orphans would be coming to live here; he thought that most of them must be at the mission in the city and that they would all be boys. Whether there would be room for girls as well at some point was another question he couldn't answer. He was sure there would be classrooms, and lessons, and chores. And mass, most probably every day.

If Vittorio might be here, with the priest?

Jack answered without hesitation. Vittorio was gone away with the Mullen family, who loved him and would care for him.

Anna wondered what the girls were imagining about the interview to come, if there had ever been opportunity for them to talk to a priest outside of religious services. Because she had spoken to this particular priest. She had told him about these girls who had survived so much, and in turn he had gone to the Mullens.

The letter Anna had written and rewritten had never been mailed. Or more to the point, it had found a different target. Anna had not been able to explain the whole series of events to herself until Margaret brought out Rosa's exercise book, every page filled to the margins with careful lettering.

Rosa had been eager to learn to read, and Margaret had worked with her every day. She was just far enough along that she could work out short, simple sentences. Mornings she would glare at the newspaper as if it were holding back secrets she was determined to discover. She would point out words she knew, and ask about others. And she did the work Margaret assigned her, and more, every day. One of her favorite things to do was to write out her own name, along with the names of all her family, father and mother and sister and both brothers.

"She's very diligent," Margaret said. "You see she filled this notebook in a week. I said she could use scrap paper from the bins until I had time to get her another one. I should have been more careful, but it never occurred to me—"

"You're not at fault," Anna said. "And neither is she. It's not the best way to resolve the situation, but it's done now. We'll have to make the best of it."

"I'm afraid I indulge her," Margaret went on anyway.

Jack shook his head at her. "She's curious, she wants to learn. It's not a matter of giving her more sweets than are good for her. I think the girls are fortunate that you have so much time to spend with them."

It was one of the kindest things Anna had ever heard him say, and it made her ashamed to have been so dismissive of Margaret.

◆　◆　◆

AND NOW HERE they were, about to confront Father McKinnawae. When Anna thought of him she saw the unapologetic dislike and disdain he felt for her. He had warned her not to test him, and that had not been an empty threat.

He came out to greet them before Jack had brought the rig to a stop. Anna's expression was grim, but the priest smiled broadly at her, his cheeks puffing up like pink pillows.

"Dr. Savard," he said, all polite good spirits. "How very good to see you again. I thought you might stop by."

For a split second Jack had the idea that Anna was going to punch the priest in the face, as hard as she possibly could. The image was so strong in his mind that he put a hand on her upper arm—and felt the flexing of her muscles.

He held out his other hand to the priest. "I'm Jack Mezzanotte, Dr. Savard's husband. And these are our wards, Rosa and Lia Russo."

McKinnawae had a firm handshake. He barely glanced at the girls before his gaze shifted back to Jack.

"And you are a doctor too?"

"He's a police detective." Rosa spoke up clearly, without hesitation, and with none of the deference Jack would have expected. Anna seemed to have lost her voice entirely but he could feel her tension, every nerve twanging.

McKinnawae said, "An Italian detective."

"Detective sergeant," Jack said.

One eyebrow shot up as if this news surprised him.

Jack had nothing against priests, in general. In his experience some of them were harmless, some meant to do good things but did just the opposite, a few managed to help, and even fewer took joy in raising hell out of bloody-mindedness, contempt for the world, and ego.

He would have guessed McKinnawae to be one of the better sort, given the amount of work that was going into putting together the refuge for orphans, but he saw now he had been mistaken. McKinnawae worked for the most vulnerable children, selflessly, endlessly, but at the same time he was closefisted, resentful, and protective of what he considered his own. Most of all, he didn't like women and wanted nothing to do with them. Anna's coming to his office had not won his cooperation; just the opposite. He wanted her to know that she had been foolish to try to outwit him. The Russo boys were not the point, as far as he was concerned.

Anna was saying, "You told me that you would be glad to talk to Vittorio Russo's sisters, and here they are."

There was a jerking at the corner of his mouth. "Dr. Savard, did I not tell you that I have no knowledge of the Vittorio Russo you're looking for? I'm sorry I can't be of any help at all. Girls, the best you can do is to pray for your brother's soul. He was baptized, I'm sure, and so you can think of him in heaven with your parents."

Lia's mouth hung open, but Jack doubted she would have been able to produce a single word. Rosa stepped a little in front of her sister and said, "Yes, he was baptized. But he's not in heaven. He went away with a family—" She looked over her shoulder as if she could see the house where the Mullens had lived. "And you know where he is, don't you."

The complacent smile froze for the briefest moment, and then McKinnawae's gaze focused not on Anna, but Jack.

"In my experience, Italian children are polite and respectful to their priests. I would have expected better."

"All right," Jack said, working hard to keep his tone neutral. "That's enough. Anna, please take the girls for a walk. I need a half hour here, and then we'll be on our way."

Rosa looked at him with a calm acceptance that he found harder to bear than tears would have been. In Italian she said, "He doesn't care. He won't help."

She walked away beside Anna without looking back.

38

Elise fell asleep waiting for Anna and Jack to get back from Staten Island, and woke Sunday to a drizzling rain. The girls were in the hall talking to Margaret and Mrs. Lee.

Rosa's tone was matter-of-fact. "I'm not going to church. Not until my brothers are found and maybe not then. Tonino keeps asking me in my dreams why we are staying away, and I tell him about that priest who stole Vittorio."

Elise drew in a surprised breath, and held it so as to hear what came next.

"But Lia can go if she likes," Rosa said.

"No." Lia said. "I won't go too."

"You won't go either," Margaret corrected.

"That too. Either," said Lia.

"Well, then," Mrs. Lee said, all business. "That's not a little thing, but we'll talk about it later today. We'll be off, Mr. Lee and me. You girls get the table set for Sunday dinner before we get back. And no peeking at the roast, we don't need any more burnt fingers."

Lia said, "Can I go over to Weeds to play with Skidder?"

"Not until you've had your breakfast," Margaret said. "Let's go do that now."

With that Elise realized the time; she was running very late and would have to skip breakfast and hearing about Staten Island, too. Whatever had happened yesterday had not paralyzed the girls with anger or sorrow, and that would have to be enough for the moment.

As she half trotted, half walked to the hospital juggling an open umbrella, her satchel, and the banana Mrs. Quinlan had pressed into her hand in lieu of a proper breakfast, she thought back to herself at

Rosa's age, and what would have happened if she had announced she was leaving the Church.

Her mother and aunts would have laughed at such an announcement. If she had persisted, there would have been more serious repercussions that had to do with the paddle that hung on the pantry wall. And after that?

The confessional, to start. She would have to explain herself to Father Lamontagne. The idea was odd enough to make her smile. Father Lamontagne had been a sweet old man who had lived a long and difficult life. He would have listened patiently, and then changed her mind for her in the gentlest but most persistent way.

Not that leaving the Church would have ever occurred to her to start with. She had liked going to mass; the Church itself felt like an extension of home.

Now Rosa had announced—what? A rejection of the Church, or God, or both? Somehow she couldn't imagine Mrs. Quinlan or anyone else in the household of freethinkers taking exception. They would ask questions, certainly, but disapproval seemed as unlikely as a whipping.

On the short walk to the hospital Elise passed four different churches: Presbyterian, Baptist, Dutch Reformed, Episcopal, and right next to the New Amsterdam, St. Mark's. She knew where to find a Friends' Meeting House, and not far from there, Scotch Presbyterian, Lutheran, and a Jewish synagogue. There were at least fifteen different Catholic parishes in the city, each with church and chapel, rectory, convent, and often a school, as well. New York was crowded with places to worship, but in the house on Waverly Place only the Lees and Margaret went to church with any regularity, and not to the same church, either.

The biggest surprise thus far—and she must believe there were more to come—was that Bambina and Celestina went to temple once a month or so. Every other Italian Elise had ever known or heard about was Catholic—as Catholic as the pope—but half the Mezzanottes were Jewish, while others seemed to be nothing at all.

She should have been shocked and worried about her own immortal soul in this hotbed of cheerful heretics; a year ago she likely would have had just that reaction. Now nothing seemed so simple. She had no basis on which to make judgments about the Mezzanottes. She hoped they would do as much for her.

◆ ◆ ◆

AT HALF PAST five Jack slipped out of bed, grabbed his clothes, and dressed in the hall, determined to let Anna sleep on. Despite a long day of traveling in damp clothes while dealing with distraught children, she had had a restless night. It was after three when she finally slipped into a deep sleep. He knew, because he hadn't slept well himself, aware of every chime of the mantel clock from the parlor.

John McKinnawae had robbed them both of a peaceful night's sleep, and Jack was sure there would be more such nights. Then at six in the morning a runner from Mulberry Street had knocked on the door with a message. The chief was calling a meeting at seven about the Campbell and associated cases. Associated cases. They were in for it now.

◆ ◆ ◆

FOUR DETECTIVES AND two patrolmen were gathered in Chief Baker's office, including Oscar and himself. Jack counted four case files spread out on the table and knew the names on the labels without looking: Janine Campbell, Abigail Liljeström, Eula Schmitt, and Irina Svetlova. More folders sat in a pile front of Oscar, the looks of which filled Jack with dread.

"I've got three more likelies and one possible," Oscar was saying.

One by one he went over the cases that fit the profile, all of them ferreted out of death certificates going back six months. Mariella Luna, Esther Fromm, Jenny House, and the one uncertain case, a Jane Doe. All of them had died of peritonitis following an illegal abortion, and all of them had died hard.

The three who had been identified were married to successful men with substantial incomes; they had well-appointed homes, servants, abundant and expensive wardrobes, and somewhere between two and six healthy, well cared-for children. They were all between twenty-five and thirty-five years old. Jenny House had died at her home on Gramercy Park; Esther Fromm and Mariella Luna, both from out of town, had died in rooms at the Astor and Grand Union hotels. Jane Doe had been dead on arrival at Women's Hospital.

Baker said, "We'll need new postmortems on all of them. Sainsbury, get going on the exhumations. I want shovels in the ground no later than noon. Maroney, do you have a forensic specialist in mind?"

"Nicholas Lambert at Bellevue, if he's willing. That will save some time, as he did the Liljeström autopsy and we won't have to bring the remains back from Buffalo. And he's good."

"Go talk to him today. We have to get moving on this before the newspapers pick it up. Larkin, what about the letter?"

Michael Larkin was the youngest detective in the room, but he was not looking his age. His eyes were red-rimmed and bloodshot, his skin mottled and doughy. The thing was, he might be fighting a hangover complete with sour stomach and a headache, but his voice and hands were steady. It was nearly impossible to knock a Larkin down; even harder to keep him there.

"I've got a draft." He slid a piece of paper down the table toward Baker, who took it up and held it at arm's length to read. In ten seconds flat he was scowling at the man who had written it.

"Christ on the bloody cross, Larkin, do you know any lady who talks like this?" He cleared his throat and read. "'I write to you in utter despair, a foolish girl taken in by the promises of a rake.' Reading penny dreadfuls in your time off, Larkin?"

Oscar handed Baker another piece of paper. "Maybe this will work."

This time the captain read aloud from the start. ". . . regard to your advertisement . . . if your medical practice . . . hygienic, modern . . . prepared to pay a premium . . . respond with particulars."

He grunted. "That's more like it. Larkin, get it postmarked first thing tomorrow and into the right post office box. Then set up a rotation to stake out the lobby. I want to hear from you every couple hours."

• • •

TURNING THE RIG north on Second Avenue toward Bellevue, Jack said, "I could have used you yesterday, talking to that priest."

Oscar had been brought up Catholic and still went to mass when he was sober enough on a Sunday morning. He had no illusions about priests and was generally hard to shock, but he frowned when Jack told him about the Mullens and McKinnawae.

"I don't know what I was expecting," Jack said. "But it didn't occur to me that he could make the whole family disappear, like a magician's rabbit into a hat."

The muscles in Oscar's jaw began to tick and roll, but his tone was even. "A trickster of the first order, and him not even a Jesuit. I'm sorry for the girls, but it's a miracle you got as close as you did. I don't suppose Rosa sees it that way."

They rode along in silence for a while. Jack glanced at his partner and said, "Lia is calling me uncle and Anna auntie."

"And Rosa?"

"Don't know if she is even talking to us," Jack said. "Remains to be seen."

◆ ◆ ◆

ANNA WOKE IN stages, like a swimmer drifting toward land until the water itself pushed her out into the waking world.

Three things came to her all at once: she was alone in bed in a quiet house, which meant that Jack had left for Mulberry Street without waking her, the rotter; the winds that had battered them all Saturday had subsided, but left behind a hypnotic rain as soft and warm as new milk; and she had a cold.

She barely got the handkerchief out from beneath her pillow before she produced a triplet of wet sneezes.

After a day of travel in damp clothes the head cold was no surprise, but it was something of a catastrophe in purely practical terms. Until her symptoms had gone, she could not see patients or even step foot in the hospital. A head cold was not a real threat to an otherwise healthy, well-nourished person, but it could be the end of someone whose health was already compromised. And she hated colds, the fuzziness of mind and head, the impertinence of a body that would not obey simple commands. The oddest thoughts came to her when she had a cold.

She hoped the girls had escaped this, and somehow knew that she needn't worry about Jack. Lying in the bed they shared, half-asleep, sniffling, she willed him healthy and untouched while he did whatever detective sergeants did on a Sunday morning.

Now she had to get up and talk to the girls. To pretend yesterday was just a bad dream would only make things worse. But it would not be easy.

Dressed and armed with three fresh handkerchiefs, she made her way through the quiet house toward the kitchen and heard the distinct rhythm of Mrs. Cabot's Down East accent: clipped in some places, r-sounds swallowed whole, while in others words were stretched to the breaking point and tacked back together. There was some debate going on about Skidder's breakfast.

"Lia, my dear, no honey for Skidder."

"Why?" Lia, sincerely curious, as ever.

"Because he's already sweet enough."

Anna smiled, imagining the look on Lia's face as she puzzled this through. Then she got right to the crux of the matter.

"Am I sweet enough?"

"You are mighty sweet but maybe you could do with a little more honey. Wipe your nose, dear—but on your hankie."

The girls sneezed, one after the other. Anna supposed it was inevitable.

Mrs. Cabot was saying, "Now, what were you telling me about that priest fella on the island?"

Rosa said, "I don't want to talk about him."

"I do," said Lia, sniffing. "He has a red face, and white hair, and he smiles a lot but he's mean. He didn't like us. He wouldn't tell us where he hid our little brother."

Anna opened the door and all three of them turned toward her. Lia's thoughtful expression gave away to something else, comfort or relief or some combination of the two. Anna's throat constricted, but she forced herself to breathe and then to smile.

Rosa's expression was far more solemn, but yesterday's open hostility was gone.

"Welcome to my infirmary," Mrs. Cabot said. "Dr. Savard, your nose is as red as a lobster."

"Lob-stah!" Lia echoed, and sneezed.

"Sit down, I've got dry toast and my special fever tea with honey and lemon."

It took some time to negotiate breakfast—Anna gave up on the idea of coffee in the face of Mrs. Cabot's stern disapproval—but in the end she sat across from the girls with a cup of tea in her hands and a plate of dry toast between them. She had wanted Jack here for this conversation, but now it seemed that this was the better way. It was something she needed to do on her own, without worry about what he was hearing or what he thought about it.

"We should talk about Vittorio," she said. "And about Tonino, too, and your parents. We have to tell stories about the people we love who go away. It's the best way to hold on to them. Don't you think, Mrs. Cabot?"

"A-yuh," Mrs. Cabot said with a quiet smile. "No better way."

"You don't talk about your people," Rosa said. "Auntie Margaret says you never do."

"I didn't, that's true. But I think it was a mistake not to. We should tell the stories and then write them down."

"I don't know where to start," Lia said.

"We can take turns," Anna said. "I'll tell you first about the summer I was three years old, when my parents died."

"Three is too little to remember," Rosa said, with a certain disdain.

"It is too little," Anna agreed. "And I can't say what I really remember and what I only remember because Aunt Quinlan told me the story. But I remember how I felt, and that's the important part."

Her voice was calm and without tremor, but Lia got up from playing with Skidder to crawl into her lap. With the little girl's solid weight in her arms, Anna sent herself back to the summer when everything changed.

◆ ◆ ◆

DR. LAMBERT WAS in the middle of a postmortem when they got to Bellevue, so they went outside to wait in air that smelled of recent rain and the sea.

Jack had almost gotten used to the smells that clung to Anna's clothes when she came home from the New Amsterdam—strong soap and carbolic, denatured alcohol, all with an undercurrent of blood and bile. Bellevue had all that times ten because they took anyone who came to them, men and women and children, the sickest and poorest and least likely to survive. The outdoor poor.

Outside, leaning against a wall warmed by the sun, Jack watched as people came and went out a side entrance favored by staff. A crowd of younger men, students or interns, appeared, looking like a company of soldiers fresh from the battlefield. Jack caught sight of a familiar face just as Oscar saw him too.

"Dr. Graham!"

Neill Graham's head jerked around toward them, his expression less than friendly.

"He doesn't recognize us," Jack said.

"Sure he does. Look at him trying to make a pretty face. He may just manage it by the time he gets over here."

Jack studied the younger man, seeing exhaustion and irritation. Medical students worked impossible hours for little pay; in the same situation Jack knew that he would be less than sociable. He could tolerate a bad mood, but there was something sour in Graham's expression.

"Detective Sergeants." Graham stood in front of them but left his hands in the pockets of his very grimy tunic, and rocked back on his heels. "I don't think you want to be shaking my hand today. Not until I've soaked it in carbolic for a couple hours."

"Hard shift?" Oscar asked

He blew out a breath. "Long. Forty-eight hours, and maybe two hours' sleep. Only two surgeries I was allowed in on because in case you didn't know, this place"—he jerked his chin toward the hospital—"is staffed to the roof with students who can buy preference. Today there was a Caesarean—only three done last year in the whole city, but instead of that I was stuck dealing with the usual garbage that comes through this place. People who don't have the sense God gave an ant, real deviants."

Oscar said, "That bad. Did you lose a patient?"

"No. The work stinks, but I could handle it with my eyes closed. Some of the patients would be better off dead, to my way of thinking. You two know what it's like dealing with whores."

You couldn't be a cop and take offense at plain speech, not if you wanted to get anything done. Conversation in the station house was often far worse, but there was something in the way Graham used the word *whore* with a lip-curling disgust.

He was saying, "I'll be glad to see the last of this place." He turned his head to scan the hospital windows.

"You headed someplace else?" Oscar's tone was light, friendly, encouraging.

"There's a surgery position opening up at Women's. That place is like a palace compared to this cesspool."

Oscar said, "Competition must be stiff."

Graham's whole face contorted. "That doesn't worry me. You know I've got twice as many hours in the operating room as anybody else who's applying. They know what I'm worth at Women's. Somebody from the staff—I won't name names—told me. He said I had a brilliant career ahead of me. Women's is my next stop, and then who knows? London, Paris, Rome." His smile broadened, full of satisfaction.

"And no poor people at Women's," Jack observed.

"They've got a charity ward," Graham said, a little insulted. "But there are only so many beds and that means you can pick and choose among the ones who come begging and only take the interesting cases. This place—" He glanced up at the hospital. "The scum of the earth."

"And still you managed to get good training," Oscar said.

Graham shot him a suspicious look but relaxed when he saw nothing but mild curiosity in Oscar's expression.

"There's work enough, but I hate having my time wasted on the cases that come in here. Truth be told, I don't much like examining any woman—any honest surgeon will tell you that. But with whores, it's like rooting around in a bucket of filth, up to the wrist in sludge. The last one I saw today, she looked forty but I doubt she was more than twenty, the worst case of the clap I've ever seen, and she was still working, still spreading her legs for coin. Imagine the degenerate who would pay for the privilege."

"Huh," Jack said. "Correct me if I'm wrong, but you'll be examining females at Women's Hospital too."

He jerked a shoulder. "They won't be crawling with lice and crabs. It's the best place in the country—maybe in the world—for the kind of surgery that interests me. The only thing that interests me. And mostly I'll be operating, anyway. And doing research. Some of the most important advances in the field come out of Women's. I've got a few ideas. You never know, I may end up revolutionizing surgery."

Jack said, "Sounds like you've got your career planned."

Graham gave a soft laugh, his mouth working like a twist of gristle. "There's always room at the top, as my mother used to say. I put in forty-eight hours here without sleep, easy as falling off a log."

His head swung toward Jack and the expression he normally wore—alert, sharply observant, constrained by respect and convention—was back in place.

"So what brings the best of the New York Police Department detective squad to Bellevue on a damp Sunday morning?"

Oscar produced his widest, least sincere smile. "Ask me no questions and I'll tell you no lies."

"Not another case like the Campbell woman."

"Why would you think that?" Jack said.

He shrugged. "Can't think of much other than murder that would bring you up here. It's not like you have room in the jails for all the rutting drunkards we see here. Inbred idiots." Graham hesitated, waited for some kind of response, and then cleared his throat.

"Nice to see you again, I've got some sleeping to catch up on."

"Give Mrs. Jennings our regards," Oscar said.

Neill Graham studied Oscar for a moment, nodded, and walked away.

◆ ◆ ◆

ON THE WAY to Nicholas Lambert's office Oscar said, "The little shit. And there he's been under our noses the whole time."

Jack was thinking the same thing. "He made my skin crawl. You like him for the Campbell case, then."

"To my mind it was as good as a confession."

"There's still the pesky matter of evidence."

Oscar shrugged that fact away. "He hates women. Hates examining them but he wants to spend a career cutting them open. He's a braggart of the first order, the kind who thinks he can do anything. To listen to him there was never a more talented doctor put on earth and everybody recognizes him for a genius, except when they're duping him out of surgeries that should be his. He can work two days without a nap and he's put out that he couldn't get more than two hours last night. He can't keep track of his lies. And don't forget, Jack my boy, he assisted in the emergency surgery on Janine Campbell. He works an ambulance a couple days a week. That's worth looking into, at least."

Jack remembered Anna talking about that at the inquest, and he remembered the way Campbell had described her when he testified. In sober but complimentary terms. Now he wondered if that had all been an act.

"If it was him who did Campbell, he found an unusual way to return to the scene of the crime without raising suspicions," Jack said.

"We should have thought of it," Oscar said. "Mrs. Stone wasn't in the bedroom when he went in to examine Janine Campbell. Maybe she recognized him, but we'll never know now. And who but a surgeon can take a knife to a woman, do his worst, and get away with it?"

"He was sizing us up," Jack said. "We'll have to be careful not to scare him off. He could disappear and start all over someplace else."

"Oh, no," Oscar said. "I'm not having that. I won't be happy until he steps on that trapdoor and falls straight into Satan's loving arms."

◆　◆　◆

AS THEY HEADED downstairs to Lambert's office, it was like walking through an invisible curtain into a swamp, the air both cooler and almost dense enough to eat.

"Neill Graham," Oscar muttered. "Putting his hands on women." He shook his head in disgust.

Nicholas Lambert was a wiry, athletic fifty-year-old with a full head of dark hair and a short-cropped beard to match. In stark contrast his complexion was very pale and as fine as a child's. Like Anna's, his hands were red and swollen.

"More than one good surgeon has given up practice because of dermatitis," Lambert said, with the slightest trace of an accent. He had been aware of Jack's study of his hands, but he hadn't taken offense. "An unfortunate but unavoidable side effect of the antiseptic method."

Oscar huffed, surprised. "Why antiseptic when you're cutting on the dead? What harm can you do?"

"That's not the issue," Lambert said. "Some diseases outlast death. The microorganisms that cause smallpox, for example."

"A dead man can give you smallpox?"

"Or cholera, or hepatitis. Other diseases too. The antiseptic methods are the first line of defense, and that's why my hands looked like boiled crabs. The odd thing is, I grew up on a dairy farm, and my father and brothers have hands that look only slightly more swollen and red than mine."

"My wife has the same problem," Jack said.

Lambert paused, a lifted brow indicating curiosity but an unwillingness to ask intrusive questions.

Maroney hooked a thumb in Jack's direction. "He married Anna Savard of the New Amsterdam."

"Ah." Lambert smiled, started to speak, and stopped. Started again, and cleared his throat. "Congratulations. Best wishes."

Jack nodded. "You haven't found a way around the dermatitis?"

"Fifty years ago they were experimenting with gloves made of sheep's cecum in Germany, but nothing came of that. Now with the vulcanization of rubber, things might move more quickly. Dr. Savard's hands are sensitive to carbolic, I take it. Before you leave, remind me to give you something for her to try. But I don't think you've come here to talk about dermatitis."

Jack said, "You did the Liljeström postmortem. Did you read about the Campbell case in the papers?"

Lambert leaned back, half sitting on the edge of his desk, his arms folded. "I did. And I wondered about the similarities. You've got more cases like those two?"

"More than a few, maybe," Oscar said. "But we need a forensic specialist to look at all the bodies. We're hoping you would be willing to do repeat postmortems on all of them, and right away, as soon as we get them exhumed."

Lambert bent over slightly, as if to study his shoes. When he looked up again his expression was somber.

"It's hard to imagine a lot of women dying like that."

"What we're hoping," Jack said, "is to keep it from happening again."

Lambert nodded. "I'll talk to the director and get permission. How much can I tell him?"

"Nothing," said Jack. "Except we've requested your help on some difficult cases. Nothing about any possible connection to the Campbell or Liljeström deaths."

"Who suggested me, if I may ask?"

Oscar shifted uncomfortably, but Jack liked the question, and the man who had thought to ask it.

"Anna. She considers you the best forensic specialist in the city."

"Very good of her. But if these cases are connected you'll want an alienist to go over the evidence. A physician who can speak to the mind of the man who would act on such impulses."

Oscar said, "That would be our next step, after the postmortem reports. Can you start right away?"

"It would go faster if I had some assistance. I've got a couple of students who would be glad of the work."

Oscar frowned. "Better not to involve anybody else, if it can be avoided."

Thirty seconds passed by while Lambert continued to study his shoes. When he looked up, Jack saw that he was far too intelligent to be so easily misdirected.

"You've got a suspect here, at Bellevue?"

"No suspects yet," Jack said. "That's why we're in a hurry. Whoever's behind this, he won't stop until he's made to stop."

"I see your point. Most likely I can manage on my own, but if things do get out of hand, could I call on Dr. Savard?"

"Sure," Jack said. "I don't know what she'll say, but you can ask."

At the door Lambert hesitated. "May I ask a personal question?"

Jack tensed a little, but nodded.

"Is the other Dr. Savard—"

"Savard Verhoeven," Jack supplied.

"Thank you. I understand she's gone to Switzerland with her husband. Do you have any word on how Cap is doing?"

"He's stable," Jack said. "His spirits are good. Sophie is content."

"I think of him often," Lambert said. "His father and mine were good friends—we come from the same town in Flanders, and I liked him. If you have the opportunity, please send my regards and best wishes."

◆　◆　◆

ON THE WAY back to Mulberry Street, Oscar watched Jack for about ten seconds too long.

"What?"

"You're lucky you got to Anna before he did. He's a doctor, a friend of a close friend. No hair up his ass about women doctors. Polite, intelligent, and he likes her. Did you see the way he smiled when her name came up?"

Jack made a sound in his throat that was enough of an answer, even for Oscar. His partner took a cigar from his pocket, bit off the end, and spat it over the side of the rig into the street. Grinning the whole time.

⋄ ⋄ ⋄

ELISE WAS IN the garden when Jack came through the back gate, and for once there was no sign of the little girls.

"You're the only one who escaped Staten Island without a head cold," she told him. "The girls are confined to their beds for the day, and none too happy about it."

"How does Rosa seem to you?" he asked.

Elise lifted a shoulder. "Some of the fight has gone out of her. It makes life easier but it's sad too, to see such resignation in a little girl."

"I'm wondering if she's relieved. Not that she'd admit to it, or even recognize it," he said. "But she did something astounding, almost unheard of. Even if the end result was not what we hoped for, she should be proud of herself."

"She should," Elise agreed. "But she can't, right now. She needs time. Did you realize that Anna has been confined to bed, too? Mrs. Cabot has got her boxed in."

"No escape attempts?"

"Not yet, but you'd better hurry."

⋄ ⋄ ⋄

HE TOOK OFF his shoes and went upstairs in his stocking feet, meaning to be thoughtful but hoping to fail, in a small way. And Anna didn't disappoint, calling out as soon as he reached the upstairs hall.

"Mezzanotte." Her voice cracked and wobbled. "Stop tiptoeing around and come in here."

At the foot of the bed he took stock.

"You're losing your voice and that means for once I have the advantage. I might even win an argument."

Her expression softened, and then she laughed, a soundless huffing.

"Sleep," he said. "We can talk later."

"I've been sleeping most of the day. Sit down and tell me about your meeting this morning."

She stared at him until he gave in with a sigh and sat down on the edge of the bed.

"Not so close." She pointed to the chairs by the hearth. "Sit over there."

He dragged the chair closer to the bed, obeying and not obeying. Sitting down, he remembered the tin in his pocket and retrieved it.

"What's that?"

"Nicholas Lambert gave it to me for you, for your hands. For dermatitis."

"Why would you be talking to Nicholas Lambert about my dermatitis? And when was this?"

"Earlier today. Because he was talking about his own, and so I mentioned it."

She curled her fingers in a hand-it-over gesture, but he shook his head. "It can wait until you're feeling better."

"Don't coddle me. Tell me about this meeting with Lambert. What did you need to talk to him about? Oh, wait. It's about the Campbell case, isn't it. Is it?"

So he told her.

•   •   •

AT FIRST IT seemed she hadn't understood him, but the color rose in her cheeks as if she had been slapped or insulted. Which, Jack supposed, she had been.

"Seven or eight women." She shook her head. "All like Janine Campbell. How are they similar?"

He gave her what she needed: described the overlapping circumstances, age and marital status, social standing, childbearing history, autopsy findings.

"He won't have to redo the Campbell or Liljeström postmortems, but the others he'll start with tomorrow. They've already started on the exhumations."

Anna leaned back against the pillows. "I can't grasp this. I can't believe something like this is really happening. Somewhere nearby there's a doctor or midwife or—I don't even know what to call such a person—who kills women because they don't want to have children."

"More children," Jack said. "All of them already had children."

"That's even worse, in some ways. A woman who wants to be finished with childbearing has no right to live." Her voice cracked.

He picked up a cup, half full, and handed it to her. For once she drank without wrinkling her nose. Then she let him smooth the sheets and adjust the blankets. All the time he wondered if he should mention Neill Graham, when he had so little concrete to offer.

Something in Graham's tone of voice, the way he turned his head, the curve of his mouth, the connections he made between *whore* and *woman* and *filth*. There was something very wrong with the man, but he would have to keep that to himself for a while longer, until he had more concrete evidence to offer this woman who was a scientist before she was anything else at all.

He sat with her while she drifted off to sleep. He was about to get up when she roused.

"If Janine Campbell was the first, that would mean that there was one victim a week for eight weeks. Did they all happen on the same day of the week?"

Even in the middle of this god-awful case, she made him smile. "Did you think like a copper before I married you, or has that rubbed off?"

There was something almost shy about her smile, as if she wasn't sure this was a compliment, and if it was, whether she had earned it. But she waited for him to answer.

"We'll be more able to answer that question once Lambert is finished with the postmortems." And then he said, "Oscar thinks Lambert likes you. I think he's probably right."

Now her smile shifted to plain disbelief. "Don't be silly. He doesn't know me."

"Maybe he knows you better than you imagine."

"Oh, I see," Anna said, blinking sleepily. "This is that argument you think you can win because I'm losing my voice. And you know what, I'll let you have this little victory. As wrong as you are."

39

WITHOUT REAL WORK to do, unable to read because of a headache, awash in honey and lemon tea, Anna's mind kept running off to Staten Island. Certain pictures came to mind and wouldn't be banished: the priest's smug expression, satisfied because he had managed to keep the children apart; the way Rosa had stood looking out at the sea, her shoulders rounded in surrender; Lia's wet face and the small hiccups she couldn't control. Their brother was truly gone and out of reach. Rosa had failed to do that one thing her mother had asked of her; they had no hope of finding Vittorio, and still not even a hint about Tonino.

And Jack, standing there in the middle of the half-built orphan asylum.

In theory Anna understood that he was capable of violence, and committed violence in the course of his every day. She knew too that he was capable of controlling his temper, but she saw what it cost him to keep his anger in check.

When they drove away from Mount Loretto, McKinnawae was standing just where they left him, his wrists crossed at the small of his back, his expression blank. Sometime, not today, she would ask Jack what he had said to the priest. When she was sure she wanted to know.

When she wasn't thinking about Staten Island, it was the story she had told the girls on Sunday morning that plagued her. Now that she had opened that door, it wouldn't be closed again so easily. During the day she drifted in and out of memories distorted by time and sorrow. She wondered now if her memory was faulty or if she had managed to really tell the story, to be factual and even blunt. She somehow managed to tell the truth, but not the whole truth.

With Jack she would have to say out loud those things she had kept locked up inside herself for more than twenty years. The terrible things she had never spoken aloud, not to her aunt, or Sophie, or even with much clarity or precision, to herself.

◆   ◆   ◆

Mrs. Cabot fed Anna broth, soft-boiled eggs, tea and toast. When she wasn't bringing something to eat or refilling Anna's teacup, she was at hand with compresses. The smell of camphor oil on warmed flannel was comforting and effective both, wrapped around her throat. She sweated through the bedclothes and sheets and then sat by watching as Mrs. Cabot changed it all so that she could go back to sleep in a cool, sweet-smelling cocoon.

All day while Anna was being pampered, Jack slept on a narrow bed in a room down the hall. When she woke in the later afternoon, she forgot for a moment why she was in bed in the light of day, alone. Then she swallowed and the ache in her throat—much better already—reminded her.

Jack was gone again, back to Mulberry Street to work on the Campbell case. On Thursday she would go back to her own patients and students, to staff meetings and consultations. She glanced at the stack of journals waiting to be read, turned over, and went back to sleep. To dream about the family she had lost, and the one she might make, with Jack.

40

WHEN JACK CAME home at six on Tuesday morning he found a note on the banister where he could not possibly miss it: *Don't you dare go to sleep until you come talk to me.*

He went up the stairs at a trot, half expecting her to be asleep and wondering if waking her would make her more or less cranky. The simple truth was, he wanted some time with his wife, whatever her mood. The door stood open and showed him Anna sitting up in bed, reading. She hadn't heard him and so he stopped to watch her for a moment.

She had tied her hair back and out of her face with a wide silk ribbon not equal to the task of subduing the riot of waves and curls. While she read—a medical journal, of course—she wound a finger through a long loose curl, tugging. There was noise from the street and the flutter of the curtains in a fitful breeze, but all her attention was on her reading. If he could paint, Jack thought, this was the painting he would want: Anna in sunlight, reading.

During the day sometimes the memory of her came to him as unanticipated as a flash of lightning: Anna underneath him, shoulders thrown back, throat arched, her gaze fixed on his as he inched her closer and closer to letting go. It had never really been clear to him before Anna, but he understood now what an act of trust it was, what a gift she gave him when she surrendered. Now the simple sight of her made him forget the weariness etched into his bones. He shook himself out of his daydream, and she looked up.

"There you are. Come talk to me."

The ribbon in her hair was a deep copper color that somehow brought out the green in her hazel eyes. He would tell her so; he wanted to tell her so, but she would fluster and turn away.

He said, "You're better."

"Almost."

"You don't sound so much like a seventy-year-old cigar fiend."

First one dimple, then the other. "What a lovely image."

He laughed and sat down on the opposite side of the bed, canted to face her.

"I think I'll be able to go back to work on Thursday," she said. "That leaves two days, and I promise you, I'll go crazy if I have to stay in this bed the whole time."

She picked up a teacup from the bedside table, wrinkling her nose at the taste. "I've never understood the concept of laziness. Doing nothing all day is torture."

He said, "Maybe this will help," and put a folder on the bed, a little grubby on the edges, Oscar's handwriting scrambling over the surface like ants. "I thought you might want to see what Lambert came up with. I brought copies of the Liljeström and Campbell reports and the three he finished last night. He hopes to get the last three done by tomorrow morning."

The smile she gave him took his breath away. He wondered what else would make her smile like that. Diamonds? A trip to London? A hospital of her own?

"Anna."

She looked up at him.

"What do you like to do for fun?"

Confusion flashed across her face. "What do you mean, for fun?"

And there, exactly, was the heart of the matter. Anna's heart.

He said, "When you have an hour or a day to yourself and no deadlines and no place to be, when you can please yourself. What do you do?" And then: "This isn't an exam. There's no right answer."

"But there's always something that needs to be done."

"This is a hypothetical question. All work done, everything sorted, people looked after, no deadlines. A day free. What would you like to do with that time? What would make you happy?"

"I'm not sure I like this hypothetical question. Is there a trick in it somewhere?"

He leaned over and kissed her forehead, damp and cool. "No. Never mind, it was just a theory I was testing."

She was frowning at him, but he could almost see her attention drifting back to the folder in her hands. He had his answer: for fun, Anna liked to think about medicine. She liked many other things: coffee and high places, little girls laughing, flower gardens and the sea, but fun was a difficult concept. The stories she told about Sophie and Cap when they were children made him think she once had been able to be spontaneous, but somewhere along the way she had forgotten what it felt like to simply enjoy herself. Outside their bed, at least, she didn't seem to understand the concept.

She was reading the first report and had forgotten that he was standing there.

He tried to catch the yawn that overwhelmed him, and failed. Instead he got up and began to strip. Jacket, tie, collar. With one hand he started unbuttoning his shirt while with the other he dropped a suspender over a shoulder. Then he saw the look on her face. Astonishment, maybe. Amusement tinged with irritation.

"What?"

"Mezzanotte. You're standing in front of the windows. Open windows, curtains drawn back."

He waited, raised a brow.

"What would you say if I stood in the windows and stripped for the whole neighborhood to stare at? You'd be shocked, wouldn't you?"

"*Surprised* is more the word that comes to mind. Um, maybe also a little . . . engaged."

Her jaw dropped open and then closed with a click. "Don't change the subject. Explain to me this compulsion you have about walking naked around the house."

He draped his trousers over a chair back and came to sit on the bed, his legs stretched out before him and his hands folded over his middle.

"You know, Savard, for a credentialed doctor and surgeon you can be very prudish."

She bristled, which was what he was after. And then she surprised him.

"Did it ever occur to you that I don't want to share you?"

He let out a bark of a laugh and she poked him with one finger, hard.

"In some parts of the world women wear dark veils every day, regardless of the weather," she told him. "Because their husbands don't want other men looking at them or coveting them. It could work the other way around, too. In theory."

He ran a finger from her throat to the first button of her chemise, and she shivered.

"How do you know about the habits of veiled women in other parts of the world?"

She sighed in mock irritation and put the folder aside. Jack was quite pleased with her about this, but he didn't let it show.

"You still don't understand what kind of place the New Amsterdam is. Poor women come in all colors and shapes and fashions. I've treated women from places you've never heard of."

"You think?" He made a rake of his fingers and slid them through a strand of her hair. "I was always good at geography. Try me."

"Wait." She jumped up and ran down the hall to a room still filled with unpacked boxes. Because she was wearing a chemise and nothing else, he quite enjoyed this small interruption. She came back at a more measured pace, with a very large book in her arms. "My atlas. This way we can check each other." She dropped it on his lap.

"Careful," he said, shifting uncomfortably. "You are gambling with our progeny."

She climbed up on the bed and sat back on her heels, her hands folded in front of herself. "I had a patient from Abyssinia last year."

There was something compelling about Anna in a mood like this, absolutely determined to win a battle of wits. He'd draw it out as long as he could.

"If I'm not mistaken," he said, "Abyssinia borders on the Mediterranean Sea in the north and the Red Sea in the south. The Nile runs the whole length of it. You've got to do better than that to trip me up, Savard. I was always good at geography."

"And languages."

"That too." What he wanted to do was to get rid of the atlas she had taken back to hold in front of her like a warrior queen's shield and then tumble her, cold or no cold.

He said, "Does it have to be a country?"

"As opposed to what?" she wanted to know. "Continents?"

He shrugged. "States. Counties, shires. Provinces. Cities."

"Suit yourself. But stay within the realm of fair play."

"But first you go on until I miss one."

"Fine," she said, composing her expression. "Basutoland."

"Africa," Jack said. "If I had to guess, the far south, one of the British colonies probably. I'll guess near the Cape Colony."

She put on her most disinterested expression, tilted her head to one side.

"Khiva."

"Spell it."

"K-H-I-V-A."

"You had a patient from Khiva?"

"I'm setting the questions, Mezzanotte. Answer, or admit defeat."

"Don't know."

She narrowed her eyes at him. "I think you do."

That made him really laugh. "Why would I lie?"

"To stop the game. But you've missed a question and it's your turn to ask me."

He tugged on a strand of her hair. "If you insist. Brunei. Spelled B-R-U-N-E-I."

"*Ei* is the word for egg in German."

"That's your answer? Brunei is a—state or principality in Germany?"

"Not an answer. It was a guess."

"I'm feeling magnanimous. One more try."

She tapped her forehead with one knuckle. "Wait. It's coming to me. Brunei is a Swiss canton on the Austrian border."

He wrestled the book out of her hands and dropped it over the side of the bed, which made her squawk.

"That's a valuable atlas."

"I've got a bigger one. Lift up." He tugged at the hem of her chemise, caught beneath her knees.

She slapped his hands away. "No."

"No? Why not?"

"I need a reason?"

"I'll give you a reason," he said, tugging harder. "I'm rewarding you for that stunning example of a bluff. There's no Swiss canton called Brunei. Now are you going to lift up?"

"No." She was trying not to laugh.

"Well, then." He shrugged. "I'll have to peel you like a banana."

She didn't try very hard to stop him and the buttons were no challenge at all. The thin muslin slid off her shoulders and down her arms to stop at her elbows. With her breasts looking at him cheerfully Jack said, "I've got an idea for a different kind of geography quiz. And this one I'm pretty sure you'll win."

• • •

"TELL ME," ANNA said a half hour later, still trying to catch her breath. "Do people just stop doing this when the real heat starts next month?"

She felt him smiling, but he rolled to one side so the breeze from the window could wash over her. "Is that better?"

"I wasn't complaining. Do people stop in hot weather?"

He said, "Don't tell me you've forgotten the bathtub."

Anna giggled, and was surprised at herself for it.

Jack lifted his head to peek at her, gave a low sound of satisfaction, and dropped it again.

"So," he said. "You were telling me about men covering up women to ward off the interest of other men. You want me to wear a veil and robes?"

Anna took a journal from under her pillow and began to flap it like a fan. "I'm considering it." And then: "You know the strangest thing about being married?"

He lifted his head again, one brow raised.

"The playfulness. I never anticipated that, and now it makes me sad to think I might have gone my whole life without it. Did you expect it to be like this?"

"I hoped, is the way I'd put it."

"But how did you know to hope for it?"

"My parents," he said. "They are affectionate with each other, and my brothers have that too, with their wives. Each in his own way." He thought for a moment. "Some more successfully than others."

"Is that an Italian thing, do you think?"

He wiped a trickle of sweat from his brow. "I couldn't claim that. You remember Giacalone the tailor."

"Now that you remind me. 'Why did you kill your wife?' in Sicilian."

He grinned at her. "We are an emotional people, in all directions."

"From the stories I think my parents were affectionate," Anna said. She was quiet, but he could hear her thoughts spinning, and he understood.

"I have an idea."

"Not another geography quiz."

"Not right now. I'm wondering why you don't write down what you want to tell me that you're having such a hard time talking about."

Her surprise was genuine, and it struck him again how intelligent people could be robbed of all ability to think rationally when it came to matters of the heart.

"I can try," she said. She sat up. "Maybe today when I'm done reading the reports. You need to sleep now."

She tried to roll out of bed, but he stopped her.

"Stay with me ten minutes," he said.

With the light breeze from the window shifting over their damp skin, every nerve in his body still vibrating, he put his face to her scalp to draw in her scent, and fell asleep.

⋅ ⋅ ⋅

ANNA BEGAN TO drift off too, but five minutes later she sat straight up in bed with her hands pressed to her mouth.

"What?" Jack sat up too. "What?"

Her eyes were very round.

"Anna," he said firmly. "What is it? A nightmare?"

"My cervical cap," she said. "I completely forgot my cervical cap."

Her eyes raced back and forth as if she were searching for something. Then she drew a deep breath and held it for three heartbeats.

"I think it will be all right. The timing is good."

"Good? For what?"

"Ovulation. Or rather, the lack of it. I'm at the end of my cycle, not in the middle. Promise me we won't lose our heads like that again."

"Anna," he said, brushing a curl off her damp cheek. "We'll get carried away plenty, but I promise I'll ask about the cervical cap first."

She nodded, yawning. "Good," she said. "I should get up now or you really will catch my cold."

That made him laugh. He was still laughing when she slipped away, and left him to his dreams.

• • •

WHILE JACK SLEPT Anna read the postmortem reports, making notes and charts until she could no longer deny that there was a pattern. She had been so sure that Janine Campbell had tried to operate on herself, because she couldn't imagine anyone, man or woman, purposefully injuring another human being in such a blatantly cruel way. She was no stranger to violence, to gunshots and stabbings, beatings and burns. Men were endlessly inventive when it came to hurting women, she understood this; and still here was the evidence that she was neither as worldly or cynical as she had believed herself to be.

It all made her miss Sophie more acutely. There was so much to miss about her cousin: the sound of her voice, the way she hummed when she went about some household chore, her dry sense of humor. Anna missed all those things, but just now, sitting with the autopsy reports spread out in front of her, she missed Sophie's medical mind most. As diagnosticians they complemented each other, and Sophie would have had useful observations that Anna missed entirely.

• • •

IN THE AFTERNOON Jack got up to start his day, and Anna said as much to him. "As I have to do without Sophie, can I ask my cousin Amelie her opinion about the autopsies? She has more experience than Nicholas Lambert and I do, even put together. Something here might trigger a useful association."

Jack liked the idea, so she wrote out a case-by-case summary along with her own observations, and put it all in an envelope that she addressed to her cousin.

"Ask Ned to mail it for you," Jack had suggested.

Anna made a sound into her teacup that she hoped he would take for agreement. The truth was, she had a small plan. An innocent plan, really. One that was unlikely to turn up any new information and thus, she told herself, best kept to herself for the time being.

Except Elise came to call in the early evening, and Anna remembered there was another mind available to her. She lacked experience, but that might even work to their favor; clear-sighted and without prior assumptions, Elise might see something.

She debated with herself while Elise talked about what was going on at Roses: Mrs. Lee had declared the little girls to be healthy again, freeing them to bounce around the house and garden like frogs on a griddle for the entire afternoon. Margaret had predicted tears before bedtime and Aunt Quinlan had made a rude sound to that idea and called the girls to her.

"They wanted to come see you, but your aunt said they had to give you another day."

Anna wanted to hear the stories Elise had to tell, but her mind kept turning back to the reports.

Elise was saying, ". . . reading a story by Mark Twain that had everybody laughing." And then: "Are you tired, shall I go?"

"Not in the least. Really. How are things at the hospital?"

It was like offering water to a man in the desert. Elise told her about the surgeries she had observed in the last week, stopping to ask Anna questions and to consider the answers.

"Do you think you might want to take up surgery?"

Elise didn't have to think about her answer. "I'm more comfortable on the other end of things, working with the patients directly. I like the challenge of . . . figuring out what's really wrong. Diagnosis."

Anna said, "That was the impression I had, so I'm wondering if you might find it interesting to read these postmortem reports I've been looking at." She put her hand on the folder.

Elise's whole posture changed. "I've never seen a postmortem."

"That's why I thought you might be interested." She gestured to a chair. "Sit down, let me explain."

♦   ♦   ♦

ELISE TOOK AN hour to read through the reports, and then she sat looking out the window for a good while. The day hadn't yet begun to wane, though it was already eight. People were drawn outdoors by the light and the fine weather, the silky touch of a warm breeze.

Somewhere in the city was a man who had caused the deaths of at least five women and maybe as many as eight, without anyone taking notice. He went about his business without interference because he showed an unremarkable face to the world. Unless he walked down the street with a bloody knife in his hand, he could go on just as he had started: an apple that looked solid until you bit into it to find your mouth full of worms.

She turned to look across the room. Anna was sitting in the corner of a sofa, her cheek against her hand while she read. She sensed Elise looking at her, and met her eye.

"Thoughts?"

"A few observations, but I doubt they're significant."

"Go on. Don't leave anything out."

This felt like a recitation in the lecture hall. Elise organized her thoughts and started.

"This doctor—I think he must be a doctor, given some of these details—started to perform these operations with two goals in mind. He wanted the patient to die in terrible pain, but he wanted the death itself to take place out of his sight.

"With Mrs. Campbell he was too violent, and with Mrs. Liljeström he was so fast that he damaged an artery and she hemorrhaged immediately and bled to death. So neither case satisfied him. But in the third, fourth, and fifth cases he had settled on a procedure that gave him the result he wanted, and then he was exacting. The incisions are all in the fundus between the uterine horns and spaced evenly, like tick marks on a tally sheet: one, two, three. All of them are angled to cut into the intestines to a depth of about two inches. The instrument was not sterilized, and it might even have been purposefully contaminated. That seems likely, given how quickly the infection took hold and spread."

She looked up from the report in front of her. "Shall I go on? I have just a few more thoughts."

Anna said, "It's useful to hear someone else's interpretation, so please do."

"I was thinking of how a patient is prepared for surgery of this kind. If these women had marks on their arms and legs that indicated they had been forcibly restrained, would Dr. Lambert have noted that?"

Anna's brows rose sharply. "Why do you ask?"

"Because if there were no restraints, he must have used anesthesia. The natural impulse would be to twist away from the pain. I'll tell you what I think probably happened."

She got up and walked back and forth for a moment to gather her thoughts.

"I think this person must be someone who is very well established.

Or at least, has that appearance. He presents himself as a highly educated medical authority, with broad experience. He won't be very young, and his fees will be exorbitant. Do you happen to know—"

"Yes, the fees were very high, between two hundred and three hundred dollars."

It took a moment for Elise to make sense of such a large number.

"So these women would expect someone with a professional demeanor," she went on, more slowly. "Someone severe, and a little frightening, but not unkind. I'm not being clear. Do you know what I mean?"

"The strict but benevolent father," Anna said.

Elise was feeling a little more comfortable now, and she let the story come out in the way she imagined it.

"The patients will have high expectations. He must have some kind of medical office or clinic, treatment and operating rooms and the right equipment, everything in good working order and well maintained. A pleasant waiting room, and there must be an assistant or nurse, certainly. Someone to help the patients undress and dress again, and someone—maybe the same person?—to administer anesthesia.

"He does this horrible thing, but then he wants it out of his sight, because he's feeling vulnerable, maybe, or superstitious, or just guilty. He might be worried about evidence, I suppose. To get her out of his office as quickly as possible he will have to administer a good amount of laudanum, so that she's far away when she realizes that something is very wrong. There are other autopsy reports coming?"

"There will be," Anna said. "By the end of the day tomorrow. Would you like to see those when Jack brings them home?"

This question felt very much like a quiz. She wondered what Anna wanted to hear and decided that it didn't really matter. She told the truth. "I'd be very interested if I can be of help."

"I think you can," Anna said, and finally she produced a smile. "It's immodest of me, but I take some pride in how quickly you're learning to think like a doctor. And now I'm going to tell you a secret. Ready?"

"Um, yes."

"If you feel like you're being tested, you are. In medicine, at least. If that's the case, don't watch the person who asked the question, for two reasons. First, the more you look at that person for signs of approval, the less likely you are to see any facial expression at all. Second, don't be afraid of silence. It's an old trick to use silence as another kind of test. It's a way to determine how confident you are of your answers. If you don't know, say so. If you do know, say that, and stop talking."

Elise couldn't quite keep from smiling.

"Go on," Anna said. "Say what you're thinking."

"I'm thinking you remind me of some of the nuns."

Her mouth twitched at the corner. "Anyone in particular?"

Feeling a little light-headed, Elise stood up and walked to the door. She chanced a look at Anna, who had one brow raised.

Elise said, "Yes." And left the room without looking back over her shoulder.

41

DRESSED TO GO to the shops, Anna told Mrs. Cabot that she would be out for an hour.

Mrs. Cabot said, "Hmmm."

Anna said, "I'm just going to the post office." She might have tried to show her dimples, but the housekeeper had already proved herself immune.

Mrs. Cabot said, "Ned will be by any minute. I'll send him to the post office for you."

Anna didn't need Ned along on this outing. She wasn't entirely sure herself what she hoped to accomplish, a fact that would be immediately obvious when he started asking questions.

"I need the exercise," Anna said in a tone that any one of her students would recognize as: *enough.*

"I don't like it." Mrs. Cabot was more like Mrs. Lee every day.

"My cold is almost completely gone," Anna countered. "It's seventy-two degrees with a light breeze, the sun is shining. The fresh air will do me good."

•   •   •

IN FACT, THE air and the exercise did her a great deal of good. It was such a relief to be out of doors that for a few minutes Anna walked at a steady pace feeling nothing but the sun on her face and an odd contentment.

She turned onto Ninth Street and picked up her pace, picked up her skirts, and stepped around the worst of the rubbish in the street. The smell of ripe trash in the sun was unavoidable in New York in the summer. In fact, that meant summer had really arrived, in Anna's mind.

At the next corner she stopped, fishing in her pocket for coins for an old couple, the man holding out a tin cup. He smiled up at her with such obvious pleasure that she was taken aback for a moment.

"It's Dr. Anna." He peered up at her from the rolling platform that did the work of his missing legs; another veteran, one who had survived the worst and was still here, managing from day to day. He elbowed the woman next to him. "Sary, it's Dr. Anna. You looked after our grandson when his knee went bad in February. Pavel Zolowski, if you recall. Our girl Judy married a Polack, you see. You came out to tell us how things stood after you fixed Pavel up."

"I remember," Anna said. "Of course I remember. A very lively boy. How is he?"

"Right as right can be," said the old woman. Her eyes scanned back and forth, sightless but still seeking.

Anna would stay and listen if they wanted to tell her about their grandson, but she asked no intrusive questions; the poor had every right to their privacy and dignity. After a moment she put coins into the old woman's hand directly, smiled at her husband, and took her leave.

◆　◆　◆

IT WAS EASY to get turned around among the market stalls; the aisles were narrow and the crowds shifted in unpredictable ways that seemed designed to halt her progress. Most of the market sellers fell into one of two categories: the overly friendly, loud-voiced but engaging seducer—she passed one who was juggling spoons while he flirted with passersby—and the irascible, curt ones who always had the best merchandise.

She found her way to the little post office on West Tenth Street and mailed the letter to Amelie, then made a plan.

First, a turn around the market. She bought some boiled sweets, a few yards of silk gauze that she rolled into a sausage shape that fit into her reticule, a card of pretty carved shell buttons. She studied ducks hanging in the butcher's window and shoes in the cobbler's. On Greenwich a clerk walked back and forth in front of the milliner's shop, showing off the newest fashion and trying to draw passersby in for a look.

When she had made a full tour of the market Anna crossed Sixth Avenue again and went straight to Smithson's.

It had been a very long time since she had last been in the apothecary, but it seemed to Anna that nothing had changed: sets of scales hung from the ceiling, heavy wood counters and glass-fronted cabinets, a wall of small drawers with printed labels, jars arranged in neat rows on deep shelves. Even early on a summer day the gaslights were turned up high, to combat the gloomy, tunnel-like atmosphere of Sixth Avenue over-hung by the elevated train.

A younger man was busy topping up a china canister from a far less attractive stoneware crock. Anna couldn't see the names from where she stood, but the sweet-sharp tang of bitter orange—*Aurantii cortex*—hung in the air. There was mint, too, and less pleasant but familiar smells, some chemical, some botanical.

A woman came into the shop from a back room, and here was proof that things had indeed changed.

Not a clerk, by her demeanor or dress. Smithson had sons; this might be a daughter-in-law, or a granddaughter. She was neatly and very fashionably dressed in a suit of dark gray summer-weight wool with a tasteful bustle and a waist cinched down to no more than twenty inches. A black velvet band around her neck was held closed by a jet mourning brooch, small but very pretty.

"May I help you?"

"Yes, I hope so." Anna came closer. "I am trying to get in touch with a midwife who used to work in this neighborhood, but no one seems to know where she's gone. Do you keep in touch with local midwives?"

"We do. Within limitations."

Anna skated right by that conversational opening. "Her name is Amelie Savard."

The cool blue gaze focused on something behind Anna, and then came back to her.

"I'm sorry, I can't help you with that." She seemed to remember her manners just that easily. "I'm Nora Smithson. My husband is the apothecary."

"It's been a very long time since my last visit," Anna offered. "I was away in Europe for a good while."

The secret to successful lying, she had observed over the years, was to stick with just that part of the truth you needed.

Mrs. Smithson said, "You might remember my father-in-law. He retired last year. May I say without presuming—if you are in need of a midwife, there are a number who work with us who have excellent reputations. Would you like a copy of the list we keep?"

Mrs. Smithson smiled at her in the way women sometimes smiled at newly expectant mothers. Anna was glad to be spared the necessity of lying outright.

"I would. Yes, please."

"If I may suggest," she went on, her voice lowered. "You might consider a physician. There are specialists in women's health who also have excellent reputations, and attending privileges at one or more of the local hospitals. Medical science had advanced beyond midwifery."

"Ah." Anna hesitated, unsure how to proceed. "Would you have names—?"

This earned her a very sincere smile. "Of course. I'll give you both lists."

She turned away to take something out of a drawer; turning back, Anna saw that she had more to say, and was looking for an opening.

"Is something wrong?"

"No. Well, not exactly. May I ask, where did you hear the name Amelie Savard?"

This Anna had prepared for. "Neighbors are very kind with advice about greengrocers and butchers and dry goods stores, and I heard the name from an elderly lady who lives next door. She said that Mrs. Savard was an excellent midwife."

Mrs. Smithson was chewing delicately on her lower lip. "Does this neighbor have children?"

Anna paused, thinking, and decided to depart from the truth in this much. "I don't actually know. They would be middle-aged, if she does."

Another small nod. "Despite what you were told, Amelie Savard was not a midwife."

Anna raised a brow, as much invitation as she could trust herself to give.

"She was an abortionist in the model of Madame Restell. You have heard of Madame Restell? She lived in a mansion on Fifth Avenue."

"Ah," Anna said. "I haven't kept up with the laws."

"There are still abortionists about," Mrs. Smithson said. "But they don't come in here. They wouldn't dare. We alerted Mr. Comstock about the Savard woman, and she left town, just like that." She snapped her fingers.

It would not do to show emotion at this moment, no matter how blatant the lies and misrepresentations about her cousin. But neither could she leave it completely alone.

"I wonder what a lady does when she has too many children, and no way to feed them. Do the physicians on your list help in that kind of situation?"

Color rushed up Mrs. Smithson's face so quickly that Anna was taken aback.

"If you came here for that purpose, you have indeed come to the wrong apothecary. I suggest you leave now."

She reached out to take back the two sheets of paper in Anna's hands, but Anna saw her purpose and stepped back from the counter.

"You mistake me," she said, firmly. "I am not looking for an abortionist. I asked a question, and you have insulted me on that basis. Do you regularly abuse and condescend to your customers?"

"I—I—" A hand crept up to her face and then pressed into her mouth. Through her fingers she said, "I apologize. Most sincerely. I overreacted and I apologize."

Anna stayed where she was, her expression frozen.

"It's a sensitive subject. I do apologize, Mrs.—"

"Apology accepted." Anna made her voice as cold as she could. "And now I wish you a good day."

◆　◆　◆

ANNA HATED WISHING people a good day. She found it insipid and insincere, and never used the expression. Except just now. Because if she hadn't said *I wish you a good day* she would have said something far more colorful. She would have called Mrs. Smithson a lying, sanctimonious bitch. Anna said it now in her head.

Now at least she understood why Amelie had given up her midwifery practice. Hundreds and hundreds of children delivered safely, mothers sustained and kept healthy, and all that was left of the goodwill accumulated over those years was this one idea. If Mrs. Smithson had started talking about the color of Amelie's skin Anna would have called her a bitch, and worse.

As soon as she was around the corner and out of sight, she began to shake. Her hands trembled so that at first she couldn't even get the lists she had been given into her reticule. Then she stood quietly and made herself take three deep breaths.

When she looked up she saw the little coffeehouse that sat on the corner where Greenwich, Christopher, and Sixth Avenue converged opposite the Jefferson Market. Before the war she had come here sometimes with Uncle Quinlan. He liked the tobacconist on the next block, and so she would come along first thing and they would have breakfast together. As far as Anna knew, the place had no name, and never had. She sometimes heard it called the Jefferson Market coffeehouse or the blue coffeehouse, and sometimes the French coffeehouse, because the owners had moved down from Montreal and spoke French to each other.

The idea of going home to more chamomile tea was insupportable. Anna crossed Sixth Avenue once again, stepping quickly out of the way of a dray and then a cab, waiting while a stream of people descended from the elevated train platform. She thought again of home. She thought of coffee, and was newly resolved.

It was a small place, very busy, very plain. The wife took her order—coffee and toast—and didn't seem to recognize Anna, which was what she had hoped. It would be very unfortunate if Mrs. Smithson came in here at exactly the wrong moment and heard someone call her *Dr. Savard*.

The coffee was served in the French way, in a cup like a bowl, milky and slightly sweet. Anna sipped and watched people coming and going, up and down the stairs to the train, across Greenwich to the market, across Sixth to the shops. Two roundsmen came in and were greeted congenially; news and a few bad puns were traded. There was talk of a robbery on the next block, windows broken but little of worth taken. An old man found dead in Knucklebone Alley, another man had lost his job at the refinery, and a third, disgusted with the city, had packed up his family and moved to Ohio.

In the half hour she took to drink her coffee people came and went: more police, shoppers, a doctor she recognized from the Northern Dispensary just down the street. He didn't notice her and she couldn't remember his name.

Three finely dressed older men came in, all of them in shining good health, polished and buffed. One had a walking stick with a jewel embedded in its head. Anna guessed them to be judges from the district courthouse behind the market. They were sure of themselves in this less-than-first-class neighborhood, but then, who would dare rob a judge surrounded by police officers? Anna had known some very handy children who could have managed to pick such pockets, but the cane would be harder to nick.

She counted out fifteen cents for her toast and coffee, added a nickel for a tip, made sure of her reticule, and left, inclining her head to one of the judges, who bowed from the shoulders. As she left the coffeehouse another stream of people came down the stairs from the elevated train platform. Businessmen and lawyers, most likely on their way to one courtroom or another; an irritated middle-aged woman with three school-age boys, and at last one elderly man, moving slowly. His cane was well used and not for show. Step by step he felt his way down, his posture exacting.

There was something in his face that spoke of joint pain, barely kept within the bounds of what a person could tolerate and stay upright. Anna knew this look from her aunt and felt a swell of empathy. She wondered if his hips were the problem, or his knees, or both.

He must have felt her gaze, because his head came up and he looked at her directly. One corner of his mouth twitched and then curved downward, as if he had seen something objectionable. It was not surprising that he'd take offense; medicine had instilled some very bad habits, and one of them was staring at people trying to diagnose what might be wrong. She had been staring. She hesitated, wondering if she should speak to him or if that would make things worse. Turning away she felt him watching her, repaying her in kind.

A glance over her shoulder showed him still standing on the stairs, one hand on the banister. As she looked his frown deepened and he thumped with his cane, very deliberately. Once, twice, three times, like the gavel of a judge.

She put the old man out of her mind, and Mrs. Smithson immediately took his place. Of course she would have to tell Jack about their conversation and she considered how best to do that while she walked. The plain truth was the best option; she had let her curiosity get the best of her.

That thought was still in her mind when she got home, ready to confess, and found that Jack had been called back to Mulberry Street and wasn't expected before early Thursday morning, most likely when Anna had already left for the hospital.

Her mood deflated, she ate a bowl of Mrs. Cabot's broth and a few crackers, drank what seemed like another quart of tea infused with honey and lemon, and took a few minutes to write a message for Ned to take to the New Amsterdam: she would be back at work tomorrow at half past six.

"I'm going to go sleep for a few hours," she told Mrs. Cabot. "But call if someone needs me."

There's was a half smile that Anna already recognized as Mrs. Cabot's quiet opposition.

"Oh ayuh," she said. "That's just exactly what I'll do."

◆ ◆ ◆

WHEN JACK GOT to Mulberry Street he found Maroney, Sainsbury, and Larkin sitting around the table listening to Nicholas Lambert, who was going over his notes on the rest of the autopsies.

So Jack leaned against the door and listened, his chin on his chest.

Lambert was saying, "Of the eight cases, the first two are significantly different, but there are similarities enough to group them all together as the work of one person. I have to write up the last three reports and a summary of my findings, but I thought you'd want to hear this much right away."

Oscar said, "It's good to know what we're dealing with. Any ideas about the person responsible?"

"Do you mean who it might be?" He shook his head. "It could be anyone. Whoever is doing this must have learned how to present a normal face to the world. The most I can say is that this is the work of someone familiar with human anatomy, and well versed in how to cause maximum damage and pain. Whoever he is, I hope he steps in front of an omnibus before he gets around to harming another woman."

When he had gone they sat staring at each other for a long moment. Interviews with cabbies, hotel employees, hospital staff had all come to nothing, and neither had the letters written to the doctors advertising in the newspaper. This thought was still in Jack's mind when Sainsbury looked up and said, "This may be a stupid idea."

To All Ladies Resident in the City or Environs:

Be warned. An unidentified person claiming to be a physician has been advertising in all the newspapers offering his services to ladies who are seeking what is sometimes called the restoration of nature's rhythms or the removal of obstructions. This person may sign himself Dr. dePaul or use other names. He is being sought by the police in connection with a number of homicides of a particularly heinous nature. For your own safety, do not communicate with anyone advertising such services unless the physician provides valid references from both patients and colleagues. Any information about this person should be directed to Detective Sergeant Maroney at Police Headquarters on Mulberry. A private citizen has made funds available to reward individuals providing information that leads to apprehension and conviction of the guilty party.

They talked about it for an hour, discussed the fine points and how to deal with what would certainly turn into a badgering by the press.

A runner came to the door. Jack took the message slips, read them, and then raised a brow in Oscar's direction.

He said, "You want the good news or the bad news first?"

"Will we be able to tell the difference?"

"Probably not."

"Then surprise us, go on."

"There's a man downstairs, Richard Crown, a brewer. He came in looking for his wife who fits the description of our Jane Doe. And we've got another one. Mamie Winthrop on Park Place—"

Oscar let out a low but heartfelt moan.

"—who died at home this morning from what her husband is calling medical malpractice."

Larkin said, "Tell me that's not Albert Winthrop you're talking about."

"And just when things were starting to slow down," Jack said. "At least we won't bore each other to death."

Jack left Oscar and Larkin to question Richard Crown and headed uptown to Park Place. He hadn't been in the neighborhood since the day Sophie and Cap left for Europe, though he had told Cap he would keep an eye on the house. He asked the cabby to pull over, paid him, and got out.

The house was closed up, the windows shuttered. He checked the locks on doors front and back, examined window frames, and, satisfied, set off for the Winthrop place. He was halfway there when he heard a patrolman's whistle behind him and turned to see that he was being pursued not just by the cop, but two men. *On the hunt*, was what went through Jack's mind. He waited, hands in pockets, until they caught up.

"That's him," said the shorter of the two men. "Nosing around the Verhoeven place, ready to break in. Arrest him."

The patrolman had the good grace to look embarrassed.

"Fred," Jack said. "How've you been?"

"Fine, Jack, we're all in good shape. There's some confusion here, Mr. Matthews—"

"No confusion," said Matthews. "I saw him with my own two eyes. Now arrest him."

Fred Marks was a friendly guy, well liked on the force, well thought of on the streets, but he wasn't much for confrontation. He stayed on the job because his mother's sister was married to the mayor, but they kept him out of trouble by assigning him the easy duties that would normally go to the men ready to retire. Now his good-natured face took on a scarlet tinge.

Marks said, "Mr. Matthews, this is Detective Sergeant Mezzanotte out of headquarters on Mulberry Street."

"I don't care if he's the pope, he was trespassing."

The second man said something in a low voice, and Matthews turned on him. Jack saw now that they were father and son.

"I never heard anything so ridiculous in my whole life. Like the Belmonts would let a wop look after anything. Like setting up a cozy bed for the fox in the middle of the henhouse."

Jack had had enough, but he let Fred give it another try. "Mr. Matthews, I'm sure Mr. Verhoeven is glad to have you keeping an eye on his property, but you're mistaken here."

"Let's go home," said the younger Mr. Matthews. "You've done your duty, Father."

Matthews looked like he was getting ready to make a citizen's arrest, or more alarming still, to try to wrestle Jack to the ground. Jack held up one hand and with the other he got his shield out of his vest pocket and held it up. "Get in touch with Conrad Belmont," he said. "He'll tell you what you need to know. Now if you'll excuse me—"

He wondered what Anna would say if he told her about this, being accused of trespassing and attempted burglary on a bright summer day. She'd be mad, and so he'd keep it to himself. In the twelve years he'd spent on the force things hadn't changed much, but he was older and could keep his temper in check where Anna would not.

He was still thinking about this when he crossed the street to get to the Winthrops' place. It couldn't really be called a house, this monstrosity in redbrick bulging with cupolas and towers, carved marble facings, wrought-iron balustrades, velvet draperies at the windows, and a front door that would have been more suited to a dungeon.

There was no sign of reporters, but he erred on the side of caution and walked around to the back of the house through the stable courtyard. The kitchen door opened and closed, letting out a single swell of sound: female voices raised in alarm, frustration, fear. From farther away a man's voice was raised in anger, too garbled to make sense of it.

Jack pushed through the crowd of servants and stable boys, put his shoulder to the door, and forced his way into the crowded kitchen. A wiry woman who was just tall enough to bite his elbow stood in front of him, a wooden spoon in her fist and murder plain on her face.

"Are you the doctor who cut up my mistress and left her to bleed to death?"

"No," Jack said. "I'm the cop who's going to track him down and see that he hangs."

A grim smile divided her face in two, but her eyes were wet and her hand trembled when she took his wrist. "This way, then. Up those stairs."

She talked so fast he only caught parts of the story she was trying to tell. Mrs. Winthrop had gone to see a doctor and come home half-dead.

"She's a spiteful thing, mean as snakes. But nobody deserves to die like this, tore up like a fox at the end of a hunt."

"Wait," he said. "She's still alive?"

"She is, but just barely."

"Conscious?"

"In and out."

"I need to talk to her."

"I expect you do," said the cook. "But you'll have to get past Sir Albert first."

Jack wondered that the cook felt free enough to call Winthrop by a nickname he must surely hate and decided she was past caring. Mamie Winthrop might be a wretched employer, but something about her had gotten the cook's sympathy.

She pointed to a set of double doors and started to turn away.

"Tell me before you go, is there anybody in the house she takes into her confidence? Anybody at all?"

"Lizzy," said the cook. "Her maid. If not for Lizzy the missus would be dying in the back of a cab or in a filthy hospital somewheres, all alone."

A break, finally. The first real break. He said, "Where is Lizzy now?"

"Packing her things. Fired."

"Don't let her leave," he said. "If you have to tie her down, keep her in the kitchen until I come to fetch her." At the look on the cook's face he said, "If you want us to catch the man responsible for Mrs. Winthrop's state, you'll keep her here for me to talk to."

He waited for her nod and walked through the doorway into a sitting room that was crammed full of furniture, the flocked wallpaper barely visible under dozens of paintings and mirrors. He stepped around a sculpture of an Egyptian goddess, a set of couches upholstered in silk, a standing lamp in the shape of a heron with ruby eyes, through seating arrangements too delicate to bear the weight of anything larger than a cat, and arrived finally at the open door.

The stench in the room was familiar: infection, blood, human waste. Two men, almost certainly doctors, stood beside the bed, their heads bent together while they talked. Someone had pulled a sheet over the shape in the bed, blinding white but for the drops of blood that blossomed on the lower half.

Alfred Winthrop was on a stool on the far side of the room, bent forward, his palms on his knees. There were rings on every finger, like extra knuckles of metal and stone. An older woman stood beside him, dressed as though she were going to a ball or royal reception. Her jewels were around her neck and hanging from her ears.

Jack stepped into the room and closed the door behind himself.

• • •

NOTHING WAS EASY with old money, and the Winthrops were some of the oldest and richest of the Knickerbocker set. Lawyers came, surveyed the situation, and advised Alfred Winthrop to let the coroner's office take charge of his wife's remains, talking in low tones about inquests and investigations. A few well-chosen words and Winthrop dropped his protesting and even agreed to answer a few of Jack's questions.

No, he hadn't known his wife was *enceinte*, and she certainly had said nothing to him about a doctor's appointment; ladies did not share such personal information, not even with a husband. They had been married four years and had no children, had wanted no children while they were still young and had so much of life to experience. They had made many plans for travel over the next year, and now it would all have to be canceled.

To Jack it seemed Winthrop was more worried about gossip than upset about his wife's death. That might be heartless and shallow, but there was nothing illegal about it.

Hardly a half hour after Jack sent for him, the coroner arrived. In another neighborhood the wait could stretch out into days, but not on Park Place. Coroner Olsen was new and intimidated by the casual display of wealth; without much effort Jack convinced him that this was a case that had to be handed over to Dr. Lambert at Bellevue.

He anticipated some trouble from the lady's maid, who would balk at the idea of being questioned at police headquarters. Instead he found her in the kitchen with two satchels, ready and eager to leave. Her life as a servant in a fine house had just ended; no one else would hire the young woman who had played some role, however how small and innocent, in Mamie Winthrop's death. The harm was done, she told him, and a few hours in a police station would make no more difference.

Jack observed her as the cab fought its way through traffic, jerking to a stop again and again, the cabby raising his voice to curse at a newsboy, a cart driver, another cabby who slowed him down. The woman he judged to be in her midtwenties—very young for the position she had held—stared out into the city with a blank expression.

The word that came to mind was *comely*: even features, fine skin, and she was perfectly groomed and dressed for her station, which was to say her clothing was of good fabric, expertly tailored, without ornament or lace. Not a speck of dust or a pulled thread to be seen.

He asked a few questions and she answered without hesitation or posturing so that by the time they walked into the detective squad room he knew the basics: Elizabeth Imhoff, called Lizzy; she was twenty-five years old, born in the servants' quarters of the Winthrops' Provincetown estate to a kitchen maid. A family by-blow, which meant, she told him with little emotion, that she had just been fired by her half brother. She had known him all her life, and he sent her off without a kind word or a reference.

Her future was dark. Unless she had a beau waiting, a man who was ready to marry her and keep her, or she knew someone who would hire her to clerk in a shop, her options were limited. Women of Mamie Winthrop's standing could and usually did bring maids over from France or England, but instead she had agreed to taking on a family embarrassment. He didn't know what to make of that, but he would have to find out.

◆ ◆ ◆

OSCAR WAS WRITING down his notes on the interview with Richard Crown of Brooklyn, who had identified their Jane Doe as his wife, Catherine, and who had gone away to arrange for her burial looking himself close to the grave.

Now he sized up Lizzy Imhoff with a single glance, got up to greet her and shake her hand—she had a natural dignity, something Oscar appreciated—and showed her to a chair.

The squad room was noisy with overlapping conversations about the day's biggest event: an especially stupid thief known to his colleagues as Half-Peck had tried to rob an opium den armed with a knife that wouldn't cut butter. It hadn't occurred to him that the owners might have weapons of their own, a lesson he had learned the hard way but would never need again from his slab in the city morgue.

"Let's get a cup of coffee," Oscar said, and set off without waiting for agreement. Jack brought up the rear, watching Elizabeth Imhoff walk, the way she held herself, the things she looked at. Her calm was unusual, almost off-putting, but he supposed she must still be in shock. Within a span of a few hours her life had been pulled out from under her.

Once they had settled into a booth at MacNeil's, Jack saw that her hands shook a little. Not completely made of ice, then. It just remained to see how she responded to Oscar's interrogation.

She listened to him ask the most general question possible—what had happened to Mrs. Winthrop—and returned with a question of her own.

"How far back do you want me to go?"

"Start by telling us a little about her," Oscar said.

She gave a soft laugh. Shook her head in apology, and laughed again. "I'm sorry, the question just takes me by surprise. I thought everybody must know Mrs. Winthrop, given the way gossip moves. But I suppose that it's a fairly small circle who would pay attention."

"She had a reputation, then."

"Yes," said Miss Imhoff. "She had a reputation. The simplest description is probably all you need. She was spoiled, as most women of her class are. But she was also cruel."

"To you?"

"To everybody. Her husband, her mother, her friends. If you can call them that. She was terrible to people on the street, to anyone who was less than beautiful, and to most beautiful people as well. And to the servants, all of us." She paused. "I'm not sure how this is relevant to her death."

"We'll get to that. How did she treat you? Did you like working for her?"

"God, no."

"Glad to be shut of her, then."

"She's dancing with the devil. The satisfaction I get from that idea will only last as long as my savings."

Jack leaned back a little, twisted his head from side to side to relieve the start of a cramp, and waited.

After a full minute Oscar said, "You know, we can ask questions and drag it out of you bit by bit, or you can just tell us. Wait, have you had anything to eat today? You are looking peaked." Without waiting for an answer he waved one of the MacNeil boys over.

"Scrambled eggs, toast, bacon. And keep the coffee coming." Oscar tilted his head at Miss Imhoff, and she nodded.

◆　◆　◆

WHEN SHE HAD some food in her stomach and her color had improved, she started talking. The story wasn't all that unusual or surprising: Mrs. Winthrop had been free with her affections. Over the four years of her marriage there were five lovers that her lady's maid knew about, simply because Mamie Winthrop took no pains to hide her indiscretions within the walls of her rooms.

"And the husband?" Oscar asked.

She gave a little half shrug. "They went for days without seeing each other at all. They didn't argue, they just . . ." She paused. "They didn't seem to enjoy each other's company."

"So no children at all," Jack said.

"A son, from her first marriage. She was a widow when she married Mr. Winthrop. The boy lives with his grandparents in Boston."

Her tone never wavered as she told the rest of it, which said to Jack that she was very much in control of her emotions. As would be necessary in the Winthrop household. "Over four years I believe there was one miscarriage, and I know there were three operations. All of them were performed by the same doctor. I don't know why she didn't go back to him," Miss Imhoff said. "He might have been out of town or retired, I suppose. She didn't tell me."

"Did you go with her to those earlier appointments?" Jack asked.

"The doctor came to her. People came to her."

"And why not this time, do you know?"

"She left it almost too late. I think she was tempted this time, to have the baby and keep it, but then she decided she wanted to go to Greece. I know that because the modiste was called in and they spent an afternoon discussing the wardrobe she'd need in Athens in the spring. The next day she sent for the doctor to put things right, that's the way she referred to the operation. She was not happy to find out he wasn't available."

"She discussed this with you."

"Oh, no. She discussed it with her mother while I was in the room. She was furious when it turned out that none of the doctors she sent for would agree to do the operation. They all said it was too dangerous, past a certain point. But she wouldn't take no for an answer."

Jack concentrated on taking notes. In his experience it was best to leave the witness feeling as unobserved as possible.

"In the end she did find a doctor," she went on. "She was put out that he wouldn't come to the house, but he had the better of her, and she knew it."

"Do you know what he charged, what his fees were?" Oscar asked this crucial question in a casual tone, but she hesitated.

"If you don't know, just say so."

She said, "I saw her counting out the bills before we left. It was more than three hundred dollars, but I don't know how much exactly."

Oscar prompted her, gently. "So you went with Mrs. Winthrop to her appointment."

"Only part of the way. The doctor was very specific in his instructions, and she didn't want to chance scaring him off. She was supposed to come alone."

Jack said, "That strikes me as odd, that she'd take such a chance. It could have been a trap of some kind."

Miss Imhoff's expression was almost amused. "She took a pistol with her. She grew up with guns, apparently. Her father taught her to shoot when she was a child."

Not that it did her any good, Jack thought.

"Do you know how she found this doctor?"

It was a crucial question, and the answer was disappointing. "I assume she got his name from one of her friends. Rich women trade in information."

Jack took down the essentials as she reconstructed the day for them:

At eight in the morning they left the house, in Mrs. Winthrop's personal carriage, with just the driver, a family retainer who was more than seventy. On the way Mrs. Winthrop had talked to her about a gown she wanted to wear to dinner the following weekend.

"She thought she'd be able to attend a dinner?" Oscar sounded surprised.

"Well, yes," the young woman said. "She was thinking this time would be like the last, and the time before that. It never occurred to her that it might go wrong."

"And where did the carriage take you?"

She said, "This is a little odd to admit, but I don't know the city very well, though I've been here since I was very little. We're not allowed to wander. I can describe the place the carriage stopped, if that will help. There was an elevated train station across from a day market, and a large courthouse just behind that. Kitty-corner from the market there's a little coffee shop. She gave me a dollar and told me to wait there, and then she walked away. Two hours later when she hadn't come back yet I was getting worried. Then I realized that the carriage had left. For a minute I thought Mrs. Winthrop had gone to a lot of trouble to be rid of me, but then the carriage came around the corner. I'm guessing she asked Cullen to meet her on a different corner at a different time, but I never got the chance to ask her."

"We'll talk to the driver. Cullen, you say."

She nodded, turned her face away to clear her throat.

Jack asked, "When you got into the carriage, what was your first impression? Do you think she was under the influence of some drug or other?"

"She stank of laudanum," Miss Imhoff said. "So I think that's a fair guess." Her tone was clipped, almost cold.

"Did you happen to see where she went—in what direction she went when she left you?"

"No. To be truthful I wasn't all that concerned. Not until I saw the condition she was in afterward. As soon as we got home she took some laudanum and then went straight to bed. Gave me strict orders, she was not to be disturbed for any reason. At five o'clock I was to bring a tea tray, but I should come in and put it down silently, within reach, and then leave again."

"And did it happen like that?"

She shook her head. "At five I brought the tray in, but she was in the lavatory. I could hear her retching. I waited a bit to see if she'd call for help, but she didn't. I went back in about two hours later, to get the tray and bring fresh towels."

She stopped and studied her hands for a moment.

"I'm not sure how to describe the rest."

"In as much detail as you can manage," Oscar said.

Another minute passed. She cleared her throat, and then she started, more slowly. "She was barely conscious when I came back. The bed was bloody, and there was a very high, keen smell. Like a wound gone bad. She had gotten sick again, but right there in bed. So I said I would call for her doctor, and she woke up then and said no, it would pass. She'd be recovered by morning."

"Do you think she believed that?"

The aloof expression she had maintained for so long began to slip. She swallowed visibly and shook her head. "I don't know."

"What happened next?"

"Nothing. She let me stay. She wanted laudanum, and I gave her as much as I thought was safe. Then I lied and said the bottle was empty. She let me change the bedsheets"—another difficult swallow—"but she kept bleeding and she passed a lot of . . . I never imagined that the human body could produce such—" She shook her head.

"That's enough, I think, Miss Imhoff. Did anybody come to see her? Her mother, her husband?"

"Not that evening. Not until the next morning when I sent for the doctor. She wouldn't respond to me, and I felt I had no choice. Things moved very quickly after that. Her mother sent word to wake Mr. Winthrop—his rooms are on the other side of the house—and he came in just as the doctor arrived. He sent me out and told me to collect my things and be gone or he'd have me arrested."

She looked directly at Oscar, the question plain on her face.

"You've committed no crime," he said. "There's just one more thing we need from you for the time being. We'll take a short drive, and after that if you like I can introduce you to a Mrs. Adams. She has a boardinghouse for ladies, very reputable and well kept. No doubt you'll sleep for twelve hours after the day you've had."

Oscar presented himself to the world as gruff, no-nonsense, unsentimental, iron fisted, but he was also generous and protective with people who were in trouble they had not earned. The wonder of it was that he had not lost those traits after so many years on the job. Jack hoped he could only do half as well over time.

◆　◆　◆

HE TOOK OSCAR home to Weeds for some supper and a quiet place to talk over the day. Coming in through the stable—empty, as they kept no horse or carriage—they stepped out into the garden and Oscar stopped.

"Well, look here," he said, spreading out his arms and turning. A dancing bear.

"Now look at this. I could live right here, out in the open."

Jack was pleased with the garden, though he hadn't had much of an opportunity to sit in it.

"Mr. Lee and my father put their heads together. They sent three wagons of earth and plants, conscripted the cousins, and this is the result."

They turned at the sound of the rear door, to see Anna standing there. She looked a little sleepy, a pillow crease in one cheek, her hair escaping its pins.

"I expect you spend most of your time indoors," Oscar said under his breath, and Jack elbowed him, hard.

• • •

MRS. CABOT SERVED her ragout of pork cooked in port with apples and prunes. Anna had to smile at Oscar's expression, as if he could not believe his good fortune.

"Mrs. Cabot kept house for a family who employed a French cook," Anna told him. "This must be one of the recipes she took away with her."

Over coffee and a plate of cookies Jack said, "We've had a busy day, but we're still on duty until morning."

"You just came home for your supper," Anna said. "But I'm glad you did. I'll be leaving for the hospital before you get in."

Oscar cleared his throat. "We have another victim."

Anna felt her expression freeze, but she took in a deep breath, picked up her coffee cup, and asked, "Exactly the same?"

"In the essentials," Jack said. "Nicholas Lambert will do the postmortem, but there's little doubt in my mind. Oscar?"

He shook his head. "But we did get some information this time, from the lady's maid. You remember the advertisements you found in the paper, the ones that mention Smithson's?"

Jack said, "What's wrong? All the color just drained out of your face."

"Smithson's?" Her voice wavered a little. "What about it?"

"There's a coffeehouse just opposite, do you know it?" Oscar asked, his tone wary.

"Yes," Anna said. "I used to go there with my uncle Quinlan when I was very young. And—" She looked first Oscar and then Jack in the eye. "I was there today."

＊　＊　＊

BY THE TIME they had exchanged stories—Jack got out his notes both to be sure of the facts and to add Anna's observations—it was eight o'clock. She started at the chiming of the hall clock.

"I thought you had to go back to work?"

Oscar raised both brows and tucked in his chin in what she thought was mock surprise.

"What is it you think we're doing?"

"Oh," she said. "I hadn't thought of it that way."

"Your parlor is far more comfortable than the squad room, I'll give you that."

Jack said, "And it smells better."

"I should hope so," Anna muttered. "Is it too late to go to Jefferson Square right now? Just to get a sense of how things are laid out, and where Mrs. Winthrop might have been going."

"Possible, but not the best idea," Jack said. "You were there this morning; we were there a couple hours ago. If someone involved in this case happened to see us there again—together—it might well send them packing before we've even figured out who they are."

"You think that's possible?"

Oscar said, "Probable, even. And after tomorrow almost certain."

Jack took a folded piece of paper from his notebook and handed it to her. "This will run in five newspapers tomorrow."

Anna skimmed it, and then looked at them. "This might help reduce the number of women who go to him, but how could it help in identifying him?"

The two men glanced at each other. "We have a suspect," Oscar said. "We'll be watching him."

"Can I ask who it is?"

"No." Jack's tone was firm.

Oscar scowled at him. "Come on, man. She's up to her eyebrows already. And if I have to remind you, she's been behind most of the useful information we have."

"I know that," Jack said shortly.

Anna said, "Oscar, I know what this is. What we have here is the Brooklyn Bridge."

The look on his face was almost comical, and so she explained.

"I wanted Jack to take me to the top of one of the arches," she said. "This was before it opened. We had a philosophical disagreement about the boundary between protectiveness and paternalism. I think this is a similar situation."

Oscar was trying not to grin. "And how did that turn out?"

"Not in my favor," Anna said. "But this time it will."

• • •

THEY TOOK A break while Oscar went back to Mulberry Street to collect some materials. Jack took Anna's hand and led her outside to sit in the garden.

"Something Oscar said made me realize we aren't taking advantage of this." He gestured around himself. "I keep meaning to look into putting together a pergola. Would you like that?"

Anna lifted their linked hands and pulled him toward a small bench at the far end of the garden.

She said, "This will do for the time being. So, you're going to have to convince me about Neill Graham."

He considered for a moment. "Tell me first why you're so sure he's not involved."

"These women may each have been desperate in her own way, but none of them was stupid. They had money—some more than others, but all of them were well off when compared to the average. They had households to run—and you know what that entails." She drew a breath and held it for a few heartbeats.

"A woman like this, with money and position, a woman who isn't stupid isn't going to hand herself over to a twenty-one-year-old intern. That kind of woman wants nice offices and treatment rooms and all the latest medicines and instruments. She wants anesthesia and laudanum and a physician with many years' experience. She wants decorum and white hair and distinction and manners, and she's willing to pay for all those things. Graham is polite and solicitous, but I can't see

Janine Campbell or any of the others simply handing over a pile of money and then surrendering to his care. Have I convinced you?"

"Not yet," Jack said. "But then you weren't there when Graham told us what it was like to examine poor women. There was—revulsion, even hatred, in his whole demeanor. And his keen interest in the Campbell case and the others—there's some kind of connection."

"I take you at your word," she said. "After talking to Mrs. Smithson today I wouldn't be surprised if she were connected too. I have no idea how. Is there one simple scenario that pulls together all the small pieces?"

"That's what we're working on. Look, here comes Oscar with his maps and the rest of the case file. Anna."

She looked up at him, waiting.

"Promise me something."

That made her laugh. "Just like that? You want carte blanche on everything, or just one thing in particular?"

"I want you to promise me you won't go digging around Jefferson Square anymore on your own."

Anna grabbed his earlobe and pulled, ignoring his yelp to plant a kiss on his cheek. "That's a deal," she said. "I won't go back there on my own. Satisfied?"

His brow pleated itself when he scowled, as he was doing now. "Savard," he said. "I know you, and you've got something up your sleeve."

"I will not put myself in harm's way," she said. "I know very well that I'm out of my depths. I'm not foolish, Mezzanotte. What I am, what I've got up my sleeve, as you put it, is anger. I can't remember ever being so angry."

He studied her face for a long moment, and then nodded. "Let's go see what Oscar's got."

42

THE NEXT MORNING Jack caught up with Anna before she had reached Cooper Square, took her Gladstone bag, and held out his free arm; he raised a brow at her until she took it.

"I said I'd be home in time to walk you to work."

"I wanted to get an early start. And you need to get some sleep, Mezzanotte."

Mornings Anna was often on edge, but there was something more to her mood this morning. They had spent a good part of the evening poring over the surveyor maps of the Jefferson Square area, compiling a list of buildings within three blocks of the coffeehouse and Smithson's where a doctor might have offices. It would take days for the officers assigned to the case to canvass all of them, but that was the next and necessary step. That, and a new and more intense look at Neill Graham.

He said, "You didn't sleep well."

"Not especially."

"I wondered if this would happen."

She rounded on him, her brows drawn down. Ready to be irritated; almost, Jack thought, eager to be irritated. "What would happen?"

"You with your quick doctor's mind and quicker surgeon's hands are finding the slow pace of the law frustrating."

They stopped at a corner to let an omnibus pass, wheels screeching on the rails. When they had crossed the street Anna looked up at him.

"I had a dream," she said. "I don't usually remember my dreams, but this one woke me and I was damp with sweat. After that I couldn't sleep any more at all."

He waited, but she didn't go on. "You don't want to tell me about the dream."

"I think I have to tell you about the dream. It goes onto that long list of things I need to talk to you about."

Jack was tired too; they had been called out to a street fight after midnight, stevedores and sailors bent on breaking each other's heads. He thought about telling her this story and decided it would wait until they were both in better moods.

In front of the New Amsterdam he gave back her Gladstone bag, brushed a curl off her forehead, and kissed the corner of her eye so that her lashes fluttered against his mouth.

"You're not easily spooked," he said. "But I'd be surprised if this case didn't give you some bad dreams."

She seemed to relax a little, her forehead pressed to his jaw. And still she looked unhappy, distracted, overwhelmed. He didn't like any of it, and there was nothing he could do for her in the here and now.

"I didn't dream about the case," she said finally. "It was about my brother. I dreamed he came to apologize to me, and I hit him in the head. With a hammer. But he was a ghost and he just stood there looking at me as if I'd disappointed him."

Jack heard himself draw in a sharp breath. "We need more time to talk about this," he said. "But I don't mind telling you that I thought that when you got around to telling me about Paul, the story would be something else entirely."

"I know." She touched his cheek with her gloved hand. "I think that's why it's been so hard for me to talk about it. Everybody expects a story that I can't give them."

"Anna. I'll take whatever you've got."

She smiled then, something almost regretful in her expression.

"We'll talk tonight." She went up on tiptoe to kiss his cheek and he turned his head to catch her mouth. A soft, warm kiss; in need of comfort herself, she tried instead to comfort him.

He kissed her back, possessively, hungrily, to remind her who he was.

•   •   •

THE OPERATING ROOM was one place where Anna knew she could drop everything and clear her mind. There was a simple hernia to be done, an operation she did day in and day out, but she was looking forward to it. Then she turned into the hall and saw Archer Campbell waiting outside her office door.

Two thoughts went through her mind at that moment: first, that it would be childish and silly to run away; and second, there were times when she really did have use for a hammer.

"Dr. Savard." He dragged his hat off his head with a reluctance that spoke volumes. "Can I have a word?"

"Mr. Campbell. No, you may not. I have to be in surgery in five minutes. I'm just here to leave my wraps."

She unlocked the door and went in, locked it behind herself, and took a moment to catch her breath. Then she went on as she had done every morning for as long as she had come to work at the New Amsterdam: she took off her hat, changed her shoes, and exchanged her shirtwaist for a fresh tunic and put on a full apron over that. The whole time she was aware that Campbell was still in the hall, waiting.

She thought of Mabel Stone in the little cottage by the sea. She thought of Janine Campbell's four boys, children she had never seen but could imagine nonetheless: if not healthy, then healing.

As soon as she opened the door Campbell stepped toward her, close enough that she could make out ale on his breath. She had faced down drunken husbands and belligerent mothers, and she resolved to face down Archer Campbell. She put her arm straight out, her fisted hand against his shoulder, and pushed him away.

"Mr. Campbell," she said. "You are inappropriate."

His hand closed over her forearm. She spun around and jerked free in one motion, and they stood looking at each other. She could hear her heartbeat echoing in her ears, and every nerve was twanging like a fire bell.

"You will talk to me." His voice went husky and she saw his pupils dilating with an almost sexual response to her rejection. She thought of one quick jerk of the knee and how that would take the look off his face.

"I want to know where Mabel Stone is," he said. "Don't tell me you don't know what I'm talking about. I saw you go into her place that night with the detectives, and the next day the Stones were gone, both of them. There's no word of them, and nobody knows where they went. Except you. You know, don't you."

Anna looked him directly in the eye for a count of three. She said, "Mr. Campbell. Leave this building and never come back. Never approach me again or I will swear out a complaint."

"Haven't answered my question, though, have you? That's as good as a confession in my book. You'll talk to me, unless you like the idea of a search. You'll never know when it's coming, but I can guarantee you, Comstock will find what he needs to send you to prison."

In some part of her brain Anna realized that he didn't know she was married, or to whom. The thought made her smile, and her smile made his whole face contort with rage. *This is what his wife faced every day,* she thought. *This is what she lived with for years.*

A small group of people came into the hall. An orderly, too busy flirting with the nursing students to take note of anything else, and behind them, Elise. She pushed her way through the others and broke into a trot.

"Dr. Savard," she called. "Do you need help?"

"She does," said Campbell with a wide rictus of a smile that displayed graying teeth. "But not from you."

His eyes moved over Anna, roaming over her body to stop on her face.

"You're no woman a man would want as a wife. I doubt you even know you are a woman." His grin flickered on and off. "But then old maids can be surprising. All those juices stored up with no place to go."

There was a distinct buzzing in her ears and she seemed to be watching the scene from a remove. She felt no fear or even disgust. The most she could muster was a clinical interest, wondering what an alienist would make of Campbell.

"I could show you what goes on in a man's bed—"

Then Elise Mercier stepped forward with both fists raised and delivered a blow to Campbell's middle that deflated him like a pin to a hot-air balloon. All the breath in his lungs left him in a rush, the smell of oysters and ale hanging in the air as he collapsed to the floor, hacking and fighting for air.

It all happened in seconds, and then everyone was staring at Elise. The look on the orderly's face was distinctly admiring, but the nurses were shocked and, Anna thought, a little frightened.

Elise studied Campbell, writhing on the ground and gasping for air.

"He'll be all right. More's the pity," she said to no one in particular. Then she realized that everyone was looking at her, and she produced a small, crooked smile. She said, "Six brothers."

That seemed to satisfy them all. The orderly crouched down to get hold of Campbell by the collar of his jacket and yanked him to his feet.

"Would you be wanting to call the police, Dr. Savard?"

Anna shook her head. "Just put him out on the street, please, Jeremy. I need to get to surgery. Nurse Mercier, I suggest you soak that hand in cold water before it begins to swell." But she smiled at Elise. "Later I'll try to remember to remind you about the prohibition on violence inside the New Amsterdam."

◆　◆　◆

ELISE, SOAKING HER hand, was still angry enough to spit, but she was also deeply apprehensive. Bullies did not stand down so easily, especially not when they had been bested by a girl. Walking home from the New Amsterdam might not be the best idea. Not for herself or Anna. She wondered why Anna had not sent for the police, if there was something unspoken that stopped her.

After a while she dried her hand, flexing each finger and making a fist. No serious damage, but then punching Campbell's middle had been like burying her fist in half-risen bread dough. She thought for a long moment, and then went to find pen and paper.

◆　◆　◆

JACK HAD COME to the conclusion that the one advantage to working the night shift was Mrs. Cabot's determination to feed him to bursting when he got up in the early afternoon. Today he was served a spicy beef hash along with a wedge of onion pie, a dish of preserved green peas dressed with mint and cream, and a bowl of banana pudding.

When he protested she poured him more coffee and put another slice of onion pie on his plate. Then she went off to answer a knock at the door and came back with a note.

Dear Detective Sergeant Mezzanotte,

I write to say that this morning a man called Archer Campbell came to the hospital and spoke very rudely to Dr. Savard in the hall outside her office. Very rudely. Because I feared for her safety I stepped in and delivered a shovel hook as taught to me by my brothers. I intended this for his liver, but it landed on his diaphragm instead. He was not seriously hurt, but he may swear out a complaint against me. More disturbing, I fear he may also seek revenge toward Dr. Savard or me or both of us, and thus this note.

To be clear, I didn't hear the conversation between them and I don't know what it was he wanted, but he wanted it very badly.

Yours sincerely,
Elise Mercier

His first stop was the New Amsterdam, where he found Joshua Abernathy behind the porter's desk.

"Dr. Savard didn't want us to call in the police," he told Jack. "I would have done it anyway, but I figured you'd be along."

He didn't have much to report beyond the fact that Campbell had snuck in while the porters' shift was changing, at about six. "I didn't see him come in, but I made sure to see him out." The surly expression gave way to a wide smile. "He was still coughing and wheezing. I hear Nurse Mercier walloped him proper, right in the breadbasket."

"She sent me a note, worried about Campbell hanging around looking for a chance to get his own back."

"Same thought occurred to me," said the porter. "If you hadn't shown your face by four, I would have sent a note on my own."

"Has he been hanging around?"

"Not that I could see. But there's no shortage of dark corners to hide in, if he's determined."

And that was the question. Jack could imagine Campbell desperate and foolish enough to do about anything.

•   •   •

FROM THE NEW Amsterdam he went straight to Oscar's boardinghouse on Grove Street. It was a big, comfortable, and orderly house where troublemakers didn't last a week, because Oscar saw to it. For his help the landlady gave him use of the parlor, where Jack found him with a newspaper and a cigar in a sea of smoke.

He sat down across from him and handed over Elise's note.

"Oh ho." Oscar put the paper down and read.

Jack said, "How close are you to sorting out the last of the bonds?"

Oscar had taken the bonds on as a project, converting them to cash at different banks, a few at a time, and sending the money to Little Compton by registered messenger. The scheme was both elaborate and fraught with pitfalls, but Oscar lived for that kind of challenge.

"Just three left," he told Jack now. "Not too many or too few. Just right. I'm looking forward to this."

◆　◆　◆

WHEN THEY SAT down to dinner at Aunt Quinlan's table for the first time in almost a week, Anna was prepared to be asked a million questions about everything from Staten Island to Mrs. Cabot's magical head-cold tea. Instead there was only one subject under discussion: the upcoming trip to Greenwood. The Mezzanotte family celebrated the twenty-fourth of June every year with a huge party, and the combined Quinlan and Savard households were invited to join them. Margaret had other plans she couldn't change, but the other adults were almost as excited as the little girls to be getting out of the city.

Even the Lees were coming. Jack had announced his plan to show Mr. Lee around the farm and greenhouses right from the start, which put Anna in a difficult spot. She tried to explain the problem: "Mr. Lee never leaves Waverly Place except to visit their son and his family, and he's just four blocks away. He always has the same excuse, that somebody has to stay to look after the property. Properties, now."

But Jack had gotten a particular look, one she had learned to recognize as unvoiced disagreement. The next day he introduced a young patrol officer he liked and trusted to the Lees. With their approval Jack hired him to stand watch while they were gone. Mrs. Lee was so touched that for once she couldn't find a single thing to say, but Aunt Quinlan didn't hesitate; she pulled him down to kiss one cheek while she patted the other. Anna wondered why they had never thought to do something similar in the past.

So they were going to Greenwood. Anna knew they had put the visit off too long already and that nothing short of an earthquake would be an acceptable excuse for staying away. What she couldn't explain to herself was how nervous the whole thing made her until Aunt Quinlan pointed out that a big party with a lot of people would be easier than a small supper where she had everyone's attention.

"We need to get an anniversary gift," Aunt Quinlan said now. "How many years have your parents been married, Jack?"

He stared at the ceiling while he subtracted. "Massimo was born on the twenty-fourth of June in . . ." He looked at his niece, who was waiting for this question.

"Eighteen forty-four."

"So they were married on the same day in eighteen forty-three; that would be forty years ago."

"They don't want presents," Chiara added. "We don't give a lot of presents." She said this a little wistfully.

Anna was thinking about forty years of marriage, what that might be like in the year 1923. If there would be children and grand-children and a party. She thought sometimes about children, a subject Jack hadn't yet raised in any serious way. Why that might be was unclear, and not something she wanted to contemplate just now.

"What are you thinking about?" Rosa asked her. "Your face is all scrunched together."

Anna started out of her thoughts. "I was thinking that I'd like more of that apple cobbler, unless somebody else has beaten me to it."

"Your appetite is restored," her aunt Quinlan said.

"After days of toast and tea and clear broth, I could eat the table-cloth."

The girls found this very funny, as if they hadn't had the same diet for days.

Margaret said, "What time are you leaving on Sunday?"

The discussion shifted to the logistic challenge of getting them all to the Hoboken ferry in time. They were a party of—the girls counted on their fingers, noisily, and came up with the astonishing number of ten, counting Bambina and Celestina. Eleven, if Ned came too, as the little girls were hoping. The plan was to leave Sunday morning and return to Manhattan late on Monday.

"Are there beds for all of us?" Aunt Quinlan asked again.

"Yes," Chiara said, smiling broadly. "Room enough."

Rosa was asking Chiara about the Mezzanotte grandchildren; she wanted names and ages and maybe even a chart that would tell her who got along and who didn't. It seemed now that Rosa had survived the trip to Mount Loretto and the shock of losing Vittorio. She had always been a serious child, and now just enough of that had lifted to see what might become of her if she could learn to let her brothers go.

She wasn't healing, that was the wrong word. She was coming to terms with loss. As Anna had never been able to do.

◆ ◆ ◆

SLEEPLESS, RESTLESS, IMAGES and snatches of conversation tumbling through her head, Anna decided that she would go read in the parlor. In the day the room was sunny, but there were gaslights, and a good chair, and a rug to put over her legs if the room was chilly.

Though Jack was a deep sleeper she moved very quietly, swung her legs over the side of the bed, and sat up.

"Savard."

She lay back down again. He rolled to his side and yawned at her. The curtains weren't closed all the way, so that she could just make out his features by the faint light from the streetlamp.

"I didn't mean to wake you."

"Why not?"

"Because you need your sleep."

"So do you." He ran a hand down her arm. "The tension is rising off you in waves."

"I'm going to go read until I'm too tired to stay awake."

"Not yet," he said. "Just rest next to me."

His hand traveled up and down her arm, the lightest of touches.

She said, "I don't want to talk about that dream."

He hummed at her, his broad fingertips barely brushing along her skin. When she was about to say that it was no use, she would go read in the parlor, he made a soft shushing sound.

"I have a question that isn't about your brother, and I want you to think about it before you answer."

She drew in a deep breath. "All right."

"Why did you feel so drawn to Rosa as soon as you met her?"

Others had asked her this question, but she had never answered it truthfully because, she knew this much, she didn't know the answer. She thought back to that day in the church basement in Hoboken, all the frightened and anxious and angry children and Rosa, holding on with all her strength to her brothers and sister. As if they were all that kept her afloat. She was going to find her father. She had promised her mother. She would keep the family together, come what may. Anna had listened closely and watched her face, knowing that none of those things would happen. They were orphans and Italian, and they were about to be tossed into a whirlwind.

She said, "I was that determined too, once upon a time. When the telegram came saying Paul had been wounded in battle I tried to run away. I thought that if I could get to Virginia and find him in the army hospital he would get better."

"How far did you get?"

"Not very. Uncle Quinlan caught up with me at the corner, on my way to the omnibus. I was six years old. I screamed and kicked and bit, but he never scolded me. He just carried me home to Aunt Quinlan and they sat with me while I howled.

"That evening Uncle Quinlan left for Virginia. Later Auntie told me he would have gone under any circumstances, but I still think that he went for me. The irony is that Paul was dead before Uncle Quinlan got there, but there was no way he could have known that and so he went around the field hospitals, asking. That's how he caught typhus. He died not two days later and they both came home in coffins."

Jack seemed to hesitate. "You blame yourself for your uncle's death."

She turned on her side to look at this man who was her husband. "I blame Paul. I blame Paul because when our parents died he swore he would always take care of me and never leave me, that when he grew up he'd have a house and we could live there together. And just three years later he broke his word and went to war. He was the most important person in my world. He knew that, but he left me to go to war when he promised he wouldn't, and he died when he said he wouldn't, and he took Uncle Quinlan with him. Uncle Quinlan was the only father I remembered.

"Everyone thinks that I was mourning my brother. That I'm still mourning him, but that's not true. I was consumed with anger. I couldn't say his name, I didn't want to see his likeness, I hated him for leaving me. And I couldn't say that, not to anyone. Not even to Aunt Quinlan. It was unsaid until Sophie came, but she understood without words.

"All these years people tiptoe around me when the subject of my brother comes up. It's almost funny, sometimes. And the thing is, I've tried to stop, but I can't feel any other way."

She drew in a breath like a hiccup and turned away to lay an arm over her eyes. Her whole body was shaking, but she was powerless to do anything but let it happen. She was afraid to look at Jack, sure to see disappointment and disapproval where there had been no doubt.

＊　＊　＊

JACK MADE HIMSELF take three deep breaths and reached for her. She came to him trembling, pressed her face against his shoulder, and wept.

When she was quiet he said, "I don't know if it would be any comfort to me if I were in your place, but I can guarantee that your brother died thinking of you and full of regrets. You were so young, Anna. He was young too, but old enough to know that he had failed you. He made promises he couldn't keep because he thought that would make you happy."

She swallowed hard. "All these years I was so angry at him, so unforgiving, and then I went and did the same thing to Rosa that he did to me."

Jack sat up, pulling her with him, holding on to her shoulders so he could look into her face, tear streaked and swollen.

"You are too rational a person to really believe that. You promised to look for the boys, and you've done that. You're still doing that. Rosa doesn't hate you. Anna, Rosa and Lia will love you for as long as they live."

He pressed his mouth to her temple. "And so will I."

43

Rosa came to breakfast on Friday morning, without Lia. She stood very formally before Anna, her expression almost sorrowful as she put a folded piece of paper on the table.

"Will you read this, please?"

Anna could feel Jack watching them, but she kept her gaze focused on Rosa.

"Now?"

Rosa nodded, the muscles in her throat working hard as she swallowed.

Anna spread the single sheet open. Rosa had written from margin to margin, each letter carefully formed and spaced.

Dear Mayor of Annandale Staten Island New York,

*I write to ask whether you have living in your town Eamon and
Helen Mullen, and their two children, a girl and a baby boy. Mr.
Mullen is a blacksmith. If you know of them I would very much like
to learn their address in order to write them a letter. Thank you.
Yours sincerely,*

> *Rosa Russo*
> *18 Waverly Place*
> *New York NY*

Anna finished reading and handed the sheet of paper to Jack. Rosa was staring at the floor, her head bent. She was trying so hard to be a grown-up, it wouldn't do for Anna to start crying.

"Rosa."

The small face came up, slowly. Misery and determination fought for the upper hand.

Anna said, "You'll need a three-cent postage stamp. I've got some in my desk."

After some discussion they came up with a plan. Every week Rosa would write to another town, one she chose from the atlas she found in the parlor bookcases at Roses. One week she would write to a town in New York, the next in New Jersey. Anna would provide the paper, envelope, and postage stamp.

Margaret would help her with the wording, consulting now and then with Aunt Quinlan and the others. Rosa could continue writing these letters for as long as she liked.

Rosa asked Jack a question that another man would have had trouble answering. "Do you think I might find them this way?"

He reached out and put a hand on the crown of her head. "I've seen stranger things happen."

Elise came in as Rosa left.

"I'm about to leave for the hospital," Anna said. "If you want to walk with me you should get your things."

"I will," she said. "But I wanted to be sure you saw this."

She put the *New York Post* on the table in front of Anna, and Jack immediately got up to come around and read over her shoulder.

NEW YORK POST

LATE EDITION

ARCHER CAMPBELL IN CUSTODY

STOLEN BEARER BONDS FOUND IN HIS POSSESSION

Acting on an anonymous tip, Detective Sergeants H. A. Sainsbury and M. P. Larkin of the New York Police Department yesterday searched the home of Archer Campbell at 19 Charles Street and found a number of stolen bearer bonds. Campbell resisted arrest and sustained significant injuries in his struggle with the detectives. He sits now in the Tombs awaiting arraignment.

Just weeks ago Campbell appeared in court to testify in the inquest into his wife's sudden and tragic death. At the same time the couple's four young sons disappeared without a trace and are still missing. The city mourned with Mr. Campbell for the loss of his family, only to find that their sympathy was ill placed.

The bonds found in his possession were just three of a larger issue of fifty. The Boston and New York police will interrogate Campbell in an attempt to uncover the location of the rest of the bonds.

"The Boston police tell us this was an older robbery," Detective Sergeant Larkin told the *Post*. "It's possible the rest of the bonds will never be recovered."

It took a great deal of stern self-discipline, but Elise never asked about the newspaper article; she kept all her questions to herself and ignored the burn of curiosity in her throat.

Instead they talked about Regina Sartore's surgery, which Anna had missed. To Elise Anna's many questions felt something like an exam that she hadn't studied for, but she answered with what turned out to be satisfactory detail. Finally she got up the nerve to ask about a different matter, almost as difficult as the newspaper article.

"Has there been any progress in the postmortem cases we talked about?"

Anna glanced at her in surprise, as if she had already forgotten the long conversation of just two days ago. Then her expression cleared.

"There's been another case," she said. "And a little forward movement. A witness who has some information the detectives are pursuing. Did you find the cases interesting?"

"The circumstances are terrible, but the discussion was interesting. Did the detectives agree that the doctor must be well established, and considered trustworthy?"

At that Anna smiled. "Just the opposite. They have a suspect. An intern, very young and untried. I'm not sure why exactly but they are as sure about him as I am convinced that you have the right of it, and they should be looking for someone older."

They walked in silence for a while, and then Elise said what came to mind.

"Why couldn't it be both?"

◆　◆　◆

ON THE WAY out of the squad room a runner brought Jack a message that he opened and read on the spot.

Oscar waited, worrying the end of his cigar. "Well?"

"From Anna. It says, 'Why are you assuming there is only one doctor? Could it not be the man you suspect as well as a more established physician, the two working together? Elise suggested this to me, and it makes sense.'"

"I can see where this is going," Oscar said dismally. "Those two are after our jobs."

This time they found Neill Graham's landlady up to her elbows in soapsuds, but she was all good cheer, made offers of tea and cake, begged just a moment while she changed her apron.

When she had finally settled on the very edge of a sofa, Oscar smiled at her. "Mrs. Jennings. We're just trying to tie up some loose ends on a case, and we were wondering if you might answer a few questions for us."

She had the bright dark eyes of a robin, but the way she was chewing on her lower lip gave her nervousness away.

"Well, now," she said, her hands fluttering. "You know I'm not the youngest anymore, and my memory sometimes fails me."

Jack caught on before Oscar. He introduced them both and left all details about their last visit unstated. It seemed possible that Mrs. Jennings had no memory of their earlier meeting; Anna wondered if that would work for or against them.

Mrs. Jennings seemed relieved not to be scolded, and sat up even straighter, an eager schoolchild wanting to please the teacher.

"We have a few questions about one of your boarders, Neill Graham. We are trying to locate his family, but without luck. Do you happen to know where they live?"

Vague enough, he hoped, to start her talking.

She knotted her hands in her lap. "Oh," she said, "Neill Graham. A very good boy, very orderly, never late with his rent. Never tries to sneak girls into his room, which you must imagine, happens often with young men like these medical students. The things I've seen, I could make the seven sisters blush, I'm sure of it."

She paused as if she had lost track of the subject.

"Neill Graham," Oscar said gently.

"Oh, yes. Dr. Graham. No, he never has girls in his room, or I've never caught him at it, I should say. Young men do have their urges. But he's never been any trouble."

"Do you know if he has any family nearby, or any close friends who might come to visit?" Oscar leaned back, as relaxed as a Buddha, radiating calm acceptance of whatever she wanted to tell them. It was the only hope they had of getting anything useful from the conversation.

"Family. Family. A sister, I think. Or a brother? A brother-in-law. Yes, a married sister, she comes by now and then and brings him things, new shirts and socks and such. He never seems very happy to see her, but then brothers and sisters often quarrel. She was a very elegant type, tall and slim, but no furs or jewels. Spoke to me very politely and didn't even blink when her brother was short with her."

"And her name?"

The small dark eyes opened wide. "Sure, she has one. I don't recall what it was he called her, she came in a fine carriage."

"You don't have any idea of her family name?"

"Well, Graham, of course."

"Pardon me, Mrs. Jennings, but didn't you just say she was married? Did her husband come to call with her?"

"He waited out in the carriage."

"Did you catch the brother-in-law's last name?"

"No, I don't think I did. Shall I ask Dr. Graham when he comes in?"

"It's really not important," Oscar said. "No reason to bother Dr. Graham with it. If you happen to remember anything else about his sister, would you drop us a note at police headquarters? We'll come again if you recall something new." He fished a card out of his vest pocket and passed it over to her.

"I'll try, but my memory does sometimes fail me. Oh. Dr. Graham's sister might be a baker's wife, she smelled of anise. Might that be of use?"

"It might just," Oscar said.

On the porch Oscar shook Mrs. Jennings's hand with great formality.

As he was turning away he seemed to remember something—it always amazed Jack that no one ever saw through this little ruse—and came up with one last question.

"How often did the older gentleman visit?"

Mrs. Jennings smiled apologetically. "I can't say. It wasn't very often, and always on Sunday. Not a talkative man, the kind who don't heap praise on a child. Or anybody, for that matter."

"And his name?"

"Don't fathers and sons always have the same last name? Dr. Graham, I suppose."

"Wait. I'm confused. Neill Graham's father comes to call, is that right?" Oscar's voice came a little hoarse: a hound on the scent, Jack thought.

"Not very often," said the landlady.

"And his father is a doctor, like he is. How do you know that he's a doctor?"

She nodded eagerly, as if she had finally come across something that might please him. "He carries one of those doctor bags. I've been boarding medical students for many years, and I'd know one of those bags anywhere."

◆　◆　◆

JACK SAID, "SHE could be wrong on both counts. The old man might not be Graham's father, and even if he is, she could be mistaken by the bag."

"No," Oscar said. "She had it right, except I think the man she remembers was the grandfather she mentioned last time. An older doctor, established, experienced, trustworthy. A woman paying him a visit would be assured by all that. Once she's under, she doesn't know who actually does the operation, does she?"

Jack shook his head. "I don't know. It feels too pat, like a big bow on an empty box."

"Do you have a better idea where to start?"

The ultimate argument. When you were stuck, you worked the clues.

◆　◆　◆

THEY SPENT THE rest of the day interviewing clerks at hospitals, clinics, and dispensaries from one end of the island to the other, jumping in and out of cabs until they came across a driver they knew and hired him to drive them for the day. So far no one had any memory of a Dr. Graham who met the landlady's description; getting a hit going about it like this was unlikely, but they plowed on.

Jerking through traffic from St. Luke's to Women's Hospital, Oscar raised the subject of Archer Campbell.

"Does Anna know they booked him?"

Jack shook his head.

Oscar said, "He doesn't realize how lucky he is to be sitting in the Tombs where you can't get at him."

"He can't make bail," Jack said. "So he's safe where he is for the time being."

"Unless you want to grease old Fish's palm, so we could pay Prisoner Campbell a visit."

"I admit it's tempting. But Anna wouldn't like it."

Oscar stroked his mustache thoughtfully. "All right," he said. "We'll table it. For the moment."

In the late afternoon they went back to Mulberry Street with just three names: Michael Graham, house physician at the Protestant Half-Orphan Asylum, Ulrich Graham, on the faculty at the Eclectic Medical School, and Andrew Graham, who had a small practice near Stuyvesant Square. None of them old enough to be Neill Graham's father or grandfather, but they'd have a look anyway. They'd find something to eat and start calling on hospital night porters. Most of them liked to talk, all of them were bored, and they saw a lot.

What Jack wanted to do was to go home to Anna, to stay close so she didn't start to imagine that the things she had told him in the night were weighing on him. As if anything could make him think less of her. He wrote her a note, one that he put in an envelope and sealed.

> Anna my love, I'll be very late but it's your own fault. The suggestion
> you made earlier today has us rushing around Manhattan looking
> for that second doctor, and we're making progress. Oscar thinks
> you're after his job. I ask myself now every day how I got so lucky.
> Love you, J.

◆　◆　◆

ALL DAY LONG Anna wondered if she had imagined the newspaper article about Archer Campbell, a question that could have been answered by a short trip to the corner where six different daily newspapers could be had for pennies each. She could read the news in German, if she pleased, or Italian, or Yiddish. And then as soon as the opportunity presented itself, she had some very specific questions for Jack and Oscar.

But she didn't go get a paper, not so much because she conquered her disquiet but because she had one emergency after another that kept her in the operating room. It began with a woman whose hand had been caught up in the machinery at a steam cleaners, mangled and scalded both. There was no choice but to amputate, which meant that she was robbing the woman of her livelihood. She explained this to her husband, still young enough that he had very little beard, and watched his eyes fill with tears that he blinked back furiously.

Elise was serving as the circulating nurse that day, and was doing a very good job ignoring the stares and whispers that came her way. They were referring to her as the little nun with the hard fist. Apparently Anna wasn't the only one thinking about Campbell's visit.

"I hear you were assaulted in the hall yesterday," Judith Ambrose said when they were scrubbing in together. "A red-haired demon, the story goes. Nurse Mercier came to your rescue with a very professional one-two punch."

Anna had to laugh. "She says she was taught how to fight by her brothers."

"She's a tough one, all right. Let's see how she handles this sad mess."

The patient was a woman of about thirty, a charwoman so strong that it took three orderlies to restrain her. She was howling, a terrible mournful wail that cut right to the bone.

"You can't have my baby." Her voice was tear-clogged and hoarse. "You can't, you can't, I won't let you."

Judy Ambrose crouched down so that the patient could see her face.

"Mrs. Allen. Listen, please, Mrs. Allen. Your baby is no longer alive. Its heart stopped beating at least a month ago. I'm sorry for your loss, truly sorry, but we have to think of your health now. The medicine we've given you will help you deliver the child. Don't fight it, please. If you don't deliver the child you'll get very sick and you will die of blood poisoning."

"No, it's not dead." She strained against the restraints, her whole body arching into a contraction. When it passed she said, "I feel it kicking. Just leave it be, just go away and leave me alone. Please."

Anna finished scrubbing in and saw that Elise was watching this exchange very closely. She was biting her lip as if to keep herself from speaking.

"Elise?"

"Just a thought."

"Go on."

"She might be comforted by prayer. If someone prayed with her for the soul of her child. Can a priest be called?"

"You don't want to pray with her?"

Elise put a hand to her lower face and shook her head sharply.

"Then find someone who will," Anna said. "We're about to get started here."

• • •

NOT A HALF hour after the conclusion to Mrs. Allen's labor Anna was scrubbing in again, this time for a slack-faced young girl who refused to give a name. Her problem was easily diagnosed.

Elise said, "This seems to be a common . . . ailment."

"Women who are desperate do desperate things," Anna said. "You will see a lot of this, I'm sorry to say."

"I thought I understood about poverty."

"You still don't. You won't, until you start going out with the visiting nurses. That's where many women give up medicine."

"Not men?"

Anna looked at this young woman who showed so much promise, who learned so eagerly and quickly, and who still was completely unprepared for the trials to come.

"Primarily women. Few male doctors will visit patients in the worst of the tenements. I don't know of any who treat the outdoor poor unless they come to a clinic. I personally think that all male medical students should be required to pay home visits to the poorest and most desperate for a month at least, but nobody asks my opinion." She managed a small smile. "So let's see to this girl. I think her case will take a happy ending." She stopped herself.

"That's entirely the wrong word. What I mean is, we will probably be able to save her life."

◆ ◆ ◆

ON THE WAY home she stopped to buy a variety of newspapers, and then sat on a bench in the small cemetery behind St. Mark's to look through them. She found mention of Archer Campbell's arrest in all of them, the articles prominently placed. There was no new information beyond the fact that he had been arrested when three stolen bearer bonds were found in his possession. The gossip rags were speculating on his role in the disappearance of his four sons. In that they were entirely wrong, and also absolutely correct.

The names of the detectives were familiar, for the simple reason that Jack had introduced her to both Michael Larkin and Hank Sainsbury the last time she had been to police headquarters. They had been both polite and terribly awkward, because, Jack told her later, they had no experience of respectable women in their squad room and feared the wrath of Maroney if they failed to meet his standards of proper behavior.

She thought of Archer Campbell sitting in the Tombs. With his visit to the New Amsterdam he had crossed a line of no return, in Jack's view of the world. She asked herself if she should be objecting for moral or ethical reasons. Then she thought of Mabel Stone and four little boys, and decided she should not.

44

SHE SAID, "DON'T you have a full day planned?"

Jack's arms tightened around her waist. "You owe me a rainy Saturday in bed."

"I might debate that, if it were raining. But it's not. Jack."

"Heartless wretch." Just a mutter, but she heard it and she knew without a doubt that he was already asleep again. It was a trick Anna knew too; she had learned it out of necessity during her training. Somehow that made it easier to rouse him again. She pressed a hand to his shoulder.

"Jack. Don't you have to go in?"

His eyes opened. "I didn't get in until three hours ago."

"That late," Anna said. "Did you make some progress on the case?"

He rubbed a hand over his jaw and the beard stubble made a sound like a scrubbing brush on brickwork.

"Three doctors named Graham so far, none of them fit the bill. We talked to maybe ten night porters. Later today we'll go to the registry office and have a look through the books." He yawned and stretched, opened one eye, and waggled both brows at her.

"Come here."

"Oh, no." She danced away, grabbing up her robe.

"You woke me not once, but twice. Now you must face the consequences."

She slipped out the door and ran, and he came along after her, grumbling, struggling into his robe. In the dining room she said, "Why are you following me?"

"Now you're fishing for compliments," he said, and gave another great yawn.

• • •

AT THE TABLE he showed her the text of the advertisement they were going to run in the newspapers. Anna read it while she buttered her toast.

She said, "So the idea is that if you can't stop him right away, you might be able to slow him down?"

"At this point we have to warn the public."

Anna reasoned that if this announcement in the newspaper frightened one woman away, it was worth the effort and expense. "But what if it makes him angry, what might that mean? Would it make him—strike out more often?"

"My sense is that it won't make a difference," Jack said. "I think he's picking up his pace anyway, and that may mean he's getting sloppy. I've been wondering ever since we interviewed Mamie Winthrop's maid. She gave me the impression that women like Winthrop don't have trouble finding a doctor to solve this particular problem, if the price is right and it can be handled privately. Is that true?"

"Nobody talks about it, but yes, probably. This is one of those areas where physicians say one thing publicly to protect themselves, but then do what they must in the patient's best interest."

"Or for their bank balances."

She nodded, stiffly. "There are unscrupulous physicians, as there are unscrupulous bankers and factory owners and police. Can we talk about something else?"

Just then Mrs. Cabot brought in the mail, a letter from Amelie on the very top.

"Apparently not," Anna said, and opened it while Jack began to look through the rest of the mail.

She said, "She sent a newspaper clipping with a note. We're supposed to go see a woman called Kate Sparrow who lives on Patchin Place; she's got a market stall where she sells sewing supplies, buttons and ribbons and such. I know her stall, but where is Patchin Place?"

"Just across from the Jefferson Market, off Tenth. What's the clipping?"

Her gaze still on the letter, she handed the newspaper article over.

"From the *Morning News*." He swallowed the last of his coffee and read aloud.

SHOCKING TESTIMONY DURING THE CAMPBELL INQUEST

LADY DOCTORS PROVIDE SALACIOUS DETAILS IN A PUBLIC FORUM

OUTRAGE IN THE GALLERY

Yesterday the jury of physicians hearing evidence in the Janine Campbell inquest heard testimony from Dr. Anna Savard and Dr. Sophie Savard Verhoeven. Questioning of Dr. Savard Verhoeven was particularly sharp and often accusatory in tone.

"She may be a lady of unusual intelligence," commented a juror who wishes to remain anonymous. "But she is still a woman and a mulatta, and unsuited to the practice of medicine."

In questioning Dr. Savard Verhoeven, Anthony Comstock of the New York Society for the Suppression of Vice criticized the deceased's behavior and declared that in pursuing an illegal operation Mrs. Campbell had reaped the terrible harvest of her sins against the laws of God and man. In the testimony that followed the jury and gallery heard details of the Campbells' marriage that were so personal in nature that Dr. James Cameron, a retired physician, left the courtroom in an outrage.

"Such topics violate all rules of decency," he told reporters outside the Tombs. He went on to quote the second book of Timothy, verses 11–12, "Let a woman learn quietly with all submissiveness. I do not permit a woman to teach or to exercise authority over a man; rather, she is to remain quiet."

When asked whether his admonition was meant for the deceased Mrs. Campbell or the Drs. Savard, Dr. Cameron said: "Both."

Jack said, "She underlined the name of the doctor they quote, James Cameron. In the margin she wrote: 'He's not dead after all.' What does that mean?"

Anna felt as if she had been struck hard in the stomach.

"Anna, is this the old man who bellowed at the coroner and then stomped out of the courtroom?"

"I think it must be. Do you remember what he looked like?"

Jack shrugged. "Frail, bent. Very proper, old-fashioned. Walked with a cane."

"Yes," Anna said. "Of course, the cane." She looked at him directly and knew that she could not hide the disquiet she was feeling. "I saw him, this Dr. Cameron, just the other day, but I didn't recognize him. It was when I came out of the coffeehouse across from Jefferson Market."

One of his eyebrows peaked, and she knew she had his entire attention. "Go on."

"He was coming down from the el platform. I suppose I never really looked at him in the courtroom, I was so focused on Sophie on the stand. But he looked at me as if he knew me and didn't like what he knew. I remember now, there was another letter he wrote, to the editor at the *Tribune*."

Jack stood up and walked across the room and then back again to sit down where he started. "Tell me what your cousin said about him when you saw her."

Anna closed her eyes to concentrate, and then recounted what she remembered: *a man more bent on purifying women's souls than saving their lives.*

"And she said he was old when she knew him, and was probably dead. He's so frail, Jack. I find it hard to imagine him operating at all. And why would a woman who can afford to pay three hundred dollars settle for him? A steady hand is the very least a woman would want."

Jack said, "They had resources, but don't forget that all of the women we know about lacked connections. Some of them were from out of town, others were from overseas, a few were isolated for other reasons. Mrs. Schmitt's husband is a Baptist minister, for example. None of them could go to sisters or cousins or aunts for advice on what doctor to consult. Now I wonder if we wasted a day looking for Neill Graham's father or grandfather. I need to roust Oscar and get moving on this."

He turned back suddenly. "This Kate Sparrow, she may not want to talk to us without you."

"I could meet you there at noon, unless I have an emergency. And if it won't be too long."

He came around the table, leaned down to kiss her cheek. "Good." He took a moment to look at her, his eyes moving over her face.

"Sometimes your eyes are brown and gold and green, and sometimes they seem mostly brown. Sometimes green. How do you do that?"

She tugged on an earlobe. "It's a secret I dare not divulge."

He smiled against her mouth when he kissed her, and then they both went off to get ready for work. The small bit of breakfast Anna had managed to get down lay like a lead weight in her gut.

◆　◆　◆

ELISE HAD SAVED her time off without a specific plan for how to use it, until the trip to Greenwood came up. Even such a short trip—they would be gone overnight—was exciting. On Saturday morning she woke thinking that she had three full days, and committed herself to using the time to best advantage. She started the day by airing bedding, changing sheets, sweeping and dusting and polishing her way through all the bedrooms.

Mrs. Lee came marching upstairs, wanting to know if Elise was trying to put her granddaughter out of a job, or if she was just set on working herself to death.

"Let me," Elise said. "Please let me. There's enough to keep Laura Lee busy."

Mrs. Quinlan steadfastly refused to accept any payment for board and lodging, but Elise needed to contribute in some way for her own peace of mind.

"Save your money," the old aunt had said when Elise offered to help with household chores. "You'll have expenses in medical school, even with a scholarship."

Today while she worked Rosa followed her around, helping but mostly asking questions. Because, she pointed out, Elise knew more about the Catholic Church than anyone else in the house, which Elise herself had to admit was true.

So she answered questions about the Church hierarchy, about the pope and the archbishops and bishops and priests. Rosa wanted to know about nuns, and who was the boss of nuns, and if nuns and priests had to go to confession, and what if a priest or nun did something really bad?

Nothing Elise said seemed to satisfy her. The little girl wanted justice, and Elise could give her no such promise.

After lunch when the girls went upstairs for their naps, she raised the subject with Mrs. Quinlan.

"She trusts you," Anna's aunt said. "Do you find her questions distressing?"

Elise thought for a moment. "I wouldn't say her questions distress me. It's just that I left that life behind. Or I'm trying to. Not because I hold a grudge, as everyone seems to think. I have no grounds to be critical of the Church."

Margaret pressed her lips together hard. Trying not to say what she thought of the Catholic Church, but sending the message anyway.

"I have no personal grounds," Elise amended. "That doesn't mean I don't see that harm has been done—is still being done—to others. To Rosa. She wants me to be as angry as she is."

"Maybe you should be," Margaret said. "Maybe you will be, as time passes and you think things through."

"Maybe that's true," Elise said, hearing the strain in her own voice. "Maybe I will feel that way some day. But right now I don't have the time or the inclination to put the Church on trial. I need every bit of energy I can muster for the challenges ahead of me."

After lunch Elise put Margaret and Rosa and the Church out of her head and settled down with her books and notes. There was an elderly woman at the New Amsterdam whose heart was failing, and she needed to understand more about what was happening to her.

Anna's copy of *Descriptive and Surgical Anatomy* was well used, the binding loose and the covers a little warped. A whole army of paper strips populated the pages, each with notes written in a small version of Anna's hand. She took the heavy book on her lap and it fell open of its own accord to page 570 ("The Lymphatic System of the Thorax") to reveal a spray of rosebuds that had been pressed there for safekeeping.

In the first moment she had the odd but undeniable sense that she had opened someone else's love letter. Then she reminded herself that Anna had given her leave to make full use of her medical library and so allowed herself to study the rosebuds, small and just partially open. Their scent lingered, faintly musky sweet.

The pages of the book itself were protected by tissue paper on one side, and on the other a large card of thick, cream-colored paper. Without disturbing anything she could make out some of the printing: an invitation to a masked ball.

A hundred questions presented themselves, when and where and mostly, why. Anna Savard didn't seem to have any interest in high society, but she had attended this masked ball. Anna and Jack at a fancy ball was such an odd idea that she had to smile.

It felt like a love letter, Elise realized now, because it was a kind of wordless declaration. Anna Savard, who presented herself to the world as an educated woman with no need for or interest in frivolities, was also a young woman who pressed flowers for sentimental reasons. She could be both people, at once, and that very thought made Elise understand something she had been blind to.

As a little girl she had never seen people courting or falling in love, and in the convent she had been taught to think of such things as shallow and unnecessary in a purposeful life. But there was something here in these few pressed flowers that spoke very powerfully to the contrary, and in a way that surprised her.

She laughed at herself, falling in love with the idea of love, and still, she spent a long time studying the rosebuds before she remembered what she was about and turned to an illustration of the chambers of the human heart.

• • •

PATCHIN PLACE WAS a narrow lane that opened off Tenth Street, lined with cottages leaning together like crooked teeth. As soon as Anna turned into the lane, a plump little woman popped out of a doorway and gestured them closer.

"There you are," she said. "Amelie's cousin Anna, the doctor, is that right? I had a letter from her saying you were to drop by. And with two detective sergeants, as big as houses, both of you. Hope I've got enough food—"

"Mrs. Sparrow," Anna said. "I'm very glad to meet you, but you really don't need to feed us."

Behind her Oscar cleared his throat.

"Nonsense," said Kate Sparrow, ushering them in. "My Mary has got charge of the stall for a couple hours, so I had time to cook. I like to feed people. I was just tickled pink to get a letter from Amelie; the least I can do is feed you after all the good service she did me over the years."

When she had arranged them around her table to her satisfaction Mrs. Sparrow set a huge pot on a trivet between them, added a basket of bread and a jug—ale, by the smell—and passed around thick crockery bowls and spoons.

"Now eat," she said. "And I'll talk. Just set me off in the right direction. Amelie said you wanted to know about old Dr. Cameron, is that right?"

Oscar seemed to be struck dumb by the scent from the stew pot, so Jack spoke up.

"That's right. We're just trying to track down background information, anything you can tell us."

Anna said, "Amelie thought he had died some time ago."

"And well he should be dead," said Kate Sparrow. "Eighty-three, by my reckoning, and so frail a breeze could put him off his feet. Now, I'll get to that, but first I want to hear about Amelie. She didn't say much in her letter but that you would be coming to call."

While Jack and Oscar concentrated on Kate Sparrow's lamb stew, Anna talked about her cousin. The storyteller's price must be paid.

"Amelie told me once she learned midwifery from her own mother, way up north in the mountains, when she was a girl."

Anna said, "Her mother was my great-aunt Hannah. They both attended my mother when I was born. Mrs. Sparrow—"

"Kate. You must call me Kate."

"Kate. Amelie said you could tell the detective sergeants about a Dr. Cameron."

Kate's expression sobered. "I can tell you about Cameron. If you really want to know."

"We need to know," Jack said.

She spread her hands flat on the table and studied them for a moment. "The word that comes to mind is *severe*. Old Testament severe. Quoted the Bible to women in travail, wanted to hear them pray out loud. Now, to be fair, he knew what he was doing. Rarely lost a mother. But the man never smiles, not even after he's put a healthy baby in its ma's arms."

"Did he ever strike out? Was he violent?" Oscar asked.

"You mean with fists? I don't think so. The man has a temper, but it was all talk, fire and brimstone. A girl expecting a baby without a husband, you could hear him shouting down on the street if the windows were open."

"He's still in practice? Delivering babies?" Anna heard her tone and wished she were better at hiding what she was thinking, but Kate Sparrow didn't seem to notice one way or the other.

"Don't see how he could," she said. "Weak as a kitten. But he does go in and out of that old office of his, pretty much every day."

When Oscar asked for more specific information about Cameron's office, Kate Sparrow led them out onto the street, and from the corner she pointed out a building at the intersection of Tenth and Greenwich. "Second floor," she said. "Side entrance."

They went back to their lunch and Jack started where Oscar had left off.

"Do you see women coming and going as well, women who might be patients?"

She shrugged. "It's a busy corner, and he's not the only one with an office on the second floor. I do see his granddaughter, because she takes him lunch every day. I notice her crossing Sixth Avenue because she's always lost in her thoughts, and many times she's come close to getting herself run over. It's almost funny, the way she looks up and scowls at the driver, like he was in her way. But now that I think on it—"

Anna gave her an encouraging smile.

"Nora hasn't passed by for two days at least. Maybe he's laid up."

Oscar said, "So Cameron has a granddaughter—"

"Nora Smithson," Kate said. "A beauty, tall and slim with hair like corn silk. She married the oldest Smithson boy, just last year. She used to work with her grandfather but now she clerks in the apothecary, does Mrs. Smithson, as she's called nowadays and don't nobody dare forget and call her Nora. The whole family's like that."

She wrinkled her nose as if she were smelling something unpleasant, and that made sense to Anna. She remembered Nora Smithson's condescending and judgmental manner all too clearly.

Anna glanced at Jack. "Could I have a couple of minutes alone with Mrs. Sparrow, do you think?"

When the men had shut the door behind themselves, Kate Sparrow grinned widely. "I was hoping you'd send them away. Can't really talk about some things, not with men thinking so loud in the background."

Anna managed a smile. "My feelings exactly. So if I can be blunt—"

Kate leaned forward, nodding.

◆　◆　◆

OSCAR BOUGHT A paper cone of peanuts and they walked over to the corner to look at the office building Kate Sparrow had pointed out. Like most of the buildings in the neighborhood it had seen better days; rain and weather had scoured most of the paint from the boards and the roof sagged. But on the ground floor a cobbler, a leather goods shop, and a confectioner were doing brisk business. Every window in the top two floors advertised a business in bold black paint on glass: dentist, bookkeeper, sign painter, textile importer, employment agent, dressmaker. It wasn't until they rounded the corner onto Christopher Street that they found what they were looking for: another entry, and above it a window identifying the offices of Dr. J. M. Cameron on the second floor.

They were debating whether to go up and have a look when the door opened and a woman came out, slender and fairly tall, carefully groomed and dressed, a fringe of almost white-blond hair just visible under the brim of her bonnet.

Oscar tilted his head toward her and took off in pursuit, leaving Jack to finagle his way into the doctor's office on his own. He went up the stairs at a trot and walked along a dim hall until he stood in front of Cameron's office at the far end. He knocked, waited two beats, tried the knob, and found it unlocked, and no wonder: inside the small waiting room was empty, without a single piece of furniture.

From an inner room he heard a scuffle of feet and a head poked out from around a corner. A younger man with a salesman's smile. "Hello! Hello, come in. Are you here about the ad?"

"I was looking for Dr. Cameron."

The smile froze and then melted away. "Dr. Cameron's retired," he said. "Last week. He was the first tenant when the building was new, almost fifty years ago and now he's retired."

He came forward and held out his hand. A dry, firm grip and the smile was back in place. "I'm the landlord, Jeremy Bigelow. Don't suppose you might be in the market for office space? Great setup for almost any business. Waiting room, office, two rooms for storage or client meetings or whatever—"

"I suppose I could have a look while I'm here," Jack said, and followed along.

The rooms had been scrubbed and painted, with only the vaguest smells left to indicate that this had been a medical practice. While Bigelow talked about square footage and foot traffic and the neighborhood, Jack looked out the window onto Christopher Street, wondering if Cameron had really retired, or if he had gone into hiding.

Bigelow wanted to know if he could show Jack anything else of interest.

"Would you happen to have an address for Dr. Cameron?"

Bigelow did not. "But his granddaughter is at the apothecary just across from the el station—" He jerked a thumb over his shoulder in the right direction. "Nora Smithson. She could help you, I'm sure."

On the street Jack found Anna and Oscar waiting, Anna looking very grim and Oscar irritated.

Anna said, "I have to get back to the New Amsterdam. If you come with me we can talk in the cab."

♦ ♦ ♦

TRAFFIC WAS JUST as congested as Jack expected it to be, but for once it would work to their advantage. It took ten minutes to get to the corner of West Ninth, just enough time to share the bad news.

Oscar said, "Two steps forward, ten back."

Cameron had left the city only days before, on his way to Philadelphia, where he would be living with a nephew and his family. His offices had been vacated before Mamie Winthrop's operation and death.

"No surgical instruments in Cameron's office?" Anna asked Jack.

"Cleaned out, every bit of it. I looked into the closets and the water closet, no luck. What did Mrs. Sparrow have to tell you?"

"Cameron was the one who forced Amelie out of the city. He went to Comstock with stories of a mad abortionist who was killing women, and he named Amelie. There wasn't any evidence because"—she looked at both of them intently—"there wasn't any crime, but Comstock made her life impossible and Nora Smithson started spreading rumors. Kate thinks that Cameron was mean to the bone, but not murderous. And not capable of operating. His hands are palsied."

"That's what his granddaughter said, that he hadn't had a patient in years. Kept the office out of stubbornness and pride." Oscar didn't seem to be frustrated, but then he had been pursuing cases like this for years, and had learned patience.

"Does she have any medical training, the granddaughter?" Jack asked.

Anna said, "No schooling, but she was his nurse for years until she got married and moved over to the apothecary."

They looked at each other for a few moments while the cab jerked to a stop and drivers let their displeasure be heard.

"Now what?" Anna said, finally.

"We go back to sorting through records and interviewing people," Jack said.

"And if there's another victim this week?" she asked.

"Then we'll know for sure that Cameron wasn't involved," Oscar said. "Or that he's still here, set up someplace else in the city and in hiding."

"Or that the responsible party has been tipped off," Jack added.

Anna asked, "He might just stop?"

"No," Oscar and Jack said in one voice.

"He's got an urge," Oscar said. "Whoever he is. He may go quiet for weeks or months, but he won't give up. Maybe he'll go away and start over, in Boston or Chicago. There's no way to know, but we do have another lead."

"You're still thinking of Neill Graham as a suspect," Anna said.

"Hard not to," Oscar said. "You'd think so too, if you heard him talking about operating on women."

"Things never tie up as neat as you'd like," Jack said, touching her arm. "Or as fast. Nothing like surgery."

She gave him a lopsided grin. "So I'm learning. Why don't you just take Graham in for questioning?"

"Because we haven't got any proof at all, and if we tip him off he'll disappear."

"That wouldn't do at all," Anna said. "Not at all."

"No reason to give up now," Oscar told her. "Not when it's just getting interesting."

* * *

IN THE LATE evening Jack forced himself to put aside thinking about the case so he could give in to the inevitable. He turned his mind to packing for the short trip to Greenwood. Anna's valise was already packed and she had stretched out on the bed with one of her endless medical journals.

Rumbling through the closet, he muttered to himself about the number of coats and vests and pairs of trousers he had accumulated. His sisters meant well but had gotten into the habit of treating him like a mannequin, something that would hopefully stop now. Right at this moment the problem was that he was not just going home tomorrow, but he was taking Anna home with him for the first time. That seemed to require something more than the casual clothes he normally put on to go to Greenwood.

Anna had hung out a summer gown of many thin layers, overlapping in some places and pinned up in others. It was cut loose, like all her clothes, with a square neck that would show a great deal of bosom and her long neck. He was pulling a suit out of the wardrobe when there was a knock at the door.

"Sorry to bother you so late," Ned called. "But there's something you will want to hear."

Jack might have sent him away, but Anna pulled on her robe and tied it while she opened the door.

"Is there something wrong?"

"No. But I talked to somebody who recognized Tonino from my description."

* * *

THE STORY WAS quickly told: Ned had run into an old friend with the improbable name of Moby Dick.

"He apprenticed to a cobbler in Harlem five years ago or more. Hadn't seen him since he moved. He was down here to show his bride his old haunts."

Anna tried very hard to harness her impatience, but Jack did not. He made a twirling motion with his hand and Ned wagged his head from side to side in acknowledgment.

"We were just talking, you know, and I mentioned I was looking for this Italian kid. Moby didn't know anything about him, but his girl did. She's a teacher at the deaf school.

"Hope, that's her name, says they've got a little boy about six or seven years old, black hair, blue eyes, but he's deaf. So it's probably not the kid you're looking for, but I thought I'd mention it. If you want me to go up there and have a look, I can."

They were silent for a moment, and then she said, "I can't remember Tonino ever saying a word to me. Did you hear him talk, Jack?"

Jack had not. "But if he were deaf Rosa would have said something."

"Children who have suffered a shock sometimes stop talking. They might believe he's deaf, when he's just ignoring everything and everyone. Out of self-preservation."

"Or he might be deaf," Jack said.

They looked at each other, and Jack saw something flash across her face, sudden insight or determination or both.

"We could go tomorrow, if we leave early enough."

Jack took a deep breath, and then another. "That's what we'll have to do. But we can't say anything to the girls."

"Or Margaret," Anna agreed. "Or anyone. Another disappointment so soon would be very hard on the girls. Aunt Quinlan has a saying at times like this. 'Don't go looking for trouble, it will find you soon enough without you shouting out an invitation.'"

Anna lay awake for a very long time, thinking of the very nature of trouble or bad luck or whatever name you wanted to use. More than that, she wondered why the idea of finding Tonino should strike her as trouble. In the end she fell asleep thinking of Rosa, who wanted this brother back so very much. She had such high expectations of what it would mean to be reunited with him, when in fact the boy she remembered was gone, even if they brought him home with them tomorrow.

45

AT SEVEN JACK went to hitch Bonny to the Rockaway for the last-minute trip to the school for the deaf. Anna followed, yawning into her palm. She had been determined to get a good night's sleep and had failed almost completely.

In the stable Bonny nickered at Jack and presented her head for rubbing. Another female under his spell, Anna thought and then watched as he snuck a lump of sugar out of his pocket and pressed the flat of his palm to her mouth.

"I saw that."

He winked at her. "Jealous?"

Anna made a face at him and went off in search of Mrs. Lee's coffee, walking through the garden. If she was really fortunate, the girls would be off with Margaret for what she called their morning constitutional. Otherwise she would be overwhelmed with questions about her plans for the day, none of which she could answer honestly.

With the door and windows all open the smells that came from the kitchen reminded Anna of Thanksgiving, an odd thing for the last week of June. Mrs. Lee had been cooking and baking for days, and had prepared so many things to take with them to Greenwood that Jack had arranged for his cousins to transport it all in one of the shop delivery wagons. Now Mrs. Lee was in a rush, putting the finishing touches on everything from a ham to an assortment of pies.

Anna said, "We don't have to bring enough food for the whole crowd, Mrs. Lee," and recognized her tactical error before the last word was out of her mouth.

Mrs. Lee lowered her chin to her breast to peer at Anna over the top of her spectacles and delivered one of her lectures, short and to the point: She, Anna Savard, brought up in this very kitchen and reminded every day since she was three years old the importance of good manners, should realize that the Weeds and Roses folks could not call on the Mezzanottes empty-handed.

While Anna listened she poured herself a cup of coffee and milk and tried to look repentant.

From her spot at the kitchen table Aunt Quinlan said, "Leave her be, Anna. You know she's not happy unless she's feeding people. And don't you look pretty. Where are you two off to this morning, anyway?"

"It's a secret," Mrs. Lee said. "Jack came by earlier to ask Henry could they take the Rockaway. Detective work."

Anna hooked a warm roll from a pan that had just come out of the oven, and jumped back before Mrs. Lee could smack her hand.

"It's not a secret," she said. "But it's too complicated to explain just now."

"Is that so." Mrs. Lee's expression narrowed.

"I promise to tell all later," she said, and pressed an impromptu kiss on the old lady's cheek.

"Get on with you." Mrs. Lee flapped her hands, but she was smiling. "I got work to do."

"A calf to butcher? A last-minute ten-layer cake?"

"Anna," her aunt said. "If you can spare a few minutes, I had a letter from Sophie yesterday."

Anna sat down, her mood gone.

"I know how you're feeling," her aunt said. "It takes courage to open Sophie's letters. So let me just tell you, Cap is stable. That low-grade fever is still hanging on, but his spirits are good. He doesn't complain about food or even treatments, and sleeps a great deal."

"And Sophie?"

"You know your cousin, she doesn't write about herself."

"Stories to tell about the folks in the village—" Mrs. Lee interjected. "Ignorant as they are."

Anna looked up in surprise, and her aunt explained.

"Sophie wrote about a little boy asking if he could see her tail."

"The ignorance of it," Mrs. Lee said. "She shouldn't have to contend with such meanness of spirit. She should be home here with us where people know her worth and don't insult her asking can they see her tail. You would never let one of your children talk to a stranger like that, Lily, and you know it."

When Mrs. Lee called Aunt Quinlan by her first name, she had come to the end of her patience.

"I want her home," Mrs. Lee went on. "But to get her here we got to lose Cap. I'm always wanting to ask you, Anna, will Sophie be home by the end of the summer, but I stop myself. It would be like asking when will it be that Cap passes over."

Anna had to swallow very hard to find her voice. "She went of her own free will, Mrs. Lee. She went gladly, because she wants and needs to be with Cap. No doubt it is odd and sometimes uncomfortable for her, but Sophie won't let anything get in the way of caring for him, you know that. If it makes you feel better, sit down and write her a letter and say what you're thinking."

"I'ma do just that," Mrs. Lee said. "First thing we get home."

"And now I have to go. I'll see you all at Greenwood." Her voice came a little hoarse.

"What about your satchels?" her aunt asked.

"On the back porch. Ned will fetch them when the wagon comes." She glanced around the kitchen, but bit back a smile. "For all this."

"You won't be late." As close as her aunt came to issuing a command.

"Of course not. We'll be there in the late afternoon."

"Late afternoon?" Mrs. Lee shook her head. "Where you going to eat between now and then? One of them little cafés where they serve out stomachache as a first and last course? Is that how you look after your husband? I swear."

While she talked she grabbed up things and stuffed them into a marketing basket. Then she thrust it at Anna. "Lunch."

Anna was still smiling to herself when she got back to the stable and found that they were set to leave, Bonny stomping to announce she was eager to be on the road. Jack's face was already damp with sweat, but he looked pleased with himself.

"There's Ned," Mr. Lee said, pointing with his chin. "He's unsure about coming along today. Just so you know."

Mr. Lee had decided that Ned belonged here, that was obvious to Anna. She wondered if Ned realized as much.

Jack called out in Italian, his tone easy, but Ned's face contorted in mock terror.

"Didn't do it," he called back. "Wasn't me."

Coming up to him Anna gave him a gentle push. "Stop pretending to be an outlaw."

"I think I'm insulted," Ned said, rubbing his shoulder.

Jack said, "What else do you know about Moby Dick's wife?"

Ned's look of surprise was genuine. "Well, let's see. She's from an old Dutch family in Harlem, don't remember her maiden name. You headed up to talk to her?"

"Maybe," Jack said. "She goes by Hope March, Mrs. March?"

"That would be Moby's moniker when he's plying his trade, Richard March."

"And she teaches at the school for the deaf, you're sure of it."

"She teaches knitting and sewing and such to the girls."

Anna said to Jack, "Stop interrogating him." And to Ned: "Do you happen to remember anything else about the boy she mentioned to you, beyond his hair and eye color?"

Ned glanced down at the ground, scuffed the cobblestones with his heel, hesitating.

"Spit it out," Jack said. "Whatever it is."

He shrugged. "She said the kid was simple, you know. Slow. Like a lot of deaf kids, his brains got scrambled somewhere along the way. But she wasn't mean about it. Moby always was a softhearted mope, they suit each other that way."

"There's more than one softhearted mope in this story," Anna said.

"What if it is him?" Ned wanted to know.

"We'll bring him home," Anna said. "And your friend's wife will get a reward. But Ned, don't say a word to anybody, especially not the girls."

Now he looked insulted. "I wouldn't hurt those girls for the world."

Anna touched his shoulder. "We know that. Are you coming to Greenwood with us?"

Jack had started to turn away, but he stopped to glance at Ned. "You're invited, in case you need reminding."

"Do your sisters know that?" Ned asked him.

Jack grinned. "I guess we'll find out."

⋄   ⋄   ⋄

TRAFFIC WAS LIGHT so early on a Sunday morning, which was a very good thing considering how far they had to go. The New York School for the Deaf and Dumb was well out of the city at 165th Street, an hour and a half away in good traffic. Alone she would have had to take at least two trains, with long waits in between connections.

She leaned back and felt herself relaxing. For the next little time they had nothing to worry about, and only themselves to amuse. She said, "You are a useful creature."

Jack gave her a long, thoughtful glance. "Am I supposed to return the compliment, or will that irritate you?"

"You know how useful I am," she said. "I can't really cook, at least not the way I'd need to cook to keep you fed. I don't clean, I barely sew, I've never done a full load of laundry."

"I can't do any of those things either."

"But you can hitch a wagon, and clean a gun, and repair a broken window. You mended the strap on my shoe, built a coatrack for the front hall. I believe you could have done most of the work on the house yourself, with sufficient time. You negotiated the purchase too. No, unless you need surgery or dosing I'm very much useless. There's a term in German that suits me exactly. I'm a *Fachidiot*. I know a huge amount about one thing, and I'm idiotically uninformed about everything else. It's a good thing we have household help or you'd be going to work hungry, in wrinkled clothes."

"We've had this discussion before," Jack said. "And we can keep having it, until you believe that I like what I've got and I'm not going anywhere. Your brother was a boy in a bad situation and he let you down. That's not me, and you know it."

"Not everything is about my brother," she said, a little huffily.

He glanced at her, his expression cool. "Not everything," he said finally. "But this is. Stop trying to talk me into giving up on you. It won't work."

Anna wanted to protest, but she remembered quite suddenly a conversation with her aunt, and not so very long ago. She had predicted exactly this, that Anna would try to isolate herself from Jack. The thought struck her with almost palpable force, and it took a few minutes for her to regain her composure. For the first time she had the idea that with Jack's help she might someday come to understand the boy her brother had been and to forgive the decisions he had made.

"You're right," she said finally. "I've been testing you without even realizing it. I apologize."

He glanced at her, his expression guarded at first. Then he smiled and took her hand, raised it to his mouth, and kissed her knuckles.

"You know," he said. "We don't have to go to the school today. It's waited this long. How about a picnic in Central Park instead? We could let Bonny stretch her legs and then go sit by one of the lakes."

It did sound like a very good idea, and she said so. "But I think we have to do it today, Jack. It would be a week or more before we get another chance."

◆ ◆ ◆

HE ASKED HER about the school for the deaf, and Anna told him the little she knew. "They have an excellent reputation. I've never had a patient from there, but Sophie has and she liked the place. The children are well looked after and there were no signs of abuse."

"You think a lot about the welfare of children."

Anna's head came around quite quickly. "Does that surprise you, given the work I do?"

"Not in the least. I'm going to ask you something, and I don't want you to get mad."

"Not a very hopeful start," she said, but she produced a single dimple, which he took as encouragement.

"I'm wondering if there are many women who would rather not have children, if they had a choice."

"Are you asking about me?"

He shook his head. "I've been thinking about Janine Campbell and the others."

Her gaze shifted and lost its focus. She was letting her mind lead her, following whatever images and words and ideas it presented. Many of them beyond his understanding.

She said, "Really you want to know if women are mentally destined to become mothers. I think the answer is no. It's primarily a matter of what a girl is raised to believe is right and normal. I'm sure there are many women who would prefer not to have children, but few of them are honest with themselves about that. They know of two ways to be female: to marry and raise families, or to never marry and forgo children. The third and fourth possibilities are not something any woman would plan for. Infertility is a terrible burden for some, but worse still—"

"Children born out of wedlock."

"Yes. I've seen young girls so devastated by news of a pregnancy that they would rather die. Some of them do choose to die; you know better than I do about the bodies that wash up on the riverbanks. But if a woman chooses not to marry and chooses to never have children, she is branding herself in a different way. Even if she has an income and can do what interests her, she is still seen as suspect. Unnatural. In the end few people are strong enough to reject what society expects of them."

"You might have done that," Jack said.

"I would have done that," she said. "If not for Hoboken. But I am very odd, Jack. You know that. I'm an unusual person in an unusual family."

"Part of why we suit. We have that in common."

Her expression was solemn. "That's not entirely true. A man has the freedom to choose not to marry. No one would have thought you unnatural."

He couldn't contradict that statement. His mother would have been sad, but none of his brothers or friends would have made an issue of it. At the same time there would be suspicions, in some quarters.

Anna said, "In general men are free to find comfort and companionship where they please. So long as they don't flout expectations openly."

She often surprised him, and he was beginning to understand that she always would. The way her mind worked was still a mystery and would probably remain a mystery, at least in part, but there was another trap that he fell into: he forgot how much experience she had in the world of things most women never were exposed to. In a city like New York, a physician could not be innocent or naïve.

They had never talked about sex except as something they shared, in the privacy of their home and bed, but that didn't mean that she was unaware. He wondered if she was thinking of Oscar, who had never married and would never marry.

"The 'confirmed bachelor.'" He used the euphemism and saw that he had understood her correctly. But she wasn't thinking of Oscar, or at least, not in this instance.

She said, "Uncle Quinlan would never have married, if he had had the choice as a young man. His affections were elsewhere, with one of Aunt Quinlan's cousins, actually. But it was impossible, and he married the girl his family chose for him. He met Aunt Quinlan at the funeral of that cousin he had loved as a young man. Later when he was widowed he proposed a marriage of convenience, I suppose is the term, and she moved down here."

"You mean they never shared a bed."

"Yes, that's what I mean. They were the closest of friends, and they supported each other through very difficult times." She paused, her gaze still speculative. "Is that the subject you wanted to raise, when you asked about women who don't want to have children?"

Jack said, "Now I'm not sure exactly what I was asking."

She shifted in her seat to look at him directly. "I have never been drawn to other women."

"Anna!"

She gave him a cool look. "You never wondered?"

"I can say with all honesty that it never occurred to me. I saw you as desirable and my sense was, you felt the same way about me."

Finally, she produced a smile. "Oh, I did. After you put those rosebuds in my hair I couldn't get you out of my mind. So you *are* asking me about children." She studied her clasped hands for a moment. "I never thought very much about having children because I didn't expect to have that opportunity. Now I think I do want to have a child or two of my own. With you. I think I'll be ready next year, if you're ready. And if you are still willing to have a wife who is a mother and a practicing physician and surgeon, all at once. It can be done. Mary Putnam is going to be my role model. A physician of the highest rank, and a wife and mother. And of course, exhausted, all the time."

She made him laugh. "You being exhausted is not in my plan."

"And you intend to have your way."

"You have grasped the essence of my character. Do you know why I raised the subject just now?"

"I expect it has to do with my first visit to Greenwood," she said. "And the questions that will be coming my way."

◆　◆　◆

WITH THE SUN in her eyes Anna couldn't quite make out Jack's expression, but she caught the change in tone. Discomfort, maybe even reluctance. "Go on," she said. "I'm listening."

"People will be cornering you with personal questions, you're right. But there's another subject that will be raised, and I wanted to make sure you knew the particulars before you hear about it. About Celestina."

"Now you've surprised me. Go on."

"You know that she goes to temple a few times a month on the Sabbath?"

"I'm aware, yes. Bambina goes too, doesn't she?"

"Less often. Bambina goes to please Mama. Celestina goes to please herself."

Anna smoothed her skirts, thinking. "I confess I have no idea where this is going."

"Then I'll get to the heart of it. Celestina had a marriage proposal, from the rabbi of her congregation."

In her surprise Anna found nothing suitable to say, and so she asked the obvious question. "When was this?"

"A couple days ago. She told me about it yesterday."

"And what did she say to him?"

"She put him off."

"She didn't refuse him?"

"Or accept him."

Anna thought for a moment.

Jack said, "You just did that humming thing. What are you thinking?"

"I'm wondering about this—what's his name?"

"Nate Rosenthal."

"Mr. Rosenthal—"

"Rabbi Rosenthal."

"Does she love him?"

He glanced at her, his mouth quirked up. "She doesn't say."

"But she didn't refuse him outright."

"No. I think she would have accepted him, if not for—"

"Bambina. She thinks the rabbi is not good enough for her sister. She doesn't approve."

"Why do you come to that conclusion?"

Anna raised an eyebrow, and he inclined his head in acknowledgment.

"Yes, all right. She doesn't really approve of anybody. She doesn't like Nate Rosenthal because he's forty. A widower with two little girls. Or at least, that's her official stance."

Anna had seen sisters who loved and valued each other, sisters who tore at each other out of jealousy and spite, and everything in between. She and Sophie had never fought the way sisters sometimes did, and never took each other or the value of their connection for granted. There didn't seem to be any rhyme or reason to the way these things worked.

She thought of Bambina as someone who was difficult to live with and drew most of the attention to herself. If Celestina found this unfair, she hid her feelings well.

Jack said, "You don't like Bambina."

"There are things I don't like about her," Anna said. "She can be narrow minded and judgmental, and it will take a long time for me to get over the way she treated Sophie. Assuming for a moment that she has changed her mind and her manners in that regard. But she's very young and bright and ambitious, and she's frustrated. I think the best thing for her would be to live on her own for a good while."

The look he shot her way was pure surprise tinged with irritation. "When this subject first came up I told you that it's not acceptable for young Italian women to live alone. It's just not done."

Anna pushed out a soft breath. "Listen before you reject the idea out of hand."

"Anna—"

"Listen," she said again. "There are some excellent boardinghouses for young women, extremely selective, in very good neighborhoods and with spotless reputations. They aren't cheap—the one I'm thinking of is six dollars a week for room and board—but no male visitors are allowed, not even relatives, except in the parlor, and then only chaperoned. I know of two women doctors who live in a boardinghouse just across from Gramercy Park. I've even visited them there. It's beautifully kept; the food is excellent. It's run by an elderly couple. She's a Quaker and he's a retired police officer. As far as I know they've never had any kind of incident or trouble—but you could, you should inquire at the station, couldn't you?"

He shrugged in reluctant agreement.

"You act as if I'm suggesting she go live on the moon."

"But what would she do with herself all day long?"

Anna resisted the urge to laugh at him, this disgruntled and overprotective and—it had to be said—clueless older brother. "She could continue with her sewing and embroidery, or she could teach, or here's an idea and it's one you really should consider. She could learn something else, study something that interests her and take up a career of her own choosing. Bambina is difficult and demanding because she's unhappy, and she's young and selfish enough to demand that her sister keep her company in her misery."

Anna forced herself to stop talking. Jack would think about this idea if she allowed him the time he needed to do that.

"She'd be alone," he said finally.

This time she did let out a small laugh. "Alone? She would be within a short walk or ride of us, your aunt Philomena, Celestina in her new home, and your many, many cousins. I still haven't figured out exactly how many cousins you have, by the way. She would also have friends her own age, young women she could go to concerts or lectures or for walks or to the theater with. Living among other young women who have careers might make a very large difference in the way she sees the world. You think she would reject the idea out of hand?"

He shrugged. "That's not what worries me. What worries me is that she'll like the idea, and my parents will forbid it. Then Celestina is worse off."

Anna put her hand on his thigh and felt him start in surprise. It was a bold thing to do in public, even with so little traffic on the streets—but she meant to startle him. "What if I talked to your mother about it? If she agreed, could she win your father over? At that point the subject could be raised with Bambina."

He shook his head and let out a half laugh. "Go ahead and talk to Mama if you can get her alone for a quarter hour." He covered her hand with his own and squeezed. Anna gave him a smile, wondering what exactly she had gotten herself into.

•   •   •

TRAFFIC PICKED UP but they still made good time. Broadway became Bloomingdale Road and houses grew farther apart, interrupted now and then by churches, dairy farms, hatcheries, horse pastures, warehouses, nurseries. This far out of the city every building was surrounded by parks: the Leake and Watts Orphan Asylum, the Insane Asylum, the Colored Orphan Asylum all looked like pleasant places to those who kept their distance. Anna, who had visited many such places when she was in training, knew better.

But they did look wonderful from the road. They drove past the Convent of the Sacred Heart in an ocean of green that stretched from 130th to 135th Streets, and then the Hebrew Orphan Asylum, one place Anna had never been but Sophie had, making rounds with Dr. Jacobi. Jack turned left on 155th and right on Eleventh Boulevard, passing Audubon Park; and turned one last time left onto a half-built road to arrive, finally, at the New York School for the Deaf and Dumb.

Anna had expected something quite small, and was surprised to see four large, well-kept buildings arranged in a quadrangle. The road approached from the rear, and as they circled around to the front entrance the landscaped grounds opened into a larger field where children were playing with a ball. The whole of the property was surrounded by woods, the kind that offered cool shade in the hottest months. A breeze came from the Hudson, which must be just beyond the woods.

Jack said, "From a distance you wouldn't know anything was different about them."

She followed his line of sight to the children.

"I thought there would be more of them," he said. "It looks like they'd have room for at least four hundred students."

Anna watched for a moment as they drew closer. Deaf or hearing, children were fearless; boys climbed onto a tree stump to fling themselves into space as though gravity had no authority and deserved no respect. A small group of girls stood in a circle playing cat's cradle, all eyes intent on the hands of the two girls who were competing. There were children playing like this everywhere in the world, but few of them would be as silent.

"I would guess that most of them go home for some part of the summer. It's not an orphan asylum."

"Which raises a question," Jack said, just as a gaunt man of about sixty stepped out of the front doors of the school. There was a woman with him who Anna guessed must be his daughter, so strong was the resemblance, from the line of the jaw and nose to the color and texture of their hair. Neat, orderly, like schoolteachers everywhere; reserved, but not unfriendly. The two waited as the carriage came to a standstill and Jack helped Anna down.

She looked up at them, using a hand to shield the sun from her face. "Hello. We were hoping to speak to the director, if he's available on a Sunday."

"That would be me. Alan Timbie." He came down two steps to shake hands, gesturing to the young woman to join him. "This is my daughter Miranda, one of our teachers. We are expecting the Humbolt family, but you aren't the Humbolts, are you?"

They introduced themselves and then waited as Alan Timbie turned to his daughter and they had a conversation in sign language.

To Anna and Jack he said, "We have a new student arriving within the hour, but I can talk to you until they come, if you like. I'm quite curious about what brings a New York Police Department detective sergeant to our door."

They sat down in a waiting room while Jack described Tonino, saying nothing of his circumstances beyond the fact that he had been separated from his family. Anna watched for some reaction, but the director's expression revealed nothing but polite concern. When Jack had finished Timbie nodded.

"We have a boy here who fits your description, but I don't think he's the child you're looking for."

Anna said, "Could we see him, just to be sure?"

He showed them to a large common room with open windows on two walls that faced a small wood of birch trees. There was a young man signing to a group of three boys while a fourth boy sat by himself with a picture book in his lap. About seven years old, he seemed on the face of things to be healthy: his color was good, his cheeks rounded, he was dressed appropriately for the season, his clothes neat, if much mended. His hair had been dampened and parted and combed into submission, furrowed as neatly as a newly plowed field. He was staring blankly at the book in his lap, like a child on the verge of sleep.

Anna felt Jack's attention focusing on the boy and the shock of recognition, exactly like her own. Tonino Russo, without a doubt.

The director was saying, "We call him Jimmy. I don't believe he can hear you, but please talk to him, if you like."

Jack cleared his throat and called across the room in a voice gone slightly hoarse.

"Tonino. Your sisters are looking for you. They miss you."

Nothing. Not the slightest shimmer of recognition. Jack nudged Anna's arm, gently, and she tried, piecing the Italian together carefully.

"Rosa has been searching for you everywhere. Lia asks for you every day."

The boy turned his face away.

Jack walked toward him, quietly, slowly, and then crouched down, his hands on his knees. Now the boy did look at Jack. He took in his features, watching his mouth as he talked, his voice lowered so Anna couldn't make out what he was saying.

Tonino looked at him with a kind of detached politeness, nothing of hostility or interest in his expression.

"He's not a difficult child," said the director to Anna. "If you can make him understand what is expected of him, he complies without complaint. But he isn't quite in the world, if I can put it that way. He's hiding in his head. It's not a medical term—"

"But it's very apt," Anna said. "He doesn't try to communicate at all? He can't be provoked?"

The director shook his head. "Not that any adult has ever observed."

"Mr. Timbie," Anna said. "This is the boy we've been looking for. He doesn't speak English, which explains at least in part why he doesn't try to communicate. The shock of losing his parents and then being separated from his sisters and brother has wounded him in a very fundamental way."

Jack came back then, his hands shoved deep into his pockets and his expression troubled.

"Let's go back to my office," the director said. "I'd like to hear the whole story in detail, and we can discuss how to proceed from there."

Walking away from the classroom, Anna took Jack's arm. She said, "Children are resilient. Rosa and Lia will draw him out. It's not too late."

Jack put his hand over hers and gave a grim smile. "I'm glad to hear it."

Anna thought, *But you don't believe it.*

• • •

It took a good while to tell the whole story, from the time the Russo children had lost their mother and been surrendered to the church by their father, what had happened at Hoboken and then at the Christopher Street ferry terminal, and finally the long weeks of calling on asylums and agencies and offices in search of the two Russo boys.

"Then we heard indirectly about a boy fitting Tonino's description through a Mrs. March."

"Our teacher, Mrs. March? Hope March?"

Anna nodded. "And here we are."

Mr. Timbie had been taking notes during the whole conversation, pausing now and then to ask for a clarification. His manner was professional, courteous, and opaque. At the same time he reminded Anna of Jack when he was thinking like a police detective: there were things going on beneath the surface that he would not divulge until it suited him.

Jack said, "I have a question for you, if I may. How is it you ended up taking in an orphan? This is a school, as I understand it, and not an orphanage. Or do I have that wrong?"

"We board most of our students, and have some space for charity cases. Deaf children, orphaned deaf children especially, don't do well in asylums, and so we agreed to keep him when the police officer brought him to us on the first of May, I believe it was."

Anna glanced at Jack and he put a hand over hers where it rested on the arms of the chair.

"You're sure of the date?"

"I can check the records, but I know it was in the first few days of May because he came right after two of our older students left us. Otherwise we wouldn't have had room. Why do you ask?"

"Tonino went missing on the twenty-sixth of March," Anna said. "Where was he before he came to you?"

"I have no idea," the director said. "I'm not even sure which police officer brought him to us. The gap in time is troubling." He looked at them and then down at his notes and then went on, almost reluctantly.

"The boy is scarred. There is evidence that he was beaten severely on his back, from knees to shoulders. Just barely healed, most of the lash marks."

Jack spoke up, and Anna was glad because she could not.

"He was examined by a doctor?"

"Yes, our resident physician. Dr. Warren. He's not here today, or you could talk to him directly. Tonino is better nourished now and less anxious than he was when he arrived, but not much less. We do what we can, but in cases like this—"

"We understand," Anna said. "Far too well. I am on the staff at the New Amsterdam Charity Hospital, Mr. Timbie. We see children who have suffered every kind of abuse and degradation."

Jack said, "You must agree that together we are well suited to care for a child with a history like Tonino's."

"In theory, yes," the director said. "But it does bother me that the boy doesn't seem to recognize you. You still want to take him?"

"We would like to take him," Anna said. "Being reunited with his sisters is probably the best way to reach him, now."

"Then there is paperwork to be done," said Timbie, getting to his feet. "It must be handled according to the law. You may start while I'm checking in the new student."

• • •

MR. TIMBIE SENT for a notary, arranged for paper and ink and pens, collected forms to be filled out, and went off to greet his new student. Anna paced the room while these arrangements were being made, stopping to look at framed diplomas on the wall. Mr. Ambrose Timbie had graduated from the National Deaf-Mute College in Washington, D.C., some fourteen years ago. His diploma had been signed by President Grant, which struck Anna as very odd.

"Our son, Ambrose," said an older woman as she came into the office, followed by Miss Timbie with a tea tray. "He was in the first graduating class at the National College, and now he is the head teacher here at the school. Both our children are deaf, you see."

"Rubella?" Anna asked.

Mrs. Timbie nodded. "We nearly lost them both, but you see how well they have turned out." She put down the papers she was carrying and signed briefly to her daughter, who grimaced.

"I embarrass her," said Mrs. Timbie with an affectionate smile. "Now, while you're filling out papers, I thought you might like some coffee."

◆　◆　◆

ANNA SAT ACROSS from Jack, and they began to sort through the paperwork. For a good time the only sound was the scratching of pens.

"They want a statement of purpose. I think they are asking whether we plan to adopt him legally."

Jack said, "That same question applies to Rosa and Lia."

"Of course. I suppose I've been waiting to resolve the situation with the boys before raising the subject. It's a little odd," she said. "Not an hour ago we were talking about the possibility of a pregnancy next year, and now we're talking about three children ages five, seven, and nine, all at once. I was aware from the start that it would come to this, but I made that decision before—"

"You fell in love with me."

She forbade herself to flush. "Yes," she said. "Before you fell in love with me."

Jack smiled, a lopsided affair.

"Really," she said. "This is a conversation we must have, for everybody's sake, before we sign legal documents."

"All right," Jack said. "Write this down. 'We are ready and willing to legally assume all responsibility for the care of Tonino Russo, as we have done for his sisters Rosa and Lia.'"

Anna smiled at him. "You sound like a lawyer when you want to."

Jack's whole lower face contorted. "You do know that coppers don't take that as a compliment, right?"

She put down her pen and set the page aside for the ink to dry.

"Jack, what if he refuses? What if he won't come with us?"

"I suppose we'd have to leave him here until we can come back with the girls. That might be the best way to handle it, even if they do give us permission to take him."

"It might be," Anna agreed, "but it goes against the grain."

◆ ◆ ◆

MR. TIMBIE WAS still busy with the new student and her family when they finished the paperwork, and so they went out to find the stable boy who had taken charge of the carriage. They retrieved Mrs. Lee's basket and ate in the shade of a stand of dogwood trees, talking of nothing in particular. Because, Anna reckoned to herself, the most difficult decision had already been made. They would take the boy away with them, all the way to Greenwood where he would be reunited with his sisters and, at the same time, plunged into the Mezzanotte family summer party.

When she mentioned to Jack that the circumstances would almost certainly overwhelm the boy, it turned out he had been thinking the same thing.

"I have an idea," he told her. "I think we can arrange a quieter reunion."

They set out at two, Tonino sitting between them as quietly and unresisting as a doll. All the Timbie family had hugged him and wished him a good journey, signing and speaking and signing again, determined to get their message across despite the boy's numb regard. In the end they passed up a small satchel and watched as Jack turned the Rockaway around and they started out. Tonino left the school without a single backward glance.

Anna determined that it was best to talk to the boy as she would to his sisters, and so she started slowly, telling him about Rosa and Lia and how surprised and happy they would be to see him. She did this in a combination of English and Italian, with Jack stepping in to help her with vocabulary, and adding words of his own.

Within a quarter hour the boy fell asleep, leaning into Anna. She took this as a good sign.

"On some level he recognizes that he can trust us," she said to Jack. And: "You don't look convinced."

He shot her a sidelong glance and shrugged.

"Sleep is the only way he has of escaping," he said finally.

Anna understood his cynicism. It was a defense mechanism, one she had to adopt in her own work. For a police detective a cynical turn of mind would be even more necessary. In fact, Tonino had suffered in ways they might never really understand, and his recovery would not be simple or quick: that was the most important truth.

But the boy had a chance. A good chance, not just because of his sisters, but because Aunt Quinlan and Mrs. Lee would concern themselves. It was hard to imagine two women less alike, or more attuned to each other and to the people around them, each in her own way. They had both comforted children through terrible loss; Anna owed them her life and sanity. She would let them lead the way with Tonino.

Then something else came to mind. "Jack. We will never make the three o'clock ferry."

Even in the best traffic, the trip from the school for the deaf to the Christopher Street ferry terminal required far more than an hour, and they still had to stop on Waverly Place to unhitch Bonny and then find a cab.

"Oh ye of little faith. There is more than one ferry, you know."

He had a backup plan, of course.

"My faith in you is boundless," she said. "It was the traffic in the city I was worried about."

They turned onto 135th and there was the Hudson like a broad, muscular arm thrusting from north to south. The sight of the river made her follow its path in her mind, moving backward in time to her grandmother and great-grandmother. They had both traveled the river as young women, deep into the endless forests where they made lives for themselves. Not easy lives, but full. Her own journey was very different, but she had the sense now that it would be far more complex and challenging than she had imagined even a few months ago.

Jack left the carriage to arrange for passage on a steam barge, but Anna stayed where she was with the sleeping child leaning against her. She could see Jack standing in the doorway of the shack that served as an office, talking to an elderly clerk in a dusty bowler hat and a mustache twisted at the ends into funny little horns. By the way they were talking it was clear that this was another one of Jack's many acquaintances. The fact that her husband knew so many people didn't really surprise her anymore, but the connections were sometimes mysterious unless he thought to explain to her.

He came back to the carriage and gestured for Tonino. Anna passed him down carefully, a warm bundle of boy. He was wearing short pants and his legs were sturdy and tanned by the sun; her fingers slid over the welts on the back of his thighs and he twitched and let out a small hitching breath. Then he was safe in Jack's arms, and he turned his whole body toward the solid wall of chest. Anna wondered if he was dreaming of his father or if someone else had hurt this child so badly that even in the full light of day he escaped into sleep rather than face those memories.

Anna got down without help. The ferryman came to lead Bonny onto the barge, and they walked behind.

•   •   •

WHEN THEY REACHED Fort Lee at half past three Tonino was awake, alert but quiet. His eyes moved restlessly from Jack to Anna to the people who walked along the river promenade. Ladies in elaborate Sunday best, their skirts pinned up and pulled back and wrapped, pleated in some places and twisted in others; Jack was always put in mind of his sisters playing dress-up as little girls, when they put on every piece of clothing they could find. He supposed there was more to it; in fact, he knew there was more to it, from listening to them talk as they paged through Madame Demorest's *Fashion Monthly*, but it was not something he missed. Anna's far simpler approach appealed to his own tastes.

His sisters were on his mind, or he would not have noticed the fashions on parade. His sisters, his mother and aunts and sisters-in-law, all the women who would be at Greenwood to welcome Anna into the family.

Anna said, "Why don't you put Tonino down?"

But the boy was comfortable. He should be at ease and unafraid, and that meant he couldn't be dumped into the middle of the chaos at Greenwood.

"Here's the carriage," he said, as if that were an answer.

When Anna was seated Jack helped Tonino up to his place between the two of them.

He said, "Here's the plan. When we get to Greenwood, I'm going to leave you at the mercantile while I go to the farm to get the girls. I think it would be best if they see each other in a quiet setting." Then he repeated a shorter version of the plan to Tonino in Italian. The boy didn't seem to be listening, unless you paid close attention. Anna saw it too.

"Have you noticed that he sits a little straighter when Italian is being spoken? As though he's hearing a familiar sound from far away. Jack, please make sure he understands that you're coming back for us. He should never have to wonder where we are."

• • •

JACK SPENT THE forty-minute trip to Greenwood pointing things out, first in English, then in Italian. An inn where George Washington had supposedly spent the night; a turn in the road where Jack had upset a wagonload of earth at the age of sixteen, and the teasing he took for that still; a grove of apple trees that had once been part of a larger farm, all of them bent and warped by age so they resembled a herd of gnomes; a farm where his mother bought her poultry. As the village got closer he told stories about particular families, like the Carlisles in an old stone farmhouse, though they did no farming at all; the schoolteacher's house in the shape of a saltbox; and the school itself, where he had learned to read and write and play mumblety-peg along with his brothers. He pointed out the doctor's place, the churches, a barber, a blacksmith, a lending library no bigger than an outhouse. A small, neat town on a sleepy Sunday afternoon in late June.

They stopped in front of a building that seemed to be an inn, a restaurant, and a dry goods store all under one roof.

"The mercantile," Jack said. "Let me introduce you to Rob, and then I'll be off."

Anna passed Tonino down, and then took the hand that Jack extended, letting out a soft exclamation when he slipped his arm around her waist and swung her to the ground.

She said, "How much farther to the farm?"

"Depending on how long it takes me to get the girls, I should be back here within the hour. Just enough time for you to settle your nerves."

"If I'm nervous about anything—" she began.

He leaned over and kissed her temple. "You don't have to explain. Not to me."

She relaxed against him for the barest moment, and then turned to usher Tonino into the mercantile.

But the boy stood aside, his whole body tensed as if for flight. Something had frightened him, but what? Jack saw all that and handled it without the slightest hesitation.

He said, "Let's see what kind of ice cream Rob has today."

It was one way to test Tonino's hearing—and his English—but he gave no sign that he had heard or understood.

A voice came out of the shop, rough with age or tobacco.

"Did I hear a Mezzanotte asking for ice cream?" An older man came out of the shadows, wiping his hands on a rag the size of a tablecloth.

"You heard right," Jack said, walking forward to shake the man's hand. "How are you, Rob?"

"Surprised. You've got a lady with you. Don't think you've ever brought one by here before."

Jack said, "I've never had a wife before."

Sparse white brows climbed high on a freckled forehead. "You don't say. I heard a rumor, but I wasn't going to bite until I saw the proof. And here she is."

"Anna Savard Mezzanotte," Jack said. "Or Dr. Savard. This is Rob Carlisle. He runs most everything in the town of Greenwood. And he makes the best ice cream in twenty miles."

"The only ice cream," corrected the older man. "But I've got a batch made with the first of the strawberries, maybe the best ever. Can I offer you a dish? And that young man hanging back by the carriage, he's welcome to a dish too."

"I have to go run a quick errand," Jack said. "Rather than bore Anna and Tonino I thought I'd leave them here to sample your ice cream. Tonino's a little shy—"

"He can have his outside," said Rob Carlisle. "In fact, we all can. Nothing like ice cream on a warm summer afternoon, sitting in the sun."

◆ ◆ ◆

THERE WAS A picnic table on a patch of lawn beside the mercantile where they sat down with their ice cream, but just as soon as Rob picked up his spoon a dray pulled up, spilling children in every direction while a mother called warnings after them.

"Duty calls," Rob said. He sighed dramatically over his untouched ice cream and then looked at Tonino. "You watch that for me now, will you?" And without waiting for an answer he scuttled off to take care of his customers.

At first the ice cream seemed to puzzle Tonino. He ignored his spoon and used one finger to poke the small mound, studied what he had found, and with some reservations, stuck the finger in his mouth. His expression went from neutral to deeply suspicious, his whole face contorting into a frown. With that he looked so much like Rosa that any doubt of his identity was banished.

For the next few minutes he just watched Anna eating her ice cream, his eyes following the spoon from dish to mouth and back again. His own dish remained untouched and so when Anna finished hers, she very deliberately reached for it.

For the first time she saw some emotion move over his face. His hand darted out to pull the dish back, and he bent his arm around it like a fortress.

"There you are," Anna said. "Very nice to meet you again, Tonino."

With great solemnity he picked up his spoon and dug into the melting ice cream. He never took his eyes from her or his arm from around the bowl as he shoveled the tremendous spoonful into his mouth. He swallowed with an audible gulp, licked his lips, and dug back in. Table manners were the last thing that worried her, but Anna thought of Margaret, and wondered whether he would adore her, as most little boys seemed to, or resent her instruction.

◆ ◆ ◆

FROM INSIDE THE mercantile came the sound of children quarreling. Tonino inched away on the bench, taking both his and Rob Carlisle's dishes along. Anna watched him and tried to read from his expression what he was feeling. Who had caused him such pain that he would withdraw from the world so completely?

As watchful as he was, she saw his eyelids begin to droop. Anna found herself holding back a yawn, but Tonino just put his head down on the table and fell asleep. He slept like an infant, in a world that Anna could hardly imagine. There would be nightmares, almost certainly, and behaviors more typical of a much younger child. Mothers came to her often in despair over bed-wetting and thumb sucking, expecting solutions when she had less experience with such things than they did. Along with Sophie she had had long discussions with Aunt Quinlan and Mrs. Lee, who between them had raised ten children and dealt with every challenge imaginable.

Anna would do her best, but she would depend on the two women who had raised her to lead the way, and on Margaret. There would need to be a very frank discussion at the start, where all the adults in the two households worked out some ground rules. As they should have thought to do when the girls came. But there were far worse things for this boy than a household full of adults dedicated to his welfare and happiness.

The sound of the rockaway pulling up in front of the store roused her out of a half doze. Anna resisted the urge to jump up for fear of startling Tonino and saw that he was awake, all his attention focused on the carriage.

Jack had seen them, but Lia and Rosa were so wound up in a difference of opinion that they took no note. That meant that Jack hadn't told them where they were going, or why. Now he made a small movement with his head that Anna understood as a request that she wait. A reasonable course of action, for any number of reasons, and still, perspiration broke out on her throat and face. Suddenly she was sure they had made a mistake, that this wasn't Tonino, or that this was not the Tonino the girls were looking for. That they would be frightened by the changes they saw in him.

Lia was turning to Jack to engage his support in this newest disagreement with her older sister when she caught sight of Anna. A smile broke out on her face and disappeared almost immediately as she took in the boy. It was the blank look on Lia's face that made Rosa look around herself.

The girls rose so slowly that they might have been puppets being drawn to a standing position. In a sudden explosion of movement they made to jump from the carriage, but Jack had been prepared for this and he held on to them both, talking rapidly.

Rosa twisted at the waist to look at her brother.

"Tonino!"

The boy, reserved and watchful, studied the girls in the carriage as he might have studied a painting of some creature out of his sphere of experience. His sisters had disappeared once before; maybe he had convinced himself that he would never see them again. Or, it occurred to Anna, he could be angry to have been left behind and alone.

Jack helped the girls down and they came flying toward the table, both of them calling his name and weeping.

Anna thought of encouraging him, of telling him to go to them, but some instinct made her hold back. To intrude now might be disastrous. The boy was so tightly wound, so tense, that she could almost feel him vibrating.

Then the girls came to a skidding stop in front of their brother. Anna moved out of the way, and Lia climbed up on the bench to take her spot while Rosa took the other side. Anna couldn't see Tonino's face because they had their arms wrapped around him. They were talking more quietly now, their voices hitching and catching.

There was no sound from Tonino. He was trembling, and his face was wet with tears, but he didn't seem able to bring forth a single word. Anna walked over to Jack and leaned into him.

"Did you ask the girls about—"

"I asked if he was as good as Lia at telling stories, and they had a discussion that made it clear that he can hear and speak."

It was almost bad news; if he were deaf, the challenges would be clear-cut. But a boy who simply would not or could not talk was a much more difficult puzzle.

When she thought she could not stand one more second of not knowing, the three children shifted a little on the bench, and a single hand—a little rough, browned by the sun—came around to rest on Lia's narrow back, and patted.

Anna realized then that she had feared the worst: that he wouldn't want to see the sisters who had mourned him. And here was proof that she was wrong: whatever he had endured, the boy he had been—the brother he had been—was still there. Torn and fearful and angry, but enough himself to touch his sister gently. He patted Lia's back to comfort her, and took the comfort the girls offered him in turn.

◆　◆　◆

THE THREE CHILDREN sat on the rear carriage bench pressed together and very quiet. Anna had still not heard Tonino say a word, but then the girls had asked him no questions, as far as she could tell.

They whispered to him now and then, and twice Lia gave a low giggle, but otherwise they had closed themselves off, cocooned together. She wondered if they had told him about their father, and decided that they had not, and did not know how to share this news.

For a moment Anna felt the same light-headed sense of unreality that overcame her after an important exam. She would have liked a few hours to catch her breath, but another exam was before her. All the calm reserve she had drawn around herself simply leaked away, and she shivered.

Jack took the reins in one hand and with the other he took her forearm. The dress she wore had wide sleeves of a light batiste, secured with a single button at the wrist. With a simple twist Jack opened the cuff. He pulled back her sleeve to run his fingers down the skin of her inner arm to trace the creases on her palm. Every nerve in her body snapped to life, and she pulled her arm away, laughing.

"Do you think I'm so easily distracted?"

"I know exactly how easily distracted you are," he said. "But this is as much as I dare, under the circumstances. Do you remember the stories about us swimming in the river on the hottest summer days? This is the river. We could follow it to the farm if we were on foot." Something in his tone aroused her suspicions and Anna turned to study his profile.

"I have no intention of swimming, Jack."

He raised one eyebrow at her as if this were a challenge. Which, she supposed, it was.

She said, "Tell me how the houses are laid out. Give me a picture."

He told her in his usual spare way: there were five houses in a rough half circle, set far enough apart and with fruit trees planted between them to provide some privacy. The biggest house, the one in the middle, belonged to his parents. They would eat all together at a long table under the pergola, with a view of the orchards and greenhouses. And they would sleep in the room he had had as a boy.

He shifted a little, and Anna poked him. "You've never had a girl in that room before, have you?"

"Define what you mean by *had*." He closed his free hand around hers before she could poke him again. "Of course not. The only females who have ever stepped foot in that room are my mother and aunts when they helped with the housework."

"Your sisters?"

"Only upon pain of death," he said grimly.

"You had a room to yourself?"

He shrugged. "It's a big house. When we had family parties I had to share with cousins. You won't mind sharing the bed with Pasquale and Pietro, will you?"

"Very funny."

He bowed from the shoulders. "You haven't met them yet, so you don't know how funny."

He was in a good mood. They had done the impossible in finding Tonino, and fulfilled at least half of the promises made to Rosa. And he was proud to be bringing Anna home to his family.

If only there weren't so many of them. Anna had devoted a good amount of time to learning names: his brothers, their wives and children. Between Chiara and Jack she had learned enough about each of them to give her a firm footing.

She said, "I'm ready to do battle to establish my place in the pecking order. It will be a bit of a challenge, but then my Italian isn't very good, so I won't know if I've succeeded or not."

•   •   •

JACK HAD GIVEN strict orders to everybody—sisters-in-laws included—about how to greet Anna.

"You make her sound like a timid rabbit," said his aunt Philomena. "I know your Anna, there is nothing timid about her. She is a strong woman and can hold her own."

"That is true," his mother said. "But we still don't want to overwhelm her on her first visit." And his mother's word was final. There would be no mob to greet them. Anna's aunt Quinlan and the Lees had been welcomed with all the good cheer and respect Jack expected, and would serve as a bit of a buffer between his wife and his female relatives.

From ahead came the sound of children caught up in some game, and the cousins had gotten out their instruments. Fiddles, a clarinet, a trumpet, an accordion in comfortable harmony. Women called to each other in Italian and English about bowls and dishes and children who needed attention, dogs in the way, the need to wipe a table. Jack only heard this in some corner of his mind. The bulk of his attention was focused on Anna and the children sitting behind them.

Rosa and Lia were talking to Tonino in a galloping whisper. If they never heard Tonino's voice again, Jack thought, it might be a simple matter of never having the opportunity to get a word in edgewise. He glanced over his shoulder to make sure the boy wasn't overwhelmed, and saw with some relief that he looked content, if a little glassy-eyed. As anyone would be, with such a sudden change in fortune.

As Jack brought the Rockaway to a halt everyone turned toward them.

Anna's aunt Quinlan laughed out loud at the sight of them.

"Tonino?"

Rosa jumped up and threw out her arms. "Yes, this is our brother Tonino. Aunt Anna and Uncle Jack found him for us."

◆ ◆ ◆

FOR SOMEONE WHO could name every bone and muscle, every gland and nerve in the human body, Anna told herself, it shouldn't be difficult to attach the names she had already memorized to the faces around her. Especially as the women were all sitting together, and she could look from face to face without apology.

Chiara's mother, Mariangela, was very tall, while Carmela, married to the second oldest son, was very slight and hardly taller than her nine-year-old son. Susanna, daughter of the famous band director, had lost an eyetooth, but her smile was wide and genuine. The two youngest of the sisters-in-law—Benedetta and Lucetta—were more of a challenge; they looked so much alike that they might have been sisters. For the moment Anna would have to depend on the color of their skirts to distinguish them. How that would work at the dinner table she had no idea, but that was a problem for another time.

They sat in the fragrant shade of a grape arbor with the low buzz of honeybees not very far off, and together they made a study of Anna. They weren't mean spirited about it; they spoke English, asked straightforward questions, and listened to her answers. And still Anna was reminded of the way a group of women passed a newborn back and forth to admire it. They saw everything, she knew very well: her posture, her features, the way she held her head, the tone of her voice, the dimples that she used to such good advantage. They watched her talking to the older women and to their children, and judged each for herself how well Anna met the challenges.

She didn't have to pretend to like children. She didn't even have to pretend to admire these particular children; they were all healthy, well mannered—at least under the watchful gazes of mothers and aunts—and curious. Like children everywhere they ran the full gamut, from the painfully shy to the very bold.

As her aunt was leaving to rest before dinner Mrs. Lee leaned down to talk into Anna's ear. "And not one of them asked could they see my tail. Good, hardworking people. Kind at heart."

• • •

THE CHILDREN TOOK her on as a project. The little ones climbed into her lap to show her their battle scars. She examined and exclaimed over skinned knees and scabby knuckles, admired the muscles the boys put on display, and declared herself very much interested in a tour of the best trees for climbing, the wild blueberry bushes, the rabbit hutches, the prize sow, the two foals in the pasture, a collection of pennies, a map of Italy, or their grandfather's photograph of Garibaldi, signed by the man himself.

Before they got very far with this long list of chores, it was time to get dinner on the table. Anna offered to help, but was refused quite firmly. Instead while the sisters-in-law went off Jack appeared and spirited her away.

"Intermission," she said in a mock whisper.

"That bad? You need rescuing?"

"Oh, no. It was very pleasant. And informative. Where are we going?"

"Grand tour."

As soon as they were out of earshot she asked, "How am I doing, do you think?"

"I told you you'd win them all over, and you did."

"Women with children are easily charmed," she said. "Admire their offspring and you've won most of the battle. And they are healthy, your nieces and nephews. Healthy and full of life."

"My mother will be pleased to hear that."

Anna thought of Carmela, one of the two sisters-in-law who had emigrated from Italy, and whose English was least fluent. But she was also very bright, it seemed to Anna, and somewhat unexpectedly, the kindest and most friendly of them all. And she wasn't well. There was nothing specific Anna could tell Jack, but she did voice her concern.

"I wondered if you'd notice about Carmela," Jack said. "Mama worries about her."

"My guess is that she's anemic," Anna said. "That can be addressed with diet, for the most part. If she asks me I'll examine her, but I have to wait for her to ask."

One brow lifted. "That's not likely."

"It might be easier than you think," Anna said. "She has struck up a friendship with Elise, and Elise can be quietly persuasive. I'll talk to her about it later this evening."

Jack said, "I noticed that too, about Elise. I wouldn't have imagined them as especially suited."

"Female friendships are sometimes very mysterious," Anna said. "But a true friendship between women is the strongest bond of all. Where is Elise, have you seen her recently?"

Jack made a low rumbling sound in his throat. "I saw her walking down toward the orchard with Ned."

"Oh." Anna considered this. "Just the two of them?"

He nodded. "Bambina was standing just there—" He pointed. "Watching them go."

Bambina, who never hesitated to find something about Ned to criticize. Anna said, "There's a line from Shakespeare that comes to mind, something Aunt Quinlan says now and then. 'Methinks the lady doth protest too much.'"

"That's what I'm afraid of," Jack said. "But here's an idea. Let's forget about all that for an hour. No talk of Bambina or Ned or anybody else. Just for an hour, while I introduce you to my favorite places."

But then he started, he admitted readily, in the biggest of the greenhouses, which was not his favorite place. Rows of pots stretched out, as carefully ordered as a regiment of soldiers.

"There must be five hundred of them," Anna said.

"Closer to seven hundred fifty," Jack said. "And I've had my hands on every one of them."

At her surprised look he said, "In March when it's time to sow the seeds we're all pressed into service. While you were on your way to the island with the girls to see their father buried, I was here, up to my elbows in loam and manure. Next year you'll be here too, right next to me."

"Will I?" She lifted a shoulder. "There are worse ways to spend a day."

"And better ones," he said, and pulled her into the shade of a shed, where he pressed her up against the wall and kissed her breathless.

◆ ◆ ◆

THEY ENDED THE tour by collapsing to the ground under a pear tree. In a month's time, given rain and sunshine, the small hard fruits would be ready to fall, gravid with juice, into a cupped palm. Things changed so rapidly, sometimes it took her breath away.

"That was a deep sigh," he said. "Exhausted? Unhappy? Both?"

"Not unhappy. Not at all. I was just thinking how quickly things change, but sometimes for the better. Not always for the better, of course." An image of Janine Campbell came to her, unbidden. She hoped that Janine's boys were healthy and learning how to be happy.

Jack ran his knuckles over her shoulder. "It's not a sin to leave your patients behind for a few days."

"I know that. Or let's say, I have learned that." She looked back toward the house, where someone was banging on a bell with great abandon.

"The dinner bell," Jack said. "Time to get back."

He stood up and offered his hand, pulled her to her feet.

"So what's next?" she wanted to know. "What will we be doing?"

"Eating," he said. "For hours we'll sit around the table and watch the kids run themselves ragged until they're tired enough to be rounded up and scrubbed down and put to bed. The cousins will play their instruments and if Mama has had enough wine, she'll sing and make all of us sing with her. We'll toast Massimo's birthday, and my parents' anniversary. The old stories will get told, about how Mama and Pa met. Every couple has to tell that story, and they'll want us to tell ours, too."

She must have made a face, because he laughed and squeezed her hand. "I'll take care of that, no need to worry."

"Oh, I'm sure you'll tell a story," she said, trying not to grin.

"Then we'll eat some more and talk some more. A little before sunset—about three hours from now—we'll walk over to that rise"— he pointed—"and watch as the longest day of our year comes to an end. How does that sound?"

"Good," she said. "So what are you going to say about how we met?"

"You'll have to wait and hear it for yourself."

"I think I had better come up with a contingency plan."

"You think I'll embroider the truth?"

"Jack," she said, rubbing her face against his sleeve. "You're a lot like your sisters that way. Everything has to be embroidered, or it's just not finished."

◆   ◆   ◆

DINNER WAS NOT quiet, but quieter than Anna had imagined. There were two reasons: the food demanded attention, and when voices did start to rise and conversations to cross, Jack's mother would half stand up, her palms on the table, her arms straight, and cast a gaze over her family. Conversations settled down again to a steady patter.

At the next table the children made far more noise, and no one seemed to mind. Aunt Quinlan pointed this out, with some satisfaction.

"I wish Margaret were here to see that boisterous, happy children can in fact grow up to be reasonable adults. No straightjackets or corsets required."

There were spots of high color on her cheeks, which could be attributed to the strong red wine she was so clearly enjoying, or simply to the fact that she was content. More important, she was holding a fork without any hint of pain, and eating with an appetite.

"You like it here," Anna said to her aunt. "It reminds you of home."

"I suppose it does remind me of Paradise," said her aunt. "In all the ways that matter most."

"You grew up in a town called Paradise?" Elise looked intrigued at this idea.

"I did," Aunt Quinlan told her. "Long ago and far away. Now almost all my people are gone from there. Time is a river, my girl. Don't ever forget that. Don't any of you forget that." And she smiled at Anna, to take the sting out of the truth.

◆ ◆ ◆

LATER, WHEN IT was their turn to tell the story of their first encounter, Jack stood up and put a hand on Anna's shoulder while he talked.

Jack said, "I walked into the church basement and there she was, in the middle of examining a little boy, a baby, really, who was sitting on her lap with his hands fisted in her jacket, as if she were all that kept him from drifting away into deeper waters. And she was just that. Then she realized that some of the children weren't vaccinated, and how angry that made her. So she marched right up to a dragon of a nun—Elise will back me up, just ask her—and scolded her. She took up for those children like they were her own and she wouldn't back down. And I knew it was her, the one I thought I'd never find. A strong woman, a smart, beautiful, uncompromising woman, and sure of her place in the world."

His mother was smiling at Anna. "And what did you think when you first saw our Jack?"

"I heard his voice before I saw him and I thought, *Oh, there's a priest come to help.* And then a little later, when I did look at him and saw him smiling at me I thought: *He's a priest. How sad.*"

◆ ◆ ◆

WHEN THE FIRST hint of twilight slipped across the sky just an hour later, Anna sat with Jack on the rise that overlooked all of the farm and the countryside beyond. They were alone, and not alone: the elder aunts had shepherded all the children off to bed, but the grown-ups were nearby, scattered over the hillside in twos and threes. Now and then a voice came to them, cajoling or scolding, singing or laughing.

An earthy, clean scent rose up from the ground as it gave up the day's heat, mingling with punk-stick and wood smoke, the pennyroyal and sweet everlasting and wild bergamot that grew along the edges of fields and pastures. All the smells mingled together to float on a breeze that rose and fell like the sea.

She let her eyes roam over the farm buildings, the hothouses and greenhouses and barns and the apiary. The river wound its way along the fields to disappear into a small pond where the reflected blue of the sky began to give way to deeper reds and pinks and oranges all limned with gold. Colors so saturated and alive Anna imagined them falling to layer on her skin like flower petals.

In a silence threaded with whip-poor-will song and the low buzz of bees Anna tried to reconstruct the afternoon for herself.

She said, "I never once saw him talking."

Jack pushed out a deep sigh that ruffled the hair on her nape.

"Not a word," she said. "Though the girls never gave up petting and hugging and whispering." Tonino hadn't resisted, but neither had he shown any particular response.

"Rosa came to me," Jack said. "She doesn't understand why he won't talk to them. I wasn't sure what to say except that he needed our patience and understanding."

"I wonder if we'll ever know where he was for those weeks."

Jack shrugged. "Maybe. He might be able to tell us himself, once he starts to believe that he's safe."

Just after dinner Anna had gone to check on the children where they slept in a single broad bed, Tonino tucked in between his sisters. Rosa's breath hitched a little, a serious child even in sleep, no doubt making plans that would put everything right. She dreamed of a world in which little brothers were whole and unscarred and full of stories that came tumbling out like a stream over rocks. *Time is a river.*

"If he had come to us with broken bones I would know what to do for him. As it is I feel helpless, but I can't let the girls see that."

"Or Tonino," Jack added.

"He'll come back to us when he's ready," she said, mostly to herself, and kept back the logical next thought: *if that day ever comes.* She could be sure of Sophie coming home one day, but Tonino was another matter.

"We'll do our best for him," Jack said. And that had to be comfort enough, because it was true.

Anna said, "This has always been my favorite and least favorite time of year. On the cusp between the light and dark. *Dusk* always strikes me as the wrong word."

Jack rubbed his cheek against her temple. "It's funny that you should say that. When I was young I couldn't understand how it could be that light and color flooded the world even after the sun disappeared. Later I understood the geometry of it, that the sun drops below the horizon by a few degrees—but still, it has never seemed like enough of an explanation. It's more than light and color, and it lasts for such a short time. And here it is now, do you feel it?"

They sat in the trembling light, Anna cradled against Jack to feel the beat of his heart against her spine, separated by nothing more than a few inches of muscle and bone. Caught in the gloaming, suspended in the gilded hour, she saw herself in a landscape of years stretching into a horizon she had never dared imagine for herself.

When the light was gone and the first fireflies rose in the fields she said, "Thank you, Jack. Thank you for bringing me here to see this."

The night came gently and still she shivered in his arms.

"Time to go in."

Anna meant to agree, but instead she produced a great yawn. With a laugh he lifted her to her feet, and then up into his arms.

"Jack. I can walk."

"Of course you can." He started toward the house, his breath stirring the hair at her temple.

"It's too far, Jack."

"Anna Savard." He shook his head at her. "When will you stop thinking of yourself as a burden?"

All at once she was aware of the beat of his heart and the scent of his skin, of his strength and the tender weight of his regard. Of the eternity of stars overhead and the rising moon and the pulse of the earth. All at once. All in harmony.

"Now," she said, surprising herself most of all. "I think I'm ready to do that now."

ACKNOWLEDGMENTS

As ever, I am very thankful for the friends and colleagues who took the time to read drafts of this novel and provide feedback. They include my super-agent, Jill Grinberg; my original, home-again editor, Wendy McCurdy; Cheryl Pientka and Katelyn Detweiler at Grinberg Literary Management; and Penny Chambers, Jason Kovaks, Frances Howard-Snyder, Patricia Rosenmeyer, and Audrey Fraggalosch. Penny listened to me read the whole novel out loud, word by word, some parts more than once. Don't know what I'd do without her.

Readers and friends active on Facebook and on my blog were instrumental in putting together a list of phrases in a whole army of Italian dialects. Thanks to every one of you.

Jason Kovaks rescued me from the quicksand of nineteenth-century legal documents, while Drs. Carl Heine, Janet Gilsdorf, and Margaret Jacobsen answered a lot of questions about medical matters in general.

Any mistakes or misinterpretations are mine alone.

Finally, I am thankful to my husband for his support and patience in difficult times, and to my daughter Elisabeth. Who is.

AUTHOR'S NOTES

The more things change, the more they stay the same.
Jean-Baptiste Alphonse Karr, 1849, *The Wasps*

(or in other words)

The past is never dead. It's not even past.
William Faulkner, 1950, *Requiem for a Nun*

TWO THINGS:

The idea for this novel originated with my paternal grandmother, Rosina Russo Lippi, born in 1882, the first daughter and eldest of four children of immigrant Italians employed in the silk factories in Paterson, New Jersey. When she was about eight, her parents died or disappeared; there is some inconclusive indication that they were living in Brooklyn twenty years later with an additional six children. How the first set of children were separated from their parents is one of many mysteries.

I've never been able to track down where the four oldest Russo children were for the first years they were orphaned or abandoned or lost. I do know that the only boy was eventually sent west on the orphan trains and later died in a factory explosion in Kansas. My grandmother's youngest sister, an infant, was adopted, while she and her sister May were eventually taken into the Mother Cabrini home for Italian orphans, where they grew up and lived until they married, both before age twenty.

My grandmother had ten children who survived into adulthood, and she died at age seventy-two in 1955, six months before my birth. In accordance with Italian custom, I was named for her. This rather mundane fact is actually more complicated than it might seem. Here's the thing: No one was ever really sure of her name.

It is spelled phonetically on her baptismal record; on marriage, birth, and death certificates it appears as Rosa, Rose, Rosie, or Rosina, with a surname that varies just as widely: Russo, Russ, Ross, and Rose. Her children each had a different story about her name and origins. The first seed for this novel was planted when my aunt Kate told me her version: *Your grandmother's name was Rose Rose, and you were named after her.*

It was in researching my grandmother's life that I first began to think about Manhattan in the 1880s, and to imagine a story. This is not my grandmother's story, which is still to be discovered, but one of my own making.

Second: To really understand Manhattan in 1883 you have to forget the Manhattan you think you know. In 1883 there was no Ellis Island, Statue of Liberty, Flatiron Building, Times Square, or New York Public Library, to name just a few landmarks. Transportation was limited to walking, horse-drawn or steam-driven vehicles, elevated trains, and the growing railroad system. In 1883 gaslight still dominated; electric light had just begun to replace gas streetlights, and very few buildings had made the switch. The telephone was on the horizon, but in 1883 a telegram was the only way to move information quickly from place to place.

This novel was a research-intensive undertaking. Some information about that research that might be useful to those interested in the history or who are dedicated fact-checkers:

I will admit to a weakness for maps, and a particular weakness for the David Rumsey Map Collection (davidrumsey.com), which was especially useful in reconstructing Manhattan as it existed in 1883. Since that time streets have disappeared and morphed, while others have been renamed. The map of the city is further complicated because in a relatively short period of time public transportation went through multiple incarnations: elevated train lines went up and came down, dozens of railroads vied for street space and custom, and the first of them were dropped into tunnels to run underground, a precursor to the subway system. In a similar way real estate boomed as the city moved northward; Manhattanites didn't hesitate to tear down elaborate structures less than fifty years old if there was a potential for profit in replacing them with something else.

What you find here are the original names and locations of buildings, businesses, institutions, intersections, residences, elevated train routes and stations, restaurants, schools, and everything else, in as far as I was able to document them.

The exceptions are first, the residences of fictitious characters: I'm sorry to say that you shouldn't bother to go looking for the Quinlan, Savard, Maroney, or Campbell homes or the Mezzanotte shop, greenhouses, or farm, because they never existed. Also, I should point out that I've appropriated a block on Waverly Place just east of the original building that housed NYU for my fictional purposes. In 1883 this block was mostly commercial in nature and home to merchants who specialized in all kinds of clothing.

The New Amsterdam Charity Hospital is also fiction, and was never to be found in Manhattan.

With very few exceptions, the names of real people have been changed to allow me more interpretive license. This is especially the case where the historical record is lacking. For example, Father John McKinnawae is a highly fictionalized version of Father John Drumgoole, who established the Mount Loretto Orphan Asylum on Staten Island and the Catholic home for orphaned boys at the intersection of Great Jones Street and Lafayette; conversely, the head of the Foundling Asylum (known still as just *the Foundling*) was in life (as she is in the novel) Sister Mary Irene, of the Sisters of Charity. Dr. Mary Putnam Jacobi was a real person, one who deserves to be widely known, married to another physician, Dr. Abraham Jacobi, whom some think of as the founder of modern pediatric medicine. All other physicians are fictional.

Anthony Comstock's public actions and life history are drawn from newspaper accounts, contemporaneous tracts and books, and historical scholarship. However, the people he hounded and drove to suicide—something the Weeder in the Garden of the Lord (a title he gave himself) bragged about—have been fictionalized.

The Comstock Act is not fiction. All of the incidents mentioned in the story—including Anthony Comstock's antics in and out of the courtroom—are based on the historical record, in particular on newspaper accounts.

I was especially careful about advances in medical science, because some of the most important discoveries—the nature of infection and the importance of sterile techniques, for example—were not instantaneously accepted or practiced; just the opposite. The story of President Garfield's death is not included here in any detail, but it is worth looking up, if only to get a sense of how slowly some things changed. Candice Millard's *Destiny of the Republic: A Tale of Madness, Medicine and the Murder of a President* (2011) is an excellent place to start.

Young people today (finally, I'm old enough to use that cliché) seem to have no real conception of how bad things were for women and, more important, could be again. The problems women faced in 1883 are not exaggerated here. However, please note that I am not claiming that all women were unhappy. Far from it, but not quite far enough. Some things to remember:

1. There was a period of several decades where male physicians were free to experiment with new procedures, no matter how specious the theoretical underpinnings, with little or no oversight from their peers or the law.

2. Women who did not adhere to the ideals of the time, whose interests and behaviors were considered abnormal and unnatural, were sometimes committed to hospitals and asylums, and in extreme cases they were subjected to castration and female circumcision. This came about in part because the men who ruled their lives decided that the female reproductive organs were the source of insanity. The aspects of the story that touch on these subjects are based on medical texts and medical journal articles of the time, as well as on current academic research. Readers familiar with the time period and subject will wonder why there is no mention of Dr. J. Marion Sims, who for decades was considered the father of modern gynecology until historians looked more closely. His absence from this story has to do with his absence from New York during the novel's time span; I am not and should not be construed as an apologist, nor would I rationalize his systematic violation of the rights of women, free or slave, white or black, in his care.

3. Women were just beginning to get access to higher education. In large cities there were women's medical colleges, but it was a good while later that they were admitted to the traditional institutions. Research on the early history of women physicians and surgeons

comes from a wide variety of sources, most especially from Regina Markell Morantz-Sanchez's work on Mary Putnam Jacobi and Mary Amanda Dixon. Susan Wells's *Out of the Dead House: Nineteenth-Century Women Physicians and the Writing of Medicine* was tremendously useful. Other authors whose work in this area I found invaluable include Arleen Marcia Tuchman, William Leach, and Judith Walzer Leavitt. Sources differ on the numbers, but in 1883 about twenty African American female medical school graduates were practicing in the United States. Sophie's history is inspired in part by the life stories of those indomitable women.

4. Nineteenth-century attitudes toward and understanding of sexuality and reproduction and the politics of birth control and abortion are hugely complex topics. Especially helpful in sorting through the murk were Timothy J. Gilfoyle's *City of Eros: New York City, Prostitution, and the Commercialization of Sex, 1790–1920*; Linda Gordon's *The Moral Property of Women*; G. J. Barker-Benfield's *The Horrors of the Half-Known Life: Male Attitudes toward Women and Sexuality in Nineteenth-Century America*; and George Chauncey's *Gay New York: Gender, Urban Culture, and the Making of the Gay Male World, 1890–1940*. These are crucial works I went back to many times.

Legal aspects of birth control and abortion are based on modern historical research and nineteenth-century books, journal articles, and newspaper accounts. Especially useful were academic works by Andrea Tone, Leslie J. Reagan, James C. Mohr, and Timothy J. Gilfoyle. Andrea Tone's "Black Market Birth Control: Contraceptive Entrepreneurship and Criminality in the Gilded Age" (*The Journal of American History* 87.2:435–59) provides an excellent introduction to the topic.

Here I must clarify something: those who would be considered socially progressive by modern standards were not infallible. In fact, some beliefs shared by otherwise rational and educated people are distinctly shocking. For example, Malthusian theory was quite popular in the late nineteenth century. In this view of things, society is threatened when population growth outpaces economic stability; thus increase in population has to be restricted, if not by disease, famine, or warfare, then by moral restraint and intervention. This boiled down to a simple formula: the white middle and upper classes needed to reproduce more, and the immigrant poor—mostly Irish, German, and

Italian at this time—had to reproduce less. In some quarters the disabled and those seen as otherwise impure were added to the list of those who should be discouraged or prevented from reproducing.

This is a highly simplified characterization of the theory of eugenics, but something like it was adopted by many social progressives and liberals in the late nineteenth century, including Theodore Roosevelt, John Maynard Keynes, Woodrow Wilson, Bertrand Russell, Alexander Graham Bell, George Bernard Shaw, Harry Laughlin, H. G. Wells, and Margaret Sanger.

This is one of the hardest things for a historical novelist to pull off: to tell a story based on facts that will be distasteful and off-putting to modern readers. Whether I have pulled this off is not for me to decide.

Regarding matters of law: the investigation of crime, the structure of the police department, the coroner system, and the conducting of inquests and court cases is based on contemporaneous works on the New York Police Department such as A. E. Costello's 1885 *Our Police Protectors: History of the New York Police from the Earliest Period to the Present Time*. More recent historical studies were also consulted, including popular nonfiction works on crimes of the period such as *The Murder of the Century: The Gilded Age Crime That Scandalized a City and Sparked the Tabloid Wars*, by Paul Collins.

I researched poverty, the homeless (referred to in 1883 as *the outdoor poor*), and orphaned or abandoned children through newspaper articles, annual reports issued by charities both religious and secular, and contemporary academic research.

Volume five of *The Iconography of Manhattan Island, 1498–1909*, a monumental six-volume work by Isaac Newton Phelps-Stokes (1915), was a primary source, along with some of the more general publications, which include (in no particular order) the second edition of Kenneth T. Jackson's *Encyclopedia of New York City*; *New York 1880: Architecture and Urbanism in the Gilded Age* (1999) by Robert A. M. Stern, Thomas Mellins, and David Fishman; Thomas Beer's *The Mauve Decade*, Part II (1926); *Lights and Shadows of New York Life* (1872) by James McCabe; Donna Gabaccia's *From Sicily to Elizabeth Street: Housing and Social Change Among Italian Immigrants, 1880–1930*; and *Daily Life in the Industrial United States, 1870–1900* by Julie Husband and Jim O'Loughlin.

A number of history blogs are run by people who are passionate about the city and who are generous with their knowledge and research. Ones I consult regularly include *The Bowery Boys*, *Abandoned NYC*, *Daytonian in Manhattan*, *Ephemeral New York*, *Forgotten New York*, *Gothamist*, and *Untapped New York*. I look forward to seeing what these websites come up with, day by day.

I am in the process of writing a sequel to *The Gilded Hour*; for more information about both books, please visit thegildedhour.com or my author blog at saradonati.com.

Sara Donati

Sara Donati is the international bestselling author of the Wilderness series, which includes *Into the Wilderness*, *Dawn on a Distant Shore*, *Lake in the Clouds*, *Fire Along the Sky*, *Queen of Swords*, and *The Endless Forest*. *The Gilded Hour* follows the story of the descendants of the characters from the Wilderness series. Visit the author online at thegildedhour.com and saradonati.com.